Brothers a

Bebe Moore Campbell is the author of *Your Blues Ain't Like Mine* and the *New York Times* bestseller *Brothers and Sisters*. She is a commentator for National Public Radio and a contributing editor for *Essence* magazine. Her articles have appeared in numerous publications, including the *New York Times Magazine*, the *Washington Post* and *Ebony*.

She lives in Los Angeles with her husband, Ellis Gordon Jr. They have a daughter, the actress Maia Campbell, and a son, Ellis Gordon III.

Brothers and Sisters

Bebe Moore Campbell

ARROW

This edition first published in the United Kingdom in
1999 by Arrow Books

3 5 7 9 10 8 6 4

Copyright © Bebe Moore Campbell 1994

The right of Bebe Moore Campbell to be identified as the
author of this work has been asserted by her in accordance
with the Copyright, Designs and Patents Act, 1988

First published in the United Kingdom in 1995
by William Heinemann

Arrow Books
Random House UK Ltd
20 Vauxhall Bridge Road, London, SW1V 2SA

Random House Australia (Pty) Limited
20 Alfred Street, Milsons Point, Sydney, New South Wales
2061, Australia

Random House New Zealand Limited
18 Poland Road, Glenfield
Auckland 10, New Zealand

Random House South Africa (Pty) Limited
Endulini, 5a Jubilee Road, Parktown, 2193, South Africa

Random House UK Limited Reg. No. 954009

A CIP catalogue record for this book is available from the
British Library

Papers used by Random House UK Limited are natural,
recyclable products made from wood grown in sustainable
forests. The manufacturing processes conform to the
environmental regulations of the country of origin

Printed and bound in the United Kingdom by
The Guernsey Press Co. Ltd, Guernsey, Channel Islands

ISBN 0 7493 1993 3

*To the healing of Los Angeles
and all of God's wounded children*

Acknowledgments

Lots of people helped me. I appreciate my husband, Ellis, for rooting for me while I was down in the trenches and for helpful criticism. Thanks to my mother, Doris C. Moore, for her insightful first read. Thank you, Delia Fance, for all your help. And thank yous to my agent, Lynn Nesbit, and my editor, Stacy Creamer, for hard work and support.

Brothers
and Sisters

The flames of April came out of season.

There is a time for burning in Los Angeles, months when devastation is expected and planned for, and blazes attack with the power and cruelty of old enemies. August. September. These are the city's appointed months of conflagration. But the fires of April were not weather. They chose their own time, creating destruction that spared no one. Long after the flames were quelled, the city was still smoldering, and even those whose lives were cooled by ocean breezes felt the heat.

I

When Esther Jackson looked up from the stack of slick new hundred-dollar bills she was counting inside the tellers' cage of the downtown branch of Angel City National Bank and glanced out the plate-glass window, the black woman inhaled sharply. 'You're out of balance,' she said woodenly to Hector Bonilla. Her English was clipped, as precise and well enunciated as that of any television news anchor.

The quiet teller standing next to the thirty-four-year-old regional operations manager watched her with eyes that slowly widened as he saw her begin to squeeze the bills in the fist her hand had become. Esther was looking beyond the short brown man, across the downtown street. Three of the Los Angeles Police Department's finest, all white, stood in front of two black boys, who were sitting on the side-walk. Esther felt a quickening in her chest as she watched the scene. *Better not touch them!* The words roared through her body. The diction in her head was as slurred and textured as the South Side Chicago neighborhood she'd grown up in.

Hector saw her lips become a thin, dangerous line.

Cops just stopped them for nothing, she fumed. But of course there was a reason. The usual reason. *Better not touch them!* She wanted to shout the words across the street, even though the youths in question looked like gangbangers. She could see their baggy pants and earrings, their hardened faces and snarls. But so what? If they were white and dressed like that, the cops wouldn't have bothered them. They have a right to look angry, the way the police hassle them every damn minute, she thought. If this weren't broad daylight, damn cops would probably drag those boys off somewhere and beat the hell out of them. Beat them like they did Rodney.

Esther felt her chest tighten as her mind replayed the infamous video and she envisioned the circle of white men in uniform, their batons swinging viciously against the black man cowering on the ground at their feet. She let the money fall on the counter as her hands began to shake above the pile of bills. For a moment, she wanted to do what she'd felt like doing only five months earlier. When she heard the not guilty verdict in April and saw those four grinning white faces on her television screen, she'd wanted to smash them and anyone who looked like them. And now here it was September, and she still felt so overcome with rage that she couldn't breathe.

White folks.

'Whatsa matter, Esther?' One glance across the street and Hector knew precisely what was bothering Esther, but it was after five o'clock. He wanted to go home.

Esther looked at him without appearing to understand what he was saying.

Hector brushed his thin black mustache with his index finger, a distracted, nervous gesture. He moved closer to his boss. 'You look very angry.' His Salvadoran accent made his words soft and musical.

Esther closed her eyes, trying to calm herself by forcing the air in and out of her lungs. When she looked through the window again, the policemen were gone and the black boys were swaggering down the street, their hard lopsided gait made up of equal parts youthful bravado and simmering rage. The setting sun's rays glinting off the large picture windows of the neighboring skyscrapers flashed and flickered like the conflagration that had raged in parts of the city five months earlier. But this time the flames were inside

Esther's head, and the truth was, she didn't know how to extinguish them.

'I'm okay,' she said. She shook her head quickly, as if the anger she felt was just so much soot caught up in her hair, then she smiled quickly at Hector. 'Let's tally this again and see if we can get you in balance.' Work always soothed Esther. Her efficient fingers flipped through the bills. As she counted rapidly and accurately, she felt herself calming down. 'We'll find it,' she said, her head bent over the money as Hector hovered above her. Tellers were always out of balance. There was often missing money to be accounted for. For Esther, discovering the error was as exhilarating as working a challenging crossword puzzle. The reward was in the completion.

But determined as she was to focus only on the money, her anger seemed to seep inside her fingers, knotting them like ropes. In frustration, she yanked each bill from the pile and slammed it down on the counter: *nine hundred, ten hundred, eleven hundred* . . .

'Are you still here?'

Hector and Esther looked up simultaneously at Mallory Post. She smiled at them both, but the longer she looked at Esther, the fainter her smile became, until at last it disappeared. Esther's frown was like a flashing yellow light. Seeing the anger in Esther's eyes, the thirty-six-year-old white woman hesitated, then, almost involuntarily, took two steps backward. But I haven't done anything, she thought.

Esther could see the warmth in Mallory's eyes, could feel the sticky Valley Girl sweetness radiating from her. She looked in her face and saw an easy childhood: all smiles and lemonade and green lights. Her mind drifted; she thought of her own Chicago youth and the daily drive to the very white North Side, to a place where ivy clung to bricks and old traditions died hard deaths. 'You children are going to have opportunities your father and I never had,' her mother had promised her and her brother.

Facing Mallory, she thought of the girls at the private school, the ones who didn't give her the silent treatment or steal her homework that first hard year. She remembered the ones who were always full of friendly curiosity and wide smiles like Mallory's. Every time she opened her mouth to speak, a look of amazement crossed their faces. In the schoolyard one day, a girl had asked her, 'Can you sing like Diana Ross?'

She had trembled in front of that pale child, not knowing what to say. Only when Esther saw her walk away did the venomous retorts begin to gather in her mind. They gathered for years. Now, as she faced Mallory, the hateful accumulation was overflowing inside her.

Blazing dark-brown eyes glared angrily into pale-gray ones. Esther didn't know why, but just looking at Mallory intensified her anger. The women's contrasting moods only underscored their physical differences. Esther was tall, with heavy breasts, slim hips, a behind that jutted out into a rounded curve, and long, muscular legs. Tina Turner legs. She was a voluptuous Beauty of the Week, more suited for a red rhinestone string bikini in the centerfold of *Jet* than for a bank. Standing next to Mallory, the dark-skinned woman seemed strong, and even her clothes – the carefully blended ensemble of Anne Klein II skirt, Ellen Tracy jacket, and Jones New York silk blouse, the plain black Ferragamo pumps with leather soft as a baby's bottom – made her look coordinated and powerful.

Esther was a woman whose beauty hinged on her state of mind: the happier she felt, the prettier she became. Under certain circumstances, her face took on a look of incandescent radiance, but at that moment, her smooth cocoa-colored skin seemed dull. Her pleasant round face, which usually reflected carefully monitored professional congeniality, was filled with tension. The large eyes that stared into Mallory's weren't bright and clear but brimmed with hostility. Her full lips, so beautiful when they were smiling, were bunched into a puffy protrusion. And Esther's short, dark hair, usually meticulously coiffed and painfully perfect, seemed violently disheveled now, as though a ferocious wind had blown through it.

Just looking at Esther's wild hair, Mallory self-consciously patted her own straight mane; it was dyed the color of wheat and just grazed her shoulders. From time to time she considered going back to her natural brown shade, but she thought the blond brought out the color of her eyes. Besides, the decision to tint her hair had been hers alone, and she equated being blond with being in control. It was the feeling she most often craved, especially now, as she felt the heat of Esther's unseasonable anger, flickering like a flame between them.

Mallory's face was narrow, and her nose and lips were thin, giving her a delicate prettiness, an aura of fragility. Of medium height, she had dieted herself to the kind of anorexic slenderness seen on Beverly Hills mannequins. Except for the Clinique blush she wore, Mallory's skin was the palest of ivory, the result of both her self-imposed exile from the sun and the temporary trepidation she felt looking into her co-worker's bitter eyes. Had she done anything to offend Esther? she wondered uneasily. She felt at fault somehow, although she couldn't for the life of her figure out what she might have done to upset her colleague so.

'Hello, Mallory,' Esther said slowly. Her face assumed a calm, pleasant air; her words, once again, stood at attention. The change was so abrupt and dramatic, it was almost as though she'd become someone else. She shook her hair a little, and every curl fell into place. 'Hector is out of balance. Exactly one hundred dollars is missing,' Esther said finally. 'You do know Hector, don't you?'

Mallory nodded. 'Hi, Hector.'

The bank teller gave a slight nod. 'How are you?' he asked softly. He took a deep breath and looked into Mallory's eyes and then immediately looked away. He'd never been introduced to the white woman formally, although sometimes they said hello to each other. Mallory was a commercial loan officer. Hector rarely had contact with people from her department, although he knew that the lenders were considered far more important than tellers or anyone in operations, even his boss. Standing next to the slender white woman, he thought of his homeland and how the poor never dared to look the important people in their eyes, especially when they begged them for money. Some things never changed: in El Salvador as in Los Angeles, the important people were usually blancos.

'I have to start interviewing for a new teller next week,' Esther was saying in impeccable news anchor English. 'We really need to get somebody else in here soon. Hector has practically been holding down the fort. He's really motivated, and he won't be in the tellers' cage for long.' She looked at him and smiled.

Hector's head was bent over the money, recounting it carefully, but Esther could see his lips curl up with pleasure as he listened to her words.

The black woman's hostility was evaporating. 'I found it, Esther,' Hector said suddenly. He held a hundred-dollar bill in one hand and the money tray in the other. 'It got stuck in the drawer.'

Esther let out a short chuckle and took the bill Hector handed her. In a way, she was disappointed. She loved being the one who found missing money. 'Thanks. I'll see you on Monday.'

'Good night,' Hector said, nodding so low to both women that he was almost bowing. Esther watched as he passed through the large glass front doors. Outside, a young

10

woman with brown skin and long black hair was waiting for him. Hector took her hand, and they walked down Spring Street together.

Mallory moved closer to the black woman. 'Didn't you tell me you had a date?' she asked.

Esther's face softened, and her full lips parted. Dimples the size of acorns accented her smile. Her teeth were large, white, and perfect. She'd forgotten that she'd told Mallory about her date. She usually tried not to talk about her personal life at work. 'It's a blind date, and if you knew my friend Vanessa, who arranged it, you'd know why I'm not in a hurry to get there,' she said, chuckling a little.

Mallory smiled eagerly, warmed by Esther's laughter. The woman has the most amazing mood swings, she thought. One minute she looks like she could eat nails, and the next, she's as sweet as can be. 'So go on your date, *honey*.'

'I just want to count this money one more time, *honey*.' Both women smiled at the private joke. Honey was what the branch manager, Charles Weber, had called all the women who worked for the bank until Esther began confronting him with a sweet: 'Are you talking to me? But you said "honey." That's not my name.' Mallory had followed suit, secretly angry with herself for having endured her boss's sexist indignities for so long.

'One hundred, two hundred . . .' Esther slowly, methodically thumbed through the bills, enjoying the slick feel of the money as well as the routine of settling the accounts.

'You don't trust Hector?' Mallory asked lightly.

'It's not that,' Esther said, without taking her eyes off the bills, without losing her place. 'It's just . . . it's just that I'm ultimately responsible.' She smiled with satisfaction, both at the knowledge that she was in charge and because of the pleasure she felt when she completed the tally and the numbers finally agreed.

Mallory watched Esther silently. She was somewhat in

awe, knowing that the black woman would have counted and recounted the money a hundred times and stayed all night if necessary to make the numbers come out right. Such devotion to duty was mystifying to her. So many times she'd wanted to tell Esther that she wouldn't earn brownie points for working when no one was watching her, but she never did, because she sensed that her comments wouldn't make a difference. Every once in a while, she had the inkling that Esther's seeming commitment to the bank wasn't anchored in dedication or even ambition; she was driven by darker forces, which Mallory couldn't fathom. She watched as Esther took the money into the large vault in the rear of the operations section. 'Now really,' she said when Esther returned, 'it's time to go home. Remember, I want to hear about your date on Monday.'

'Have a good weekend,' Esther said. As she rushed out the door, she thought of the inaugural meeting of Women in Banking nearly a year ago, when she and Mallory first met.

The white woman had stood up in the middle of the session, her expression intense and angry, to declare that the women present should demand seed money for their fledgling organization from the top male executives at their respective banks. 'They could think of it as out-of-court settlements of a class action suit charging them with creating and maintaining an industry-wide glass ceiling.' When the other women laughed nervously, her voice rose higher. 'I'm dead serious. We deserve the money.'

Esther was struck that night by the incongruity of Mallory's rage. Anger didn't seem to fit her. Her contorted mouth and loud voice were like a costume she'd put on. Her fury was opera, full of theatrics and falsetto notes that she sustained only until the curtain came down.

Mallory was easy enough to talk to, and they seemed always to end up sitting together during meetings. Once or twice they'd gone for coffee afterward. Still, Esther was surprised when immediately after the riots, the white woman approached her about coming to work at Angel City National. 'There's an opening for a regional operations manager, and I think you'd be perfect,' Mallory had told her.

Esther was appreciative but not interested. She held the same position at Federal already. Operations was the stepchild of the industry: the lowest pay, the least prestige. She wanted to get into lending, where the financial rewards were greater and where her M.B.A. would be respected. 'Look, Mallory, thanks for thinking about me, but I got into operations because when I made the switch from retail two years ago, it was the only available opening at Federal. But my goal has always been to become a lender, and the word I'm getting is that within the next year or so, Federal will let me make the switch. I'm not going to jeopardize that for a lateral move at Angel City.'

'Listen, I know you want lending, but there are some things you need to consider. First of all, I didn't just say operations manager, I said regional operations manager. The downtown branch is the regional center, the largest in the area. Four other banks report to us. The operations managers in all those banks would report to you, and in addition you would serve as branch operations manager for the downtown office. That's a hell of a lot more responsibility than you have now. If you do well, and I know you will, I think you'd be in operations a year at the most and then you could make the switch to lending. And I'm sure this position pays a lot more than you're making now.'

'Let me think about it,' Esther said.

Esther came to Angel City's downtown regional headquarters a month later. During the first four months she fired two tellers, streamlined the branches' safety-deposit box system, and improved employee morale. There were nights when she didn't get home until after ten o'clock, barely time enough to go to bed and begin the process all over again the next day.

'Listen,' Mallory said one evening, 'you don't have to put in such long hours. Nobody expects it.'

'I'm having fun,' was her reply. It was true. She always woke up eager to begin her day. The prospect of meeting with her staff, assigning tasks, delegating responsibilities, and attending to the thousand and one nitpicking details made her adrenaline flow.

But the reward she expected was slow in arriving. Esther's attempts to find a mentor who would help her make the transition to lending were just as frustrated as they were at her old bank. Her boss was out of the question. Charles Weber knew banking inside out, but Esther didn't want to risk the kind of close contact a mentor-protégé relationship called for. Charles was a better conduit for women who were willing to sleep their way to the top. Mallory gave her several leads, including the regional branch manager at the Valley headquarters branch, which included the area just north of the city, as well as several senior lenders in her own department. Esther dutifully and enthusiastically approached each one of the white men Mallory recommended. One by one, she took them all to lunch and, over an expensive meal, attempted to sell her intellect, her integrity, her financial acumen. Each nodded and seemed to listen intently, but after she made her follow-up calls and sent her thank-you notes, she never heard from a single one. They refused her subsequent invitations to lunch politely but firmly and avoided eye contact when she happened to meet them in the bank or on the elevator. Their message was clear: If Esther had a future in lending, they didn't see it and they weren't going to help her claim it.

'Vagina envy,' Mallory snapped, when Esther reported on her progress or, rather, its lack. 'They're such sexist pigs. These men are so goddamned intimidated by women. God,

14

it's just amazing.' Mallory's face turned a deep shade of pink, and she flailed her hands in exasperation. 'That's why women need to own our own banks and businesses. The old boy network is still in control.'

Esther nodded as Mallory's flimsy operatic anger puffed out her cheeks and hardened her eyes. Yes, the old boys are sexist pigs, she agreed. But did this little Valley Girl really think sexism was her only problem?

'What do you expect?' her brother Stanley, a lawyer in an all-black firm in San Diego, said when she called for his advice. 'Do you expect white people to help black folks get more power? Shi-it. They don't want you there in the first place. I hope you know that.'

'Well, it's like we always told you: you have to work twice as hard as white folks to get half as far,' her mother said when her parents called from Chicago. That credo of upwardly mobile Negroes had permeated her childhood, along with 'Lift Every Voice and Sing' and the Twenty-third Psalm. Hearing the words again, Esther realized both how powerfully they were pressed into her subconscious and how little control she had over the toll they took on her life. 'After all, you're qualified. Your father and I did our best to help prepare you and your brother. You're not some affirmative action reject. Now, if you want to become a lender, you just have to outwork them, that's all there is to it.'

Listening to her mother, Esther recalled the ball of fire she'd always been. It was her mother who announced one night at the dinner table that she thought it would be a good idea for her and her husband to go to college. 'Your daddy just doesn't realize what he's capable of,' her mother used to whisper to her. She got the applications from Chicago State, filled them out, and, despite his protests, dragged her husband along, until one day, to his great surprise, he began getting better grades than his wife. He eventually went to law school and passed the Illinois bar the first time he took the test. For eight years, her mother and her father had worked full-time jobs and attended classes at night. Esther smiled to herself. Her mother thought hard work was the answer to most of life's dilemmas.

'Listen,' her mother continued, switching to her chirpy voice, 'have you started redecorating your house yet? I've clipped some pictures from *House Beautiful* that I want you to think about for your living room.'

'Okay, Mom.'

'And, sweetheart, have you met any nice professional men? I— '

'Anna, hush,' said her father on the extension phone.

'Who you telling to hush?' her mother snapped back good-naturedly. 'Esther, you need to get out. Join some coed organizations. Join a church. Go where the men are.'

'You finished?' her father muttered. A lawyer and a brass-tacks pragmatist who believed that for every problem there was a peremptory solution that could be outlined in definable steps, he'd been clearing his throat repeatedly. It was the noise he always made when he was deep in contemplation. Esther could see him stroking his tiny pointed goatee. The image made her smile. 'Didn't you say your human resources person was a black woman? It's her job to match people with jobs. Give her a call. She may be able to suggest something.'

Esther had followed her father's advice, and now, as she rushed into Patti's, a small, popular restaurant near the city's music center, she peered around the dim room, searching for Michele Coleman. She saw her sitting in the front, near the bar. 'Sorry I'm late,' she said as she sat down. 'One of the tellers was out of balance.'

'No problem,' Michele said. She was a good-looking woman in her late forties, slightly overweight but still very

16

attractive. 'I'm hearing good things about you. You've really turned that department around, you know that? People are talking.'

Esther smiled. 'Thank you. I'm enjoying the job a lot. A lot . . .'

'But . . .' the older woman said.

'But I want to go into lending.' Esther blurted out the words, then described her frustration in seeking a mentor, while Michele nodded sympathetically and sipped her bourbon. ' . . . so I seem to be drawing a blank, and I thought you might be able to point me in the right direction, or at least tell me where I'm going wrong.'

'Listen,' Michele said, setting her empty glass on the table. 'I have no wisdom to give you, Esther. You and I are the highest-ranking black people at this branch, and before you came, I was in the trenches alone. Some of the old guard just aren't thrilled about either one of us being here.' She laughed softly. 'See, when white folks reach what they consider to be their mountaintop, they don't want to look over and see us. How can they have achieved as much as they think they have if they look up and see some black folks there doing the same thing? The neighborhood can't be that good if we're there. The country club can't be that exclusive. And my God, if one of us has the same job, well, they must not be as smart as they think they are. They're becoming schizophrenic because the Japanese outperform them. They will lose it completely if they have to believe that you or I can do the same things they can.' Her eyes darted around the room, and then she leaned in so close that Esther could see where her gray roots needed a touch-up. 'You did not hear this from me,' Michele said, her eyes glazing over a little bit. She whispered softly: 'The scuttlebutt is that there are going to be some changes pretty soon. The Community Reinvestment Act folks have been breathing down Angel City's neck since the riots. The regulators are saying that the bank isn't investing enough in South-Central and the East Side, which we know is true. Any black person or Latino who asks for a loan just gets his feelings hurt. Kirk and Mallory and the rest of the white lenders always find a reason to turn them down. Always.'

'Mallory?'

'Yes, Mallory. There isn't one person of color in her entire loan portfolio. Maybe some Asians, but you know they consider them honorary white folks. Anyway, Preston Sinclair is feeling the heat. He's going to have to do something to get the regulators off his back. The man does not like bad press. He plans to make Angel City look more like America, if you get my drift, which may be beneficial to you. In the next six months or so, somebody may come on board who is willing to bring you along. Just wait it out, that's my advice.'

Esther nodded silently, not commenting on Michele's analysis of the loan department's casual racism. She didn't want to admit to herself that she felt hurt that the black woman thought of Mallory as one of the main perpetrators.

Michele's words hadn't cheered her, but as she walked from the restaurant to the parking lot, Esther still had hope, only now she pinned it on the corporate largesse emanating from the thirty-fourth floor. If Preston Sinclair was going to institute change, she just prayed that he would do it soon. Regardless, she was going to find a financial chieftain who would not care that she was black or a woman, who would be her mentor, take her under his wing, and guide her right into lending. One day she would put together the deals and approve black folks' loans, so that they could own a piece of L.A. If she had to work harder, well, she'd been doing that all her life.

Crossing Spring Street, Esther felt a full blast of dry September heat. The air smelled hot and musty, like a stale casserole reheated again and again. In the distance, a brown

18

ring of smog had settled over the city, stuck halfway between the San Gabriel Mountains, to the north, and the sky, hovering like a grimy halo. The temperature had been in the upper nineties and low hundreds for the last three weeks. The night before, on channel 7's eleven o'clock news, the preternaturally tanned weatherman had predicted another blistering weekend and advised children, old people, and those with respiratory problems – was there anybody who didn't fill one of these categories? – to stay indoors. The city looked as parched and dust-bowl dry as the midwestern farm towns so many of the older white transplants had fled during the Depression. The grass on vacant plots was like straw, and in the hills north of the city, fires had been raging on and off for days.

Esther sighed as she reached the edge of the parking lot; she could feel a trickle of sweat rolling down her back. There had been no rain since April, and sometimes the heat and drought felt as deliberate as a punishment, as if the sky above the city were purposely withholding the water that would wash away what was floating in the foul air. Nervous residents were mindful that the recent big earthquakes had occurred during dry, hot weather – the Shake and Bake, people called it. She was from the South Side of Chicago, born and bred in a place where all hell could and did break loose but the ground, at least, stayed put. In Los Angeles, she had learned that she couldn't even trust the earth beneath her feet. All she could do was memorize the emergency measures: stay calm; check for injuries; clean up dangerous spills. It was good advice for all disasters.

The strain of standing in the heat for even a short while showed on the faces of the people waiting for their cars in the parking lot. There was a uniform look of irritation and exhaustion in the eyes of the men and women assembled around the attendant's booth, as if the drought, the Santa Ana, and the fires had taken up residence in their minds.

19

Esther got in line behind a short Asian woman and two white men who were waiting at the small red booth in the center of the lot for Luis, a thin, neat man in a blue uniform, to give them their car keys. One of the men waved at her, and Esther smiled back, recognizing him as someone who worked in her building. She'd shared a table with him once at lunch when Patti's had been crowded. She thought his name was Dan.

Standing there, nodding toward Dan, she mentally immersed herself in the cool water of her swimming pool. The pool was what she liked best about the house she'd recently purchased. For the last few weeks she'd had a dip almost every day after work. Looking at her watch, Esther realized that she wouldn't have time to swim and then do her hair. Once her hair got wet, she'd have to wash, blow dry, and curl it in order for her to look presentable. She'd soak in a cool bath instead, she decided. That would feel good. She'd sip fresh lemonade – there was a lemon tree in her backyard – while she sat in the tub. Esther tried to think of the cool drink and relaxing bath and not of the evening that lay ahead. She wasn't going to waste her emotions on a man she hadn't met, and as she stood in line she assiduously repressed forbidden thoughts of happily ever after.

'Can you believe this weather?' Dan said, stepping out of line to talk with her. He had a booming, jovial voice and sounded like Willard the weatherman. The Asian woman smiled and moved to the right, so that Dan had an unobstructed view of Esther. 'And the air conditioner in my car is on the blink.'

'Oh, no,' Esther said sympathetically.

'I've got to drive all the way to Moreno Valley in this heat. That's at least an hour's—'

Esther didn't know whether it was the unmistakable apprehension that suddenly filled the man's eyes as he looked beyond her, his pronounced intake of breath, or the awful engulfing odor that made her spin around.

'You looking good, sistuh.' The voice was as loud and insistent as a boom box with the volume turned all the way up. Months-old funk and stale urine clung to the hot, dry air between her and the black man who stood grinning at her a few feet away from the parking attendant's cubicle. She could hear the shuffle of feet as the rest of the people in line moved away from the two of them. Without looking up, Esther knew that the distance that abruptly loomed between her and the other commuters was something to be measured not in inches but in fear. The man's hand was stretched out. She could see the dirt caked underneath his curved fingernails, the filth embedded in the lines of his palms. She looked at his face; beneath the grime, he was a nice-looking man. He resembled her uncle Donald, her father's brother; they had the same hopeful smiles. 'Could you spare me . . .'

Esther looked around and saw that her former lunch partner was staring at the two of them, although when she glanced in his direction, he looked away. Shame slammed into her belly like a punch. Why did the man standing before her have to be black, stinking, and in need in front of people who were none of the above? Talking that 'sister' mess! Esther glared at the homeless man, wanting him to disappear. Then she looked at Dan, who had stepped out of line and was steadily backing up as close to the parking attendant's booth as he possibly could. As he moved away, he pulled his hands through his thinning hair in a compulsive and repetitive gesture that made him look helpless and frantic. Like a brush fire picking up momentum, Esther's anger spun away from the derelict and burned toward the white man, whose eyes were wide and filled with fear. She had a sudden urge to slap Dan's face. Did he really think the filthy, pitiful creature standing in front of them intended to

21

do him harm? Jesus Christ! She felt drained and tired. The air was unbearable. 'Sister . . .'

'Here,' she said, handing the man a dollar. She glared at the people around her and then, almost defiantly, gave him another.

'God bless you, sistuh,' the man said. For the first time, Esther noticed that below his left eye was a mark shaped like a cauliflower. He turned away before she could tell whether it was a scar or a birthmark. Esther watched the back of his tattered coat drag the ground as he disappeared down Spring Street.

'Poor guy,' Dan said to her, moving back in line after the vagrant had left. He shook his head and affected a sympathetic expression. 'Poor guy.'

His voice was weak, sounding like every parody of a white man that Richard Pryor or Eddie Murphy had ever done, a thin, nerdy voice, full of high SAT scores and devoid of soul. Without warning, the heat rose inside Esther again. Dan's face suddenly seemed a pale, featureless mask. What the hell do you know about it? she thought. Take your scared white ass back to Moreno Valley.

The leather seats of Esther's silver BMW were burning up. She could feel the heat coming through her skirt, scorching her thighs, and as she headed onto the Harbor Freeway, going south, the initial hot blast from the air conditioner only made her sweat more. Still, she could feel herself loosening up, molting the skin of her North Side corporate persona, slipping into the comfort of her South Side soul.

The voice of Luther Vandross blared out from KJLH. Esther sang along, not caring that the 110's lanes were clogged with cars. She inched along for a mile or two, unable to pick up enough speed to make the air conditioner spew out anything other than more heat. The news came on after Luther finished. 'Meanwhile, campaigning in Indiana, Democratic presidential nominee Bill Clinton promises to make health reform his number one priority.' The reporter's intonation gave way to the candidate's southern twang, capsulized in a sound bite. 'What America needs . . .' She switched her dial to V103 and tried to let the droning beat of the rappers make her forget that she was hot and stuck in traffic, but after she heard the word 'ho' for the third time and 'bitch' for the second, she turned the music off.

Esther maneuvered her way into the far right lane and turned onto the Santa Monica Freeway, heading west. The traffic was lighter, and she managed to pick up speed; the air conditioner finally kicked in. After a few miles, she got off at the Cranston Boulevard exit. The broad avenue that ran between two black-middle-class bedroom communities was still scarred from the violence of April 29. It was a wide, rough-around-the-edges street, nowhere near as tony as even the mid-city part of Wilshire Boulevard, let alone the Beverly Hills stretch, but it had a proud, self-sufficient air. The neighborhood had been all white up until the late fifties, when upwardly mobile Negroes broke through the borders of South-Central and Watts and began moving into the area en masse. Cranston needed a good sweeping in some places; in others it was spotless. The shops along the route were mostly mom-and-pop businesses, along with fast-food restaurants and some chain stores. There were one or two car dealerships and several unoccupied buildings that used to house similar businesses before the economic slump shut them down. As Esther drove along the boulevard, she tried not to look at the hulls of burned-out stores or the razed earth where the buildings had finally been torn down. Funny what had survived and what hadn't. Not one of the six wig stores that lined the avenue had been touched, much to Esther's chagrin. She had dreamed of torching them herself long before the unrest; they ghetto-ized the neighborhood. She passed by the site of the chain drugstore where she used to have her prescriptions filled.

Gone. Less than a mile away, another from the same chain had been destroyed, as well as an Auto Track on the same lot. There were stores along the street that had suffered only a few broken windows. Most were untouched. The two closest 7-Elevens, one on Slauson and the other on La Cienega, had been burned but were on their way back. Already the new prefabricated structures were almost complete, and bright signs attached to the wire fence proclaimed: WE'RE COMING BACK! as though the occupants had moved to Miami and then changed their minds. In all the madness of April 29, none of the recreational facilities had been touched. Neither the bowling alley nor the theater had been disturbed. The new mall, the jewel of the neighborhood, survived unscathed and as Esther passed by it, she felt both anger and resignation. The two department stores offered goods that were mostly inferior to the quality sold in similar stores on the West Side, but bad as they were, the neighborhood needed them. Housing prices had plummeted in most of the city, and if the mall became a casualty, values would decline even more in the neighborhoods surrounding Cranston. A huge wrought-iron fence bordered the mall; many people believed it had deterred looters and as businesses began to rebuild, some were erecting gates as a precautionary measure against future outbreaks of civil unrest. The reasoning was that steel was an adequate barrier to rage.

Rage was what had greeted Esther that day in late April when she returned home from work. As she turned off the freeway, a bottle grazed her front tire. She looked up, and a crowd was gathering along the sidewalk. The space around them seemed to vibrate in wavy lines, like the air surrounding a mirage. But the people were real. Their screams of anger, their cries of fear, were real. And so were the fires that consumed building after building. Even after she got home and shut all her doors and drew the curtains, she could still smell the smoke. The sirens screamed all through the night.

Now, as Esther waited at the red light, the air around Cranston was calm. Two blocks before her turn, she pulled into a strip mall. The entire parking lot was enveloped in the sweet doughy scent of freshly baked goods that came from Diamond Donuts. Esther parked right in front of the small shop.

Inside the crowded store, three old black men were sitting at a table in the corner. Every time Esther came into the store, they were huddled there, sipping coffee, and conversing in loud, animated voices.

A plump Korean woman who looked to be in her fifties was leaning over the counter, listening to the men. On the wall behind her was a panoply of eight-by-ten glossies, the same collection of stars and wannabes that adorned the walls of half the cleaners, doughnut shops, and barbershops in the city. Dolly Parton. Cher. Prince. All were autographed to Hyun and Henry, in the same scratchy handwriting. Below the photographs on the floor, in a solitary corner, was a small table covered with a red cloth. A bowl of fruit, a plate of doughnuts, and two burning candles were placed on it. The owner straightened up when she saw Esther. 'How are you today? May I help you?' She pronounced each word very carefully and slowly, then smiled in the same painstaking manner. Her head bobbed just slightly as she spoke, as though the gesture was an unwanted habit she couldn't break.

'Three apple bran muffins,' Esther said, pointing to the ones she wanted in the case. The woman plucked them out with a pair of steel tongs and dropped them into a small white paper bag, which she handed to Esther. Esther gave her a five-dollar bill.

'Thank you,' the Korean woman said. Her polite acknowledgment gave no hint that she distinguished Esther from any of her other customers. There was no real warmth in the smile that never left her face, just the desire not to offend. The boarded-up window behind her was a constant reminder that she was in a new land with new rules. She placed the change carefully in the palm of Esther's outstretched hand, not on the counter, as she would have in Seoul. 'You have nice day – evening,' she corrected herself quickly, then put her hand up to her mouth and giggled.

A red Buick was blocking her in and Esther had to wait a few moments before the driver moved his car. The lot was so crowded she had to inch her way onto Cranston. Just before Esther reached her turn, a huge billboard loomed into view. The background was a vivid, oceanic blue. The picture of a premature black baby with bark-colored toothpick arms and legs, his shrunken torso filled with needles and tubes, seemed to leap out at her. His tortured body, so obviously struggling to stay alive, was a warning to pregnant drug addicts, but the caption's caution seemed aimed at the beleaguered city: HE COULDN'T TAKE THE HIT.

Esther entered another world when she made a right turn up the hill. The area known as Park Crest was the center of black-middle-class life in Los Angeles, although some whites lived there still – mostly older people who, for whatever reasons, hadn't joined the exodus to the suburbs in the late fifties and early sixties. There was also a trickling in of younger whites: yuppies who had discovered the neighborhood after the *Gazette* did an article on it several years before. Esther left behind the littered boulevard and was surrounded by verdant hills, elegant Spanish stucco homes, and gardens filled with roses, impatiens, bougainvillea. Lemon and orange trees decorated the lawns, and the sweet scent of the fruit and flowers hovered in the air. Yet despite its pristine beauty, the neighborhood was on guard, like the rest of the city. The lawns that decorated each charming house were dotted with signs from various security companies – American Security, Westex, Home Security – all proclaiming the same bold warning: armed response. The signs were as much a reminder as the Mercedeses and BMWs that sat smugly inside each attached garage: the residents of Park Crest were people with something to lose.

As Esther's BMW climbed the hill to her own street, she passed retired neighbors: older black women mostly, who were watering their lawns. The kids from the end of the block were storming the wide street in a bicycle squadron. She began to feel cooler, lighter. She had looked at houses in other areas, but the sellers all seemed to want more money for far less house. She'd gone to an open house for a place on the West Side that wasn't bad, but she hadn't seen any black people on the block. The residents weren't rednecks but middle-class, fairly liberal whites, who might even have welcomed her, but when she tried to visualize herself having a barbecue and inviting the neighbors, she wondered how comfortable she would feel. She wanted to live in a place where she could be her South Side self.

Esther pressed the Genie button; the garage door opened, and she drove in. By the time the door came down she was already in her kitchen. Standing there, she was filled with exhilaration. Her own home! She could hear the washing machine and dryer going. The house smelled like Pine Sol. 'Lupe!' she called. Her housekeeper came on Fridays, and sometimes she stayed late. Esther walked upstairs to her bedroom.

'I'm here, Missy Esta,' Lupe answered. She was ironing in the smallest of the three bedrooms, her long black braid swinging every time she lifted the iron. She smiled, revealing a gold tooth.

Esther sighed. It was on the tip of her tongue to remind her housekeeper not to call her Missy, but she knew that the woman was uncomfortable with such informality. Instead, she pointed to her watch. It was after seven o'clock. 'Go home,' she said to Lupe, who immediately showed her the unironed clothes left in the basket.

'Next week,' Esther said. 'Oh, Lupe, wait a minute.' She reached inside the small closet and pulled out two shopping bags filled with outfits she no longer wore. 'Do you want these?'

Lupe didn't look inside. 'Thank you. Thank you,' she said, taking the bag. 'You very nice.' The dryer on the service porch next to the kitchen shuddered as it stopped, and the floor shook a little. Esther howled and jumped up with alarm. Lupe gazed at her in amazement.

'Missy Esta, you scare?'

'No. No. I . . . uh . . . Look at the clothes. See if you like them.'

Esther watched as the brown-skinned woman examined the skirts and pants and blouses. She remembered how, when she was little, her grandmother used to bring her bags of dresses and sweaters: hand-me-downs from the children of the white woman she worked for. Even though they were usually nice things, she recalled feeling embarrassed when she wore the old clothes of white children she didn't know. Now, standing in front of Lupe, she wondered what the woman really thought about accepting her used things. The words zigzagged through her mind in a guilty pattern: I have become Miss Ann.

But Lupe seemed pleased. 'Thank you much,' she said over and over, until Esther was embarrassed. She was anxious for her to go home. The woman her grandmother worked for would talk on the telephone and sip coffee or watch television while the black woman cleaned. 'Umphumphummph! Lazy heifer,' her grandmother would say, fuming even as she distributed the children's clothing her employer gave her. 'Doesn't even have the decency to go shopping while I scrub her nasty floors.' Esther didn't feel comfortable relaxing while someone else was cleaning her house.

After Lupe left, Esther made herself a pitcher of lemonade with lemons from her own tree, then poured herself a glass. She liked being in her house when it had just been cleaned. The Spanish stucco had been built in 1928 and still had the original mahogany floors and oak baseboards and trim. On Fridays the wood was polished to a dazzling sheen. For a moment, she leaned against the kitchen counter and enjoyed the beauty and fresh cleanliness of the room. Everyone who visited Esther was amazed to learn she'd been there only a few months. She completely organized the place the first week after she moved in. The books were on the shelves, the CDs in their case, and every picture was hung as though she'd lived there for years. Of course, the house needed to be modernized, she thought, as she stood in the old-fashioned kitchen. This is project number one, she decided. Esther looked at her watch again. She had to get ready.

Only when she was sitting in the tepid bubble bath that smelled like jasmine, sipping the rest of her lemonade, did thoughts of the impending date intrude. As she stretched out in the water, Esther allowed herself the luxury of hoping for the best. Suppose the man was fine? Suppose he was fine, tall, intelligent, successful, and ready to commit? What if they liked each other instantly and he was a great kisser and a wonderful lover? She could feel the soft mushies creeping up her spine. 'Stop that!' she told herself loudly as she stepped out of the tub.

After she dried herself, Esther stared at her nude body in the full-length mirror in her bedroom. Her dark skin glistened over her flat stomach and round behind, but Esther shook her head in dismay. Jesus, my butt is the size of New Mexico, she thought glumly. And my breasts! Elsie the Cow. *He* probably likes women the color of the inside of almonds, women with hair that cascades down their shoulders and blows in the wind, and with pert little titties that stand at attention. Why in the world had she let Vanessa arrange this fiasco? The thought, familiar and painful, filled her mind like a migraine she'd been expecting: He won't like me.

2

Esther was dressed in a navy-blue suit and low heels, pacing and fuming, by the time the bell rang. She'd been waiting for an hour. When she opened the door, Elizabeth Taylor's Passion was scenting the night air, and Vanessa Turner stood before her like a perfumed exotic bird.

'Hey, girl,' she said a little breathlessly, giving Esther a bright smile and a tight hug that immediately dissipated her friend's anger.

Vanessa didn't so much walk through the door as fly in, her long arms extended like wings, her fingers cupped to beat against the air, to grab onto anything that came her way and continue soaring. She was brightly dressed in orange, purple, yellow, and red, a long, flowing costume that was, as was the case with most of what Vanessa wore, unlike anything Esther had ever seen. Her skin was reddish brown, and she was tall and slim, with high cheekbones that seemed to be sculpted. Enormous gold hoops decorated her earlobes, and a waterfall of light-brown hair cascaded down her back. Esther felt as drab as a sparrow standing next to her. 'Now, don't be mad,' Vanessa said, before Esther could open her mouth. 'Charmaine took forever to tighten up this weave,' she said, patting her hair. Suddenly she let out a little squeal and jumped up and down several times.

'What? What?' Esther was already smiling in anticipation of whatever adventure Vanessa was about to describe.

'On Monday I'm auditioning for the love interest in Denzel's new movie.'

Esther laughed. Vanessa eyed her friend with the same cheerful, self-assured expression that had characterized her demeanor through three up-and-down years of auditions, callbacks, and rejections. She always carried herself like an actress who already had the gig. 'I'm ready for the big time,' is what Vanessa told her three years ago when she moved to Los Angeles from new York after costarring for eighteen months in a hit Broadway play. And although she'd resorted to temping on several occasions, Vanessa still moved under the aura of a true believer. She held fast to the dream that L.A. would deliver.

'I'm claiming this role,' she announced, still smiling. Esther laughed again. Vanessa claimed all the roles she tried out for. The ritual had something to do with karma or divine right or, maybe, both.

'Well, girlfriend, I hope you get it,' Esther said.

'Be all up in Denzel's arms. Chest to breast. Lips locked. Oh, God, I hope there's a nude scene.'

The two women laughed.

'Enough about that,' Vanessa said, peering at Esther. She began frowning. 'Why do you have on a suit? You're not going to work. Put on something else. Please. Please. Please.'

Esther followed Vanessa as she ran up the stairs to her friend's room and opened the closet. All the clothes were lined up in perfect color-coordinated order. She shook her head. 'Damn, you are the neatest heifer on the planet.' She flipped through several business suits in muted colors. 'Who dresses you? Nuns "R" Us? Where's the spandex? Where's your see-through stuff?' Vanessa asked. 'If I had your boobs, they would be on display, girlfriend. You hear me?' She looked at her friend again. 'You need to sport some cleavage.'

Esther didn't have anything transparent, but Vanessa was satisfied with an olive-green miniskirt and a matching jacket. An ivory bustier was revealing enough to earn her approving nod. 'There you go. If you got it, flaunt it. If you don't, wear ruffles. Now, where did I put my ruffles?' Vanessa giggled. She turned to Esther. 'At the end of this evening, you are going to be kissing my feet. This brother is fi-i-i – yi-i-ine. Matriculated at Mandingo Warrior High School. And he's a *nice* brother too. Unlike some reptiles, who shall remain anonymous.'

Esther was grateful that the doorbell rang, so that she didn't have to respond to the reference to Mitchell Harris. She knew that tonight's blind date was part of Vanessa's strategy to discourage her from getting back with him.

Esther could smell the Armani before she opened the door. The two men trooped in, one behind the other, and the taller one handed Esther a bottle of Chandon champagne. The shorter man gave Vanessa a hug.

'Watch the weave. Don't bend the weave,' Vanessa said. The taller man's mouth dropped open. 'Now, you didn't really think this was my hair, did you? Felton, I know you know better. Nobody has this much hair but that tramp Barbie Doll. Anyway. Esther, you know Felton. And this is your very own blind date, Rodney Simpson. Rodney, this is Esther Jackson.'

Esther stopped chuckling and smiled at Felton. She was about to extend her hand to Rodney and say hello, when Vanessa said, 'What do you think, Esther? Didn't I tell you that you were meeting the great-great-great-great-grandson of Kunte Kinte? Look at those lips. Oooh, he likes you too; I can tell.' Vanessa turned to Esther's date. 'I told you she was built.' She whirled around and faced Esther. 'He said you had to have big legs or he didn't want to meet you. Yeah, he's one of those body-parts men. Didn't ask nothing about your IQ. Here, hand me that bubbly. See,' Vanessa said, looking at Esther and nodding to Rodney, 'this Negro has class. Let's have a little toast before we get this party rolling. I'll get the glasses.' She bustled into the kitchen.

'I refuse to be embarrassed,' Esther said to Rodney and Felton.

'They know I'm a wild fool,' Vanessa shouted from the kitchen.

Esther shook her head and smiled. 'I'm glad to meet you, Rodney,' she said. 'Nice seeing you again, Felton. Won't you guys have a seat?'

The men sat down, and the silence in the room engulfed the three of them. Finally, Rodney said, 'You have a very nice place. Vanessa said you haven't been here too long.'

'Just three months.'

'You look really settled.'

And you look really good, with your little sweet Hershey bar self, Esther thought. Why was he staring at her like that? There was something wrong with her hair. She smiled, her fingers already inching toward her head. 'Excuse me,' she said.

She dashed into her bedroom and patted her hair. Looking in the mirror, she didn't see an elegant woman in an olive-green suit. She saw a skinny adolescent girl with more barrettes than braids, hair that no amount of greasing or pressing or coaxing could persuade to grow. Bad hair. Nappy hair. 'Got as much hair as dust on a jar,' the boy said that day as she strolled past the candy store. She was eleven, walking alone to buy a Baby Ruth, anticipating the sweetness of the chocolate in her mouth. She wore a red dress, she recalled, and a red hair ribbon carefully pinned to a tiny, tiny braid. The boy and his friends screamed with laughter, and she kept walking, looking straight in front of her, until everything, everyone around her was a blur. Even now she could feel the shame that stung her eyes when she walked by that screaming throng of schoolboys, trying to pretend that she didn't care.

A certain practised hardness stole into her eyes, dulling them a little, as Esther gave her hair a final pat and adjusted the collar of her silk shirt. When she looked into the mirror, the skinny girl was gone and in her place stood a woman layered in Donna Karan, bathed in Carolina Herrera, shielded by fourteen-carat-gold earrings and a diamond tennis bracelet, a protected woman, totally insulated.

Esther returned to the living room just as Vanessa came in with a tray holding four glasses of champagne and a crystal bowl filled with potato chips. 'This child is so organized. Everything is in its proper place. It's disgusting,' she said, grinning at Esther.

'Why can't you copy your friend?' Felton said with a laugh.

'Divas do not clean house, baby,' she said, passing out the wine. She lifted her glass. 'To love,' she said.

'Aren't you rushing things?' Felton asked.

'I'm talking about you and me.'

'Aren't you rushing things?' he repeated.

Vanessa pouted. 'Dis me in front of my friends. Well, I love me, even if nobody else does. And if you don't want to toast to love, toast to my residuals.' She pulled a check for $437.53 from her purse and held it up. 'To Kellogg's Corn Flakes,' she said, kissing the check.

The two couples laughed and then clinked their glasses together. 'Was that the cereal commercial you did last year?' Esther asked.

'Yep. Corn flakes have been the cash cow of my career. I wish I could get another gig like that. Soon.'

As Esther leaned over to toast Rodney, she got a better look at him. He was good-looking: muscular, nice fade haircut, thick mustache, straight white teeth, big juicy lips. And she had a feeling that what was hiding under his jacket was the basketball butt of Life.

Lawdhamercy.

Rodney opened the door of the big black 300 Mercedes for her, and she slid into the passenger's seat beside him. Esther closed her eyes and inhaled the odor of the expensive leather interior. It smelled new. She wondered what kind of work he did. They could take some trips together, maybe drive up the coast to Carmel. Slow down, she told herself. Slow down. But the soft mushies were rising up inside her, swimming haphazardly toward her heart like intoxicated sea creatures. Sitting next to Rodney, her nostrils filled with new leather and Armani, she could feel all the pent-up frustrations and loneliness inside her. Why couldn't he be the one? Was that so much to ask for? She stared at Rodney as he drove. Slow down, she thought, but she couldn't. If he had a house, which he probably did, they could sell both of their homes and get a bigger place, one of those really huge mansions in Hancock Park. Or a little mansion. She could feel a soft, pulsating warmth crowding under her left breast. She sighed and yielded completely. One thing was sure: their children would be beautiful.

The restaurant was in the marina, and the line seemed to stretch to the Valley. After adding their names to the waiting list, the two couples found an empty table in the bar and ordered a carafe of Chablis. 'So where are you from? Originally, I mean,' Rodney asked her.

'Chicago,' Esther said.

'The Windy City. Traded all that snow for the balmy breezes?' He grinned at her.

'I traded all that snow for earthquakes, Santa Anas, smog, drought, torrential rains . . .' They both laughed. 'Where are you from?'

'Watts.'

'A native.' Well, he must have pulled himself up by his bootstraps. The thought was comforting.

'I'm a rare breed.'

'I guess last April must have been like déjà vu for you?'

'You mean the riots?'

'The rebellion,' Felton said, bending his head away from Vanessa and toward Rodney. 'It was a rebellion, man.'

'Whatever. The end result was the same. It tore up the neighborhood.' He turned back to Esther. 'Yeah, it was déjà vu. And I hate to sound pessimistic, but the same thing is going to happen to South-Central that happened to Watts.'

'What's that?'

'Nothing, that's what. A lot of promises and then nothing. Rebuild L.A. Shi-it. Excuse my language. That's a joke. White folks are going to come in, pass out the money to other white folks, give a little to the Asians, give two cents to the Latinos, and we'll end up with nothing. Again. Because the banks aren't going to loan us money to start businesses in our own communities, and that's what it's going to take to turn this mess around. And I don't care who gets in next – Bush, Clinton, or that little sawed-off sucker from Texas. If they're not talking about fostering economic development in the black community, they better get used to America being on fire.' He signed and looked at Esther. 'Look, I don't feel like talking about this tonight. Makes me too mad. Felton tells me you work in a bank. What do you do?'

'I'm the regional operations manager,' she said, trying not to sound as smug as she felt. But she was proud. Even if she wasn't in lending, how many black women were regional anything? 'What do you do, Rodney?'

'I drive a bus for the city.'

'Oh.' Esther felt a shiver under her left breast and then an empty numbness. Whatever magic the evening had possessed suddenly evaporated. A bus driver. 'Oh.' She could feel her smile cracking her face into two even parts.

'What are you two whispering about? Rodney, are you getting fresh?' Vanessa leaned across the table.

'Fresh as I can.' He grinned at Esther and reached for her

hand. Esther leaned away from him and placed her two fists in her lap.

By the time the waitress showed them to their table, there were definite gaps in Esther and Rodney's conversation; by the time dinner was served, they were barely speaking.

'What's up with you?' Vanessa hissed when the two women went to the bathroom after they ordered coffee.

'Not a love connection,' Esther said.

'I don't need to be Chuck Woolery to see that. You can still talk to him.'

'We really don't have anything to talk about. Listen, why don't we cut this short?'

Half an hour later, Esther was lying in bed, switching the channels on her television listlessly. She settled on a rebroadcast of the ten o'clock news. The Latina coanchor's face was somber as she described the kidnap-rape-murder of a thirteen-year-old from Pasadena. There was a picture of a blond girl with an angelic face, followed by live footage of her distraught parents. Then the Latina announced that two suspects had been arrested. Lord, please don't let these fools be black, Esther said to herself. She held her breath as an on-the-scene reporter who was standing outside the county jail described the men arrested. Finally, she saw the two suspects as they were led into the jail. They were both white. Thank you, Jesus, Esther thought, changing the channel. The telephone rang just as she was about to settle into *Live at the Apollo*.

'You gotta answer a few questions, girlfriend,' she heard Vanessa say. 'Now, didn't you think Rodney was fine? Answer me that.'

'Yes.'

'Wasn't he nice? Well-mannered? What the hell is your problem?'

Esther sat up and propped her pillow against the headboard. 'He was fine. He had nice manners. Good conversationalist. I'm just not interested.' Saying those last words made her feel safe, strong, and protected.

'What! What are you talking about? Why not?'

'Vanessa, the guy drives a bus.' Her voice was businesslike.

'Wha-a-at!?'

'No romance without finance: that's my motto.'

'You've got to be kidding. That's your priority for making a relationship work? He has to make a lot of money?' Vanessa was almost shouting.

'Hey, he didn't want to talk to me unless I had big legs. Don't lecture me on my values. Rodney's not what I'm looking for,' Esther said.

'And just who are you looking for? Mitchell Harris? King of the Assholes?'

'What's wrong with wanting to be with someone who has goals and aspirations that are similar to mine? Listen, I've dated Mr. Blue Collar. I've dated Mr. Starving Actor. I've even dated Mr. Unemployed. I'm sorry, the Jackson University for the Remedial Training of Brothers with Potential is closed. No more mismatches. This isn't about Mitchell Harris. It's about me knowing what I want.'

'Bullshit. This is all about Mitchell the M.D. You saw that big-ass house and long car, all those credit cards, and swore you were in love. The only problem is he has fifty eleven other women.'

Esther winced. 'Vanessa, I did not like Mitchell *just* because he had money,' she said wearily. 'I really cared about him, and I think you know that.'

'And I think I know where all your caring for him got you. You're not even going to give Rodney a chance?' She groaned. 'You're so-o-o bourgie.' She started chuckling. 'I mean, I guess the projects where you grew up had gold numbers over the door, huh? I bet your great-great-granddaddy worked *inside* Tara. I bet your high-yella

grandmama did the hootchy-kootchy in the Cotton Club.'
They both laughed.

'It's not a matter of being bourgie. I know what I want,
and I'm not lowering my standards. Period.' My standards,
Esther thought proudly. Mine.

'Esther, you're sitting up in the bed, all by yourself, about
to plug in your hand-held vibrator, talking about you're not
dating a man who is fine, has good sense, and likes your
Anne Klein-wearing ass, just because he drives a bus? How
do you know he's not going to law school at night?'

'Even if he is, he still has to play catch-up. I want a
man who is matching me or doing better, preferably much
better.'

'I mean, okay, you don't have to marry the man, but
shoot, you could have some fun. Fun, Esther. It's what
you're supposed to have when you leave the white folks at
the bank.'

'You're about fun. I'm about business. No romance without finance.'

Esther could imagine Vanessa shaking her head. 'You are
hard on the brothers. Did you ever think that you might
enjoy letting the right person catch up to you?'

'The right person is way ahead of me. And this conversation is over.'

'Well, I guess I'm scared of you.'

The two women were silent. 'I wonder how Rodney
affords that Benz,' Esther said.

'He must be doing a lot of overtime.'

'Or else he's one of the founding members of the Men
Who Sleep in Their Automobiles Society.'

'That's cold.'

After Esther hung up, she tried to fall asleep, but she
couldn't turn off her mind; she kept thinking about Mitchell
Harris, with his soft brown skin and soft brown eyes, with
his strong dark hands. Esther could feel the soft mushies

rising up in her for the third time that evening. She closed her eyes. She didn't want to think about Mitchell Harris, or the five on-again, off-again years they'd had together. Years filled with other women, broken dates, and fractured promises. Yo-yo love, Vanessa called it. 'The relationship is all in your head,' her friend told her again and again. Each time she said it, Esther would get furious. She'd hang up the phone or stomp out of her girlfriend's apartment. But sometimes, when she was alone, she'd find herself on the verge of admitting that sleeping with Mitchell wasn't the same as having a relationship. Now she was finally resigned to a life without him. She hadn't heard from the man in at least six months, probably more. The last time they'd been together was when they bumped into each other at a party and he ended up going home with her. When she woke up alone, she swore on her grandmother's grave that she'd never see him again.

She might not have Mitchell, but whoever she did hook up with had to have as much going for him as she did, and that meant having two degrees, owning a home, having money in the bank and future plans. She didn't give a damn what Vanessa said: Bus drivers need not apply.

Esther turned off the television and slid under the covers. She was tired; her muscles ached as though she'd been in a fistfight. No romance without finance, she whispered to herself over and over. When she placed her head against the pillow, she felt relief as sweet as a first tear.

3

'Can't you stay a little longer?' Mallory whispered, pressing her head into Hayden Lear's bare back. She was so accustomed to begging him for more of his time that she felt unashamed that the hope that flowed inside her was stronger than her pride.

Hayden sat on the edge of her bed, smoking a cigarette. His bony shoulders were hunched, and his brows came together in consternation. He didn't answer her question. He never did. She circled Hayden's chest with her thin, girlish arms. 'Please,' she said. The word echoed in her head as though they were going through tunnels, passing through steel and years. She rubbed his arms and groped for his hands. The hard circle of gold that he wore pressed against her fingers.

Hayden stood up. 'Don't be a child,' he said. He turned away. He never looked at her when she begged him to stay.

Mallory lay back down on her bed and stared up at the ceiling. She could hear Hayden dressing quickly. She smelled his cigarette; the smoke would linger long after he'd gone. She felt his lips as they brushed across her cheek. They were dry and rigid. 'I'll call you,' he said.

'C'mon! Move it!' Mallory muttered as she leaned her head outside the window of her Lexus, trying to determine just what was holding up the Monday morning traffic, which was going south on the 101. Her words were soon swallowed up by louder, more profane shouts, which whizzed around the line of stalled cars like bullets. Vibrating through the thick, heavy air were the flat, nasal radio voices of 'Ken and Bob,' the streety bantering of the black cohosts on V103, and the loudest salsa Mallory had ever heard in her life. The music, the engines, and the horns made her head ache; the smog and gasoline fumes stung her eyes. She ducked her head back inside and soon was listening to herself grumbling, until she stopped in midsentence to stare at the back of a highway sign poised at least twenty, maybe even thirty feet in the air. It was covered with squiggles and wiggles; not letters, just angry, inarticulate symbols. Death-defying graffiti! For a moment she forgot about the commuter hell she was trapped in. How had anyone been able to climb to the top of the sign and make such a mess of hieroglyphics? There were no stairs or ladder. She tried to visualize young black or Latino boys (gangbangers, every single last one of them) coming out to the 101 at – what? – 4:00 A.M., hoisting themselves up the poles that led to the signs. Or did they bring ladders? Why was it so important, these screaming letters that made everything look so dismal and hopeless? She took a last look at the swooping symbols. They seemed to throb with life. Each one was like a raised fist, beating against the world. As she passed under the sign, Mallory couldn't help but shudder, remembering that she'd seen the same kind of angry scribbling on a wall less than three miles from where she lived.

A little farther on, Mallory discovered the cause of the delay: lookyloos were slowing down to watch policemen talk to three black teenage boys wearing bright golden hoops in their ears and oversize jeans and shirts, who managed to look menacing even as they stood with their hands locked behind their necks. Good, they caught them, she thought as she sped past. These were the animals who defiled public property and shot innocent bystanders. They were just like the pigs who beat Reginald Denny. Just thinking of the helpless white man being dragged from his truck, for no reason, no earthly reason, except that he was white, made Mallory tremble with fear. She couldn't get that tape out of her mind; it gave her nightmares. Oh, sure, it was awful, just awful, what those cops did to King. Totally unnecessary! But King was a convicted felon, and he was running away; if he had cooperated, he wouldn't have been beaten. Police didn't beat people without provocation. The four cops were just doing their job, trying to protect innocent people, and now they were going to suffer for the rest of their lives. She'd read that two of them were about to lose their homes because of their legal fees. But those monsters who attacked a completely innocent man would probably have their defense paid for by the NAACP or the city. They didn't have any reason for attacking Reginald Denny, except that he was white. And black people had the nerve to call all white people racist. Mallory shuddered as she took one last glimpse at the hoodlums. Couldn't they just kill each other, without messing up everything around them, without hurting other people?

Mallory gasped, horrified as she recognized that she was mouthing her father's bigoted reasoning. She could still remember how her father rushed out and found a realtor and put their house up for sale the same day the first black family moved into Park Crest, their old mid-city neighborhood. 'We're not living around coloreds,' her father said, his face red, his mouth contorted. 'They're dirty. They steal. And they bring down property values.'

For years, she thought of 'coloreds' as a disease. But when some were bused to her high school in the San Fernando Valley, she met one or two black girls she really liked. 'A few of them are different,' her mother whispered, admonishing her not to tell her father about her friendships and, of course, not to think about bringing any of the Negro girls to their home. Mallory knew better than to tell even her mother that she thought one of the black football players on the school's team was unbelievably cute. Still, her father's words had marked her. The thought of venturing anywhere near Park Crest filled her with fear.

She stared at the graffiti. She didn't want anyone to die. She didn't. The young boys who fought in gangs and covered every conceivable space with graffiti didn't have dads in the home or proper guidance. They needed care and attention. Recreation centers. Something.

Mallory looked below, onto the streets of Hollywood. Beyond the squalid residential area lay Sunset Boulevard and the gleaming dome of Capitol Records. She took a lipstick from her purse and put color on her tense lips. In her rearview mirror she could see a young Latina in the Honda behind her, her beige cheeks dusted with blush, her stiff blue-black bangs swooping upward like frozen butterfly wings; she was diligently applying lipstick too.

Mallory felt the heat when she opened the door of her white Lexus in the parking lot across the street from Angel City National Bank. Nearly eighty-five degrees, and it was just seven-thirty. Yet even as she stepped out into the sweltering air, her shoulder bag and briefcase swinging by her side, she had to admit that it was cooler in Los Angeles than in the San Fernando Valley, that sprawling furnace of a suburb that she'd just spent forty-five minutes traveling from. At least if she lived in the city she could wipe out the commute, she thought. She shook herself a little and then brushed away the strands of blond hair that fell in her face. What in the world had made her think about that? Living in the city was out of the question now. Nobody wanted to live in Los Angeles; everybody wanted to get out.

Mallory put her things on the roof of the Lexus, then slid her hand inside her jacket, prying apart the beige cotton suit coat and the silk blouse that seemed plastered to her back. When she had finished, she was dismayed to see that the front of the straight skirt she wore was creased with tiny wrinkles. God only knew what the back of her jacket looked like. She pushed aside the bangs that clung to her damp forehead, then retrieved her briefcase and purse. She stared at her diamond-studded gold Rolex much longer than was necessary, then touched it gently with her index finger. He can give me everything but himself, she thought. Mallory felt tears, like hot pinpricks, stinging her eyes. 'Don't start. Don't start. Don't start,' she said aloud. It was too early in the morning to cry about Hayden Lear.

She looked around at the parked cars. Where was Esther? They were both early birds, and most days they left the parking lot together; the camaraderie was a pleasure that Mallory was more dependent upon than coffee to get her going in the morning, especially on days like this, when she felt so empty. It was becoming harder and harder to go to bed with a man in her arms and wake up with no one. Her little finger patted the rim of her left and then her right eye, carefully wiping away the tears so as not to smear her makeup. She looked around again. Esther always said something that made her laugh. If the events of April 29 had taught her anything, it was that the world needed human kindness and friendship. Well, she was doing her part to make the world a better place. As Mallory began heading toward the exit, she spotted Esther's silver BMW turning into the lot. She waved wildly, buoyed by the surge of energy and happiness that suddenly flowed through her.

Mallory waited at the parking lot exit, admiring Esther as she walked toward her. The black woman wore a navy suit, matching shoes, and a pale-pink blouse. She's always so impeccably dressed, Mallory thought. And what a body! Why couldn't she have an ass like hers? She smiled as Esther approached.

'How did it go?' she asked. Esther gave her a blank look. 'Your blind date.'

'Oh, that,' Esther said, her voice flat. 'Not a love connection.' She looked at Mallory, trying not to think about what Michele had told her.

'Aww.' Mallory felt surprisingly disheartened. She'd thought of Esther over the weekend and pictured her having a good time.

Esther couldn't help smiling. 'You were expecting a wedding?'

Mallory laughed lightly. 'No-o-o. I just wanted you to like each other and have a good time. Fall madly in love. Have passionate safe sex in the parking lot of the restaurant. And *then* have a wedding. Is that too much to ask?'

Esther was laughing before she could stop herself. 'Well, if it's any consolation, he was okay. I'm just picky,' she said with a sigh as they reached the entrance to the bank.

'I figured as much.' Mallory was almost reproachful.

Esther tilted her head and looked at her. 'Oh, you did?'

'Esther, you're gorgeous. You're bright. You're fun. And you're not seeing anyone. You must be playing hard to get.'

'A good man is hard to find,' she said, then quickly averted her eyes. But the dearth of professional black men wasn't a topic she'd ever discuss with Mallory.

'No, dear. That's: A hard man is good to find.' The two women laughed uneasily. Mallory wondered what the sudden awkwardness between them was about. Sometimes, without warning, Esther would get a look in her eyes that was like a bridge she couldn't cross. She glanced down at her skirt. 'Do you have your steamer?' she asked.

'In my office.'

The two women passed through the empty lobby, walking by the vacant tellers' stations. The bank didn't open to the public until ten o'clock, although most of the staff arrived by eight-thirty. Outside the picture window, both women could see several people awaiting their turn at the ReadyTeller. Esther's office was located at the end of the bank's central area; the outer wall was made of glass, so that she could observe the tellers and service representatives at their duties. Esther unlocked the wooden door, and Mallory followed her inside.

The black woman reached into one of the drawers of the teak desk and pulled out a small steamer, which she plugged into an outlet on the wall. A few minutes later, Esther approached Mallory with the steamer in her hand. 'Pull your skirt away from you so that you don't get burned,' she said.

Mallory did as she was told but still felt a burst of hot air across her thighs as Esther guided the steamer along her skirt. When Mallory looked down, the wrinkles had disappeared.

'We don't want you wrinkled for the staff meeting, *honey*,' Esther said.

Mallory groaned. 'Oh, God. I forgot.'

'How could you forget? It's Monday.' Esther stared at Mallory. Pampered little Valley Girl. Esther knew that *she* couldn't afford to forget one single detail. Despite the sudden resentment she felt, she made her voice sound normal. 'You're not having any problems, are you?'

'Problems? You mean, besides a major recession? You mean, besides the fallout from a major riot? You mean, besides the fact that the entire department has been under the gun since April twenty-ninth? We're supposed to be doing these special interim loans to businesses that will eventually qualify for federal funding, and I've been trying to meet with some guy from the rebuild project who is going to set up a process so that we can identify those with legitimate needs, but every time I try to meet with him, he cancels. So consequently there is no process in place and we've been winging it, which isn't my fault, but a course Charles isn't going to see it that way.

'Some of my clients are really in trouble. I have a lot of Koreans. I have this family, the Rhims. They owned a paint store that got torched. They are way underinsured, and I don't think they're going to qualify for government assistance, because they look a little too good on paper. The husband said he was seriously thinking about going back to Korea. It's so sad. They're such hardworking people.'

'A lot of hardworking people lost out during the civil unrest,' Esther said, thinking about what Michele had told her. She tried to make the words glide smoothly off her tongue, but she ended up flinging each one at the white woman like a tiny rock.

Mallory winced. She wanted to ask Esther, 'What did I say?' but instead she forced her words to tiptoe around the rising indignation that had suddenly stiffened Esther's lips and hardened her glance. 'Yes, the entire city lost out,' she said carefully, trying to keep her tone even and light and free of the resentment she suddenly felt. Why did she always have to watch her every word around Esther?

Esther swallowed the small, hard lump that suddenly clogged her throat. It wasn't good to get so angry, to lose control; Mallory didn't mean anything. She had to watch herself. Mallory was a political ally, even if she wasn't a friend. 'Do you have a written plan?'

'Are you kidding?'

Esther looked at her watch. The meeting won't start for another hour. Write something down. Anything. You know Charles. He's not going to read them, but if he sees you referring to notes, it will make him feel secure.'

'The man is such a jerk,' Mallory said with a sigh.

'Yes, well, we can't do anything about that.' Esther drummed on her desk with a pencil. 'I'll give my report first and I'll drag it out; that way there won't be much time left for you. Besides, Charles will be so busy getting on Kirk's case. God, I hope he closed that Winthrop deal. I'm not in the mood to see a massacre.'

'Poor Kirk,' Mallory said.

'Is there a history behind Charles's hostility? What does he have against the guy?'

Mallory gave a short laugh. 'You mean, besides the fact that Kirk has hair and he's two feet taller and ten times smarter than Charles? Get real. Com-pe-tition, that's the—'

They turned simultaneously toward the voices coming from the lobby. Looking through the glass wall of Esther's office, they saw five men and one woman, all white, standing in front of the elevators.

'They finally put a woman on the board,' Mallory said. There were layers of pleasure in her voice.

Esther saw Mallory's smile, a smile that invited her to be happy about the lone woman too, a smile that said they shared some great victory. She searched for the proper North Side response: That's really great! Gee, how about that! The phrases drifted too quickly for her to catch hold of. What gurgled up in her throat was a familiar sound, not even a word. It wasn't North Side; it was deep South Side and didn't belong in Angel City. But the intonation, handed down from her mother and grandmother and other powerful ancestors, couldn't be stopped. 'Umph.'

Mallory's shoulders jerked. The startling noise sounded like a grunt, but she discerned the disdain, sensed even malice. But when Mallory stole a look, the black woman was smiling at her. Looking at Esther, she thought: It's almost as if she's wearing a mask.

4

Preston Sinclair, the fifty-three-year-old president and board chairman of Angel City National Bank, stood at the large picture window that took up nearly an entire wall of the thirty-fourth-floor boardroom, waiting for the members to arrive. His reflection showed salt-and-pepper hair, thinning drastically. There were circles under his watery hazel eyes, deep lines that ran from the corners of his nose to his mouth, which he was noticing for the first time. He rarely looked at himself. Preston Sinclair was not a details man. What Preston cared about was outside himself: the business of the day, in all its macro glory.

He held a month-old copy of the *Los Angeles Business Journal*. On the front page was a picture of a young black man named Humphrey Boone. The president peered at the headline with the intensity of one who was reading it for the first time, when in fact he had the words memorized: 'Commerce's Humphrey Boone Clears Way for Hospital Expansion Financing.' He scanned the article below, which stated that the private placement loan for Lebanon Hospital, a 'prestigious West Side institution,' was the largest single financing of a California medical institution in history. How the multimillion-dollar private placement loan had come into being was part of what intrigued Preston Sinclair. The paper said that the hospital was reluctant to finance its expansion efforts with a regular bank loan because of the high interest. Boone, who specialized in private placement loans, had overheard the executive director of the hospital talking about the dilemma facing the institution. They'd both been in the steam room of an exclusive downtown men's athletic club, and Boone, clad only in a towel, introduced himself to his fellow club member, who later admitted to a reporter that he was somewhat taken aback at the unorthodox approach. But in the locker room, Boone gave him his card and persuaded him to come to lunch. The rest was financial history. Boone, the article said, managed to place the loan with one of the largest insurance companies in the West, for considerably lower interest than a regular bank would have charged. As the 'middleman,' Commerce Bank of New York wound up with almost two million dollars in fees. In the picture, Boone was smiling with the hospital's executive director and the head of the insurance company that made the loan. The three men held up a white towel, presumably the one Humphrey Boone had been sporting that day in the steam room.

Black wunderkind, Preston thought every time he thought of the article. By God, there was a man who knew how to think on his feet. And what credentials! Boone was a Yale graduate and a Rhodes scholar, and in addition to all his professional accomplishments, the article cited his membership in at least half a dozen civic organizations. He was also president of a black bankers' group. Preston had saved the article because he was drawn to people who made a difference, especially those who attracted favorable press when they did it. The press could make or break careers. Important careers. The banker folded the paper carefully, walked over to the long table in the center of the room, and put it at his place. Humphrey Boone was in his plans.

As he paced around the table, Preston's eyebrows furrowed into one long line of irritation and his lips curled downward in a frown. The boardroom had recently been renovated, and the huge picture window was an addition. A damned waste of money, he muttered to himself. Almost an entire wall had been knocked out, when shelves and bookcases, places to put things on, useful things, were what was needed. A piece of art, investment art, would have made better business sense. Spending money so that people could look at scenery! If people wanted a view, they could go to the mountains. He rubbed his chin vigorously. Might as well toss the dollar bills out the damn window: $243,000 worth of renovations was exactly the kind of wasteful spending in the corporate sector that the *Gazette* might decide to cover in a front-page exposé. His own office was absolutely palatial. A real monstrosity of excess. The refurbishments had been initiated and approved of by his predecessor – one of the last in a long line of the man's foolish, spendthrift decisions – but he would be the one looking like a greedy fat cat should reporters ever come after him. Why, only last week, in the paper's left-hand front-page column, reserved for in-depth analysis of a variety of subjects, some hotshot had written a detailed examination of the professional and personal lifestyle of the flamboyant multimillionaire businessman David Tate. Preston sighed. Now, there was a man who'd elevated indiscretion to an art form.

From the street below, the muted sounds of sirens traveled upward. In spite of himself, Preston Sinclair peered out the window. He could see clear to the Pacific, and the sight of the sparkling blue water in the distance was surprisingly soothing, almost hypnotic. He seldom took the opportunity to appreciate the beauty of Los Angeles, and he was amazed to discover how peaceful he felt as he gazed out at the sea. Looking at the ocean was almost like going to the beach, something he hadn't done in years. Los Angelenos had the reputation for being laid-back surfers, but the truth was that they were as workaholic as their New York counterparts. For a moment, he felt as weightless and free as the long-distance runner he had once been. The sirens wailed again, longer, louder, and more insistent this time, screaming over the vast metropolis, that jungle of palm trees, buildings, cars, and people that lay just east of the ocean. The searing sound pierced through the tranquil tableau. Preston turned away from the calm water. As he looked at the city below, it was all that he could do to keep from trembling. High up as he was, he knew that he wasn't immune to the chaos in the city streets. Preston was suddenly filled with frightening memories, the kind that weave nightmares. Five months ago, he had stood at the same window and watched Los Angeles burn; he'd been smelling smoke ever since.

Even from the relative safety of the thirty-fourth floor, the possibility that each faceless person was carrying a concealed weapon made Preston clench his teeth. L.A. was a virtual arsenal. The gangbangers had looted thousands of dollars' worth of AK-47s and Uzis during the riots, and now the gun dealers were doing record-breaking business selling firearms to petrified people intent on saving their lives and property should violence break out again. Profiting from fear, Preston thought, shaking his head. There was no honor in that. Bel Agua, where he lived, was as full of weapons as Armageddon. The national guard had scarcely quelled the rioters before panic, as thick and choking as smog, began spreading again. No one would be safe if – true to rumors circulating – mobs of young black and brown men soon took to the streets once more, leaving the ghettos and coming to *their* neighborhoods.

As he stood by the window, Preston thought of how nervous Claire, his wife, became in the days after the looting and violence. She came to him crying that Sunday evening, after things had settled down in the city, and told him that she wanted to go home, home to Indiana. Indiana! He nearly choked when she said that. 'Claire,' he'd told her, 'we're not the kind of people who run away. There is a solution to these social problems if we approach them with a modicum of business sense.' He reminded her that he was earning more than a million dollars annually. 'People don't make that kind of money in Indiana.'

His wife calmed down then. She was a clearheaded, rational woman, always had been. Not a lot of flash, but then what good did blond hair and lipstick do a man over the long haul? Secretly, he'd always wanted one of those tall, razzle-dazzle, big-busted women with pale golden hair, but long ago he realized that women like that didn't come cheap. They had to be wined and dined. They required presents and constant attention, those bosomy blonds. And they weren't good for the image of a man who still had places to go, mountains to climb. Blonds could be the ruination of a man. Claire was a bargain, a sensibly priced woman, never too demanding. After the boys got older, she busied herself with her volunteer work, something to do with hospitals, he thought. And now that the kids were away at school, she . . . Preston rubbed his chin. Was she still with the hospital? He really didn't know exactly what Claire did to fill her days. He smiled to himself. Whatever she was involved with was certainly all right with him. She was like blue-chip stock: steady, predictable, and valuable, the best business decision he'd ever made.

Preston walked away from the window and trailed around the long rectangular table, rubbing his hands together. It was unusual for him to think about his wife while he was at work, or to be so meditative; he was a man who rarely stood still. Early in his life he trained himself to make and execute decisions simultaneously. Certainly in the eight months since he'd accepted the presidency at Angel City there hadn't been much time for reflection. He was too busy running from one branch to the next, from one department to another, to meeting after meeting, in an attempt to get to know the managers and learn the inner workings of the bank, to attune himself to the nuances of its corporate culture so that his job would go more smoothly. One of the first things that had to be dealt with was the Community Reinvestment Act, the federal law requiring banks to reinvest in the communities that provided them with deposits. During his predecessor's tenure, the bank had received a warning from the enforcing agency, a precursor to an unsatisfactory rating. The first week on his new job, Preston personally reviewed the records pertaining to the CRA and was appalled to discover how very negligent the former administration had been. Angel City's record for lending money in even the downtown Latino barrio, only a few miles to the east, was way below the federal standards; in South-Central, their history was even worse. As a businessman, he could understand the poor record. It was a fact that blacks and Latinos simply didn't have the credit needed to get loans. He couldn't blame his lenders for turning them down. Still, in the current tense climate in Los Angeles, public knowledge of Angel City's record was an invitation for bad press. The bank couldn't afford that, and neither could he. He had plans.

Preston had built a successful career based on making things happen, moving from bank to bank, climbing higher and higher with each new position. His latest coup had been his appointment as chairman of the board. These days, his charge was simple: to stay the course for Angel City, as profitable and honorable a course as was possible during recessionary times of bank failures and closings. At a relatively young age, he had the power and prestige he'd been working for all his life. Not that the presidency and chairmanship of Angel City would be the pinnacle of his achievements. Oh, no. Angel City was his last rung on this particular career ladder. Preston still had ambitions. Politics! That little jug-eared Texan had the right idea, even if he didn't have a snowball's chance in hell of getting to be President this time around. Perot was creating his own destiny, and that's what Preston intended to do. He dreamed of being governor of California. He certainly had the connections, and the financial backing wouldn't be a problem. His closet was free of the skeletons that had ruined so many recent candidates. He'd always walked a tight line.

But instead of basking in his current success and reveling in his future plans, Preston was uneasy. Log Angeles was already in the grips of a severe depression. The aerospace industry was reeling, and so were the companies which serviced that behemoth. Businesses were leaving town, and the riots had made cities like Raleigh and Phoenix look increasingly attractive to investors. Banks were only as solvent as the economic climate that surrounded them. What would happen to Angel City if another riot broke out? And what would that mean for his future? These were the questions that had plagued him in the last five months. In the wee hours of the morning, when the sky was dusted with the color of roses, his eyes were still open, his mind was busily humming, seeking a clear, precise answer that made good business sense.

As part of his 'hands-on' presidency, Preston had called an unprecedented meeting in late May at the South-Central branch. The ostensible reason was to talk with managers about the problems the branch was having, including a rash of robberies and a below-par real estate loan portfolio. But he also wanted to assess the type of talent, or lack of it, at the South-Central branch.

Preston had thumbed through a report while his driver took him down the 101S. It was all there in black and white. Bank holdups had increased all over the city at a phenomenal rate. The other Angel City branches had their fair share, but none could compare to the hits South-Central was enduring: they had been robbed five times in the past year. That's outrageous, Preston thought, shaking his head. During the last robbery, the security guard was taking an unauthorized break, smoking in the men's room. A customer had been shot and killed. The family was suing the bank for ten million dollars. The insurance premiums were now astronomical. Preston shook his head. Something absolutely had to be done. He was so immersed in going over the papers in his briefcase that he didn't look out the window until the chauffeur was parking the car. When the door opened, he was startled to see standing in front of him a group of black teenage boys and one or two men who appeared to be in their twenties. They were staring at the car, glaring at him, fury and aggression dripping from their eyes. He felt a sudden chill and lowered his head as he passed them and went into the bank.

The conference room at the South-Central branch was smaller than his office. The room had been scrubbed and polished in his honor; the wood floors, windowsills, and conference table were gleaming. In the center of a small table in the corner there was a huge bouquet of roses, dahlias, gladioli, and baby's breath. Mints in cut-glass crystal bowls were placed strategically. Still, no amount of window dressing could camouflage the shabbiness of the place. South-Central was the oldest branch of the bank, and it showed. The floors were worn, the walls needed painting, the table was scarred, and the drapes on the windows were ancient. Anyone could see that South-Central was the bank's bastard child.

The five managers seated around the table looked as though they were about to explode with tension. Preston knew that he was the cause of their nervousness – it wasn't every day that the president came calling. Looking around the table, he felt a curious rush of blood, a kind of throbbing in his temples. Preston dropped his pen. Several people made a move to get it, but he waved them away and bent down to pick it up himself. No sooner had he retrieved it and settled himself than he dropped it again, under the table this time. The pen rolled near one of the women; he almost touched one of her dark legs as he reached for it. Preston hit his head on the table as he attempted to get up. 'Is this the beginning of a bad day?' he asked the black senior loan officer sitting next to him when he was finally back in his chair. They both laughed uneasily. By God, he did feel tense, a little constricted. While gripping his Mont Blanc with his right hand, he loosened his tie slightly with his left, but he didn't get the relief he expected. His palms were sweaty; he almost dropped the pen a third time. He placed it carefully in front of him. When he looked around the table again, Preston experienced the same sense of being threatened, being in danger he had felt when he passed the group of thugs outside the bank. He tried to recall what he'd eaten that day; he was a little nauseated. What is the matter with me! He looked around the table again; five pairs of dark eyes in five dark faces stared back at him. He trembled violently. The people assembled looked at him expectantly. Snap out of it, he commanded himself. These are my employees! He flexed his fingers and nodded toward each person, taking deep breaths, until he felt himself grow calm and steady. 'Let's get down to business,' he said.

The boys were still there when he returned to the car. Their insolent eyes seemed harder, their smirks more vicious than before. He forced himself to look at them, to nod curtly. 'Good afternoon, gentlemen.' They didn't answer, but he could see the shadow of surprise in their eyes.

One of them called out, 'Nice ride, man,' as he got into the car. Another said, 'Hey! Hey! I need me a loan! Can I get a loan?' He watched them out of the back window. Their sinewy bodies moved like oil as they leaped into the air and slapped five before they came crashing down to the pavement on their huge athletic shoes. As the car pulled away, he thought: They are the ones who tore this city apart, and now they are just standing around with nothing to do.

As the freeway loomed into view, Preston mentally tallied all the black people he knew. There was a friend in graduate school. Well, not exactly a friend. He really barely knew the fellow, although they spoke occasionally. Early in his career, he shared an office with a black man. Raymond Kendall. They hadn't communicated in years. When they lived in Indianapolis, he and his wife employed a woman to look after the children. She lived with them for three or four years. What was her name? He placed his briefcase on the seat beside him and slumped back in his seat, his brow furrowed in contemplation. Later, when he got back to the office, he was still trying to remember.

That evening, after he sat down to dinner, he asked Claire, 'Do you have any black friends?'

She looked startled; her pale forehead creased as she contemplated the question. She was silent for a minute. Claire took more pains with her looks than Preston did. She had her hair dyed a frosted blond shade, went on diets, and worked out. Still, she was a rather plain woman, whose only outstanding physical attribute was a good set of teeth. She smiled at Preston. 'Well, there's one of the nurses at the hospital. Betty. We joke a little and talk from time to time. And there's Marcia; she's a docent at the same art museum with me. A lovely person. Her husband is a physician. But of course they aren't friends. They're more like acquaintances.' After a pause, she added casually, 'The boys have black friends.'

'They do?'

'Oh, yes. There was a black fellow in Robbie's fraternity. And Pres . . . well . . .'

'What about Pres?' He looked at his wife.

She sighed. 'Pres dated a black girl for about a year. They broke up a few months ago.'

'He did? Why didn't you mention it to me?'

'He asked me not to tell you. I guess he thought you'd be upset.'

'Why did he think I'd be upset?' His voice rose a few octaves.

'Well, naturally you'd have been upset. I figured that it would blow over, and it did. I think Pres was just rebelling. Although I must admit, she was a beautiful girl.' She seemed to go into a trance for a moment. 'Very exotic-looking. She wore her hair the way so many of the black girls do, a lot of little . . . uh . . .'

He looked at her blankly.

'Oh, you know. The little . . . They sort of twist the hair into little . . . It's very attractive.'

'You met her?' Preston felt miffed that his son's exotic beauty hadn't been presented to him.

'At parents' weekend last spring. You were working.' She said the last with her lips compressed, her arms folded.

'Were you upset?'

'Of course. And even after I met her and could understand the attraction, because she was so beautiful, so refined and nice, I was still absolutely terrified. Ah! What do they call those things? Braids. Braids.'

Preston gave her a blank look. Finally, he said, 'What were you afraid of?'

'Why, that they'd get married and have children, of course.' She almost added, 'little mocha-colored children,' but decided not to, because she thought it sounded rude. 'Isn't it strange how a white person and a black person are only capable of producing black children, how white just gets wiped out. That's scary, when you think about it. Of course, Robbie dated a Chinese girl his first year.'

'Really?'

Claire laughed lightly. 'It was a phase, I think. He was terribly sexist then. I believe he was looking for someone who'd wipe his feet with her hair. The girl turned out to be more on the order of Connie Chung.' She paused. 'They're just so different from us.' Seeing Preston's confusion, she clarified herself: 'Black people, I mean. Although Betty and Marcia are absolutely lovely. But then I know them.'

'Would you feel uncomfortable being in a group of black people by yourself, say five people.'

'Well, I don't know. That would all depend. But, darling, why are you asking me all these questions? Did something happen to you today?'

Preston shook his head. 'Let's say grace.' They bowed their heads. The slow words were a habit from his childhood, a ritual that he'd been unable to break even though he hadn't been to church in years. He found that saying the blessing was a soothing exercise, often the most peaceful interlude in his day.

Absolutely nothing had happened, he told himself as he settled down after dinner at the computer in his study. Briefly he imagined a reporter from the *Gazette* at the South-Central meeting. 'Bank President Perspires and Drops Pen in the Presence of African-Americans and Latinos! Under Pressure, Bank President Admits Minorities Make Him Physically Ill.' The next thing he knew, Phil Donahue would be sticking a microphone in his face. Or Oprah! He'd never get to the governor's mansion with that kind of headline. He'd just been a little out of sorts, a bit woozy, that's all. He wasn't a fearful or nervous kind of person. He judged each man on his own merits, by the content of his character. Or her character. He leaned back in his seat and stared at the room around him. The walls were covered with plaques, resolutions, pictures of him with important people. There's no more wall space, he thought, suddenly weary. As he sat perfectly still, a kind of emptiness washed over him, like a wave knocking him down. Where on earth would he display the rest of his life?

At the bank the next morning, Preston told his secretary to ask Bailey Reynolds to report to him. Five minutes later, his right-hand man was sitting in front of him, smiling amiably. Bailey was the only one of the four executive vice presidents he'd inherited from his predecessor. A seasoned officer of the bank, he flowed smoothly into Preston's regime, changing camps as easily as most men switch hats. Bailey was a man for whom following orders seemed to be a higher calling. Preston was suspicious of him at first, suspecting that the very friendly exterior that he presented to the world couldn't possibly be sincere, but Bailey had never given him reason to doubt his loyalty. He had to admit that he couldn't have asked for a better number two man. Preston could tell that Bailey's mind began ticking the instant he asked him for a racial breakdown of the bank's employees. Numbers, statistics, and the endless minutiae that the business often demanded were Bailey's forte; he was a details man.

'Certainly, Preston,' Bailey said evenly. Given an assignment, Bailey carried out his work promptly and efficiently. Within two days, Preston had a copy of the report on his desk; it confirmed what he'd seen with his own eyes. The bank employed some black and Latino tellers and customer reps, but with only a few exceptions, the decision-makers were all white and mostly male. Except for South-Central. He set down the statistics and leaned back in his seat, stretching out his legs under his desk. Why, Angel City was practically segregated! It wasn't the numbers that shocked him but the fact that they were so blatant, so easily discovered. If the *Gazette* ever focused on this . . . He stood up. He had to hire a black senior manager. When those teens on the corner saw that there were people like them who could make it to the top, perhaps they'd be less inclined to throw their Molotov cocktails, and the business climate in Los Angeles would improve. He took a deep breath and

63

sat down, feeling satisfied and strangely vindicated. Would a man afraid of blacks and Latinos make that kind of commitment? he asked himself. Of course not. His dad would be proud of him. For a moment, Preston saw his father's wizened face, his gentle eyes, felt his hands on his shoulders. The old man was still preaching the gospel every Sunday in the little Baptist church in Preston's hometown. And he believed every word he preached. 'Son,' he had told Preston when he was a boy, 'the Lord called me to be a good shepherd. He touched my heart late in the midnight hour, and now the gospel has taken over my life.' My father would have been happier if I'd become a penniless do-gooder, Preston thought. But he wasn't weighted down with any of his father's high-minded and cumbersome principles. His father's fruit had fallen far, far from the tree. The gospel would never take control of Preston's life. He'd made his choice years ago, when he ditched Sunday school and bought lemons and sugar with his offering. He sold drinks to other backsliders, only blocks from the church. The money in his palm inspired him like no hymn he'd ever sung. Ah, sweet profit. When he discovered the perfidy, his father read the Book of Acts to him in a solemn, even cadence, all to no avail. When he left home, Preston stopped going to church altogether. He preferred to worship at the feet of the only true God he knew: his own ambition.

Preston turned away from the picture window when he heard the voices in the hallway. He strode to the heavy wooden door and flung it open. 'Hello. Hello. Glad to see ya.' His flat midwestern voice boomed out as he greeted each person, pumping hands, slapping backs, and grinning from ear to ear with the exuberance of a candidate running for office. Preston was happy to see the people assembled in the oak-paneled room. He rubbed his palms together excitedly as he watched them fill their cups with coffee and choose from an assortment of fruit-filled Danishes that had been placed on silver trays on a long antique buffet near the window. He was impatient with chitchat, yet he respected the importance of it, and in the few minutes before the meeting began, he went from member to member, inquiring about health and spouses, children and even grandchildren, even though he was eager to plunge into the agenda.

By ten of nine, the last straggler had come in, and by nine o'clock, Preston took his seat at the long oak table and cleared his throat. In a second, the room was completely silent. Preston quietly surveyed the people at the table. 'I'm glad to see that some of this city's leading citizens could tear themselves away from the pressing matters of politics to come help me take care of the more mundane matters of banking,' Preston said with a wide smile. The board members chuckled, knowing that Preston was obliquely referring to the role the assembled hoped to have in choosing the city's five-term black mayor's replacement. After all, their quiet decisions and signatures on generous checks had heralded the ascendancy of more than one political candidate. Since the current mayor's announcement of his plans to retire (long overdue, most thought), they had been busy. The Angel City National Bank meeting was a mere pit stop on their crowded agenda, a breather in the constant round of political gatherings where they organized, strategized, and set the stage to financially fortify the man who would best serve their interests and possibly the city's.

The laughter died down, and Preston welcomed everyone. He asked the lone woman, newly installed at the last stockholders' meeting, to stand, and they all applauded her. Some of the applause was merely polite. To Preston, Amanda Parker's presence was essential. He had his own opinion about women in business, but with the majority of the bank's stockholders being female, it simply wasn't good policy not to appear to include them in decisionmaking.

Amanda was the first of several female additions he planned for the board, once he pushed some of the old-timers out. 'We're all glad to have you working with us,' Preston said. 'You have our full support.' This last was a warning. He had no patience with illogical people who clung to the past. Personal idiosyncrasies and biases had no place in business. If it made good business sense to do something, why then, it had to be done.

They went through the agenda quickly, passing over the old concerns in less than an hour. Preston stood up, anxious to plunge ahead with the new. 'I'm going to be blunt.' There were chuckles from one end of the table to the other, since Preston was known for not mincing words. 'As you know, Angel City is an equal opportunity employer, at least on paper. It's recently come to my attention that we need to extend our commitment to equal hiring into the upper echelons of power in this institution. There isn't a single black, Latino, or Asian senior manager in any of our branches, with the exception of South-Central. I am committed to changing that.'

The room was silent for a moment, and Preston could see the king-makers on the board pursing their lips and pressing their fingers together. Finally, from the end of the table, one of the oldest members said, 'We're living in very unstable times. The city's a powder keg. No one is saying that minorities don't have a legitimate beef, but the economy is bad. We have to be very careful about the message we send.'

'Be more explicit,' Preston said.

'We don't want to give the impression that affirmative action is the guiding force at Angel City. If you do so, you'll create a moral problem of gigantic proportions.'

'You're saying . . .' Preston made small looping circles with his hands.

'That if white males' – he nodded toward Amanda and smiled apologetically – 'feel that they are being displaced

66

solely because they are white, this bank is going to see some lawsuits.'

'I'm not talking about displacing anyone. I'm talking about bringing in highly qualified people.'

'What you are trying to achieve is admirable. Admirable,' said another of the older members. 'The problem is that you've got to go very slowly.'

'I don't think we've got that kind of time. Unless these people are allowed to participate fully in the system, unless we conduct a business that includes as opposed to excludes, how in the name of heaven can we expect them to feel they have a stake in this city?' Everyone around him was still, and Preston realized that he'd been shouting. Where on earth had that emotion come from? He pushed up the wire-rimmed glasses that had slipped down the bridge of his nose.

'Excuse me, gentlemen.' Amanda Parker's tone was soft and just a bit tentative. As she spoke, she raised her voice a little at the end of each sentence, so that it seemed as though she was posing questions. 'As I see it, the issue isn't whether or not to hire a senior minority manager – we absolutely must do that – but how to maximize that occasion for the good of Angel City. I think this could be a wonderful opportunity to create goodwill for the bank. The right person, of course, could generate quite a bit of media interest.'

Preston felt his rib cage pressing into the table as he nodded vigorously at Amanda. 'Now, that's an interesting thought,' he said. 'Very interesting.' He unfolded the newspaper at his elbow. 'I think I have a highly qualified candidate.'

Thirty-three stories below, in the first-floor conference room, Charles Weber's right eye began to twitch in evenly spaced intervals. The regional branch manager's right foot, which was crossed rigidly over his left knee beneath the conference table, had been jerking spasmodically for the last five minutes. Esther, noting the combination of physical symptoms in her boss, took it as the final warning it was: Her allotted time was up; any further delay would be to her own jeopardy. There were other signs. The people around her wore the glazed expressions of catatonics. No one had asked any questions in the last ten minutes. Only Mallory was alert, following her every word with rapt attention and a clear-eyed expression of gratitude. Esther felt curiously detached from the woman's appreciation; it was all in a day's work. She knew that Mallory would have done the same for her. They were business allies if nothing else. Esther finished up her assessment of the teller situation just as Charles cleared his throat and rose slowly from his seat, his thick, short body expanding like the funnel of a tornado. He bellowed, 'I think we get the complete picture, Esther.'

Charles sat back down and glanced at the clock on the wall. Very carefully, he gave the front of his head a delicate scratch with the polished nail of his bejeweled pinkie. His hairline was rapidly disappearing behind his ears, and to compensate, he combed the strands from the back of his head forward, swirling them around his denuded pate in an attempt to camouflage Mother Nature's betrayal. He had recently divorced, and in the aftermath of his separation he had acquired not only a pinkie ring but a gold bracelet, which dangled slightly below the cuff of his Italian suits. His jewelry was a piercing scream amid the silent, unadorned style of the bank. Esther could only suppose that he felt so secure in his position that he believed his unorthodox fashions would be tolerated. She had to suppress a giggle every time she looked at him. The New Joisey mobster goes corporate, she thought.

'Well,' Charles said, his voice calmer, 'I'm glad to know

68

that we will have someone on board by . . .' He looked at Esther, letting his eyes linger on her breasts.

Esther narrowed her eyes until they were like slits and made her glance as hard as flint. 'No later than the end of this week. Is there something wrong, Charles?' she asked in a loud, clear voice.

Charles looked away. 'Good. That's good,' he said.

Esther watched as Charles nodded toward Kirk Madison, who sat at the opposite end of the table. 'And now for the Madison report,' he said tersely. He sucked in his belly and thrust out his chest. His glance was challenging. 'Did you complete the loan evaluation for the Winthrop deal? This loan has been taking what – four months?'

Kirk unfolded his arms, opened the folder in front of him, pulled out some papers, and leaned forward. At thirty-eight, he was still boyish-looking, even when his face showed tension and anger that he couldn't mask. His hair was neatly, though not stylishly, cut; he still wore suits that were vented in the back. 'The main holdup has been the client's inability to furnish me with the financial roll-up for last year,' he said. Looking down, he brushed a piece of lint from his jacket.

'Four months is a lot of time to have gotten no further than you have,' Charles said gruffly.

'I've spoken to the client several— '

'You're going to need to do more than speak to the client, Kirk. Otherwise, the deal is dead in the water. You ever think about giving the guy an ultimatum?'

'The client is a woman. Mrs. Baker.'

'Jesus. No wonder it's taking so long,' Charles said. His laughter boomed around the room. Esther watched as Donald and Jim from the loan department chuckled. Kirk, glancing nervously at Mallory and Esther, joined in for a few seconds, then plowed ahead eagerly as Charles continued to enjoy his own joke. 'I've given Mrs. Baker until the end of this week. The reason I've been sticking with this is that she looks like a good risk and the bank can earn nearly – well, exactly – $628,023.48 in fees and interest payments. I think this deal is worth putting in some extra time.' He looked anxiously at Charles.

Damn, if he were a puppy he'd be wagging his tail, Esther thought.

'Well,' Charles said coldly, 'I want to see some closure on this by the beginning of next week. I tell you what: you arrange a meeting with the three of us sometime within the next five days. Check with me first about times.'

'Charles, I don't think that's necessary at this point,' Kirk said.

'Just set it up,' Charles said.

Kirk rattled off some other information about loans that were in the works, trying to hide his humiliation with glib academic references. Esther waited for further attacks from Charles, but the older man had turned toward Mallory and was smiling at her.

'I'll just rush through this as quickly as I can,' Mallory said, glancing casually at her watch. She pulled out a piece of paper and began reading, describing what she'd done to accommodate the number of her small-business customers seeking new payment plans. As she read, Charles's eyes never strayed from her breasts, although from where he was sitting, only Mallory and Esther could see his eyes. When Mallory looked up, he met her glance with a smirk.

Esther tried to contain the anger that was welling up inside her. She caught Mallory's eye and sent her a strong telepathic message: Wipe that Barbie Doll smile off your face and confront the bastard.

Mallory reddened, then turned away. She put her head down and pulled the paper closer to her eyes, so that her face was hidden. She read faster, her words running into each other like frightened rabbits. She had almost completed her report, when Charles stood up. He pointed to his watch. 'That's fine, hon – Mallory.' He playfully slapped his face.

As they left the meeting, Mallory whispered to Esther, 'Maybe we could all put our money together and hire a hit man.'

'Don't ever look away from him when he does that to you. Roll your eyes at that mothafucka— ' Esther stopped, realizing how 'street' she sounded. It wasn't the language for work. Around white people, her language had to be precise enough to let them know that she was as verbally adept as they were. Then they could whisper among themselves that she was 'so articulate,' which was to say that they were amazed that she spoke as well as they did.

But Mallory was staring at her with intense interest. 'What do you mean, *roll* my eyes?'

Forgetting to be careful, Esther said, 'Stare him down. Like this.' She pressed her lips into a tight, mean line, narrowed her eyes, and blinked them open and shut, each time making her stare harder and poking out her lips more. Then she let her eyes travel across Mallory's face in one mean, sweeping glance.

'Co-ol.' Mallory pronounced the word like a Valley Girl. She made two nerdy syllables of what should have been one syllable and came down hard on the *l* instead of slurring it.

'That's called nonverbal communication.'

'Who taught you how to do that?'

Esther started to say her mother and grandmother, but no, she definitely didn't want to get into all that. 'A survival tool I picked up along the way.' She laughed lightly as Mallory continued to look at her in an open and curious manner. 'Do you think that Kirk realizes he won't be rewarded for being a good boy?'

No sooner had she uttered the words than Kirk appeared at her side. 'Hey, you guys,' he said, nodding to each of the women. Before Esther could respond, Kirk turned to Esther and said quickly, 'Operations has been looking great since you took over. You're doing such a fine job,' he said. 'You've got the greatest people skills.'

Esther sighed. He said the same thing practically every time he saw her. 'Enough already,' she wanted to say. But she smiled at Kirk and stood chatting for a few minutes before he excused himself.

'He's just trying to be nice. He likes you,' Mallory said quickly as Kirk walked away.

'Of course,' Esther said.

'He does go a little overboard,' Mallory said. 'Thanks for covering for me.'

Esther shrugged.

'Don't look now, but you are being watched,' Mallory whispered.

Esther turned. Across the room, a man she judged to be just shy of six feet, with skin the color of biscuits and a neatly trimmed mustache, was smiling at her. All of her. He was wearing a Western Express uniform. The navy-blue shorts clung to the tightest, roundest ass she'd ever seen and revealed calves that belonged on a basketball court. Mandingo Warrior, Esther thought, thinking of Vanessa's term. She sniffed disdainfully and marched into her office. Moments later, when she glanced out her glass wall, he was still staring at her.

5

'Girl, you're not dressed yet?' Vanessa asked when Esther answered the door in her pajamas the following week. 'I thought we were going to run.'

'We are,' Esther said, stifling a yawn and closing the door behind Vanessa, 'but you don't have to be so daggone cheerful about it.'

Vanessa stretched her arms above her head and stood on her toes. 'I have to be fit if I'm going to be Denzel's woman. I have to have leg muscles and quads for those romantic close-ups.'

'You are a truly sick woman,' Esther said, laughing in spite of her fatigue.

'No. Listen. I'm going to get this part. It's down to fifteen of us now. I always knew I could make it in this town.'

'Fifteen people?' How, she wondered, could Vanessa be so excited about such long odds.

'Do you know how many people auditioned for this part? Every sister in Hollywood, maybe a hundred women. The Dreadlocked Diva herself went out for the role. So to make a cut like that is fantastic.'

'Oh, that's great,' Esther said, giving Vanessa a tight hug.

'Girl, affection is cool, but you have the morning mouth of life. How about a quick shot of Listerine for the road?'

At five-thirty, the early chill of the dawn pushed away the last vestiges of sleepiness in Esther as she and Vanessa stretched in front of her house. After a few minutes, they started jogging. Vanessa followed Esther's lead. For the first fifteen minutes they ran through the flatlands of the neighborhood, starting off slowly, almost haltingly, doing more talking and laughing than running, then they picked up a steady sprint as they passed the elementary school and the tiny park in the center of the community. The scent of oranges, lemons, roses, and gardenias mingled in the heavy, sweet air. The city was waking up as they ran. Esther could see bedroom and kitchen lights, people in bathrobes opening their front doors to retrieve their morning papers. On every street the whirring *chchchchchchchch* of the automatic sprinklers doused lawns and flowers, giving what the sky would withhold for at least another month or two; the women had to run in the road to avoid getting wet. Sometimes Esther could smell eggs, toast, and bacon cooking from the houses they passed and hear voices from open windows. She wondered what it would be like to cook breakfast for her family, to see her children off to school, to kiss her husband goodbye.

Esther relished the wind in her face as they left the flatlands behind, and she appreciated the strain she felt in her legs as she took the gently angled hills. Her heart pumping, the sweat beading up and then pouring down the sides of her face, energized her. They got into a rhythm, offset by shrieking crows, as they passed through the clean, wide streets. Their bodies were soaked by the time they had reached the first of several rolling hills and the running had become more strenuous. Vanessa began panting. They both fell silent as they concentrated on getting up the really steep incline – the Big One, they called it – which suddenly loomed in front of them like a ninety-degree angle. As Esther climbed, her breath came in ragged spurts and her ears began to hurt a little inside. The strain in her calf muscles became one solid ache, and when she looked around, Vanessa was faltering too. Every time she breathed, Esther felt as though someone were jabbing an ice pick in her chest. She kept lifting her legs and putting them down, even when she wanted to scream. 'All right!' Esther called out jubilantly when she and Vanessa reached the top. They hovered near each other, catching their breath, enjoying their exhilaration and closeness, the mad way their hearts were pumping.

The sun was shining, and already Esther could feel the heat rising. Running always cleared her mind, and now, as she strode home, she could see her day spread before her like a road jammed with traffic. She clicked off her appointments in her head.

'What are you thinking about?' Vanessa asked. 'You look so intense.'

'Work,' Esther said. 'I've got a lot to do today.' She saw that Vanessa was looking at the house next door to Esther's, which had had a Sold sign stuck in the lawn for several weeks. A huge moving van was being unloaded. 'Looks like you've got new neighbors,' Vanessa said. Standing on the sidewalk, watching the moving men, were a white woman, a black man, and a beige little girl with the wildest, crinkliest hair Esther had ever seen. Flames leaped into the pit of her stomach. She sucked her teeth in disgust and scowled.

'What's the matter?' Vanessa asked.

Esther sighed. 'Why do I have to wake up every day and see some brother and his white woman?'

'Girl, don't trip,' Vanessa admonished her. 'Go over there and introduce yourself.'

But Esther shook her head. She waved as Vanessa drove away, then she went into her house, slamming the door behind her.

At eight-thirty that morning, Fred Gaskins, one of the four operations managers from the downtown branches and the only male in the group, leaned across the conference room table, his face contorted, his eyes bulging, until his nose was almost touching Esther's. 'You mean to say that you want us to give the tellers a two-hundred-dollar limit on check-cashing approval? Whose idea is that? Is that *your* idea? That's the most ridiculous thing I've ever heard!' His cheeks turned redder and redder.

The remnants of Esther's runner's euphoria rapidly dissipated in the face of such overt hostility. She could feel her shoulders converging with her neck and her fingers clenching the pencil she held in her hand. She tapped her foot rapidly against the back rung of the chair. This was not the first time she wanted to reach across the table and squeeze Fred Gaskins's fat little neck, but she managed to smile and keep her voice low, even as the decibels in his kept rising. You insubordinate, Bart Simpson-looking asshole, I'm not letting you make me lose control, she thought, wishing she could scream the words at Fred.

'What about it seems ridiculous to you, Fred?' asked Esther. There wasn't a trace of emotion in her voice or expression.

Two of the women managers waited, their faces impassive, but a third, Dorie, was smirking, her thin lips pressed together in pure delight at the simmering feud she was witnessing. Esther had realized from the first time she met them that Dorie and Fred were in cahoots. They each thought they should have gotten her job, and even though they had always competed with each other, they were united in their resentment that an outsider had swept in and taken the plum that belonged to them. Especially since that outsider was a black woman.

Fred retracted his nose an inch. 'That's giving way too much power to entry-level people. I feel that my authority is being eroded.'

'Fred, every time your tellers have to come to you for your approval to cash a check, that takes you away from something more important. This move will ultimately enhance your position, by freeing you to exert your authority in more meaningful ways.' Esther spoke softly.

'Obviously, you're not down on the front lines often enough to know the caliber of people you want to allow to make these kinds of important decisions,' Fred said with a sneer. 'Some of them are so fresh off the boat, they can barely count in English, the others come from substandard high schools in South-Central.' He spat out his last statement as though it were something nasty-tasting in his mouth. One of the women flushed and looked at Esther sympathetically.

Esther counted to ten silently before she spoke. 'Fred, I'm convinced that where a person comes from has nothing to do with his ability to count. But,' she said in a soft, sweet voice, 'perhaps it does reflect upon your ability to judge character if you've chosen to surround yourself with incompetent people. Are you trying to tell me something about your skills?'

'You still haven't told us who approved this,' he said, glowering at her while he settled back in his chair.

'Fred, I approved it, and I assure you the idea went through all the proper channels before it became policy. My understanding is that it will be instituted throughout the branches within the next three months.'

'My God, not South-Central, I hope. Can those tellers count to two hundred?' he asked. Dorie giggled.

Esther wanted to scream 'Fuck you!' in Fred's face. She could taste those words as they burned her throat. Instead she said quietly, 'The new two-hundred-dollar maximum will be instituted in the downtown branches two weeks from today. I hope that's clear to everyone.' Esther looked directly at Fred.

'I've got the bank's interest at heart,' Fred said loudly.

'I assume we all do, Fred,' Esther said. 'If there are no other questions, let's adjourn. I'll see you all next month.'

She managed to exchange the pleasantries that were required after such meetings and even made a funny comment about the presidential elections. It was hard: hard not to take the coffee she was drinking and hurl it at Fred, the little asshole. But she could be cool. Being cool would get her into lending, where the big deals were made and the rewards were greater. But when she heard Fred call out, 'Affirmative action will be the death of this country,' it was all she could do to keep herself from going straight for his jugular.

Back in her office, Esther closed her door, hurled her briefcase into the corner, collapsed into her chair, and brought her fist crashing down on her desk several times; the sound was like a bomb detonating. The motion released some of her pent-up tension but did nothing for her aching head, which had begun throbbing halfway through her meeting and now was reaching a crescendo of pain. Feeling around in her purse, Esther grabbed a bottle of Tylenol; she quickly chewed and swallowed two pills without water. Damn! She pounded the desk again as Fred Gaskins's words came back to her: *Affirmative action will be the death of this country.* She wanted to go find him right now and scream at him, 'I am qualified to do this job, and that's why I have it!' God, what she wouldn't give to be able to file a complaint with EEOC, but if she ran crying racism every time an asshole like Fred said something about South-Central or affirmative action, she'd only be cutting her own throat.

When Esther left the bank that evening, her stomach was making the same kind of noises her car made right before it was time to be serviced. The air was thick and hot. Looking around her, she silently prayed that her scarred, homeless friend wasn't around. Since their first encounter, the man had become a regular at the parking lot; right now she just wasn't in a charitable mood.

Esther was nearly home when she decided that she didn't feel much like being alone. She turned her car around and headed back down Cranston toward her friend Vanessa's.

Vanessa lived in a peach-colored apartment building on the edge of Hancock Park, the mansion-laden, predominantly white community that lay east of Beverly Hills and north of Park Crest. The story was that Nat King Cole had integrated the neighborhood in the fifties, at the height of his popularity, much to the horror of the white home owners, who, when they approached him about buying back his property, allowed that they enjoyed his singing very much. There still weren't a lot of black families in the vicinity, but the influx of those who followed the smooth crooner served notice to the older residents that black Los Angelenos would no longer remain banished in their allotted southern quadrant of the city.

'Who is it?'

Esther stepped back from the entrance to Vanessa's building and peered up at the small second-floor patio until she saw her friend peeking out of the sliding glass doors. 'It's me.'

The buzzer sounded, and Esther opened the door. Just inside it, an old white woman, her head full of silver hair, peered uneasily at her. Esther was about to say hello when she saw the fear in the blue eyes. My God, she thought, she's scared of me. She was so shocked that for a moment she didn't move. To her surprise, tears began gathering in her eyes. Standing there, she was eight years old again, sitting alone at a table in the lunchroom of the North Side school because no one wanted to eat with her. The pain was so familiar. Just as quickly she felt herself begin to be filled with the rage she'd felt earlier that day. I'm not going to snatch your purse, you old bat, she thought, glaring at the woman.

'Hello,' Esther said finally, in a tight, hard voice. 'I'm going to visit my friend Vanessa.'

The fear vanished from the woman's eyes. 'Oh, you know Vanessa!' Esther could hear her sigh of relief. She smiled.

Esther didn't smile back.

Vanessa's apartment door was open. Esther entered and began picking up the newspapers and magazines that were scattered around the floor. As she straightened up, she could still see the frightened blue eyes, could still feel her own burning anger. Vanessa literally jumped out from behind the door and threw her arms around her friend's neck. 'Quit cleaning up! Girl, I'm so glad to see you. I was going to call. Guess what? I got another callback!'

'A call who?' Esther asked in a dull voice.

'Another audition for the Denzel movie,' Vanessa squealed, holding on to Esther's shoulders and jumping up and down. 'My agent just phoned me ten minutes ago. It's down to five people.'

'Five? Go 'head, girl.' They slapped palms lightly.

Vanessa began waltzing around the room, holding up the edges of her silk hot-pink bathrobe. As she twirled, her woven tresses spun out from her head. 'I am scared of me, girlfriend,' she sang over and over.

'Congratulations,' Esther said when Vanessa stopped whirling. She momentarily forgot about Fred Gaskins and the old woman and let herself feel happiness for Vanessa. 'So when do you go back?'

'Next week sometime. Eeeeeeeeeeeee!' She stamped her feet. 'Okay. Okay. I'm calm now. I'm cool. You want something to drink? Cranberry juice? Diet Sprite? Wine?' She stopped abruptly. Her face became suddenly solemn. 'You know, I could really play the hell out of this part. I could be the bomb, and that's no lie. I just want the chance.' She turned her face up to the ceiling. 'I claim this role.'

After Vanessa poured them both a glass of wine, they

toasted the callback. She stared into Esther's face. 'What are you looking so evil about?' she asked.

Esther grunted a little. 'When I was coming into your building, this old white woman took one look at my black face and got scared. And that pissed me off.'

Vanessa smiled as she settled herself in a chair on the small patio. 'Oh, you're talking about Helena. That's my girl. She brings me dinner sometimes. She's real sweet. How'd you scare her?'

'I think she thought I was going to snatch her purse.'

Vanessa chuckled. 'She probably did. Girlfriend is real nervous around strangers.'

'Real dumb too. What kind of mugger wears a business suit and high heels. Who did she think I was, Willie Horton in drag?'

Vanessa chuckled. 'She's just jittery. She's cool once you get to know her.'

'I don't need to get to know anybody who's scared of all black folks. I get tired of them being so scared of us all the time. Wears me out. What has happened to white people? They used to have guts. They'd be out there exploring strange lands, declaring war, conquering people, going into outer space; they weren't scared of nothing. Now the sight of one black person gives them heart failure. They need massive doses of Valium.' She shook her head, ignoring Vanessa's laughter. 'I'm serious. I know they're scared of crime. Hell, I'm scared of crime. Yeah, there are black people who will rob you, rape you, kill you but we don't do *most* of the crime in America. So how did we get the reputation of being the only criminals in this country? All these serial killers running around mutilating coeds are white. All these damn cult leaders, burning people up, are white. Charles Manson. Jeffrey Dahmer. White. You don't see us shooting our parents for the insurance money.'

'Get real. Black people have done everything you've mentioned,' Vanessa said.

'But white people do every damn crime we do, and they don't get the rep. I'm calling up Jesse. Forget about civil rights. Who does white people's public relations? We need a damn ad campaign.'

Vanessa shrugged. 'I think *you* need the Valium, girl-friend,' she said. 'I've lowered my expectations of my white brothers and sisters. Helena has redeeming qualities. Now, it is true that she is scared of strange black people, but she's very kind to me.'

'In other words: can we all get along?' Esther said, her lips curled up in a sarcastic grimace.

Vanessa shrugged. 'In other words, Helena isn't into burning crosses, and sometimes she cooks me dinner. She's cool.'

Esther poured herself another glass of wine. She shook her head. 'You're a little more charitable than I am. I'm sorry, but if your first thought is that since I'm black I must be a thief, then we can't deal.'

'Why should her thoughts be my problem? If I dwell on Helena's racism and Joe Blow's racism, that's all I'm ever going to think about. I'll always be thinking about white folks: what they did to me, what they're getting ready to do to me, what they haven't thought about doing to me. I won't be thinking about what I want to accomplish and how I can do that; I'll be thinking about white folks. I'll always be angry, and that's giving them too much power in my life. If I have to overlook some racism to stay sane, then hey, I will,' Vanessa said, plucking Esther on her knee.

'Well, thank you, Miss Good Karma. Miss New Age.'

'Hey, black folks need to get new. We've been running those same old tapes in our head about the mean old white folks for too long. If we can't find it in our hearts to love white folks, the best thing we can do is ignore them.'

'How in the hell can you ignore white people?'

'You have to focus on you. Every morning, go to the mirror and say, "My color is my joy and not my burden."'

'Oh, please,' Esther said, throwing up her hands.

Vanessa shrugged. 'Anyway, what's happening with you? Rodney asked about you.'

Esther rolled her eyes, still holding on to her anger.

Vanessa said, 'I don't know why you won't give that boy some play. Just a little. I heard he has a great big johnson and can really do it.'

'Not interested. No romance without finance.'

'You're an evil heifer. How are you ever gonna find somebody?'

Esther's response was a short laugh accompanied by a slight shrug. She changed the subject quickly.

It was nearly nine o'clock by the time Esther got home. She took out a cup of plain yogurt from her refrigerator, sprinkled it with raisins and sunflower seeds, and sat down at the kitchen table, scanning the *Gazette* as she ate her meal. When she finished, she went upstairs, put a Jane Fonda tape in her VCR, and began exercising. Halfway through her workout, she stopped and sat on the floor, rubbing away the burning sensation in her thighs. When the sharp pain dulled, her entire body seemed to go limp. She took a bath, then climbed into bed. Just before sleep claimed her, Vanessa's voice echoed in her mind: How are you ever gonna find somebody? It was a question that made her writhe with sweat and grapple against her strangling sheets as the night dragged on.

6

The loan department of Angel City National Bank occupied the entire midsection of the first floor of the downtown building directly in front of the beleaguered real estate branch, which was slowly sinking under the weight of the biggest depression in housing anyone could remember. If the operations department, located in the front, was the bank's stepchild, the lending side, home of an elite corps of highly trained technicians who proudly possessed the requisite M.B.A.'s, was its favorite son. In lending, unlike operations, privacy was prized and each spacious office came with opaque walls and a large oak-veneer door, complete with a lock. There were six of these doors, and on a Wednesday morning a little before eight, Mallory pressed her body against the wall outside the largest and most imposing of all the offices, the working quarters of Charles Weber. The door in question wasn't locked, was, in fact, cracked just wide enough to allow Mallory to see the branch manager and senior loan officer standing by his desk, both fury and panic etched in his trembling jaw. 'You heard me!' he screamed. 'The son of a bitch has had me transferred to South-Central. Said it's for the good of the bank to ensure racial diversity in our workforce. Can you believe this shit! Hell, no, I'm not going!' Mallory could see him circle his desk, like a wildcat about to spring. 'It's all part of his big restructuring plan; the entire system has been affected. It's like busing for the M.B.A. set,' Charles said bitterly. 'That son of a bitch. If Preston Sinclair wants to be the Emperor of Diversity, I'll be damned if it's going to be at my expense. I'm not going to take this. I'll sue for reverse discrimination. There's no way in hell I'm going to work in that jungle.'

The next thing Mallory heard was the sound of Charles slamming down the receiver. She headed straight to Esther's office. The news she had was too good to keep.

That same morning, Preston Sinclair was being interviewed by a very bored *Gazette* reporter. In the days since April 29, the newspaper had developed a voracious appetite for 'post-riot' stories, especially ones enhanced by the promise of the ever elusive happy ending the city was seeking. Hope was what Los Angeles wanted to read about, and the paper's headlines attempted to package this too rare commodity in words that began with *re*: 'recovery,' 'renewal,' and, of course, 'rebuild.'

'In summation, as the first prong of our Diversity Program, we are lending one of Angel City's senior managers from our downtown branch to the South-Central branch for an unspecified length of time. This is the initial step toward a full-fledged exchange of managers who work in areas of high minority concentration with those who work in communities that are less, uh, diverse. What we hope to accomplish ultimately is not only an enhancement of skills for all managers but the development of mutual respect for the diversity that is represented at Angel City National Bank.' Preston's smile was a flourish, an exclamation mark.

The reporter frowned and adjusted his glasses. This non-story certainly didn't deserve a photo, but his editor was insisting there be one.

'This way, Mr. Sinclair.' Preston turned toward the photographer and leaned forward in his chair. In his eyes was a look of such earnest sincerity that he appeared more like a minister of the cloth than a powerful executive. In fact, his expression was the result of years of imitating the pious mien of his father as he preached from his Sunday pulpit. What he was never able to mimic was the burning devotion and humility that were the heartbeat of his father's soul. Preston found that in most cases, few people could tell the imitation from the real thing. Certainly not the stoop-shouldered, bespectacled reporter the *Gazette* had sent over. Preston's smile was pure zirconium as the photographer snapped the first picture, but when he began circling, looking for an angle for a second shot, the thought occurred to Preston that he might be squandering an opportunity, a superior photo opportunity, as it were. Several weeks from now he hoped to announce that Humphrey Boone would be joining the Angel City National Bank team in a newly created position that would make him the highest-ranking minority in the organization and probably in the city. He didn't want to jump the gun, of course, but he was making the black man the proverbial offer he couldn't refuse. When he made that announcement, he wanted his picture and Boone's on the front page of the business section. Only now he wondered if the *Gazette* would run another illustrated article about him so soon after this one. The flash popped several more times, and then Preston rose, extending his hand first to the photographer and then to the reporter, who was checking through the notes he had scrawled so furiously during the interview. Preston hesitated, then smiled again. He gave the young man a pat on his back. 'Great questions. Very sharp. Ve-e-ery sharp.'

'Just one more thing, Mr. Sinclair,' the reporter said. There was something so smug about Angel City's president that he felt he deserved a curve ball. 'There are many minorities, and white women as well, who assert that American corporations are racist institutions that limit their progress because of their gender and the color of their skin. Does the new program at Angel City National hope to address some of the inequities inherent in your institution?'

Let's see you squirm, the reporter thought. He held his pencil aloft and eyed Preston.

The zirconium smile reappeared automatically. Admit nothing, Preston silently reminded himself as he searched for just the right response, something weighty and, well, gubernatorial. He stared into the reporter's eyes until the young man looked away. 'The United States isn't a perfect country. Its institutions reflect that imperfection. The important thing is not to point a finger at flaws but to attempt to correct them. There is no room for a glass ceiling at Angel City National Bank.'

A decent quote, the reporter thought. Not great. But decent. 'Now, young man, my assistant will be calling you with another story in a few weeks,' Preston said, holding the door open.

'I look forward to that, Mr. Sinclair.'

When Preston was alone again, he pounded on the desk with his fist several times. 'Yes!' He was carving out his political persona: a fiscally conservative, moderate Republican who believed in giving everyone a fair shake. And he wasn't just being self-serving, he told himself, as he thought about the Diversity Program he was creating. The new policies were for the good of the bank. They made good business sense. That was all he asked of anything.

On her way to Esther's office, Mallory passed the coffee machine and saw Kirk Madison pouring a sickening amount of sugar into his cup. From several feet away, the shine on his thick cordovans almost blinded her. When he saw Mallory he waved and then motioned her over.

Kirk reminded Mallory of a big, overanxious puppy, forever nipping at the heels of whoever he thought had dog biscuits. 'Have you heard that Charles is being transferred?' he whispered, barely able to contain his glee.

Play dumb, Mallory told herself. 'No!' she said, trying to look surprised. 'Are you serious?'

'I hear he'll be gone in a couple of weeks.'

'Is it a promotion or a lateral?'

He looked around him before he spoke. Satisfied that no one was listening, he said, 'He's going to the South-Central branch. That sounds like a demotion to me.' He winked at Mallory and then grinned. Mallory could tell that he believed he was the natural successor to Charles's position. She tried to envision Kirk as her boss. At least he had a wife – presumably he wouldn't come to work horny every day. She'd stand a better chance of advancing under Kirk than with Charles, and maybe Esther could finally come over to the loan department. She felt guilty that the black woman hadn't been able to make that switch. Might as well get in a good word now.

She leaned over the coffeepot and whispered in Kirk's ear: 'I hope you get his position. You deserve it.' Kirk beamed. Mallory smiled somewhat seductively, even though she felt like gagging. As hard as she tried not to do it, flattering a man came so easily to her, and there didn't seem to be a feminist alternative that could get the same results.

The door to Esther's office was open. 'Excuse me, Esther. I didn't mean to interrupt. I have superb news,' Mallory said, stepping inside and closing the door.

Esther looked up and then leaned back in her seat.

'I thought you might like to know that Charles is leaving downtown. He's being transferred to South-Central.'

Esther's body lurched forward. 'What!'

'Let's have a drink after work, and I'll give you the details.'

Esther nodded.

The waitress at Patti's had a terrible perm, Mallory noticed as she and Esther followed the middle-aged woman toward the rear of the dim, quiet restaurant. Across from them, at another table for two, a pair of women, one black, one white, sat drinking wine and talking softly. As Mallory watched, Esther nodded and said, 'How are you doing?' to the black woman, and they smiled at each other.

'Dinner?' the waitress asked, looking directly at Mallory as she handed menus to the two women.

'Just drinks,' Esther said. Her voice was firm, business-like, and Mallory detected a trace of annoyance. 'What are you having, Mallory?'

'Oh, I'm celebrating, *honey*. I'll have champagne,' Mallory said.

'Two,' Esther told the waitress, who nodded.

'So,' Esther said, after the waitress left.

'So,' Mallory echoed.

'He's really leaving. Hallelujah!'

The two women giggled.

'He is on his way to head up the South-Central branch for an indeterminate length of time,' Mallory said. 'From what I understand, this is part of Angel City's new program aimed at enhancing diversity at the bank. They're supposed to be planning all kinds of managerial exchanges to balance the personnel racially. I understand they even plan on instituting racial awareness and sensitivity classes.'

'Who's responsible for all this?'

'I hear that it's coming from the very, very top,' Mallory said.

'Sinclair?'

'Evidently he's committed to change,' Mallory said.

'Do you know who's replacing Charles?' Esther asked.

Mallory shook her head.

'If it's an exchange, does that mean that his South-Central counterpart is coming downtown?'

Mallory pondered Esther's question. She started to say

that she didn't think anyone at South-Central, the smallest branch in the system, would have the experience necessary to handle downtown, but she thought her words might sound to Esther like a put-down of that branch or maybe of the people there, even though that wasn't what she meant. But if Sinclair was genuinely committed to the diversity campaign, there was a chance he had that kind of shuffle in mind. The thought of some manager from South-Central getting preferential treatment over her bothered Mallory. After all, women had been denied opportunities for centuries.

'Hey, why so glum?' Esther asked. 'We should be celebrating. I'd like to propose a toast.' Esther raised her glass. Mallory picked up her drink, and their two glasses clinked. 'To the end of Charles Weber,' Esther said.

'Hear! Hear!'

'May I get you ladies anything else?' Mallory looked up to see the Frizzball smiling at her.

'We'll have another round,' Esther said.

When the drinks came, they again toasted Charles Weber's departure, then lingered awhile, sharing office gossip for nearly an hour. The more they laughed, the more Esther felt herself relaxing.

'You care for another round?' Frizzball asked, adding up the total as she spoke.

'No, that's it,' said Esther.

The waitress nodded at her, finished her calculations, and placed the check on the table directly in front of Mallory. Before Mallory could reach for it, Esther snatched it away with fingers as curved and violent as an angry cat's. 'I'll take it,' she said sharply.

Mallory's pale-gray eyes met Frizzball's blue ones, and each silently posed the same question: *What's the problem?* Esther seemed suddenly furious, but Mallory was afraid to ask why. Moments later, when the two women across from them collected their purses and rose to leave, the black woman patted Esther's shoulder very quickly as she walked by. Esther shook her head. Mallory realized then that the black woman knew what she and Frizzball didn't know and could never know without asking.

Esther slapped her gold card on the little plastic tray. The waitress took it and disappeared. Mallory sat stiff and silent in her chair, trepidation rippling through her throat. She wanted to ask the question, but she was afraid that the look of outrage in Esther's eyes would intensify and begin to encompass her. But they could never be good friends unless she was willing to risk her feelings. Mallory leaned across the table. 'Esther . . .'

The laugh she heard came from a few tables away, yet it seemed closer, much closer. The heavy male chuckle was so familiar. She felt a slow burning agony creeping through her body, as the strong laughter was echoed by giggles as frail as lace. Mallory spun around. Hayden Lear sat at a table, drinking with a middle-aged woman – his wife!

'Mallory?' Esther asked.

'Hayden.' Mallory's voice was a whimper. 'Hayden.' People at the closest table stopped talking to turn and look at her. Mallory pushed back her chair. Her entire body was trembling. She was crying as she began to walk toward the laughter, toward the table in the back where Hayden Lear sat with his arm draped casually across his wife's shoulders. His wife, who didn't understand him. His wife, who didn't like sex. Mallory took another step, and a body, as strong and impenetrable as a wall, stood before her.

'No-o-o, girlfriend. Girlfriend-n-nd! Now, let's not act a fool in here.' Mallory felt Esther's fingers circling her wrists, clamping down on them like handcuffs. She let herself be led toward the door.

Mallory heard Hayden's laughter until she was outside and her own sonorous wailing drowned out the sounds in her head. She followed Esther, unaware of where she was going, until she heard the car door open and found herself sitting in the passenger's seat of Esther's silver BMW. She covered her face with her hands and bawled. She wasn't aware of how much time had passed; she just knew that her own crying was the only sound she heard and that the pressure from Esther's fingers around her shoulder was as steady as her own heartbeat.

'I must look a mess,' Mallory said when she finally stopped crying. Esther handed her a tissue, and she wiped her eyes and blew her nose. 'Thanks.'

'You okay?'

Mallory nodded. Then she began sobbing again. When she was able to stop, she said, 'I'm sorry. I'm sorry.'

'It's okay.'

'That was Hayden Lear.' Mallory giggled a little. Everything looked blurry and out of focus. 'I think I lost my right contact,' she said dully.

'It's probably in your eye,' Esther said. She sidled up close to Mallory and peered into her eye. 'Look up. Look down. There it is. Work it down with your finger.'

Mallory rotated her closed eye until she felt the contact slide into place; blinked until everything was in focus. 'He was my first boss, my mentor, and we've been having an affair for the last four years. The woman he was having such a great time with is his wife; I met her a few years ago. She's the bitch who's never there for him. Well, she seemed very much there this evening.'

'Listen, Mallory, you don't have to— '

'He says he's going to divorce her,' Mallory said. 'He says that all the time.'

'Girl, they all say that,' Esther said softly. 'Look, this isn't any of my business.'

'I love him. And I know that he loves me. I know that eventually we'll be together,' Mallory said fiercely.

'I see you are living the life Aretha sings about,' Esther said with just the trace of a smile.

Mallory gave her a blank look.

' "I Ain't Never Loved a Man," "Chain of Fools," "Dr. FeelGood." Never mind. It's a black thing; you wouldn't understand.' The words just slipped out.

'What?'

'Nothing.' She was sorry she'd spoken, that she'd crossed a line. Now she wanted to get back to the other side.

'Tell me.'

'It's just an expression.'

'Because I'm not black, I don't understand certain things about black people?'

'Something like that. No offense.'

Mallory spoke softly. 'I'm not offended, Esther. Hayden was the first man who believed I had abilities. You got that when you were a little girl, I can tell. You're very self-assured. My family didn't expect anything from me other than that I be a pretty little girl and then a pretty big girl and then somebody's wife. I was smart, but that didn't matter to them. They didn't encourage me. Hayden did. He helped me get promoted into lending. I was just floundering before I met him. I owe him so much.'

'You don't owe him a damn thing, Mallory. He's getting his. He's taking your youth, your time, your faith, your self-esteem.'

Mallory shrank away from the fervor in the black woman's voice. 'I know he is,' Mallory said, her voice trembling. She began whimpering and then sobbed again.

Esther leaned over and put her arms around Mallory's shoulders. Lawdhamercy. She rubbed her back until Mallory was quiet again. Theirs were the only two cars left in the parking lot, and the sky around them was almost dark.

'I better get going,' Mallory said. She really didn't want to leave.

Her car was only a few steps away, but Esther drove her to it. She watched Mallory as she unlocked her door and got in the Lexus. She heard the motor and was about to drive off, when Mallory honked her horn and rolled down her window. The air was still hot and gritty. 'Esther, I want to ask you something. When you were angry in the restaurant, was *that* a black thing I wouldn't understand?'

The light was on in Mallory's car, and Esther could see the kindness and concern brimming in the white woman's gray eyes. She turned away. 'It was nothing,' she said. 'See you.' She rolled up her window and drove off.

Mallory watched the silver BMW as it turned out of the lot. Nothing? She recalled the set of Esther's mouth, the fire flashing in her glance, the way her hands snatched the check away. Nothing? She doesn't trust me. The words revolved around her mind in slow, faint circles. Mallory sat in the dark for a moment, thinking. Behind her, the Los Angeles skyline had an eerie yellow cast. Below her, the earth beneath the city put off trembling for yet another day. She doesn't trust me. As Mallory drove out of the lot, she wondered what it would take before Esther *could* trust her.

7

On Saturday, Mallory stood outside her parents' home, the house they fled to when they escaped the onslaught of colored who began encroaching upon Park Crest. The four-bedroom ranch with its picture window in the living room was identical to the surrounding houses in Arroyo, one of the many suburbs that sprang up in the fifties and early sixties after neighborhoods in the city began to integrate and industries began to relocate farther from Los Angeles. More than once since she'd grown up, Mallory had parked her car in the wrong driveway, only to discover her mistake when she reached the front door. Her own town house was less than twenty minutes away, but she came to her parents' home only when she was summoned.

It was barely past noon, but already the temperature was in the nineties, at least ten degrees hotter than in the city. But the heat in Los Angeles was not only weather. Only that morning, Mallory had turned on the news and heard that fighting had broken out between black, Latino, and white prisoners in one of the city jails. As she turned off the radio, once more the specter of Reginald Denny, his crumpled white body sprawled in the streets of South-Central, rose in her mind. Were such attacks going to become common? She shuddered.

Now, at her parents' door, Mallory felt removed from the problems of the city. The thick air around her was clogged with bits of ash from the fires that were still roaring in the Angeles Forest, not ten miles away. As she looked into the heavy sky, she didn't see one bird. During the heat wave, her parents' automatic sprinklers came on early every morning, but as Mallory looked at the front lawn, there was no indication that the grass had been watered at all. The entire neighborhood seemed scorched, as though an invisible, fire-breathing dragon had gone on a rampage.

For as long as Mallory could remember, her mother was constantly redecorating their house. She could see that it had been painted since her last visit. Peering through the large picture window, she saw new carpeting and drapes.

Mallory pulled the brim of her Lakers cap down low on her forehead. She had her key, but she rang the bell three times before it dawned on her that no one was coming to open the door because everyone was already out back for the barbecue. As Mallory walked around the house, the scent of the flowers was every bit as strong as the odor of steaks and chicken sizzling on the grill.

'Mallory! Sweetheart! Oh, you're so ski-i-iny.' Her mother hugged her, held her long enough and tightly enough so that Mallory could smell both her Chloé and her Scotch. She pulled away first, as she always did when her mother embraced her. 'Oh, sweetheart, you didn't get dressed up. Daddy will be so disappointed.' She whispered the last, her voice tinged with a slight edge of apprehension, of hysteria, the voice of a woman who asked how much she could spend, who looked over her shoulder as she whispered into the telephone.

Mallory smiled at the older woman. She was wearing a plaid shirt with piping along the shoulders, a buckskin skirt with fringes, brown leather boots, and a cowgirl hat. Her dark eyes were framed by deep lines, and the tilted hat didn't totally cover her gray hair. She looked like an aging Annie Oakley. 'Mallory's here,' her mother called out gaily to the rest of the people. Glancing around the yard, Mallory saw that her father, her brother, Jonathan, and his wife, Sharon, as well as the neighbors from either side and across the street, were all dressed in Western style, the usual theme of her parents' Columbus Day barbecue. 'Go tell Daddy you forgot,' her mother whispered. Mallory could see her silent message in her eyes: Ask him to forgive you.

'I forgot it was Western, Dad. Sorry,' Mallory said to her father as he barbecued. He was a big man, a hulking John Wayne type, whose size had always made her feel small and insignificant. She stood in front of her father, as stiff and wooden as a puppet. He was wearing a sky-blue shirt that had fringes hanging from the sleeves. Over that was a fake-suede vest with a tin star pinned to the flap just below his BUSH FOR PRESIDENT button. Strapped to his waist was a holster bearing two huge guns. For a fleeting moment, Mallory wondered whether or not they were loaded.

He was standing over the grill, a huge, barrel-shaped contraption, spreading barbecue sauce on the steaks and chicken. His big hands moved back and forth in a fluid rhythm. Her father's hands always seemed to be wrapped around something, holding something. They'd never held her. She had to stand on tiptoe to brush his cheek with her lips. He didn't bend down, but he did turn and look at her, taking in her khaki shorts and white T-shirt in a quick, dismissive glance. 'It was a small thing to remember, Mallory. Your brother didn't forget,' he said. He didn't stop what he was doing to return her kiss. Mallory squinted as plumes of smoky air blew in her direction. She felt a scream racing to her throat, but instead swallowed hard, as she often had to do when she came home.

'I'll go say hello to everybody,' she said softly. Her father didn't respond. She walked across the yard, feeling lost and lonely. Only her father could make her feel so. She remembered a Parents' Night when she was in the fifth grade, Jonathan in the first. She held her mother's hand, her excitement growing like a flower in her chest as they neared her classroom. She had a spelling test with a bright gold star on it tacked up on the bulletin board. The teacher had posted her A+ math test in the back of the room, and on the side, under the window, her science project was on display; she'd received an A+ for that too. As they approached her class, her heart was pounding, because her father had never come to Parents' Night before, not when she was in the first or the second, the third or the fourth grade. More than anything, she wanted her father to see her beautiful papers, to hear the lovely things her teachers had to say about her. She wanted him to know that she was smart, that she was in the advanced section. Her mother knew all these things; her mother came to the school every year. Maybe if her father discovered what a good girl she was, what a bright girl, he would pay more attention to her. Maybe he would muss her hair, the way he did Jonathan's. Perhaps he would ride her on his shoulders too. And so, as they neared her classroom, she began running, pulling her mother by the hand, rushing them toward the open door, praying that once they were inside, the magic would happen. But they didn't go inside the door to her class; instead, they walked right past it, down the hall to Jonathan's classroom, where they sat until the bell rang to warn them that there were only ten minutes left of Parents' Night. Her mother and father left her brother's classroom, and she could remember their shoes scraping against the cement floor as they trudged down the hall to her room. Her hair kept falling in her eyes and mouth as she ran, because she was laughing. And then she heard her father's heavy footsteps stop, and he told her mother to go ahead, that Jonathan was tired. He would stay with Jonathan. He said, 'Go on. Go on. We'll meet you at the car.' She remembered the way her heart lurched in her chest, hammering away so hard it hurt to breathe. She wanted to scream at her mother, 'Make him come. You make him come see my stars.' But her mother nodded in a way that was barely a movement at all and took her by the hand, and once again it was just the two of them. She wore a blue dress with flowers on the bodice that night so long ago, and what Mallory remembered most deeply about her fifth-grade Parents' Night was how dark the blue of the flowers became when they were wet.

As she neared the canvas-covered brick patio, Mallory could hear the neighbors' voices rising in debate.

'Aww, he's a crackpot, a rich, big-eared crackpot. He's got as much chance of being President as a snowball in hell.'

'Well, I like him. This country needs a businessman.'

'How's running a business gonna help him when Saddam Hussein declares World War Three. I tell ya, we need to stick, with Bush. Give the man four more years and he'll straighten out the economy.'

She heard her brother's voice. 'What I want to know is who's gonna stop all these wetbacks from coming in here and getting on welfare with the blacks? That's the man I'm voting for.'

'Mallory,' her brother called out as soon as she was near. He was tall, like their father, and had to bend down to hug her. His dark, spiky hair smelled like coconut. He had been born after her father had four daughters with his first wife and another with his second. She'd seen her half-sisters three times during her childhood: the same number of times her father saw them after his divorce. He had no need of daughters after his son was born. It didn't matter that Jonathan was in and out of jail and on and off drugs. He was the chosen one; she was one of five disappointments. She begged for her father's love; her brother squandered it. 'Somebody get Mallory a beer,' Jonathan said loudly.

Mallory, who hadn't seen her childhood neighbors in months, greeted everyone, pausing to hear stories about their families, to answer their careful questions about the life of a thirtysomething-year-old woman that didn't include marriage and little ones. She was chatting with her sister-in-law when warm fingers grasped Mallory's wrist and gently pulled her away. 'Hi, stranger.'

'Susan!' The two women hugged tightly for a few moments.

'I never see you anymore.' Her friend Susan pouted just a little.

The accusation stung, not because it wasn't true but because Mallory had been dreading it so much. She thought of Susan as her best friend, but they didn't get together very often anymore and Mallory had broken the last two dates they'd made. 'Oh, don't fuss. You know you still love me,' she said playfully. Then she bent down and kissed the two small girls who clung to each leg of Susan's jeans. 'Hi, Pumpkins.' She looked up at Susan, who was smiling. 'God, they're really getting big.'

Two sets of big brown eyes stared back at her without blinking.

'How's the big-time executive?'

Mallory stood up and faced Phillip, Susan's husband. His lips managed to curl into a smile, but his eyes were cold. He moved closer to Susan and put his arm around her in a way that forced her to turn her body toward him.

What a jerk, Mallory thought. The smile she gave him was just as phony as his; her eyes were every bit as unfriendly. 'What can I tell you, Phillip? I'm making more money than most men I know. I'm happy.'

Mallory smirked inwardly as a brief shadow crossed Phillip's face and dimmed his smile. Gotcha, you little asshole.

But Phillip's eyes gleamed maliciously. 'I don't know, Mal,' he said. 'While you're making all that money, your old biological clock is just ticking away. You'll never catch up to Susie. Did she tell you we're expecting another blessed event?'

'Phillip!' Susan said. 'I wanted to tell her myself.'

'Sue will never have a fancy-schmancy career. She's just a good old-fashioned girl,' Phillip said, still smiling. He raked his fingers through his short brown hair.

'Congratulations,' Mallory said softly. I'll have babies, she told herself. She looked at Susan, who averted her eyes. What could she be thinking of! The last time she'd talked to her friend, she was planning on going back to school, getting her degree. They'd discussed her goals for hours, and Mallory had carefully advised her where to apply, what courses to take. And now she was pregnant. Again.

'Gotta get me a boy,' Phillip said. He put his hands on his wife's belly and squeezed it softly. The gesture was so intimate that Mallory looked away in embarrassment.

'Phi-i-il.' Susan pushed his hands away. But there was pleasure in the eyes that met Mallory's, a smug satisfaction that Mallory felt was designed to elicit envy. And she did envy Susan. She had a family.

The loud, tinny sound of a triangle being hit with a metal mallet permeated the yard. Mallory looked toward the barbecue grill. There was a table next to it, and her mother was standing there, arranging the side dishes of potato salad, baked beans, corn on the cob, rolls and pitchers of iced tea and lemonade. 'Come and get it, partners!' her father called out, his voice deep and harsh.

'Hon, would you get me a plate? And make sure the meat's medium,' Phillip said. 'I'll watch the kids for you.'

'It was an accident,' Susan whispered as they walked toward the food.

'Look, I think it's really great,' Mallory lied. 'You're such a wonderful mother, Sue. Really, I think it's great.' How, she wondered, could her friend be so passive?

Susan grinned at her, and Mallory realized that she was actually happy to have another baby with her jerk of a husband.

'If the new baby's a boy, I'm finished. I told Phil I'm

getting my tubes tied.' Susan giggled. 'Of course, he hit the ceiling. The man is crazy about kids. His business is doing really well, so . . . Can you believe that Lindsay will be going to school next year? So tell me who you're seeing, Mal.'

Mallory hesitated. She always meant to tell Susan about Hayden, but somehow she never did. Listening to her friend chatter about her third baby, about schools and her husband, she felt the way she often did around her: they lived in two separate worlds. 'I'm dating several guys. Nothing serious. The job, my career, keeps me so busy. I have a lot more responsibility these days.'

'You're so glamorous, Mal. So thin. I'll never be thin again.' Susan slapped her thick thighs with her palms. For a moment, Mallory relished her friend's envy. But at the same time, when she looked at Susan's red hair and freckles, her sweet, childlike face, she remembered their days as girls. There was a time when neither one of them could imagine life without the other. There was so much she wanted to tell her.

'Let's go talk in my room for a few minutes,' Mallory said, grabbing Susan's hand.

'I have to fix Phillip's— '

'Oh, come on. He can survive for a few minutes.'

The house was blessedly cool, thanks to central air-conditioning. Mallory's old bedroom had been turned into a kind of office-gym, but her old twin bed was still there and from force of habit that's where Mallory led her friend.

'I ran into Steve McPherson last week,' Susan said, settling herself in one corner of the bed across from her friend.

Mallory squealed at the mention of her high school boyfriend's name. 'Oh, God. How's he doing?'

'He looks great. He asked about you.'

'He did? What did he say?' Mallory pressed against

Susan's arm. Steve McPherson. My God, she thought. 'Is he still married?'

The door creaked as it opened. The two women looked up at the same time. 'Hey! Here's Mommy. She's talking with her executive girlfriend. I guess she doesn't care that her family is starving.' Phillip stood in the doorway. He had one little girl in his arms, and the other was holding his hand. The children were crying softly.

Susan got up from the bed and took the youngest child from her husband. 'What's the matter?' she cooed.

Mallory watched as the baby put her arms around her mother's neck. Sue swayed a little to rock her, and the whimpers quietened down. Mallory wondered what it would feel like to have that kind of power, to touch a child and have her tears disappear. She felt an ache in her back where her spine was pressed up against the hard wood of the headboard. 'Come on,' Susan said to Phillip. She looked back at Mallory and smiled wistfully. 'I'll see you outside,' she said.

Susan and Phillip's footsteps were soft on the carpet. When Mallory couldn't hear them any longer, she let her head fall back against her pillow. She opened a window. The aroma of barbecued beef and chicken and the sound of Hank Williams singing 'Your Cheating Heart' wafted up. Her mother's laughter floated across the yard: a mildly hysterical blend of coughing and cackling that meant she'd had one Scotch too many. Mallory looked at her watch. In ten minutes it would be three o'clock. At three o'clock she would do what she always did on these occasions: what was required. She'd go downstairs and eat her father's barbecue and pretend not to see her mother getting drunk. And when she couldn't pretend any longer, she'd go home.

There was a telephone next to her bed. Hayden was probably on the golf course now. That's how he spent his Saturday afternoons. Even if he were at home, she couldn't call him there. Tears welled up in her eyes. She pinched her arm as hard as she could. Don't you dare cry. Don't you dare. Mallory thought about how she'd bawled in Esther's car. For a fleeting moment she wondered what the black woman was doing on a hot Saturday afternoon. She wished she had her number; she wished she had her strength.

From the bedroom window, Mallory could see the smoke still rising from the barbecue grill. Her mother looked happy, standing next to her father behind a table that was crowded with all the good things she'd cooked. Her mother was spooning food onto Jonathan's plate. Mallory heard her father laugh for the first time that day as he told her mother, 'Give the boy more.'

Mallory closed the window. Already the oppressive heat from the still, heavy air had seeped inside the small room. Ten minutes, she told herself. In ten minutes she'd go down.

8

The storms finally came at the end of October, unexpectedly early and more plentiful than people who'd lived with almost five years of drought had expected. The truth was, many Los Angelenos had given up believing in rain or at least in its transforming powers. The drought had been so long and severe, rain was but a distant memory. But what fell from the clouds was torrential, nothing like the half-hearted sprinkles of the recent past, which had dampened little more than spirits. The dark clouds that suddenly filled the sky were of biblical proportions, and the storms lasted for days and nights. People were lulled to sleep at night by the rhythmic pounding of the water coming down hard on their roofs. They heard the downpour lashing against their windowpanes and woke up to find a drenched dawn, with a sky that still wasn't clear. Grass that had been brown and patchy turned a lush, brilliant green. Camellias and begonias doubled in size, the leaves on jade plants swelled until they almost burst, and the boughs of lemon and orange trees were bent over with the weight of their fruit. The outline of the downtown skyline, a smoggy mystery to residents of Los Feliz, Pasadena, and Hollywood during the hot spell, was suddenly 'the view' proud home owners boasted of.

But even before the water in the city's reservoirs rose to surpass the satisfactory level, the same people who only a few months earlier had prayed for rain began to wish it would go away. The storms were inconvenient, even dangerous. L.A. drivers slid across slick streets and highways, crashing into walls and each other. The wet weather was bad for many businesses. Car washes were closed for days at a time. Not only were the owners grim but hordes of mostly Latino workers were idle. Even the red-light hucksters, those new brown-skinned immigrants who hustled oranges, peanuts and bananas at freeway exits, stayed home on rainy days. Mudslides in the hills buried homes and people. More than once an unfortunate child was swept away when he attempted to swim in a storm drain.

One week of rain was all it took to forget the drought, the fires, the fear of a water shortage; Los Angelenos shed their newly acquired conservation habits as though they were an unnecessary layer of clothing. They did what came naturally: ran their faucets while they talked on the telephone; let the water flow freely as they brushed their teeth; flushed their toilets after a single pee. Everyone admitted that they needed the precipitation, yet no one really valued it. The truth was, the waterlogged city reminded residents too much of the places they'd left behind – Houston, Oklahoma City, New Orleans. They had come to Los Angeles for sunshine and shirtsleeve weather, for good times. Watching the rain from their houses, they were as disgruntled as children banished to their rooms. They wanted to go outside and play.

The Saturday morning before the presidential election, Esther stood in front of the oval picture window that overlooked her front lawn, sipping a cup of hot peppermint tea, staring at a fine, steady drizzle. She remembered how she and her brother, Stanley, used to stand in front of the picture window in their parents' home on snowy Saturday mornings, looking out at their front lawn, itching to get outside to be with the kids from their neighborhood. Their mother never allowed them out while the snow was actually falling, but as soon as the last flake hit the ground, they took to the streets.

After their parents sent them to the white private school on the North Side, it was only on Saturday that she and Stanley had a chance to play with other black kids. These Saturdays were all the more precious since the two of them had been ostracized by many of the neighborhood children the entire first year they attended private school. The whispering commenced almost as soon as their absence at their old school was noticed, but the real ugliness began when they opened their mouths. The proper English that was the requisite language of the posh North Side was the South Side's enemy tongue. 'Trying to be white,' some of the children said, taunting them. No matter how many times she and Stanley denied the accusation, their persecutors wouldn't relent. Trying to be white was an unpardonable sin. Then and now.

'Envious. Little evil things are just envious,' he mother exclaimed. 'Don't pay them any mind. You all are going to be somebody, and they're not.'

Her mother's words were more sobering than soothing. The thought that black people could be divided into those who would be important and those who would not hadn't occurred to Esther before. She wanted to be somebody, but she didn't want to be set apart. She could count her white friends on two fingers. Where was she supposed to fit in? But when she asked to return to the public school, her parents said no.

During their second year at the white school, a small miracle occurred. Much to their surprise, the same neighborhood children who taunted them and beat them up the year before welcomed them back into the fold with open arms. What turned the tide, Esther discovered, was her running into one of her tormentors at the corner grocery store. Perhaps feeling guilty, the older girl started a conversation, and while the two children were talking, Esther innocently told her how much she and Stanley hated going to private school. That confession had the effect of magic and traveled throughout the neighborhood in record speed, and only hours later, the same children who had kicked their asses were ringing their doorbell, asking if they could come out and play. Suddenly it didn't seem to matter that Stanley and Esther 'talked white'. What was important was that they identified as black. Stanley was clueless as to what had brought about the change, but Esther was far more perceptive and vigilant in making sure that the mistreatment and ostracism they had suffered never resumed. Whenever she had a chance, she brought up the topic of her hated banishment to the white school. Subtly, she shifted the blame to her parents, who began to acquire a reputation among the neighborhood children as merciless ogres who forced their children to go to private school when they really wanted to go to the neighborhood school like everybody else. When she could manage, Esther sobbed out the entire story for maximum effect, always emphasizing, between her tears, that her loyalty would always remain with the neighborhood.

Esther looked away from the rain and felt rumblings in her stomach. She went into the kitchen to fix herself some breakfast. Opening the cabinet where she kept baked goods, she was dismayed to find no apple muffins. Then she remembered that between dinner and a movie with Mallory, she hadn't had time to make her usual Friday night trip to Diamond Donuts. Esther decided to jog to the store, even though she hadn't run in nearly two weeks. After changing into her sweats and tucking her hair under a Bulls cap, she took a five-dollar bill from her wallet and ran out the door.

Esther was so intent on keeping her head down that she didn't realize there were people on the sidewalk until she was about to run into them. She raised her eyes just in time to see the white woman and her wild-haired child.

Between them was a fat poodle. She stopped short, narrowly missing knocking down the little girl and almost squashing the miniature dog. She bent down and put her arms around the little girl's shoulders. 'Oh, I'm sorry,' Esther said. 'I wasn't looking. Did I scare you?'

'Oh,' the mother said, smiling eagerly, 'she's okay. No harm done. Sarah, say hello.'

'Hello,' the little girl said obediently.

The woman smiled broadly and stuck her hand out toward Esther. 'I'm Carol Linton, and this is my daughter, Sarah. We just moved in not too long ago.'

She's not pretty and she's overweight, Esther noted with satisfaction. If a brother has to pick a white girl, he could at least get someone who looks halfway decent, instead of some homely heifer no white man wants. They stood in the rain, not saying anything for a moment, then Esther reluctantly took Carol's hand. 'I'm Esther Jackson. I live next door.' She started to say 'Welcome to the neighborhood,' but the words refused to come out.

The front door opened. 'Honey,' the man called. He nodded toward Esther in a friendly way. She couldn't quite manage a smile.

Two homely nerds, Esther thought to herself as she began jogging. *Honey.* She mimicked the sound in her head. *Honey. Honey. Honey.* The anger that rose up inside her went to her head immediately, and she could feel her temples throbbing. Why do they bother me so much? she wondered.

The rain started coming down harder just as Esther reached the doughnut shop. Inside, the aroma of coffee and the sweet, yeasty scent of baked goods made Esther even hungrier. Trays of glazed, powdered, and jelly doughnuts glistened behind the glass showcase. On the other side, an array of blueberry, carrot, apple, and bran muffins were on display. Ahead of her was a woman with a small boy who seemed unable to choose what he wanted. The Korean woman leaned against the counter.

The woman and boy finally made their decisions and, clutching their goodies, made a dash to a white Mazda parked right outside the shop. When the Korean woman turned to Esther, her high-wattage smile seemed to intensify. 'Good morning. May I help you?'

'Hi,' Esther said. 'Let me have three apple bran muffins, please.'

She glanced around. The corner table, which was usually occupied by old black men, was empty. Esther pointed to the table and said, 'I see that your regular customers didn't come today.'

'Huh?'

'Where are the men who sit there?'

Esther saw a glimmer of understanding in the woman's eyes. She shook her head. 'Don't come in rain.' The shop owner leaned into the counter. 'Every day come, drink one cuppa coffee. Stay all day. Talk. Talk. Talk.' She shook her head in such a way that Esther couldn't tell whether she was happy the men had stayed away or lonesome for their company.

As Esther watched, the shop owner put three muffins in a small white bag. Esther handed her a five-dollar bill, but to her surprise, the woman put the bag behind her back and shook her head. 'No Laker, no muffin.'

'What?' Esther leaned closer and could feel her waist pressing against the counter. 'What did you say?'

The woman pointed to her Bulls cap. 'No Laker, no muffin.'

Esther started laughing. 'I'm from Chicago.'

'Ah, Chicago. Michael Jordan. Pretty good. Pretty good, Michael Jordan. Okay, okay, Chicago, I give you muffin.'

'What's your name?' Esther asked.

The woman looked surprised. 'Hyun,' she said softly.

'I'm Esther.'

Esther waited for her change, looking out the window as the woman opened the cash register. She was going to get soaked jogging back home. She wondered whether or not the cap would keep her hair dry. Damn, she didn't feel like doing her hair. Behind her, she heard the door of the shop open.

'Hello, Esther.'

Her stomach contracted as though she'd been punched, even though the pain she felt wasn't physical. She wanted to bolt through the door, but she couldn't move. Esther didn't need to turn around. She hadn't forgotten his voice, his laugh, even his smell. Don't be smiling, she thought. And don't touch me. 'Hello, Mitchell.'

But of course he was smiling. And the first thing he did was to take her hand. She could still feel his fingers after they slid away from her palm. She forced herself to look at him, to take in his faded jeans, the matching jacket, the Gucci loafers with leather soft as butter. God, he looked good, she thought. He wasn't wet, even though he didn't have an umbrella. But then every obstacle had always gotten out of Mitchell's way, even – apparently – rain. She didn't want to look at him, but she couldn't stop. His hair was different, shorter. She remembered the feel of his rough, crinkly curls, the taste of them against her tongue. She began trembling, a slight, rocking movement in her knees, imperceptible to anyone but her. 'How have you been?' he asked.

'I've been fine, Mitchell. I'm at another bank. Still trying to get into lending.' She was talking too fast, saying too much, but she couldn't stop babbling. 'Everything okay with you?'

'You look good, Esther.' His eyes were so dark she couldn't see his pupils.

She giggled a little, laughter she couldn't control. 'It's

111

great seeing you, Mitchell.' She hoped she didn't sound nervous. She wanted Mitchell to think that he didn't have an effect on her anymore.

'Wait a minute. Don't go yet.' He turned toward the Korean woman. 'Give me half a dozen blueberry muffins. I'm in a hurry.' It was his usual take-charge voice, a tone that didn't allow for excuses or questions. When he had his bag, he looked toward Esther and said, 'Where are you staying these days? You still in the same place?'

She shook her head. 'I moved. I bought a house right up the street in Park Crest.'

'Home owner, huh? Congratulations. Are you listed?'

'No.'

'Well, I want to call you. I'll take you to dinner. There's a new place on Melrose. You'll love it.'

'I'll call you,' she said quickly, because she could feel the pin-prickly edges of the soft mushies, trying to invade her consciousness. She looked out the window. It was raining hard, but she needed to get home. Now.

'Didn't you hear what I said? I want to take you to dinner.'

She heard, all right: she excited him, he wanted her, but only for the moment. Oh, he would take her to some fancy place, wine her and dine her, call her a few times, and then disappear. Esther knew the dance well; she wasn't going for it this time. 'I've got to go,' she said. 'Good seeing you, Mitchell.'

Good girl, Esther, she told herself as she rushed out the door. Good girl! The rain felt soft and a little warm as it ran down her cheeks. She shoved the muffins inside her sweatshirt and began to run. She was so intent on getting home that she didn't hear the car slowing down behind her. Only after the horn blared so suddenly that she jumped and the bag of muffins fell onto the sidewalk did she look up to see Mitchell's Jaguar sitting next to her at the curb. He rolled the window down a crack.

'Esther, let me give you a ride.' The gleaming gold from his watch hypnotized her.

'I—'

'Woman, get in the car.'

She got in the car.

'Why didn't you tell me you needed a ride at the doughnut shop?'

Because I don't trust myself around you, she thought. 'I wanted to run,' she said.

Mitchell smiled at her. 'I won't bite you.'

'Said the snake.' The words came out fast. Her eyes flashed when they met his, and her lips twitched until she couldn't hold them together anymore. They laughed hard and long together, and every time they thought they'd come to the end of it, they found themselves going into yet another spasm, gasping for breath even as their knees brushed and their fingers touched accidentally. All the while Mitchell was driving, Esther held her head up and looked out the window, thinking how happy her mother would be to see her riding in such a fabulous car with such an obviously prosperous man.

By the time they reached her house, they were still chuckling, although calmly, quietly, the joke just an excuse for their eyes to linger over each other. 'So are you going to invite me in?' he asked easily. 'I'd love to see your house.'

Esther opened her mouth to object, but Mitchell said, 'You can't tell me it's not clean. I know you too well, Ms. Compulsive. Maybe we can eat our muffins together, like old times. You're not going to send a brother out in the rain, are you?'

The garage was built for two. Mitchell's Jag slid in easily next to her BMW. 'Excuse me for a minute,' she said as soon as they were inside. She looked terrible, she thought, as she raced up the stairs. She ran into her bedroom, took off her grubby sweats and put on jeans and a tight white cotton blouse. She took the Bulls cap off and fluffed out her hair, then ran into the bathroom, sprayed herself with Clinique Elixir, and put on a little red lipstick, all without letting herself wonder why she was changing her clothes for Mitchell.

'Damn, baby, you'd give eyesight to the blind,' he said when she reappeared. 'Show me around.' They started on the second floor, and she walked him through the three bedrooms and two baths describing the kind of renovations she planned for each room, feeling good that he was with her, that her Saturday afternoon no longer loomed before her like an empty road. They went downstairs, beginning in the living room and ending up in the kitchen. 'It's a great house,' Mitchell said, and she felt good hearing the approval in his voice. They were standing by the kitchen table, and for a minute Esther didn't know whether to ask him to sit down or not. Then she felt his chest press into her back, the heat so sudden and penetrating that she had to step away.

'I was serious about the muffins. You have any orange juice and coffee? Not instant.' He grinned at her, and she laughed because his breath, so close to her neck, tickled. And because she suddenly realized that she hadn't been alone with a man in her own home since she bought it. She tried, but she couldn't stop herself from laughing, from tingling, and, she suddenly realized, from hoping the dumbest, most futile hope of all: maybe he's changed.

'I've learned how to make coffee,' she said, getting some drip grind from the closet.

'You have today's paper around here?'

Esther was placing the muffins in the microwave. 'It's right behind you on the counter.'

'I can't reach it,' Mitchell said. She glanced at him; he hadn't turned around. 'Would you get it for me, baby?'

She walked over to the counter and picked up the paper and handed it to him. 'Thanks, baby,' he said.

When the coffee was ready, she poured out two cups and placed one in front of Mitchell and the other on her place mat. He didn't look up; she had to ask him to lift his paper so that she could set down the muffins in front of him. She placed the strawberry jam and butter on a little plate in the center of the table. She sat down and he asked her – still without looking up from the paper – if she had any orange juice. She got up and poured him a glass. By the time she handed it to him, he was already eating.

Esther sipped her juice and her cooling coffee, nibbled at the muffin, no longer warm, and gazed at Mitchell. He was looking at the sports section, and from time to time he would grimace and grunt. Finally, he set the paper on the floor and reached for another muffin. 'Would you put some butter on that for me?' Esther cut it in two parts, slathered butter on both, and handed them back to Mitchell. 'Any more coffee?' he asked.

She took his cup over to the pot, poured another cup, handed it to him, and sat down, feeling a slight tightness in her jaw. 'This coffee is good, baby,' Mitchell said. 'If we were together, would you make me a cup every morning?'

She could feel her smile breaking up her tension. She knew she was grinning like a fool, the hope in her eyes as naked and bright as a neon sign, but she couldn't help it. Yes, she would make him coffee, pour it in his cup, hold the coffee up to his lips or spoonfeed it to him, whatever he wanted, because it felt so good to have him with her. 'Sure I would,' she said softly.

'Come here, baby,' he said in a voice that was used to making commands, used to being obeyed. He shifted the chair around slightly, so that Esther was able to ease herself onto his lap. Then he took both her hands and held them in one of his. He put his other hand on her neck and pulled her face close to his. 'How come we aren't together anymore? I miss you. You're good for me.' She felt his lips on her neck, and then her face was full of his kisses. Each wet spot lit a tiny flame inside her. Esther pulled her hands away from his and grabbed the back of his head, letting her fingers rake through his crinkly hair, kissing him harder and harder, until their tongues were caught up in a Luther Vandross slow drag, full of heat, rhythm, and sweet pressure. Beneath the table, their thighs opened and closed around one another. They rocked into each other's groins and slowly began sliding down the chair and onto the floor.

Outside, the rain was coming down in thick, heavy sheets. Under the table, Mitchell's fingers were pulling at her bra, and then she could feel his lips sucking and licking. She reached for his arms to hold her; she wanted to be held and kissed for just a little while. Mitchell kissed her lips again, very quickly. Too quickly. Instead of placing his arms around her neck, he suddenly shifted his weight on top of her and pulled his mouth away from hers. Before she could say 'Wait,' he was inside her. 'It's all yours,' he whispered.

'Oooh,' Esther managed to say. 'Oooh,' she said again, louder. Louder still, her final theatrical moan blended into Mitchell's thunderous, culminating groans. As he collapsed onto her, Esther's neck was rigid; the muscles in her back were tense, and the hands she placed behind Mitchell's neck were knotted into two fists. As she lay on her back, observing the clothes that were scattered across the kitchen floor, Esther knew that she had made a mistake, one that she was already regretting. She looked over at the man lying beside her. Mitchell was softly snoring, oblivious to the cold floor. You asked for this, she reminded herself sternly. He was the same old Mitchell, the same old selfish Mitchell. And she was the same old fool.

His eyes opened suddenly. He pulled her close to him, brushed his lips against hers, tweaked her nipples, and looked at his watch, all in one languid, careless motion. 'Wow,' he said, stifling a yawn. 'I had no idea it was this late. Get me another cup of coffee, baby.'

Fifteen minutes later, she watched the back of Mitchell's Jag disappear over the hill on her street. The last thing she saw was his vanity license plate: MVH MD. When she closed the drapes over her living room window, the afternoon stretched before her, as bare and forlorn as a tree in winter.

She cleared the kitchen table and put the breakfast dishes in the dishwasher, feeling all her soft, mushy hopes crumpling up inside her like a paper doll that someone had stepped on. On the counter, in a small bag, were the muffins that Mitchell had left behind. Esther wiped the crumbs off her counter and then swept the floor and watered the purple African violets that were in pots on her windowsill. She went from room to room, dusting, wiping, rearranging, until there was nothing left to do, not one piece of lint she could pretend to pick up. As she stood in the middle of her living room, Esther began whimpering, softly at first and then slowly building up to a crescendo of sobbing. She cried for nearly fifteen minutes, and when she stopped, her head felt light and her eyes hurt. Okay, she told herself, you are over this. You are over this right now! But there were a few more tears in her, and they trickled silently down her cheeks. The house around her, so neat, so obsessively clean, was oppressively empty.

She just wanted to talk to somebody. She went upstairs to her bedroom and began dialing Vanessa's number, but hung up the phone on the second ring. Vanessa would know by her voice that something had happened, and she didn't want to have to explain to her about Mitchell. She thought about Mallory then. A vision of the blond woman storming

117

across the restaurant floor toward her lover, ready to make a scene, came to her, and before she could talk herself out of it, Esther had her telephone book in front of her and was dialing Mallory's number.

The lilting hello startled Esther. In the background she could hear guitars, a man's twangy voice singing 'Achy Breaky Heart'. Holding the phone, she felt as though she had dialed the wrong number and was connected to a stranger. She slowly lowered the phone toward the receiver.

'Hello. . . . Hello?'

With a deep breath, Esther put the telephone back to her ear. 'Mallory, it's Esther.'

'Oh.' There was such a rush of warmth and happiness flowing with her words, such obvious pleasure in her voice, that Esther was instantly cheered.

'I just called to say hi.' She tried to sound vivacious, to make her voice bright and sunny, all the while wondering why she had called Mallory, of all people. Mallory, with her Valley Girl voice and her sun-streaked hair that rode the breeze like a carefree kite, had no wisdom she could use. 'Listen, I don't want to keep you . . .'

'Esther, you don't sound like yourself. Is something wrong?'

Esther was too astonished to speak.

'What's the matter?' Mallory's voice was soothing, a gentle invitation to talk.

Esther hesitated. Then all the words rushed out in a jumbled, nervous bunch. 'This morning I ran into an old boyfriend, someone I was in love with but swore I wouldn't see again. One thing sort of led to another. He came home with me and we had sex. And now I feel like a complete fool.'

'And afterward were there skid marks on your floor from him leaving so fast?'

'You know him?'

'I know that guy. Men. Can't live with them; can't put them out on the curb when you're done. What the hell. You want to whine? Cry? Plot your revenge?'

'Whining is good.'

'Okay.'

'Why did he do that to me? Why did he come over and screw me and leave? Why couldn't he spend the afternoon at least, take me out to dinner, and *then* never call me?'

'Number one: He's not a nice guy. Number two: You let him.'

'Why did I let him? Why?'

'Don't feel bad, Esther. It's just one of those things. He caught you in a weak moment, a horny moment. Next time you'll be stronger. Listen to me: the blind leading the blind!' She started laughing and didn't stop until long after Esther had joined in, long after they both felt much better.

The city braved Election Day with umbrellas and raincoats, tracking mud into the residences of grim-faced citizens who now had second thoughts about allowing their homes to be used as official polling places. As drivers skidded and swerved on that rainy Tuesday, talk show hosts bantered with callers who insisted that the downfall of America was imminent if their candidate lost.

After Esther finished voting that morning, she switched on her car radio as she headed toward work. The voice of King Clever blared inside her car. 'Amerifriends, we are losing ground. Our rights are being eroded as we speak. Affirmative action activists, welfare rights advocates, feminists, AIDS activists, they are all encroaching on our rights as red-blooded Americans. And I tell you, we need to do something before it's too late. By God, I hope today isn't the beginning of too late.' On that ominous note, Esther switched the station. King Clever wasn't speaking to her.

The rain was coming down in soft, feathery wisps as

119

Esther turned onto Cranston. The wet weather had slowed the progress of the clean-up efforts on the block, and as she sped along the boulevard, Esther was dismayed once again at the many burned-out hulls and damaged stores that remained from the time of civil unrest. She couldn't help but think about all the pristine West Side and Valley neighborhoods where April 29 had left no mark. Not two feet away, a large crowd of young black teenagers was standing quietly at the bus stop. Their arms were weighted down with books. For some reason she couldn't explain, the sight of them warmed her and made her feel hopeful. Esther let out a small sigh. As her silver BMW zoomed onto the freeway, she felt drained, even as she was on her way to begin her day.

Esther stayed in her office the entire morning, working on a personnel report. She enjoyed evaluating her employees, appraising them in a systematic way. From time to time, she glanced through the glass partition or opened the door and stood just outside, listening and watching to make sure things in operations were running smoothly, that everything was functioning in an orderly manner. Each time she checked, she saw that Hector and the three other tellers were working steadily, with pleasant smiles on their faces. Customers were being attended to in a reasonable amount of time.

Toward lunchtime, when Esther glanced over at the cage, the lines were beginning to get longer; she could see that two of the tellers had gone on their break. She was about to tell the assistant operations manager to help out until the lines got shorter, when she heard a piercing scream, followed by frightened shrieks. Looking through the partition, she saw a black boy, not more than sixteen, dashing wildly toward the entrance, his footsteps rapid and frantic. One of the heavy glass doors flew open, and the youth, skinny and fast, raced through. As he was running out, the Western

Express deliveryman, his arms full of mail, was coming in. 'Hey . . . ,' he said as the youth collided with him, sending letters flying all over the courtyard. In seconds, the boy was gone.

A middle-aged black woman standing in one of the tellers' lines was screaming, 'My money, he took all my money.' As Esther rushed toward her, she could barely hear herself think.

'What happened?' she asked Hector, who seemed to have leaped over the tellers' cage.

'The woman was holding some money in her hand. And a boy, he grabbed the money and ran,' Hector said.

'Call the police,' Esther commanded.

The woman was still shrieking, ignoring the people around her, who tried to quiet her. 'One thousand dollars,' she cried. 'Oh, my God! Oh, my God!'

Esther heard a woman behind her say, 'Where the security guard? He supposed to be protecting people. The bank should pay you!'

Oh, Lord, Esther thought. She walked up to the woman and put her hand firmly on her arm. 'Excuse me, ma'am. I'm Esther Jackson, the regional operations manager. I know you're quite upset, and I wonder if you would mind stepping into my office. Right this way.'

The crying woman whirled around to face Esther, who was still gripping her elbow. She was a small, buxom, pecan-colored woman; her dark eyes were red from crying. 'I think the bank should be liable. I was standing right here in line, about to make a deposit, and a thief comes and snatches the money right out of my hands. What kind of security do you people have?' The woman was sniffling and coughing as she spoke.

'If you wouldn't mind stepping into my office,' Esther said quietly, squeezing just slightly on the woman's elbow.

The woman snatched her arm away. 'I demand to see the manager,' she said loudly.

Esther said quietly, 'I am the manager.'

'The real manager.'

Esther swallowed. 'I am the real manager.'

'Humph!' The woman eyed her suspiciously. 'Well, that man just stole a thousand dollars from me, and I want this bank to replace my money.'

Realizing that the woman was enjoying the audience she'd attracted and wasn't about to take the discussion into a private office, Esther tried to get her to lower her voice by whispering, hoping that she would get the message. 'Miss, I'm quite sorry about your loss. I can understand how upset you are, but the policy of Angel City is that it isn't liable for the theft of any money not deposited in an authorized account.'.

The woman raised her voice several decibels. 'Whatchu mean, authorized account? I was in the damn bank. Where the hell was the security?'

Esther held her breath. Hector was quickly and efficiently getting the lines back in order. The people were openly gawking. 'Security guards aren't required to intercept robberies,' Esther said with a great deal more calmness than she felt.

'Well, what the hell do you have security guards for if they're not supposed to stop robberies?' The woman placed her two plump hands on her hips; her neck started swerving back and her bottom lip protruded. Esther read the signs and knew that an explosion was imminent. She stepped backward just as the woman opened her mouth and bellowed: '*I want my damn money!*'

Lawdhamercy.

'You ain't no manager,' the woman said suddenly and venomously.

'I beg your pardon.'

'You heard me. I told you I want to see the real manager.'

Lord, Esther prayed, please don't let me go off on this woman. Please help me not to get ignorant and act a fool in front of my employees. She lowered her voice to a whisper that only the woman in front of her could possibly hear, and then, without changing her expression, which was one of professional concern, she could feel herself crossing over an emotional line, pressing a mental button. Without anything discernible taking place, the South Side of her personality blew through her like a harsh, grit-filled wind. Her neck automatically started bobbing, and when she looked down, her two hands were placed firmly on her hips. 'Let me tell you something, sister,' she hissed through teeth clamped together so tight there wasn't space for air. 'I don't know what you mean by a real manager. If you're looking for a white man to solve your problems, I'm sorry to disappoint you. Now, I am the regional operations manager, not only for this bank but for four other downtown branches. If you can't handle someone who looks like you being in charge, then I'll be happy to refer you to another bank.' The two women stared at each other, their eyes as hard as two pairs of dice.

Please, Lord.

Esther heard a slight noise. She looked to her side, and the Western Express man was standing next to her.

'May I say something?' he asked the woman. His voice was straight from a Barry White album, basso profundo, the kind of low, gravelly tone that was created for phrases like 'Right on, right on.' The woman closed her mouth. He had everyone's attention. 'Now, I know you upset, but look at this logically. If you was waving a fistful of money in 7-Eleven and the same thing happened, would you expect the store to pay you back? Of course not. And they have security guards there too. But I been ripped off before, and I know how that feels. Here. I hope this will help a little.' He handed her a twenty-dollar bill. Then he turned to the rest of the people in the two tellers' lines and said, 'If anyone is interested in helping this lady out, she sure would appreciate it.' —

Several people came over and handed the woman money – some ones, a few fives, and even a couple of tens and twenties – which she immediately put inside her purse. 'Thank you for at least trying to help me, which is more than the *manager* did.' She gave Esther a long, mean stare. 'You didn't have to get nasty. Think you so important,' she said, her tone surly. 'If y'all can't protect my money, I ain't coming back here no more,' she said.

'If you would like to close your account at this time, I'd be happy to help you with that,' Esther said. The woman glared at her then turned away abruptly as two policemen approached them.

Thank you, Lord, Esther said to herself. She answered the officers' perfunctory questions and listened as the woman described her assailant. In less than five minutes, the woman and the police were gone. After they left, she surveyed the area quickly to make sure that the two lines were moving, and then she walked back to her office. The minute she sat down, there was a light tap at the door. 'Come in,' she called out.

The Western Express man crossed her office floor in two steps and placed several letters on her desk. 'You got away so quick, I didn't give you your mail.' He was an average-looking man, she thought. Just a regular light-brown-skinned brother with a nose that took up a lot of his face. His hair was a neat fade. His smile, though, gave her the sensation of walking into a brightly lit room, of being in the midst of a festive occasion.

'You could have left it out front, where you usually do,' she said.

He leaned over her desk. 'You handled yourself real good

out there. I just thought things were about to get out of hand and that you needed a little help from a man.' He smiled.

Esther felt a frosty wind blowing through her. 'Listen, Mr. . . . uh . . .'

'Tyrone Carter.'

'Mr. Carter.'

'Call me Tyrone.'

'Mr. Carter. I didn't need your help. I was managing the situation quite well alone, thank you. And if you don't mind, I'm very busy.' Esther lowered her head and began reading her report. She didn't look up for a good five minutes, but when she did, Tyrone Carter's megawatt smile was blinding her again.

He said, 'I like your style. Can I take you to dinner this Saturday?'

'I'm busy.' She said this in her coldest, deep upper North Side voice.

Tyrone Carter shuddered. 'Just got a little chilly up in here.' He threw back his head and laughed.

The sound was so exquisitely inviting that before she could stop herself, Esther was laughing too. But not for long. 'I'm really sorry, Mr. Carter,' she said, recovering her composure, 'but I am busy on Saturday and I'm busy now.' She gave him a long look without a trace of a smile.

'All right, Ms. Jackson.' He walked to her door and was about to leave, when he turned to her and said, 'I'll ask you again.'

Before she could say 'Don't bother,' he was gone.

Esther closed her eyes. That Tyrone Carter was a real clown. She was almost sorry she had to be so stern, but she knew she wouldn't be doing the man any favors by encouraging him.

When she opened her eyes, Charles Weber was standing in front of her. 'Oh, Charles,' she said, suddenly flustered.

As much as possible, Esther avoided being alone with her boss, especially since his days downtown had become numbered.

The office scuttlebutt was that Weber had contacted every head-hunter in southern California in an attempt to secure a new position, all to no avail. With each passing day, Charles had become increasingly resentful and hostile. After several meetings, members of his staff whispered that they smelled alcohol on his breath. By the time Charles finally accepted the fact that he was truly on his way to South-Central, he also had to endure the news that Kirk would be taking over his old position, at least in an acting capacity. This last news seemed to push him to the very edge, which is precisely where he seemed to be perched as Esther gazed into his bloodshot eyes. 'Tell me everything that happened,' he said. He was swaying just enough to make Esther realize he'd been drinking.

After Esther finished her account of the robbery incident, Charles sighed heavily. 'You should have had her sign a waiver, releasing the bank of all liability.'

'Charles, the woman was in no mood to sign anything,' Esther said evenly, her tone news anchor perfect. 'I made it perfectly clear to her that Angel City wasn't liable in any way.'

'Did you get her name and address?' His piggy eyes rested on her breasts, and now his tongue protruded slightly from his mouth.

She hardened her eyes and stared into his. You little asshole, she thought. 'No, I didn't, Charles. The situation was pretty chaotic. The woman was quite upset and—'

'That's just my point,' Charles shouted. He stepped closer to Esther, and now she could smell the liquor, although just faintly. 'She could be contacting a lawyer as we speak. You should have gotten her name and address and had her sign a waiver.'

'Charles,' Esther said softly, 'I really don't think we're going to hear from that customer again, and if we do, I think that the legal department can easily handle any claims she might make.'

'I'd hate for this mismanagement of a situation to have to go into your personnel file.' He leaned closer to her. 'Is that, uh, a new perfume you have on? Do you smell like that all over?' He grinned at her, revealing a bit more of his tongue.

Esther could feel the rage pulsing through her body, making her head pound. She wanted to slap his face so badly that her palms were itching. At the same time, logic told her that in a few days this man would be out of her life for good. 'Charles . . . ,' she began, stepping backward and hoping that she would say the right words.

The door opened again and Mallory came in, her face moist and rosy, as though she'd been running. 'I just heard what happened. My God. Are you okay? Oh, hello, Charles.'

Charles straightened up, and his lizard's tongue darted inside his mouth. He nodded curtly toward Mallory, letting his eyes linger on her breasts just long enough to make her begin to twitch with anxiety. 'We'll talk later,' he told Esther, then he left.

When the door closed, Mallory turned to Esther. 'What's wrong? Did he say something to you?'

Esther hesitated for just a moment, but her rage was too volatile to contain. 'That asshole! He was in here asking about the robbery, and then he tells me I mishandled it because I didn't get the woman to sign some stupid waiver that doesn't exist and wouldn't it be a shame for that to go in my personnel file, and by the way, that perfume you're wearing is turning me on!'

'He did the same thing to me. Two of my loans are in trouble; both the clients were burned out during the riots, and Charles is trying to make everything my fault. He

127

threatened me too. And he tried something similar with Sandra. Ever since he found out he's going to South-Central, he's been trying to intimidate women by holding their personnel files over their heads. He's out of control.'

'Do you think he's serious?'

'He's upset about his transfer. He's trying to take it out on someone. Whether he'd really put anything negative in our personnel files, I don't know.' There was anger in her voice, but Mallory raised her hands in a helpless gesture of frustration. 'So what happened during the robbery?'

'Some kid snatched a thousand dollars out of a customer's hands and ran out the door. The woman got hysterical and demanded that the bank replace the money.'

'I heard that people started giving her money.'

'When I was talking to her, the guy who delivers for Western Express sort of butted into the conversation. Well, actually, he was trying to help. He did help. He convinced her that the bank wasn't liable and then he gave her twenty dollars and asked other people to give her some money too.'

Mallory raised her eyebrows. 'A hero!'

'I wouldn't exactly call him that.'

'*I* would. A hero with great buns.'

'What?'

Mallory peered out the glass partition. 'You don't think he's got great buns?'

Esther glanced into the operations area. Tyrone was staring into her office, and when she looked his way, he smiled. He did have a nice body and a great smile. 'Well, Baby got back,' she said absentmindedly.

'What'd you say?' Mallory's eyes, crinkled around the edges, were filled with puzzlement. 'Baby's got what? You mean he's got a nice back? Like, a broad, strong back?' Mallory searched her friend's face for a clue. 'No, you don't mean that.'

Esther suddenly chuckled. Ever since she and Mallory

had started calling each other on weekends, she seemed to be constantly explaining things to her and revealing more of herself in the process. The first time a piece of her carefully monitored blackness slipped out in front of Mallory, she was startled, she so seldom dropped her guard. But gradually, when she was with Mallory, the South Side, that carefully hidden neighborhood full of righteous anger and gut-belly laughter, that place of southern cooking and Baptist churches, that place of sorrow and dreams, would no longer stay put. 'It means he's got a nice butt,' she said finally.

'A back is a butt?'

'A back is a butt.'

'Baby got back,' Mallory repeated in her high, whiny voice. She sounded like Murphy Brown trying to do gangsta rap. 'Why are you laughing?'

'Does the term "cultural dissonance" mean anything to you?' Esther took another look into the operations area, just in time to see Tyrone heading for the door. Why was she wasting her time staring at a glorified mailman? She turned back to Mallory, her face suddenly becoming somber. 'Listen, we've got to deal with Charles.'

'What do you mean, "deal with Charles"?' Mallory asked. She seemed both startled and fearful.

'I mean, I'm not letting him ruin my future,' Esther said. 'I think we need to confront him, Sandra, you, me. We all need to walk into his office and tell him that we're united and we aren't going to take his bullshit. That if he so much as writes one word in any of our personnel files, we'll all charge him with sexual harassment. Do you think that Sandra will come with us?'

'I don't know.'

For the first time, Esther heard the tentative quality of Mallory's voice. 'You're coming, aren't you?'

Mallory sighed. 'I . . .'

Esther looked at Mallory. Ever since she'd gotten to know her, she'd realized that her staunch feminism was a veneer she used to cover her fearfulness. 'I'll do most of the talking. You just be there.'

Sandra declined their invitation to join them. She said that Charles's bark was worse than his bite; she didn't feel it was necessary to confront him face-to-face. She knew how to handle him, she told Mallory. They were over-reacting.

The two women arrived at Charles's office right before noon. Charles rose from the chair behind his desk when they entered. 'Have a seat,' he said. Despite the redness in them, his eyes were alert, wary. Lord, please put the right words in my mouth, Esther thought as she sat down.

'Charles,' Esther said, her voice sounding loud and almost strident in the silence of the office, 'Mallory and I would like to discuss a matter of grave importance to us.'

'I don't have a lot of time right now,' he said, waving his hand as though he were telling them good-bye.

You better make time, fool. Esther's hands began to ball up into two tight fists. 'This won't take long,' she said. She took a deep breath, then stood up, opened her hands, and put them on the desk. She leaned across it so that her face was directly in Charles's. 'Today you hinted that I mishandled this morning's robbery and that you were thinking about putting a negative evaluation of my per-formance in my personnel file. Then you told me that I smelled good and asked me if I smelled that good all over. Am I remembering the sequence of events?'

'I don't know what the hell you're talking about.' Charles's voice was calm, but his face had grown red and contorted. He looked ready to explode.

For a moment, even Esther felt like retreating. Don't be a punk, she told herself sternly. Punk. Punk. Punk.

Mallory eyed Esther, desperately wanting the black woman to back down.

Esther took a deep breath and moved in closer to Charles. She could feel his breath on her face. 'I think you do. Mallory certainly knows what I'm talking about. Isn't that right?'

Mallory managed to nod. 'Yes,' she said, her voice squeaky and thin.

Esther's voice got louder, stronger. 'And so does Sandra Grossman. In the last several weeks we've all been the recipients of your threats and . . . sexual harassment.' She wielded those last words like a weapon; Charles began to slump in his seat. 'Neither Mallory, Sandra, nor I are interested in sleeping with you, Charles. We don't want to date you. Is that clear? You will be with us for another week, and during that week we don't want you staring at our breasts or our hips. We don't want you licking your lips at us. We don't want you calling us anything but our names. Do you understand me? Now, if my or Mallory's personnel records are changed, we'll go straight to Kirk and we'll be discussing some of your other offensive and highly suggestive remarks. Do I make myself clear?'

As Esther was speaking, Charles remained subdued; he acted like a defeated man. But as soon as she had finished, he sprang out of his chair like a wild dog on the attack, the gold pinkie ring and dangling bracelet sparkling as he waved his hand back and forth. 'I never heard such a crock of shit in all my life,' he snarled. 'Who do you think you're talking to, some stupid kid? I never harassed either one of you.' He stalked across the room until he stood directly in front of the two women. 'You girls are looking for action, that's your problem,' he said with a sneer. 'You wish I would look at you. You've been coming on to me. Both of you. And when I do the write-ups, don't think I won't include

131

that bit of information as well.' He smiled, a triumphant grin full of malice. 'Am I making myself clear?'

Esther stole a glance at Mallory and saw that her face was as pale as a piece of paper. Absolutely bloodless. Her own heart was pounding, frantic little thumps. She could feel rage coursing through her body. Her mouth was full of burning words. She knew she should take a deep breath and regain control, but she didn't want to calm down. She wanted to go off. Before Esther could stop herself, she put her left hand on her hip, craned her neck to the side, and pointed her right finger at Charles's face, almost touching his nose. 'Fuck you, you bald-headed, polyester-suit-wearing, potbellied, drinking-on-the-job, two-inch-pudding-dick motherfucker. Let me make myself crystal-damnclear: I know some guys who'd take your little pale, flat ass out for a hundred bucks. And I have a hundred bucks. Now,' she said, getting right up in Charles's face, so close her eyes began to cross, 'if you put a negative review in my personnel file, or any of our files, you'd better take a damn bodyguard with you when you go to work and when you go home at night. If you think I'm playing, try me.'

She was panting when she finished, and her head felt light. Charles's shiny moon face was red; sweat was beading on his hairless pate. He opened his mouth to speak but could only make a faint gagging sound. Esther knotted her hand into a fist and slammed it into her other palm. Charles jumped back at least two feet. 'It's been great talking with you,' Esther said. 'You just remember what I said. Do not try to fuck with us.' She nodded toward Mallory, who, appearing nearly as frightened as their boss, looked at Charles and then at Esther. For a fraction of a second, it seemed as though she didn't know whose side she was on. But then she slowly stood up and followed Esther.

Neither woman said a word until they were inside Esther's office. Mallory cleared her throat and said in a high, whiny voice, full of wonder and just a little fear, 'Do – do you really know people like that?'

Esther tilted her head and watched Mallory as she fidgeted with her fingers. 'Like what?'

'Like – like you told Charles about. Men who would hurt him.'

Esther peered into Mallory's face and saw Barbie the Innocent. For a minute, she wanted to slap her more than she wanted to hit Charles. 'What do you think, Mallory?'

The white woman shrugged her shoulders and shook her head. Had she said something wrong? 'I don't know.'

'Mallory,' she said tersely, 'it's straight out of *The Godfather*.'

Mallory's head jerked a little, as though Esther had hit her. She stood there feeling stupid and a little ashamed, but at least she understood the anger in her friend's face. 'I didn't mean . . . I just wish I could be that angry and show it. But where did all that . . . all that come from?'

'Ghetto 101.'

Mallory moved forward eagerly, her bright-gray eyes like headlight beams searching in the dark. 'Do they have that at Cal State?'

Esther looked at Mallory's sincere face and burst out laughing. Mallory looked momentarily stricken, as if she'd been slapped, then the tiniest giggle escaped from her lips and she began to laugh too. Esther leaned against the wall with her head thrown back, her hunched shoulders shaking in a jerky rhythm. Each time they tried to stop laughing, the two women only had to look at each other to start up again.

'What do you think he's going to do?' Mallory asked between bursts of laughter.

'I have no idea.'

'Suppose he still puts that stuff in our files?'

'Oh, yeah? He'll wake up with a horse's head in his bed. Shi-i-it.'

They fell against the glass partition, their bodies bent over and spasmodic, laughing so loudly, so wildly, that they didn't even notice the customers turning to stare at them.

9

By the time Charles was about to be transferred to South-Central, he was barely speaking to either Mallory or Esther. The silence was fine with both of them, especially since Michele Coleman revealed to Esther that nothing had been added to either of their personnel files. Both women turned their attention to the series of activities that were designed to solicit employee participation and goodwill for the bank's new Diversity Program.

Several weeks earlier, all department heads and managers had received packets of information about the new program, which they were instructed to disperse and explain in detail to their employees. Staff meetings were called to discuss the three-pronged plan, which included a series of monthly two-hour 'diversity awareness' sessions to be led by industrial psychologists on Friday afternoons; the formation of a mentor program, in which certain minorities and women were chosen to be paired with a senior executive, whose charge was to show them the corporate ropes and help them learn to climb them; and, finally, the managerial exchange plan, in which Charles was the first and probably the most reluctant participant.

Most of the white male managers at Angel City voiced their outrage initially only in the men's room, where, lined up in a neat row, they grumbled about reverse discrimination. That attendance in the diversity awareness sessions was mandatory rubbed some the wrong way. Various senior executives were disgruntled that they would be forced to mentor people not of their own choosing. And as for the managerial exchange program, did that mean that someone from South-Central was going to take Charles Weber's place, they all demanded to know. Ridiculous. There was no one in that branch who had the experience or the qualifications.

In hushed tones, many of these same men, the majority of whom were among the most highly paid workers in the bank, cursed Preston Sinclair. 'A sellout!' they grumbled. 'Is he going to have the checks printed in Spanish?' 'Is he going to let some homeboy run the damn organization?' In frustration, they closed their office doors, turned on their radios, and forgot their sorrows with King Clever.

Kirk Madison might have become one of the talk show host's devotees. He certainly found the man informative and enormously funny, although a bit of a hard-liner. But Kirk didn't have the inclination to tune in, since Sinclair's new programs benefited him directly. He had been appointed acting regional manager. He intended to do everything in his power to see that the post became permanent.

Farewell parties at Angel City Bank were ordinarily quiet affairs: usually lunches that were confined to one hour and attended by the outgoing employee and his or her immediate group of co-workers. But because Preston Sinclair saw Charles Weber's transfer to South-Central as the launching of the new Diversity Program, the word was sent down that a little more fanfare was in order. For that reason, spouses were invited as well.

The gathering was held, not during lunch, but after work on a Friday evening at Billy's Grill, a local eatery and watering hole that was not far from the bank. In another break with tradition, all the department employees were invited, from the tellers to the executives. It was a cross-section of the bank that didn't usually interact during working hours, let alone socially.

Kirk was standing by the bar when his wife came in. She was wearing a paisley print suit that fit too snugly around her wide hips. As he watched her searching the crowd for him, he wondered just how long it had been since he really looked at Sheila. Could that lumpy, waddling woman be his wife? The two kids, back-to-back, had ruined her shape. Before the babies, she'd been a thin person who liked to swim and bike and take walks. Now she was a fat matron with graying hair and tiny lines around her mouth, and not from laughing either. She was barely thirty-five, he thought glumly. What the hell would she look like at forty? Peering around him, he found it hard not to compare her with the sleek professional women flitting near the bar in their fitted business suits and low-heeled pumps.

Their original plan was for Sheila to work and pay the bills while he attended medical school, studying to become an orthopedic surgeon. Back then she was his champion, making him coffee when he had to hit the books until all hours, urging him on when he felt low. The truth was, it had been Sheila's idea for him to study medicine. She was the one who got the applications and actually filled them out; she even applied for financial aid. She did it all on the promise of a glorious future, a Beverly Hills future, an ocean-view future. When they still had the dream, everything was easy between them: easy to talk; easy to divide up the workload; easy to make love.

And then he flunked out of medical school, right at the end of his third year. When he failed her, the easiness between them disappeared.

Several of his former classmates had formed a very successful orthopedic surgery corporation. They and their families were now luxuriously ensconced in what could best be described as Beverly Hills Yupdom: part of the thirtysomething crowd that the old guard residents of the flats of Beverly complained about so stridently in the

West Side section of the *Gazette*. Buying up older homes on decent-size lots and then tearing down the original structures, they had erected garish monstrosities that dwarfed the surrounding residences. Every holiday season, his former classmates threw a party, and he and Sheila went. He dressed carefully for the event; after all, he wasn't a failure. 'Banking is great!' he would tell them, his voice booming jovially through the crowd. He smiled the entire time he was there; when he left, his jaw was actually in pain. Was it his imagination, or did his old friends seem to patronize him? With each year, their recognition of him seemed to grow dimmer and dimmer, as though his name were in their computerized invitation list but they could no longer recall the reason for his being there, or even who he was. Each year, he swore it would be the last time he attended. The valet parking. The Dom Pérignon and caviar. Waiters everywhere. Vulgar excess, that's all it was. And on top of everything else, he was forced to do protracted penance afterward, as he saw the silent disappointment in Sheila's eyes. She didn't say it, but he knew what she was thinking: If only he'd finished medical school.

The thing that hurt most was that he knew he was smarter than any of those guys. He'd had bad luck during his third year, that's all. If his professors had only been reasonable and let him take some makeup exams. Maybe if his name had been Goldberg, they'd have given him a break. He and Sheila had already received the invitation for this year's big bash. He had absolutely no intention of going. The next time he saw those phonies would be at *his* mansion.

Kirk took a big swallow of beer and watched Sheila searching for him in the crowded room; he took care to avert his eyes just as she spotted him.

By the time his wife reached the bar, Kirk could hear her panting a little, and there were faint beads of perspiration

138

glistening on the lines of her forehead. 'Hi,' she said, giving him a quick, dry kiss. She glanced around her. 'Not a bad place. There's the waiter, Kirk. I'd like a white zinfandel,' she said, smiling at him.

By the time Sheila had her drink, the gathering had been hushed to silence as Bailey Reynolds strode to the front of the room. Kirk listened as Preston Sinclair's right-hand man gave an energetic five-minute pep talk on the Diversity Program. 'We may have come over on different ships, but we're all in the same boat now,' Bailey proclaimed in a happy, booming voice.

'God help us,' one of the men standing near Kirk said with a groan. 'He's quoting Jesse Jackson.'

When Reynolds called for Charles Weber to come forward, there was a smattering of applause. Kirk gloated inwardly when he distinctly heard someone say, 'I'm surprised he can walk, the way he's been tossing back those Stolys.'

Charles's expression, as he made his way to the front of the crowd, was that of a man on his way to his mother's wake. With his pinkie ring and gold bracelet gleaming, he said a few quick words about his wonderful time at the downtown branch, his perfunctory monotone punctuated with just enough slurring to start a ripple of elbow nudges going around the room. As Charles walked back into the crowd, he passed by Kirk and gave him a hard stare with his bloodshot eyes. 'It's all yours,' he said tersely.

'Why does he look so angry?' Sheila asked when Charles walked away.

Kirk didn't answer right away. Instead, he turned around and watched his former boss maneuver his way through the crowd. He was walking straight toward the bar. God, what a lush! Kirk wasn't the only one looking. Mallory and Esther were standing at the bar, sipping what appeared to be white wine, when they noticed Charles approaching them. Kirk watched as Esther, her eyes like two brass knuckles, put her drink on the bar and turned to face Charles. As she stepped forward, her hands were coiled into tight fists and her face – God, her face was like a killer's. Charles took one look at her, appeared to hesitate for just a fraction of a second, then abruptly pivoted and headed for the door. What the hell was that all about? Kirk turned back to his wife, who was tugging at his sleeve. 'You didn't answer my question, Kirk,' she said.

'He's angry because it's my turn now. He's on the way down, and I'm on the way up.'

Sheila's eyes seemed to brighten. 'Kirk, you *have* to become the permanent regional branch manager,' she said softly. Smiling sweetly, she held out her empty glass. 'I'd like another one, please.'

Kirk heard the urgency in Sheila's voice and felt annoyed. He didn't need his wife to tell him that to make it big at Angel City, he had to turn his temporary appointment into a permanent one. *Nobody* had to tell him that.

Nothing had prepared Kirk for the volume of work that he inherited. For the first few weeks, he plodded through fifteen-hour days. The real estate department was in the worst shape. Kirk discovered multimillion-dollar properties that were thousands of dollars in arrears, for which fore-closure action hadn't been started. In cases where such proceedings had been initiated, only a preliminary letter had been mailed, months earlier, with absolutely no follow-up since. Because of the drop in interest rates, the bank had been swamped with literally hundreds of applications for refinancing home mortgages. Beleaguered lenders were juggling a workload of nearly three hundred loan appli-cations, trying to play a never-ending game of catch-up. To his horror, Kirk soon discovered that some of the appli-cations were months old. Worse, there seemed to be no system in place to process them. In the days that followed Charles's departure, the niggling details of bank management that his predecessor had failed to attend to took up all Kirk's time. He erected a huge flow chart right above his computer, depicting all the work that needed to be done. Slowly and methodically, he set up a series of systems for dealing with the various forms of overload that were plaguing Angel City.

Kirk came early and left late. By the time he got home, Sheila was usually asleep, and he barely had the energy to get into bed beside her.

At the end of each day, he crossed off his accomplishments with a bright-red pencil. Gradually the flow chart turn more and more scarlet. This position is mine, he told himself; it belongs to me. What he needed was a way to get the attention of the very top, a chance to impress upon Preston Sinclair and his executive sidekicks, in a way that was irrefutable, that he was one of them. That he belonged.

The idea of how he could make the top brass notice him came to Kirk after he'd been in his new assignment for several weeks.

'I hate to stick you with this,' Kirk said to Mallory when she came to his office one afternoon in early December.

'What am I getting stuck with?' Mallory asked. She looked slightly curious and a little amused.

'The Diversity Program will be launched in a couple of weeks. I need for you to oversee the efforts for the various departments. I want you to appoint a chairperson for each department and make sure they all set up their groups, have their meetings, and do the requisite follow-up work.'

'No problem,' Mallory said evenly.

Her expression didn't reveal whether she was putting Kirk on or was truly happy about the assignment. She had a kind of Mona Lisa smile, he thought, really quite intriguing.

'I'm so glad you're in this position, Kirk. Everyone can see the difference you're making already. Morale is much higher.'

'Thank you. I want the program to be a success. I think it's absolutely necessary that everyone feel he or she has an equal shot at the top.' He said this as though he were reciting for a final grade.

Two weeks later, the first diversity awareness workshops were held. Mallory and Kirk made the rounds, sitting in on each of the departmental sessions. In one of them, a black woman showed slides of individuals from different races. After each slide, she asked the group what they thought about the person pictured, whether or not he or she was good, bad, intelligent, could sing or dance. They were supposed to say the first thing that came into their minds. There was one picture of two men, black and white. They both wore jeans, had beards, and stared straight ahead with hard little eyes. Kirk's initial thought was that the black man looked like a robber and the white guy looked like a college kid, maybe a surfer. He tried to talk himself out of both assumptions and asked himself why a hairy black man was more frightening than a white one. Which one of these men will hurt you? the facilitator asked. No one in the room raised a hand.

Mallory leaned over, giving off faint wafts of some sweet scent that tickled Kirk's nose. He could smell her pepper-minty breath when she whispered, 'Maybe we ought to get to the next session.'

'Well, I know where she's going, but frankly, I think it's a little condescending,' Mallory said once they were in the hall. 'I mean, maybe if we were in Mississippi or somewhere like that, she'd need to teach us not to judge people based on skin color, but that's really not an issue for the folks gathered in this room. I think people just need to get to know each other better. Become friends.'

'That's it,' he said quickly. 'When I was on the football team in high school, half the team was black. We all got along.'

Mallory nodded. 'What high school was that?'

'Sergeant, in the Valley.'

Mallory clapped her hand over her mouth. 'We used to play you guys. I went to Belcher. I was a cheerleader.'

He could picture her as a slim, leggy cheerleader.

'No kidding. When'd you graduate?'

'Seventy-four.'

'I came out in seventy-two. I'll bet we were at some of the same games.'

'Amazing. Anyway, I understand that this diversity thing is an issue that Preston Sinclair is absolutely passionate about.'

It was while they were walking to the next group that Mallory's words sunk in. The Diversity Program, as mindless as Kirk thought it, was important to Preston Sinclair. Why, he wasn't quite sure, but for now it didn't matter. If he wanted to impress the president at this point in time, the quickest way to do it was through diversity.

Kirk didn't go home after the last session, as he had planned; instead, he returned to his office. Sheila's puffy face stared at him from an eight-by-ten frame; everywhere he went in his office, her eyes seemed to follow him, like a constant reproach.

Kirk leaned way back in his chair, remembering what a former colleague had once told him: Help a powerful man get what he wants, and you make a powerful friend. He closed his eyes and tried to think of what could be motivating Preston Sinclair. Was he an honest guy with integrity who truly believed in racial harmony and fair play? He dismissed that thought immediately. That type dies in the Peace Corps, he told himself. What did the man want? he asked himself, closing his eyes even tighter. He thought about some of the changes that had occurred since Sinclair's presidency began. Several older board members had been replaced by women: he recalled the pictures in the *L.A. Business Journal* of three smiling women and a beaming Sinclair. When Angel City Bank gave a $25,000 check to the United Negro College Fund, Preston's picture appeared in the business section of the *Gazette*. He was photographed again when the Diversity Program was announced. His every accomplishment was accompanied by his picture in some newspaper or magazine. He was even in *Our Town*, pictured dining out at one of the trendy restaurants that monthly never stopped writing about. The man is a media freak, Kirk thought. Preston Sinclair was a man after a good photo opportunity. Well, Kirk was going to give him one.

Nearly a week later, Kirk sat at a table in one of the city's downtown restaurants. Seated across from him was Bailey Reynolds. He searched Reynolds's face, studying his eyes for some indication, any hint that would reveal just how much he could trust the man. Angel City was as cutthroat as any other corporation, and despite the older man's genial manner, Kirk knew that he hadn't gotten as far as he had just by being nice. But if he couldn't rely upon him, who would be his conduit to the thirty-fourth floor so that he could get the attention he needed?

While Kirk was fitfully pondering his options, Reynolds reached into the basket that the waiter had placed on the table and plucked out a roll. 'Kirk,' he said as he buttered his bread, 'you're doing an admirable job.' He broke off a small piece of flaky pastry and popped it into his mouth with fingers that seemed naturally curved. He continued to smile even while he was chewing. 'Everyone knows that you inherited a less than perfect situation, and we're aware of the yeoman effort you've made to turn things around. You're a man who gets things done, and I don't mind telling you that you're being watched. Just keep up the good work.'

Now it was Kirk's turn to grin. So they were watching him! Wasn't that another way of saying they were grooming him? 'The hard work you've seen is simply my way of letting everyone know that I'd like my present appointment to be a permanent one. I'm capable of a great deal more, sir,' Kirk said.

The older man fastened his hard black eyes and his steady beam of a smile on Kirk. 'Call me Bailey.'

'In fact, I invited you to lunch to share with you an idea I've been thinking about.'

Reynolds's smile stretched out to jaw-breaking proportions. He was a pragmatic man. One of his great strengths was that he knew his limitations better than anyone. His job, which he did well, was to carry a hatchet at all times and make sure that the victims didn't see the blow coming and no blood was ever seen by unsuspecting bystanders. He wasn't creative. He wasn't an idea man. But he appreciated talent in others and had come to depend upon using what bits and pieces of genius strayed his way to ensure his own survival. Leaning across the table, his bread poised in midair, he said, 'I'm listening.'

'I don't have to tell you that ever since the riots, a lot of attention is being paid to the way minorities don't get mortgage loans. Now, you and I both know that Angel City standards apply to everyone equally. The reason blacks and Latinos are turned down is because they don't qualify. I thought that in the current climate, it would be a positive step for Angel City if it inaugurated a Minority Mortgage Loan Program, which creates special qualifications for potential home buyers who are black and Latino. The program could help satisfy the Community Reinvestment Act folks, and the bank would get favorable press. We might get the endorsement of some powerful person from the minority community.'

'Does anyone come to mind?' Bailey said.

'There's that minister who's always in the paper. Reverend Rice.'

Preston Sinclair would like the idea. 'That sounds promising. Why don't you talk with Reverend Rice? See if he'd be willing to give you his support.'

Two days later, in the early evening, Kirk stood outside the Solid Rock Baptist Church, a massive brick edifice that took up an entire city block. He felt a thin prickle of terror skitter down his neck like a frightened spider. Spilling out of one of the church's basement doors was a long line of ragged men and a few women. They all bore the air of disheartened refugees. For as long as he could remember, he'd heard nightmares about neighborhoods like this one. The stories and the fear were well founded, he thought. The fires of April 29 had been proof enough of that. Kirk just didn't understand that kind of rage. Okay, okay, it was wrong for the cops to beat Rodney King, although, c'mon, the guy had to have been doing something. Cops didn't go around beating people for no reason. But for the blacks to go on a rampage, burning and looting – that was just crazy, plain stupid. And then the way they beat that Denny guy, dragged him out of his truck and beat him, four against one. Could have been anybody. Anybody. He looked around him, nervously eyeing every dark face he saw, looking at their hands just in case they were packing a brick – or worse.

'Reverend Rice isn't here just yet. He's talking with the homeless in the church basement. I'm Mrs. Rice.' The woman who stood before Kirk in the cramped reception room didn't look like a minister's wife. She was about thirtysomething and had a sultry, exotic kind of beauty that was decidedly more worldly than spiritual. The dark skirt

146

she wore ended just above her pretty knees. She extended her hand, and Kirk saw the vivid red of her fingernails. 'Was the reverend expecting you?'

'Yes. I have an appointment. I'm Kirk Madison from Angel City National Bank,' he said, shaking her hand. He tried not to sound impatient. People who were late annoyed him.

'Well, he'll be here soon,' the woman said placidly. 'Why don't you have a seat over there.' She nodded toward several plain wooden chairs lined up around the wall. Kirk took a seat and instantly regretted that he hadn't brought a paper with him at least. To make matters worse, he was starving. He hadn't eaten breakfast or lunch. And the whole building seemed to be filled with the delicious aroma of fried chicken. 'Is that food I smell?' he asked the woman somewhat tentatively.

'They're feeding the homeless in the basement.' She glanced at him, her eyes filled with concern. 'Are you hungry?'

'Oh, no. No, no.'

'I can have a plate sent up here.'

'No. Really. I'm fine. Really.'

Nearly twenty minutes later, Reverend Odell Rice barreled into the room. By his side was a boy who looked to be about eight years old. As soon as Rice entered the space, it seemed full, almost crowded. He was a big man, with expansive gestures. He kissed his wife on the cheek. 'How's it going, Juanita?' The woman murmured something, and the two of them laughed. Reverend Rice then turned to Kirk. 'Mr. Madison? I'm Odell Rice.' The minister had one of those deep, 'Ol' Man River' kind of voices, and standing before him, he appeared to be no more than forty-five, a lot younger than he looked in the newspaper pictures and even on television. As senior minister of one of the largest black congregations in the city and executive director of the Los

Angeles branch of the oldest civil rights organization in the country, Reverend Odell Rice was in the news a lot.

Reverend Rice led Kirk into his office, a room only slightly larger than the reception area. The boy, whom Kirk assumed to be his son, silently followed the minister and sat in a chair in the back. The walls were literally covered with plaques, awards, and citations of every description. Kirk counted at least four certificates of appreciation from the mayor and three resolutions from the Speaker of the Assembly. In addition, there were pictures of the minister with numerous city and state officials, even a photo of him with the President-elect. 'Well, Mr. Madison, I want to hear more about your idea. I was intrigued by what you told me on the telephone,' he said, taking a seat behind the desk.

Kirk leaned forward in the hard wooden chair. 'It's really quite simple, Reverend Rice. Along with everyone else, the people at Angel City National Bank were quite devastated by the, uh, events of April twenty-ninth. As responsible corporate citizens, we're committed to providing ways in which minorities can participate in the American dream.' As his voice droned on, Kirk stole a quick glance at the clock. My God, he thought. It was almost seven. He definitely didn't want to be in South-Central after dark. He heard a cracking sound from out on the street and jumped a little in his seat. His words floundered, momentarily suspended in air.

'Just a car backfiring,' Reverend Rice said blandly. 'Gunshots are louder, a little sharper.' He smiled broadly, revealing a huge gap between his front teeth.

'Well, uh . . .' Kirk took a breath and mentally condensed his fifteen-minute spiel into three minutes. 'At Angel City Bank we believe that the best way to achieve the American dream is through home ownership. Therefore we are offering a special program that will enable potential first-time

148

minority home buyers to purchase houses with little or, in some cases, no money down.'

'And how can I help you?' Reverend Rice asked.

Kirk leaned slightly forward in his chair. 'Well, we were hoping that once you learned a bit about the program, you might be moved to endorse it. And of course, with your status in the community, we hoped that you might be able to help identify and steer some potential buyers to us.' He smiled.

A sudden hardness filled the minister's eyes. 'Look in your computer files. You must have lists of all the qualified black folks you've turned down for loans,' he said coldly.

'Excuse me.' Kirk felt his face grow red.

The reverend stood up. He really was quite a big man. 'Look, Mr. Madison, I appreciate Angel City's sudden largesse. Truly I do. But you and I both know that the reason fewer black people own homes in L.A. is because banks make it impossible for them to qualify. And let's not talk about business loans. Angel City is one of the worst offenders in the city. You all don't even loan Asians any money.' He laughed, a loud, crackling sound like bullets popping. He leaned toward Kirk. 'Are you in lending?'

'I was.'

'How many black clients did you approve?'

'I don't quite . . .'

'Nobody comes to mind? Mr. Madison, if we're going to play ball, let's determine the rules of the game, shall we? Now, Angel City obviously wants to change its image. Fine. You guys want a public relations coup, but you need my help to get it. Well, my help doesn't come cheap, Mr. Madison; I have terms.'

Kirk was startled. He hadn't expected the minister to make demands. 'Such as?' he managed to ask.

'Solid Rock needs a three percent – that's right, three percent – loan for the apartment buildings just west of here.

We plan to turn them into low-income housing. We'll need a renovation loan at the same rate.' He paused long enough to search Kirk's shocked face. 'Hardball, Mr. Madison. Only game I play.'

Kirk swallowed several times, trying to recover. Of course he'd want something. The man wasn't a fool. 'What's the asking price for the property, Reverend Rice?'

'Nine hundred thirty thousand. Another five hundred for renovations.'

'Will it appraise out?'

The minister raised his eyebrows.

'Well, let me see what I can do.'

'There's something else, Mr. Madison,' Reverend Rice said. 'Home mortgages are fine, a good step, but if you want people to have a stake, they need to be in charge of their own neighborhoods.' His deep voice suddenly rose, and he stretched his arms open wide. Kirk was afraid to look at him, and at the same time he was afraid to turn away. 'They need to own the businesses in their own communities, not be sold to by a bunch of outsiders and foreigners who don't respect them. Let's make Angel City's commitment a two-pronged affair that includes low-interest business loans. And I'm talking about qualifying people without the usual bullshit. I'm sure you know what I mean.' He lowered his voice and his arms and smiled. 'Now, when the building is completed and, say, the first new business in the black community has been successfully opened, that will be a real ribbon-cutting ceremony, Mr. Madison. The mayor, whoever he is, will be there. Lots of dignitaries. And, of course, bank officials. You. Your boss. Very important that your boss be there, eh, Mr. Madison?' Reverend Rice paused, then added, 'Of course, we'll have to call a press conference. You'd like that, wouldn't you, Mr. Madison?'

Conniving bastard, Kirk thought, looking into the minister's composed face. He managed a stiff smile. Actually, things had gone rather well. It was always good press to loan money to a church, and in times like these, to lend money to a black church was the best kind of human interest story. And the part about business loans, why that wasn't a bad idea. Reverend Rice's project might work in their favor. A press conference. Great! That would certainly appeal to Preston Sinclair. And Sinclair should be grateful. He smiled to himself, then stood up and extended his hand. 'Yes, I would, Reverend Rice.'

When Kirk stepped outside the church, he was almost swallowed up by the line of people wending their way into the church basement. There must have been nearly three hundred of them. The men were frightening: dark and lean and desperate. A few were Latino, but most were black. Hopelessness seemed to be coming out of their pores, along with the horrible stench of bodies that smelled as though they hadn't been washed in months. Who were all these people? he wondered. Where on earth did they come from? And then he saw, through the open basement door, tables stacked with clothing. Others with toiletries and blankets. And other tables with hot food. He remembered what the minister's wife had told him. It was a feeding program for the homeless. Inside, black men and women called out directions and kept the lines flowing. Kirk felt fingers tapping on his back. He whirled around and faced a toothless old black man. 'Say, mistuh, you in line?'

Kirk fled to his car, jumped in, and took a deep breath. Everything in the surrounding night seemed to be leering at him. He sped down the dark street, toward the freeway.

After driving two blocks, he came to a dark corner and hesitated. Right? Left? Each way seemed wrong. In the gloom, he didn't recognize any landmarks. He was about to turn right when in his rearview mirror he saw a car coming up swiftly behind him. Before he could veer away, the dark sedan had crashed into the back of his new Lexus!

151

Kirk jumped out and raced to the rear, crouching down to see the damage. Lucky. The fender appeared to be barely dented. He was about to turn around and walk to the driver's side of the other car – he had a few choice words to say – but he felt the gun in his back.

There were two men, close enough so that he could smell the beer they'd been drinking. Or maybe it was malt liquor. He'd read somewhere that black people drank an inordinate amount of malt liquor.

'Give it up, motherfucker!'

The words were like a hard uppercut. The air seeped out of him. He didn't move.

'Your fucking money! Gimme that watch!' a voice shouted.

Kirk pulled his wallet out of his pocket, then took off his watch and placed them in the outstretched palm in front of him. Just let me go home, he thought. Don't hurt me.

'Where your car keys?'

'What?' Kirk whispered weakly.

'Something wrong with your ears, motherfucker?'

'They're in the ignition,' he said slowly. Kirk scratched the back of his neck self-consciously, then watched as a short, stocky figure got in his car and sped away. The car behind him took off in the same direction. He heard both drivers laughing as they drove away, shouting into the street, 'You been jacked, motherfucker. You been jacked.'

Reverend Rice was standing on the stage in the basement, in front of the crowd of homeless people, when he saw Kirk come in. His son was next to him, mimicking the older man's wide-legged stance. From where the minister stood, he took in Kirk's pale face and the terror in his eyes, and he knew there had been trouble. At the moment, though, the problems of the people gathered in the room were foremost in his mind. The smell was overwhelming. He knew that many of the men and women in front of him hadn't bathed in days. He held up a roll of paper towels in one hand and a bottle of glass cleaner in the other. 'Brothers and sisters, I told you some time ago that I didn't believe in giveaways, that I believed in people standing on their own two feet. Solid Rock's ministry isn't about giving you a fish dinner; it's about teaching you how to fish. We're going to begin phase two of the program here. It is about self-help. Tonight we will be giving out paper towels and glass cleaner, jumbo garbage bags, as well as shopping carts. These items have been donated by Louie Markets. You have a choice: you can take the glass cleaner and paper towels and clean car windows; you can use the shopping carts to collect bottles and cans, which can be redeemed for cash at the church every evening at six o'clock; or you can use the paper bags to clean up strip mall parking lots. At the back of the church, we also have T-shirts for you with the church logo, which will identify you as part of this program. In the near future, we will be giving out graffiti-removal solution, and that will be another source of revenue for you. Starting tomorrow, dinner will cost twenty-five cents, you will pay for it with the money that you earn. We will give you free work supplies for three months, and then we'll begin to charge a small fee for these items. As I've said in the past: America isn't the land of giveaways. Some of you blame the white man, your ex-wife, or your old supervisor for your current condition. Let me tell you something: The Lord ain't interested. No matter what adversities I've experienced, my God tells me to get my behind up and get on with it. If your God tells you to wallow in your own misery, to blame the white man, blame your ex-wife, blame your old supervisor, you're worshiping the wrong God. Now, some of you are struggling with the demons of alcohol and drugs. We have programs for those of you who truly want to be free. Some of you can't read. That's nothing to be ashamed of. The shame is in not improving yourself when you have the opportunity. We have a literacy program that will teach you. Just see Mr. Simms at the back of the church, and he can sign you up. Brothers and sisters, your fate is in your hands. Take responsibility for your own lives. Let us pray.'

After the prayer, Kirk made his way to the front of the church. He was about to pass out from fear and the terrible odor that was pressing in on him. Reverend Rice walked over to him, followed by the boy. 'What's wrong, Mr. Madison?' he asked.

'I was robbed,' Kirk said weakly. 'They took my car.' His body weaved a little as he spoke.

Reverend Rice grabbed Kirk's arm. 'Watch yourself, now. Let's go over to my office. We'll call the police. Would you like some water? Something to eat?'

Kirk shook his head. The minister held him by his elbow, steering him past the crowd and out the door. 'Well, Mr. Madison,' Reverend Rice said as they walked up the steps to his office, 'do you think Angel City might want to add a special low-interest car loan to the program?'

IO

Preston Sinclair had known Bailey Reynolds long enough
to know when he was genuinely happy and when he was
smiling out of habit. One look at his right hand man's face
revealed a false joviality. Preston leaned forward. 'Well?' he
said. 'Tell me what happened.'

'Preston, Humphrey Boone isn't interested in coming to
work for Angel City. Michele Coleman, our human
resources person, spoke with him. I spoke with him. This
isn't a marriage for him. There are plenty of other candidates,' he said smoothly, holding his curved fingers in his
lap, 'and I've compiled a list of five: three black men, one
Latino, and an Asian woman. I had Michele put out some
preliminary feelers, and from what she told me, they are all
highly qualified. My suggestion is that we begin the selec-
tion process with one of these people.'

'Describe them to me.' Preston listened attentively as
Bailey, after pulling a folder from his briefcase, smiled his
way through a litany of facts about each prospective
employee. He wondered why Bailey was selling so hard,
pointing out the virtues of each of the other candidates with
an intensity that bordered on passion. The slate of aspirants
all had impeccable banking credentials, but none of them
seemed to belong to any civic organizations. They weren't
known outside their field. They just didn't have star quality.

'Call Humphrey Boone and tell him that I'd like to meet
with him,' Preston said.

Bailey's mouth hung wide open for a few seconds before

he filled it with a smile. 'Certainly, Preston. I'm sure that would make a difference.'

'I want to get with him as soon as possible. Today. Tomorrow. At his convenience.' He was surprised at the intensity he felt. If Bailey noticed his excitement, his only comment was a silent one, a slight nodding of his head, a faint 'no problem' smile.

Later that evening, Preston took a sip of chilled German white wine as soon as Claire finished pouring it for him. It was slightly sweet and very good. 'Wait for a toast,' she chided, snuggling next to him on the sofa in the large family room.

She extended her glass to her husband's and clicked it against his merrily. Preston thought the gesture surprisingly frivolous. Claire was usually a very serious person. 'To being parents again,' she said with a laugh. Above them, on the second floor, they could hear their sons, Robbie and Pres, their loud voices booming from room to room. They were home for the holidays. Preston glanced at Claire. She seemed younger, her face relaxed and happy as she sat drinking the wine. The boys always had a cheering effect on her.

They heard the clatter of two pairs of footsteps on the stairs. Listening to his sons, Preston was amazed at how much noise they made. The house was usually so quiet after he got home from work. He and Claire weren't big on conversation. After nearly twenty-five years of marriage, they seemed to read each other's moods without saying anything at all. At least Preston didn't feel the need to talk. But when the boys were around, the house was filled with conversation and laughter. Preston liked to dream of all the wonderful things they would accomplish. He had plans for them, big plans. They would have entrée into the most prestigious business circles. If he could become governor, why, one of them might well become President. Whatever they wanted, he was going to help them get it.

The boys bounded into the family room, smelling like shampoo and cologne, their thick brown hair blown dry. Preston noticed that his wife began smiling as soon as they appeared. 'We're going out,' Pres announced, looking at his mother. He was the older of the two boys, although Robbie was taller. God, they were handsome, Preston thought, watching them. And things were so much easier for them than they had been for him. He was grateful for that, that his money and success made everything so simple for them. What was his father ever able to give him, except a sermon and some worn-out platitudes?

'Where are you going?' Claire asked.

'Hanging out with some friends, not too far from here.' Pres stood very close to his mother, so that it seemed natural when she rubbed his arm while he was talking to her.

'Which car do you want?' Claire asked. The boys had flown in from the East Coast, leaving their vehicles behind.

'Who's got the gas?' Robbie quipped. His mother let go of Pres's arm, reached out, and swatted at him. Robbie tousled her hair very gently. 'Look at Blondie,' he said jokingly.

Preston stared at his wife's hair. To his surprise, it did seem lighter, more golden. Very beautiful, he thought.

'Take my car,' she said. 'You know where the keys are. Are you going to see Bill and Adam tonight? Did they get in yet?'

'Yeah, they're back. They'll be there.'

'How about Amber and Hollie and the Grueber twins? Are they around yet?' She spoke to both boys but looked particularly hard in Pres's direction.

Preston listened. He didn't recognize any of the names his wife was rattling off. He felt annoyed and oddly lonesome.

157

'Claire, would you get me some more wine,' he said, a bit peevishly.

'In a minute, darling,' Claire said. Preston thought he detected a slight edge to her voice. Not unpleasant, just an edge.

Pres grinned at his brother and pushed back a stubborn lock of brown hair that kept falling forward onto his forehead. 'Do you think that last was a legitimate question or just a neat way to exercise her right to be nosy?'

Claire chuckled merrily.

'Oh, it was definitely an in, Pres,' Robbie said. He was grinning also.

'And if we answer it, what will be the next question, Rob?'

'Oh, she'll say' – he pursed his lips together in a perfect imitation of his mother, and his voice went up an octave – 'And do you think either of you boys are going to take any of those beautiful girls out while you're home?'

'Then what?'

'Then she'll say, "By the way, did you boys receive that copy of 'The 20 Safest Condoms' that I sent you?" '

'Then what will she say?'

Rob tilted his head slightly and put his hand to his mouth as though he were about to whisper. ' "By the way, are you boys carrying your condoms? You know they are of absolutely no use to you at home in your drawer." '

The boys laughed and Claire giggled, then crossed her legs demurely. 'Naturally, as a mother, I have a few concerns.'

Preston listened in amazement. The idea of his wife sending Pres and Rob lists of rubbers was shocking. Not that he disapproved; he supposed that the times warranted such drastic precautions. He was happy that she'd done it. Still, it seemed totally out of character for Claire to be so brazen. He peered at his wife and was struck by the brightness of her hair. Why hadn't he noticed it before? He stared at the three of them, huddling together, like a football team about to make a play, while he stood on the sidelines.

The two boys said good night to both their parents and started for the garage. Preston watched them as they walked away from him. 'You boys have fun,' he called out. It was an afterthought. He had no idea of what they called fun.

There were young people running in and out of the house throughout the holidays. Preston continued to go into the office, but Claire insisted that he come home early. 'I want you to have time with the boys,' she'd say, with an urgency that increased as it got closer to Christmas. Time with the boys. The words felt familiar, like an old hat found in the bottom of a trunk. Preston made several attempts at conversation, but Pres and Robbie never really seemed to have time to talk, with all their coming and going. Robbie was especially busy. Every night he zoomed off to some party, not to surface at home again until sometime the next afternoon. But Preston did manage to have quick exchanges with him about the car, about school. Once, Robbie was telling him what he thought about the new President, when the phone rang and Claire gaily called out his name; Robbie fled from his father with an alacrity that was almost uncivil.

Pres was much more subdued and harder to approach. After attending an initial flurry of parties and get-togethers, he settled into being a homebody, watching television in the family room, listening to music, or chatting with his mother in the kitchen. One night Preston walked in on his older son and found him sitting contemplatively in the dark living room. The drapes were open; he seemed to be staring at the moon. 'Pres,' he called softly, as he turned on a lamp. The sudden stream of bright light revealed the palpable outlines of melancholy etched in his son's face.

Seeing the boy's pain seemed to stir a kind of quickening panic inside him. Preston could feel his heart thundering in his chest. He couldn't imagine his son being unhappy. For a moment a sense of absolute desolation washed over him. He walked out of the room, resolving then to take both boys aside, have a few words with them. That's what he'd do.

But of course he didn't. There was no time. Robbie and Pres left for their respective schools the day after New Year's. And in the few days before, for one reason after another, he just couldn't connect with them. In the car on the way to the airport, there wasn't enough privacy to have a man-to-man talk with his sons, and somehow everything else he wanted to say to them never got said. Claire talked a great deal in the car and while they were all waiting for the plane, but Preston mostly listened. When they began boarding, he stood back and watched while the boys kissed their mother, and then he gave them a clumsy hug, an awkward affair because he ended up attempting to put his arms around both of them at the same time and of course the boys were different heights, and so he held one under the arm and another just above the waist. He could feel them trying to wriggle out of his grip, but Preston held on to them. He slipped his arms up and down until they stopped squirming, until they were still, and he was going to squeeze them, but the plane was called then and they finally did pull away and ran toward the gate. Claire waved to them and blew kisses. Preston stood rigidly with his still hands that were holding on to nothing.

II

The Wednesday after New Year's Day, Humphrey Boone stood inside his gargantuan walk-in closet and paused in front of a long row of suits. He chose a navy-blue pin-striped Armani, one of three in his wardrobe of thirty-plus Italian-cut work uniforms. He usually rotated his suits, putting the last one worn at the end of the line, so that he never wore the same outfit more than once in any given month, a device that freed him of having to make last-minute fashion decisions. On special occasions, he broke his routine. Today was special. He turned to the other side of his closet and eyed several rows of shoes, searching among the nearly fifty boxes for his newly purchased navy Ferragamos. As he scanned each container, he looked in the upper-right-hand corner for the descriptive label he affixed to each new pair of shoes he bought. The labeled shoes were stored with others of the same color and category: dress, casual, sport, evening. The system worked very well, and it usually didn't take Humphrey a long time to dress.

Today he was a little late. Shoes and suit in hand, he backed out of the closet and slid the door closed. It was nearly six forty-five, and he had an eight-fifteen appointment with Preston Sinclair at Angel City's downtown branch. He hadn't even begun his morning routine. The water in the shower was already running as Humphrey stepped inside. The shower lasted exactly thirty minutes, during which time he soaped himself and rinsed off seven times and vigorously scrubbed his fingernails with a small brush. He shampooed his short hair – four sudsings – which

161

he did every morning, and applied an instant conditioner, letting it remain in his hair for five minutes before he rinsed it out. When he stepped from the shower, he smelled like sandalwood and coconut. He lotioned his body from head to toe with a thick white cream that was made by a French company and cost twenty-five dollars a jar. Humphrey couldn't stand being gray and ashy, and he'd found that the French lotion was the only thing that worked, other than Vaseline, and he certainly wasn't going to use that. His Vaseline days were far behind him.

Humphrey put a small bit of gel and a tiny dab of Duke hair conditioner in his palm and rubbed his hands together, then massaged the mixture into his scalp first and then all over his hair. He'd experimented for a long time to find out which preparations gave his hair a softer appearance. He didn't want to look as though he had a Jheri curl, all wet and drippy like some ghetto gangbanger, but his hair was very kinky and he thought it needed a lot of moisturizing. His natural hair offended him; he believed that without the creams and conditioners it was too nappy. As he carefully combed and brushed his hair, he avoided looking in the mirror. He shaved the same way, looking only at his cheeks and chin, hating the razor bumps he saw. He poured after-shave into his hands and slapped his cheeks and chin briskly. Then he splashed on a little cologne in the same scent. He brushed his teeth carefully and then gargled for about five minutes before he applied a very strong anti-perspirant. Profuse perspiration was a problem for him, and in his position he couldn't afford to have body odor. He couldn't afford to be anything less than totally presentable and acceptable at all times. Grabbing a towel and drying himself, Humphrey rushed into his bedroom. He'd ironed his shirt the night before, even though it had come directly from the laundry and hadn't been worn. The ironing was a habit, as was shining his shoes, which he did every Thursday night while he watched television. He dressed quickly and then gave his bedroom a fast survey. His bed was made, and nothing was out of place. He hated the sight of disorder. Grabbing his briefcase, which was on the floor, leaning against his bed, he hurried out the door. The case was made of fine black leather and on the outside were his initials, monogrammed in gold. The feel of the leather was always reassuring to him.

As he turned off the Marina Freeway in his shiny Mercedes SEL 500, he thought about the interview he was about to have at Angel City National Bank. Ever since the *Gazette* ran the story about his role in the Lebanon Hospital private placement loan, his telephone had been ringing off the hook with job offers. This wouldn't be the first meeting he'd had since April 29, and it probably would be exactly like the others he'd gone on: a colossal waste of time, another White Man's Post-Riot Guilt Trip. He was in vogue, and he knew it. Ever since the riots, every major bank in Los Angeles had called him in for a 'spook by the door' position. But when it came to salary, responsibility, and perks, none of them were offering anything to tempt him. Angel City was smaller and far less prestigious than the New York money center where he was employed, and it was probably even more racist, he thought. Might as well sleep with the devil I know, he mused. If the white boys where he worked didn't like him, at least they respected him and knew enough not to mess with him. To go someplace new, he'd have to form new alliances and constantly watch his back. As he veered off the exit for the Santa Monica Freeway heading east, he almost reached for the car phone to cancel the appointment, but he stopped himself. An interview with the president of a major bank was not something to take lightly. A black man in corporate America couldn't afford to insult anyone.

Humphrey was a bit surprised when the assistant told

him that the meeting had been changed from Preston Sinclair's office to the boardroom. He took the elevator to the thirty-fourth floor. The machine ascended smoothly and effortlessly, with little noise and scarcely any vibration. He was grateful for the swift ride, because sometimes elevators frightened him. When the doors closed, he often felt panic welling up inside him, scraping through his throat until he wanted to scream. But today he didn't have time to be frightened, and when he got off, another assistant met him in front of the elevator. She walked with him toward two huge oak doors and knocked sharply. He heard a man's voice, and the woman poked her head inside the door. 'Mr. Boone is here, sir,' she said.

Preston Sinclair was standing to greet him. 'It was good of you to come, Mr. Boone,' Preston said, extending his hand. Boone was taller than Preston had imagined; he was at least six-feet-two, maybe six-three. Humphrey Boone was a sinewy black racehorse of a man, whose sharp eyes seemed to take in everything at once. He exuded class and sophistication, from his close-cut hair to the smooth gloss of his expensive leather shoes. He had the look that Preston was after: the look of leadership. 'Sit down, please. Is there anything I can offer you? Coffee, tea, juice?'

'No, thank you. I'm honored to meet you. It's not often a man is interviewed by the CEO of the fifth-largest bank in the state,' Humphrey said easily. He glanced around the room. It bespoke old money. The man was trying to impress him, but why?

'Especially when you've made it quite clear that you're not interested in our offer.'

Their eyes met. The black man held the stare and smiled mildly. Here's one who puts his cards on the table, he thought. This might be interesting. 'Well,' he said finally, 'as I said, I'm honored. And,' he added, 'I'm here.'

Preston leaned forward just slightly and caught a subtle

whiff of aftershave. Nothing too perfumy, just a bracing, clean smell. The man had the whitest teeth he'd ever seen in his life. He wondered if they only appeared that way because of the contrast they made with his very dark skin. 'I read about your work with Lebanon. That was very impressive. When I hear about highly credentialed people with awesome track records, I want them on my team. Mr. Boone, I want you on my team.'

'I'm flattered, Mr. Sinclair, but as you must know, I specialize in private placement loans. I know that Angel City occasionally does them, but not at the volume or the, uh, level that I'm used to. I've got some long-range goals, and Commerce is willing to be very accommodating.' Tell me what you want, what you're willing to do, so I can get the hell out of here, Humphrey thought.

Sinclair nodded. So far Humphrey Boone hadn't told him anything that he hadn't expected to hear. 'I'm very interested in your goals, Mr. Boone. Tell me, are you from Los Angeles?'

'Yes, I'm one of the rare native sons.'

'I see. And what do your parents do?'

Humphrey shifted in his seat. 'My mother is a teacher and my father is a lawyer.' He rubbed his hand across his mouth.

'Is your father with one of the firms in town?'

Humphrey had to hold back a laugh. What black man old enough to be his father was a member of any established white firm? 'Private practice,' Humphrey said.

'And you weren't interested in following in your father's footsteps?' Preston smiled mildly.

'No. I knew early on that I had no legal talents. Banking has always intrigued me. Five years from now, I'd like to be a regional senior vice president in charge of private placement,' he said, easily segueing into the topic he knew that Preston was steering him toward. Are you going to help me get there, white boy? Humphrey wondered as he stared into Preston's dough-colored face.

Preston rose abruptly and walked over to the picture window. For the first time since he had come to Angel City, he forgave his predecessor his excesses. From the thirty-fourth-floor picture window, that colossal paean to profligacy, a man could see himself as master of all he surveyed. That was precisely the image he wanted Humphrey Boone to have of himself. 'Mr. Boone – Humphrey – have you ever seen the view from this high? Come take a look.'

The black man walked over to the window, wondering what the view had to do with why he was here. But as he stood and looked out at the city, he had to admit that the scene was spectacular, truly breathtaking.

'You've been kind enough to share your goals with me; allow me to tell you some of mine,' Preston said. 'First, let me give you a brief bit of background. I've only been president of Angel City for a year. In the beginning of my administration, I set some goals, the usual bottom-line barometer of success. And then the riots happened. I don't mind telling you it caused me to do some soul-searching.'

Here it comes, Humphrey thought. He smiled benignly, trying to mask the cynicism he knew was filling his eyes. More we-shall-overcome bullshit.

Preston stole a quick look at the black man standing next to him. He thought he heard Humphrey sighing, but they were far enough apart that he couldn't be sure. 'Yes, soul-searching,' he repeated. The phrase was one his father used quite a bit, and as soon as those words were out of his mouth, he saw the old man in his ministerial robes, leaning against the pulpit, his eyes filled with humility and pious sincerity. 'Mr. Boone, I'll be frank with you. Angel City National Bank has a lot of minority customers. African-Americans, Latinos, Asians, all kinds of people, walk through our doors every day and trust us with their money.

What we don't have is a lot of minority employees, at least not many with decisionmaking power. In these days and times, that's an untenable situation, and I mean to rectify it.'

'That's admirable, Mr. Sinclair. I sincerely wish more people in your position felt the same way.' Humphrey gave Preston Smile Number 101 from the Catalog of Corporate Negro Smiles, the same curve of teeth and lips that he'd flashed on countless other white men who wanted to impress him with their liberal credentials.

Preston hesitated, trying to figure out what he was sensing from the man who nodded at him so pleasantly, listened to him so attentively. The air between them was charged with something that bordered on anger but didn't have its fire, that resembled sadness but lacked its depth. Preston looked at Humphrey again and felt a resistance so strong that it was impossible to misinterpret it. God, the man doesn't believe a word I'm saying, Preston thought. The revelation stunned him.

Preston was speechless. But only for a moment. He envisioned the photograph of Humphrey Boone and him in the *Gazette*. The caption would read: 'Angel City President Names Black to Top Post.' That mental picture was the incentive he needed to plunge ahead with vigor. 'I've instituted a Diversity Program here at the bank, which is a three-pronged program. . . .' He spoke with the enthusiasm of a candidate on the stump and watched for a telltale flicker of interest in Humphrey's eyes.

There was none. Humphrey had heard it all before. Diversity Program! God, every company in Los Angeles has one, and what difference have they made? In a minute he is going to offer me some window-dressing job with no responsibility, no potential for growth, no . . .

'The program is off to a rousing start and will serve as the foundation for some fundamental changes in this institution that I hope are going to have a truly profound impact

167

on the city's social structure. What I feel will enhance the Diversity Program is for employees of all races to know that at Angel City there is no glass ceiling. The top rung of the ladder is available to those who work hard. That's why I wanted to speak with you, Mr. Boone. I feel that Angel City has a unique opportunity to offer you. I am prepared to create a position for you. Several weeks ago, our regional manager was transferred to South-Central as part of the Diversity Program. The four downtown branches all reported to him. They numbered some two hundred people, and he oversaw a multimillion-dollar budget. We've had someone in an acting capacity since he left. What I'm proposing is that you take over that position and, in addition to those duties, oversee and expand the existing private placement program at Angel City. We could set up a bonus system commensurate with what you've been earning. Does the idea of creating something all your own excite you?'

Regional manager? Start and manage his own private placement program? Humphrey tried to monitor the rising excitement he felt. 'I think everyone dreams of forming something useful and lasting,' he said cautiously.

Sensing a change in the air, Preston plowed ahead. 'In addition, we are in the discussion stage of instituting a minority lending program. This would be a twofold affair. Angel City would offer low-interest mortgage and business loans to applicants who wouldn't qualify using our normal system. As I said, this is a program in the planning stages, but if we adopt it, that would be your baby as well. Let's be frank, shall we. What are you making now? A base salary of – what? – $100,000, maybe $115,000, with a very generous bonus structure. You earn about $160,000 or so a year, give or take a few dollars. You're paid handsomely, and you deserve every penny. You've done well, Mr. Boone. But how many deals can you rely on in this market? Your dealmaking skills are superb, but you lack management experience. I'm offering you a chance to broaden your skill base.'

A sixth sense told Humphrey to mask his interest. 'Mr. Sinclair, with all due respect, I'm not lacking in opportunities at Commerce. They respect my talent. And as you say, I'm well rewarded. They are also aware of the direction I'm interested in going in. Why should I jump ship?'

Preston sensed it was the time to play his trump. He leaned over the table and looked Humphrey directly in his eyes. 'You'll never be president of Commerce.'

With more than a little satisfaction, Preston saw the dark eyes widen, blink rapidly, and then open even wider. He had Humphrey's attention now, Preston noticed. His undivided attention.

Humphrey laughed mildly and kept his sharp dark eyes focused on Preston's face. 'Are you offering me the presidency of Angel City? Is that what you're saying?'

'Absolutely not. At the moment, the job is taken. But I am in a position to make a promise: If you accept my offer and if you do the job that I believe you're capable of, I'll groom you for the presidency.

'I know what you're thinking, Mr. Boone. Why would I go out on a limb like that? Well, I've had you thoroughly researched; I've spoken with every boss you've ever had. You see, I'm a risktaker, but I don't take foolish risks. You, Mr. Boone, appear to be a sure thing.'

Humphrey attempted to respond, but he couldn't speak. For the first time since he'd been in corporate America, a white man had surprised him.

'I'm fifty-three years old,' Preston said after Humphrey remained silent. 'I've been in banking for more than twenty-five years, and it's been good to me. But I have other aspirations, other options, which I plan to exercise within the next three, no more than five, years. I want to leave behind me not only a replacement but a legacy. I'm asking you to consider being that.'

'Mr. Sinclair, as I said, I'm very flattered that you're interested in me, but I want to be very frank with you. Commerce has given me a great deal of autonomy and a chance to move forward at a rather accelerated pace.'

'They've given you golden handcuffs, that's all.'

'I beg your pardon?'

'You're making money; you're not making progress. There's a difference.' He patted Humphrey on his shoulder several times and then extended his hand. 'Mr. Boone, why don't you think about your future and give me a call in a week.'

Humphrey took a last look out the window. Far below him, the city looked like something that could be controlled, even conquered. 'I want to thank you for your interest. I've enjoyed our chat, and I'll be in touch,' he said.

Humphrey could barely make it out of the room without jumping up and clicking his heels. President! He forced himself to calm down. He didn't know Preston Sinclair from a hole in the ground. The man might mean what he said, or he could be blowing out hot air.

When the doors of the elevator opened on the first floor, Humphrey was dizzy and light-headed. The elevator had descended so rapidly that for a moment he felt almost drunk. He walked toward the front entrance with the quick steps of a dancer. In a place deep within him, he felt acknowledged and validated, as though someone had just handed him a trophy.

He knew the parameters for a black man in banking were narrow; there were lines that couldn't be crossed without intimidating people who could topple him. If there was anything that scared white folks more than a black man with a gun, it was a black man in a suit. He'd learned to work beneath a glass ceiling, knowing that if he pressed against it too hard, he'd crack his skull. He'd seen it happen to others. He'd watched fast-tracking brothers climb up the ladder helter-skelter, zooming, only to get stuck on the middle rung or, worse yet, knocked off the ladder altogether. It was the reason he planned to leave Commerce eventually and start his own business. Entrepreneurship was the only way a black man could really succeed in America. It was how Jews had made it and how the Koreans were forging ahead. The Fortune 500 would always be the province of men with his credentials but not his color. As he pushed open the glass doors to a smog-filled Los Angeles morning, he felt a surge of power. Walking to the corner, he felt something within him stir, a part of his dormant soul wake up and say maybe. Maybe. Humphrey chuckled a little as he waited for the light to change. If Preston Sinclair was conning him, for whatever reasons, at least that white boy knew the right things to say.

Hours later, the Solid Rock Baptist Church Manhood Training Council gathered in one of the many small meeting rooms in the lower level of black Los Angeles's most renowned house of worship. As Humphrey Boone stood before a group of fifteen black boys, he drew his first calm breath of the day, although there was nothing serene about the group he faced. Ranging in age from nine to twelve, the boys hailed from the southern quadrant of the city and were rounding the curve into manhood at a dangerous speed. 'At risk' was the euphemism most commonly associated with them. Looking into their brown faces, Humphrey remembered his own accelerated boyhood. His was not the privileged childhood, with two educated parents, that he'd described to Preston Sinclair – a lie he'd concocted years ago to make himself fit in – but a battle for survival in South-Central. Every scar on the dark faces before him echoed his own ancient confrontations with the demons of the street. He had won those battles, armed with nothing more than his mother's steady hand on his shoulders, the guidance of one or two teachers who saw his early promise, and his own inner yearnings and fragile faith that life could be better, even for black people. But the boys before him were at greater risk than he had ever known. His father was a shadowy memory, but his mother had been made of steel. Some of the boys sitting before him couldn't even claim their mothers, because crack had a stronger hold on them than any maternal instinct.

Humphrey had been a volunteer mentor for the pre-teen boys for three years, beginning when Reverend Odell Rice, a fraternity brother of his, enlisted his assistance with ministerial persuasion. 'We've already lost a generation. Black boys are going down the slippery tubes to hell if brothers like yourself don't step in and give them some guidance. And don't give me that "I don't have any time" bullshit. Make time.'

'And you're supposed to be a man of the cloth,' Humphrey said, laughing. 'Cussing like that.'

'Damn straight. Lord said I could be myself.'

'Why don't I just write you a check, Odell?'

'Do that. Great big one. And then bring your black ass along with it on Wednesday, and I'll give you your crew.'

Humphrey gave a sigh of resignation. 'How much time are we talking about?'

'Two hours, one night a week, for one year.'

'Man, I— '

'You got time to make money for the white man, you got time to save your own kids. I'll see you next Wednesday.'

As he stood in front of the room, looking into the eyes of the ten-, eleven-, and twelve-year-olds who appraised him, Humphrey felt like a combination teacher and father, which, in fact, was what he was. The first few months he had worked with boys he resisted that role, but now it fit comfortably. In truth, he enjoyed working with the 'young men' and even allowed himself to hope that he was making a positive difference in their lives. He cleared his throat, and the noise died down. 'Okay. Last week we discussed our emotions,' he said. 'Does anybody remember what emotions we talked about?'

Reverend Rice had given him a 'curriculum' when he began mentoring, telling him to feel free to expand it. Humphrey liked to think of himself as giving his boys life skills, the kind of guidance he remembered needing when he was as young and at risk as they were. During some sessions they played basketball in the church's gym. Other times he instructed the boys to bring in their homework, and the night turned into a tutorial class. Many of the kids were behind in school, but there were a few who were startlingly brilliant. There were boys in his group who were salvageable and some, he knew, who would be lost. He remembered how Reverend Rice gave him his charge: 'I want you to arm them with the tools they need to get through the drug trade and the gangbangers. Build their self-esteem to the point where they see another way.' It was a hard job then and it hadn't gotten any easier in the three years he'd been mentoring.

When that night's session was over, Humphrey was just about to leave when he saw Reverend Rice. 'Hey, man,' the minister said, shaking his hand. 'I really appreciate what you're doing, brother.' He saw that he was embarrassing Humphrey. 'Listen, I want to ask you something about banking.'

Humphrey looked at him expectantly.

'What would it take to start a bank?'

Humphrey laughed. 'A lot.'

'Like what?'

'Money, because I assume the person or group would be buying an existing bank. Then you need a board. You need people to run it. And they'd have to be approved by the feds. It's not easy. Why?'

'A white man came in here not too long ago, talking about my endorsing a program Angel City National is starting that would offer minorities low mortgage loans. I told him they ought to offer low-interest business loans. Then I got to thinking the hell with Angel City. Why shouldn't we have our own full-service commercial bank. What do you think?'

'I think it's a lot of work,' Humphrey said with a laugh.

'Yeah, well, everything that's worthwhile is a lot of work.'

'Think about it.'

'Damn straight,' Odell said, as he walked away. 'I'ma do that.'

As he drove back to the Marina, Humphrey felt drained. He mulled over the evening's discussion, seeing in his mind the faces of the boys. He thought it was good, using Adam and Eve and the apple as an example of when to say no to yourself. They got that. Yeah, he thought, as he began to smell the ocean, just say no.

12

Esther's head was bent over the papers she held as she walked down the hall to the employees' lounge. A cough, hard and deliberate, forced her to look up. She turned to let the person pass and found herself confronting a smiling Tyrone: Mr. Basketball Butt. 'How you doing, Ms. Jackson?'

Right on. Right on.

She hadn't spoken to the man since the robbery, although she'd caught him staring at her once or twice. Facing him in the otherwise empty hallway, Esther suddenly felt trapped.

'Oh, you not gonna speak to me?'

His Barry White boom box of a voice was tuned down low. God, what an irritating person, she thought. But even as she thought it, she knew it wasn't true. The man wasn't exactly annoying; he was just persistent as hell. 'Hello, Mr. Carter. How are you?'

'I'm just fine, thank you. And how is your day progressing? Did you capture any robbers yet?'

Esther had to suck hard on her bottom lip to keep from smiling. 'Well, I haven't seen any today, but if I do I'll let you know.'

'Yes, please do that, Ms. Jackson. I would just love to come to your rescue.' He gave her a sly glance and a smile she ignored. Without being aware of what she was doing, she watched him go into one of the offices. Ass almighty. Damn.

When Esther returned to her office, there was a sealed envelope on her desk, with her name printed neatly on it.

175

Inside was a card with an African man and woman staring into each other's eyes. She opened it and read: 'Please have dinner with me this weekend.' It was signed: 'Mister Carter.' He'd actually spelled out 'Mister.' Esther chuckled. There was a telephone number under the signature.

That's what she got for smiling at him. She sighed and tossed the card into her wastepaper basket. When her prince came, he wouldn't be delivering the mail.

'I think you should go out with him,' Mallory said calmly that afternoon, when she and Esther were eating lunch at Patti's.

Esther's mouth was full of tuna fish salad; she almost choked. 'You think I should what?' she managed to say.

Mallory took a sip of the black coffee she always ordered with lunch. 'I think you should go out with him.'

'Would you go out with someone like him?' Esther's breath was coming out in short, jagged spurts.

'I've gone out with truckers, plumbers, unemployed actors, you name it. My only requirement is that the man I date be a jerk.' She gave a cryptic smile. 'Why were you looking so angry just then?'

Esther ignored the question. 'Give me three good reasons for going out with him.'

'Number one: He's compassionate. That was a really nice thing he did, giving that woman money and even trying to help you out with her. I know it came off a little sexist, and maybe it was, but at least his behavior says he's a helpful, take-charge kind of guy. Number two: He's not playing games with you. He likes you and he asked you out. Number three: He has the best buns in town. And number four: You're lonely, Esther. You haven't gone out with anyone since your friend fixed you up with that blind date. That was like a couple of months ago. You need to have some fun and affection. Besides, you're attracted to him. I can tell.'

'I am not attracted to him. And I don't see how you could suggest that I date someone who delivers mail to our office. I mean, you're Miss Politics.'

'I didn't say you have to go broadcast the news to everyone. Adults can be discreet. My entire relationship is built on discretion.' She sighed, and her face suddenly seemed shadowed.

'How are things going?'

'We were supposed to go to Santa Barbara last weekend. His wife was out of town. I waited for him to pick me up on Friday night and he never showed up, never called. Nothing.' Three seconds passed before her first tear fell. 'Let's drop this,' she said, wiping at her eyes.

'Can't you just stop seeing him?'

'I have tried to stop seeing him so many times, it's ridiculous.'

'Maybe you need some help. It's okay if you can't do it alone. Maybe there's some psychological reason that you're so attached to him.'

'Oh, that. I'm attracted to unavailable men because my father was a cold, distant shithead. So I find men who are cold, distant shitheads and try to work out my childhood issues of abandonment.' Mallory laughed. 'What else do you want to know?'

Esther shook her head. 'When you're ready, when you're strong enough, you'll let him go.'

'Yeah,' Mallory said softly. She took a sip of coffee. 'Tell me something. The truth. Whole truth, nothing but. Why were you so angry at first when I said you ought to go out with the Western Express guy?'

'I was surprised, that's all.'

'No, you were angry. Would you please just tell me. I know it has something to do with my being white.'

Esther hesitated. Then she sighed. 'I thought that you thought black women didn't have standards for choosing a man. That because I was black and he was black it was a love connection, even though I'm more educated and I make more money.'

Mallory sighed. 'Look, from now on, would you tell me whenever I offend you, or if I say something... something...'

'Racist?'

Their eyes met. 'Yes. That. Let me know, please. I want us to be friends. I've always wanted that.'

'Okay.'

'And give Mr. Fun Buns a chance.'

Esther shook her head. 'Seriously, he isn't my type.'

13

'Say, Cody, what do you do when a woman you like won't go out with you?' Tyrone sat on a narrow bench in front of his open locker at work. It was nearly six o'clock, and he and Cody Phelps had pulled their mail trucks into the company garage only a few minutes earlier.

'Find another woman, man. Life's too short. Stuff like that usually don't work out.'

'Stuff like what?'

'When you're chasing her and she's running away as hard as she can. Like I said, life's too short.' Cody stepped out of his uniform and laid his navy pants across the bench. He jerked a comb through frizzy curls that were the color of bricks.

Looking at him, Tyrone wondered why he bothered to ask for his advice. Cody was still a young boy, barely twenty-three. What could he possibly know about women, especially sisters? Ordinarily he didn't ask other guys for personal advice, especially about women, but he had trained the fire-haired white boy when he joined the company eighteen months ago, had driven around the city with him day in, day out, until he knew his route. Being cooped up with another person, with only breathing room between them, Tyrone was amazed at what they talked about, the things they confided to each other. Deep secrets. Family stuff. They played a lot of chess too, and Tyrone always won. Once Cody got his own truck, they didn't see each other as much. But ever since they'd spent that time together, he often found himself running things by Cody.

And in this case, Cody was probably right: If he was smart, he would forget about Esther Jackson. A woman like her was into sophisticated guys, brothers with two and three degrees. Doctors. Lawyers. Benz Brothers. He sighed, thinking that if he'd finished college, he'd have been that kind of man. Tyrone got up abruptly.

'Where are you on your way to, man? Want to go get us a couple of forties? There's a place not too far from here.'

'Nah. Maybe some other time.' Tyrone took a quick look at his watch. 'I have to go over to the place where I order my T-shirts. There's a bazaar coming up soon, and I have to get in a supply.'

'Man, you work harder than James Brown,' Cody said, laughing a little.

Tyrone watched silently as Cody put on his Lakers cap and turned the brim to the back. He put his uniform in a khaki duffel bag and stepped into some jeans that were two sizes too large and sagged around his waist. Tyrone couldn't help chuckling. Dude looked like Doogie Howser, the Crip.

'What are you laughing at?' Cody asked.

You, with your wannabe self. 'You gotta be the strangest white boy on the planet.'

Cody flinched a little, then shrugged his shoulders. Without a trace of a smile, Cody extended his hand to Tyrone, slapped a high five, and then gave him a black-power handshake that was topped off with a clenched fist. 'Watch out for women who play hard to get, man.'

'That's the only kind I like.'

On the first Saturday in February, L.A. was raining. Beneath the downpour, the city trembled, shaken by the rumblings of a new trial. The four white policemen were about to face another set of charges, another judge, another jury. Televisions blared old evidence, old lies, and old tapes, which rekindled flames that Los Angeles thought it had banked the year before. Each station competed with others to show the most controversial footage of the previous trial in order to position itself as the ratings winner during the upcoming one. Hate flowed throughout the city like lava. Sale signs proliferated all over town as people attempted to flee from their troubles. In schools and prisons, blacks and browns rumbled for tiny parcels of dying turf. Inmates brandished homemade knives and American-made hatred. They went for the gut and the jugular. Even after the bodies were taken away, the scent of blood was still in the air.

Dainty drops filled delicate puddles just enough to rinse away the smog and chase away customers. Solid Rock Baptist Church's Annual Black History Month Bazaar was officially declared a washout at three o'clock. Vendors grumbled under the huge canvas top that covered the church's parking lot as they packed up their food and merchandise. Tyrone was among the grim-faced merchants. Before him, spread out on a long wooden table, were piles of T-shirts emblazoned with every Afrocentric expression known to mankind, from FREE AT LAST, FREE AT LAST to BY ANY MEANS NECESSARY. In eight hours he'd sold twenty-three of the five hundred he ordered. As he packed the boxes, the word 'nonreturnable' resounded in his head like the weary refrain of an old blues tune.

He was loading the last box into the trunk of his Audi when he felt a heavy hand tapping him on his back. He turned around and faced Reverend Odell Rice. The older man had been his pastor when he was younger and his parents made him attend services. Technically, he still was his pastor, but Tyrone hadn't been to church in years. He always liked the amiable minister, and now, as he approached, Tyrone smiled. Reverend Rice handed him an envelope.

'What's this?' Tyrone asked.

'Under the circumstances, we're returning your vendor's

fee,' the minister said. 'We had good publicity; the weather just didn't cooperate. I'm sorry for any inconvenience. We're planning on having the African Family Reunion at the end of the summer. I hope we can get you to come back, Tyrone.'

'I'll come back if you buy a T-shirt, Rev. This is just your size.' He pulled out a bright-gold one that read: YES, I'VE BEEN BLESSED. 'Regular ten dollars. I'll give it to you for eight.'

The minister grinned, then reached into his back pocket and pulled out a five-dollar bill and three faded ones. 'You know, you always were a little hustler. Wasn't it you who sold candy bars on the bus that time the Sunday school took a trip to the desert?'

'Yeah, that was me.'

The minister chuckled. 'I mean, you waited until we got good and hungry, then whipped out those candy bars and jacked up the prices.' He shook his head. He peered into Tyrone's face. 'I sure would like to see you sitting up in church one Sunday.'

Tyrone looked down at his shoes. 'Well, I'll have to arrange that.'

'If there's anything I can do for you, or if you ever need to talk to someone, you just come see me, Tyrone.' There were so many young brothers with potential, Reverend Rice thought. He saw a spark in Tyrone's eyes. 'A salesman like you ought to have his own store.'

'Well, I'm working on that, Rev,' Tyrone said, passing him the T-shirt. For a moment, he saw himself enrolled in college, taking business courses. But when the moment passed, so did his vision.

The minister's eyes brightened with interest. 'That a fact? Well, I'm working on it too. You come see me when you're ready to get that store. Maybe I can do something for you.'

Tyrone mumbled something as he left. The truth was,

he'd never even thought about owning a store. Oh, maybe he'd imagined what it might be like, but he never really sat down and gave the idea serious contemplation. He wasn't thinking about it now. What was on his mind was the fact that the merchandise was nonreturnable and billable in thirty days.

As Tyrone cruised down Cranston, he looked for a likely corner to set up shop, which is what he always did when the bazaars and other vending events didn't pan out. The rain had stopped, but the streets were slick and wet. He hated selling on corners. He had to keep one eye out for customers and the other out for cops. There was a Muslim hawking newspapers and bean pies in front of the huge liquor store located across the street from the billboard with the crack baby, and he decided against sharing the spot. One, because cops were always drawn to liquor stores, and two, because he couldn't stand looking up and seeing that puny, wasted baby. Instead, he chose a corner two blocks to the north, directly in front of the mall. Pulling onto a side street, he parked his car. Then, on Cranston, he set up a card table with a kente cloth cover; he put the shirts on it and opened a folding chair. Next to his display, he placed a carefully printed sign that said: BELOW ROCK BOTTOM PRICES in huge red block letters. He could feel the hustling spirit begin to take him over the moment he sat down. His soul was singing the salesman's song: Sell! Sell! Sell! The adrenaline was pumping through his veins. 'Come on and get a bargain. Who's looking for a bargain?' he called out to the passersby. Three women were walking toward him. 'Come on and make these T-shirts happy, ladies. You know this cotton wants to get next to your skin.'

The women giggled and stepped over to the table to look. Each of them bought a shirt. 'Thank you, ladies,' Tyrone called out as the women left. He looked up and down the street, searching for customers. Like an old-fashioned huckster, he delivered a custom-fit, rapidfire sales pitch whenever anyone came near. More often than not, the person ended up buying a shirt. He stayed on the corner for several hours, until the bean pie man had disappeared and the streetlights came on. Reluctantly, he boxed up his goods and packed them into his car, wishing the daylight had lasted a little longer. Thirty-eight shirts. Not bad for less than two hours' work, but that still left him with more than four hundred nonreturnable items. He'd have to check around and see if any events for vendors were coming up anywhere in the city.

His apartment was less than a mile away, in the section just east of Park Crest, a neighborhood of neatly clipped lawns, two-bedroom bungalows, and well-kept duplexes. By the time he lugged in the boxes to his second-floor apartment, Tyrone was tired and sore. He took off his clothes, leaving them right in the middle of the bathroom floor, ran a hot bath, dumped in half a box of Epsom salts, and then sat down in the steamy tub. He stretched out as far as his lanky body could go and finally felt his legs go limp. He soaked for at least thirty minutes. When he got out, he turned on the radio to KJLH and fell asleep listening to Sade's sultry crooning.

He was awakened nearly two hours later by the ringing of the telephone. His friend James's harsh voice blared in his ear like a car alarm. 'Party time! Party time!'

'Huh?' Tyrone said groggily.

'Wake your black ass up,' James yelled into the phone, 'and get over here. There are some fine women waiting for you.'

The bed felt wonderful, he thought after he hung up the phone. His shoulders were tired from lifting boxes. He really didn't feel like driving all the way out to Carson for a house party. But it would be good to see his friends and have a few beers. Maybe he'd get lucky and sell some shirts.

184

The first person he saw when he stepped inside the house was his ex-girlfriend Sylvia. She looked fine as usual, but she was the last person in the world he wanted to see. Not because they'd parted under a cloud of acrimony, but simply because they didn't seem able to stop trying to patch up what needed to stay broken. Yo-yo love. He didn't want to get started all over again. As he was looking at her, she turned around and saw him. She jerked her head a little, the way she did whenever she was startled, and then gave him a little wave. As soon as she looked away, he eased into the kitchen. There was a bid whist game going on. His friend James was standing over the players.

'Aww, shit. Here come Willie Loman, y'all. I mean Beau Willie Loman. What you got in the bag, man?' James called out. He was leaning against the refrigerator, a Corona with a twist in one hand; he held a woman's hand in his other. 'You better not be bringing anything in here to sell, I know that.'

Tyrone started laughing.

James shook his head. 'Nah, man. Take that mess right back to your car.' James turned to the people in the kitchen. 'This Negro can't even come to a party without bringing something to sell. Need to call you Tyrone Avon Carter. What you got in that bag, you goddamn money grubber?'

'Mind if I make myself comfortable?' Tyrone said, moving the salt and pepper shakers from a nearby counter. He spread his kente cloth over the space, then set the T-shirts out in two orderly rows. Next to them he placed his sign, BELOW ROCK BOTTOM PRICES.

'Ain't this some shit? I know you giving the house ten percent. I know that.'

'Gotta give the house a cut,' Tyrone said.

'Well, what are y'all waiting for? Get your wallets out,' James said.

Tyrone stayed in the kitchen for at least an hour. A small

woman with long fingernails and big hips started giving him the eye after she abandoned the whist players. Tyrone began giving it right back to her. She's cute, he thought, looking at her hips. 'You see anything on my table you like?' he asked casually.

'I see something behind your table I like,' she said, and then licked her lips. Slowly.

Hello.

Nicole was a good dancer, and on the fast numbers they really clicked. But when Babyface started crooning his slow, lovesick melodies, they couldn't get the rhythm together. He stepped left and she stepped right. They bruised each other for about three numbers, and then he led her off the dance floor and back into the kitchen. The air was spicy with the odor of barbecue and potato salad. She talked a lot, mostly about her class of third graders. There were thirty-five kids in her room, and after an hour had passed, Tyrone felt he knew each one intimately. When people came in to buy a shirt, he was happy for the interruption, but the woman stayed right beside him. Wouldn't budge.

'Mr. T-shirt strikes again.' He looked up, and Sylvia was smiling at him. He was almost glad to see her. Out of the corner of his eye, he saw Nicole press her lips together tightly and move closer to him. 'Uh, Sylvia, do you know Nicole?'

Sylvia's eyes widened, and her upper lip wrinkled just a fraction of an inch. She's pissed off, he thought. 'Nice to meet you,' she said icily.

'Nice to meet you too,' Nicole said.

The three of them made the smallest of small talk, while the two women glared alternately at each other and at him. Tyrone felt as if two gigantic boulders were pressing against him. Finally, Sylvia said, 'May I speak with you privately, Tyrone?' Her voice was loaded with malice.

She had barely pulled him out the kitchen door before

she was hissing and snarling. 'Is she the reason we broke up?'

'Sylvia, I just met the woman.'

'Right.'

'Look, if this is all you want to talk about, we're not going to have a conversation.'

The light from the kitchen illuminated Sylvia's perfectly round and very hostile face. The tear that rolled down her cheek seemed almost electric. But he was used to her tears and other let's-start-over tricks. 'Sylvia,' he said wearily, 'we ain't doing this. We're not good for each other, we ain't going to be together, and I'm going back inside.'

Before he could cross the kitchen threshold, another woman was by his side. He looked down and saw grape-colored skin. Long legs. Hair like thick ropes. She put her hand on his arm. 'You feel like dancing?' Her heavy breasts seemed to move whenever she spoke. They sang a siren song, those breasts did. Tyrone looked away.

'I think I'll sit this one out, sweetheart.' He was ready to leave. He collected the remaining shirts on the table – he'd sold twelve – folded up his kente cloth, and put everything in two plastic bags. 'James,' he said, when he found his friend on the dance floor, 'I'm outta here.' He placed twelve dollars in his friend's hand. 'Don't spend it all in one place.'

'Peace, my brother,' James said, tucking the money into his pocket.

As he crossed to the front door, a thin, buck-toothed woman reached out and touched his arm. 'He-e-ey! Don't I know you from— '

He shook his head almost violently and continued his trek to the door. Tyrone didn't feel truly safe until he was in his car.

The In Town bar was crowded, and Esther made several attempts before she caught the bartender's eye to order her second glass of white wine. She twisted the ruby-and-diamond ring on her finger around and around. The ring had been a college graduation present from her parents. She played with it when she was nervous. She glanced at her watch. She'd been waiting for Vanessa for exactly thirty minutes. The bartender handed her the wine and Esther extended a five-dollar bill, but he shook his head. 'The gentleman sent it with his compliments,' he said, indicating her benefactor with a nod of his head. Esther followed the motion and found herself regarding a man across the room who could only be described as a clone of Quasimodo. She said hastily, 'Oooh. Wel-l-l. Tell the gentleman thanks, but I'm meeting someone.' She pressed the money into his hand.

The bartender nodded.

'Hey, mama. You sure are looking mighty good.' Her seatmate, a small, greasy man, smiled at her, revealing not one but two gold teeth.

'How are you?' she said weakly, looking around for another seat. There were none. Esther had a sudden gasping sensation, as if she couldn't catch her breath.

'Fine thing like you out here by yourself. This must be my lucky night.' The gold was blinding her.

'No-o-o,' Esther said quickly, panting a little. 'I'm meeting someone any minute now. Any minute. Soon. Very soon.' She looked around the room in a distracted, almost hysterical manner.

The man nodded, and a slight spritz of Jheri-curl juice sprayed over her. Everywhere she turned, men were smiling and winking at her. One blew her a kiss. I will stare into this glass of wine until they come, she told herself. She breathed slowly.

'Esther!' Vanessa was making her way toward the bar. She was wearing pants, Esther thought, but the green-pink-and-purple outfit was so loose and chiffony that she really couldn't tell what her friend had on. She smiled, waiting for the dates to appear, until she realized that she was looking at them. Standing next to Vanessa were two fi-i-ine men: tall, muscular, and impeccably dressed.

And white.

Esther barely heard the introductions. She was conscious enough to nod her head, stick out her right hand, and smile. Around the bar, the same men who'd been looking at her with naked desire now gave her contemptuous glances.

At her suggestion, the two couples moved to a table near the rear. Drinks arrived, and they began chatting. When she thought enough time had passed so that she wouldn't be considered rude, Esther said, 'Vanessa, I need to go to the rest room. Would you come with me?'

The door to the ladies' room had barely closed when Esther said to Vanessa, 'Why did you bring them? You know I don't date white men.'

'You know what? You got too many rules. You don't date poor men. You don't date white men. You must want to be alone. Relax. It's not a date,' Vanessa said simply.

'What do you mean, it's not a date? We're at a club; we're having drinks.'

'Let me put it this way: *They're* having a date. We are not having a date.'

Esther looked at her blankly.

'Work with me, people,' Vanessa said.

Esther made a small noise, a fraction of a scream. 'They're having a date . . .'

'With each other. Relax. They can dance their asses off. Anyway,' she said, sighing, 'I didn't get the part; I'm not going to be Denzel's woman. Bobby and Paul are fellow actors, and they're just trying to cheer me up. We did a show together.'

'Oh, I'm sorry, sweetie.' Esther actually did feel disappointed.

Vanessa gave her a look of the gravest incredulity. 'Don't

worry about it. I'm up for another part. I'm going to play Eddie's woman. I know I'm going to get this one.'

Esther stared at Vanessa without speaking.

Paul and Bob stood up when they returned to the table.

'Now let me get your names straight,' Esther said, determined to be personable for Vanessa's sake.

'I'm Bob Cappuletti and he's Paul Petrucelli,' Bob said quickly.

'Are you guys from Los Angeles?' They didn't really look gay, Esther thought to herself.

'Nah. We're just a couple of Italian guys from Brooklyn,' Paul said. 'But don't worry, we're not in the Mafia. We have no ties to the Gambino or the Gotti family.' He stood up. 'Excuse me, I left something in the men's room.'

'Behind the toilet,' Bob whispered, in a perfect imitation of Don Corleone.

Vanessa was laughing before Esther realized that the men were doing a parody of *The Godfather*. She started chuckling too.

Bob and Paul were a comedic tag team; as soon as one ended a funny story, the other began one. The two men regaled the women with tales about life in the industry, and after a while Esther was laughing too hard to feel uncomfortable. When a fast song came on, they all got up and danced. Paul and Bobby were good dancers, and the four of them stayed out on the floor for almost an hour. When a slow song came on, the two couples returned to their table and ordered another round of drinks.

'Well, if it isn't Ms. Jackson.'

Esther looked up into the smiling, slightly mocking face of Tyrone Carter. 'Oh, uh . . . uh . . .'

'Mr. Tyrone Carter,' he said easily.

She laughed in spite of herself. 'Yes, of course. Tyrone, I'd like you to meet Vanessa, Bob, and Paul.'

Vanessa smiled and nodded. The men shook hands.

'Do either of you gentlemen mind if I steal me a quick dance with Ms. Jackson?' Tyrone asked.

Vanessa's arched eyebrows rose just slightly; Esther looked surprised.

'We'll be watching,' Paul said.

Tyrone led her to an open space on the crowded floor. They found their rhythm easily and began swaying in synchronized rocking, not too fast, not too slow. 'So,' Tyrone finally said, when the song was just about half over, 'I see that you really are busy on Saturday nights.'

Here it comes, she thought. But Tyrone only smiled, and when the song ended and was quickly followed by a slow number, he wrapped his large fingers around her wrists and gently pulled her toward him. Esther slid easily into his arms. His neck smelled soapy and fresh.

'So did you come with them?'

'No, I met them here. I drove.'

She has the prettiest eyes, he thought. For a minute, he remembered Cody's advice. What did that fool know? Go for it, he told himself. 'Well, if you'd like to, uh, reconnect with your culture this evening – you know, get in touch with your roots – I'm getting ready to roll over to Rick's over on Wilshire. Why don't you meet me there in thirty minutes?'

Esther didn't say anything. He is pleasant, she thought. He's nice-looking. He's sane. He's the postman, she reminded herself. 'I don't think so,' she said.

Tyrone walked Esther back to her table. He nodded toward her friends. 'Thank you. Good meeting everyone. Oh, before I leave you good people, may I interest you in a T-shirt?' He pulled two shirts from a plastic bag and held them against his chest. One said: IT'S A BLACK THING, YOU WOULDN'T UNDERSTAND. The other had the infamous picture of Malcolm X holding a rifle and looking out the window, and it read: BY ANY MEANS NECESSARY.

'What do you think, Bob?' Paul asked.

' "It's a Black Thing," ' Bob read. 'Oh, I've got to have one. I can't wait to stroll into Stage with that on.'

Tyrone smiled as he accepted the money and handed Bob the shirt. 'Good night.' To Esther he said, 'I hope to see you again soon.'

'So who was that?' Vanessa kept her eyes on the man as he walked away.

Paul and Bob's heads were turned too.

'He's the Western Express man. He delivers mail to my office.'

'How can I get on his route?' Vanessa said with a sly laugh. 'Just kidding, girlfriend.'

Esther gave a little sniff. 'I barely know him. And you know he's not my type,' she said, turning her head just slightly.

Tyrone put the last forkful of chicken and french fries in his mouth and took a large gulp of 7-Up. As he chewed, he glanced at his watch. His last look, he told himself. He'd been in the restaurant for nearly an hour. The woman wasn't coming. Cody was right. On to the next one. He handed the waitress his money, put a dollar next to his plate, and headed for the door.

It was only half past midnight. Traffic zoomed by, but as Tyrone walked down the block to his car, there were no other people on the street. The February night was cool and crisp. The sky was dark and clear and the air around him was so peaceful that he almost felt safe. The city could do that sometimes, lull him into believing he had nothing to fear. But the Los Angeles he knew was full of surprises, of sudden winds, fire. The entire place could shudder and shake and destroy with no warning whatsoever. Tyrone looked around him, alert and wary. Well, the night hadn't been a total waste, he thought as he reached his car. At least he'd sold some more shirts. Tomorrow he would find out if there were any festivals going on. He mentally calculated how many shirts he'd gotten rid of and how many more he had to sell to pay off the bill that would be due in less than thirty days. Deep in thought, he slid his key into the lock, unaware of the car that was pulling up behind him. He didn't hear the door open and shut or the clicking heels on the pavement. He turned around only when heard, 'Tyrone?'

Esther Jackson smiled at him. 'Oh, you're leaving,' she said. He could tell that she felt a little embarrassed. He was really surprised that she'd come at all. What a beautiful mouth!

'No,' Tyrone said quickly. 'I mean, are you hungry? We can go back inside.'

'Well, I am a little.'

When they sat down at a table inside, Esther's stomach began to flutter. She'd had three such nerve attacks on her way to Rick's, after increasingly dramatic and even histrionic urging from Vanessa, Paul, and Bob. As she faced Tyrone, she wondered once again why she was here, although the longer she sat opposite him, the more the flutters in her stomach subsided. 'So,' she said. He had the roundest, clearest eyes she'd ever seen.

'Glad you made it. Didn't think you were coming.'

'Neither did I.'

'So I guess you— '

'Got hungry!' Esther said.

Tyrone smacked his jaw with his hand in a playful manner. 'Woman just dissed me!'

A young Latina waitress came and took Esther's order. She returned within ten minutes with a plate of fried chicken wings, potato salad, biscuits, and a glass of orange juice. Esther picked up a wing with her fingers and chomped down on it. She chewed silently for a few moments, peering around the room. She was so intent upon her food that when she finally looked at him, she was surprised to see that Tyrone was laughing at her.

'What's so funny?' she asked.

'Girl, I see a whole different side of you.'

'What do you mean?'

'I mean, when I see you at the bank in your little tight-fitting business suits, you are Ms. Corporate Jackson. And now here you are eating wings with your fingers at Rick's in the middle of the night. You full of surprises.'

Esther's greasy lips glistened in the dim light of the restaurant. 'I'm just a sister from the South Side.'

'Chicago?'

She nodded.

'Well, you're working out with that chicken. How do you do with ribs?'

'I don't eat red meat.'

'Health-conscious, huh? I don't eat red meat either. You only get one body. Hafta take care of it.'

'You sure do take care of yours.' The compliment slid off her tongue before she could censor it.

'Thank you.' He leaned back slightly in his chair. 'You're in very good shape yourself. I'm sure your date thought so.'

'My date? Oh.' She laughed. The tiny mean streak in her told her to let him wonder, but Tyrone looked so genuinely troubled that she blurted out the truth: 'It wasn't a date. Those guys were my girlfriend's buddies. They're gay.'

She saw that Tyrone looked strangely relieved. 'I was wondering how I was going to break it to you.'

They both began laughing.

'So now that I know that Bob and Paul aren't my competition, who is?'

She had begun to feel comfortable sitting across from Tyrone, but his question put her on guard. She took a quick swig of orange juice, wiped her mouth with a paper napkin, and looked around for the waitress. She would pay her own bill.

Tyrone put his hand lightly on her wrist. He could see her lips twitching nervously. 'Am I getting ahead of myself?' he asked.

She turned to him and was about to say, 'Yes, you are,' but Tyrone was no longer paying any attention to her. His eyes – round and bright with alarm – were focused on the door, where two men were entering. His glance swallowed them whole. Young. Latinos. Long hair. Mean faces. Both were carrying guns. Tyrone felt his body tense up. 'Just be cool,' he said softly. 'Just be cool. Don't panic, baby.' He saw the fear welling up in her eyes, and he slid his hand across the table and grabbed her fingers. She could feel him pulling off her ring. He looked into her eyes. 'It's gonna be all right, girl.' She nodded mutely.

'This is stickup, everybody. Put your wallets and your jewelry on the table,' the taller one yelled out. He spoke with a thick Spanish accent. 'Don't try nothing, and nobody won't get no hurt.'

Tyrone and Esther laid their wallets next to their plates and placed their watches beside them. Almost immediately a gun was sticking in Esther's face, touching the tip of her nose. 'You ain't got no gold necklace? No rings? Lemme see you hands,' one of the men demanded. Esther held her hands in front of her. They were shaking violently. She turned her face so that he could see she wasn't wearing a gold chain.

'Take it easy,' Tyrone whispered to her. 'Everything will be okay.' A low moan seeped through her throat. The man snarled something in Spanish and went to the next table.

Esther turned as the shorter of the two guys scrambled behind the counter to the cash register. His voice blared through the silent restaurant. '*Give me the fucking money!*' he screamed. Esther's head jerked involuntarily with every word. The clerk, a small black man with a boy's face, was too frightened to reply or even to open the cash register. The Latina waitress began whimpering and mumbling in Spanish. Tyrone looked at her – she was standing by their table – and said very quietly, 'Stay calm. Just don't panic.' He repeated the same soothing words over and over again. A tremendous wave of trembling rattled through Esther's body. She felt light-headed and dizzy, as though she were about to faint. 'Be cool. Be cool. Count from five hundred backward. It'll be over within a few minutes,' Tyrone whispered, taking her hand. She gripped his fingers tightly, too afraid to let go; she began counting.

'*Give me the fucking money!*'

The thief's voice was louder and angrier. Esther watched in horror as he began shoving the clerk. There was a sudden loud popping noise. The black man screamed, and his body fell to the floor with a heavy thud. Beside her, the Latina waitress began to sway. One of the men screamed angrily in Spanish at the other, who quickly snatched open the cashier's drawer and emptied the money into a paper bag. Both men ran out the door, then took off down the street on foot.

Tyrone stood up. 'You all right?' he asked her. Esther barely managed to nod weakly. The waitress was still shaking. Tyrone gave the thin brown woman's arm a tight squeeze before he rushed behind the counter, where the clerk lay on the floor. The small black man was groaning as blood trickled from his arm. 'Where's the phone, man?' Esther heard Tyrone ask.

The police and the ambulance arrived together. The medics declared the clerk's wound superficial but took him to the hospital anyway. The officers questioned the other customers briefly and then turned their attention to Esther, Tyrone, and the waitress, who had begun to cry hysterically. Esther sat woodenly, trying to answer the police but unable to focus on their questions. As hard as she tried, she couldn't remember anything about the thieves: not how they looked, not what they were wearing, not even what they said. All she could recall was the dark steel shoved against her cheek, pressing her nose. When one of the officers asked her what the men had taken, she was silent for a long time, trying to picture exactly what was in her wallet. Finally, she shrugged. 'I don't remember,' she said.

'She's kind of traumatized,' Tyrone said. He took her hand in his.

Tyrone, on the other hand, remembered everything. He gave the police detailed descriptions of both men, even including moles and facial scars. The entire time he was talking, he patted Esther's hand and sometimes rubbed her arm.

One of the officers told them they could leave. Tyrone took Esther by the arm and walked her to the door. Still woozy with shock, she leaned against him for support as they stepped onto the street. The sirens had attracted a small crowd. 'Hey, what happened?' an older man asked.

'Robbery, man,' Tyrone said tersely. 'They shot the cashier.'

'They kill him?'

'No.'

'Useta be so easy living here.' The man looked at Esther's distraught face, reached out, and patted her shoulder. As he did so, she jumped. 'Did you feel that?' she asked Tyrone.

'What?'

'I thought it was an earthquake.'

'You're just nervous,' he said.

'This place don't make no sense,' the man said.

When they got to their cars, Tyrone faced Esther and put his hands on her shoulders. 'Look, you're still real shaky. I think I should follow you home. Where do you live?'

Still in a daze, Esther told him her address, waited for him to get into his car, and then took off. Tyrone pulled up to the curb in front of Esther's house as she drove into her garage. He was expecting her to wave and for the automatic Genie door to close, but instead she got out of her car and stood in the garage, waiting for him to join her.

'Would you come in, please?' she asked when he was next to her. Her eyes were glazed with fear.

Without taking off their jackets, they sat at the table in the breakfast room for a few minutes. He looked around. 'You want some coffee or tea or wine or something?' he asked finally.

'Yes.'

'What?'

'Peppermint tea. It's in the cabinet. There,' she said, pointing toward the kitchen.

Tyrone went into the kitchen, and soon he returned to the breakfast room with two steaming mugs. Sugar and honey were in the center of the table. 'You want something in your tea?' he asked.

Esther nodded her head.

'What? Honey?'

'Yes,' she said softly, and Tyrone poured honey into her cup.

They sipped the tea, not saying anything for a few minutes. When Tyrone looked out the window, rain was beginning to fall, softly at first and then gradually harder. 'I'm still scared,' she said. 'You're so calm. You act like stuff like this happens every day.'

He chuckled tersely. 'Baby, this is L.A.'

'Yeah, you're right.'

'How much money did they take from you?'

She shrugged a little. 'Not much. Maybe thirty dollars.'

'Any credit cards?'

'No. I left them at home.'

'That was lucky.'

'How much did they get from you?'

Tyrone chuckled. 'Seven dollars.' He held out his leg, pulled up his jeans, then reached into his sock and pulled out a wad of money. 'My daddy is from Mississippi, and he told me, "Son, when you go out partying, always put your money in your sock." So here's two hundred dollars that those fools didn't get. Oh,' he said, reaching into his shirt pocket, 'this is for you.' He placed her ring on her finger.

'Thank you. I didn't know what you were doing when you grabbed my finger like that.'

'Thought I was kinda weird, huh?'

Esther smiled.

'As soon as I saw those guys, I knew what was going to go down. You live in L.A., you have to be ready for anything. This must be the fourth or fifth robbery I've been involved in. Once two guys held up my truck because they thought I was carrying money. Idiots. I'm like, "Does it say Brink's on this truck?" I've walked in on robbers in my apartment.' He shook his head and stood up. 'I'm going to go and let you get some sleep. I'll call you tomorrow. Maybe we can go out.'

She felt panic welling up inside her. Her fingers wrapped around Tyrone's wrist. He saw the fear in her eyes before she spoke. 'Would you just stay a little longer?'

He sat back down.

'When you said you were going to leave I got scared.' Her eyes were filled with tears. She didn't bother brushing them away. 'I could feel that gun; it touched my nose.'

He reached across the table and took her hand. 'It's okay. Cry it out. It's okay.'

She whimpered for a few moments, sounding more like a child than a grown woman. He wanted to hold her, but instead he tightened his grip on her hand. After a while she stopped crying and sipped her tea.

'Are you hungry? You didn't get a chance to finish eating.'

She shook her head. Tyrone looked around the room they

were in and out into the kitchen. It flashed across his mind that she probably owned her home. He was renting his duplex. In a secret place inside him he felt the chill of intimidation, but he was too tired to give in to it. 'You have a nice house. I always liked this neighborhood. You been here long?'

'Less than a year,' she said dully.

'Where's your VCR? You got any videos?'

They sat in the family room and watched *Do the Right Thing* and part of *All About Eve*, until they began to doze, leaning into each other.

'You need to go to bed,' he said. That same dark panic slowly filled her eyes. He hesitated. 'Are you still scared? Do you, uh, do you want me to walk you upstairs?'

She nodded.

The hall light was on, so Esther didn't turn on the lamp inside her room. Fatigue and fear battled inside her. She and Tyrone stood at the edge of the door. 'Tell me what you want me to do,' he said.

She tried to speak, but her voice faltered.

'You're shaking,' Tyrone said softly. He pulled her to his chest and held her tightly, patting her back as if she were a small child. She felt safe.

Finally, she said softly, 'Could you just lie on the bed next to me?'

Tyrone sighed. For a fraction of a second, he thought she might be playing some sort of seduction game. But when he released her, the light from the hall illuminated the stark terror in her eyes. He took her hand and said, 'Yeah, I could do that.'

She stretched out on the bed, and he lay down beside her. She fell asleep within minutes.

Esther woke with a start a few hours later, the memory of the gun nightmare fresh. When she sat up, her breathing came hard and fast. She gagged a little. In another minute, she knew, she'd be screaming. Then she heard the voice beside her, the strong, soft bass. 'I'm still here,' he said.

Right on. Right on.

14

Tyrone looked for Esther as soon as he came into the bank on Monday morning. He had a light load, only four packages, and none of them were addressed to her. It was early; there weren't any customers in line yet, and what he wanted to do was run through the place yelling her name, but he knew he had to be cool. Discreet. He couldn't wait to see her again. Before he left her house, they'd made a date. When he was lying next to Esther in the wee hours of the morning, thoughts of the holdup weren't what kept him awake. Every time he tried to close his eyes, Esther would shift her body next to his. He'd feel her cool, sweet breath in his face, smell the faint scent of her perfume, and hear her moan. He stayed awake all night, just watching her.

As he glanced around the bank, he saw a black man emerge from the elevator, accompanied by a white man who couldn't seem to stop smiling. The brother caught his eye. The charcoal-gray suit he wore hung on his tall, thin frame as though it had been made for his body. A suit like that cost eight hundred dollars, maybe more. Tyrone could tell that everything the black man wore was expensive, including the briefcase he carried, with his initials, H.B., in gold. He was one elegant brother, the kind of dude who had a wallet full of gold cards. He probably drove something fast and sleek, a Benz, maybe a Jag. And sitting beside Mr. Debonair, in his slick, shiny ride, was a woman like Esther. Tyrone's mouth went dry.

Esther didn't see Tyrone until he was leaving the bank. The sight of his strong body was enough to make her want to call out his name, but of course she didn't. Instead, she watched him through the glass wall as he walked toward his truck. Looking at him, she remembered his scent when she lay next to him. After the ordeal of the robbery and staying up half the night, he still smelled fresh and clean, like new wash. He's the mailman, she reminded herself. She turned back to her work.

By the time Esther passed through the narrow hall that led to Kirk's office, later that morning, she'd emptied her mind of all thoughts except her strategy. Only a few days ago, Mallory had suggested that she approach Kirk about becoming a lender. Since he was the acting regional manager, the idea was sensible, but something held her back. She'd been rejected too many times by white men she thought might help her; she didn't want to set herself up for another failure. But after mulling over the matter, she decided on a more subtle approach. She wouldn't push; she'd just plant a seed. Let him know that she was interested in lending. She had to make Kirk feel comfortable with her first. Then, in a couple of weeks, she'd invite him out to lunch and get into a deeper discussion of her goals.

As Esther sat stiff and straight in front of Kirk's desk, she tried to wipe away the memory of the robbery, to ignore the migraine that had set in on Sunday morning and refused to go away, and, at the same time, to mask with a congenial smile the discomfort she felt whenever she was around her new boss. Being with Kirk always made her feel a little queasy. He would single her out, shower her with smiles and warmth, sometimes touch her arm in a collegial way to emphasize a point, but his manner always seemed artificial to her, as though he were trying out for the role of the Great Emancipator in a college play. Esther leaned forward in the chair. 'Kirk, I know I've told you this before, but I'm very pleased that you're the new regional manager. You've made a remarkable difference in a very short period of time. If I can assist you in any way, just ask me.'

'Well, you certainly have operations running smoothly, Esther. I've been at this bank for five years, and you've outperformed everyone else who's been in your position.'

'Thank you. I'm very happy with my job. Of course, eventually' – she put a bit of emphasis on the word – 'I'd like to expand to other areas of banking.' There, she thought; that was just enough. To her surprise, Kirk responded without hesitation.

'Really? What did you have in mind?'

She hoped her surprise wasn't apparent. 'I want you to know that what I've done for the operations side, I can do for the loan department.'

Kirk's countenance slowly changed, interest shifting to sympathy. 'Esther, I'm going to be honest with you. Mallory told me about your desire to be a lender, and quite frankly, I can't promise you anything. In the first place, you are such an outstanding operations manager that I don't have anyone who can replace you. Secondly, there aren't any openings for a lender right now. I wonder if you've thought about your goal in a practical manner. Do you realize that you'll have to take a cut in salary? You'd be coming in as a novice at an age where most of the lenders are somewhat seasoned. And there's a, uh, certain mentality that goes along with being a lender. I'm not sure you have that kind of hard edge.' He stood up, smiling blandly. 'You're such a nice person.'

Esther was too stunned to speak. What Kirk was telling her was that he didn't think she was qualified to be a lender. Anger, pure South Side wrath, full of alleys with broken wine bottles, crept up her back like a flame following a fuse. She wanted to explode, but instead she looked around the office. She was on the North Side of a whole different town.

After taking several quick breaths, she smiled. 'Well, as I said, I'm happy where I am at present.'

Kirk touched her arm softly. 'I don't want to leave you with the impression that the case is closed on this. I just wanted you to consider some things. We'll uh, keep the dialogue going. And by the way, I've approved your request to hire another teller. How's that?'

Esther nodded her head enthusiastically and gave Kirk an upper-upper North Side smile. Keep the dialogue going, she thought. She knew what that meant: she'd have to tap-dance a little harder.

Kirk walked her to the door, opened it for her, and put his hand on her shoulder. Esther tried not to cringe. 'Mallory told me you were the victim of a holdup this weekend. I'm sorry to hear that. How are you feeling?'

'Still a little shaky,' she admitted.

'I was carjacked at gunpoint several weeks ago, and I tell you, I don't think I've ever been more frightened in my life. And the aftermath was in some ways worse than the actual robbery. If you need some time off, take it.

'I don't blame my assailants, of course. They were two young black men. Probably unemployed. I was in South-Central at the time. I had a meeting with Reverend Odell Rice at Solid Rock Baptist Church. It happened a couple of blocks from the church.' His eyes were glowing with empathy and goodwill. 'Maybe if there were some decent programs for youth – and of course the public schools need a complete overhaul. I mean, with the conditions that the black community has to live in, what can anyone expect? If they catch those guys, I just hope they won't deal too harshly with them.' Even as the noblesse oblige oozed out of his pores, Kirk managed to sneak a quick look at his watch. He had a very important meeting scheduled. He opened the door wider.

Give me a damn break, Esther thought. A wave of nausea

churned through her belly. 'Well, if they find the guy who stuck a gun in my face, I hope he gets the chair. I guess I'm just not as forgiving as you.'

'Well. We'll talk,' Kirk said pleasantly. He wasn't surprised that the black woman wanted to get involved in lending, but, he thought, she was much more useful in operations. After all, that department had the most diverse workforce in the bank, and what better person to be at the helm than a black woman? Lending probably seemed glamorous to her, but she wasn't really qualified, and God only knew how long it would take to train her. She'd probably give away the bank. Some good-looking black guy with a line yea long might waltz in, and that would be it. A lender had to be sharp, perceptive: someone like him.

Bailey Reynolds announced his entry with a quick, hard knock. For the past few months, the older man had dropped by frequently, usually to remind Kirk that he was being watched, which to Kirk's ears was the same as saying he was being groomed.

Today the ebullient Bailey wouldn't even sit down. 'No time! No time!' he said, beaming expansively. 'Just wanted to let you know that your memo about the foreclosure sales was received and the president is ecstatic. To unload twenty-eight properties in this climate, in less than six weeks, is nothing short of extraordinary! Keep up the good work! Mr. Sinclair is very pleased.' He winked and nodded his head at Kirk. 'Ve-e-ery pleased,' he added.

'And the Minority Loan Program?'

Bailey smiled and rubbed his nose with his curved fingers. When he spoke, his words came quickly. 'Yes. I was getting to that. Seems there was something in the works already. Your idea sort of overlaps one that the president had already concocted. As you know, diversity and fairness are issues that are close to the president's heart. But Mr. Sinclair was pleased that you were thinking along those lines. Very pleased.' Bailey didn't look at Kirk as he spoke.

Kirk tried to hide his disappointment. He had thought that the Minority Loan Program might put him over the top. 'Well, I hope the president is aware of my desire that my position becomes permanent.'

Bailey's eyes shifted just slightly, a movement Kirk saw but dismissed. The older man smiled broadly. 'I think I can say that you're headed in the right direction.' Bailey glanced at his watch and murmured, 'Ooops, running late.' He shook Kirk's hand and gave him a quick slap on the back. 'Don't worry. Preston Sinclair believes in rewarding excellence.'

There were a thousand and one projects he needed to be working on, but for the moment Kirk let his exultation spread from his head to his toes. He stared at Sheila's picture. Her plump cheeks seemed to be engorged with unspoken accusations. But Sheila was wrong. His former med school chums were wrong. Kirk wasn't a loser.

He was on a roll. Last week he'd purchased two suits, at six hundred dollars each. They needed to be picked up today. He envisioned himself wearing them. They were both silk-wool blends. Ordinarily he would consider such an exotic fabric too ostentatious for the bank, but the suits were cut severely, and the total effect was very understated. He hadn't meant to buy two, but the salesman kept telling him that a man in business, a man with a career to make, needed a couple of suits like that in his closet. After all, he was on his way up. Pretty soon he'd have to get a mink for Sheila. Funny how people didn't notice how heavy a woman was if she was swathed in mink. Kirk thought it over and decided that the man was right. Today he was acting regional manager, but soon he would be the regional manager. Maybe today Bailey Reynolds hadn't told him in so many words the news he craved, but he understood his smiles and winking and back patting. He knew exactly what Bailey was telling him.

He was headed for the big time.

Two days after her conversation with Kirk, Esther was smiling at a young man sitting across from her desk, who could have passed for Alex Keaton in *Family Ties* – except for the tiny hole in his ear. The hole didn't have an earring in it, Esther noted, and the man was dressed conservatively, in a dark suit and tie. His shoes were shined, his fingernails were clean, and his hair was short and shiny. David Weaver, Esther read from the résumé. A nice *Family Ties* name.

'So, David, it says here you've been with Security for two years. Why are you considering leaving?'

He sat up straight. His face was smooth, as though he'd never shaved. Just the tiniest amount of peach fuzz on his upper lip. But his serious expression was filled with earnest determination that almost seemed out of place in one so young. 'I'm looking for a position that will offer me some mobility. There aren't many opportunities to move up at Security.'

'What kind of opportunities are you looking for, David?'

'Well, I'd like to become a service representative in a reasonable amount of time. And then I'd like to be able to go to school at night and get into management. Ultimately, I want to be a middle-market lender. That's always interested me.'

'Do you know TIPs? That's not the computer system Security uses, is it?'

'I know it,' David said, leaning toward her eagerly. 'I took a class at night.'

'How do you feel about working for a woman, David?' She watched his face intently.

He chuckled easily. 'I'm working for two already. I got

married last year, and my wife just had our daughter two months ago. And my current boss is a woman.'

Esther smiled. Stable. The guy is stable. She thought of D'Andre Lang, the last teller she'd hired, the one she'd recently fired. His earring had appeared after he took the job, and so had a number of other little peccadilloes. Like two-hour lunches and his penchant for flirting with the female customers. And then there was that odor that clung to him after he returned from his lengthy breaks – decidedly herbal.

And naturally he was a brother. She'd gone out of her way to hire him – against her better judgment – and what had it gotten her? It took all her effort just to do damage control, so that Charles never found out just why D'Andre was dismissed.

It was always so much easier for the Keatons' baby boys, she thought, looking into David's smooth face. Not that the young man seated before her couldn't mess up, but even if he did, somehow the full weight of his mistake wouldn't fall on her doorstep. He was one of theirs. She thought about Kirk's words, a hint really, telling her that the case wasn't closed on her desire to be a lender. Just hiring someone white would earn her points. And she needed lots of points to move into lending.

She rose and extended her hand. 'I've enjoyed chatting with you, David. I'll be in touch soon.'

'It's been a pleasure talking with you, and I look forward to hearing from you,' David replied.

After he left, she said softly, 'He's bright. He's ambitious. He'll make me look good.' She repeated the words over and over until they were a mantra that left no space for other thoughts.

By six o'clock that evening, Esther felt drained. She'd had a headache ever since the morning after the robbery; the pain had increased exponentially when she met with Kirk.

She had thought that getting back to the bank would help her forget about her Saturday night ordeal, and when she was immersed in her work during the day, she was able to put everything out of her mind. But when she was just sitting at her desk, as she was now, her hands would start to shake. Worst of all, whenever she closed her eyes, even for a moment, she could feel the steel tip of the gun pressed against her nose. She was too exhausted to stay at work any longer, but the thought of going home to her empty house, of sleeping alone in her bed, made her heart pound and her palms slippery.

Esther was so absorbed in weighing her options, she didn't realize that Mallory had come into her office. When she saw her friend suddenly standing before her, she jumped. 'Oh, I didn't mean to scare you,' Mallory said soothingly. 'I just wanted to ask you how the interview went. I saw the young man as he was leaving. What'd you think?'

'Very sharp. He's the best one. I'm going to hire him,' Esther said dully.

Mallory walked around the desk and hugged her friend. Esther put her arm around the white woman's thin waist and clung to her for a minute, a gesture that surprised them both. 'Poor baby,' Mallory said. 'You're still freaked out, aren't you?'

'Every time I think about what happened, I get terrified. Am I going to be scared for the rest of my life? God, I hate this feeling.'

'When somebody sticks a gun in your face, it's kind of a memorable experience. But,' Mallory said, speaking more slowly, more carefully, 'after a while – you know, weeks, maybe months from now – if you don't feel better, you might want to think about seeing somebody. Aren't there victims' assistance programs to help people recover from the trauma?'

210

'I don't know. All I know is I'm scared to sleep in my own house. I spent Sunday night with Vanessa, but I can't stay there again. She only has one bed, which wouldn't be so bad if we were the only ones in the bed. But Vanessa puts everything in her bed: her stupid cat, books, newspapers, everything. That girl is so junky.' For the first time in several days, Esther laughed a little.

'You could stay with me. I don't have a cat, and I'm sort of compulsively neat.' The words slipped out before she had time to think. Once they were spoken, she felt happy.

'Oh, no. I . . .' Stay at her house?

Mallory took her hand. 'Please. You can stay as long as you need to.'

At her house?

'Please.'

'I'll have to go home and get some things.'

Esther got lost several times after she turned off the 405. The streets were dark; she couldn't read the signs, and she made so many wrong turns that it was nearly nine o'clock before she reached Mallory's. When she saw the sign announcing the town houses, she wanted to shout hallelujah. Nice, she thought, as she turned into the new subdivision. There was a guard station in front, and Esther waited patiently for the security man to phone Mallory. For about an eighth of a mile, she followed a road bordered by a huge expanse of sloping lawn, fringed by palm trees, roses and azaleas, and birds of paradise. She passed a tennis court and an Olympic-size swimming pool. Really, really nice.

Mallory was already in her bathrobe by the time Esther rang the bell. When she opened the door to let her friend in, she had a mug of coffee in her hand and her hair was wet. 'I was beginning to worry,' Mallory said.

They stood in an entryway that was almost the size of Esther's family room. In front of her was a winding staircase. To the right was the living room, large and sunken, with a sofa and a love seat covered with expensive fabric. On her left side was a dining room with a long glass-and-brass table. The wood on the floors was bleached. The color scheme was earth tones. Everything was straight out of *House Beautiful*. Esther couldn't help thinking how impressed her mother would be if she lived in a home like Mallory's, the kind of place that she and Mitchell could have together.

'Your house is gorgeous.'

Mallory shrugged. 'I'll show you where you're going to sleep. You can put on your robe and get comfortable.'

Esther hung up her clothes and stashed her toiletries in the adjoining bathroom. How can she afford all this? Esther silently wondered. She made $65,000. Mallory couldn't make much more than $75,000. She admitted to herself that she was envious, but she was also curious and a little suspicious. It's not your business how much her house cost, she reminded herself.

Esther took off her clothes and put on her pajamas and robe. She thought about rolling up her hair but decided to do that later, when she was ready for bed.

Esther followed the scent of food into a large, bright kitchen with an island counter in the center of the room. The walls were covered with flowered wallpaper and were coordinated to match the curtains. Mallory was standing at the stove, taking a pan full of steaming chicken out of the oven. The small table under the kitchen window was set for two. The place mats matched the curtains. In the center of the table was a bowl filled with salad, another with two ears of corn, and a small plate with several rolls on it.

'I'm starving,' Esther said. She added, 'You need any help?'

Mallory shook her head. 'Just sit down.' She took out a

212

pitcher from the refrigerator. 'Is ice tea okay? There's no caffeine in it.'

'That's fine.' Esther eyed the room approvingly. 'I love this kitchen. Mine is so old-fashioned. The first major renovation I'm doing is to gut it and start from scratch. This island is great.'

'Where do you live, Esther?'

'Park Crest. Do you know where that is?'

'I used to live there when I was a child,' she said.

'You're kidding. Small world,' Esther said.

Mallory didn't mention that she hadn't been back to the neighborhood in years, that the thought of so much as visiting the place was frightening to her. She wondered how Esther could live there. Mallory placed a platter of chicken on the table, sat down, and began eating right away. Esther bowed her head and said a quick grace. She always felt self-conscious when she was the only one at the table giving thanks. When she raised her head, Mallory was staring at her. 'It's been so long since I did that. I think the last grace I said was "God is great, God is good, and we thank him for our food."'

'Well, I guess I won't be seeing you in heaven,' Esther said, laughing quietly. She took a bite of chicken. 'This is delicious, Mallory.'

Mallory stood up and turned on the radio, and the kitchen was filled with soft New Age music, as soothing as meditation.

As Esther listened, she swayed just a little. 'God, I'm so glad I came. If I were at home, I'd be jumping at every sound. I hate feeling that way.'

'Give yourself time.' Mallory took their empty plates to the sink. When she came back to the table, she set down a bottle of pinot noir and two glasses. Esther poured them both drinks. 'To your serenity,' Mallory toasted. They each took a sip of wine. 'So,' Mallory said, putting her glass down, 'how was the date? I mean, before the robbery. Is the guy from Western Express nice?'

Esther's face softened. 'Yeah, he's really nice. But it wasn't exactly a date. I ran into him in a club, and then arranged to meet at the restaurant later.'

'That qualifies as a date. Are you going to go out with him again?'

'Just listen to you. Such a matchmaker. Well, this will make you happy. We're supposed to go out again on Saturday.'

Mallory smiled. 'I had a good feeling about that guy.'

'No, you had a good feeling about his butt,' Esther said with a laugh.

'That too. Speaking of which, did you happen to get a closer look at it?'

They both whooped.

When they settled down, they finished their wine. Mallory cleared the rest of the dishes, refusing her friend's offer to help. Esther began reading the copy of the *Gazette* that lay on top of the island counter. From time to time, she would say, 'Listen to this,' and read aloud to Mallory.

When the kitchen was clean, they took their wineglasses to the family room and turned on the television. Mallory's TV had a superwide screen. Esther was aware such a television could cost almost three thousand dollars. How can she afford all this? she wondered again.

Mallory turned on the channel 7 news, then disappeared for a moment, before returning with nail polish, remover, cotton balls, and an emery board on a small tray. 'Well, if you're going to do your nails, I'll set my hair,' Esther said. She went to the guest room and brought back her comb and rollers and a scarf. She settled herself on the sofa next to Mallory, who poured more wine in their glasses.

The pungent odor of polish and remover wafted through the room. Mallory watched Esther do her hair. 'That's why your hair always looks so great. I haven't rolled mine since I was a little girl,' she said.

'Honey, if I didn't put my hair up at night, even Charles Weber wouldn't give me any play.' Esther made a funny face. Just then the doorbell rang. The women looked at each other, then Mallory rushed toward the door, her eyes filled with expectation.

Esther quickly finished tying up her scarf and was about to hurry to her room when she heard a male voice, reeking with displeasure, say, 'You have company?' It was a father's stern reprimand.

She heard Mallory's voice, lower, childlike: 'I'd like you to meet her, honey.'

Esther instantly recognized the man from that night in the restaurant: Hayden Lear. He was expensively dressed. One glance at his leather coat, and Esther knew it felt as soft as rose petals. She also knew the answer to her questions about Mallory's luxurious house.

'Hayden, I'd like you to meet my friend Esther Jackson,' Mallory said nervously. 'Esther, this is Hayden Lear.'

Esther extended her hand, and Hayden shook it quickly. 'I didn't realize that Mallory had company,' he said in the same hostile, accusatory tone. He scarcely bothered to look at Esther but instead gave Mallory a cold, imperial stare.

Mallory's in love with an asshole, Esther thought to herself.

And it was love that plainly shone on her friend's face. Love that, despite her obvious anxiety, made her gray eyes soft and warm when she looked at Hayden. Love that compelled her to rest her hands on his arm and on his back and to stand as close to the angry man as she dared.

'I'm pleased to meet you,' Esther said evenly. She thought about apologizing for being in rollers but immediately decided against it. Let him apologize for being an asshole. 'I'll say good night.'

About an hour later, Esther was lying in bed, grateful that she was relaxed and sleepy, that when she closed her eyes she didn't see guns or feel cold, hard steel. She was almost dozing when she heard little yelps like a small puppy whining. She sat up in bed and listened. The noises were coming from Mallory's bedroom. Then she heard Mallory laughing, a soft gurgling sound, and the yelping started up again.

The next morning, Mallory was awake before her alarm sounded. She woke up the way she did on all the mornings after Hayden had been in her bed, her fingers groping toward where he'd lain but finding it, so warm only hours earlier, cold now. Hayden never spent the night.

Mallory reached over and turned off the alarm. It wasn't quite five-thity. She put on her robe, went next door, and knocked on the door.

'Esther,' she called softly as she stepped inside. 'Esther.' She went over to the bed and called her friend's name again. Then she shook her. 'Hey,' she said when Esther opened her eyes. 'Time to get up.'

Esther jerked her body upward and leaned on her elbows. 'What time is it?' There was panic in her voice.

'Don't get excited,' Mallory said soothingly. 'It's not even five-thirty. Did you sleep well?'

Esther sat up. 'I went right to sleep,' she said. 'Is there a safe place to run near here?'

'Sure. I'll go with you.'

Mallory and Esther did stretching exercises for about five minutes before they jogged to the track that bordered the tennis court. There were other early birds out running, and Mallory waved to several of her neighbors. Some of them stared at Esther in an open, curious way as she and Mallory began sprinting down the path. Mallory had to work hard to keep up with Esther's long strides. They circled the quarter-mile track twice; by the time they were finished, both women were wiping their necks with the towels they'd brought. 'That was good,' Mallory said as they trudged back to the house. She could smell her own musky funk mingling with Esther's sweaty scent. 'So what did you think of Hayden?' she blurted out. Her own words surprised her. She never talked about Hayden to anyone, but saying his name aloud to Esther, she felt good, suddenly free and weightless. She stole a quick look at her friend's face. She could tell that Esther was searching for a way to soften her criticism. 'You can say it, honey. I already know that he's an asshole.' Mallory laughed at Esther's shocked face.

'If you feel that way, why are you with him?'

'Glutton for punishment, I guess. I don't know.' She was silent for a moment, as if she was mulling something over in her mind. 'He gives me a lot of money,' she said softly. She looked at Esther for a reaction. 'He bought me my house.' To her surprise, her friend didn't seem shocked.

'You're not with him for money. You're in love with him. He's absolutely wrong for you. You know that, don't you?'

'I've known it from the very beginning.'

'So what's the hook? He's not good-looking. And don't tell me it's the money.'

'Well, don't underestimate the money,' Mallory said with a smile. 'Cash can be very seductive. My parents were far from rich.'

'Is he great in bed?'

'We've had some great moments there, I must say that.'

'But the sex isn't what keeps you coming back for more.'

Mallory shook her head. 'I grew up in a house where women were nothing. When my brother was born, it was like the second coming. Nothing was expected of me. I was smart, but my parents never encouraged me. I mean, I went to college because my high school counselor talked me into it. I met Hayden eight years ago, when I first became a lender. He's one of the owners and board members of

217

the first bank where I worked. He told me that I was the smartest woman he'd ever known and that my brains turned him on. He paid attention to me. He listened to me more than any other man I've dated. We became lovers and, well, things got easier for me at the bank. He says he's going to divorce his wife and marry me. And I'm stupid enough to believe him.'

She'd always thought that she would feel ashamed if she told anyone the details of her relationship with Hayden, but there was something about Esther's calm face that radiated understanding and empathy. She's not judging me, she thought. Walking back to her house, Mallory felt almost giddy; she gave Esther a quick hug.

'Girlfriend, you deserve someone better,' Esther responded.

'I guess I don't believe that. You want to know something? Hayden isn't the worst man I've ever been with, not by a long stretch. This is the way it's always been with me, Esther: I always choose the wrong man. Always.' She reached out and squeezed the black woman's hand. 'I'm really glad you came to stay with me,' she said.

By the time they got back to the house, it was nearly six-fifteen. Mallory drank a cup of coffee, and Esther had orange juice and toast. They both showered and dressed for work. As they were leaving, Mallory said, 'Why don't you come back tonight? We can take one car to work.'

Esther spent three nights at Mallory's house. They were nights of languid contentment, filled with New Age music, intense Scrabble games, relaxing dinners, and plenty of conversation. They spoke of their childhoods and their families. They talked about work and love and friendships, as they put away the dishes or did their nails. Sipping red wine, they confessed to each other that the size and shape of their breasts dismayed them, that no amount of exercising seemed to firm the flab on their thighs. They laughed way into the night. Esther's memory of her ordeal at Rick's didn't fade away completely, but reliving the experience became much less intense, much more manageable. When Esther got into bed at night, she was able to fall asleep easily.

On their last evening as roommates, Esther and Mallory went shopping at the mall near Mallory's house. They wandered around one of the many exclusive boutiques. At one store, Mallory went to look at blouses and Esther looked in the Anne Klein II section. Earlier, an Asian saleswoman had come up to them and disappeared when they told her they were just browsing. Now, as Mallory looked through the blouses, she saw the woman staring at Esther, watching her carefully as she looked at the expensive outfits. Twice she approached her, hovering near the black woman as she lingered over the racks. At one point, Esther frowned at the woman. Mallory looked away.

After their shopping, they went to an Italian restaurant. The place was small and crowded. The waitress who led them to their table was young, her thin face sallow, as if she hadn't seen the sun in weeks. 'Is this okay?' she asked Mallory, who turned to Esther for her approval before nodding. 'Let me tell you about the specials,' she said, her eyes riveted to Mallory's face.

When she finished rattling off the dishes, Esther asked her pointedly to repeat the second offering. The girl hesitated, her dull eyes wandering around the room for a moment. When she spoke, she again addressed Mallory. Esther said, 'Excuse me, miss, would you mind looking at me when I ask you a question?'

Mallory watched as the flustered waitress rubbed her hands together anxiously before facing Esther. Mallory felt sorry for her. The girl didn't mean anything, she wanted to tell Esther, but she didn't say a word, simply stared into her napkin as the waitress rattled off the specials again and then fled from the table.

Esther hit the table with the flat of her hand.

Mallory began carefully: 'I don't think she meant to insult you, Esther.'

'Mallory, she meant it. And she'll mean it when she comes back and hands you the check. They always mean it.'

Mallory could feel her face flushing. 'I'm sorry. I— '

'You don't have to apologize. You didn't do anything.'

'I guess I just don't notice things like that.'

'Why should you notice it?' There was no anger now, just weariness. 'Everywhere you go in this country, you look like the people in charge. And the people in charge assume that you're okay. And they assume just the opposite about me and anyone who looks like me. You don't have to go on a guilt trip on my behalf, but if you want to be my friend, you need to understand that I run into people like that waitress every day and they always piss me off. Most of the time I don't say anything, but the feeling builds up inside, like steam. And every once in a while, I blow my top. That's what you need to understand.' Esther took her hand away from the table. The tension that had been crawling up her shoulder blades like a spider was suddenly gone. 'I'm okay now,' she said.

But Mallory wasn't. She was confused. 'This may sound dumb, but why do you want her to give you the check?'

'Because I'm treating you. And because when I come into a restaurant I want the person who's waiting on me to feel that I can afford to be there, that I'm not some supplicant from the Union Mission who lucked up on a free meal. Hell, I carry American Express Gold.'

The busboy came and filled their water glasses and put bread and butter on the table. Esther took a sip of water and sucked on an ice cube. A moment later, the waitress returned. 'Have you decided?' she asked Mallory.

'Yes, but I think you'd better ask my friend first. She's doing the ordering, and she'll be paying for everything with her gold American Express card.'

Esther opened her mouth, and the ice cube flew across the table like a projectile, landing in the center, where it spun around and around until it disappeared.

15

V103 blared into the silence of the tiny bedroom on Tuesday morning, flooding the air with Patti LaBelle's highest notes. Five-thirty. The first thing LaKeesha Jones did after she reached out from under the sheets and blankets and flipped off the alarm switch was to examine her nails. She'd had acrylics put on the night before, and she wanted to make sure that she hadn't messed them up while she was asleep. When she looked down at her fingers, the nearly inch-and-a-half curved flaming-red nails were intact; the rhinestones inserted on each baby finger were exactly where they had been the night before. She took a deep breath. The air was clogged with the stale odor of fried chicken, fish, and pork chops that always permeated the apartment. Shaking the sleeping three-year-old who lay next to her, she said softly, 'Dang, Man, you sleep through anything. Get up now! Mommy has to be someplace.' The boy didn't move, and she sat up and pulled the covers back. Her son's plump dark-brown legs were curled up under him so tight she couldn't even see his toes. But she did see the wide wet spot circling out from beneath his bottom. 'Dang, Man. You peed the bed. Get up! Come on now! I gotta wash you up and change these sheets. Boy, wake up!' She reached over to his side of the bed to make sure that the trash liners she'd placed there had protected the mattress. At the same time, she saw her son open his eyes. He immediately began crying, even as he tried to climb into her arms. 'Wait a minute, Man,' LaKeesha said. But the more she tried to push him away, the harder he tried to sit in her lap. Exasperated, she put the sheet down and instinctively raised her hand to smack his legs, but she stopped herself. 'Come here, Man.' She let her son climb into her lap and began rocking the boy in her arms for a moment. 'What you crying about?' LaKeesha whispered. 'Something scare you?' As she talked, she could feel herself growing calmer. She always had to remember what she'd learned at her parenting class: not to hit her child. She kissed the little boy's forehead.

'Me scared,' the child said, snuggling against his mother.

'Aww, you just jiving me, you little pee-pee stinkpot.' She tickled the fat little belly that protruded from the too small undershirt he was wearing. Man began giggling. LaKeesha gave him another quick kiss.

'We gotta get up.' Still carrying him, LaKeesha slid away from the edge of the bed next to the wall, yanked off the bottom sheet, and got out of the side that faced a small, dilapidated dresser, which contained their clothes. There was scarcely enough room on the floor for the two of them to stand without bumping into the worn-out piece of furniture, but the bedroom was painstakingly neat and clean. Man's and LaKeesha's clothes were hung up in the closet; books were arranged in an orderly row in a corner; and there wasn't a speck of lint or dirt on the dull gray carpet or the bureau. The only decoration in the cramped room was a *Boyz N the Hood* poster that was taped to the wall above the bed. An unframed GED certificate was tacked over the dresser.

Grabbing Man's hand, LaKeesha opened her bedroom door and led him across the narrow hall to the bathroom. Inside, the paint was peeling, and the faded linoleum, once a brilliant lime green, had separated from the floor in spots. The shower curtain was half on and half off the rod, and there was no toilet paper. Eight dingy-looking towels and washcloths were hung wherever there was room: on the racks behind the shower, over the ledge of the tub;

several were thrown over a mashed-in wicker hamper. Eight toothbrushes lay in a heap behind the faucets on the sink. LaKeesha looked at the mess and tried to ignore it, then closed the door, turned on the shower, and took off her nightgown. She quickly undressed Man and adjusted her 'do rag,' a screaming purple-and-pink scarf that preserved her hairstyle during the night. Peeking into the mirror, she carefully pushed back the few strands of hair that had managed to escape from the scarf, then she and Man stepped into the shower. She soaped herself, then her son, and while they were rinsing, she washed the boy's soiled underwear and sheet, wrung them out, and hung them on the shower curtain rod. The rest of the family would have to push it aside when they showered. 'Get out, Man,' she said, when they were finished. She grabbed her son, lifted him over the edge of the tub, and placed him gently on the floor. Then she stepped out beside him. She took one of the towels and quickly dried the boy and herself; she brushed his teeth, then hers.

LaKeesha cracked the bathroom door and yelled out, 'Get up, y'all. Get your behinds up,' until she heard her two younger sisters and their children stirring. 'Angelique! Shoni! Come get these pills!'

In a few minutes two brown-skinned teenage girls, fifteen and sixteen, their eyes glazed over with sleep, stumbled toward LaKeesha. Both girls wore their own do rags, braids hanging beneath the scarves. Angelique and Shoni stuck out their hands as if on cue for LaKeesha's daily dispersal of their birth control pills.

'I don't know why I gotta take this pill and I don't know why I gotta have a drawer full of condoms,' Shoni, the youngest, whined. 'I ain't doing nothing. Me and Malik don't even go together no more. I don't have no boyfriend, Kee-sha.'

'Girl, you ain't been without a boyfriend for more than

two days in your entire life. Look, I told you before, if you're gonna do something, you have to be protected. I don't want you to get AIDS, and ain't no more babies coming into this house.'

Shoni held the pill in her hand and chewed on her lower lip.

'Girl, you better take that pill. I ain't playing with you,' LaKeesha said.

Shoni sucked her teeth and then popped the pill into her mouth.

LaKeesha turned to the older girl. 'Angelique, fix toast, oatmeal, and orange juice for everybody. Have it on the table in fifteen minutes.'

'There ain't no orange juice,' Angelique said sullenly.

'Milk, then.'

'Ain't no milk.'

'Give everybody water.'

Watching her sisters walk back down the narrow hall, LaKeesha felt older than her twenty-one years. She could already hear their infant daughters wailing inside the small bedroom Shoni and Angelique shared with their grandmother and their babies. LaKeesha tried never to go into her sisters' room; it was a complete jumble of baby clothes and diapers, not to mention their own things. There were so many little outfits on the floor, it was impossible not to step on something. LaKeesha attempted to get her sisters to organize their possessions, but they seemed to prefer living in chaos.

Shoni and Angelique had become pregnant at the same time, giving birth to premature, underweight girls within days of each other. Stupid, just plain ole stupid, that's what LaKeesha called them when they told her they were having babies. 'Y'all see how hard it is raising Man. And don't even think them boys gone help you, 'cause that would make you bigger fools than you already is!'

In a way, she blamed herself for setting a bad example. But then so had her mother. She couldn't remember the last time she'd seen any of their daddies. Didn't even know where their pictures were. LaKeesha tried not to think about her father, because when she did she became filled with the kind of sadness that came crashing down like an old-fashioned venetian blind and shut out the sun and the flowers. The gray, drab world inside was so lonely, so hurting.

LaKeesha knew how it was when her sisters got with their daughters' fathers, because she knew how it was with her and King, Man's father. When she thought about it, her loving King wasn't even about King, at least not his whole self. Really, she only wanted pieces of him, just a portion of him to wrap herself up in so she'd feel safe. She wanted his strong arms and hands mostly, but not when his fingers were groping for her breasts or probing up inside what was between her legs. She just let that happen so she could have the other feeling: his hands lying heavy across her shoulder, circling her neck, playing with her hair; arms that held her when she was crying; deep voice that said, Be all right, girl. Not the wild, wet tongue kisses, but his lips pressing against her forehead, her cheek. Feet running to do for her. What she craved from King was what her sisters needed too. Deep inside their boyfriends was the daddy part. They were looking for what was missing from their lives; they ended up with babies.

Angelique and Shoni refused to have abortions, wouldn't even discuss the idea. 'I want somebody to love me,' Angelique told LaKeesha, and Shoni nodded in silent and unwavering agreement. The older girl could only shake her head. Dumb! Dumb! Dumb!

Not that she hadn't been just as stupid. Couldn't nobody tell her nothing either. She was so full of love and dreams when she discovered that she was pregnant. Thinking King was gonna marry her and take care of the baby. Believing he was gonna quit gangbanging and dealing, get a job, buy them a house and come home every night. And the baby. The baby was supposed to love her and always be there for her. Well, she found out the hard way that babies are the ones who need the attention. And they don't care if you're tired or broke. They just keep on needing, and you have to keep on giving.

'Be still,' she snapped, as Man wiggled on the toilet seat. 'You do anything yet?'

He grunted loudly and screwed his face into a frightening grimace. 'I did it.' He grinned.

But when LaKeesha investigated her son's claims, there was nothing in the toilet bowl but water. Man giggled wildly; the thought of fooling his mother was too uproarious to contain. She sighed, then took a birth control pill from the pack and swallowed it. 'Come on, boy.' She grabbed her naked son around his middle and carried him down the hall to their bedroom.

A few minutes later, there was a knock at her door. When LaKeesha opened it, her grandmother, a thin, tired-looking woman, was standing in front of her, holding a cigarette between two skinny fingers with swollen knuckles. She let the ashes fall into the top of a mayonnaise jar she carried in her other hand. 'Your mama still on the living room floor where she fell out last night,' she said flatly.

LaKeesha pulled a bright-yellow and green Gap Kids shirt over Man's head, ignoring his yelps of protest, then helped him step into matching shorts and a pair of bright-yellow Nikes. Her son's father didn't give her money regularly, but he was very generous about providing outfits. He wanted his child to look good, in the baby gang-banger tradition; feeding him was another matter. 'You look nice, Man,' she said. Then she turned to her grandmother. 'She wet?'

'No,' her grandmother said, the smoke coming out of her mouth in tiny puffs.

'Leave her butt right on the floor, Mother,' LaKeesha said.

'Just don't make no sense,' the old woman muttered, speaking more to herself than to her grandchild. 'Useta be a nice-looking woman.' She shook her head, and wisps of gray hair fell against the sides of her face. She got in with them bad men. One right after the other. They wasn't no 'count, not a one of them.' She drew herself up. 'Now, my husband took care of his children. Took care of his children till the day he died. Now alla y'all got babies and ain't got no husbands. This family going backwards. Your mama come in here, round two or three, justa carrying on. And then when I told her—'

'Mother, I don't have time for all that,' LaKeesha said wearily. She picked up a brush from the top of the bureau and began taking quick, vigorous swipes at Man's hair. The boy needed a haircut; the zigzag lines the barber had cut in were almost completely covered with new growth. La-Keesha looked in a plastic dish on the bureau and picked out a miniature diamond stud earring. She crouched down next to the small boy and pushed the jewelry into the tiny hole in his ear. Getting Man's ear pierced was King's doing. He wanted the boy to have holes in both his ears, but LaKeesha felt so guilty when she heard Man screaming, as the woman in the jewelry store pierced the first earlobe, that she wouldn't allow a second. After she and King broke up, she used to think about letting the hole close, but no matter how long she didn't put an earring in, it stayed open. 'Mother, would you give Man some breakfast while I get dressed.' LaKeesha poked her head out the door. 'Angelique,' she yelled, 'breakfast ready?'

'In a minute,' her sister hollered back.

The grandmother eyed the clothes that were carefully laid

out on LaKeesha's bed, taking special note of the black heels and purse. 'Where you on your way to? Gone see your caseworker?'

'Uh huh.'

'What you getting so dressed up for?' She eyed her suspiciously.

'Kee-sha! Ain't no butter,' Angelique called from the kitchen.

'Go next door!' she yelled. 'Mother, please feed Man. Can't even get dressed without everybody wanting a piece of my mind,' she muttered. She slammed the door behind her grandmother and son as they left. What would it be like, she wondered, just to be somewhere where there ain't a whole bunch of commotion every damn minute?

LaKeesha opened her closet door, stood in front of the cracked, narrow mirror that hung there, and unwrapped her head rag. What seemed like hundreds of tiny braids cascaded down her back. She was trying to get her hair to grow, and several people had told her that braids helped. She reached in the drawer and pulled out a can of TLC oil sheen, closed her eyes tightly, held her breath, and began spraying until the mist encircled her head. When the spray had settled, the young woman carefully dusted her face with a walnut-colored powder, lined her eyes in black, and applied a vivid red lipstick. She put on dark stockings and then carefully slipped a black dress over her head; it got stuck at her hips, and she yanked it down.

LaKeesha couldn't help grinning when she saw herself in the narrow mirror. She wasn't pretty, she knew that, but her short dress fit her in all the right places and showed off her muscular legs. She looked good. She placed her hands in front of her and then spread out her fingers so that her perfect acrylic nails could complement her outfit.

When LaKeesha opened her bedroom door, the odor of scorched oatmeal made her clap her hand over her nose.

That Angelique! It was the second time this week that she'd burned the breakfast. 'Sure hope that doesn't taste as bad as it smells,' she grumbled as she slid into one of the rickety kitchen chairs. Shoni, the two babies, Man, and her grandmother were crowded around the small table. Behind them, the sink was filled with dishes from the previous night as well as some from this morning. Paper and plastic bags had fallen from a haphazard stack at the top of the refrigerator to a cluttered heap on the floor.

LaKeesha tasted a spoonful of oatmeal from her bowl, made a face, put her hand on her heart, and then slumped into her chair. Man and Shoni giggled.

'I only burned the bottom,' Angelique said, her lower lip poked out. 'This is from off the top.' The same defiant lip began to tremble dangerously, and then, without warning, the teenager slammed the pot of oatmeal on the table.

'Gir-r-rl!' LaKeesha shouted, jumping up from her seat. 'I was just playing with you.'

'How I'm spozed to cook breakfast for everybody, watch my baby, and get ready to go to school? How I'm spozed to do that?' Angelique wailed. She began to sob.

LaKeesha walked over to her sister and put both arms on her shoulders. 'Aw, girl, don't cry.' She hugged her. 'Why you didn't ask Mother or Shoni to hold the baby?'

'She wanted me. She always wants me,' Angelique said, her sobs coming in waves like hiccups.

'It's okay, Angie. It's okay,' LaKeesha said.

Angelique pulled away from LaKeesha's embrace. Her thin fingers flailed the air helplessly. 'I don't even have time to comb my hair.'

'You ain't got to comb your hair. You got braids, fool!' LaKeesha said. Shoni and her grandmother laughed, and then even Angelique joined in.

After breakfast was finished, their grandmother took over the two babies, and Angelique and Shoni rushed to their bedroom to dress, gather up their books, and sneak out of the house to school before their daughters realized they were gone. 'Y'all do your homework?' LaKeesha asked, standing in the doorway of her sisters' bedroom. The two girls looked at each other, their lips twitching, then turned to face LaKeesha.

'We didn't have none,' Shoni said, averting her eyes.

'You a didn't-have-none lie,' LaKeesha said.

'We got a free period. We'll get it done. Don't worry, Mother-r-r,' Angelique said with a giggle.

'You better get it done. And listen— ' But before she could finish, her two sisters pushed past her and bolted from the room. They rushed down the narrow hallway to the living room and ran out the front door. LaKeesha followed them to the doorway and then watched as they scrambled down the steps that led from their apartment to the street. Her two sisters ran, looking over their shoulders at her and laughing.

She had to chuckle to herself. That's the way they should be, she thought, watching Angelique and Shoni racing down the block, their braids flying, their faces lit up with happiness. Then she frowned, as she saw her sisters stop at the corner and proceed up a street that led away from the school. She was racing out the door before she stopped herself. She could catch them, she thought, march them right up to school, but what good would that do?

A few minutes later, LaKeesha was standing at the front door again, holding Man's hand. 'Mother, we're about to leave,' she called out to her grandmother. She heard a slow, muffled sound, like a rock being dragged across the ground. When she looked up, her mother was standing in front of her. Annie's hair was wild and tangled, her too small dress was stained and wrinkled, and her bloodshot eyes were lit up with unmistakable venom. She looked fifty, although she wasn't even forty. 'Where you think you going?'

There was a fight in her mother's voice, LaKeesha realized, a nasty, name-calling, down-in-the-alley free-for-all. She took a backward step and watched her mother sway a little, then lean against the wall to balance herself. LaKeesha could smell the harsh, grainy odor of malt liquor from across the room. She could feel her own tears stinging her eyelids. Why this morning?

'Go lie down, Annie,' LaKeesha said, her voice sharp and much stronger than she felt. She looked at her watch. Damn! She didn't have time for no mess this morning. Why couldn't her mother just sit her behind down and be quiet? 'There's coffee in the kitchen. Why don't you go get you a cup? I gotta go someplace.'

'I don't want no goddamn coffee. Shi-i-it.' She studied her daughter's outfit and careful hairdo, then her eyes brightened with malice. 'I know where you going. Think you gonna be somebody, don't you? Well, you ain't nobody.'

'Okay. Well, I'm going.' LaKeesha opened the door. Bright sunshine poured into the small, dim apartment. She moved toward that light. 'C'mon, Man.'

Her mother took a tentative step away from the wall, her body wobbling like an off-balance globe. She inched toward her daughter until she was only a breath away and then gave her a dazzling smile, warm and inviting and full of apologies. 'Baby,' she said.

Confronted with this maternal contrition, LaKeesha drew in an indecisive breath and stayed put for a moment. Her mother's smile filled her with the kind of wild hope she'd left on the door of the A.A. meeting hall nearly a year ago when Annie refused to go in. LaKeesha let go of Man's hand and turned toward her mother, instinctively trying to claim a tiny piece of warmth and kindness from the woman who had long ago relinquished any claims of motherhood. For the first time in many years, LaKeesha realized that she missed the mother she'd lost. 'Mom,' she said.

232

Just that quickly, the smile was gone, and Annie's rheumy eyes held not a trace of kindness. LaKeesha shrank back just as her mother threw up on the worn gray carpet. When she had finished gagging, she turned to LaKeesha, her lips twisted in perverse satisfaction. 'Now you clean it up.'

LaKeesha looked at her watch and then at the puddle of vomit in the middle of the living room floor. Damn! She heard her nieces screaming in the kitchen and saw her son watching her quietly. 'Man, sit down on the sofa!' she commanded, then ran past her mother into the kitchen, where her grandmother was sitting at the table drinking coffee, smoking a cigarette, and watching the two little girls. From under the sink, LaKeesha retrieved a small bottle of ammonia, a scrub brush, and a bucket, which she filled with hot water; then she rushed back to the living room. Her mother, propped precariously against the sofa, watched as her daughter scrubbed the rug with wide, hard swipes, holding her body away from the water and vomit so that none would get on her dress.

As she was scrubbing, LaKeesha heard her mother crying, and despite her anger, she stole a look in her direction. Poor Annie. She finished quickly, then gathered up Man. There was more fear than anger in her mother's eyes as she watched LaKeesha open the door. 'You gonna be getting that Mother's Day check till the day you die, just like the rest of us,' she whispered. She lifted her hand toward her daughter, her fingers spread apart and curved, as though she were clutching something. It looked to LaKeesha like a claw, trying to grab her and pull her back.

'No I'm not, Annie,' LaKeesha said softly. She tightened her grip on Man's hand. 'C'mon, baby. Mommy has to go somewhere.'

The air outside was cool. Along the wide boulevard, people waited for the bus that would take them to work. LaKeesha saw several girls walking, large backpacks filled with books over their shoulders. Now, why couldn't Shoni and Angelique be like that? she wondered. Why couldn't I? Around her, some shops were beginning to open. They were mostly mom-and-pop stores owned by Koreans, but there were also a couple of black merchants. LaKeesha waved at the owner of the shoe repair shop as she passed it.

'You looking real nice today,' the man who waited on her at the cleaner's called out as she passed. LaKeesha smiled and waved her hand. She ducked her head inside Man's barbershop and said hello to his barber, then continued her trek. Outside the High Noon liquor store, older men were clumped along the sidewalk like patches of weeds. As she and Man passed by, LaKeesha heard them swapping stories and lies, from time to time taking a swig from the paper-bag-covered bottles. One man just stared vacantly into the bright-blue sky. The High Noon was one of the few businesses along the strip that could claim to be riot survivors. When the burning and looting started, the liquor store's Korean owners, two families, stood guard with rifles. Looking inside the store, LaKeesha wished the place had burned down. She saw the owner with his stiff, spiky hair and unsmiling face. Old nasty thing, she thought, thinking back to the time she went inside and he followed her around. Walking up on me like I'm getting ready to steal some of his mess. She had stormed out and hadn't been inside the store since before Man was born. In fact, she didn't go to any of *their* stores.

Passing some of the burned-down buildings, LaKeesha couldn't help remembering how she'd had to stop her own two sisters from taking part in the looting. She was coming back from somewhere with Man when the trouble hit. It seemed that one minute the sky was clear and the next smoke was everywhere and the whole world was gray. She just wanted to get home, take her son out of all the madness and smoke and flames. She didn't want Man to get hurt, and

234

she knew she couldn't get hurt, because then who would take care of him? She was running toward home, away from all the craziness, when she saw Angelique racing out of a restaurant with five boxes of rolls; Shoni was right behind her, carrying at least that many cartons of raw, frozen chicken, their eyes full of the kind of delirious happiness they used to feel when LaKeesha took them to Disneyland or Magic Mountain. Angelique rushed up to her. 'Kee-sha, girl, go get you something.'

She slapped Angelique as hard as she could and punched Shoni in her chest. 'Put that shit back or I'll beat both your butts right here on this street,' she told them. They whooped and hollered, talking about she was crazy, everybody was doing it, but in the end they did what she told them to do. Even now she didn't know why she hadn't joined in that day. Everywhere she looked, people were running and laughing, pushing and snatching for chicken, gym shoes, gold chains, liquor, soap powder, anything they could grab.

But most of the people hadn't gone berserk. Some of the owners of the mom-and-pop stores that lined Normandie were screaming at the mob, their hands raised into tight fists. Others were crying. The ones she couldn't forget were the regular everyday folks who didn't own anything except the neat little bungalows that lined the side streets. They stood silently along the boulevard, watching the looters. Old ladies and men, shaking their heads. Mothers and fathers, who grabbed their children and took them into the house, slamming their doors behind them. Pulling down the shades so they wouldn't have to see. They're ashamed, she had thought, and in that instant she was too. She grabbed her sisters by their arms and pushed them past the hordes, not stopping until she got home.

Now, as LaKeesha and Man stood outside the neat white bungalow, the events of April faded from her mind. For the third time, LaKeesha knocked on the door. It looked like all the others along the narrow street. The lawn was freshly clipped, and rosebushes and impatiens bloomed along the side of the house. Only the small sign above the bell distinguished the place. It read: SOUTH-CENTRAL ALTERNATIVE EDUCATION CENTER.

LaKeesha heard the jangle of keys in the lock, and then the front door swung open. A short, cinnamon-brown man, his large belly covered by a T-shirt that read: PEACE ON THE STREETS, opened the door. A small boy, no more than three or four years old, clung to his pants leg. 'I'd a been here sooner, but it's kind of hard walking with four legs, if you know what I mean,' the man said, laughing a little. 'How are you, Keesha? Hey, Mandela. How ya doing, buddy?'

'Hello, Mr. Clark. Man, what you say?' LaKeesha asked.

Man hung back until Mr. Clark scooped him up in his arms and hugged him, and then he began to giggle. 'Come on back,' the older man said. 'Betty wants to see you.'

They passed through a modestly furnished living room and dining room. There was nothing memorable about the house except for an amazing array of photographs of children. There were pictures everywhere – on walls, on the mantel, on the dining room table, on top of the buffet, even fastened to the refrigerator in the kitchen. Everywhere were the faces of the infants, toddlers, preteens, and teens who had passed through the Clark home.

LaKeesha had met Mrs. Clark when she was in her eighth month of pregnancy. She was shopping in the grocery store and had just given the lady at the register her food stamps, when a sweet-faced woman with a neat gray natural handed her a card. 'Sister, if you're going to be a mother, you need to be educated. Call this number after your baby is born,' she told her. Then the woman took her telephone number. A few weeks after Man was born, she called LaKeesha. She kept calling until she came to her first class. That was when LaKeesha learned that the Clarks were former teachers

236

who'd opted for early retirement in order to start their own educational program. In that first class, surrounded by the other teenage mothers, LaKeesha heard Mrs. Clark say out loud that she was smart and that she was going places. She was going places! After that, the older woman didn't have to call, because nothing could have stopped her from coming.

Children's voices were singing in the back room. 'A is for Crispus Attucks, first to die in the revolutionary fight. B is for Benjamin Banneker, he designed the city of Washington just right . . .' About ten children were seated in a circle on the floor of what had once been the sun porch of the home and was now the preschool. The Clarks' garage had been converted into a center for after-school tutoring for the GED exam. They brought in professionals to teach computer skills and vocational courses as well. The center charged no tuition. The couple operated on donations, a small city grant, and their personal savings.

Mrs. Clark sat in the middle of the circle. She stood up when she saw LaKeesha and Man. 'Keep singing, brothers and sisters. Papa Clark is listening.' The husband and wife exchanged places, and Man sat down among the children as the song continued. LaKeesha blew her son a kiss and then followed Mrs. Clark into the kitchen. The small woman grabbed the girl by her shoulders. 'Where have you been, sister? I expected a call from you. How was the interview?'

'That's where I'm going now,' LaKeesha said.

Mrs. Clark stood back and looked at her for several seconds. LaKeesha could feel her taking in her dress, her braids, the heels and black stockings. Then she looked at her hands. LaKeesha held them out, proudly showing off her new inch-and-a-half acrylic nails. When she looked at Mrs. Clark, she couldn't tell what the woman was thinking. One minute she thought she wanted to tell her some kind of bad news, but the next minute the teacher was smiling at her and squeezing her hand. 'The instructor told me you were the best bank teller trainee in the class,' Mrs. Clark said. 'You're smart and you're going places. I know you'll do just beautifully.'

Esther stared at the scrolling figures on her computer screen. It was hard to comprehend that people could be so careless about their finances that they forgot they had money in the bank, but as she reviewed the dormant accounts, a task she undertook every few months, the evidence was indisputable. In the downtown branch alone, there was nearly three million dollars in accounts that hadn't been active in months, sometimes years. Two million, nine hundred thousand and seventy-eight dollars, to be exact. She logged in the amount. Of course, some of the holders of the accounts were deceased, but in those cases, she would have thought that relatives would come and claim the cash. All that money going to waste. She shook her head.

Esther heard a soft knock at the door. She looked at her watch: nine-thirty. She had completely forgotten about her appointment. Well, the interview wouldn't take long. She'd already decided that she was going to hire David Weaver. 'Come in,' she called.

The door opened slowly, and a young, dark-brown-skinned woman stood in front of Esther's desk. Their eyes met, and Esther could read in them the girl's uncensored surprise. Esther realized immediately the reason for the startled look in the young woman's eyes: she hadn't expected another black person to be interviewing her.

Two months earlier, Angel City had formed a partnership with the city's social service agency. The bank was obligated to interview a certain number of welfare recipients who were involved in a job training program, although they weren't obligated to hire them. Today's interviewee was Esther's first from the program. Office scuttlebutt said the candidates were pretty poorly qualified.

Esther found the girl's astonishment amusing. Why, the child couldn't even speak. 'Were you expecting someone else?' Esther said.

'Oh, no. Well, I—' The girl stopped, and they both laughed. 'I'm glad it's you,' she said, and they chuckled again. 'No, I mean, like, it makes me feel good to know that one of us is the boss. You know what I mean?'

'Yes, I know what you mean,' Esther said. The girl seemed a little awkward. This was probably her first job interview. Esther felt a twinge of guilt, knowing that her mind was already made up. Thinking, she probably needs a job worse than old Alex Keaton, Esther extended her hand. When the girl shook it, Esther could feel her fingers trembling like a frightened kitten; then she felt something hard and sharp cutting into her palm. She looked down. Good God! Long. Curved. Bright Red with a capital *R*. And rhinestones were embedded in the pinkie nails. Genuine Hootchy Mama fingernails. 'I'm Esther Jackson. Thank you for coming. Sit down, La . . . La . . .'

'LaKeesha. LaKeesha Jones.' She talks so proper, La-Keesha thought. Just like a white woman.

LaKeesha sat down in the chair near the desk. Esther gave her a quick once-over. The dress was too tight and too short, but not awful. The girl's face was pleasant, even though she wore too much makeup. The braids, well, they weren't the proper hairstyle for a black woman who wanted to get ahead in business. 'Tell me a little about yourself, LaKeesha,' Esther said. 'Have you had any teller experience?'

LaKeesha took a breath, trying not to be nervous in spite of the way Esther was looking at her. Her eyes were like fingers lifting her collar to check for dirt. LaKeesha attempted to concentrate. She'd been through a number of practice interviews. She paused, remembering what Mrs. Clark had told her: Look the person straight in her eyes; smile a lot; speak clearly; sell yourself; don't be nervous. But Esther's language, each word so precisely enunciated, was erecting a brick wall between them. There was nothing to be nervous about, LaKeesha told herself. She smiled at Esther. 'I just, like, finished the South-Central Alternative Education Center's bank teller program. I was, like, you know, number one in my class. . . .'

An around-the-way girl if ever I saw one, Esther said to herself as she listened to LaKeesha describe her course work and a month-long internship at one of the city's banks. 'The manager wanted to hire me, but they didn't have no openings at the time.'

Esther flinched at the double negative. 'Well,' she said, getting a word in, 'it certainly appears that you've been well trained. Tell me about the school you attended.'

'See, I dropped out of high school after I had my baby. Then I met this lady named Mrs. Clark; her and her husband run the school, and so she talked me into going there to get my GED. She has a contract with the city to train people, so after I got my GED, I decided that I wanted to take the bank teller course, because, well, I'm on the county and I want to get off.' LaKeesha sat back in her chair. She hadn't meant to talk so much, to get so personal. Mrs. Clark told her to be professional. Maybe she shouldn't have mentioned being on the county. She looked at Esther's black suit, the shiny low heels, and all that gold jewelry she wore, not the kind that screamed at you but a nice quiet gold. And words came out her mouth so sharp they could draw blood. She probably thought she was white, sitting up in her own office, being everybody's boss. She shouldn't have said anything about being on the county.

A baby, Esther thought. She could just hear the phone

240

calls, the excuses: the baby is sick; the baby-sitter can't make it. Hiring a single mother with a baby – because of course she wasn't married – was asking for trouble. She looked at LaKeesha, who was staring at her uneasily. 'Do you know TIPS?'

LaKeesha grinned. 'That's what we was trained in.'

Esther scratched the back of her neck. The child wasn't ready for prime time, and the bad thing about it was that she probably had no idea just how deficient she was. Esther thought fleetingly of what that asshole Fred Gaskins would say if he were listening to her conversation with LaKeesha. He'd say that LaKeesha was another product of a *substandard high school in South-Central.* She could just see the operations manager, his fat little lightbulb head bobbing back and forth, his bantam chest heaving in and out. Fred Gaskins can go to hell, she thought to herself. She glanced at her watch; ten o'clock. 'Come with me, LaKeesha. I'd like to see what you can do.'

Leading the young woman out the door to the operations area, Esther guided her past the customer reps' desks, around to the back of the tellers' cage. There were five people on duty. Hector Bonilla smiled in his usual polite manner as soon as he saw the two women approaching him. 'Hector, I'd like you to meet LaKeesha Jones. Hector, LaKeesha and I have been chatting about the possibility of her becoming a teller here. I'd like for you two to work together for an hour or so, and then I'll come back for you, LaKeesha. Hector, may I see you for a second?'

Esther walked the young man a few feet away from his station. 'Listen, I want you to really pay attention to how LaKeesha works. Look at the way she deals with customers, how she handles money, and how well she knows TIPS. I'll talk with you later, all right?'

'Yes, Esther,' Hector said, nodding his head so vigorously that his straight black hair rippled over his forehead. In the eighteen months that he had been with the bank, Hector had proved himself to be a good worker, stable and serious. He always came early and stayed late. Esther knew she could depend upon him for a fair assessment. She might not hire LaKeesha this time, but if the girl had decent skills, she might consider her when there was another opening.

One hour later, Esther stepped outside her office, caught Hector's eye, and motioned him over. In a few moments, he appeared at her door, and she ushered him to a seat inside. 'How did she do?' Esther asked.

'She is very good worker,' Hector said solemnly, his dark, serious eyes looking straight into hers. 'She is polite to customers. She is accurate with money. She knows the computer system too. I didn't have to tell her very much at all.' His smile was as earnest and diffident as he was.

'Thank you, Hector. Would you tell LaKeesha to come to my office, please.'

'Well, Hector told me you did very well,' Esther said after LaKeesha settled herself into her chair. The young woman beamed. Esther asked her a few questions about the transactions she'd just made. Finally, she stood up and extended her hand. 'I've enjoyed chatting with you, and I'll be in touch.'

LaKeesha stood up. 'My grandmother, she lives with me and she keeps my baby, even if he's sick, so you don't have to worry about that.'

Esther nodded her head. 'Well,' she said, opening the door just a little wider, 'that's just fine.'

She felt the girl's eyes on her. 'Just fine,' Esther repeated, waiting for LaKeesha to leave.

The young woman stepped toward her. 'I know I can do a good job for you. I'll come on time. I know how to be a good worker. I can smile at the customers and be polite and hand them their money. I want to work.' She knew she was talking too much, that she should just leave, but the words seemed to be bubbling up from some spring. 'My whole family's been on the county for as long as I can remember. I didn't tell none of them where I was going, because I didn't want to get their hopes up. I want to be a good example for my younger sisters. They need to see somebody working.' She paused and stood up straighter. 'If I don't get this job, would you just please call me and, like, tell me what I did wrong, so I won't make the same mistake on the next interview? Because if I don't get this job, I'm gonna get me a job from somebody.'

Esther hesitated a moment, then closed the door. 'Sit down,' she told LaKeesha.

'First of all, get rid of those fingernails. This is a place of business, not a nightclub. Second, your dress is too tight and too short, and your heels are too high. Third, you're wearing too much makeup. Fourth, your grammar is poor. It's "I didn't tell *any* of them," not "*none* of them." And don't say "like" so much. And another thing: get rid of the braids. I think they're beautiful, but when you're working for white folks you want to fit in, not stand out.' Seeing the distraught look on LaKeesha's face, Esther spoke a little more gently. 'Now, everything I'm telling you can be corrected. It's up to you.'

'If I change all those things, will you give me a job?' LaKeesha's expression was eager, hungry.

'I can't promise you that,' Esther said quickly, 'but I believe that if you make those adjustments, somebody will hire you. And don't think in terms of a job. You have to think about a career.'

LaKeesha's eyes, which seemed to grow larger and more hopeful every minute, didn't leave Esther's face.

'You need to think: I'll start as a teller, then I'll become an operations assistant, then I'll get in the operations training program, and then I'll become an operations manager.

That's the kind of mind-set employers want to see in an employee.'

LaKeesha's face brightened, and she stood up. Before she realized what she was doing, she was hugging Esther and mumbling in her ear: 'Thank you, sister.'

Esther felt the word even more than she heard it. There was obligation in that word. And she didn't want any part of that.

She pulled away. 'Don't ever call me that here,' she said quickly. Esther watched as LaKeesha passed through the bank and out the door. Even after she left, the musky odor of TLC oil sheen spray clung to the air in the room. Esther knew the odor well; it was her scent too.

Esther closed her eyes. She could see herself making those fast deals. Lending millions just on her say-so. If she played her cards right, maybe she could be the one who'd transcend the glass ceiling. Every once in a while, they let somebody black slip through. Why shouldn't she be the one?

Esther walked around her desk with her hands clasped together in front of her and then behind her. She pictured LaKeesha's face, the yearning in her eyes. No, no, no! She wouldn't sacrifice her career in the name of racial solidarity. Forget it. She was going to pick up the phone and hire an acceptable white boy, with acceptable grammar and short fingernails, because that was the right move to make. The smart move.

Sister.

That and a dollar won't even get you a ride on the bus.

Esther picked up the telephone.

16

Tyrone dialed the number one last time from the pay phone in the locker room of Western Express. After three rings, Esther's familiar voice recited a short taped message, complete with background vocals by Chaka Khan. He hung up the telephone. He'd left his name and number when he called her on Monday. She had yet to contact him. He hadn't even been able to catch a glimpse of her in the bank, as he usually did, because his route had been temporarily changed. Of course, she might have called him already and not left her name. A woman like that was busy, he reminded himself. He'd been out at Venice Beach most of the day Sunday, trying to unload some T-shirts. He didn't have a vendor's license, and it was illegal for him to sell his wares at the beach, but in between ducking the cops, he managed to peddle nearly forty shirts. And he planned on spending some of his profits on Esther Jackson on Saturday night.

'Hey, Cody,' he said after he hung up the telephone. The white man was sitting in front of his locker. He had a copy of the *Gazette* in his hand and was glancing at the front page. 'Where do you take a woman if you want to really impress her? A nice place.'

'Never spend money on women, man. Just backfires. They start getting gold-diggeritis, turn all yellow and shit. Nasty. Best place to take a woman is to your mama's house for dinner. That way you haven't spent any money and she thinks you're serious about her. Taking a woman home to your mama is automatic pussy. I mean, you ain't even got to ask for it. Honeys meet your mama, their legs just fly open.'

Tyrone looked at Cody sideways, then shook his head. Perched on top of the crinkly red curls was a red-green-and-black X cap. 'See, that's why you don't have no woman.'

'What are you talking about? I got plenty of women, man,' he said, as he watched Tyrone walk toward the door. The black man waved his hand without turning. 'Hey! Hey! I got plenty of women, brother man. Hey! The back of your hair is looking pretty tacky. Let me trim it for you.'

Tyrone turned around, and Cody was holding electric clippers in his hand. 'Now, how in the world can a white boy cut my hair?' He laughed.

'I know how to cut your hair,' Cody said. If Tyrone had been looking, he would have seen resentment filling his eyes, but he was already walking away.

When Esther heard the doorbell ring Saturday evening, a full two hours before her scheduled date, she thought for one horrified moment that Tyrone had arrived early. But she opened the door to Vanessa, who stood there grinning. 'Did someone call for a wardrobe consultant?' she said breezily as she sauntered into the house.

'What is this, prom night? You came to see me get dressed?'

'Your last date was the prom. Now, darling, I'm here to serve you. Zip you up. Button your buttons. Tease your hair.'

'No,' Esther said, laughing, 'you're here to try and make me show my breasts to the world. Go home to your cat.'

'Not the two entire breasts. Give me some credit. I have class. Just a little cleavage. If I could get some cleavage out of my A cups, believe me, I would have me a line down the middle of my chest. I can't, so I live vicariously through you. Now show me what you're thinking about wearing.'

246

'I'll show you what I'm going to wear.'

Vanessa soon talked Esther out of the conservative white pantsuit and into a hot-pink bustier with matching pants and a rhinestone-studded cream-colored jacket, a frivolous outfit that she'd bought on a Saturday shopping expedition with Vanessa.

When Esther was dressed, Vanessa looked at her approvingly. 'Tyrone is going to fall madly and passionately in love with you.'

'I'm not ready for that,' Esther said with a giggle. 'How's show business?' she asked, as she put on her makeup in the bathroom. Vanessa lay stretched across the bed.

Vanessa's voice brightened. 'Oh, I got a commercial,' she called out cheerfully. 'Dr Pepper. It's national.'

'Congratulations!'

'And I have a callback for the part where I'm Eddie's girlfriend. Anyway, my agent thinks I have a very good shot. So . . .'

'Life is good!'

'Life is always good!'

They heard a sudden piercing wail outside Esther's bedroom window. Running to look, they saw that the little girl next door had crashed her bicycle into her parents' garage. She was crumpled on the ground, her little shoulders racked by sobs, her wild, wiry hair sticking straight up in the air. Within minutes, her mother and father rushed outside, murmuring soothing words of love and comfort. The white woman scooped up the child, while the father attended to the bike. The little girl must have been more scared than hurt. She stopped crying and let herself be led into the house.

Esther felt a sudden pang as she watched the quiet exhibition of family devotion.

'What's up with minigirlfriend's hair?' Vanessa asked, after the family disappeared inside.

Esther shrugged.

'Did you make friends with them yet?'

'I have no intention of getting involved with those people,' Esther said coldly.

'Every time you look at them, you get mad. They have power over you. Reclaim your power.'

'Thank you, Miss Good Karma.' Esther rolled her eyes. 'Listen, Vanessa, I want to ask you something. What would you do if you had to hire someone and your choice was between a highly qualified white guy and a qualified but has-some-problems sister?'

'Be more specific.'

Esther made a face. 'I've got to hire a new teller. Last week I interviewed a young white guy, and he was perfect. Experience. Knowledgeable. Good appearance. Could hit the ground running. So I think to myself that he's the one. Then a few days ago, this sister comes in. Dress is a li-i-ittle tight, a li-i-ittle short. Girlfriend has the acrylics of life. We are talking Love That Red assault weapons. Okay? She is knowledgeable and competent but has no work experience, because she has been on the county all her life. And of course, she do be talking that Shenaynay talk. So. Anyway, sisterwoman doesn't quite stack up to the white guy. She can do the work, but she'd require an— '

'Adjustment period.'

'There you go. And the entire time I was interviewing her, I knew that I wasn't going to hire her. But then, when she was leaving, she starts telling me how much she needs the job and that her entire family is on welfare, and I just felt, like, you know . . .'

'Guilty,' said Vanessa.

'No. No. Guilt I can handle. I feel disloyal, as though I am about to – drumroll, please – betray the race.'

'You know you can get your NAACP membership revoked for that kinda shit. Plus, you won't be able to get

248

into any more Luther Vandross concerts. Plus . . . you won't be allowed to do the Electric Slide and you will lose the ability to digest collard greens and hot-water corn bread. Sistuh, are you sure you want to sell out?'

Esther sighed. 'Thank you for your sensitivity and deep insight. I can't tell you how much better you've made me feel.'

'You know what?' Vanessa said as Esther walked her to the door. 'You trip too much about race. It's just eating you up. You need to learn how not to be black.'

Esther raised her eyebrows.

'Just *be*, girlfriend. Learn to just *be*. Repeat after me: 'My color is my joy and not my burden.' You need to say that every day.'

'Yeah, right,' Esther said.

After Vanessa left, Esther had just enough quiet time to try and figure out just why she had agreed to see Tyrone again. He didn't have any money, that was for sure. And not much in the way of prospects either. But she remembered that when she woke up early that Sunday morning, sensing a scream was right at the tip of her throat, his hands were warm and strong around her body. She remembered lying next to him and feeling safe, the way she felt around her father and her brother. She thought about Tyrone during the robbery, the calm way he attended to her and the waitress and the cashier, how he moved quickly and efficiently, without panicking. He took charge, she thought to herself. He took care of me. A warm sensation rushed through her, and even though she tensed her body and shook her head, even though she said no, over and over again, the heat was still there, pulsating and circling her heart. She held herself very still, knowing that the soft, mushy heat that fanned out from her chest was a kind of beginning.

That same warmth washed over her an hour later, when

Tyrone stepped inside her door, greeting her with a hug that was full of his fresh, soapy scent. Esther knew the gesture was meant to be a casual one, but feeling his body, she was transported back to the last time he had put his arms around her – in the aftermath of that awful night at Rick's. In her doorway, she held on to him longer that she had meant to, and when Esther let him go, they were way past casual. 'Hey,' he said, stepping away from her slightly but not removing his arms. 'Hey. It's gonna be all right.'

He walked her to her living room sofa, his arm still around her shoulder. They sat down. Tyrone put his hands on her upper arms, squeezed them a little, and turned her body so that she was facing him. 'Here's the way it is. I'm not your kinda guy, Esther. I know that. You have a lot of education. You got an important job. When you be dreaming about Prince Charming, he ain't driving no mail truck. I ain't your kinda guy. You're into me now because of what happened, because when everything went down so fast, I did what was necessary and I kept you calm. Maybe you think I saved you. I didn't, and I don't want you fantasizing about what happened or about me being some kind of hero and then one day you wake up and realize that, hey, I ain't what you made me out to be, because by then I'll be hooked, see. See, I'm not your kinda guy, but you're my kinda woman. I like you. I been liking you for a long time, ever since I first seen you in the bank. I think you're fine. I like your hair, and I love your dimples, and your eyes are beautiful. I love how you're built. I be watching you, girl. You're a good boss. You make those people want to work hard for you. And you don't mind taking a chance, like coming to Rick's to meet me. I think you a bad sister, Esther. And I would like to get to know you better.'

When he finished speaking, Tyrone could still hear his words echoing off the walls, or so it seemed. His voice was so loud, maybe too loud. He wondered how he sounded to an educated woman like Esther. Perhaps if he'd gone to college he could express himself better.

'Tyrone,' Esther said.

He shook his head. 'Don't feel like you're on the spot or anything. Let's go out and have a good time. And we'll see what happens.'

Esther judged Tyrone's beige Audi to be at least six years old. It was immaculately clean and so newly polished that she could see her face in it under the streetlight. For a moment, she thought about Mitchell Harris's new Jag and felt a twinge of regret. People looked at her in a certain worshipful way when she stepped out of a car like that, and it carried over to how they treated her when they realized that she was with Dr. Harris. She hadn't spoken to Mitchell since that rainy Saturday she met him at the doughnut shop, although she had thought about him. But when she climbed into the Audi, the same fresh, clean odor that clung to Tyrone permeated the air enveloping her. Mitchell faded from her mind.

'Do you like Jamaican food?' Tyrone asked her as he started the car.

She nodded.

'If you don't, mon, we can go someplace else.' He was grinning, but his smile didn't mask the concern in his eyes.

'I like it.'

The Jamaican restaurant wasn't far from her house. It was a small and cozy place, replete with spicy aromas and the lilting patois of Kingston and Montego Bay, spoken by diners and staff alike.

The place was vibrating with reggae. The entire Marley clan, both deceased and living, was well represented. Tyrone drummed to the beat softly on the table with his fingers, while Esther did a sort of limbo dance, shaking her shoulders down toward the tabletop and then back up again.

The waitress laughed out loud at their antics when she brought them their meals: two heaping plates full of jerk chicken, peas and rice, a sweet fried bread, fried plantains, and mixed vegetables. Esther bowed her head quickly to say grace, but when she did, Tyrone reached across the table, took her hand, and bowed his head too. They danced and swayed as they ate their dinners, the music growing louder with every bite. Tyrone clicked his fork against his plate and blinked his eyes in time. Esther started laughing and couldn't stop.

They were still dancing when they left the restaurant. 'Obviously, we need to take our party to an appropriate place,' Tyrone said as they got into his car.

The club was located in Venice, not far from a neighborhood on a canal. Esther could hear the loud music from the street. Tyrone paid the five-dollar cover charge, and they went inside. The interior was dim and crowded and smelled like sweat, stale perfume, and cigarettes. Tyrone took her hand and led her into the thickest part of the throng. They stayed there dancing for nearly three hours straight.

'Girl, you wore me out,' he said when they were sitting in the car, down the street from the club.

'No, you wore me out.'

Tyrone turned the key in the ignition but didn't start the engine. Luther Vandross's sweet tenor filled the car, and Tyrone and Esther sang along, as they rocked a little to the music. Esther fished around in her purse until she found a tissue, then wiped the perspiration from her brow. She sighed. 'That felt so good. I've been so busy at work. I've been interviewing tellers all week.'

'Did you choose one?' Tyrone's fingers twirled around a lock of her hair.

Esther pulled away and turned to face him. 'It's between a white guy and a sister.'

'No brothers applied?'

'A couple. They didn't have the experience.'

'Well, then, hire the sister.'

'It's not that simple. The white guy is a little sharper than she is. She's not' – Esther looked away from Tyrone – 'she's not polished. I have a new boss, and everything I do is being scrutinized.' She felt a twinge of conscience as she exaggerated. 'If I hire this sister and she screws up, it'll make me look bad, and then I won't be able to do some of the things I want to do.'

Tyrone began stroking his chin with his thumb and forefinger. 'I don't know. I'm not a manager, so maybe I don't have a full understanding of what you're talking about, but I know this: White folks hire white folks. Jews hire Jews. Chinese people hire Chinese. Some brother with a Ph.D will apply for a job, and a white man will tell him he ain't qualified and then turn around and hire some white boy with a GED. I feel like a black woman in your position ought to try to bring in as many black folks as possible.'

'Somebody white hired me, Tyrone. I mean, suppose the black folks aren't qualified?'

'They hired you because there is an equal opportunity law that makes them hire you. We're talking about a teller. A teller, not no brain surgeon. I mean, can she do the work?'

'Oh, that's not the problem.'

'Well, what is the problem? Help the sister out a little bit. Polish her up.'

Esther nodded, more out of frustration than in real agreement. He doesn't get it, she thought. He punches a time clock and goes home. He doesn't have to worry about office politics. For the first time all evening, Esther felt the differences between her and Tyrone. Luther's song ended. She felt Tyrone's fingers in her hair.

'How old are you?' he asked.

'Thirty-four. How old are you?'

'Twenty-eight.'

Esther's eyes blinked rapidly, and she made a small, unintelligible noise, as though she'd accidentally swallowed a piece of ice.

'Does it bother you that I'm younger?'

She nodded. 'Yes.'

'Why? You look good. Nobody will ever know. Break some rules, honey. Okay?'

She laughed a little. 'All right.' She shook her head again.

'Hey. So it's okay if I call you Mommy?'

'Don't make me hurt you, boy,' she said, shaking a fist at him.

Tyrone grabbed her hand and put it around his neck and she put her other hand there and he smiled at her and said, 'I've been thinking about your lips all week long.'

This isn't going to work, Esther thought. She felt his hands on her back then, and then he was leaning across his seat, attempting to press his body into hers and not be impaled on the stick shift between them. His lips felt hard and then soft and then mostly warm. His mouth was closed, and she enjoyed the pressure of his kiss, the pucker and pout of it, the way he moved his face back and forth, so that her lips were completely covered by his. Then he opened his mouth and she opened hers and she could feel his tongue gliding over her teeth and licking the roof of her mouth and tasting her gums. Everywhere his tongue landed was sweet and hot all at once, and when she kissed him back she seemed still to be dancing, to be writhing and twisting, trying to get closer to his sweetness.

He put his hands on her neck, then touched her shoulders. His fingertips, hotter than his tongue, made her arch a little when they pressed into her back. He didn't fumble or grope. He knew just where his hands were supposed to be, how his fingers were supposed to feel when he touched her. He put his hands on her breasts, and she heard his breathing stop for a moment. A long time, really.

Her breasts filled his hands. He moved his fingers back and forth until he could feel her nipples stiffening beneath her bustier. He rubbed the back of his hands across her skin at the top of her cleavage. He felt her moving a little closer to him. He wanted to take his tongue and plunge it between her breasts. 'Baby,' Tyrone finally whispered into her ear, 'you so sweet. Sweet. Sweet.' Then he stopped, kissed her very quickly, and then took his hands away. He looked around on the street. He wasn't going to feel her up in public. 'Girl,' he said, as he started the car. 'Oooh, girl.'

They were quiet all the way back to her house, and after he parked the car in her driveway, neither one of them moved. Finally, he walked her to the door. 'Now, if I come in there, I'm not going to want to come out until morning. You ready for that?'

She sighed. 'Are you ready for it?'

'I been ready, girl. You the one. Think about it.'

'If we have sex, what will that mean?'

'It means that we had sex. If you like it, we'll do it again. If you don't, we won't. Baby, you in the driver's seat. Let me just tell you a few things that might help you decide: I've never been married. I don't have no children. I have no problem using a condom; in fact, I brought several. All latex. I'm HIV negative; I took my test the day after Magic made his announcement. I don't have herpes. I'm healthy and I'm ready to please. And while we're on the subject, let me just say this: I will do my best to satisfy you and also have a damn good time myself. I respond positively to the words Stop, No, More, Yes, Not so hard, Harder please. If any particular part of my anatomy ain't as well trained as you'd like it to be, ain't the size you need, fails to make it through the marathon of love we are about to engage in, if it don't do everything you want it to do, if it, like, falls down on the job in any way, I want you to know that there are other parts of my anatomy that are at your command. Hello.'

'Are you trying to talk me into something?'

'He-e-ell, yeah.'

By the time they reached Esther's bedroom, she had changed her mind two or three times, although she hadn't said anything. It was too soon. And how did she know how Tyrone was going to act once they had sex? Suppose he became possessive. What if he started some mess on the job? What the hell was she doing?

'You can still change your mind,' Tyrone said softly. He knew a nervous woman when he saw one, and Esther was about to jump out of her skin. 'Relax,' he said. 'Lie down.' He began kneading the back of her neck and shoulders until he felt her going limp. 'Now, I must warn you: this is a trick to get your drawers off.'

He felt her shoulders shaking with laughter beneath him, and when she turned her face toward him, she was smiling. God, she sure was fine. He bent down and kissed the back of her neck. 'You so pretty,' he said. Now he felt nervous, as she turned over and pulled him down on top of her. Her breasts felt good pressing against his chest. A woman like Esther, he thought, sister must have all kinds of brothers chasing her. Brothers with money and education. He could feel himself tensing up. When Esther began to pull at his pants and his zipper, he felt panic showering down on him like rain.

Esther didn't know what had made her change her mind. Tyrone, she knew, was just something to do until the real thing came along. But he was so sweet. And his lips felt good, kissing her everywhere. His hands were hot and strong, and she liked the way he held her. The more he kissed and touched her, the more she wanted him inside her.

Tyrone could feel her eagerness. But the desire trickling down her thighs was scary. What was she expecting from

him? He looked into Esther's eyes and saw the hungry passion of a woman in need of a strong loving. When Tyrone looked between his legs, his strength was fading fast.

At first Esther couldn't understand it. One minute he was rock hard, and the next he was as soft as last night's noodles. The harder he tried, the worse things got, until finally she told him to stop and they moved away from each other in the bed, retreating into their own personal silences. Then Esther said, 'Tyrone, did I do something wrong?' Her eyes, he saw, were full of concern, not demands. He wanted her to hold him, but he didn't know how to say that.

To Esther's surprise, Tyrone started laughing, a strange kind of nervous laughter she'd never heard before. 'You know, I'ma tell you the truth. Here's the problem: this really isn't my dick. My dick works every time. I didn't want to say nothing, but I'm gonna tell you what happened, okay? My dick is in the shop. That's right. What you smiling at? My dick is getting a forty-thousand-mile tune-up. This is, like, a rental dick. What's a brother spozed to do? Here I am with my baby, damn rental dick ain't working. Ain't this a trip!'

Esther moved close to Tyrone and put her arm around his waist. 'Is there anything I could do to help?'

'I don't know.'

'I think the rental dick is nervous. That's what I suspect. I think he's just all upset. Maybe I could talk to him. What's his name?'

'Brotherman.'

Brotherman was looking exceedingly dejected. Esther picked him up and stroked his head lightly. 'Now,' she said, looking at Tyrone, 'I want you to calm down. You're not here to perform. You're here to share. Just relax.' She placed Brotherman gently between Tyrone's thighs. 'We'll let you have a little rest and when you're ready, I'll introduce you to

Madam Queen.' She smiled at Tyrone, then snuggled closer. 'You want something to eat or drink?'

He kissed her on her mouth and cheeks and throat. 'I like what you said. That was nice.'

Esther put on a robe, and Tyrone threw on some jeans. They went downstairs and made popcorn, put on some CDs, and fast-danced to Janet Jackson until their faces were moist and their hearts were racing. The music slowed down, and Tyrone pulled her close enough to feel Brotherman waking up. 'I think Brotherman is ready to meet Madam Queen,' Tyrone said with a slow grin.

He stayed ready all night long.

That Monday, Esther showered, dressed, gobbled down her breakfast, scanned the *Gazette*, and then raced to the office, leaving the quiescence of Park Crest behind her. She felt tension settling around her shoulders. Across the city, in a downtown court building, the civil rights trial of the four officers was about to begin its proceedings for the day. Tonight the news stations would bombard the city with old videos and new prints. Tomorrow fresh anger might stalk the streets. Thinking of the four policemen, Esther muttered, 'Somebody better go to jail.' But the trial wasn't her only concern. As she drove, thoughts of LaKeesha Jones and David Weaver intruded like a sudden thunderstorm. She saw the black girl's face, the outlines of it as sharp and clear as a bolt of lightning. Then she saw David Weaver's fresh-scrubbed profile. Their voices seemed to drown out even the sound of Esther's own breath.

Esther was the first one to arrive at the bank. She wanted to make the telephone call as soon as possible, to hear herself speak aloud the words that would confirm her decision. She was in a hurry to get to the place where there was no turning back, where her choice was a done deal. At eight-thirty she dialed the number. In a few seconds I won't be able to change my mind, she thought. She took a deep breath when she heard the soft hello. 'LaKeesha? This is Esther Jackson from Angel City National Bank. I'd like to offer you the position. We need to talk. Can you come in this evening? Around six o'clock.'

The girl's thank you was filled with incredulity and joy. And such gratitude. 'You not gonna be sorry,' she said several times.

We'll see, Esther said to herself as she hung up the phone. For some reason she felt reassured and cheered by the girl's promise. At the very least, she thought, there will be another sister here. The idea warmed her. She allowed herself to feel the full impact of it, and in that thin space she saw a scrawny brown-skinned girl of eight, with more barrettes than hair, walking into class on her first day at the private school. She remembered standing there and feeling the eyes, so many eyes, staring at her. She took her seat and was surrounded by a sea of white faces, and very few of them were smiling.

Esther stood up and walked to the glass partition and looked out into the empty operations area. When LaKeesha came, she wouldn't be the only one anymore. For a split second she felt the joy of that explosion detonating inside her. And in that moment she realized for the first time that she'd made her decision to hire LaKeesha as soon as she'd met the sister.

17

A fierce March rain was coating the slick city streets outside the bank. Kirk liked the view inside better. From where he sat in the multipurpose room, if he craned his neck just slightly, he could get a stronger whiff of the soft, musky perfume that Mallory was wearing and, at the same time, a better look at the thin expanse of ivory thigh that the slit in her skirt revealed.

A Latino man was addressing the group. 'Picture this,' he said in softly accented English. 'You arrive for a staff meeting on Monday morning. You're a little early, and the boss isn't there yet. There are three other people, who are already seated. You approach them smiling and are about to greet them, when you notice that they are all speaking Spanish. How does that make you feel?' The employees, who were arranged in a horseshoe facing the speaker, had the collectively skittish mien of colts who wanted nothing so much as to bolt out of their confines and head for open ground. People shifted in their seats, averting their eyes from the speaker and one another, finding something in their programs to examine.

'Come on. Isn't anyone going to answer my question?' This was the tenth week of diversity awareness sessions, and as Kirk made the rounds with Mallory, he couldn't help feeling that the meetings were becoming tedious and redundant. The trainers always seemed to want to incite some sort of infantile discussion about feelings by tossing lead-ins as threatening as hand grenades. The message always seemed to be the same: all men were sexist, and all white men were sexist and racist. The poor minorities and the poor women were never at fault. They were just the victims of white men's oppression. What a crock! He hadn't oppressed anyone. What the sessions needed to do was instruct people how to compete, how not to blame other people for their own problems and lack of accomplishments. What could Preston Sinclair possibly be thinking of, wasting the bank's money in this way?

Kirk stole a look at Mallory and let his eyes wander from her throat to her breasts and then back down to her thighs. She uncrossed her legs suddenly, and Kirk raised his head. He caught Mallory's eye and indicated the door with a nod.

'What a ridiculous question,' Kirk said as soon as they were in the hall. 'It's rude when people speak a foreign language in front of others who don't understand it. I mean, that's the sort of thing that should be done in the home, not a place of business.'

'Well, I guess sometimes if it's your first language, you just sort of slip into it,' Mallory said.

He shrugged his shoulders and directed his eye to the slit in her skirt, which gapped with every step she took. Mallory was such a petite woman. Dainty was the word for her. He could probably lift her with one hand, that's how delicate she was. Such a pretty woman. 'Things are going to be changing for me here. Soon,' Kirk said suddenly, his voice low and careful. 'Just between you and me, I think I'm about to be named the permanent regional manager. In fact, I'm sure I am.' What did it hurt to tell Mallory his good news? After all, Bailey had as good as told him the job was his. He stole a look at Mallory's pretty face to see the effect of his words. At that moment, making an impression on Mallory seemed to be all he wanted to do.

Esther looked up when she heard the light tapping. The door to her office opened, and Mallory stuck her head in.

'You busy? Oh,' she said, 'I didn't realize you were in a meeting.'

Esther was seated at her desk, and a young black woman was in a chair next to her; cards were spread out in front of them. They both had the same startled expression on their faces, Mallory thought, as if she were an intruder. She felt a funny tightness seep inside her chest as she watched Esther pick up the cards with a deft, almost sneaky movement and drop them inside her desk drawer. For the first time in a long time, Mallory sensed that she wasn't welcome. Even though Esther and the young woman were now smiling at her, she still felt like a young girl watching others play in a circle game she wasn't invited to join.

'Mallory Post,' Esther said warmly, 'I'd like you to meet LaKeesha Jones. LaKeesha is the new teller I've hired. Today is her first day.'

Mallory tried not to look surprised. Esther had led her to believe that she was hiring a young man, David somebody or other. Of course, she was entitled to change her mind, if she thought she'd found a better candidate, but why this girl? LaKeesha? What kind of name was that? The young woman was neatly dressed in a medium-length black skirt and a white blouse. Her black shoes had sensible low heels and were newly shined. Tiny gold hoops were her only adornments; she didn't even wear nail polish on her short, oval-shaped fingernails. Her hair was smooth and short, a suitable style for the bank. And yet, as she observed her, Mallory thought that there was something unappealing and maybe even a little threatening about her. 'Well, welcome to Angel City,' Mallory said, extending her hand to the young woman.

'Thank you,' LaKeesha said. She shook Mallory's hand, but she looked at Esther the entire time.

There was something a little rough around the edges about her, Mallory thought. The girl didn't seem mature enough for the job. She didn't seem responsible. Watching the two black women standing so close together, she wondered how the new girl would enhance Esther's position. Not that she'd be held accountable for everything an underling did, but still, hiring someone who didn't work out could reflect poorly upon her judgment. Like that D'Andre character. What a jerk! That almost cost Esther politically, only she was able to salvage things by getting rid of him quietly, before Charles realized just how badly he'd screwed up. As she looked LaKeesha over, Mallory wondered why Esther hadn't stuck with David whatshisname. She'd seen a glimpse of him. He looked responsible; he looked qualified. This girl appeared to have a chip on her shoulder. Mallory released LaKeesha's hand.

'Nice to meet you,' LaKeesha said, her voice hardly audible.

Mallory stepped back. Her eyes met Esther's cool, steady gaze. She knows that I don't like LaKeesha, Mallory thought. The notion made her feel panicky. As if to cover her feelings, she smiled brightly at the new teller. 'I'm really glad you're here. Esther can use some help. I'm sure you'll be happy.' She smiled again, hoping she sounded gracious and welcoming.

Mallory watched as Esther put her hand on the girl's arm. She said, 'Why don't you go on back outside. If you have any questions, ask Hector. All right?'

'Thank you, Esther.' She nodded toward Mallory.

After LaKeesha left, Mallory sat down in front of the desk. 'I thought you were hiring a young man,' she blurted out.

'I changed my mind,' Esther said curtly. She put her hands on her hips. The gesture was unconscious. As soon as she realized what she'd done, she dropped her hands.

Mallory laughed nervously. 'Well, I hope she'll work out.'

She leaned forward eagerly. 'Anyway, you know why I really came by. How did the date go?'

The wave of annoyance Esther had felt initially passed. 'This is not going to satisfy every *Love Connection* fantasy you've ever had,' she said, 'but you will be happy to know that we had a great time.'

'All right!'

'He drives an old Audi, but it's clean and shiny. We went to a Jamaican restaurant and then we went dancing, and he can really dance. We necked in the car, and it was dee-vine. And then he took me home, and . . .'

'And . . .?'

Esther grinned at Mallory, who began giggling.

'And then on Sunday we went to the beach and to the movies and we had something to eat. He's really easy to be with. I mean, his grammar's not great, but . . .'

'He is.'

'He's okay,' Esther said demurely. 'Definitely not my type, but he's fun.' She looked at her friend, who was staring at her with a child's happy eyes. Esther laughed. 'Don't give me that look. We're just friends. I'm not in love with him.'

Mallory smiled her goony smile. 'Oh. Not to change the subject, but you'll be happy to know that Kirk is going to be appointed the permanent regional manager.'

'Why should that make me happy?' Esther asked.

'Because Kirk is going to bring you over to the lending side, that's why.' Mallory's face was so full of goodwill and kindlless that Esther hated to burst her bubble.

She shrugged. 'Maybe. Maybe not.'

Mallory looked astonished. 'What do you mean?'

'I mean maybe, maybe not. I talked with Kirk. I don't think he's convinced I'm lender material.'

'You just have to show him what you can do, Esther.'

'I've shown him; I've shown everybody. This department was a mess before I took over. I turned it around in less than a year. Look, I'm telling you he's not going to give me a chance.'

Their eyes met, and in that instant Esther saw that Mallory discerned her secret thoughts about Kirk. In another moment she knew that the white woman didn't believe her unspoken opinion to be valid. 'I'll talk to him, Esther,' she said firmly. 'You can't just write him off. After all, he's going to be a very important person in this organization.'

Preston Sinclair extended his right hand to Humphrey Boone, who grasped it in his own firm grip. 'All right, face front and smile,' the photographer said. The flashbulb popped, and Preston breathed a sigh full of relief and exultation. Weeks of delicate negotiating and compromising were over. Next Monday, Humphrey Boone would begin his tenure as Angel City's regional manager and senior vice president in charge of private placement loans, at a base salary of $150,000. 'Glad to have you on board,' Preston said. 'Angel City is going to be good to you.'

'I'm depending upon that,' Humphrey said.

The reporter from the *Gazette* had come earlier and asked a few questions. Preston had carefully shaped his answers so that they segued into the topic for which he wanted maximum exposure: his being the architect of the Diversity Program and the person behind Angel City Bank's hiring the highest-ranking black banker in the city. 'At Angel City Bank, we recognize that talent comes in all colors,' he said. He thought it was a highly effective statement, almost a slogan, and hoped that the newspaper would use it in the caption under the photograph.

'Well,' Preston said to Humphrey as the photographer was leaving, 'we'll see you next Monday.' He nodded toward the corner where Bailey Reynolds was sitting. 'If there is anything you need, either before that time or after you get here, please get in touch with Bailey.'

Bailey's lips curved up automatically. He nodded his head, and his hard eyes glittered as he took in the president's good mood, the way he kept his hand on the black man's back.

Humphrey picked up his monogrammed black leather briefcase and walked toward the door. 'Thank you for everything. I'm looking forward to next week,' he said.

'There's still an issue that needs to be resolved,' Bailey said softly once Boone was gone. He smiled mechanically. 'Kirk Madison has been acting regional manager for several months now. He's done an excellent job, mostly because the carrot that we agreed to hold out was the prospect that his position would become permanent. He's going to be quite disappointed.'

'Ah, yes,' Preston said. 'What do you suggest?' he asked somewhat peevishly. As much as he was able, he left the unpleasant chores to others.

Bailey shrugged his shoulders. He could tell that Preston wanted to change the subject quickly. 'Well, he was a lender before. Perhaps we can give him back his old job at a slight increase, say five to eight percent.'

'Five,' Preston said quickly. 'Take care of the details.'

'Consider it done.'

When Kirk Madison put down the telephone in his office, his hands were trembling. Yes, he said to himself. Yes. Yes. Yes. He glanced at the flow chart above his computer and saw a sea of red ink. Every line on the page represented another accomplishment. All those check marks were like a map, taking him where he wanted to go. And he was going up. He flipped open his briefcase and stared into the mirror attached to the back as he combed his hair and adjusted his tie. In twenty minutes he was going to have lunch with

Bailey Reynolds. 'There's something I want to talk with you about,' Bailey had told him. That could mean only one thing.

Bailey was waiting in a black Cadillac in front of the bank. 'We're going to the Marina,' the older man said cheerfully after Kirk got in. The Marina was a good thirty minutes away. It was the site of leisurely meals, occasions when time wasn't important. The thought of a three-hour celebratory feast just added to Kirk's excitement. He could imagine his doctor friends taking three-hour lunches. Maybe he'd run into them. The thought pleased him.

The restaurant had an open-air design and overlooked the ocean. 'Let's have drinks,' Bailey said as soon as they were seated. The waitress was young and cheerful and had sun-streaked hair. They ordered vodka and tonic.

Kirk drained his drink quickly and then inclined his body forward. 'You have some news for me about the job?'

'We'll get into that, but let's have our lunch first, shall we? The steak here is the best in the city,' Bailey said.

They both ordered the steak. 'I want mine very, very rare. Bloody,' Bailey told the waitress, who blinked at the graphic order. 'I'm from Chicago,' Bailey explained. 'I guess I can't get away from my stockyard upbringing. I just love red meat.' The woman nodded as she collected the menus. When she had gone, Bailey turned to Kirk with a wide smile. 'I know you've been interested in the status of your current position,' he said.

Kirk's fingers rested on the table. Something in Bailey's tone made him begin to grip the edge. He looked into Bailey's face and saw in an instant that his smile was cold and distant.

Bailey cleared his throat, tickled out whatever was clogging it with a series of tiny, efficient coughs. When he finished hacking, his voice had regained its original sunny cadence. 'Well, Kirk, there's good news and bad news. The

267

bad news is that as of today, a new regional manager has been hired. The good news is that we're restoring you to your original position at a five percent raise. Now, I know that you're bound to feel some disappointment, but . . .'

Later, Kirk wouldn't be able to recall the precise time when he stopped hearing Bailey Reynolds. One moment he understood him perfectly well, and the next thing he knew, the older man's mouth was opening and closing, but not a sound was coming out. Kirk slumped back against his chair and shook his head a little, in a vain attempt to both clear his ears and refocus his attention. But Bailey's mouth just kept moving, like that of a ventriloquist's dummy. Kirk went over in his mind what he thought he'd heard Bailey say, but he couldn't quite grasp that either. He picked up the drink in front of him – miraculously, another one had appeared – and drained it. When he raised his head, the power of sight, hearing, and speech returned to him.

'You're going to have to repeat that, Bailey.' His voice was a grim whisper.

'What didn't you hear?' Bailey was somewhat unnerved by the intensity of Kirk's glance and the harshness of his voice. His mind flashed to a recent news article about an employee who had gone berserk after he lost his job. A man who'd returned to his old job with a gun and shot his boss and five other people. The boss died. Come to think of it, the papers were full of stories like that. Bailey began tapping his foot against his chair leg.

'You're saying I'm no longer the regional manager,' Kirk said, his voice dull, his eyes hard and at the same time quite vacant.

'I'm saying that the greater need of the bank is for you to return to your position as a lender, with a five percent raise.' As he spoke, Bailey realized how paltry the increase sounded. At least Preston could have upped the ante to eight percent.

268

'I see,' Kirk said. At that moment, the food appeared before them. The blond waitress, chirping like a happy little bird, asked if there was anything else they wanted. Was everything okay?

Bailey poked his steak with his knife. A thin trail of pale red trickled onto his plate. 'Fine,' Bailey said, smiling. He looked at Kirk. The man looked pale, almost ill.

'Look,' Bailey said, 'I'm really sorry. I know this is rather a surprise. It's a shock to me too. I fully expected that you were going to get the position, Kirk. I was pulling for you.' It was difficult to apologize and be detached at the same time, while still appearing pleasant and amiable, but Bailey managed it. As he spoke, some of his fears dissipated, and his foot stopped kicking the chair. Kirk no longer looked enraged; he looked defeated, which was awful to see, but not at all frightening. Bailey was used to seeing vanquished men. He breathed in the savory aroma of the food that was in front of him. He really was starving. Tentatively, he picked up his fork and knife and cut off a thin slice of meat. Delicious, he thought, as he chewed. Even better than he remembered it. He didn't want to appear insensitive, so he tried not to show how much he was enjoying his food. He rested his silverware on the edge of his plate. 'Listen, things like this happen in business. You mustn't think that there are no opportunities for you at Angel City. You'll have other chances.'

Kirk nodded his head stiffly.

'Why don't you eat your lunch,' Bailey said.

They ended up leaving the restaurant much earlier than Kirk had anticipated. During the ride back to the office, the two men were quiet. As they were nearing the bank, Kirk said suddenly, 'Who's been hired to replace me, and when will he come on board?'

Bailey had been dreading both questions, hoping that somehow Kirk would be too distraught or distracted to make any practical inquiries. 'The man's name is Humphrey Boone, and he'll be starting next Monday.'

Humphrey Boone. His rival. His adversary. Kirk wanted to ask Bailey what kind of credentials Humphrey Boone possessed that had pushed out a man who managed to unload twenty-eight foreclosed properties in the middle of a recession, but he didn't know if he could keep the resentment from his voice, and he didn't want to betray his feeling to Bailey. 'I assume I'll be going back to my old office,' Kirk said.

Bailey nodded as he pulled up to the curb in front of the bank. 'Why don't you take the rest of the day off,' he said as they sat in the car.

'I've got a lot to do,' Kirk said. The men shook hands. 'Thank you for lunch.'

Kirk closed the door to his office and sat down. In a minute, he told himself, he would wake up and the nightmare would be over. He felt drained, as if he would fall down if he tried to stand up. The flow chart above his computer was a silent reminder of his long days and late nights, his high hopes. All that work. For nothing. All for nothing. He hit the back of his head with his open palm. The smack reverberated in the quiet room. He hit himself again and again and again.

Kirk's head was throbbing when he picked up the telephone and dialed his home. He wanted to talk to his wife. But when he heard her voice, he was silent. She sounded so listless. He didn't want the Sheila who was on the other end of the line. He wanted the old, sleek Sheila back, the woman whose voice was always full of laughter and enthusiasm, but that woman was lost to him.

To hell with Angel City! I'll quit. The thought rushed through him, filling his head and chest until his entire body breathed his resolution. Yes. He was going to quit.

He remembered the two beautiful suits he'd recently purchased. He considered Sheila's new health club membership and the bill for the vacation to Maui that they'd taken last year, right after the holidays, on the spur of the moment. A five percent raise wasn't going to cover everything.

To hell with the bank! He pulled up his résumé on the computer. To hell with all of them. He typed furiously. There was a job out there paying six figures with his name on it, and he was going to find it. Just the thought made him feel as though he were kicking in the door of Bailey Reynolds's office. I'll show them all, he said to himself. Fuck Angel City National Bank.

Kirk's euphoric state didn't last very long. Sheila was silent for a long time after he told her the news that night in bed. Finally, she said, 'How could you let such an opportunity slip through your fingers?'

'It wasn't my fault,' he said.

'Nothing is ever your fault,' she replied, and then turned her back to him.

By the time he got to work the next day, Kirk had his To Do list sketched out in his mind. He'd take his résumé to the printer, call two headhunters he knew, and start putting the word out, very quietly, that he was in the market. As he strode down the hall, he was so preoccupied with the tasks he'd set for himself that at first he didn't notice that no one was speaking to him, that people seemed to avert their eyes and rush right past him. But then he became conscious that the greetings he was receiving were muted, mumbled, barely audible. As Kirk turned to go into his office, a woman lowered her head, pretending not to see him as she walked by. That was odd, he thought. Putting his briefcase down, he went out to the kitchenette and poured himself a cup of coffee. Usually, at that time of the morning, two or three people would be standing there with their mugs, but not today. Kirk carried his coffee back to his office and placed it carefully on his desk. As was his practice, he pulled his copy

271

of the *Gazette* out of his briefcase, so that he could glance at the headlines before the day really got started.

The picture was the first thing he saw. Preston Sinclair shaking hands with a black man. He peered at the headline: ANGEL CITY NATIONAL HIRES HIGHEST-RANKING BLACK IN BANKING IN THE CITY. At first the words didn't connect. For a moment, looking at the photograph, he tried to figure out what position the black man would fill. How could such an important job become available and he not know anything about it? Kirk was truly perplexed as he perused the article. Everything jumped into place when he read the caption identifying the smiling black man as Humphrey Boone.

Kirk slumped in his chair. The headline played over and over in his head like the words of a hateful song that he couldn't stop singing: 'Angel City National Hires Highest-Ranking Black in History.' Those bastards. Those fucking bastards. He felt hot and achy and shook his head from side to side, as though he were in a trance. He forced himself to read further and gasped when he came to the statement that Mr. Boone would also head up the newly implemented Minority Loan Program. Preston Sinclair was quoted as saying: 'With this program, which has been endorsed by the esteemed Reverend Odell Rice, Angel City National Bank hopes to begin its long-term efforts toward turning around the conditions that led to the civil unrest of April 29.' Those bastards. Those fucking bastards.

He recalled Bailey's cunning smile. 'Keep up the good work.' 'The president is impressed.' 'Good news.' That lying bastard. It was a setup, with Bailey feeding him just enough bullshit to keep him hustling and hanging on. All they had wanted was for him to work his ass off while they wooed somebody else, who could get them some newspaper coverage. After all his hard work, they were going to hand over the job he deserved to some black guy. And they expected him to take their fucking five percent raise and go back to his old office like a good little boy. Well, they could shove it up their asses. He pictured his hands around Bailey Reynolds's throat, squeezing the smile off his face. He pictured himself putting a gun to Bailey's head and pulling the trigger.

Kirk stood up and paced back and forth. He'd never been arrested. He didn't have a record. Getting a gun would be easy. He would go buy a gun, come back and march right into Bailey's office and . . . and . . . Kirk felt a sharp pain just below his throat, and for a minute he couldn't catch his breath. His heart was hammering away inside his chest. He picked up his coffee cup, and when he looked down at his desk, there were huge dark drops over everything. He set the cup down.

Kirk felt as though he were stepping inside a dense fog; he couldn't see himself coming out on the other side. He imagined holding a gun, aiming it, pulling the trigger, Bailey's blood spurting everywhere. Then he'd ride up to the thirty-fourth floor and find Preston Sinclair and kill him too. He looked at the picture again and slammed his fist down in a puddle of cold coffee. Loser. Loser. Loser. The words seemed to come from a tape that had always been playing somewhere deep within him.

Kirk caught sight of his face reflected in the glass of one of the bright, sunny pictures of floral bouquets that decorated his walls. His hair had fallen into his face, and there was a wildness in his expression that he'd never seen before. To his own eyes he looked deranged. For a moment, he couldn't remember what he was thinking about, and then he looked at the picture again, the smiling white man, the grinning black man. All right. All right. Just calm down, he told himself. Another idea came to him, superior to the first. He didn't have to shoot anyone. Hell, all he had to do was press a few buttons on the computer, lose a few files, wipe out some accounts. Oh, he could make them suffer.

He walked around the office, jangling his keys, trying to control the conflicting impulses that were bombarding the synapses of his brain. He looked at the picture again, and as the keys in his hand clanked against each other, the jangling resounded inside his head, and he began to feel intense pain around his temples. His eyes hurt, and he felt every breath he took. He reached up and wiped his forehead. When he looked around him, the room seemed to be whirling. I've got to get out of here, Kirk thought. He took one last look at the photograph and noticed, for the first time, just how dark the black man was, standing next to Preston Sinclair. As he peered at the photo, he thought that Humphrey Boone wasn't smiling; he was smirking.

Arrogant affirmative action bastard.

He *would* buy a gun, Kirk decided in the space of time that it took him to cross Spring Street and get to his car. He didn't have time to tinker with computers; he wanted to do something now. The attendant at the parking lot was surprised to see him. 'You just get here,' he said, his words covered with a thick Spanish accent.

As soon as he got into the car, he turned on the radio. The jovial voice of King Clever boomed out. 'My Amerifriends, do you remember the way things used to be?' Kirk was too distracted to focus on what King Clever was saying from his exalted radio throne, but the tone of his voice was soothing, and for the first time all morning, Kirk felt himself calming down.

He drove to where he thought a gunshop was located, but he passed it and couldn't go back easily because of the network of one-way streets that threaded the downtown area. He made a wrong turn, and the next thing he knew, he was on the Santa Monica Freeway, travelling west. For a fleeting moment he thought about going home, but he got off at La Cienega and headed north toward Beverly Hills instead.

274

Kirk was startled as he emerged from the freeway. He hadn't been in the area in months, and what he saw bore little resemblance to what he remembered. The boulevard he was traveling on looked as if it had been shelled. Along La Cienega there were gaping holes where businesses used to be. Within the first block there were the burned-out hulls of buildings that had yet to be demolished. Farther up the street, he passed several vacant lots. What happened here? he wondered, and then, almost as soon as he posed the question, he realized that the street he was on was a casualty of the riots. The violence had come right to the edge of Beverly Hills.

Look what those people have done to our city. He pictured the dark, frenzied faces he'd seen in the news. Savages. Tearing and clawing, breaking and entering, trying to take what they didn't deserve.

'Amerifriends,' King Clever said in his soothing all-American radio voice, 'it's time that Americans get back to the values that this country was founded upon. The people who work hard deserve the rewards. That's not greed. That's the American Way.' Kirk almost plowed into the car ahead of him. It was as though the man was speaking to him. His anger drained away as he turned up the radio and let King Clever's voice fill his ears until he couldn't hear anything else. He pulled the car over and parked and listened until the show's bouncy black theme music began playing.

Kirk started the car and continued traveling north. He knew where he was going, now that he was thinking clearly. The thought of his recent vow made him cringe. He wasn't going to kill anyone. He'd been completely out of control. The best thing for him to do was leave the bank. One of the headhunters he'd heard about had an office not five minutes away from the city's most exclusive shopping mall, which was straight ahead. He'd brought his briefcase, and his résumé was inside. He'd simply see if the man was available.

As he got close to the Beverly Hills commercial district, the clean sidewalks, gaily decorated shops, and outdoor cafés gave no hint that the area had ever seen any trouble. But the mall itself, that great opulent jewel, had been under siege for several hours on April 29, before the police stormed the place and shut it down. Not two blocks from the mall, the medical offices where his former classmates practiced stretched for nearly a block. Kirk knew he was near it, but the building loomed up before he was quite prepared to see it. The structure was a monstrosity of white marble. As he stared at it, he sensed the old envious rush of astonishment, and the old question came to his mind: How had they been able to do it? If there were other questions, he couldn't bear to ask them.

As Kirk turned into the parking lot of the headhunter's building, he was completely calm. Yes, he'd leave Angel City. That was the best choice under the circumstances. Also the safest. He didn't know what he was capable of doing if he stayed.

18

Four blocks from the downtown branch of Angel City National Bank, on a rainy morning, the four police officers and an ethnically diverse jury of their peers were gearing up for yet another round of testimony, charts, expert witnesses, and, of course, videotapes. In the weeks since the civil rights trial had begun, Los Angeles seemed to tremble more and more. Already the National Guard was on alert. The thundercloud that covered the city was the color of nightmares.

But Humphrey Boone's dreams were sweet and about to come true, or so he thought as he closed the door to his new office, placed his monogrammed briefcase on the floor, and breathed a sigh of exhilaration. He wasn't paying much attention to this round of trials. What did it matter whether or not the cops went to jail? The important thing was for black people to ascend to positions of power, to be in control of their own destiny. And he, for one, was on his way. He studied his reflection in the clean picture window. For the first time in years, he looked approvingly at his wide nose, his thick lips, and his jack of spades skin. He wasn't ugly. He was okay. More than okay. He whispered aloud, 'I am the Man.'

He could smell the fresh paint. In the middle of the large mahogany desk – brand new – was a huge basket of fruit in which a bottle of Mumm's champagne was nestled. He could smell the ripe oranges through the cellophane. The card, signed by Preston Sinclair, read simply: 'The future is yours.' It was indeed.

Humphrey slipped off his suit coat and hung it on a

padded hanger on the back of the door, loosened his Hermès tie just slightly, and sat down at his desk. In another hour, he would convene his first staff meeting, a meeting for which he was totally prepared. He'd come in early because he wanted to enjoy his first hour on the job, to savor it by himself. There was nothing to do for the moment but indulge himself in his own vanity, congratulate himself for paying attention to all the signs on the highway, following the rules, dotting his *i*s, crossing his *t*s, and working three times harder than any white man he'd ever competed against. And now he was claiming his reward. He flipped on the small clock radio in front of him to KJLH. He leaned back in his richly upholstered chair and put his feet up on his brand-new desk and tapped them to a familiar beat.

The telephone rang just as Humphrey stretched out. He hesitated for a second, then pressed the button for the speakerphone. He wanted to give the impression that he was already so busy, so important, so powerful, he couldn't even pick up the telephone. 'Humphrey Boone,' he answered smoothly.

'Humphrey? That you, baby?'

His mother's flat Mississippi drawl – an accent that was still thick though she had lived half a century in Los Angeles – blaring into his palatial corporate office seemed the essence of incongruity. A chilly wave of apprehension rolled up under his shoulders. Humphrey reached for the receiver. 'What's wrong, Mama?' He felt a sense of dread, the same foreboding that was present whenever his mother called him. For as long as he could remember, his mother had brought him nothing but bad news. Hearing her voice always made him want to run. Her words sounded the way she looked: heavy and tired. Oh, Mama. Sometimes he wanted to take her in his arms. Sometimes he wished he could flee to where he'd never have to hear from her again.

'Chontelle called. The oldest boy done got himself in some more trouble. She scared to call you, because she didn't pay you back from the last time, but I was just wondering if you could let her have some money for his bail. She your sister, Humphrey. Everybody ain't had your good fortune.'

Good fortune? He bunched his fingers into a tight fist. She made it sound as if his success was something he picked up in the street one day. As if he hadn't worked two jobs through high school and two through college, straining to make good grades and take up the slack that his absent father left. Nothing stopped Chontelle or the others from doing exactly what he'd done. Nobody told Chontelle to have three babies by a high school dropout who couldn't keep a job. Why did he have to be responsible for everybody?

'Mama, I work for the bank. I ain't – I'm not the bank.' He tried to sound hard and cold, but the attempt fell flat, and he ended up merely whining.

'Baby, I know that.'

'I take care of you, Mama. Isn't that enough?' He heard his mother sighing. He'd made her feel guilty, and he didn't mean to do that. He couldn't stand the thought of his mother feeling bad. Her whole life had been nothing but hard times. He remembered how when he was small his mother would clean offices at night to augment the pittance that the state gave her after his father left. He was in charge of the other children while she was gone. He had to feed them, bathe them, and make sure they got to bed. Sometimes, after his sisters and brother were asleep, he'd wait up for her. He'd hear the bus screech to a halt at the corner, and five minutes later, his mother would wobble through the door of the tiny apartment the five of them shared, taking slow steps like an old woman, reeking of ammonia and furniture polish. He would have a plate waiting for her, and sometimes she'd fall asleep at the table before she finished eating.

'I won't ask you no more, Humphrey,' his mother said. 'It ain't fair. You got a right to enjoy yourself.' She was getting ready to cry. He could hear it in her voice.

'How much do you need?'

When he hung up the telephone, he wrote a check for $525, the $25 being the amount that the store near his sister would charge her to cash his check. He shook his head, an involuntary gesture. She couldn't even afford to open up a checking account.

What was the difference? he wondered for the millionth time. He had made it somehow, but why not them? Chontelle was on welfare, and his brother, Louis, was in and out of jail and on and off drugs. Only his youngest sister, Latriece, was self-sufficient, working as an administrative assistant in city government, but she was too busy partying and having a good time to think about going to college. He'd talked to her about getting a degree, shaping a career, but she wouldn't listen to him.

Sometimes he hated them all. Hated them for not being as smart as he was, for not being as strong. He'd blazed his way through school, earning nearly straight As. When things were horrible at home, he would open up a book and escape. Maybe that was one of the differences between him and his siblings: he always knew that things were bad, that other people didn't live the way they did. In the library, flipping through the pages of *Ebony*, he would see pictures of black people, even people as dark as he, living in beautiful homes, wearing gorgeous clothes. The fact that some of the models and subjects of the articles were his particular shade he took as a kind of redemption. He was the darkest of his mother's children, and he was darker than most of his friends. His mother lovingly called him Black Berry, but other people weren't so kind. A few of the kids in the neighborhood teased him, calling him 'Ape Man' and 'Gorilla,' but mostly he could read in their eyes that people thought he was ugly. Not everyone, of course, but enough, especially girls. So when he saw the black-skinned people in *Ebony*, lounging in their luxurious homes, posing behind the desks of their splendid offices, he believed that the photographs were a foreshadowing of things to come. The pictures also convinced him that what he always suspected was true: his family's lives were small and mean and hard. But there were other people, people who looked just like them, who were on a different path. And he trusted his mother and teachers, the coach on his basketball team, the owner of the store where he worked after school, when they assured him that the path he was walking led to success and wealth.

But when he showed the pictures to his brother and sisters, they weren't interested. Perhaps, because they were younger, they were far more absorbed in the tangible pleasures right outside their door. They listened to nothing but the call of the street. The gangs were like a magnet for his brother, Louis, who liked the instant power and street fame that such an affiliation garnered. And Chontelle was like a delicate leaf riding the winds of disaster, swayed by every hard-faced boy who called her name in a rhythm that suited her fancy. The baby girl, Latriece, was the only one he and his mother could control. Watching the streets slowly claim Louis and Chontelle was like witnessing their deaths. Humphrey blamed himself for their loss. And so, when calamities befell them, he rode in with his checkbook. 'You can afford it,' they said, when they didn't repay his loans. 'You in the big time, brother. Won't hurt you to help me out a little bit.' They were both proud and resentful that he'd succeeded. His good fortune was an accusing finger pointed straight at them, which said: I did it, why didn't you? When he bought clothes for his brother's two children or took food to his sister, they accepted it, but he knew that secretly they would have been happier had he shared their situation, so that they could all commiserate about how harsh life was, how white people always kept them down.

Damn them! Humphrey looked at the check he held in his hand. Even now, he dreamed of saving them, of becoming rich and powerful enough to swoop them all up in his checkbook carpet and bring them down gently into the land of middle-class living, not so much for the sakes of his worthless brother and sister, but because he knew that seeing their new lives would make his mother happy. His dream had always been to make his mother happy, and it had partially come true. He had bought her a house and a car. He'd gone with her the day she told her caseworker to take her name off the welfare roll. The first of every month, he sent her a stipend of $1,500. But to save his brother and sister, to turn their lives around, would take more, much more. He would have to make every moment at Angel City count.

Humphrey looked at his watch. In fifteen minutes his meeting would start, and already he felt drained. The radio was playing a fast, bouncy rap. He bobbed his head a little, as he stood up and thought about what was ahead of him. If he played his cards right, if he not only impressed the right white people but made them feel comfortable around him, who knew how far he might go. It was way too early in the game to tell whether or not Preston Sinclair would live up to his promise, but at least Humphrey meant to leave with far more than he had when he came: access to capital to start his own company. Humphrey put on his jacket and tightened his tie. He turned off the radio and tuned his mind to sharper rhythms. He could feel the adrenaline surging through him, even as he looked in the glass picture window again. What he saw made him recoil. The black face peering back at him was that of a frightened boy from South-

Central, going with his mama to get her welfare check. 'I am the Man,' he whispered. A defiant ferocity welled up within him. 'I am the Man,' he repeated, stronger this time. 'I am.'

Humphrey was staring intently at his dark image in the plate glass when there was a knock at his door. He opened it, and a white man who appeared to be his age was standing in front of him, his hand extended. When Humphrey took it in his own, the white man's palm was limp and sweaty. 'I'm Kirk Madison, Mr. Boone. I wanted to welcome you to Angel City.'

As Kirk shook the black man's hand, he felt all the rage that he'd previously assigned to Bailey Reynolds and Preston Sinclair. Looking into Humphrey's face, he saw the obscenely opulent white marble medical building that the Jews he used to go to school with owned, he saw their mansions and their slim Gentile wives. He saw a black man with the power that should have been his standing where he should have stood. He forced his mouth to smile, but his fingers trembled as he shook the man's hand.

The black man released Kirk's hand when he felt his fingers shaking. 'Call me Humphrey,' he said. 'Have a seat.'

'Well, actually, I know you're on your way to the staff meeting. I just thought I'd come by early and say hello.'

'That was kind of you.'

'You probably know that I was acting regional manager for several months before you were hired. I just wanted to let you know that I have tons of information that I can pass on to you. When you get settled, let's get together. And in the meantime, if there's anything you need, please don't hesitate to ask.'

'Thank you. I'm sure I'll do that,' Humphrey said easily.

'I'll see you in a few minutes.'

'Yes.'

Humphrey smiled to himself as the door closed. He had

met his first declared enemy at Angel City National Bank. Bailey Reynolds had told him about his predecessor, and Kirk's presenting himself saved Humphrey the trouble of seeking him out. He knew his type well. Kirk was the grin-in-your-face-while-stabbing-you-in-the-back type. He'd had to fight off that kind at every job he ever worked at, and it was about to begin again. His variety came in black, brown, and yellow as well, but in most job situations, Humphrey had been 'the only one'. At his level, he rarely encountered people who looked like him. Humphrey knew the MO. Kirk was going to withhold information and, since he had an extra vendetta, would probably give him false data too. And he probably wasn't above spreading rumors. Jesus, he thought, does it ever stop? He would simply have to watch his back and hope that there was one person among his employees whom he could trust.

By 9:05 the members of his staff had assembled in the conference room. Humphrey worked the crowd for about ten minutes, introducing himself, shaking hands, and chatting long enough to know that he was the recipient of a divided house. It was what Humphrey had expected. The expressions on the various faces revealed both curiosity and hostility toward the man who was standing in front of them. The announcement of Humphrey's arrival had reached the personnel of Angel City Bank several weeks earlier, in the form of a memorandum issued by Bailey Reynolds. The memo was immediately embellished with speculation from the office's political gossip mill as to why Kirk had been passed over in favor of a black outsider. Lines were silently drawn, and two opposing camps emerged: one group felt that Kirk had been irreparably wronged, sacrificed on the altar of affirmative action; the other opted to support management's choice, secretly hoping that their cooperation would prevent Kirk's fate from becoming theirs.

Kirk's fellow employees' sense of identification with him was so strong that Kirk didn't have to utter one word of blame or condemnation; his outrage was assumed and shared. Word had gotten out that his interviews with Beverly Hills headhunters had netted nada. The recession, the exodus of employees in the aerospace industries, the sliding real estate market, and layoffs all around town had rendered positions for bank executives scarce. But a sagging economy was one thing; to many at Angel City, the passing over of Kirk Madison in favor of a black outsider was a betrayal. Not that anyone would publicly voice an objection. Everyone was too scared to align himself with Kirk. No one wanted to tempt fate.

In the conference room, Esther sat in the front row, hardly able to contain her excitement. Just when she had been about to resign herself to the fact that Kirk would never be her ally and that she'd never get into lending through his help, he was out, replaced by a black man. And not just any black man but Humphrey Boone, the president of the Los Angeles chapter of the National Alliance of Black Bankers, an organization she'd joined nearly two years ago. With Humphrey at the helm, the group had nearly doubled in size, quadrupled its earnings, and given out five times as many college scholarships to black high school seniors as in the previous year. Although she'd met him only once, Esther admired not only his charismatic leadership but his professional accomplishments. Ambition stirred within her. For the first time since she'd come to Angel City, she felt that someone who might be a friend to her was in control. And sitting in the chair as Humphrey walked to the front of the room, she felt proud, the kind of pride she experienced when the black Olympians brought home the gold, when Jesse Jackson ran for President, whenever somebody black won on *Jeopardy*. 'Go 'head, brother,' she said to herself as she looked at Humphrey Boone.

When she had learned that Humphrey would be coming to Angel City, she wanted to share the news with Tyrone. She seemed to tell him most of what was going on in her life. They now spoke several times a week, chatting as easily as old friends.

They'd been eating pizza in her kitchen one night, laughing, as they always seemed to do, when Esther said, 'Guess what? Angel City has hired a black man to head the entire region. Isn't that great?'

Tyrone immediately pictured the sophisticated-looking black man he'd seen in the bank. 'Tall, thin brother? Real dark? Combination *GQ* and *Ebony* Man?' Tyrone put his chin between his forefinger and thumb, leaned his head to the side, raised his eyebrows slightly, striking a pseudo-sophisticated pose. 'I've seen the gentleman in question. He's quite sua-vay.'

Esther clapped her hand over her mouth to keep from spewing out pizza as she laughed.

'Maybe I can get me a loan now that we in charge. Uhh, what's the brother's name?'

Esther was still giggling. 'Humphrey Boone.'

'Humphrey? Now you know he gotsta be cool. The gangsta banker. Open up a savings account, or I'll blow your head off. I'm going in there Monday morning to see ole Humphrey.' Tyrone pretended to pick up the telephone and assumed an accent straight from the annals of *Amos and Andy*: 'This here the Homeboy Savings and Loan? I ain't got no savings, but I'se calling 'bout da loan part. I got me a little bi'ness and I needs me some money. Put Humphrey on the line.'

'Do me a favor,' Esther said, still laughing. 'Don't mention my name.'

'Yeah, Humphrey, Esther Jackson told me to call you. Yeah, brother, she know me real good. Yeah, she'll vouch for me.' He put down the receiver and said to Esther in his real voice, 'You gonna vouch for me, Esther?'

Esther smiled. 'I have to see your credit report first.'

'That's cold. Chilly, chilly wind blowing up in here.' Tyrone drew both his arms across his chest and pretended to be trembling.

Even though he was only joking, Esther regretted her quick retort. She'd learned on their second date that Tyrone had ruined his credit. He had pulled out a wad of bills to pay for their dinner at a West Side café, and she said, 'Tyrone, you frighten me, carrying so much money around. The way things are going nowadays, it's better to walk around with minimum cash and a few cards. At least you can replace the cards.'

Tyrone had sighed, and for the first time since she'd gotten to know him, he looked truly embarrassed. He hesitated and then said with a grin she could tell he didn't feel, 'I was young and foolish. Got a bunch of credit cards and ran them up to the hilt. Couldn't pay the piper, so they took my cards away.'

Esther had shrugged her shoulders and acted as though having credit cards didn't matter to her at all. But of course it did matter. She could hear her mother saying to her, 'A grown man without a Visa, MasterCard, or American Express just isn't responsible.' And hard as she tried, she couldn't block out her mother's warning.

Esther had to admit, as she sat musing in the conference room, that she enjoyed herself with Tyrone, responsible or not. In the time that she'd been seeing him, she laughed a lot, danced a lot, and felt increasingly comfortable with him. Perhaps because of the robbery and the trauma they both experienced, they skipped the game-playing phase of their relationship; they were buddies who'd been through the storm together. Tyrone had seen her when she was needy and vulnerable, and he had come through for her. And the more often they made love, the better it got. 'The man is learning my body,' she told Vanessa. Even now, just thinking about Tyrone – in the middle of the conference room, surrounded by her co-workers – she could feel heat pulsating in her groin. 'Tell me how you want to do it,' he said whenever they had sex. She closed her eyes and she could feel him inside her, his hands on her breasts, his voice whispering, 'Tell me when you're ready. I'ma wait for you, baby.'

She liked the man in bed; she liked him out of bed. It was downright scary. Tyrone Carter, she reminded herself, was just something to do.

'What are you looking so serious about?' Mallory whispered, interrupting Esther's reverie as she slid into the seat next to hers. Esther merely shook her head and patted Mallory's arm. Humphrey was walking toward the front of the room.

'What do you think about him?' Again Mallory whispered, nodding toward Humphrey as he took his place in front of the people gathered to hear him.

'I think he'll be excellent and— '

Mallory interrupted. 'I'm not talking about that. Don't you think he's good-looking?'

Esther gave her a surprised look. 'He's okay.' What was Mallory getting at?

Mallory perceived her friend's shock and said quickly, not moving her lips, 'He's everything you're looking for. He's good-looking and smart, and God knows they're paying him enough money.'

'How much?' Esther tried not to sound too interested.

'I heard his base salary is $175,000. And that he'll be getting bonuses based on the private placement loans he brings in.'

She couldn't help it: as soon as Mallory mentioned money, a picture of the Hancock Park minimansion that she

288

coveted invaded her mind. The house was a two-story brick Tudor – a rarity in California, which made her nostalgic for Chicago architecture – and appeared to be at least five thousand square feet. A Benz and a Jag were usually parked in the driveway. The vanity plates on the Benz said HISBENZ, the ones on the Jag read HERJAG. Once, when she was driving by, a confident-looking black couple in their early forties came out. Assuming them to be the owners, she said to herself, 'Everything is possible.'

She observed the man standing in front of her and pictured herself walking out the door of a mansion with him. Humphrey Boone wasn't handsome, but he exuded a panther's grace and sinewy elegance. And he radiated the kind of self-confidence and power that come from playing the white man's game and not only surviving but winning. She knew that his wallet held the magic array of plastic cards belonging to a man in charge of his life, the kind of man who would instantly win her mother's approval. You're being ridiculous, she told herself. For all she knew, the man had a woman or a wife or both.

As if reading her mind, Mallory whispered in her ear, 'He's not married. I checked.'

Esther shook her head, as if to dislodge all the ridiculous fantasies. What she needed from Humphrey Boone wasn't that he be Prince Charming: she simply needed him to give her a boost up the corporate ladder. 'Listen,' she whispered to Mallory, 'I'll be better off getting him to be my mentor than my lover.'

Mallory leaned over and said very quietly, 'Who says he can't be both? Just joking. Just joking,' she added quickly when she saw the shocked look on Esther's face.

'Good morning!' Humphrey said to the people who sat before him, balancing Danishes and coffees on their laps. Surveying them, he realized afresh that the biggest part of his job was to make believers out of his own staff. It was the

289

part that he liked best, because it was one of the few areas of work where he could take off his mask, at least temporarily, and call upon the skills he'd honed in South-Central. Sometimes he mused to himself that perhaps one of his best-kept secrets was that so much of what he'd learned growing up was totally transferable to corporate life and had, in fact, prepared him for succeeding in the white man's world. As a hungry boy he had scrounged for survival, and now as a man he was doing the same thing, in a different setting. The gangs in his neighborhood and the white men beyond the glass ceiling had never been his friends. He'd had to outrun one and outwit the other. In both places, he found that sometimes success was simply a matter of bullshitting the people with power, getting them to like him, to help him. Fooling them into thinking that he was one of them. Maybe fooling himself too. But he never felt safe, not then and certainly not now.

Humphrey smiled broadly as he addressed the group. 'First of all, I want to say that I'm glad to be here. We've got some exciting times ahead of us.' He spoke smoothly, watching, without seeming to, the reactions of everyone around him. He had dressed with extra care that morning and was smiling just a little harder than usual. Even as he stood in his clean black suit, with his wing tips shining, his perfect smile in place, enunciating for all he was worth, he could feel the tiny pinpricks of a headache sneaking around his temples.

'Angel City is stretching out in all kinds of directions, and we're all going to be a part of that. As you know by now, we've recently instituted a Minority Loan Program that will be the bank's way of revitalizing the inner city through home mortgage and business loans. I'll be talking more with you about that in the future, but for now, think of this program as our investment in peace and prosperity for all the people living in Los Angeles.'

His eyes wandered from face to face, as he spoke about the work that needed to be done in the bank. He talked about the bottom line and making their region number one. The white men with hard eyes who thought of him as the affirmative action enemy shifted in their seats. All for one and one for all, that's what he zealously pushed. He told a couple of funny stories about the mistakes he'd made in his career, and he watched as the hard eyes softened just a little. And every once in a while, he stole a look at the black woman. Her reassuring eyes were a touchstone. The entire time he stood there, she was smiling, nodding, telling him without saying a word that he was saying the right thing.

'In the next few weeks, I'll be meeting with each of you, one-on-one. We'll be getting to know each other better. I want to know your problems, as well as your triumphs. You should think of me as your managerial advocate,' he said.

Esther felt Mallory's hand squeezing her arm. She turned to face her smiling friend. 'He's really articulate, isn't he?' Mallory asked in her breathless voice.

Esther didn't bother to mask her frown.

'What?' Mallory whispered. Esther shook her head. Mallory poked her in her ribs. 'I didn't mean it like that,' she said. When Esther looked surprised, she said, 'I know what you're thinking. I'm not saying that just because he's black.' Now it was Mallory's turn to feel aggrieved. She's so damned thin-skinned, thinking everything has to do with race.

'I didn't say that,' Esther whispered.

'You were thinking it,' Mallory said firmly.

Esther frowned again, but when she looked into Mallory's indignant eyes, she shrugged. Maybe she had been overly sensitive. 'Sorry,' she said.

As Humphrey shook hands with his staff, he began to realize that a subtle transformation was already taking place, one that he knew would go through many reversals. He sensed the easing up, perhaps even the giving way of that first layer of resistance.

Out of the small throng that crowded around Humphrey, Kirk emerged. 'I enjoyed what you had to say, Humphrey,' he said, as he shook the black man's hand. People, of course, were hovering around the two men like paparazzi hoping for a scandalous shot. 'As I told you earlier, I've got a lot of notes and information for you. So as soon as you're settled, we can get together.'

'I'll call you in a little while and we'll set up a meeting,' Humphrey said, conscious of the silent group around them. 'I appreciate having you on the team,' he said.

The room was emptying out when the black woman came up to him, accompanied by the white woman she'd been sitting next to during the meeting. 'Mr. Boone, I'm Esther Jackson, regional operations manager. We met last year at the National Alliance of Black Bankers meeting. I want to welcome you to Angel City. This is Mallory Post, vice president and loan officer.'

'Please, call me Humphrey.' He shook their hands in turn.

Esther and Mallory stayed only long enough to assure him that they were glad he'd come to the bank and looked forward to working with him. Chatting with the two women, he didn't know why he assumed that Esther would be an ally. He'd been stabbed in the back at least as many times by black people as by white, maybe more. But there was something about the tall black woman that made him feel that she was not only black, she was a sister. The jury was still out on the white woman, although the fact that she and Esther seemed to be tight was a good sign.

He had a good feeling as they walked away. Both were at least potential allies. He would find out what they wanted; holding out a carrot was the fastest way to solidify a corporate relationship. He couldn't help noticing and admiring their bodies in what he perceived was a purely detached way. Nothing could screw a brother faster than sexual improprieties.

He took one last look at the black woman as she passed through the doorway. Good God! He sighed. There was nothing on the planet like a sister's ass.

19

LaKeesha looked quickly around the bank. An overweight older woman, her thick ankles lapping over her shoes, was lumbering up to the tellers' cage. She smelled like she'd fallen into a vat of knock-off Giorgio. 'Here comes your woman, Hector,' she whispered mischievously, launching into the game they played when few customers were around. 'She's smelling good for you, homeboy. She's got that love jones for you, boyfriend. I can see it in her eyes.'

There were no other customers, so LaKeesha stood back while Hector waited on the lady. Afterward, she began laughing, and Hector soon joined in. 'Okay, okay. You got me. You're not a nice girl, you know that?'

LaKeesha giggled again. 'I know. I'm a terrible person. Hey, did you bring me any papusas for lunch? I love that stuff.'

Hector opened a paper bag stained with dark grease and pulled out something that resembled a burrito, wrapped in waxed paper. The odor of beans and spicy beef permeated the air between them. He handed it to LaKeesha.

'My homeboy. Thank you. Oooh, a whole one, and it's still warm. Thank you. Thank you.' She looked around quickly and, seeing no customers or supervisors, pulled the waxed paper back and bit into the cornmeal cake, before quickly rewrapping it and putting it inside her own lunch bag under the counter. 'Oh, this is so good,' she said, chewing. 'Your mama make this?'

Hector nodded.

'You live with your mama?'

Hector hesitated for a moment. He knew that in the United States it was expected that young men his age should have their own apartments. Even young women. He didn't want the laughing black woman to think he was dependent.

LaKeesha put a hand on his arm. 'Don't feel bad, Hector. I live with my mother and grandmother,' she said sympathetically, 'and my two sisters and their kids. It's so crowded in our apartment, sometimes I can't even catch my breath.'

Relief washed over his eyes. 'Yes, I know. In the mornings, when everyone is going to work, trying to get into the bathroom . . .' He shook his head wearily, as though even the thought of such chaos tired him out.

'I'm the only one who's working in our family,' LaKeesha said softly.

Hector saw the fleeting sadness in her eyes and knew that her sisters were like so many women in their neighborhood, collecting a monthly check from the government in order to feed themselves and their children. 'I have three jobs,' he said.

'You do? You work at night?'

He nodded. 'I clean offices every night but Wednesday. That's the night I study computers. And on Saturdays and Sundays I am a security guard.'

LaKeesha shook her head in wonder. 'I wish I could do that, but if I worked like that I'd never see my son.'

'I have to work so that I can save enough money to help my mother get a bigger place for my brothers and sisters. And' – he drew a deep breath – 'I want my own place someday.' He didn't tell her that he wanted to get married.

'You and me both,' LaKeesha said eagerly. 'I have saved about two hundred dollars already. I saw the apartment I want. But I need a thousand-dollar deposit.'

'Yes, always the deposits.' Hector sighed.

LaKeesha tapped him lightly on his arm. 'Stay happy,

homeboy. We'll get there. And you tell your mama that your co-worker said she can really burn.'

Hector began laughing. 'I will tell her this. I'm going to say, "My friend says you can burn." '

'Yes, she can re-e-elly burn.' LaKeesha imitated Hector perfectly, which set them both off again. As they were settling down, LaKeesha looked up and saw Esther beckoning her from her office. 'I'll be right back,' she said.

Hector watched his dark-skinned friend go into Esther's office. Through the glass partition, he could observe the two women, their heads close together. His smile faded. Don't be angry, he told himself sternly. Be happy that you have a job. Be happy that you are in a place where bombs aren't dropping every minute. But as much as he lectured himself, he couldn't help but feel some resentment. Before LaKeesha came, Esther used to single him out and tell him what a wonderful job he was doing. She would talk to him about being promoted, but now she had time only for LaKeesha. He had seen them once or twice, meeting together early in the morning in Esther's office. The older woman held up cards, and LaKeesha repeated some words he couldn't hear. And then afterward they laughed: It was the laughter of two friends. Their mouths were wide open, and their shoulders vibrated, and Esther patted LaKeesha's shoulder. Well, what did he expect? Blood is thicker than water, he reminded himself. It was one of the few American expressions that he could remember. The black woman's future would always be easier than his. She was a citizen. There was nothing to stop her progress.

But no one would stop his either, he decided. One day he would own a house and a car, and his wife and children – only two – would wear nice clothing from Bullock's. He would have charge cards and eat in restaurants. His mother wouldn't have to scrub the floors of rich black women who lived in fancy houses. And he would take the whole family to Disneyland. But he couldn't make any of his dreams come true on a teller's salary. He needed more money, a lot more money.

Be patient, he told himself. Remember how far you've come. He thought about the countryside outside of Chalatenango in his country. He recalled the nights he couldn't sleep because the gunfire lit up the sky. Life was far better in Los Angeles, even though the two-bedroom apartment in South-Central was crowded with eight people and there was never any privacy, no place to be alone with his girl-friend, Idalia, not at his place and certainly not at hers, where twelve people lived in three rooms. But his family's apartment had a bathroom. And there was running water, hot and cold. They had electricity that went off only when his parents couldn't pay the bill. It was better, even though the gangs shot at each other and some of the black people in the building said that the neighhorhood belonged to them first. It was better, even though the whites and blacks called them wetbacks and the store clerks' faces became filled with hateful exasperation when his mother and grandmother tried to explain what they wanted in their very broken English. At his brother's high school, fights had broken out recently between the blacks and the Latinos. But even when they fought with the niggers – that's what his brother called them – even then it was still better here.

And it didn't matter to him that during the last few weeks, when he walked onto the streets of L.A., he could feel the city holding its breath as the jury decided whether or not the white policemen should go to jail. He'd long ago learned not to look for justice from either grinning politicians or courts of law. Only if powerful people wanted the police in jail would they be sent there. Their fate wasn't in his hands, but his was. Let the old woman in his apartment building pray for peace on the streets. Hector prayed for an opportunity.

Hector could see LaKeesha nodding her head at her boss. He liked the chocolate-skinned girl with the plump curving lips who loved his mama's papusas and made him laugh so hard that he got stomach cramps, but because of her, he no longer had a patron. She called him homeboy, but the truth was, they were competitors, each trying to make it to the finish line first. However much he liked her, there could be only one winner.

As LaKeesha sat down in the chair opposite her desk, Esther nodded approvingly at the conservative outfit and low-heeled black pumps she was wearing. The shoes had the kind of high-gloss shine on them that made them seem new and expensive, though Esther knew that they were neither. She had passed on to LaKeesha the 'shine your shoes' regulation that was the South Side credo of upwardly mobile black folks. Her own father had instilled the rule in her.

'Good morning, LaKeesha,' Esther said.

'Good morning, Esther. How are you?' LaKeesha looked up, smiled, and kept her eyes on Esther's as she spoke.

She had noticed during her first interview that LaKeesha had a bad habit of not looking at people when she spoke to them. Eye contact was one of the lessons the older woman had taught her. When you don't look people in the eye, they feel that you are intimidated by them – or they get the feeling that you're sneaky, she told her. LaKeesha had taken her words to heart. She now corrected herself whenever she said 'ax' for 'ask,' although she was still slipping up on the 'to be' verb, using it as a helper. This morning, as Esther quizzed her on verb agreement, there were still some trouble spots, but overall, LaKeesha was proving to be a quick study and Esther felt reassured that she'd made the right choice.

LaKeesha handed the flash cards to Esther.

'Fill in the blank for the perfect tense of 'go.' I have *blank* to see my mother.'

'I have went to see my mother.'

'Try again.'

LaKeesha's foot started tapping against the chair. Esther could see the anxiety flickering in her eyes. She was so anxious to please her. 'Just relax. Relax. You know it.'

'I have . . . I have gone?'

Esther smiled. 'That's right. You're really very bright.' LaKeesha pressed her hand to her heart. 'Oh, I forgot to show you something.' Esther took a letter from the corner of her desk and handed it to the teller, who scanned it quickly. 'It's a letter from a customer you helped. I'll pass it along to my boss. Just keep up the good work and some great things are going to happen for you, LaKeesha. You've already got yourself a fan.'

The younger woman beamed with pleasure and said, 'I told you I'd do my best.'

Esther glanced at her watch. 'Time to get back to work,' she said.

LaKeesha rose from her chair a little reluctantly. It wasn't that she didn't want to go back to the tellers' cage. She loved her job. But when she was with Esther, she felt like the little girl she'd never been. Esther praised her. She told her what to wear and what to say. For as long as she could remember, LaKeesha had always taken care of everyone else, but when she was with Esther, she felt nurtured. I want to be like her, she thought to herself as she left the older woman's office. I want to be just like her.

As LaKeesha walked away, Esther caught sight of Hector Bonilla, approaching the tellers' cage with that curious bouncing gait of his. Hector always seemed to be in a hurry. Watching him rush to his station, Esther felt a faint pang of guilt. There were only so many slots for operations assistant, and in all fairness she should recommend Hector first.

She looked at the two evaluation forms that lay on her desk. She had written up everyone else's and was putting the final touches on LaKeesha's and Hector's reports. As she stared at the documents, she felt as if she'd been caught in a lie. She wasn't lying, she reminded herself. She was merely being selective about what she chose to tell. Hector did need improvement in customer relations. She didn't say he was rude; it was just that he barely spoke to people and he rarely smiled. It was her job to report that, she reminded herself. And LaKeesha did excel in that area. Why, any number of customers had remarked about how courteous she was.

That said, she couldn't dispute the fact that Hector had helped to train LaKeesha. How could she give the trainee a higher evaluation than the trainer? Looking toward the cage at the two of them with their heads close together, LaKeesha with her dark skin and Hector with his shiny black hair, Esther remembered what she'd learned in the schoolyard at the posh private school she hated, what was the credo of the streets of South Side Chicago: Blood is thicker than water.

20

When she heard the television come on, LaKeesha looked up reluctantly from the copy of *The Color Purple* that Esther had loaned her. 'Go do your homework, girl,' LaKeesha said to Shoni, who was turning the channels.

'I done my homework. You already seen it,' Shoni said.

'I did my homework. You already saw it,' LaKeesha said.

'That too,' Shoni said. Both sisters laughed. 'Why you all the time be trying to get me to talk white?'

'It's not white; it's correct.' She didn't feel as sure as Esther and Mrs. Clark were when they said it. Sometimes she was a little afraid that she was talking white, that she could lose herself in the land where enunciation was crisp and all verbs agreed. And at home, especially on weekends, it was hard to hold on to that language of success and power. Somehow, in the cramped apartment, those agreeable verbs and starched words could easily just vanish in thin air. She would grope for them on Monday morning, and they were hard to find. 'When you go to work, you have to know the right way to speak,' she added, looking in Shoni's eyes as if she was sure of what she was saying, even though she wasn't.

'Uh huh,' Shoni said, as she nuzzled her daughter's neck. 'Oh,' she said suddenly, 'I didn't take my pill today.' She rushed to the bathroom, jostling her baby, who squealed with laughter.

LaKeesha shook her head as the thin teenager and her baby disappeared. She still wasn't used to how cooperative her sisters had gotten lately. She was fighting with them less and less about homework and birth control pills. And when she checked with the attendance office at their high school, the report was that they had been coming on time. In the months since she'd been working at the bank, they seemed to have mellowed. Angelique and Shoni's room was still a pigsty, and they could get an attitude in a minute, but lately they were responding differently to LaKeesha. 'It's like they respect me more,' she told Hector at work. 'Like, before when I told them to do something, they'd act like I didn't know what I was talking about, but now . . .'

'You the Man,' Hector said, slurring his words in a slangy cadence. The two laughed. 'No,' he said, suddenly solemn, 'it is because you have a job. They know you are responsible.'

But it was more than that, and she knew it. Her sisters had begun changing the day LaKeesha announced to the family that she would no longer be receiving AFDC. Even though she could hear the words coming out of her mouth, they didn't seem quite real. For her entire life, the only money she'd ever depended upon came from the welfare office. It was as if she were changing religions, putting her faith in another god.

'You ain't getting no more checks?' Angelique asked, her eyes bright with amazement.

Then her grandmother said, 'She getting a check from her job.'

'What if you get fired?' Shoni asked. There was fear in her voice.

LaKeesha drew herself up. 'I'm not getting fired. And if I do, I'll get me another job.'

As if to prove her competence, a few months after she'd been working at the bank, LaKeesha came home with a J.C. Penney charge card. Her sisters and grandmother gathered around her to gaze at the small plastic rectangle. The respect and admiration LaKeesha saw in their eyes when they looked at her was almost a kind of worship. There hadn't been a credit card in their home since their grandfather died, nearly fifteen years earlier. His Sears card might as well have been buried with him, because no one else in the family qualified for credit. 'Now we moving forward,' her grandmother said jubilantly.

'I'm the only one who can use this card,' LaKeesha explained, in the same stern tone that Esther had used with her, 'and don't even think about asking me can you use it. And I'm not going crazy with this either. This is mainly to get the kids clothes. If we charge a hundred dollars, the store will charge us about twenty dollars each month, until the bill is paid. And we have to pay interest. If we don't keep up with the payments, they'll take the card away and we won't be able to get any others because I'll have a bad credit report. If I pay the bills on time every month, after a while they'll let us charge more. I'll have a good credit record. Then I can buy a car.' Mother, Shoni, and Angelique's eyes began to dance, and they looked at each other and grinned. LaKeesha didn't want to say that with good credit she could buy a house. That word was too large for her mouth, but it wasn't too big for her mind. Not only did she have a Penney's charge; LaKeesha was also the proud possessor of a checking and savings account.

'Lawdhamercy!' Mother said, when LaKeesha showed her grandmother and sisters her checkbook. For all of LaKeesha's life, the family had transacted their financial business with money orders. They had to pay to have a check cashed. Now, when her two sisters' checks arrived, she deposited them into her account and doled out an allowance to them. She made them save twenty dollars out of each check and posted a running account of their money on the front of the refrigerator. 'You hafta have a goal,' she told them, again echoing Esther.

'I want me some Rollerblades,' Shoni said wistfully.

'How much they cost?' LaKeesha asked.

''Round 'bout sixty dollars.'

'Well, see, in if you save twenty dollars a month, in three months you'll have enough.'

LaKeesha didn't tell them what she was saving for, but sometimes when she was alone, sitting in the bathtub, or when she was in the bed with Man, his soft brown body curled up in a tight ball beside her, she would close her eyes and see the safe place she dreamed about. Flowers. A porch. Clean streets. A real home. Plenty of room for everybody. And sometimes, even when her eyes were still closed, the house would fade away, retreat from her consciousness like a dark shifting cloud. Houses cost so much money, and saving even as much as fifty dollars from each paycheck didn't seem to bring her any closer to buying one.

LaKeesha read her book until her grandmother called her to eat. After dinner, she ran a bath and put all the kids in together. She put plastic bowls and cups in the water and laughed as she watched Man and his cousins splash around. Drying the children and dressing them for bed, she took them into the living room and read them a story from a book she'd gotten from the library. In the background, she could hear shots being fired, from one or two blocks away. The children paid no attention to the noise, and the two girls were asleep before the story was finished; they'd both been sucking on bottles while she was reading. Angelique and Shoni came in and carried their daughters off to bed. But Man was wide awake, his eyes alert. 'Read it again, Mommy,' he said, and she did.

LaKeesha heard footsteps outside the front door. She wasn't expecting anyone. 'Go get in the bed,' she told Man, who immediately began crying. 'Boy, did you hear what I said?'

Man rose reluctantly, sniffling and whimpering as he

walked toward his bedroom. 'Stop crying. I'll be there in a little while,' LaKeesha called.

She was about to turn on the television, when there was a knock at the door. 'Who is it?' she said, trying to peek out the window. The porch light was out, and it was too dark to make out the figure standing there.

'It's King. Open the door.'

LaKeesha hadn't seen King in weeks. Months. She put her cheek against the wood and didn't speak. She could hear him breathing on the other side.

'Keesha, c'mon, girl.'

'No.' She deliberately made her voice sound harsh. He hadn't visited Man for months, and now he had the nerve to think he could just knock on her door and she'd let him in.

'C'mon, girl. You know you wanna open that door.'

LaKeesha visualized him with his lopsided grin. She couldn't keep herself from smiling too. 'No,' she said, but this time the word was softer, a whining invitation.

'Keesha, I wanna see Man. I wanna see my son.'

She felt someone touching her hand. 'Is that my daddy?'

King bellowed through the door. 'Yeah, Man, it's your daddy. Let me in, Keesha. Let me see my son. Quit playing, girl. Shit.'

When LaKeesha looked down at Man, he was crying. She opened the door, and then King was standing inside, filling up the room with his dark, rangy body. There was a long scar on his face, glazed with a keloid that cut into the laugh line on the right side and made his smile seem both happy and dangerous at the same time. She smelled malt liquor as King carried Man over to the couch, sat down, and put him on his knee. Man tugged at the brim of the red baseball cap that was perched on his father's forehead until he had pulled it off, revealing King's short, wiry, uncombed hair. He snatched the hat away from the small boy and placed it on Man's head. 'There ya go, cuz. Gimme five, Man.'

Man obediently held his hand out. When his father's palm lightly touched his, he burst into giggles. LaKeesha stood by the door, her face a hard, still mask.

'Come on over here, girl,' King said. Now that his cap was off, LaKeesha could see his dark, bright eyes. 'I see you trying to look all mean and shit. You ain't fooling no damn body. Know you glad to see me. Ain't she, Man?'

Man glanced at his mother. Then he turned to his father and nodded. King laughed out loud, and Man started giggling. When LaKeesha sat down on the sofa next to them, she was smiling.

The three of them watched television for a while. Man couldn't sit still. He bounced on King's right knee, then climbed onto the other one, squealing with delight as his father jerked his leg up and down, giving Man a roller coaster ride. 'Boy, you gone break my leg,' King said.

'He acts just like you. Crazy,' LaKeesha said. She laughed a little as she watched her son with his father. God, he was so happy. Man had been grinning and laughing ever since King walked through the door. This is the way it should have been, she thought.

After Man drifted off to sleep in his father's arms, King carried him to the bedroom and tucked him in. Once the little boy was under the covers, he rolled into a little ball near the edge. 'He need his own bed,' King said.

'Where are we supposed to put it?' There was an evil edge to LaKeesha's question, and it wasn't lost on King. He pulled several bills from his pocket and handed them to her. 'I know he need some clothes and shit,' he said.

'He needs you,' LaKeesha said quietly. 'Why you don't come around to see him more often?'

'Yeah, yeah. I'ma do that.' He sat on the bed and pulled her down beside him. With her finger she traced the scar on his cheek, remembering, as she always did when she was close to him, the way the blood had spurted out after the rock hit his cheek when they were in ninth grade. Now she glanced at his arms and saw that he had other scars, some she'd never seen before. King reached up, grabbed her fingers, and put them behind his neck. His lips were on hers before she could draw another breath.

'Stop,' she said, pulling away.

His breath was warm against her cheek. 'Who you been giving it to?' he whispered, with just a thin film of anger.

'I been keeping it to myself, okay? It's mine, ain't it?'

'Bitch, you don't wanna kiss me, you ain't gotta kiss me. I ain't begging. Too proud to beg,' he said, grinning.

'You ain't too proud to bed. That's the way the song goes,' she said, laughing, pretending she hadn't heard the word 'bitch,' even though it was hovering in the air like an evil spirit.

'Oh, is that the way it go?' His hand was around her neck, pulling her to him. When she parted her lips, she could taste the Colt 45 on his tongue. It was bitter, like so many of her memories of him. But the deeper she probed, the more familiar the taste and the terrain became. She knew the streets and alleys of King's mouth. She'd memorized his lips, and there was a sweetness in the knowing that forgave everything.

'You still love me, girl, ain't that right?' King whispered.

She had a fleeting sense of running, of racing down narrow alleys, trying to get back to safety, but she kept losing her way. With his strong hand, King was pulling her away from the main road. She was too tired to struggle. LaKeesha put her hands around King's neck. 'Yes,' she said. 'Yes.'

It was after midnight when King left. He gave her another hard kiss at her front door. She watched him walk away without asking him when he was coming back, then leaned against the jamb with her eyes closed.

'Don't you let that boy mess you up again.'

LaKeesha opened her eyes. Annie was sitting on the sofa in the dark. She could hear the liquor in her slurred tones, but she thought she heard something else. 'What did you say?'

But her mother only stared at her, refusing to repeat her words.

LaKeesha was running late when she got to the Clarks' house on Monday morning. When the older woman opened the door, LaKeesha barely had time to give Man a good-bye kiss and a wave. As she raced for the bus stop, she thought about what her mother had said. She was right. King wasn't going to do nothing but bring her down. Calling her a bitch, not even knowing it was an insult. Cussing around Man. Thinking he could go to bed with her anytime he got good and ready. King wouldn't bring her nothing but alleys and gang fights; if she got involved with him, she'd end up with a lifetime of scars. She'd slipped up. She wouldn't make that mistake again.

Waiting on the corner, LaKeesha could see the bus lumbering down Normandie toward he stop. The week she started working, she discovered that Hector lived in her neighborhood. Most days, they wound up riding the same bus, but this morning as she looked around, she didn't see Hector. Unless he'd caught an earlier bus, he was going to be late.

LaKeesha liked Hector. At work he went out of his way to be helpful, always explaining things to her. When they rode together on the bus, they talked about their dreams: how they wanted to move away from their tiny apartments, how they yearned for a room all to themselves. As Hector described the kind of house he wanted – enough space for his entire family – LaKeesha would close her eyes and visualize such a place. She soon realized they wanted the exact same house. Just as the bus slid to a stop in front of her, LaKeesha took one last look down the street. Hector was running toward her, waving; he was less than half a block away. 'Mister, can you wait just a second?' LaKeesha said, as she handed her money to an overweight black bus driver. 'My co-worker is running to catch this bus.'

He looked at LaKeesha without smiling. 'I got a schedule to keep,' he said, closing the bus doors.

Hector reached the bus just as it pulled away. Rain had begun falling, and he didn't have an umbrella. He could see LaKeesha inside, talking to the driver and pointing toward him. She looked angry. As the bus rattled toward the next stop, he took off after it, racing along the sidewalk, dodging the pedestrians in his path. When he looked up, he could see LaKeesha's face in the back window. She was laughing and motioning for him to run faster. Hector laughed too, as he raced down the street. By the time the bus arrived at the next stop, he was standing there waiting.

LaKeesha was still chuckling as Hector made his way down the aisle, past people who were chatting in Spanish, English, Korean, and the lilting patois of Jamaica, before he sat down beside her. The people around them were smiling. 'He's my co-worker,' she said to no one in particular. She handed Hector a small paper bag. When he looked inside, he saw what looked like a piece of orangy-brown pie, wrapped in waxed paper. 'That's some sweet potato pie. Bet your mama doesn't make that, huh?'

He shook his head as he took a bite. Hector wasn't prepared for how light and creamy the pie was. He'd only meant to taste a sample, to save the rest for his lunch, but once he began eating it, he couldn't stop. 'It's good,' he said. 'Thank you.'

LaKeesha grinned at him. She was a woman with a job

and a future, and Hector was part of that, an extension of her happiness. For the first time in her life, she had a co-worker. 'I got your back, homeboy,' LaKeesha said. She extended her hand to his, palm up.

Hector looked at the black woman, his mouth full of pie, his eyes full of questions. His back? Another black-American riddle. He concentrated on the other word, even as he lifted his hand and let his palm graze hers. Her eyes flashed with approval when he touched her skin. *Homeboy.* He let the word reverberate inside his head until it felt permanent and immutable, until the sound of it was as sweet as the pie in his mouth.

21

Kirk woke to the voice of the new chief of police blaring from his radio. He pictured the black man's face and bulky East Coast body as he heard him declare that the Los Angeles Police Department was prepared for any emergency in the wake of the jury's verdict. As groggy as he was, he could feel the same rush of anger he'd experienced the previous evening when he heard the decision announced: of the four police officers two were acquitted; two were going to jail. What a crock, he thought. Two decent cops, just doing their fucking jobs and now they were thrown to the wolves just to appease the homeboys. Karumph! His fist hit the pillow. What the hell was America coming to?

When Kirk looked out his window, he pulled the covers over his head and groaned like a man under the knife. The rain was just another punishment. Jesus! When it rained, Los Angeles was a city full of speeding bullets on wheels. Cars crashed into guardrails and each other with all the precision and none of the grace of hired hit men. He didn't even want to think about the mess that was waiting for him on the 405.

When he finally pulled back the covers minutes later, the first thing he saw was his wife, glaring at him. The sight of her unwashed face, her puffy eyes, framed by a tiny network of scratchy-looking wrinkles, the creases that ran from the edges of her nose to either side of her chin, was more startling than an alarm clock. 'Wha-a-at?' he said, sitting bolt upright. He moved his head back a little and peered into her face.

Jesus.

'You were supposed to bring home half a gallon of milk when you went out yesterday, and obviously you forgot. How are the kids supposed to eat their cereal?'

Kirk flinched. His wife's voice was somewhere between a whine and a shriek, a sound designed not so much to wake the dead as to make them the objects of envy. It had the same effect on Kirk as hearing a nail scraped across a blackboard. He vaguely remembered Sheila saying something about milk yesterday when he was rushing out the door on the way to his office. For the last few weeks, he'd been putting in a few hours at the bank on weekends. My God, it was a wonder he could remember his own name, let alone some damn milk. 'I've had so much on my mind, I just forgot,' he said carefully. 'Can't you make them some eggs or something? I'll pick up the milk after work.'

Sheila's swollen eyes flashed open. 'I'll just tell the kids that their father was too busy working for a bank that demoted him to think about them.' Kirk flinched. Since his return to his old job, Sheila no longer attempted to contain her fury toward him. She stomped out of the bedroom, slamming the door behind her. He glanced across the room at a small desk loaded with a haphazard stack of mostly overdue bills, and his spirits fell even further. He was behind on nearly everything. Collection agents had actually started calling the house. The insistent ringing of the telephone woke him up, interrupted him at dinner and once even during a rare occasion when Sheila consented to make love. Those harassing fiends with their bulldozer mentalities and their drill sergeant voices unnerved Kirk. The voices weren't new to him; he heard them often enough during his childhood. Back then when the phone rang, his father and mother nodded toward him, the eldest of the four children. He recalled how his father whispered each time, 'Tell them we're not here.' While his parents cowered near the door, he talked with the man – it was always a man – on the telephone. He explained slowly and softly, in his eight-, nine-, and ten-year-old voice, that his parents weren't home, that they were out of town. Later, when he spoke to the callers in the deeper tones of a seventeen-year-old, his response was perfunctory and he no longer trembled. He knew how to get rid of them quickly. To hang up and not feel afraid that whoever was on the line would rush right over to reclaim the new television, the dishwasher, the stereo component set, extravagances that his father bought, knowing he couldn't afford them. By then Kirk had sense enough to get out of the room fast after the call ended, to flee and spare himself another painful rendition of what had become his father's customary response. Because if he hesitated, even for a second, he would have to endure, for the millionth time, his father's lament as he wailed about the unfairness of management, the disloyalty of the union, how everyone was against him. Someone else was always to blame for his being out of work, or 'in between jobs,' as he liked to put it. 'I'll fix them. I'll fix them,' his father would mutter ominously. When he was little, these warnings excited Kirk and he waited expectantly for his father to make good on his threats, for the last office that his father worked at to explode and the victimizers to die in agony. But as much as his father moaned and muttered, there were no such explosions. Every once in a while he would bring home a box of paper clips, a ream of paper, an old type-writer. It took Kirk a long time to figure out that these items had been pilfered from some job that had fired his father, that his tiny heap of trinkets was the sum total of his impotent revenge. Kirk's entire childhood was spent pre-cariously poised on the brink of disaster. By the time Kirk finished high school, he vowed that he wouldn't inherit his father's financial insecurity or his cycle of scrimping and saving and splurging. But now the teetering stack of bills in his own room was like a finger pointed at him. It was déjà vu. He'd allowed himself to be seduced by all the bright perishable goodies that he couldn't possibly pay for on a lender's salary. In the weeks when he believed that he would become regional manager, he'd let his hopes outstrip his common sense. The two suits had been only the beginning. After being prudent for so long, he succumbed to profligacy like a drug. He and Sheila ate at expensive restaurants and ordered champagne by the bottle. They went to Vegas and took the kids to Disney World. For a few months Kirk felt like the carefree child he'd never been. He discovered that his father's philosophy – 'Sometimes you just have to risk a little bit, spend a little more than you have, just so you know you're alive' – expressed his sentiments exactly. And then Bailey Reynolds told him the unfortunate news. Very unfortunate, because of course he'd been betting on a favorable outcome. Now his self-indulgences had returned to haunt him, just as his father's had so many years ago.

And yet the hardest part of looking at the tiny desk in the corner wasn't seeing the mountain of bills that he couldn't pay. Perched on top of that intimidating heap of exclamatory missives was something even more painful to view: a follow-up letter from the last job interview he'd had, a rejection written in precise and polite corporatese. Looking at the letter, even from across the room, depressed him, not because the job was such a plum – it wasn't a particularly promising opportunity – but because it was the only interview he'd had that called him back for a second meeting. His only prospect had fallen through. Looking at that letter, Kirk felt his breath cut off. He was stuck at Angel City, trapped in his old office, with his old duties and his new boss. The thought of the elegantly dressed, self-assured black man induced reflections as dark and gloomy as the sky. He could hear Sheila downstairs in the kitchen, flinging pots and slamming down pans. All that noise, and he couldn't smell a thing cooking. At least his wife had a way of expressing all the pent-up hostilities she'd unleashed since his demotion. Kirk's fury was still, churning and burning inside him, seeping out only in his dreams. When he awakened with a start late at night, the only piece of the relentless nightmare that didn't drift away was the part with the gun and the blood-splattered walls. He was always holding the gun. But Kirk knew how to separate nighttime fantasies from daytime realities. David may have gone up against a giant, but after his initial rage subsided somewhat, Kirk realized that, with or without a gun, he was no match for the Goliath on the thirty-fourth floor of Angel City Bank. He wasn't going to shoot anyone. That kind of helter-skelter vengeance had to be acted out in the throes of the purest kind of insanity. Kirk was still angry, but his fury had burned down like a wick on a candle. What was left gave off light, not heat, and revealed that his case would be far better served by the coolest kind of premeditation.

He'd learned about getting revenge the day he flunked out of medical school. When his anatomy professor gave him an F, Kirk knew that the end was near unless he got him to change his mind. He arranged a meeting and explained that he misread the instructions on the final. Wouldn't he please give him another chance? But the professor was adamant: his decision stood, he told Kirk. No amount of persuasion would change his mind. When Kirk insisted on a second meeting, the professor was even colder. He was sorry, but there were standards he had to uphold. 'If you can't make the grade, Mr. Madison, I advise you to find some other avenue for your talents.'

Kirk merely nodded and left, carefully shutting the door behind him after he made sure that the lock was off. It was late in the day – Kirk had chosen that time deliberately – and he waited outside the building until he saw the professor leave. Then he sneaked back into his office and placed a five-pound bag of Colombian dope in the bottom drawer of the desk, under some papers. He called campus security and the head of the department and told them where they could find the marijuana. Kirk kept calling back for days to find out what had happened, but he couldn't get any information. When he asked, none of his former classmates seemed to know anything about the incident. Nearly a year later, though, he learned that the man hadn't gotten tenure; he felt a deep sense of satisfaction.

By the time Kirk drove into the parking lot across the street from the bank, it was raining hard. He recognized two of the tellers, a black woman and a Mexican or something (who could tell these days), walking together under a single umbrella. He couldn't remember either one's name. The black girl was new. The Mexican had been there longer.

While he was parking his car, a Mercedes pulled into a spot across from his. The car was sleek and so highly polished that the beads of rain that appeared on the hood were lined up like rows of diamonds. A foul taste came to Kirk's mouth, a sensation that only intensified when a large black umbrella opened to shield Humphrey Boone as he emerged from behind the wheel. He was wearing a charcoal-gray pin-striped suit. Kirk could see the gold cuff links sparkling just below the jacket, the black leather briefcase with the gold initials. Kirk fought an urge to lunge at the man and seize him by the throat. Arrogant bastard! The way he strode through the bank, acting as if it and everyone in the place belonged to him! Looking at Humphrey Boone, Kirk found it difficult to swallow. He couldn't believe that they were actually paying the man two hundred thousand dollars a year – that's what he'd heard. Two hundred thousand plus bonuses and perks. Kirk felt a slow burning sensation in his chest as he watched Humphrey Boone stride across the street to his office, his plush, newly painted and decorated office. Humphrey held up his arm and smiled at the

316

drivers in the oncoming traffic. Affirmative action bastard, Kirk thought. He wanted one of the cars to run the black man over, smash his body like a toy watch, but the cars stopped and let him pass. Humphrey smiled and crossed the street, nodding like a politician who'd just won the election. The burning in Kirk's stomach flared up again, making him jump a little. As he watched the black man enter the bank, he could feel all of the anger he'd previously directed toward Preston and Bailey swing in Boone's direction like a well-oiled pendulum.

At exactly eight-thirty, Kirk opened the first of several credit reports that had been on his To Do list ever since he'd come back to his old office. A deadening lassitude began engulfing him after his demotion. He was literally unable to accomplish any of the goals he set for himself. The flow chart that he'd created when he returned had not one red check mark. And as each day passed, his torpor seemed to increase. At the rate he was going, he knew his days at the bank were numbered. It was exactly the kind of enervating feeling he'd experienced just before he flunked out of medical school.

At eleven o'clock, Kirk closed the credit report he'd been attempting to read all morning, rose from his desk, shut the door to his office, and turned on his radio. It was preset to the correct station. He turned the volume down low, but loud enough for him to hear the bouncy rhythm-and-blues theme music of the *King Clever Show*. As the wahwah of the acoustical guitar faded, the host's booming voice, even turned down low, seemed to fill every crevice of the small office. 'Amerifriends,' the host began, and Kirk could feel himself believing that he really was with a friend. 'This country was founded on the principles of hard work, fair play, and just rewards. That's what made America a great nation. Americans meet on a level playing field. This is a nation where anyone can succeed if they work hard enough. And yet I'm telling you, Amerifriends, we are being held up at gunpoint by set-asides and affirmative action. There are people in this great country of ours who expect to get pref-er-ential treatment because of the color of their skin. This generation should not be expected to atone for the sins of our forefathers. If indeed they sinned. Huhhuhuhuhuhuh.' His heavy chortles warmed Kirk's heart, and he found himself joining in. It was what Kirk wanted to hear. It was what he needed to hear. For the first time all day, Kirk began to feel good, to feel understood. 'Amerifriends, as a nation, we've got to take the bull by the horns and make America great again.' As King Clever spoke, Kirk had a vision of a large bull, draped in an American flag, approaching a magnificent hilltop. He closed his eyes, and he could see himself riding that bull, charging up the hill.

'Amerifriends, we've got to seize the day! Take back what we've lost! Let this administration know that we don't want quotas and set-asides and affirmative action. That's not the American way!'

Kirk could feel a surge of excitement pulsating through his body. Take back what we've lost! King Clever was speaking to him. He had certainly lost something!

'Kirk, muhboy,' King Clever said, his voice taking on a conspiratorial whisper, 'only you can do it.' Kirk looked around the room. He actually felt another presence. 'If you want your job back, if you want the position that is yours by all that's holy, then, by God, muhboy, you've got to muster up some of that good ole American willpower and take control of the situation. Y'know what I mean?'

Kirk felt himself nodding. The voice around him was so soothing, so understanding. And then it dawned on Kirk that what he was listening to was the voice of God.

'Only you can send a message to this misguided administration and let the President know that the real Americans want our country back!' King Clever was louder now, and the words seemed to echo in Kirk's ear. 'Do you hear me, Kirk, muhboy?'

'Yes,' Kirk whispered. It was God, he was sure of it.

'You can get the job you deserve. It's the darn system that's punishing white men like you. Don't you take it lying down! You are going to fight as an American for what's rightfully yours, aren't you?'

'Yes.'

Kirk looked around. King Clever's voice suddenly boomed out of the stillness with a hypnotic urgency. 'And by the way, Kirk, do you have a copy of my book?'

Before he could answer, there was a knock at the door. Kirk looked up and shook his head a little. He felt as though he were waking up from a dream, and it took him a second before his wits fully returned. He turned off the radio and opened the credit report that he'd been working on. 'Come in,' he called out.

Mallory was puzzled. She could have sworn that she heard Kirk's voice before she opened the door. But there was no one in there with him. Kirk appeared to be studying his credit reports. 'Oh,' she said, feeling a little self-conscious. 'I thought someone was in here with you. Are you ready for the meeting?'

Kirk gave her a blank look.

'The lenders have a meeting with Humphrey Boone in a few minutes. Did you forget?' Of course he'd forgotten, she thought, staring at the chaos on his desk. Ever since he'd been sent back to lending, Kirk had become a basket case. She'd never been particularly close to Kirk, but he'd been given such a raw deal; she did feel sorry for him. Mallory watched silently as he slowly began to gather up his credit reports, depositing them in his battered leather briefcase, which was as scuffed as an old pair of shoes. 'I don't think you need to bring anything, Kirk, except maybe a notepad and a pencil.' He looked a little disheveled. She started to suggest that he do something with his hair.

God, Kirk thought, when he caught Mallory's pained expression, I must look really awful. He reached in his back pocket and took out a comb and rearranged his hair with a few quick strokes. He straightened his tie, put on his jacket, and squared his shoulders. He had to seize the day, claim the power, right the wrong. Mallory smiled at him, a beautiful smile full of compassion, kindness, and blinding light. 'Ready?' she asked.

'Yes.'

The meeting was in the conference room on the ground floor, behind the loan department. Mallory and Kirk slipped in quietly and took seats near the door. A few minutes later, Humphrey stood in front of the table. The lenders were gathered around him like a squadron of attentive privates facing their commanding officer. Except for Humphrey, everyone in the room was white. Kirk watched as Humphrey studied the people around him and then flashed a quick, penetrating smile. 'I'd like to welcome you this morning. This meeting will be brief. I know we've all got lots of work to do.

'As you know, the Minority Loan Program will be officially implemented on Friday. Since you lenders will be on the front lines, I wanted everyone to have a complete understanding of why the program was started, what it entails, and what your duties will be regarding it.'

Kirk listened as Humphrey droned on. 'I'm going to make this short and sweet. Fewer than three percent of all the home loans that we grant are given to minorities; fewer than six-tenths of a percent of all the business loans go to minorities. The Community Reinvestment Act people are breathing down our necks because of the low rate of investment in the surrounding communities. Folks, there are going to be some changes around here, and we're going to start with attitudes.'

Humphrey spoke for about twenty minutes, spelling out all the details of the program. When he had finished, he answered questions, none of which were as hostile as the thoughts of those who posed them.

'Mallory, would you stay for a few minutes?' Humphrey said as everyone was leaving. 'I'd like to talk with you about the Diversity Program.'

Kirk watched as Mallory walked to the front of the room. He'd never noticed how well defined her body was. Her legs were like a racer's, the muscles smooth and tight. He saw that Humphrey was looking at her, smiling as she came toward him, smiling when she reached him, smiling when he pulled out the chair nearest him and she sat down.

As Kirk watched them, he was frowning.

22

Preston Sinclair was nervous. The harsh megawatt light-bulbs in the makeup room of the network affiliate glared in his eyes and made him squint. 'Are you going to keep your glasses on or off?' the young makeup artist who was powdering his face asked him. She was leaning over him, and her small breasts poked into his neck every time she moved. She was very thin and waifish. Her dark hair was cut in a rather severe bob, and she smelled like roses almost everywhere except under her arms, which were raised just above Preston's twitching nose and exuded not so much an odor as the aura of sweaty men engaged in hard labor.

It had never occurred to him to take off his glasses. Why would he want to? he wondered aloud.

'Well, you ought to think about it,' the young woman said. She moved back a step so that she could examine her work. 'I mean, sometimes there's a glare with glasses.' She leaned forward a little and lifted Preston's glasses off his face. 'If you decide not to wear them, I'd better put some makeup under your eyes. Your bags are pretty bad.' She studied him in silence for a moment, then reached behind her and grabbed a tube of flesh-colored makeup. 'Maybe I'd better fix them up anyway.' She applied a dot of the foundation under his eyes, then took a little sponge and began dabbing at the makeup. She stood back again. 'That's better.' She handed Preston his glasses. 'I'm finished. You can go wait in the green room. Out that door and take a left. Second door on the right.'

The waiting room was empty. Preston sat down on the

sofa, trying to calm himself down. He looked at his watch. In less than seven minutes he would be on national television. His heart was racing in his chest. Relax, relax, he told himself. You'll be fine, just fine. All he had to do was talk about the Diversity Program and the Minority Loan Program and the fact that he'd hired Humphrey Boone to spearhead both. He took deep breaths.

Two days earlier, he'd been ecstatic when a producer for *Evening Conversation*, the highest-rated late-night news talk show in the country, called his office and asked him to be a guest. 'We're doing a program on how companies are responding to diversity in the workplace, and we've heard about some of the innovative ideas that are taking place at your bank. We'd like you to come on and share your thoughts with our audience,' the producer said. Preston agreed immediately. When he hung up the phone, he felt as though he'd just drunk three cups of strong black coffee. National exposure! The potential benefits were enormous.

As the clock inside the green room ticked away the minutes, Preston felt more and more like bolting. He was absolutely sure that he was going to make a fool of himself. He could feel his heart beating. 'Mr. Sinclair.' Preston looked up. An aide was standing by his side. 'It's show time,' the man said with a grin.

Oh, God.

The studio was freezing and was empty except for two surly-looking cameramen. The show originated in New York, and the other guests, a noted sociologist, a senator, and the president of the Urban Institute, as well as the host, were in the East Coast studio. Preston was being hooked in via satellite. The cameramen nodded at him, and for a moment he felt calm, reassured by how ordinary and working class the men appeared. They reminded him of his father's friend when he was a boy in Indiana. Their faces looked sallow under the bright studio lights, and Preston wondered if his skin was that same sickly yellow. The thin cameraman slipped a tiny microphone under Preston's suit coat and pinned it to his lapel. 'Now, you're going to look right into that monitor. That's where Martin Kirkland and the other guests will be,' the cameraman said. 'Don't worry about the camera; it will find you.' At the mention of the host, an aging Ken Doll look-alike whose name was synonymous with impeccable articulation, unflappable calm, and an IQ that was seemingly higher than God's, the reality of what Preston was about to do, the enormity of it, hit him again. He wasn't prepared, he thought in a panic. All Kirkland had to do was throw him one curve ball – and he was known for doing that – and Preston would wind up looking like a fool. No press was better than bad press; that was a cardinal rule. It wasn't too late; he could still back out. He could say he didn't feel well. He did feel sick and light-headed. Preston had his hand on the body mike and was looking around for exits, when suddenly the makeup moppet appeared in front of him, a powder puff in her hand. Before he could say anything, she removed his glasses. 'Let me get rid of the shine,' she said. She gave him a curious look and then smiled benevolently. 'Don't be nervous. There's nothing to this.' Then she leaned over and dabbed powder on his forehead and nose. One whiff of her armpits, and Preston sat straight up, his eyes wide open. Forward, he thought. 'Good luck,' she whispered as she disappeared.

'Ten, nine, eight, seven . . . ,' the cameraman said solemnly. Preston stared straight into the monitor.

'Good evening,' Kirkland said from the New York studio. 'The American economy is in the doldrums, and the American workforce is on the brink of change. Tonight we're going to explore diversity in America's workplace. We'll be joined in this discussion . . .'

Preston listened as the host rattled off the names of the

324

guests and smiled when he heard his own. 'Mr. Sinclair, let's start with you. Your bank has recently implemented a Diversity Program. Would you tell us what it's designed to do.'

Preston leaned forward in his seat. He felt clearheaded and alert, as if he'd just come from a cool dip in his swimming pool. There wasn't a trace of the nervousness that had dogged him earlier. This was an opportunity, a business opportunity. He wasn't about to squander it. 'I'd be delighted to,' he said with a smile.

From Martin Kirkland's first question, Preston was in control, so smooth and articulate he couldn't believe that just minutes earlier he'd been overwrought. He smiled. He laughed. And he cut off the other guests in midsentence with such suave ruthlessness that even the host appeared impressed. He played *Evening Conversation* right down the middle, presenting himself as a pragmatic businessman who saw that the hand that was writing on America's wall was getting browner and had to be acknowledged. He condemned quota plans but said that he hired 'carefully selected people with the highest level of competency' from a diverse group of candidates. 'America can ill afford a workforce that either excludes or includes solely because of color,' he said.

'That was good, what you said,' the makeup artist whispered when she dusted him with powder during the commercials. Preston beamed.

Preston sailed through the second half of *Evening Conversation*. His appearance was a triumph – and a harbinger of many more to come. When he left the studio, he felt that he was on the verge of something great.

That first show was the beginning of Preston's romance with the media. The following day he received a telephone call from another talk show. The next week the *Gazette* contacted him, asking if he would be interested in writing

325

an editorial. And then, several weeks after *Evening Conversation*, Preston received a call from his good friend Dan Wilkerson, a mover and shaker in the Republican National Committee. 'We haven't talked in quite a while,' Dan said amiably. 'I just thought I'd say hello. I've been seeing you on television and hearing about your work. Very impressive.'

'Thank you,' Preston said smoothly.

'Yes, indeed. A lot of people have their eyes on you, Preston. Just thought you'd like to know that. How's the family?'

'Everyone is fine. And yours?'

'Oh, fine. Just fine. Listen, gotta run. Let's do lunch soon.'

Juggling his new media schedule was time-consuming. Writing the editorial took three days, and he began to have to set aside time in the mornings to conduct interviews with various reporters so that they could see the bank in operation. To make up for the lost time, Preston worked later in the evenings. Some nights he didn't get home until after ten. The long hours didn't tire him at all; in fact, he found them invigorating. But there were moments, when his adrenaline was flowing and his mind was racing and he knew that he was winning, when he felt an emptiness engulf him that he couldn't comprehend.

Claire was usually asleep when he got in, but sometimes she woke up as he was climbing into bed. Some nights he felt her fingers brush against him; he heard her soft sighs. But his mind was too crowded with thoughts of the mountains he was scaling to respond to her subtle entreaties. He nudged her gently to her side of the bed and watched as she wrapped her empty arms around herself.

One evening in the last week in April, when the rainstorms were beginning to taper off and the night air was warmer, Dan Wilkerson called Preston moments before he was about to leave his office. He'd been calling a lot lately, and this chat was no different from the others. They mostly talked about politics. But just before he hung up, Dan said, 'There are some very important people who feel that you could help shape the future of this state, Preston.'

'Well, I take that as a compliment, Dan,' Preston said easily.

'I just thought you'd like to know that your name has come up quite a bit,' he said.

'Oh?' Preston said. 'In what way?'

'As a potential candidate for state office. Are you interested?'

'Depends on the position,' Preston said smoothly.

'Name it.'

Preston chuckled.

'I'm serious. Listen, I realize that this is awfully short notice, but a group of us are meeting tomorrow night in the penthouse at the Wilshire Arms. We'd like for you to come. It's what we call a strategy session. The lieutenant governor may drop by.'

'What time?' He looked at his calendar. He and Claire were supposed to go out to dinner at seven tomorrow.

'Seven.'

'I'll be there,' he said.

Preston was humming as he opened the front door to his house. He was expecting the usual dim lights that signified that Claire had retired for the evening, but to his surprise the house was as brilliantly lit up as the noonday sky. As Preston closed the door, he could hear a commotion of footsteps and doors slamming and high-pitched shrieks. He bounded up the stairs two at a time and ran into the bedroom. Claire was crying hysterically, while she and the maid shoved clothes into a suitcase that lay open on the bed. 'What is it? What is it?' Preston asked, rushing to her. He put his hands on her arms and shook his wife gently. 'Darling, what is it?'

She put her arms around him, but her body was jerking

so hard he could barely hold her. 'Oh, God. Oh, God. Pres was in a car accident. He's in intensive care. There's a plane in an hour.'

Preston held on to Claire, and he felt her crumple. An accident, he thought, the words dancing in his brain. Pres is hurt.

Claire held her stomach, as though she were trying to absorb a blow to her body. 'We've got to pack,' she said.

He looked at her without speaking. She saw his hesitation, and her eyes narrowed. 'You are coming, aren't you, Preston?'

They arrived in New Haven the next morning. A nurse was waiting for them at the intensive care unit. 'Stay right here,' she said quietly. She disappeared down a long, quiet corridor, and when she returned, a tall man with blond hair, wearing a white jacket, was with her.

He extended his hand. 'Mr. and Mrs. Sinclair, I'm Dr. Patterson. I want to warn you: your son is in bad shape. He's bruised and swollen. Can you handle that? Can your wife?'

'We want to see him,' Preston said.

The sight of Pres, his puffy face nearly twice its size, the skin under his eyes black and blue, a lump on his head as big as an egg, tubes attached to his nose, an IV in his arm, made Preston take in a breath that he had trouble exhaling. 'Oh, my God,' he said. Claire began crying and buried her head in his chest. Preston held on to his wife to keep her from falling.

'Mr. and Mrs. Sinclair, I'm going to have to ask you to calm down. Your son has obviously been very badly hurt. He's in a coma right now. His legs are broken. His left wrist and elbow are broken, and he's fractured several ribs. He has a concussion. We're running some tests now to see if there's internal damage, specifically brain damage. There is

328

a possibility that his spleen is bruised. There may be internal bleeding. At this point we're not sure about paralysis.'

'What do you mean?' Preston asked. Claire's moan was muffled against her husband's chest.

The doctor measured his words very carefully. 'We want to see if your son is still able to walk, Mr. Sinclair. We'll have to run some tests.'

Claire bent down over the bed and kissed a spot on Pres's forehead. She touched his shoulder lightly. 'Honey, Mommy's here,' she whispered.

Preston put his arms around Claire and closed his eyes. He bowed his head. 'Don't take him, Lord. Please don't take him.' When he looked up, Claire's round eyes were filled with silent wonder. He felt a deep calm enveloping him.

They sat in the waiting room for an hour. Preston went to the vending machine and brought them back awful-tasting coffee, which they sipped in silence. Claire's head was bowed. Preston thought she was asleep until he saw her lips moving rapidly. He thought about the television show and remembered the political meeting Dan had set up for this evening. A feeling of suspended animation seeped into his bones. He should get up and telephone his office, but he just couldn't summon the strength to make the call. Fatigue and sadness wrestled inside him. To his surprise, a tear rolled down his cheek. And then another. He lifted the cup of coffee to his lips, but his hand was shaking so badly that he put it down.

'Surely goodness and mercy . . .' Scraps of psalms and other Bible verses he hadn't thought of in years filled Preston's mind as the slow hours passed in the waiting room. 'They that wait on the Lord . . .'

'Mr. and Mrs. Sinclair.'

They stood up and faced the doctor. He was smiling. 'I have good news for you. Your son regained consciousness about ten minutes ago.' Claire let out a little sliver of a laugh. 'There is no paralysis and there doesn't appear to be any brain damage. We're still checking his spleen.' Claire reached for him, and Preston put his arm around her shoulders and hugged her. 'But,' the doctor said solemnly, 'the break on his right leg is much worse than we thought. He's going to need one, possibly two, operations and then extensive physical therapy. It will take months before he regains the use of that leg completely. But we can talk about that later. Would you like to see your son for a few minutes?'

Preston and Claire rushed into the room. Pres's swollen eyes were open, and when he saw them he smiled weakly. 'Hello, sweetheart. Everything is going to be all right,' Claire said. 'We've spoken with the doctors, and there's no internal damage. You're not paralyzed. There's nothing to worry about.'

'Dad? Is that you, Dad?' Pres's faint voice was filled with surprise; his fingers groped toward his father.

Preston took the boy's hand and squeezed. 'I'm right here, son. I'm right here.'

They stayed a few minutes more, and then the nurse stuck her head in the door and motioned for them to leave. 'We've got to go, darling,' Claire said. 'You need rest. We'll be back tomorrow.'

Robbie flew into the city the next morning. Pres underwent surgery early that afternoon, and several hours later the doctor declared it successful. Preston, Claire, and Robbie spent the entire next day and most of the evening by Pres's side. Sitting in the room, listening to his wife and sons talk, Preston felt himself yearning at times for the security and detachment of his work at the bank. His son's face was still swollen and bruised, and every time Preston looked at the deepening purple shadows under his eyes, the gashes across his cheeks and forehead, he'd feel a quickening in his heart. Claire and Robbie talked and laughed, seemingly oblivious to Pres's wounds. Preston longed to be part of the intimate rhythms of the conversation that swirled around him, but it seemed always to be just over his head, just out of reach. 'I'm going to get a cup of coffee,' he told them. But when he went outside, he simply leaned against the wall and breathed deeply, listening to his wife and Robbie talk. For the second time in two days, Preston cried.

Later that evening, when Preston and Claire were in their hotel room, preparing for bed, he said to her, 'I think I'll leave in the morning. I'll arrange for the physical therapy, and when Pres is able, you can both fly back home.'

In his mind, everything was settled. The crisis had passed. The surgery had been successful and his son's spleen was undamaged. He was of no use to Claire or Pres. It was time for things to go back to normal. He would earn the money, and Claire would attend to the children and keep the home fires burning. That was their arrangement. Back in Los Angeles, he wouldn't have to deal with the trembling fear that made him weep. At the bank, there were no emotional sucker punches. He went to the closet, took out his suitcase, and laid it on the bed. To his surprise, Claire walked over to the bed and angrily shoved the bag to the floor. 'What are you doing?' he asked in amazement.

'My God, Preston. He is your child too.' She spat the words out and then sat down on the edge of the bed. She looked utterly drained.

For a moment, Preston was too stunned to answer. In all their years together, she'd never spoken to him with such anger. 'I don't know how to do this,' he said, before he stopped to think.

Claire stood up and walked over to him. She circled her fingers around his wrist and squeezed until he winced. 'We just need you to be with us, even if your mind is a million miles away. Can you do that?'

Preston hesitated. 'I'll try,' he said.

As he lay in bed, he began praying softly to himself. The words seemed to flow from him effortlessly. He felt an enormous sense of power, and at the same time he felt a serenity he hadn't known in years.

He stayed four additional days. For most of that time, he sat in the hospital room, fidgeting and trying not to think about all the work that he needed to be doing. He tried to at least listen to his wife and Robbie as they spoke, and once or twice he joined in. Several times they laughed together at some joke, and even Pres managed a weak smile.

On the third evening, Robbie stayed with Pres while Claire and Preston went to dinner. After the meal, they returned to their hotel room. While Claire took a shower and washed her hair, Preston sat on the bed, leafing through the Gideon Bible that he found in the drawer of his nightstand. As he read through the Acts, he heard his father's voice, pious and sincere. He thought of his son, his body stiff and bruised, but alive. 'Thank you, God,' he said aloud. He began weeping.

He looked up when Claire came into the room. The sight of his wife's damp nakedness, her wet golden hair glistening, surprised him. He hadn't really looked at her closely in a long time. 'Come here,' he said. Claire sat down on the edge of the bed. She put her hands around his neck. He felt the weight of her as she began crying softly into his chest.

Later, when they were in bed, she was still clinging to him, holding on with an intensity she'd not shown in years. Preston felt a ferocious wetness when he entered her. He kept his eyes open the entire time they were making love. And so he was aware of the precise moment that his wife's face flushed in ecstasy.

Preston flew back to Los Angeles the next day. The bank seemed like a foreign city to him; the frenetic pace was strangely jarring. His assistants seemed to hover about, scarcely giving him enough air to breathe. Every decision demanded his immediate attention. There were several messages from television and radio talk shows. He could feel the adrenaline in his body attempting to surge, but he simply couldn't muster up the energy he needed to be excited. He told his assistant to inform all the media that he was overbooked at present, to please call back at a later time.

Dan Wilkerson contacted him after three days. 'The committee's still anxious to meet with you,' he said.

Each word felt like a brick going into a satchel that Preston was carrying. 'Right now isn't a good time, Dan. My son was involved in a terrible car accident. He'll be coming home soon, and I'm in the midst of making arrangements for his physical therapy.'

'Sorry to hear that,' Dan said. 'I'll call you in a few weeks.'

By the time he met with Bailey Reynolds toward the close of his first day back, a kind of luxuriant lethargy was settling over Preston, immobilizing him in ways that were completely uncharacteristic, almost unimaginable. As Bailey gave him a rundown of the major activities that had taken place in his absence, he sensed a kind of dislocation emanating from the president. There was something weakened about the man sitting across from him. His sharp bird's nose smelled opportunity wafting in the air. He smiled broadly.

'And how is Humphrey Boone making out?' Preston asked.

Bailey's smile disappeared. 'I think it's still too early to tell,' he said solemnly. 'Perhaps . . .' His brow was furrowed and his expression was troubled.

'What?' Preston asked.

Bailey smiled. He waved his hand. 'Let's just give him a bit more time. This is your first day back. Let's not load you down too much.' Today was a day for planting seeds, he thought. Not harvesting crops.

Preston gave Bailey a grateful smile. The truth was, he couldn't have absorbed anything specific at that moment. Jet lag was kicking in, and his head had begun to ache. 'You're right. Thank you. We'll get together tomorrow. Lunch at noon in the conference room. And I'd like you to set up a separate lunch for me with Humphrey, the earliest available slot.'

'Fine,' Bailey said. 'Glad to have you back.'

But Preston wasn't glad to be back. The next day he overslept. When he woke up and saw that it was after seven o'clock – he usually rose at five-thirty – he visualized himself getting up, showering, dressing, and arriving at the office, but he didn't do any of that immediately. Instead, he sank back under the covers and stared at the ceiling for a good fifteen minutes before he moved a muscle. And when he did stir, it wasn't to rush into the shower. He walked languidly into the adjoining sitting room, pulled down picture albums, and began flipping through them, gazing at photographs of his sons when they were young. The two small boys playing in the snow in Indiana were like strangers to him. He couldn't remember ever having seen the red snowsuits they wore. There were certain shots where he didn't even recognize their faces, pictures he had to look at again and again to make himself remember. He put the album away and got back into bed. There was a Bible on the nightstand. He turned to the Book of Acts.

He didn't make it into the office that day until eleven o'clock. A smiling Bailey was standing by the door when he walked in.

Several weeks later, Preston met Claire and Pres at the airport. Pres emerged from the plane in a wheelchair. The sight of the boy being pushed along by a skycap, while Claire walked behind him, unnerved Preston. All the while he was waiting for them to return, Preston had envisioned his son as strong and healthy. But Pres appeared frail, and the scabs that covered his face made him look even more unwell. Preston waved as he walked toward them. His son smiled, and for an instant he thought he saw traces of the exuberant little boy in the red snowsuit. He's going to get better, he told himself. As Preston kissed his wife with a warmth that made her blush, and then lightly patted Pres's shoulder, he filled his mind with that thought until there was no space for any other.

23

Preston and Humphrey walked the block to the penthouse restaurant, part of the La Jolla Club, Preston's private club. The early spring weather was cool, and the sun was bright; Humphrey was grateful for the crisp air. Between coming into the bank on weekends, working on the private placement deals he was trying to set up, and trying to put out the fires that constantly raged in the lives of his family, he hadn't had a chance to get out and enjoy himself. Now, as he felt the breezes against his cheek, he made a mental note to try to schedule a tennis game for the weekend.

Humphrey had been to the club before, but the elegance of the turn-of-the-century architecture, the opulence of the dark, rich mahogany-paneled walls, the beauty of the heavy Oriental rugs, the lushness of the huge urns filled with exotic flowers, the richness of the rare paintings and tapestries that covered the walls, the deference of the staff, with their Yessirs, Nosirs, and quick smiles, were always impressive. Preston introduced him to several of the distinguished-looking gentlemen who were having drinks at the bar in the corner of the room. Humphrey saw two board members from his previous bank. He tapped them on their backs, and when the men turned around and saw him, their eyes contained the startled, almost frightened looks that Humphrey knew so well. He could have predicted that surprise and fear, yet both still had the power to offend and enrage him. But he smiled quickly, extended his hand, and said, 'Humphrey Boone,' and the light of recognition immediately displaced the fear as the unknown black man and possible assailant became someone they knew, someone safe. They clapped him heartily on his back and declared how wonderful it was to see him, and then Humphrey took them over and introduced them to Preston. They chatted or a few minutes, lacing their farewells with such sincere goodwill that Humphrey almost forgave them. Almost.

White folks sure know how to live, he said to himself, as he glanced around the magnificent lobby. For of course, the hallowed halls of the La Jolla Club were for all practical purposes the almost exclusive province of white males, although immediately after the civil unrest of April 29, the first black member, the owner of a chain of parking lots throughout the city, was inducted. But as Humphrey seated himself at a table in the penthouse restaurant, he was very much aware, as was everyone else in the club, that he was the only black person in the room, other than two rather decrepit waiters.

'This is the best place in the city for veal,' Preston said, as both men looked out the window next to their table. Below them the people appeared to Humphrey like so many bright specks, jewels set into a gigantic, sparkling pendant. But instead of seeing people, Preston saw his son's swollen, bruised face. He saw his son hobbling on one limb, dragging his injured leg as he grimaced and groaned. Preston drew his hand to his mouth and bit down on his index finger. He looked over at Humphrey, who was staring at him uneasily. 'So,' Preston said a bit too loudly, 'I've been hearing great things about you. Tell me about the private placement deals you've lined up.'

Humphrey leaned slightly forward and peered at Preston. On the several occasions when he'd been with the president, he was usually on guard, monitoring his language, gestures, and references, making sure that he didn't offend in any way. He was careful not to say anything that could be construed as angry, belligerent, or militant, because that kind of behavior, even a hint of it, made white folks nervous. Humphrey was tuned in to every smile and facial tic of the powerful white man he was with, because his survival depended upon his clear-sighted interpretation of everything that crossed Preston Sinclair's mind.

Looking at the president, Humphrey realized that something was slightly off. The few times he'd been with Preston, he filled the room with his bigger-than-life energy. The man sitting across from him seemed shrunken somehow.

Preston could feel the younger man's enthusiasm as he launched into a neat rundown of the many aspects of the deals he'd created. 'The beauty of it is that I've already got several insurance companies lined up. They're all anxious to participate; it's just a matter of getting the right terms.'

'I understand that the terms will be quite lucrative for Angel City,' Preston said.

'If things go the way I think they should, we're looking at approximately one point seven million dollars' profit. More importantly, these deals will put Angel City squarely up front with the rest of the players in the private placement market. They serve to put everyone on notice that there's a new kid on the block. And, Mr. Sinclair, I want you to know that your reputation makes my job so much easier.' The praise slid off his tongue easily, but his tone reflected the sincerity that propelled it. He had to admit that Preston Sinclair was well connected and highly respected.

Preston heard the compliment, but he couldn't feel it. 'Thank you,' he said. He started to say that he was pleased to have Humphrey on the Angel City team, but he hesitated. He didn't want to sound paternalistic. They didn't like that. Just as he was about to speak, an attendant appeared and handed him a cellular phone. 'There's a call for you, Mr. Sinclair.'

Humphrey said, 'I'll just excuse myself,' and began to

stand. Preston motioned for him to sit down. Cupping his hand over the receiver, he said, 'This will just be a minute, I'm sure.' But then Claire came on the telephone, and she was crying.

'Darling, what's wrong?'

In the midst of her loud wailing, he heard the word 'surgery'. Everything around him went hazy.

Humphrey watched as Preston's cheeks began to sag and his eyes stared straight ahead without focusing on anything. Again he started to rise. This time he felt Preston's fingers grip his wrist. One look in his hollow eyes, and Humphrey knew that it was the act of a blind man, reaching out for something steady.

'Calm down,' Preston said. 'Calm down, darling.' He was aware of movement across the table from him, but everything and everyone around him had become dim. For a moment, he couldn't catch his breath or speak. He had a sense of holding on to something. 'What are you saying? What are you saying?'

But Claire could only sob out a jumbled response that he couldn't comprehend. She was hysterical. He knew that she wanted him to come home, but she wouldn't ask him. He felt guilty for not offering.

'All right. All right,' he said. He didn't ask pertinent, pointed questions but allowed himself to get caught up completely in his wife's frenzied emotions, which wasn't his style. Emotions didn't make good business sense. Not at all. But above all else, he wanted Claire to stop crying. I should leave, he thought, just go home. But his body seemed frozen. He was afraid to go home. Scared of what he'd find. Frightened of what it might mean to become a man who went home in the middle of a business day just because his wife was crying. 'You'll be all right, darling. Have a cup of tea. Stop crying.' When he switched off the telephone, he still felt as though he were with her, and it took a full minute for his heart to calm down, for everything around him to come into clear focus, and when it did, he realized that his fingers were wrapped tightly around Humphrey Boone's wrist. 'I'm sorry,' Preston said, withdrawing his hand. 'I . . . uh . . . where were we?'

'Are you all right, Mr. Sinclair?' Humphrey asked. His wrist felt a little sore where Preston had squeezed it. Preston looked pale and suddenly much older, really haggard. Humphrey had never noticed the deep circles under his eyes before. Droplets of perspiration were collecting near his hairline. His gaze seemed to be focused at some point in space. When he looked into the white man's eyes, Humphrey saw trouble etched in the creases around his eyes, in the sharp deep line between his eyebrows, the kind of trouble he'd been raised on. 'Are you all right?' he repeated. The man looked as if he could have a heart attack at any minute.

'No,' Preston said, 'I'm not.' He sighed wearily. It was the middle of a workday and he was conducting business and his cardinal rule was never to discuss personal matters at work. If the truth be told, Preston rarely engaged in an intimate conversation. 'My son, the older boy, Pres, was hurt badly in a car accident several weeks ago. He almost died.' Preston spoke haltingly, as though the words he was speaking were coming through a pipe that was rusty from disuse. As he began to speak, he realized that except for Claire and Robbie and the doctors, he hadn't discussed his son's medical condition with anyone. 'He was in a hospital back East for a while before we brought him home for physical therapy. It's not going well. My wife is very upset. She was always so self-sufficient.' He said that last as though the very idea of Claire being needy was a concept he couldn't quite grasp.

'It's not every day your child almost dies,' Humphrey said, hoping he was saying the correct thing. He smiled sympathetically. 'I'm sure he'll be all right. He's young. How old?'

'Twenty-two.'

'At that age, they still have Jell-O for bones. He'll mend. When I was twenty-four, I broke my back. I was painting the second floor of my mother's house, and I fell off the ladder. They told my mother that I'd be in a body cast for six months. I was out in less than three and back on the basketball team in four. Did he play sports in school?'

Preston hesitated. The balls of his son's childhood, small and white, orangy pigskin, round and hard, whizzed back and forth across his mind, but he couldn't place them. They were just so many catches, passes, and baskets that he'd never seen played, so many games missed. His mind fastened on the hard white ball. 'He plays tennis very well. He's on his college team. He talked about becoming pro, although frankly we discouraged that.'

'Then he's in shape. Being in shape counts a lot when the body is trying to heal. He'll be all right.'

'I haven't seen him play tennis in a long time,' Preston blurted out. The words seemed to accuse him of something. He lowered his head. 'I missed a lot of his games when he was growing up. His mother went,' he said in a barely audible voice.

The two of them were silent. A thin Latino waiter came over, but Humphrey waved him away. He didn't know how to read the president's sudden personal revelations. He still seemed pale and strangely lethargic. 'Well, my mom was the one who came to my games too,' he said smoothly. He added, 'My dad was, uh, too busy working.'

Preston searched Humphrey's face. 'Did you hold that against him?'

'No,' Humphrey said quickly. 'He had to make the money. I understood that. He made sure that my sisters and brother and I had everything that we needed. We never

341

wanted for anything.' When Humphrey tried to swallow, his throat was sore, as though the words had scraped it raw.

'My father wasn't around much either,' Preston said, 'although his absence didn't result in material comforts for our family. He was a minister. Always out and about, doing good. Every Saturday morning, he wrote his sermon. In the spring and summer, when he was finished, he'd take us kids for ice cream. When it was cold, we'd go for hot chocolate. Boy, we were a happy little band of ragamuffins.' Preston's laughter rose like the notes of a trombone and then faded. Humphrey watched as he stared off into space. 'My God,' Preston said. 'We had absolutely nothing, and we didn't even know it.'

'When it's really nothing, you know it,' Humphrey said, and instantly regretted his words. He knew he sounded bitter and angry. He tried to cover up his emotions with a smile so broad that he thought his lips were going to crack.

But Preston seemed too lost in thought to have even heard his words, let alone picked up the tone. 'We lived in a very small town in Indiana. Parkerville. The entire business district was only two blocks. The drugstore where we got the ice cream and hot chocolate was on Main Street. Parsons' Drugstore.' Preston let out a laugh. 'We made quite a little procession going down the street. Every few feet, someone would stop and greet my father. Everyone knew Reverend Sinclair. He was so well respected. People loved him.'

'Preachers' kids are usually pretty wild, aren't they?'

'In a town of forty-five hundred people, it's hard to sow wild oats. That had to wait until I left for school, but yes, I did make up for lost time.'

'Do you get back home much?' Humphrey asked, interrupting Preston's reverie.

'No. My parents are deceased. My brothers and sisters are scattered all over. I haven't been back in years. I should have taken the boys back there more often,' he said. 'They visited when they were small, but when we moved out here, they stopped going. I should have kept the connections stronger. They don't know their roots.'

'Well,' Humphrey said, 'it's never too late to find your roots.'

They both chuckled a little. The two separate sounds knotted together as tightly as a handshake.

Preston's shoulders eased down a bit, and he let his jaw muscles go slack. 'Your son will be fine,' Humphrey said, and the white man nodded his head.

'When Pres is better, I'd like you to come by the house and meet him,' Preston said. 'I'll have my secretary call you with a date.'

Humphrey was silent, as he felt the full weight of what he'd just heard. An invitation to dinner was an offer to be molded and groomed, mentored and befriended. Preston Sinclair was asking to be his friend. There was no mistaking his intent. And he wasn't asking in a calculated manner but in a moment of sincerity and vulnerability. Preston Sinclair had anointed him again. For the first time, it occurred to Humphrey that the man might be serious about helping him become the first black president of a major bank. Preston Sinclair just might be a man he could trust.

24

Mallory answered the telephone on the third ring and tried to avert her eyes from Hayden's disapproving stare; he was sitting across from her on the super-king-size bed. Hayden was watching a baseball game so intently that before the telephone rang, Mallory would have sworn that he didn't know she was in the room. But now, as she picked up the phone, he glared at her in annoyance. When a commercial came on, he grabbed her ankle and held it tight.

Who do you think you are, trying to control me? she wanted to scream at him. You haven't seen me in three weeks, and now you want my undivided attention. Mallory turned her back to him with as much spite as she could muster, which wasn't enough to make her point. As hard as she fought against it, Mallory was afraid of Hayden's displeasure. Her heart was beating as tremulously as a kitten's. She didn't want him to leave.

'Hello,' she said, cupping her hand over the telephone, so as not to disturb Hayden.

'Mal?'

'Oh, Sue.' Mallory giggled, her laughter a high trill of nervousness and guilt: it always seemed to be Sue who did the phoning, and this time she wouldn't even be able to talk for very long. She glanced uneasily at Hayden. 'How are you?'

'Like you care. I'm just calling to see if you're alive.'

'Sorry I've been so incommunicado. How's everything? How are the kids?' She didn't want to ask about her jerk of a husband, but there was no way she could gracefully not mention him. 'And Phil's doing okay?'

Susan immediately launched into a detailed account of her two daughters' progress up the growth chart, as well as a blow-by-blow description of Phillip's husbandly virtues. She babbled nonstop for ten minutes. With each mention of her family, each description of domestic contentment, Mallory wanted to throw down the telephone and bury her head under the pillow. As Susan began to describe the progression of her pregnancy, her excitement about the imminent birth, Mallory was filled with a yearning that was so deep and sharp that she almost cried aloud. She realized that the reason she never called Susan was that she couldn't bear to hear about her life.

Hayden coughed. Mallory looked over her shoulder. The game was just about over, and his team wasn't winning. As Hayden's eyes met hers, they were filled with petulance and an unspoken accusation: You should be paying attention to me. She was still half listening to Susan, laughing at the appropriate moments as her friend recounted yet another family-centered anecdote, when she felt Hayden's smooth, heavy fingers slowly moving from her ankles to her legs. He began rubbing her skin with ever increasing pressure.

'So what have you been up to, Mal?'

'Oh, not a lot.' As she searched for words, she could feel a tiny circle of heat rising from the skin that Hayden touched. When she looked at him, his sullen eyes were full of unspoken demands. I'll talk as long as I feel like, she told herself. He breezes in here whenever he feels like it and expects me to drop everything for him. I will not get off this phone until I want to, a childlike voice inside her screamed. Then, without warning, Hayden snatched away his hand and stood up. When Mallory looked at him, the set of his mouth was controlled. His eyes told her he was leaving.

Mallory hesitated for just a second. 'Sue. I'm going to

have to call you back.' She hung up quickly, so she didn't have to hear the way Sue said good-bye, her voice like a finger waggling at a naughty child.

She stood up and walked over to Hayden, put her arms around his waist, and leaned against his back. 'I don't want you to go,' she whispered.

'Well, I certainly didn't think you'd miss me. You were having such a good time chatting with your friend.'

'Don't go,' she begged softly.

They sat down on the bed. Their fingers groped at each other's clothes, and they fell back onto their sides. Hayden's mouth pressed against hers, and she opened her lips to receive his forceful tongue. She pushed him onto his back, and then she got on top of him. His mouth and tongue felt softer this way. She enjoyed kissing him, pressing herself against him. She could feel herself opening up and finding her own pleasure. Then suddenly his hands were firmly around her shoulders, like a caress at first, but as she leaned into him, he turned her on her back, got on top, and thrust himself inside her. Her anger grew as he moaned above her. When they fell apart, she began to cry like a child.

'What's the matter, honey?' Hayden asked very calmly. 'You're not doing much for my ego. I thought we just had a very good time.'

'I – I'm just emotional, that's all. It was wonderful. Thank you.' She kissed him on the cheek.

'PMS?' Hayden sighed. He straightened out the heavy gold chain that had bunched up around his neck. His body was red from lying out in the Palm Springs sun. The sight of his crimson skin intensified her anguish. He hadn't been lying under the sun alone.

'Hayden, I'm thirty-six years old. I'm tired of living like this. I want a family.' She hated her voice when she whined, and she knew that he did too.

'Can we discuss this another time?' He stood up and

walked into the bathroom. A minute later, Mallory heard the shower. Hayden sang as he bathed.

Mallory sat up on the bed for a moment, then flung herself back so hard that her head bounced when it hit the pillow. She could still hear him singing, even as she was sobbing and thinking of Susan and her two children, her belly swollen with another life, and, yes, her husband, who was a jerk but who at least belonged to her. No one belonged to Mallory.

She got up, ran to the bathroom, and snatched open the shower door. She wanted to scream at him, to call him names and curse him, but when she opened her mouth, no sound would come out. As she watched, Hayden turned around in the shower so that he could rinse himself completely, then he reached for the towel in a languid motion. His wet arm brushed against Mallory's breasts. He wiped himself off and then pulled the towel around him. He looked at Mallory, who was now sobbing, her wet, naked breasts heaving up and down. 'Darling, there's no need to upset yourself. Why do you carry on this way? Can't you be patient just a little longer?'

'I've been patient for a few years, Hayden. I'm not going to wait any longer. I'm not going to waste my life waiting for you. I want children,' she said, her voice breaking off into a sob. 'I want my own children.'

'We'll have them,' he said. 'Just be patient. Things have to be arranged. There's property involved here, a settlement.'

It was what he always said, she realized, just as the last sob she had in her dissolved in her throat. I want more. I deserve more. She opened her mouth, then closed it. Then she tried again. Her voice was very soft, like a whisper in a ballroom. 'No. It's over. Now just leave.'

Esther smiled to herself as she waited in the reception area outside Humphrey Boone's office, thinking of the conversation she and Mallory had had at lunch. Not for one second did she believe that Mallory would never see Hayden again. She laughed, thinking of the intensity in Mallory's eyes when she insisted that Esther and Humphrey could date discreetly for a year or so and then get married. 'Of course, you'd have to transfer once the engagement was announced, but you might want to have a baby right away, and then you could stay home,' she said, ignoring Esther's laughter. The girl lived for romance, and she thought every black man who crooned a tune or graced the silver screen was gorgeous. A suspicion, as lithe as a worm, inched up Esther's backbone and made her squirm. No, she thought. Don't even think about it.

'Mr. Boone will see you now,' his assistant said. She was a silver-haired woman, the color of café au lait, fiftyish and very stylish. Hired a sister, Esther thought approvingly. This boy just might be all right.

Humphrey Boone rose when Esther came in, and the odor of his expensive cologne wafted in the air around him. He smiled as she approached and gave her hand a vigorous shake when she extended it to him. His fingers felt smooth and cool, and when she glanced down at his hand, she saw that next to his skin, her own nut-brown color seemed pale.

Humphrey could feel himself being appraised. Despite Esther's professional demeanor, her gracious nonsexual smile, he knew that she was checking him out. Sisters had a way of doing that, no matter the circumstances. And whenever he was the object of their powerful female judgment, he felt as though he were a skinny fourteen-year-old again, taking that long walk across the dance floor in search of a partner. 'I ain't dancing with that ugly boy. He so dark I can't even see him.' That's what he'd heard one girl tell her friend after he walked away. And even though he realized that now black women were interested in him – all those thirtysomething sisters searching for Mr. Right – he couldn't get the ancient taunts out of his head. He knew he looked a lot better to sisters these days, with his title and salary, his Armani suits and Rolex, his Marina address and sleek automobile. Even the really pretty high-yellow ones, the blow-hair girls with the light eyes who used to turn up their narrow noses back in the day, were eager to be with him now. He knew that they wanted him, and yet that didn't allay the apprehension he felt whenever black women looked at him. The fact that they were at his beck and call didn't lessen his resentment. There was a wound inside him, where their contempt had marked him, and from time to time it festered. His memory was too long, he knew, but he couldn't shake off his past, couldn't stop remembering when he worshiped black women and they thought he was black and ugly. He still worshiped sisters; he just didn't trust them with his feelings.

He remained standing until Esther sat down in the small wing-back chair in front of his desk. She glanced around the large, sunny office, taking inventory: new paint job, new Oriental rug, new cherrywood desk. No question about it: Humphrey Boone was the man.

'I'm glad we're finally getting a chance to chat, Esther. As you might imagine, things have been quite hectic for me, and up until now I haven't had a free moment,' he said easily.

If I closed my eyes, I'd think I was talking with someone white, Esther thought, listening to Humphrey's clipped enunciation and perfect diction. She thought of Tyrone's streety cadence and split infinitives; no mistaking him for anything but a brother. Looking at the black man in front of her, she wondered about his background. Was he a blue-blood or a bootstrapper? One thing was for sure: he knew how to work the system. Humphrey was working it to death. This brother has some real power, she thought to herself, trying not to feel awed but sensing a nervous twitching in her belly. 'Well, I'm . . . uh . . .' Calm down. Spit it out, girl, she told herself. ' . . . glad we could finally get together,' she continued smoothly. She chatted easily about what a difference Humphrey was making at Angel City, then reminded him that she was a member of the National Alliance of Black Bankers. 'I have to admit, I haven't been terribly active,' she said.

'Well, I hope you'll start coming to meetings. There's a lot that needs to be done.'

The conversation was going well, she thought, as she segued into a discussion of her professional contribution to the bank. Humphrey was reserved but appeared to be listening attentively, although she did see him glance at his watch just as she was about to broach her desire to become a lender. As he turned his hand to see his watch, his college ring caught her eye. It was a Yale ring, with familiar Greek letters across the stone. The chuckle burst out before she could stop it.

Humphrey looked at her with surprise. 'What's so funny?'

Why in the world had she laughed? She knew better than anyone that just because Humphrey was black didn't mean she could get comfortable. 'Oh. I just noticed your ring,' she said. She paused for a moment, wondering about the man who was staring at her quizzically. How could she get out of this?

'And?'

'Well, I was noticing that you went to Yale and that you pledged Gamma. And I was just thinking that . . . uh . . .'

'That a "Gamma Dog" from Yale is a rare man indeed.'

She could feel a South Side wind blowing through his words.

They both laughed at the same time, and it occurred to Humphrey that it was the best laugh he'd had since he began working at Angel City Bank. 'Actually, I pledged the city chapter. There weren't any Greek organizations on campus.'

'That's my brother's fraternity,' Esther said.

'Oh, really. Did you pledge?'

'Oh, of course. Kappa Alpha Kappa.'

'Finer womanhood,' Humphrey said. There was a definite slur in his voice. 'It's a small black world.'

He flashed Esther a smile that was more 'Gamma Dog' than corporate, but it quickly disappeared, and when he spoke, his clipped enunciation was back in place. He didn't want to get caught up in the 'Negro Network Game'. He'd learned a long time ago that small talk worked against him. Humphrey knew that if they started out with frats and sororities, the next discussion would be the people they knew in common. Then it would be, 'And where did you grow up?' which always led to questions about the family. Black people generally had sense enough not to ask what a person's parents did, knowing full well that any baby boomers usually had parents who wore pink, blue, or no collars at all. But they would ask about siblings. His own brother and sisters were the last people on earth that Humphrey wanted to talk about. Besides, all the chitchat led to the same place: Esther wanted something from him. He knew an ambitious black woman when he saw one. 'Has your experience at Angel City been a good one?' Humphrey asked smoothly. There. He'd given her an opening; the rest was up to her.

The words tumbled out. 'I've had a wonderful time in operations, but I want to go into middle-market lending,' Esther said.

'Well, you're qualified.'

'Yes, I am. I have an M.B.A. from—'

Humphrey waved his hand lightly. 'I'm familiar with your résumé. And I know your reputation. You turned operations around one hundred eighty degrees.'

'Thank you.' She was surprised by how genuine his admiration seemed. She'd run into enough sexist brothers over the years to be wary. More than one had tried to sabotage her career. Maybe Humphrey would be different.

'I'll look into it. I'm not making any promises. And this won't happen overnight.' He stood up.

Esther nodded as she rose. She thought about mentioning that there were no black lenders and that almost no business loans were being made to any minorities, but she forced herself to remain silent. Humphrey probably had more stats on the loan department than she had ever seen. Besides, how did she know if black progress was important to Humphrey? People didn't rise to his heights by being loyal to the race. For all she knew, he was a King Clever devotee, a registered Republican. She was lucky he took the Gamma joke in stride. No sense pushing her luck. But something told her that Humphrey Boone would look out for her, that he was a real brother. 'I've enjoyed talking with you,' she said, and she meant it.

'Yes, Esther. We'll do it again soon. And say hello to my frat brother.'

Walking out of Humphrey's office, Esther felt buoyed. For once she felt as though someone in charge was on her side. She was so preoccupied with reviewing her conversation with him that she almost bumped into Tyrone as he was coming down the hall with overnight letters in his hand. He glanced around quickly and didn't see anyone. 'Hey, girl,' he said quietly. 'You sure look good today.' He grinned at her.

Esther looked up and down the hall before she smiled back. 'Well, thank you.'

'Listen, I— '

Behind her, the door to Humphrey's office opened. Tyrone closed his mouth immediately as he took in the navy pin-striped suit, gold cuff links, Hermès tie, and Ferragamo shoes, all in one swooping glance. Brother is clean, he thought to himself. He looked down at his own scuffed sneakers and didn't look up again.

'Esther, may I speak with you, please?' Humphrey said.

Esther was standing between the two men. 'I'm surprised it hasn't come yet,' she said to Tyrone, noticing the slump in his shoulders as her words hit him.

'I'll look for it at the office,' Tyrone managed to sputter before he walked away, but not before he heard the tall black man's crisp, college-boy English, the same language that Esther spoke at the bank. Of course the man had been to school, Tyrone admonished himself as he walked down the hall. A brother didn't get to wear suits like that without a fine education, without being really intelligent. As much as he envied Humphrey his trappings of success, what he coveted even more was what he couldn't see: his brains.

Tyrone had known practically all his life that he wasn't smart. He did well enough in his neighborhood elementary school, but after he was bused to the suburbs for junior high, he seemed to lose interest. By that time his mother was working, and it was harder for his parents to drive way out to the Valley for a PTA meeting. Some nights they didn't even bother to check his homework. After all, they told him, you're in a good school now. He seemed to hit a wall. The work was harder, and at first it seemed that no one cared whether he got it right or not. When his English teacher told him in front of the class that he was a failure as a student, it was easy to believe her. Even when he encountered teachers who took time with him, the label was still in his head. Failure. After that, he began to clown his way through school, telling one joke after another to drown out the feeling of incompetence he felt. Now, as he walked slowly down the hall of the bank, Tyrone felt like a skinny ninth grader with an F taped to his forehead.

'Esther,' Humphrey said, 'I was just wondering if you

353

were going to be coming to the Black Bankers dinner dance next Friday. I've been so busy, I haven't had time to sell my twenty tickets,' he said sheepishly.

'Oh.' She looked down the hall, wondering if Tyrone could hear her. 'That sounds great. In fact, I may be able to take two from you.'

Esther saw the roses even before she walked into Mallory's office. When she did step inside, she was bombarded by the sweet fragrance. There must have been five dozen long-stemmed American Beauties, in every color imaginable. One look at the embarrassed expression on Mallory's face, and Esther knew exactly who had sent them. 'Well, I will say this: the man knows how to apologize.' She looked at Mallory, whose bottom lip was quivering slightly.

'I know you think I'm a wimp,' she said quietly.

'No, I don't.'

Mallory shot her a 'give me a break' look.

'Well, okay, I do. But hey, I've been the same kind of fool. You just need to get stronger. I mean, these flowers are beautiful, but they're not going to last a lifetime.'

'He is going to leave her, Esther,' Mallory said earnestly. She could tell by her friend's dubious expression that she didn't believe her. 'I just feel that this time he's really going to do it.'

'I hope he does.' Esther looked away from Mallory and was quiet for a moment. Lord. Just wake up and smell the stinkweed, girlfriend, she said to herself. Wasting her time on that creep! She had the urge to put her hand on Mallory's thin shoulders and shake her until she got some sense, but instead she glowered at her for a few seconds. She felt like a bully when the white woman averted her eyes. Just leave her alone. If she wants to be a wimp, it's not my business, she reminded herself. 'Well, my meeting with Humphrey went very well. I think I may have found an ally.'

Mallory's eyes gleamed with mischief. 'You could find more than that, if you played your cards right. If I were in your shoes . . .'

'What would you do? You talk about him so much, I think *you* must like him.' Esther's words had an irritable edge to them.

But Mallory didn't notice her friend's displeasure. 'Oh, he's way too good for me. If I had a nice man I'd probably go into culture shock,' she said with a sigh.

The Friday night of the bankers' dinner dance, Esther left work early. She stopped by the bakery for her apple bran muffins. Behind the counter, the candles on the low worship table were burning brightly and a glazed doughnut, a banana, and some nuts had been set out for Buddha. She glanced at the old heads who were, as usual, sitting at 'their' table, holding their coffee cups, jabbering away. Looking around for Hyun, she finally saw the small Korean woman sitting in the corner with the old men, laughing and talking. She nodded at Esther, got up, and went behind the counter. 'Sorry. Sorry,' Hyun said. 'They telling me so funny story.' She giggled again, looked over at the men, and waggled her finger at them. Then she turned back to Esther. 'Chicago, you want six muffins today?'

She smiled. 'Yes, please.'

Hyun handed her the muffins and went back to sit with the men. As Esther was leaving, she could hear the woman's soft giggles, muffled behind the hand she held against her mouth.

Esther zoomed up the hill to her house and pulled into the garage with a screech of brakes. If she didn't get moving, she was going to be late. The banquet started at seven-thirty, and she had to pick up Vanessa. She took a quick shower, curled her hair, applied her makeup, and then put on the red silk sheath that was hanging behind the door.

The dress was a belted, low-cut refined mini that showed off all her attributes. The telephone rang, and she let the answering machine take the call. Hearing Tyrone's voice as she was on her way into the garage, she felt a twinge of guilt as she slid behind the wheel and began backing down the driveway. When he had asked what she was doing that evening, she told him she was hanging out with her friend.

I'm not married to the man, she told herself. I'm not even his girlfriend. There was no sense in feeling bad; she couldn't take him to the banquet. Humphrey might recognize him, and that wouldn't be cool. Besides, the banquet would be full of brothers and sisters with degrees and titles. Tyrone would be out of place. He's just something to do, she reminded herself.

Just as she was about to turn onto the street, she heard a rap on her window. Startled, Esther jumped a little, then turned to see her nextdoor neighbor, his face solemn, his finger pointing downward. She felt a trace of annoyance as she lowered the window. What did he want, with his jungle fever self? 'Yes?' she said tersely. 'I'm sorry, I can't talk. I'm running late.'

'You're not going anywhere,' he said cheerfully.

'I beg your pardon?'

'I hate to tell you this, but you have a flat.'

'Oh, no.'

'Do you have a spare?'

'Yes, but— '

'I'll change it for you. You look too nice to get under a car. If you'll wait a minute, I'll get my tools.'

Did she have a choice?

A few minutes later, the front door to the Linton house opened, and the three of them came trooping out. 'I brought my cheerleaders,' the man said easily in his flat, twangy voice. Boyfriend sounds like he's from hillbilly country,

Esther thought. The little girl was quiet. She stood beside her mother, sucking her thumb and twirling her wild hair.

'Hi,' Carol said. 'See you're having a little trouble.' She had the same accent. Funny, she hadn't noticed it before.

'Yes, I am. Your husband was kind enough to help me out.'

'Oh, Harold's a pretty handy fellow,' Carol said. They smiled at each other.

'Excuse me, where are you from?' Esther asked. She was afraid they were going to say Dogpatch.

'Kingsley, West Virginia.'

'Are both of you from the same town?'

They laughed. Harold, fitting on the new tire, chuckled and said, 'We're from the same street.'

Carol nodded. 'He's the boy next door.' And this time Esther laughed too, until she stopped herself.

Harold stood up, balancing the old tire with his finger-tips. 'You're all set. This one's no good. I'll just get it out of the way.'

'Please.'

Harold propped the tire against her trash can. He slapped his hands together to get off some of the dirt.

'You really saved my life,' Esther said.

'That's what neighbors are for,' Carol said.

A sudden rush of Sunday school guilt attacked Esther; she felt the urge to atone for her evil thoughts. 'I'll have to have you guys over for dinner sometime,' she blurted out. No sooner were the words in the cosmos than she wanted to snatch them back. Shit! What did she say that for? The Lintons were grinning at her as though she'd offered them the key to the city.

'We eat anything,' Harold said jovially.

Esther smiled weakly. She knew she should set a date, but instead she repeated her thanks, gave her neighbors a wave, and then rushed to her car. The Lintons, who were standing in a huddle at the sidewalk, waved gaily as she took off down the street.

Despite the fact that Esther was a good twenty minutes late, Vanessa wasn't ready when she arrived. After blowing her horn, Esther had to wait ten minutes before her friend wafted out, wearing a bright-green silk pants suit. The first thing Vanessa said when she got into the car was, 'Oh, cleavage! Go 'head, girl.'

'I'm out to catch a new career, honey.'

'Well, sometimes that's as good as a man.'

Networking was in full swing outside Ballroom A of the downtown hotel, and as Esther and Vanessa approached the crowd, they could see people scurrying like hungry rodents from one person to the next, smiling, chatting, sipping white zinfandel, passing out business cards, and then hustling off to the next person who might be able to do them some good. As was customary with most Friday night functions, guests were dressed in everything from business attire to cocktail party outfits. Some had come straight from work and even carried their briefcases. Vanessa's bright eyes darted over the crowd, pausing to eyeball flirtatiously any good-looking man who happened into range. 'So this is how the professional people party,' she said. 'Well, I see me some cutie pies up in here. Sure do. Is my weave in order?'

Esther nodded, then peered through the crowd of bankers, looking for Humphrey Boone. Tonight would be the perfect time to solidify their relationship, to impress upon her boss's consciousness that she was a friend, an ally, and definitely lender material. She didn't see the tall, dark man anywhere, so she led Vanessa, who was busy gawking at the men, to the bar and stood in line. While they waited, Esther greeted several people she knew and walked over to speak to one woman who called her name. As she was returning to the line, she caught a glimpse of a familiar-looking face, and when she turned around she saw Mitchell Harris coming up the escalator. On his arm was a woman who looked like a young Lena Horne. Esther vaguely remembered seeing her at a Women in Banking meeting. 'Oh, God,' she said. Esther could feel herself gritting down on her teeth.

'What?' asked Vanessa, turning around. Her eyes followed Esther's glance. 'Ugh! I thought you said this was a classy affair.'

'Do I look okay?'

'What are you talking about? You have cleavage. Of course you look okay. Get a grip, homegirl. And I'm telling you right now, if you start salivating over that fool, I will take you into the ladies' room and spank you in front of all the boogie sisters in there.'

But after the initial surprise of seeing Mitchell, Esther didn't feel any yearning for him at all. By the time he began walking toward her, her heart was calm. 'Brace yourself, honey,' she told Vanessa. 'He's coming over. Don't act ugly.'

'And don't you act like a fool,' Vanessa whispered fiercely. 'Pretend I'm not here,' and she turned around.

But for the first time in her long and turbulent history with Mitchell Harris, Esther didn't act or feel like a fool. 'Hello, Mitchell,' she said evenly. He was alone. Esther looked around and saw that he'd left his beauty queen on the other side of the room, where she stood rather forlornly. There but for the grace of God. She turned back to Mitchell. He hadn't lost any of his gestures. Standing in front of her, smelling good, looking good, he still had the same penetrating glance that used to go through her like a blowtorch. Mitchell managed to let his fingers brush accidentally against her bare arm. He still had his charm. But he'd lost his control. The second time he touched her, Esther stepped back. No, she didn't feel any yearning. She didn't even feel angry. Not even disgusted, when Mitchell whispered in her ear, 'You sure are looking good. Let's go out to dinner next

359

Friday. I'll pick you up at eight.' So sure of himself. She thought of Tyrone's sweet, worshipful glances. Listening to Mitchell's familiar rap, Esther felt not desire but deliverance.

'I'm busy, Mitchell,' she said with a smile.

'Well, how about the following week?'

She shook her head. 'I'm busy.'

He gave her a slight nod and said, 'Oh, I get it,' then walked away.

No, she thought to herself, I got it. Finally.

By the time they bought their drinks, the cocktail hour was over and people were streaming into the ballroom. Their table was in the middle of the room, equidistant from the door and the dais. Humphrey Boone, the other officers of Black Bankers, and a tall white man with thick gray hair were seated there. The official business moved along quickly. Humphrey gave a smooth, gracious welcome and then turned the program over to the master of ceremonies, the black weatherman from the ABC affiliate, who cracked a few corny jokes about needing a loan and then introduced Reverend Odell Rice. The reverend's 'Ol' Man River' voice boomed out across the room. 'Brothers and sisters, let us pray. Almighty God, we ask that you bless us here this evening. Bless this food of which we are about to partake for the nourishment of our bodies. Bless our souls, Lord. Bless our minds. Touch the brain power of all these fine black bankers, Lord, and let them know that they are capable of building their own institutions. And in the words of a hungry Negro in a hurry, "Good food, good meat, thank the Lord, let's eat." '

People were still laughing as Reverend Rice took his seat. No sooner had the last titter disappeared than snippets of Spanish filled the room as a highly organized squadron of Latino waiters and waitresses descended upon the tables. 'I remember a time when all the waiters working these downtown hotels were black,' an older man at Esther's table said, shaking his head. To anyone looking around the room, it was clear that that time had come and gone.

After the rubber-chicken dinner had been served, the remains of the ice cream cake dessert taken away, and the coffee poured, the weatherman introduced the lean, earnest-looking white man as the keynote speaker. He was the president and CEO of a large software company that had contributed fifty thousand dollars to the Black Bankers Alliance scholarship fund. In his speech – which was mercifully brief – he spoke of the need for corporate America to reinvest in the inner city.

'How about *in*vest,' the same older man at Esther's table whispered loudly.

Any cynics notwithstanding, the CEO's remark yielded him enthusiastic applause. Humphrey presented him with a handsome plaque, and the two men shook hands while a photographer for the city's African-American newspaper snapped their picture. The scholarship awardees, ten college-bound students, came to the stage, and Humphrey gave each one a check. Just as the weatherman was about to call Reverend Rice to give the benediction, the vice president of the organization, a tiny dark-skinned woman, announced that Humphrey was the recipient of the Black Bankers Humanitarian of the Year Award for his work with African-American youth. As everyone watched, a teenage boy, looking awkward in a dark suit and shiny shoes, walked across the stage and stood nervously in front of the podium. He spoke haltingly into the microphone. 'I am one of the many young men whose life has been touched by Humphrey Boone.' There was a slight tremble in his voice, and he looked straight ahead at the wall across from the stage as he spoke. 'I met Mr. Boone two years ago, when I was in the ninth grade. At that time I had bad grades, a bad attitude, and I guess I thought I was kinda bad.' A ripple of chuckles passed through the audience. The boy looked startled, then pleased, and began to glance nervously at the audience. 'Mr. Boone taught me how to become a responsible black man by being about the pursuit of excellence.'

'Yessir! That's all right!' the older man at the table shouted. He stood up and began applauding, and soon others joined in. The boy grinned unabashedly at the response his touching 'uplift the race' message had garnered. By the time Humphrey strode across the stage to accept the plaque, several women were dabbing at their eyes and thinking exactly what Esther was thinking: We need more brothers like Humphrey Boone.

As soon as Reverend Rice gave the benediction, he walked over to where Humphrey was sitting. 'Well, congratulations, Humphrey,' he said.

'I know this was your doing,' Humphrey said.

'Well, you have to encourage good people, especially when you have something else for them to do. I found a bank.'

'You what?'

'You heard me. Bank of Southern California wants to get out of South-Central. They want to sell three branches. They're asking a million and a half apiece.' Reverend Rice grinned.

'Obviously, they're only talking about the physical structure. What about the deposits? What about the premium?'

The smile didn't fade from Reverend Rice's face. 'Now see, that's why I need your input. I want you to be involved in this, Humphrey. Can you attend a planning meeting this Tuesday? Say around eight o'clock.'

One of the officers of the organization passed by, a man who'd been seated on the dais. Reverend Rice paused to shake his hand and take his card before turning back to Humphrey. As much as he liked Odell, he wasn't interested in getting involved in any small, three-branch black bank. He was too big-time for that. He was going to be the president of Angel City National Bank. 'Sorry, Odell. It's not where I'm going right now.'

Reverend Rice nodded. 'That's cool. I understand. Just give me my damn plaque so I can get my twenty-nine ninety-five back.' A woman was walking by. Reverend Odell stopped her, introduced himself, and took her card.

Humphrey laughed. 'You know what? You ain't nothing but a hustler with a divinity degree.'

Now it was Reverend Rice's turn to laugh. 'Damn straight. And proud of it. You know, I do the best I can, brother. I'm guilty of some sins and innocent of others. I don't drive a Cadillac. I don't mail out prayer cloths. I don't ask my congregation for a trip to the Holy Land. I don't chase after women – mainly because Juanita don't play that. The girl is from Louisiana. I eat a little fried chicken and I drink me some Chivas every now and again. And I try to help my people, the best way I know how. And what my people need is some capital.' Humphrey became aware that the minister was staring at him. 'You know, Humphrey, everything you got going for you ain't worth shit if you don't bring it home. We're going to talk again, brother. You ain't heard the last of this.'

By the time the band began tuning up, Vanessa was busy making good on all the come-hither eyeballing she'd engaged in earlier in the evening, and by the first song, she had men waiting in line to dance with her. 'Oooh, I like these little boogie brothers, Esther,' she whispered to her friend after the third dance.

The moment Esther saw Humphrey alone, she walked over to him and extended her hand. 'Congratulations.'

'Oh, Esther. Thank you.' He looked embarrassed and a little weary. 'I had no idea . . .'

'You deserved it,' she said. 'It's wonderful what you're

doing. If more black men tried to help young boys, we wouldn't have gangs.'

He shook his head. 'Don't kid yourself. It will take more than volunteers to turn around the gang problem. The boys I deal with aren't hard-core bangers; they're basically good kids who need some guidance.'

'There are a lot of good kids in gangs who need guidance. You're saving them before they go bad. That's commendable.'

'Well,' he said. He looked embarrassed again. 'Would you like to dance?'

The music was up-tempo, and they did a fast, two-step, no-name dance that was exactly what the rest of the thirty-something crowd was capable of executing after a decade and a half of nonstop workaholism. But they found their rhythm easily and flowed smoothly together on the dance floor. When the song ended, they danced to the next one, and after that they joined an Electric Slide line. Esther danced in front of Humphrey, and as she was going across the floor with the synchronized group, she missed a step. She felt hands firmly on her waist and then warmth as Humphrey spun her around to the correct position. When she looked up at him, they smiled at each other. Our children would have beautiful teeth, she thought.

As they talked a little about the private placement loans that Humphrey was working on, he tried not to look at Esther's breasts. She mostly listened and asked questions, intelligent questions, he thought. He told her about his plans for the Minority Loan Program. 'It's going to shake up a lot of people. What it boils down to is that I've created a special committee to review loan applications from minorities. I'm taking the decisionmaking power out of the hands of lenders who don't seem to be able to find it within their hearts to make loans to people who don't look like them, especially black folks.'

Esther studied the resolute tilt of Humphrey's chin. The idea of suspending the lending authority of the entire department was nothing short of revolutionary. This brother is bad, she thought.

They talked and laughed until the music stopped. When they looked around, the room was almost empty. Vanessa sat at a neighboring table, surrounded by three men. 'Well,' Humphrey said, 'we'll have to— ' He coughed. 'I'll see you on Monday,' he said, correcting himself.

'Yes.' She heard what he'd almost said: we'll have to do this again. Humphrey likes me. The thought circled her mind like a soft, mushy cloud.

25

The memo from Humphrey Boone was to the attention of all loan officers. It read: 'The attached document contains the bank's policy for the new Minority Loan Program.' Kirk slowly and carefully read every line in the thirty-five-page manuscript, and with every page he turned, his face became redder. When he was finished, he stood up and flung the papers down on his desk so hard that his Rolodex crashed to the floor. From behind the eight-by-ten frame, Sheila's accusing eyes stared back at Kirk. His shoulders slumped, and he felt his chin tapping against his chest. Jesus, what a rotten world! he thought. I've worked hard all my life, and for what? 'Dammit!' he said, looking at the scattered cards at his feet.

'Kirk?'

He looked up and saw Mallory in his doorway. In her hand was the same document he'd just finished reading.

'Have you seen this?' she asked. She stepped inside the room and closed the door. She looked as though someone had just slapped her face, and even though his head ached with anger, Kirk had to fight the desire to put his arms around her. 'I can't believe this,' she continued. 'It's like they're saying because there are so few loans to minorities, it means all the lenders are racist.'

'Didn't you know all white people are racist? Yeah, it's in the genes. Hell, maybe I should just quit my job, become a black man, and get a loan from Angel City.' His eyes were flashing.

'I mean, there are procedures, guidelines. This is a federally regulated industry. Are we supposed to just give away the money to anybody who asks for a loan?'

'As long as they're not white,' Kirk snapped.

Mallory sat down across from him and tapped on the desktop with her fingertips. 'I mean, there have been lots of minorities that I personally wanted to loan money to, but they didn't fit the guidelines. What are you supposed to do if somebody comes to you with a credit report from hell? And then whose fault is it when he defaults on the loan?' Her forehead was creased with thin lines of worry, as though she were trying to figure something out.

'Well, don't you know that if you're black or Mexican, that automatically rules out any chance of default?'

'There was a very fine black gentleman who came in for a loan last year. He owned a beauty supply company. He hadn't been in business very long, less than a year, and his TRW was just terrible because he'd ruined his credit trying to finance the business. It was just beginning to make a profit, and he needed a small loan to make some improvements in the store. He was very nice, but it wasn't possible.' Mallory's voice climbed higher and higher, until it was almost squeaking. 'He didn't qualify. I mean, I really tried to make it work, but the numbers weren't there. So does that make me a – a racist?' She actually looked as though she were about to cry, which only made Kirk angrier.

'Oh, we're all racist. All white people were born with the R gene.'

'I am not a racist,' Mallory said, her thin bottom lip trembling. 'I do not judge people by the color of their skin. I don't even see color.' Her chest heaved in and out.

'Listen, Mallory,' Kirk said, patting her hand very lightly, 'this whole business isn't about fairness or equality. It's about Humphrey Boone making a power play.' The name spewed out of his mouth like venom. 'And you know what? He's probably going to get kickbacks from some of these loans. I'll bet you that a lot of the guys who get loans are his buddies.'

That comment momentarily cooled Mallory's sense of outrage. 'Kirk, I think you have to be careful about making those kinds of accusations.' Poor guy, she thought. He really did get a bum deal. 'I think we have to have a different kind of strategy. That's what I came to talk with you about. The message I'm getting is that Humphrey thinks the entire department is composed of a bunch of racists who won't make loans to minorities just because they're not white. Maybe what we need to do is approach Humphrey and let him know that simply isn't the case. And that if he takes away our ability to process loans, he's going to have a major morale problem.'

Mallory had crossed her legs at an elegant angle. The sight of those pale, slim, beautiful legs had a tranquilizing effect on Kirk.

Mallory was glad to see that he'd regained his composure.

'You're right. I was out of line. Maybe you should approach Humphrey,' Kirk said quietly. 'He knows that I was supposed to have his job. Anything I say is suspect. And everybody else in the department is scared of him. But you, maybe he'll listen to you.' Of course he would listen to her. 'Are you going to do it this afternoon?'

'No. I've got to meet with some customers later on. I'll try to set something up for tomorrow, because I'm leaving the day after that for the Women in Banking Conference in Washington.'

'Just the girls, huh?' Kirk said with a smile. 'Planning a takeover?'

'That's the general idea.' Mallory laughed and walked toward the door.

'Let me know how your meeting with Humphrey goes,' Kirk said.

The next morning Mallory was ushered into Humphrey Boone's office by his silver-haired assistant. Her boss stood up when the white woman came in and remained standing until she was seated. He looked at the sheaf of papers she was carrying. 'I see you got my memo,' he said quietly. He'd been expecting an outcry and figured that Mallory was either an emissary for the entire loan department or just the first to complain. 'What can I do for you?' He smiled at her, noting that she didn't smile back.

'I want to discuss the memo you sent, Humphrey,' Mallory said.

'Fine. What is it that you'd like to talk about?'

Mallory felt a surge of anger pulse through her, but looking at Humphrey's face, she hesitated, asking herself the question she always asked: Did she have the right to be angry? Of course she did! She swallowed. 'I'm deeply offended by the notion that because I'm a white lender, I'm not sensitive to the needs of my minority customers.' Humphrey's dark eyes seemed to burrow into her skin like an irritating mite. His eyes were so dark. As dark as his skin. She crossed, then uncrossed her legs, alarmed that her anger was being replaced by trepidation and self-doubt. Those emotions were much more familiar to her.

'The needs of your minority customers are the same as your white ones. They both need money. And at Angel City Bank, very few minority customers, particularly African-Americans, are getting their needs met.'

'But this memo seems to suggest that because I'm white, I'm deliberately not making loans to black customers, solely because they are black.' The initial indignation had drained from her voice, and her new tone was tentative, almost tremulous.

Humphrey leaned over the desk. 'Not at all,' he said smoothly. 'I regret that you saw fit to interpret it that way.

The report simply says that while our customer base is sixty-eight percent minority, ninety-one percent of the loans we make across the board go to white people. The report suggests that something is wrong when we've got such skewed statistics, that maybe what we need is another way to look at minority loan applicants. And so Angel City Bank will have a special group of people whose sole responsibility it will be to determine the eligibility of our black, Latino, and Asian customers.'

'But you've taken away our lending authority,' Mallory said.

'Actually, what is being taken away is your ability to turn down loan applications for nonwhite customers.'

Mallory felt herself flushing.

'Do you know what it's like to be denied a loan all over town, not because your credit rating isn't as good as the next guy's, not because your business plan isn't as astute, but simply because of the color of your skin? Do you?' Humphrey asked. He watched Mallory's face turn crimson and recognized it as the first blush of guilt. It was so easy to make certain white women feel guilty. He had learned in college that there were some white girls who wanted to atone for the sins of their forefathers, who would respond to his ranting and raving about the white man's injustice with rosy cheeks and sympathy. Unlike sisters, who'd heard it all before and whose only response was a stalwart 'The struggle continues' or some variation on that theme, white girls were prone to offer their bodies as consolation prizes. He had a sixth sense about such women.

'No. I mean . . .'

'Statistics show that blacks are turned down more frequently for loans than anyone else, not only in this city but all over the country. Not only for business loans, but black people are more than three times as likely to be denied a mortgage loan as well, even when they have the ten percent

370

down payment. And Angel City National is one of the worst offenders in Los Angeles.'

'Well, I . . .' She crossed her legs and uncrossed them and told herself that she'd done nothing wrong and had nothing to feel guilty about. She'd simply followed bank procedure, that's all. That's what she was paid to do.

'There simply will not be business as usual any longer at Angel City National Bank,' Humphrey said. He wasn't shouting, but his voice was a little stronger. He could feel his words filling the room, not in volume, but in intensity. Then he softened his tone. 'Angel City National Bank is going to become the bank that is known for fair play. I'm sure you're in favor of fairness, aren't you, Mallory?'

'Of course I am,' she said weakly. 'I have never discriminated against anyone on the basis of color. And believe me, I've denied loans to plenty of white people too.'

'Nine percent,' Humphrey said. He rose and extended his hand to Mallory, who stood up woodenly and accepted his handshake. 'The Minority Loan Program will take some adjusting to, but I think it is the fairest, simplest instrument we have to bring equity and justice to Angel City. What I'm asking for is your understanding and cooperation.'

'I'm not a racist,' Mallory said. She couldn't bear the thought of anyone thinking that she based her professional decisions on the color of a person's skin. The idea made her frantic. As she shook Humphrey's hand, she had the urge to tell him about her childhood, how her dad had commanded her not to play with black children and her mother said it was okay as long as she didn't inform her father. She wanted to tell him about Trudell Simms, the black girl who was practically her best friend in high school, although they didn't see each other on weekends. She wanted to tell him that she'd gone out with two black guys and that there wasn't a prejudiced bone in her body. But most of all, for some reason she couldn't explain, she wanted Humphrey Boone's forgiveness.

Humphrey could still smell Mallory's perfume after she left. Every time he sniffed the scent, he saw her again and he was aroused as he was when she was sitting across from him, looking defensive, her eyes full of unspoken apologies as she crossed and uncrossed her pale, elegant legs.

'I don't want you to get excited,' Esther said to Mallory as they boarded the jet that would take them to Washington for the Second Annual Women in Banking Conference, 'because I know how you get, but I think I have a little crush on Humphrey. I just admire the man so much.'

Hearing Humphrey's name, Mallory thought back to the talk she'd had with him one day earlier. She hadn't mentioned the memo or her conversation to Esther. Hearing her friend say she liked the man who seemed to think that she and the other white lenders were discriminating against black customers gave her an uneasy feeling. She wondered if her incipient crush would affect the way Esther thought of her.

'I have the minihots for the man,' Esther said. 'It all began when I was in his arms.' She laughed when she saw Mallory's startled expression. 'You should see your face. It's not that serious. We were at a dinner dance together last week.'

'What about Mr. Fun Buns?'

'Oh, he's still fun, but you know Tyrone isn't someone for the long haul. He's just good for now.' As she said those words, Esther felt slightly guilty. Tyrone went out of his way to be kind to her. The night before, he cooked her dinner, and he had driven her to the airport. He wasn't just 'something to do'. In many ways, he was becoming a really good friend.

'Humphrey is quite eligible,' Mallory said. Despite her

newfound reservations about her boss, she felt herself being swept away by the notion of an office romance blooming right under her nose. 'Is he a good dancer?' she asked with a smile.

Esther nodded. 'A great conversationalist too.'

'Go for it, girlfriend,' Mallory said, imitating Esther's voice. The two women laughed.

Esther felt a surge of energy when the plane landed at Washington National. She'd spent four years attending college here and had lived in the city for five years after she graduated, so in many ways, D.C. was a second home to her. D.C., even more than Chicago, was where most of her really close friends lived. 'My girlfriend said she'd pick us up,' she told Mallory, looking around the gate area, but after waiting for a few minutes, they decided to go get their bags.

As they walked to the baggage claim area, all kinds of black men – a Nigerian in full national dress, a Jamaican with dreads as thick as ropes, three brothers in full corporate attire, and at least half a dozen skycaps – gave her the eye, and a few said, 'Hey, mama,' very sweetly as she passed.

'You certainly are popular,' Mallory said.

'I love D.C.' The ratio may be twenty women to every man, but at least the men are alive, she thought to herself. It felt good to be in a city where brothers knew how to flirt, unlike L.A. men, who wouldn't say 'Hey, mama' no matter how good a woman was looking. Except for Tyrone; he flirted just fine. Which made her sudden interest in Humphrey all the more confusing. But she hadn't come to D.C. to think about her love life. She was here to have a good time.

Marlene appeared just as their baggage arrived. She was a tiny, fairskinned black woman with freckles. Esther could feel her bones as they hugged. 'Gi-i-i-r-r-rl!'

373

'Howyoubeen?'

'What'shappening?'

'YouseenJackieanthem?'

'Yeahgirlweallhangingtonight.'

Mallory stood by the luggage and watched them, a polite smile on her face. The two friends' mouths were open and words were coming out, but the language was so strangely pitched and accented that to Mallory's ears it sounded like a kind of patois floating on a southern wind.

Marlene drove them to the downtown Sheraton, where they registered and took their luggage up to their room. When Mallory disappeared into the bathroom, Marlene turned to Esther and said, 'So is Mallory coming with us?'

'Sure.'

Marlene raised her eyebrows. 'She's not your boss or anything, is she? Can we be ourselves?'

'She's cool,' Esther said, knowing exactly what Marlene meant. 'Now, there are certain things that I must do while I'm in D.C.'

Marlene started laughing. 'You have to go to the Grille.'

'I must go to the Grille and have my fried chicken and greens and world-famous biscuits. And following that, I must go over to Georgia Avenue and have a drink or two at Traces.'

'Sister, these things have already been arranged,' Marlene said. 'The girls are going to meet us over at Traces at nine-thirty. Okay?'

'What are the Grille and Traces?' Mallory asked, coming out of the bathroom.

'Citadels of African-American culture,' Marlene said sweetly. 'Honey, you're about to experience the D.C. you don't read about in your civics book.'

The waitresses at the Grille were just as slow and friendly as ever. The tables in the cramped restaurant were all filled, so the three women sat at the counter. The first bite of her long-awaited dinner revealed to Esther that the superior quality of the fried chicken and greens hadn't declined since her days as a college student. As she ate, Esther turned and looked at the people surrounding her. The customers were a mixture of working-class folks from the surrounding community, university students and professors, and white-collar professionals who'd come to the restaurant straight from their downtown government jobs. Esther felt as though she knew everyone in the place, and in fact she did recognize one of the waitresses and several of the older patrons. She saw Mallory looking around tentatively as noisy conversations and raucous laughter, as thick as the odor of fried food, wafted through the air. Esther turned away from Mallory, chewed her chicken, and remembered her freshman year, all-night cramming sessions and pledging. In the scent of corn bread and candied yams that drifted in the air, she could smell her happy past. She put her fork down and extended a high five to Marlene. 'Da Grille,' Esther said to Marlene, and grinned. Their palms smacked together lightly.

When she turned around to look at Mallory, she saw that the tension had drained from her face. She was shoveling candied yams and fried chicken into her mouth, and the euphoric brightness of her eyes indicated that she was a woman experiencing rapture. 'Oh, God, this is so good.' She looked up at the two black women, who were staring at her in amusement. 'I'm, like, in heaven.'

'Don't hurt yourself, now,' Marlene teased. 'We don't want to have to roll you out of here with a stick.'

By the time they all finished the thick wedges of sweet potato pie that the waitress placed before them, Mallory had loosened her belt. 'I hope they have a gym at the hotel,' she said as they left. 'I need to work this dinner off immediately.'

'Child, you are not in L.A. You're allowed to gain weight here,' Marlene said with a wink.

The parking lot outside Traces was half full, as it usually was on weeknights. From the outside, the squarish, one-story brick building was unprepossessing and blended into the quiet neighborhood of brick row houses with neat porches that surrounded it. There were no gentrified pretensions about the place. It was a neighborhood bar and restaurant that drew its clientele from all over the city. Esther felt excited as she and the other women made their way across the parking lot. Traces was the scene of the date that preceded her deflowering, and ever since that time, it held a special place in her heart.

The interior, dimly lit, was divided into a bar on the left and a restaurant to the right. Mallory followed Esther and Marlene, who seemed to know where they were going. As soon as the three women turned left, she heard happy squeals as two more friends rushed toward them.

'Esther!' they said in unison. They took turns hugging her, and then, amid more squeals and giggles, Mallory heard that exotic language again. The four dark women stood in front of her, speaking the lively patois she couldn't quite comprehend. Mallory turned away from them and looked around the room. She saw one white man, sitting at a table with a black woman. The two were laughing uproariously, and when his eyes happened to glance at Mallory, he looked startled and turned away quickly.

'Mallory, I want you to meet my friends Jackie and Titilayo.' Mallory shook hands with Jackie, who smiled warmly at her with slightly buck teeth, then turned to Titilayo. She tried to look at her neck, her chest, anywhere but at the thick tangle of dreadlocks that surrounded her dark face and cascaded down her back. She had never met anyone with dreadlocks before, although she'd seen them on actors and musicians on television and in the movies. She wanted to stare at, even touch, the rough-looking squiggly snakes, but she knew that would be rude. Besides, Titilayo's face was somber, almost stern. She didn't seem friendly.

They sat down in a booth, and as the four black women chatted happily, Mallory glanced over at Esther from time to time. She'd probably prefer that I weren't here, the white woman thought. I shouldn't have come. She tried not to look at Esther's friends, because whenever she did, her eyes went immediately to Titilayo's hair. Esther would occasionally say something to draw her into their conversation, but their talk was too full of reminiscences for her to get involved.

After they had been sitting for about twenty minutes, a heavyset waitress, who walked as though every step she took might be her last, finally came over to their table. She whispered to Esther, who craned her neck in the direction of the waitress's hidden finger. 'Oh, Lord,' she said. An elderly gentleman, seventy if he was a day, waved at her from the bar. 'Tell him thank you, but I'm expecting my husband any minute.'

'I'll tell Grandpa that you're already spoken for,' the waitress muttered, limping toward the man.

Marlene, Jackie, and Titilayo chuckled as they looked toward the bar. 'Girlfriend has caught big time already,' Marlene said. Mallory craned her neck to see what everyone was looking at, but she didn't understand what was going on. Seeing her perplexed expression, Esther said, 'Pops wanted to buy me a drink. . . . Gray hair. Red tie,' she added. Mallory located the man who fit the description and started giggling.

'Don't laugh,' Marlene said. 'Social security checks make good pocket change.'

'Oh, girl, please,' Jackie said. 'There will always be a Traces; it will continue like the pyramids. And there will always be old nig—' She stopped, glancing at Mallory, who could feel her face turning red. Esther, seeming a little embarrassed, gave her a reassuring smile. ' . . . geezers hanging out at this bar, talking trash. You can set your clock by it.'

The waitress brought everyone a glass of wine, except Titilayo, who had ordered apple juice. Mallory stole a quick look at the dreadlocks, wondering how hair could get like that, wondering how she kept it clean. It didn't look clean. Well, it didn't, she told herself when she started feeling guilty for her thoughts. It looked matted and unkempt. And angry. It frightened her.

'A toast,' Marlene said, and they all raised their glasses. 'To old friends and new.' She smiled at Mallory. Their table was filled with the sound of clinking glasses. After they began to drink their wine, the conversation seemed to flow in more general directions. They talked about careers and movies. They bashed L.A., D.C., and men. From time to time, the waitress would hobble over to their table, cast her heavy-lidded eyes in the direction of some would-be lothario, and, en masse, they would send her on her way with yet another refusal. Each time they turned down a 'geezer', they would fall out in a fit of laughter and then resume their conversation. They ordered another round, and when they were nearly finished sipping their second wines, Esther leaned over and whispered to Mallory. 'You okay? Having a good time?' Mallory nodded.

'So how are things in D.C. these days? I've been reading that crime is totally out of control,' Esther said.

'Straight-up madness,' Marlene said. 'It's all drug-related, and the dealers have no consciences, no value for human life. You can get shot for just being there.'

'Did you hear about our new scandal?' Jackie asked.
Esther shook her head.

'The school superintendent for one of the counties, who is a dashiki-wearing, Afrocentric, loud-talking, save-our-children kind of brother, was arrested with a substantial amount of cocaine in his possession,' Jackie said.

'One of the secretaries tipped off the cops. Old head sister. She said that she was tired of seeing our children's educations sabotaged by incompetence,' Marlene said.

'How much cocaine?' Esther asked.

'A street value of twenty-five thousand dollars,' Marlene said.

'That's enough to sell,' Esther said. 'And so, is he in jail?'

'Out on bond and talking much shit about how the' – Jackie gave Mallory a tentative glance – 'system is out to get him because he is a powerful, uh, brother.' Her lips curled up in disgust.

'He's telling the truth,' Titilayo said.

'Oh, Titi, please. How can you say that?' Jackie said.

'Because he was trying to improve educational conditions for *our* children. You think the, uh, power structure wants to see that?'

'Yeah, Titi, I do,' Jackie said. 'I think that at this particular time on this planet, the, uh, power structure would love to see *our* kids learning as opposed to gangbanging, carjacking, selling drugs, and having babies, which our tax dollars and theirs go to support. I'm not being naive. I know I'm talking about the people who enslaved and chained us, gave us Jim Crow and lynched our granddaddies, but my guess is that even they would rather see *our* kids get high SAT scores than see them breaking into their houses. I mean, every, uh, member of the system in America isn't intent on grinding us into the dust. Most of them don't care one way or the other. And some of them actually want to help us. So I'm not with the conspiracy theory.'

Mallory sat back in her seat.

'Well, I think he should sue for entrapment,' Titilayo said. 'What a setup. The *D.C. Daily* was gunning for him.

How did he happen to get arrested and have the drugs on him? Who sold him that stuff?'

'Titi, whoever sold him twenty-five thousand dollars' worth of cocaine wasn't twisting his arm or giving out freebies. We ain't talking about no nickel bag. The brother had to save up to buy twenty-five thousand dollars' worth of dope. And now he has the nerve to talk about a conspiracy to destroy *our* leadership,' Jackie said.

Esther took another sip of wine, leaned forward, and put her elbows on the table. She stole a quick glance at Mallory, who was staring straight ahead.

'There is a conspiracy. All you have to do is see how many black men have been toppled from power,' Titilayo said, her voice quivering with emotion.

'Titi, give me a break,' Jackie said heatedly. 'The man gave himself to them on a silver platter. Did the white folks' – she gave Mallory a quick apologetic look – 'force the coke up his nose? I mean, when I elect somebody black to run my city, or represent me in Congress, or catch dogs, that's what I want them to do. I don't want them chasing women or getting high or stealing the money or bullshitting or putting their own egos in front of the needs of black people.'

'White leaders do it all the time,' Titilayo said, wrapping her dreads around her fingers. She didn't look at Mallory, who was sitting as far back in her seat as she could.

'Are we talking about white leaders?' Jackie asked. 'That's just the problem. We get these insecure brothers who want to do what the jivest white men have done, because they think that's like being equal, that the civil rights movement was all about their being able to exercise their lack of personal integrity to the highest extent of their distorted imaginations. They put their egos before the needs of the black community that entrusted them with leadership in the first place. I say fry their asses. The standard isn't John F. Kennedy or Tricky Dick. You know what I mean?

The standard is Frederick Douglass, Malcolm X, Harriet Tubman, or Fannie Lou Hamer. That's the standard.'

'Yeah, you can say all that, but the truth is, every time a black man achieves any kind of power, white people try to pull him down,' Titilayo said.

'So come up with a strategy,' Marlene said.

'When the powers that be can get one of your own to betray you? I mean, the sister sold him out.'

'She saw him doing wrong, so she told,' Marlene said.

'How much does any sister owe any brother?' Esther asked quietly. 'I mean, ultimately we all have to live with our own sense of integrity.'

Titilayo gave a little shrug and took a sip of apple juice. Esther looked at Mallory. Her eyes were wide open, and she seemed to be hanging on to every word that was being said. Hope we're not scaring girlfriend, Esther thought to herself.

'You all are so invested in being black,' Mallory said, as she and Esther got ready for bed. 'I mean, that's such a huge part of your identity, isn't it? Even more than being an American, being black comes first, doesn't it?' She didn't stop to let Esther answer, her mind was so full of her own thoughts as she replayed snippets of the conversation she'd heard in Traces. 'I mean, way back when, my family is English and French, but that means nothing to me. We don't have any customs or language from our heritage; my mother never even cooked French food. I don't have a sense of – of ethnicity, not the way you do,' she said wistfully.

'You lost your roots.' Esther smiled.

But Mallory wasn't smiling. 'Yes. That's exactly what I mean.'

'You don't need ethnicity, Mallory. You have the privilege that your skin gives you. You don't think of your color as an issue, because it's not. Sales clerks don't chase you around Saks Fifth Avenue trying to figure out what you stole because you are white. And the saleslady doesn't give a damn if you just got off the boat from Bosnia. It doesn't make any difference if you're French or English or Irish. You're white, and white people have the power in this country.'

'White people have power, but we've lost our identity. It got thrown into the melting pot.'

'Well, yeah. That's who the melting pot is for: white folks. Nobody else blends in except you all. It's for all the Italians and Germans and Swedes to jump in and claim one glorious identity. Why do you think none of the Latinos are bothering to learn English? They know that the pot's not for people with brown skin, dark eyes, and straight black hair. They know they won't mix, so they're not going to give up their culture for half the dream. Hell, if I were from Mexico, I'd ask that my kids be taught in Spanish too.'

Mallory stared at her friend's tight face. All the anger that she'd ever suspected was inside Esther seemed to be seeping out. 'But why do you sound so bitter? You don't think you're in that melting pot? Look at you. You've done so well.'

'Mallory, there are white women with high school degrees who make more money than I do. Do you have an M.B.A.?'

Mallory looked startled and then shook her head.

'I make sixty-five thousand a year. How much do you make?'

'But I've been in banking longer,' Mallory said quickly.

'This is true, but— '

'And lenders are paid more than operations people.'

'And why are there no black lenders at Angel City?'

'I don't know.'

'You think no black people have ever applied for the job?'

'I don't know. Maybe there weren't any qualified black people.'

'You mean qualified like Charles Weber? Is that what you mean? Give me a break, Mallory.'

'Well, Humphrey Boone is one of the highest-ranking employees at Angel City, and he has a lot of responsibility.'

'And it took a damn riot to get him hired.'

Mallory shrank back as though she'd been slapped. She opened her mouth, then closed it.

'And I'll tell you something else: If anything happens at Angel City, any kind of an economic downturn, guess who's going out that door first: you or Humphrey Boone? you or me?'

'You don't know that. . . .'

'Trust me. I do know that.' The black woman felt a sudden surge of relief, as though she'd been walking around with a migraine and was finally feeling the aspirin kicking in.

Mallory sighed. As Esther glanced at her, she seemed confused and unhappy. 'So I guess you think that affirmative action is the answer?'

'Do you mean affirmative action for white people or for black people?'

Mallory looked startled again.

'You think America is a meritocracy? You've had affirmative action for white folks ever since this country got started. Every time a black person couldn't get the job because he was black, that was affirmative action for white people. Every time we get turned away from the luxury apartment building and the new housing development, that's affirmative action for white people. And it's not because you work harder and you're smarter and have higher SATs. It's because you're white. So hell, yeah, I want some affirmative action for black people. I want some jobs reserved for me. I want some prime real estate reserved for me. I want spots in the best schools set aside for me. I want the Justice Department to bend the law my way.'

383

Mallory looked at Esther, saw the bitterness in her face, and felt small and weak. She thought about her meeting with Humphrey Boone, and experienced the same urgent need for forgiveness. 'You make me feel guilty.'

'Guilty about what?'

'Guilty about being white.' She knew her words sounded ridiculous the instant she spoke them; she wanted to call them back.

Esther glared at her. Ever since she and Mallory had become closer, the little things she'd always tried to keep hidden from white people she worked with were gradually slipping out. Her mask was no longer in place. She was always wondering whether or not she was revealing too much of herself. Now, as she looked at her friend, she realized that she no longer had the power to monitor herself with Mallory. She'd stepped over a line, and there was no turning back. And for the first time in a long time, when she looked at Mallory she didn't see her friend; she saw a white woman. 'If you feel so guilty, why did it take a special program to force you to make some loans to black customers?' she said quietly.

Mallory's eyes grew very wide, as if she were looking at a bullet that was coming right at her. When she could find her voice, she said, 'I don't make bank policy, Esther.'

'You and I both know it's about more than that. It's a judgment call. Pure vibes. You're in your office with a client, and after you go through the TRW and the application forms, it's about how comfortable you feel with the person. How much you trust him. You look across that desk and you ask yourself: Is this person like me? And when the person is black, the answer is always no.' The words screamed out in her mind: *Try to deny it*. She had a mental image of the frizzy-haired white waitress who refused to give her the check, of the many sharp-nosed salesladies who'd followed her around. Of all of them. And now Mallory, too.

The white woman could hear everything she always feared in Esther's voice: the full-force purity of her anger, slamming into Mallory as though she were the enemy. 'What do you want me to say?' Mallory's voice was rising, like high, fragile music. 'That I turned down black loan applicants? I did. You think I did it because they were black? That's just not true. I turned them down because they didn't meet the minimum requirements for getting a loan. Do you think I loaned money to every white person who wanted it?'

'There have been white customers who didn't have everything they needed, who were borderline. You worked with them, and don't tell me you didn't.'

Mallory winced. 'That's not fair,' she said. Esther could hear the rising hysteria in Mallory's voice. In a minute she would be crying; her lips were already trembling. Let her cry. What the hell do I care? She got in the bed nearest the window and turned her back to her friend.

They were quiet the next morning. They dressed silently, observing the curves and planes of each other's bodies out of the corner of their eyes. They were unfailingly polite, getting out of each other's way, taking turns in the bathroom. Pleases and thank yous bubbled from their lips, but not much else. At the conference, they attended the same sessions. They sat together, then drifted apart to network with other women. At lunchtime, Mallory told Esther that she was going to eat with someone else. Esther felt a twinge of loneliness as she watched her walk away. She joined two other black women, who, like her, weren't hungry, and spent her lunch hour wandering around a downtown shopping mall with them.

By the time the last session, titled 'Beyond the Glass Ceiling,' ended, Esther was hungry. As the horde of women emptied out of the hotel meeting room, she looked around for Mallory. She scanned the departing throng even as she exchanged pleasantries with friends and acquaintances. Just as the mass of people was thinning out, she saw Mallory standing next to two white women. The eyes that stared into hers were neon letters that said: Get me away from here.

Mallory felt a softness brush against her shoulder. She turned to the women and excused herself, then faced Esther. 'Listen,' they both said at the same time. They looked at each other for a few seconds.

'I care what you think about me, Esther.'

'I know.'

'I've made mistakes, but I'm not "the white people".'

'I'll try to remember that,' Esther said.

26

Humphrey parked in front of a settlement of dilapidated buildings the color of bathtub rings and sat in his Mercedes for a few minutes. He hated coming over to this side of town, his old neighborhood. He hated going to his sister's house. Five or six teenage boys were lined up outside her apartment, their bodies one long connected slouch, the very breaths they took a declaration of war. They all wore jeans that were several sizes too big; the bands of their underwear were showing. They all had earrings, and the hair of those whose heads weren't shaved completely bald was a collection of jagged lines. The hard glint in their eyes was intended to frighten. Humphrey sucked his teeth in disgust. Why couldn't they just pull themselves up! Jesus, you didn't have to be a rocket scientist to see that the people who make it are the ones who go to school, study, and work hard. Humphrey rolled down his window and spat into the street. He searched their faces, looking for his nephew. 'Bunky,' he called, 'come here for a minute.'

Frowning, his nephew detached himself from the group of boys who were staring at Humphrey or, more precisely, at his Mercedes. Bunky swaggered to his uncle's car and stuck his head in the window on the driver's side, filling the automobile with his sweaty odor.

'Wha'zup, Humptey?' He stood back a little and appraised his mother's brother and his shiny ride. 'You stay clean,' he said admiringly.

Humphrey started to say, 'If you want to be "clean" and have nice things, you need to go back to school and study,' but he stopped himself. It was an old, useless lecture. The boy had heard it before, and nothing had changed. Humphrey sighed, remembering weekends he'd devoted to taking his sister's children to the zoo and to museums, trying to be a good role model. But the older they got, the more obvious it became that he was no one-man army: He couldn't fight the streets, and they had a prior claim to his nieces' and nephews' lives. He looked into the boy's eyes and saw an emptiness so profound and inevitable that for a minute he couldn't speak. 'How are you, Bunky?'

'Hey, I'm cool. I'm straight.'

'Listen, I'm going up to see your mother. Keep an eye on my ride, will you?'

'Oh, I'ma do that. For real.'

Humphrey locked the doors and put on the alarm anyway.

'Hey, Humptey,' his sister said when she opened the door. Chontelle had gotten even bigger since the last time he saw her. He remembered when she was a pretty little girl and then a beautiful teenager, but that was before she married the wrong man and had three babies in as many years. Chontelle gave him a hug and led him to a dingy couch, moving a stack of children's clothes out of the way to give them both room. He took his jacket off and sat down carefully next to his sister. The cramped apartment smelled like hair oil and fried chicken.

'You said you were sick.' He put his jacket on the back of the sofa. He knew that she was going to ask him for money, and he wanted to expedite the business at hand.

Chontelle sighed. 'Did you move into your new place?'

He'd been in his town house for over a year, but when he talked with his mother, his sisters and brother, he always made it seem as though he'd just moved in. 'It's still a mess,' he said quickly.

'Well, I want to come over and see it when you get settled,' his sister said.

He looked nervously out the window, keeping his eyes on his car. 'Listen, Chontelle, I'm kind of on the run. What's wrong with you and what can I do?'

'Well, they think I might have what you call lupus. It's kind of like arthritis. Lotta black women get it. Your joints be aching.'

'What do you need?'

Chontelle hesitated. 'Well, they got some experimental drugs that MediCal don't cover. The doctor say it might give me some relief.' She looked at him quickly and then looked away. 'It's expensive.'

Humphrey knew a lie when he heard it. His mother told him about every ache and pain that she, his two sisters, his brother, and all his aunts and uncles ever had, and she'd never mentioned lupus. 'Chontelle, why don't you quit trying to bullshit me,' he said. 'Why do you need the money?'

Chontelle sighed. She moved in close to him and peered at his face.

'You got some ingrown hairs, Humptey. You want me to pull them out?'

He rubbed his face. His skin was irritated. 'You have any alcohol?'

Hc could feel the cool alcohol on his face as she swabbed him with a cotton ball. Then he felt the tiny stings as she tweezed the hairs that had curled into his skin. 'Humptey, I gotta pay Bunky's lawyer,' she said as she stood over him. He didn't say anything, and she continued to pull the hairs. For as long as he could remember, she'd always done this for him. Her fingers were familiar and soothing.

He shook his head even as she was tugging on his coarse whiskers. 'No. I gave Mama some money for the lawyer a couple of months ago. Get a public defender.'

Chontelle stood back from him. 'They don't do nothing. He'll end up in jail.'

Humphrey sighed. 'It's kind of inevitable, wouldn't you say? I mean, how long is he going to be able to stay out of jail, hanging with the homeboys? I'm sorry. You're my sister. I'd like to help you, but I'm not made of money.' Humphrey stood and picked up his coat.

'Humptey, I need three hundred dollars. Just three hundred dollars.'

He hated hearing her beg. Her pleading always made him feel guilty. He had nothing to feel guilty about, he reminded himself. He wasn't responsible for his sister's problems. 'Oh, just three hundred dollars.'

'Aww, nigger, you got it.' Just that quickly, the pleading had gone out of her face and the eyes he looked into were hard as bricks. Kickass eyes. They always brought out the worst in him.

'Hell, yeah, I got it. You know how I got it, Chontelle? I work my ass off for it. You should try it sometimes.'

'Well, fuck you, then. Don't wanna help nobody. Fuck you.' Her full mouth had turned into an angry sore; her fat cheeks quivered.

Humphrey put on his coat. 'I have helped you. Nobody told you to have all these kids by that sorry-ass dude. It's not my fault.'

'What you saying? I shoulda killed my kids?' she screamed, rushing toward her brother, her arms flailing. 'That what you saying? I shoulda killed my kids? If you'da been a woman, the same shit coulda happened to you, motherfucker."

'If I had been a woman, I wouldn't have had any children that I couldn't take care of. I mean, you ever hear of birth control, Chontelle?'

'Oh, yeah, Mr. Perfect. Got it all wrapped up tight, dontcha? You think you so high and mighty, just because you got you a piece a job. You talk white. You act white. But you know one thing: You ain't white, Humptey. You got with white folks and want to act like you don't understand what it's like to be black no more.'

'Being black is not synonymous with being a poor single mother on welfare, except in your head. To me, being black is working hard and moving on up to that deluxe apartment in the sky or any other damn place I want to be. Being black is living well, driving a good car, and taking a vacation to Hawaii when I feel like it. Why can't you see that? Don't try to guilt-trip me because I don't buy into the misery you've created for yourself, Chontelle. Why do I have to pay for your life?'

Chontelle waved her hands in her brother's face. 'Shi-i-it. I'm paying for yours. Oh, I guess you can't see that. You so damn smart, you don't even understand the real deal. Nigger, you where you are because folks like me threw bricks and set fires last April. Can you dig that? You think Martin Luther King set you free? Niggers burning down Detroit, Chicago, and Watts set your ass free. You can't relate to my problems? They beneath you? You think I ain't shit because I got married and had kids and the marriage didn't work out. You so disgusted with me, huh, Humptey? But when them white folks knock you on your ass, I bet you'll begin to relate then. One of these days, you gone remember exactly what it's like to be a nigger, and I hope I'm around to see it.'

The boys were leaning against his car when he got to the curb. 'All right, then, Humptey,' Bunky said.

'Take it easy. Stay out of trouble,' Humphrey said, and he sped off as quickly as he could.

The telephone was ringing when he entered his house. He picked it up on the third ring. 'Humphrey. This your mama. Chontelle just called me. How could you turn your sister down like that? Y'oughta fall on your knees and ask Jesus to forgive you, son. Turning that girl down like that, when you practically all she got.'

By the time Humphrey got off the telephone, his temples were throbbing. They were still aching as he wrote out a check for three hundred dollars. This was it, he told himself, as he put the check in an envelope and addressed it to his sister. This was the last time. But even as he made that vow, he knew that there would never be a last time. He would always have to ride in with a magic checkbook, because he was the success of the family, the only success they knew. As he stared at the check, he wanted to laugh that such a pitiful amount was the difference between life and death to his sister. Three hundred dollars. That was bullshit. His laughter sounded strangely solitary in his bedroom. If he had real money, then he could help them. He might be able to make a difference. He leaned his head back in the desk chair and slowly began banging it against the firm upholstery in a staccato rhythm. Mo' money. Mo' money. Mo' money. If he had big dollars, then he could save them all. He could bring his entire family out of the ghetto, not just his mother. It was never too late when you had real money. He could send Bunky to a military academy and put the rest of his sister's children in good private schools. He could send his sisters, even his fool of a brother, to college and pay for graduate school. Or trade school. They weren't stupid people; they just didn't know how to set goals and follow through on anything. God.

He closed his eyes, and his dream appeared to him, fully formed and alive. If he got to be the president of Angel City, that would almost be enough. What did Sinclair make? he wondered. At least $750,000 a year. That would be a beginning. He could change their lives with that. But what he was really dreaming of was more permanent than a job: He wanted his own business. He wanted to own a bank, a first-class, full-service commercial bank. Odell had the right idea; he just wanted to move too fast. Humphrey would bide his time. He was getting on-the-job training at Angel City. If he was president for about five years, he'd have all the contacts he needed to get start-up capital and investors. All he had to do to get the ball rolling, to make his dream come true, was to excel as the regional manager of Angel City. As simple as that.

But as he got into bed, thinking about the good job he needed to do filled him with panic. Earlier in the week, the first of three private placement deals he'd been working on fell through the tubes. And that was right after he told Preston Sinclair that everything was going so well. Now he was back at ground zero. His fingers gripped the smooth edges of his sheets. It was okay. Business was full of ups and downs. But he was under a microscope at Angel City. He had a lot to prove, and he couldn't afford any downs. Jesus, he was tired. He stretched down in the bed again. He hadn't really slept since he'd gotten the call two nights before from the insurance agency's representative, a little slime-ball white boy, telling him that they'd decided to pull out of the deal. And then the client backed out. Walked right after the insurance agency called. As he lay in bed, the feeling came over him again that they were in cahoots. He had that feeling right in his gut. The two white boys had gotten together and decided they didn't have to give him anything. He closed his eyes and pounded the ends of the bed with his fists. The key was not to panic, to be cool and float into the next deal. That's what that old white guy had told him at the bank where he did his first private placement loan. He said, 'Humph, they're gonna fuck with you for two reasons: because you're black and because they can. The trick is to stay buoyant and keep floating.' He shut his eyes tightly, opened his hands, and let his body go limp. 'I am the Man,' he whispered to himself. Those words usually calmed and reassured him, but this time, instead of blocking out all his worries, his magic phrase was overwhelmed by the sound of his sister Chontelle's shrieks. 'One of these days, you gone remember exactly what it's like to be a nigger.'

Humphrey reached across his desk and took the documents from the hard-looking little black woman seated in front of him. He glanced quickly at the credit report. The TRW was impeccable, as clean as a snake. Give me a goddamn break, Humphrey thought. He put down the papers and glanced at Rhonda Baldwin's tight, smug face. Jesus! He knew from the minute the woman had sidled up to him at the banquet that she was a bad check on skinny legs. When she asked to come in and talk about a loan, Humphrey tried to put her off on one of the lenders, but then it turned out that her husband was a Gamma, and there really was no way he could get out of meeting with her. But that frat brother shit could go only so far. The woman sitting in front of him was as slick as snot, and there was no way in hell he would approve a ten-cent loan to her. He just wanted to get rid of Rhonda Baldwin as expeditiously as possible. And he didn't want her coming back. Humphrey sighed. Sometimes he felt as though a call had gone out throughout the entire known African-American world: Brother with the power to give out money is in the house. And they had come, from all corners of Los Angeles and beyond, far too many of them bringing a load of bullshit with them. Of course, there were plenty of qualified people too, but they were never quite as memorable as the hustlers. During the time he'd been in banking, he'd seen his share of white slicksters – far more plentiful because they had more resources – but he didn't care about them. For some reason, it actually hurt his feelings when a brother or sister tried to deceive him.

Looking at the phony TRW in front of him, he didn't know whether to laugh or get angry. Humphrey knew that Rhonda's credit was bad enough to carry a gun. Several days after the banquet, he talked with a lender from another bank who'd dealt with her. 'I've seen some terrible credit in my day, but this woman's takes the cake. She owes the moon money. Defaulted on two bank loans. She's going to present a squeaky clean report, but don't believe it for a second.'

Humphrey handed the papers back to Rhonda. 'Ms. Baldwin, I don't know where you bought this report from, but I know it's not yours.'

Rhonda smiled broadly. She was a wiry, homely woman with thinning hair and short, nervous fingers. Her eyes seemed to take in everything while they avoided looking into Humphrey's. She ignored his remark. 'Brother, I'm trying to help the community,' she said, her voice suddenly filled with passion. She let her glance rest on Humphrey's for a moment. 'You know, I can be generous with that loan. I can spread it around a little.'

'I'm paid very well by the bank,' Humphrey said with a sigh. He added, 'Look, you don't qualify. Your credit report is phony. You have no collateral. Do I need to go on?'

'So it's like that, huh? No, *brother*, you don't need to go on. I can see that you're not going to help me. It's brothers like you that keep the rest of us down.'

The words were as familiar as flies and just as annoying. 'I will be happy to put you in contact with some venture capitalists, who might very well be interested in your idea,' Humphrey said carefully and quietly. He didn't want Rhonda getting loud and crazy in his office.

'Venture capitalists,' she said with a sneer. 'Like they're going to be interested in any idea a black woman has.'

'Look, let me be honest. You're going to have to clean up your credit legitimately before any lender or investor will even consider you. Your business proposal is well done, and you've got a strong idea. My suggestion is that you go into partnership with someone whose credit will help you qualify for a loan.' He stood up and extended his hand.

Rhonda Baldwin's lips were drawn tightly against her teeth. She looked down at the floor. 'Look, all I need is a chance.'

The begging threw him a little, made guilt gush up inside him and burn his throat. Then he caught himself. Rhonda was trying to con him. Why should he feel guilty? 'I'm sorry, Ms. Baldwin,' he managed to say. He waited briefly, and then, when it was clear that the woman had no desire to shake his hand, he withdrew it. Humphrey walked to the door, held it open, and watched as Rhonda Baldwin disappeared down the hall.

Instead of going back into his office, he stood at the door for a second. In one hour he had a meeting with another insurance official, who was champing at the bit to get in on the private placement deal he was putting together. As he thought of his pitch, the way he would word his proposal, he could feel his adrenaline pumping. And he could also feel fear, like cold, sharp claws digging into his spine. This was the second attempt at the same deal. The first deal evaporated, slipped through his fingers, even though he was clutching as hard as he could. He needed a win; Angel City didn't pay him to lose. He thought about Kirk Madison's smug face, the bland smile he gave him every time their paths crossed. He's just waiting for me to fall, he told himself. Wouldn't he just love to see me flat on my ass. How many black men got a shot like the one he'd been given? He had to win. Humphrey rubbed the back of his neck, then he closed his office door and began walking down the long hallway.

When Esther opened the door to the employees' lounge, she was surprised to see Humphrey leaning against the soda machine, drinking a Pepsi and looking off into space. The somewhat dingy room was almost exclusively the province

396

of the bank's underlings; she rarely came here herself. But it did have the only soda machine on the premises, and from the somewhat spaced-out expression on Humphrey's face, it appeared that the man needed a change of scenery almost as badly as he needed a cold drink. As Esther walked toward him, he took a last gulp and tossed the container into the trash can.

'You're not setting a very good example,' Esther said. She smiled at Humphrey's puzzled look and then reached in for his empty. In the back of the room were three smaller bins, marked CANS, NEWSPAPERS, BOTTLES. She threw the Pepsi can into the first one. 'Angel City is politically and environmentally correct,' she said, and they both laughed.

Esther hadn't spoken with Humphrey other than to say hello since the banquet more than three weeks ago. Standing beside him, she felt a kind of nervous excitement flooding her body. As she did nearly every time she saw him, she gave his body a furtive appraisal. He wasn't bad-looking at all, she thought. She smiled at him, then chose her words carefully. She didn't want to make the mistake of being too casual just because they were both black. On the other hand she wanted to begin to carve out a friendly relationship with the man she hoped would transfer her to lending. 'How's everything going, Humphrey?'

His response took her by surprise. He gave her a long, curious glance, then chuckled a little and shook his head. 'A woman was just in my office wanting a loan for an open-air fruit market she wants to put on Slauson, just east of La Brea.'

'That's my neighborhood. Good idea.'

'Good idea. Good business plan . . .'

'Bad credit.' Esther shook her head empathically.

'Perfect credit report.'

'Which she bought and paid for.'

'No question. We are talking about the cleanest, most perfect TRW that I've ever seen.'

'Black?' Esther chuckled when Humphrey nodded. 'Well, you can't blame her for trying.'

'Oh, is that right?' Humphrey gave a brief laugh, and when he heard it, he realized how tense he was feeling. 'I mean, did she think I wouldn't check?'

'Sure,' Esther said cheerfully. 'She thought you'd recommend her for the Minority Loan Program and she'd get her loan. She'd open up her business, make a million dollars, pay off the bank, get her credit straightened out legitimately, buy his-and-hers Mercedeses and a house in Bel Agua.'

'To make matters worse, her husband is a frat brother.' He chuckled again, and Esther joined in.

'The sister knew you wouldn't turn down a Gamma man's woman. I'm sure she left with a check.' 'Sister' was a word she reserved for her world beyond the bank. It felt a little strange saying it in the bank, but she was reassured when she saw Humphrey smile.

'Right.' They both felt good as they talked. Normally, Humphrey kept his professional concerns bottled up inside him, brooding when things were going badly, exulting when they were going well, but never discussing them. And Esther was always so careful around her co-workers, with the exception of Mallory, that she rarely saw the light side of any bank business. But as Humphrey and Esther bantered back and forth, they both felt comfortable and relaxed. It was only after he let his eyes stray to her face and body that Humphrey felt a new tension, which had nothing to do with Angel City National Bank.

Esther was fine; that much was clear. It was strange how his eyes, maybe even his mind, played tricks on him when he looked at black women. Esther was in front of him, and yet he saw his sister Chontelle's wide behind, the ashy patches on his sister's rusty knees, the little tufts of nappy hair at the nape of her neck. Jesus. It was Esther's voice that filled the lounge, but when he listened to her he heard his mother's harsh words: 'Boy, get your behind up out this bed' – words that probably saved his life but hard words, spoken in a hard way. His mother had been angry every day of his life, and her anger frightened him, even now. Esther was a beautiful woman, but even in the midst of admiring her, he heard loud cussing and saw food stamps and welfare checks. He saw all that, and it wasn't because he wanted to see it. He was trying not to see it. And he heard other voices too. All those beautiful cream- and cocoa-colored girls in the schoolyard, laughing at him. All those caramel girls at dances, turning him down. All those lemon-wafer girls telling him they were busy, far too busy to go out with a skinny dark boy with thick lips. He couldn't look at any black woman, not even the lightest ones, with the blowiest blow hair, without seeing his mother and his sisters and those other women in the welfare line, without smelling that odor of hair grease and fried chicken, without hearing rejection and mean laughter. They could be trying to kiss him, and he tasted hair grease and cussing in their mouths. They could be trying to love him with their bodies, but what he felt was all that grease and cussing up inside them. All that anger. And he couldn't help but compare Esther to other women, women who were pale and quiet and pretty. Women who smiled at him from big screens and small screens and magazine covers. They were always welcoming, with their dazzling white smiles. These women were never angry, and they smelled happy. This was the type of woman he needed sitting next to him in his Mercedes when the top was down. This was the kind of woman, as flashy as a bar of gold, whose streaming hair let everyone know that he was important, that he was somebody, even when he was afraid he was not. Especially then.

'Listen, great point about switching over to Wellington's for our check service. I support you fully on that,' Humphrey said.

Esther smiled, pleased to be complimented on the idea she'd raised during the last staff meeting. 'Thank you. Just trying to save the bank some money,' she said lightly.

Humphrey felt the urge to put his fingers inside her dimples. 'I'd better be getting back,' she said.

As she left the lounge, Esther could feel Humphrey's eyes on her. She wondered whether or not she should have reminded him again of her desire to become a lender, but decided that she was right to keep silent. She didn't want to go into overkill. On her way back to her office, she thought about what Mallory had said, that she could have a relationship with Humphrey and still work for him. He liked her. She could tell by the way he looked at her when he thought she wasn't watching. She thought fleetingly of Tyrone, Tyrone of the tense buttocks and silver tongue, her buddy and lover. But Tyrone was just something to do, she reminded herself. She could never marry Tyrone; the man didn't even have a MasterCard. She could build a life with Humphrey.

The May sky was still light by the time Esther left the bank that evening. Cranston showed signs of recovery. The burned buildings had been razed, and the damaged ones were being repaired. During the day, the air was split with the noise of drills and hammers, and now, in the relatively quiet evening, Esther felt a calmness as she drove down the street. Stopping at the light in front of the doughnut shop, Esther looked inside and saw the old-timers sitting at their table in the back. They looked like they were playing cards. Hyun was seated in the middle of the group, her head thrown back in laughter.

There was a speck of pink sticking in the corner of Esther's front door, and after she parked her car in the garage, she walked back outside to investigate. The pink was a note, folded neatly. 'Please come next door. There is a surprise for you.' It was signed 'Carol Linton.' Esther crumpled the note and threw it into the trash can and began walking toward her neighbors' house. She'd been trying to avoid the Lintons ever since Harold changed her tire and she spontaneously invited them to dinner, but as she rang their front doorbell, she knew that she'd have to make good on her word.

Esther could smell steak and biscuits when Carol opened the door. The white woman gave her a big smile. Their home was as nondescript and charmless as she'd thought it would be. 'Guess who's here to get her surprise,' Carol called out toward the dining room. Harold and the little girl appeared instantly, and they, too, were smiling at her. What the hell is going on? she wondered. The whole damn family looked like Moonies, all the simple grinning they were doing. 'We're just sitting down to dinner. Do you care to join us?'

'Oh, no. No, thank you.' Esther knew she should ask *them* to dinner, give them a definite date, but when she looked at the black man and his white wife, she couldn't imagine spending an evening with them.

'Harold, go get the surprise,' Carol said cheerfully. Harold disappeared, and returned with a small bouquet of daisies, carnations, and roses.

'Oh,' Esther said, taking the flowers.

'You weren't home, so the florist left them with us. Somebody definitely likes you,' Carol said. 'There's a card in there,' she added.

Esther picked out a small white card that read: 'To the prettiest flower in the garden. Love, Tyrone.'

'Oh,' she said again, and this time she was smiling.

'Well, looks like she's happy,' Harold said to Carol, who nodded. Their little girl positioned herself between her parents. She held on to her father's pants and her mother's skirt.

'Don't mind us; we're just real country, honey. West Virginia people are nosey parkers,' Carol said. Harold chuckled.

'Well, thanks for accepting the flowers for me,' Esther said.

'Oh, no trouble at all,' Carol said warmly.

No one said anything for a moment. Esther began rubbing the back of her neck. The harder she rubbed, the more it seemed to itch. Invite them. Invite them, her inner voice said. But her mouth wouldn't open. 'Good night,' she said quickly.

She put the flowers on her dining room table and stood back to admire them. Tyrone was so sweet. He was always sending her cards and giving her little quirky presents. One night he stopped by and presented her with a bag of muffins. Another time he brought her a gift-wrapped box of Calgon. Early one Sunday morning he came to her door bearing a tin of brownies that he'd just baked. They were still warm after they made love.

Esther was sipping peppermint tea at the kitchen table, when the doorbell rang. She ran to the living room, peeked out the window, and began giggling when she saw Tyrone's car. When she opened the door, he was standing in front of her, wearing a warm-up suit and holding a pizza box in one hand and a bottle of wine in the other. 'You're just full of presents tonight,' she said. She put her hands on his cheeks, leaned her body over the pizza box, and kissed him. 'Brotherman must want something.'

Tyrone grinned. 'He wants to speak to Madam Queen.'

'Oh, really,' She grinned.

She set the table in the breakfast room, while Tyrone poured the wine and cut the pizza. As soon as they sat down, he lifted his glass, leaned across the table, and tapped hers with it. 'To my baby,' he said.

'Thank you for my flowers and my dinner.'

Tyrone's eyes stared lovingly into hers. He had never meant to get so into Esther, but he couldn't stop himself. 'So how did that meeting go?' he asked.

She gave him a questioning look, and he said, 'Didn't you have your monthly operations managers meeting today?' He felt proud of himself for not only remembering the meeting but getting its title right. He was pretty sure he got it right. She liked to talk about her job, and he wanted her to know that he was interested in what she did.

'Oh, that was two days ago. It was fine.' She was surprised that he remembered.

'Did that asshole give you any trouble?'

'Who are you talking about?'

'You know, the guy you told me about who always has something to say about black people and Mexicans.'

She laughed. 'Oh, you mean Fred Gaskins. You have such a good memory.'

Tyrone didn't say anything. The truth was, he remembered everything that Esther had ever told him about her life. And he remembered how she looked and how her voice sounded when she was telling him. He could tell when she was sad, just by the way she glanced at things without focusing. Whenever she was happy, really happy, he could tell that too. 'So how was he acting?'

Esther shook her head. 'Listen, ever since Humphrey Boone took over as regional manager, Fred Gaskins has been on his good behavior.'

Tyrone felt his jaw muscles tighten when he heard the elegant black man's name, and he visualized him in his impeccable suits, with his monogrammed briefcase. He wanted to reach out and grab Esther's hand, but he restrained himself. 'Don't want anybody messing with my baby,' he said. He felt a fluttering in his stomach, like wings trying to find their way home. 'So what's happening in your department?'

It was such a generic question, he knew immediately that it sounded dumb. And he could tell from the look in Esther's eyes that he was trying too hard.

'I'm interviewing again for another teller. And I'm in the process of doing employee evaluations. At the last managers' meeting, I made the proposal that we switch to another check provider, and the bank is seriously considering it.' He doesn't know what a big deal that is, Esther thought when Tyrone didn't react to her words. 'Did I tell you I talked with Humphrey Boone about transferring me to the loan department?'

Tyrone nodded. 'He the one who makes the decision?' He could feel his throat growing tighter as he thought of the man who had more control over Esther's destiny than he did.

'He's the Man.'

Tyrone winced. 'I thought you like what you do. Why you want to go into lending?'

'Lending is more challenging. It'll open up more doors, and in the long run it will be much more lucrative. Besides, I'm not really using my M.B.A. with what I'm doing.'

Tyrone was silent. He hadn't known that she had two degrees.

Esther could see that Tyrone was surprised to hear about her M.B.A. – and a little taken aback. She couldn't expect him to know every little thing about her work, and if he couldn't get used to her having an M.B.A., she'd soon know. She reminded herself to be grateful that she had a man who brought her flowers and dinner. Maybe she should ask him about his day. How did his deliveries go? Or maybe she could ask him about T-shirt sales. In the time that she'd known him, they never went anywhere without him taking along T-shirts. Sometimes it was downright embarrassing the way he'd whip them out.

An M.B.A. Tyrone thought about the few months of community college he had. He didn't want to think about why he hadn't gone back. That was the story of his life: He had a hard time seeing things through. Might as well admit that he was scared, that he let one professor who told him that his math skills were below par chase him away. All he had to do was take the course again. Lots of people took things over, except a guy like Humphrey Boone. He probably had an M.B.A. too.

Tyrone thought about telling Esther that he'd sold twenty more T-shirts, but he didn't. The girl was dealing with thousands of dollars every day, talking about doing loans for millions. What did she care about some ten-dollar T-shirts?

They are their pizza in silence.

Afterward, they listened to music as they cleaned up. Tyrone had brought a salsa tape, and they danced while they loaded the plates into the dishwasher.

I can make her laugh, Tyrone told himself; don't take no degree to show her a good time. Their hands and shoulders touched; their hips bumped up against each other. They both started making sounds that were not quite laughter. 'You want me to work you out?' They were still dancing, only slowly, and he whispered it in her ear. When she nodded, he said, 'Go put on your sweats.'

By the time Esther returned in her workout clothes, Tyrone had moved the furniture to the side of the family room. 'I'm going to warm you up,' he said softly.

She stood in front of him and turned her head to the left, to the right, up, down, and then repeated the process all over again while he watched. She rotated her shoulders forward and then backward, and then he put his hands on them, pressing them down, then pulling them up. 'Hold it eight counts. Hold it until you feel it,' he said. He made her reach up. Higher! Higher! She made circles with her arms, small ones and then larger ones. He stood behind her, so that her round hips jutted into his groin. He grasped her wrists and had her trace circles that were larger still. Then they jogged in place, standing so close that their arms brushed against each other. Esther began to feel warm. The first beads of perspiration rolled down Tyrone's forehead. They lay down side by side on top of the large towel she had brought from her linen closet, and they lifted their legs in unison. 'Get it up higher, baby,' he whispered. She could feel the heat right under her groin. 'Is it burning, baby?' Tyrone asked. He pressed his chest against her back, and they did five more leg lifts. Then Esther felt his mouth against her wet, salty neck, his tongue against her shoulder. 'Cool-down time,' he said.

'I don't want to cool down,' she whispered, rolling on top of him.

They made love twice and didn't stop kissing even while they were putting their clothes back on. At the front door, they fondled each other so long that they began to feel new heat rising inside them. 'Stop,' Esther finally told Tyrone. She pushed him out the door, and when she closed it she was still smiling.

After Tyrone had left, Esther soaked in a tub full of Epsom salts and bubble bath. She felt sore and good at the same time as she relaxed in the warm water. Closing her eyes, she reexperienced Tyrone's lips over her body, Tyrone inside her. She felt a tiny explosion detonate, a miniature of the real thing. Sinking down into the water, she leaned her head back against the edge of the tub. Her body held memories of Tyrone, but he wasn't in her head. As she stretched out in the water she saw Humphrey, lean, dark, and elegant, heard Humphrey with his razor-sharp business mind. She imagined Humphrey Boone kissing her, touching her, inside her. Those images made her so dizzy she had to grope for the side of the tub as she stepped out of the water. Tyrone was a wonderful lover and a nice guy and there was no reason why she shouldn't continue to see him. After all, he was something to do. But Humphrey was going somewhere.

It was only ten-thirty, and she knew that Mallory didn't go to bed until after the eleven o'clock news went off. 'What are you doing, Mal?' she asked when her friend answered the telephone.

'Oh, I'm in the process of being stood up. Same as usual.'

'Oh, Mal . . .'

'No pity, please. I'm not in the mood.'

'Well, how about a little vengeance. I can arrange to have his ass thoroughly kicked by people in that line of work.'

'I want Mike Tyson for the job.' They both laughed. 'What are you doing?'

'Eat your heart out. I'm recovering from Tyrone.'

Her voice brightened. 'Oooh. Details. Details. Blow by blow. Let me at least have a vicarious sex life.'

'Oh, he was wonderful as usual, delighted every orifice of my body. And he brought me flowers, and pizza and wine.'

'Give that guy a gold star.'

'Yeah.'

'So what's wrong?'

'You know what's wrong.'

'Look. You're not going to marry this guy. You said it yourself: He's somebody nice to date. Enjoy him. Don't go through the blue collar–white collar angst. Spare yourself.'

'Mal, I think I like Humphrey.'

She could hear Mallory take a deep breath on the other end of the telephone. 'Go for it.'

'That's just what I'm going to do.'

They chatted a little while longer before hanging up. When Esther laid her head against the pillow, she felt drowsy and content. Ever since their confrontation in Washington, she was finding it easier to talk with Mallory. The odd thing was that at first she thought her rage had destroyed the friendship, that it wasn't strong enough to survive her true feelings. Now she realized that what they had before hadn't truly been a friendship, merely a relationship held together with polite talk and suppressed feelings. For the first time in her life, she trusted a white woman.

27

Bel Agua was a different kind of Los Angeles, a part of the city that never seemed touched by any of the calamities that racked the rest of the town. There were no crack baby billboards, no strip malls, no liquor stores on any corner. No graffiti. The sun was brighter; the rain fell more softly. There seemed to be no earthquakes in Bel Agua, or at least none that did any damage. It was as if the entire area were lifted up on some sort of insulated cloud. The place was protected somehow. The grass was greener. Simple as that. At least that's what Humphrey thought as he steered his Mercedes up the winding, tree-shaded roads that led to Preston Sinclair's home.

If he had stopped to get out and take a closer look, he would have seen the small cracks and tiny fissures visible in the thick adobe-style walls of the mansions he passed. Upon closer inspection, he would have noticed doorjambs that had been replastered, sanded smooth, and repainted so that they looked as good as new. But Humphrey was in a hurry as he drove west, and the brilliant sun was obscuring the finer details of his surroundings. His hands clenching the wheel of his car, he looked voraciously at each house he passed. This is what real money buys, he said to himself as he glimpsed the outlines of the fabulous estates. As president of Angel City, he could join the ranks of Bel Agua success stories. With enough money, he could install his mother in a home in Park Crest. He'd buy a house for his sister and her children, then buy an apartment building and put his brother and baby sister in that. Make them managers. His checklist of possibilities expanded with each salary increment he imagined. When he made it big, his entire family would move up. It was the American way.

As he approached the gate that led to a smaller community within Bel Agua where Preston Sinclair's home was located, he had to chuckle at the notion of a bastion of exclusivity even within the most elite enclave in the city. He said his name to a uniformed guard, who scanned a list attached to a clipboard and then waved him in. Humphrey passed private roads and swimming pools, lawns so large they looked like farms. He had heard that Preston Sinclair was a wealthy man, rich not merely from his seven-figure salary but from parlaying that financial foundation into millions from stock market deals and business ventures. As Humphrey pulled into the driveway of the magnificent Sinclair home, he knew that the rumors were true.

When the front door opened, Humphrey recognized Preston's wife from a photograph he'd seen in the president's office. 'I'm Claire,' she said, taking his hand in hers and holding it for a moment. 'You must be Humphrey Boone. I'm so honored to have you in our home, Mr. Boone.' She laughed suddenly, a thin, nervous trill. 'Oh, my,' she said, and put her hand to her neck as if to keep something from seeping out of her.

Humphrey could hear classical music – Verdi, he thought – playing in the background. 'You have a lovely home,' Humphrey said, hoping that his compliment calmed her down. He was used to white wives getting nervous around him. The trick was to talk them through it; after a while they convinced themselves they were having a big adventure. Claire recovered more quickly than most. 'Thank you,' she said. Gathering her composure, she placed her hand gently on his back. 'Come this way, Mr. Boone. Let me get you something to drink. Preston will be down in a moment.'

Claire ushered him into the living room, which was huge and awash in pastels that reflected off glossy bleached wood, and she sat down with him on a large sofa bedecked with tapestry pillows of various sizes and shapes. In front of them was a glass-and-brass coffee table, on which there were dishes of cheese and crackers, vegetables and dip, and fresh fruit. 'What would you like to drink, Mr. Boone?' Claire asked.

'White wine will be fine,' he said.

'Dry or do you like something a little sweet?'

'Dry.'

'Chardonnay?'

'That's fine.'

By the time a maid brought the wine, Preston had joined them. 'There you are,' he said, striding into the room. 'I thought I heard the doorbell. Good to see you.' He gave Humphrey's hand a robust shake. 'Glad you could make it. I see that you've met Claire. Pres will be down in a second. He's still moving slowly, but he's doing a lot better than he was a few weeks ago. The doctors are predicting a complete recovery.' Preston and Claire smiled at each other, and Humphrey could feel their mutual affection. Preston clapped his hands. 'I'll have some of what you're drinking.'

They sat sipping their wine and munching on paper-thin wafers and cheese. Humphrey could smell the aroma of food, and he thought how pleasant it must be to throw a dinner party and not be involved in preparing the meal. 'Something smells wonderful,' he said, and then complimented his hosts once more on their beautiful home.

'We've been here for nearly – what?' She looked at Preston. 'Thirteen years. It's a lovely neighborhood, although, of course, things have changed.' She hesitated. 'Crime. We've had a rash of robberies lately. The latest thing is that the robbers follow you home. Come right behind you, and when you open your garage they drive their car into yours so that you can't close the garage.' Claire shuddered, a refined little tremble. 'Of course, that's not possible here – we're a gated community – but some of our friends have been held up at gunpoint.' She sighed. 'I don't suppose it's safe anywhere anymore.' They dropped the subject of crime and began chatting about the weather and sports, the latest movies. From time to time, Claire or Preston would glance toward the steps and then at each other, with a dejected slump of their shoulders.

When he finally appeared, the boy walking haltingly across the living room floor was a thinner, paler version of his father. It was apparent that he was still in the throes of convalescence, and when he sat down, Humphrey could see that the young man was not an altogether willing dinner participant. What Humphrey saw in Pres's eyes was not unlike what was reflected in the expressions of the black boys he mentored: a reluctance to be engaged.

After Preston introduced Humphrey to his son, he said jovially, 'You're both Yale men.'

Humphrey smiled at Pres. 'Is that so?'

The boy nodded awkwardly.

'So your dad tells me that you play a little tennis,' Humphrey said. Pres looked at his father with a combination of surprise and annoyance in his eyes, then glanced back at Humphrey. 'I used to play pretty well. I don't know what I'll be able to do after I recover.' He spoke slowly in a low voice, and he kept his head down.

'I was telling your dad that I fell off a ladder and broke my back when I was your age and then went on to play college sports. What I didn't mention was that I took yoga and swimming; they were part of the therapy. There's nothing like yoga and swimming to recondition the body.'

There was the faintest flicker of interest in Pres's eyes. 'What did you play? At Yale, I mean.'

'A little basketball.'

'Oh, yeah? What position?' Pres's eyes, when Humphrey finally saw them, were hazel, like his father's.

'Forward. I played pro for a hot second. Seventy-sixers.'

Pres sat up in his chair, and there was no mistaking the interest now. 'So did you, like, want to slit your wrists when you got injured?' Humphrey could see Claire and Preston looking at each other. They seemed to be holding their breath.

Humphrey leaned toward Pres and grinned. 'Actually, it was kind of like a vacation. It was the first rest I'd had in years.'

Pres gave a slight smile. 'Sure,' he said.

'Seriously. The team was working me to death. The courses were rough. My parents were demanding. All of a sudden, everybody was bringing me ice cream. I put on twelve pounds sitting in my room and listening to Marvin Gaye for three months. Had a great time.'

The four of them shared the first real belly laugh of the evening. 'Marvin who?' Claire asked when they were quiet.

'I like Marvin Gaye,' Pres said, giving his mother a look of disdain. 'I mean, his music. I listen to "What's Going On" all the time. I like R and B, jazz, the blues. Rap. I dig all that stuff.'

A hip young white boy, Humphrey thought with amusement. They talked about music all through dinner, while Preston and Claire listened, seemingly fascinated. He couldn't remember a time when he'd ever seen Preston not taking charge; the man who sat at the dining room table with him was a stark contrast to his professional self. He wasn't nearly as intimidating. In his cardigan sweater, with his potbelly and sunken eyes, he seemed like an aging Father Knows Best, more concerned with eavesdropping on his son's conversation than in closing a multimillion-dollar deal.

By the time dessert arrived, laughter was circulating

around the table like air from an open window. They talked for a while over coffee, and then Pres and Claire excused themselves. 'It was just delightful having you here, Humphrey,' she said. 'I want you to come back soon.'

'It's been real cool, man,' Pres said, and Humphrey chuckled again to himself. He extended his hand and the younger man shook it.

'Real cool,' Preston repeated after his wife and son had disappeared. 'That's high praise, isn't it?'

'You can't get any higher than that.' The two men laughed. Preston led Humphrey back into the living room, and the maid brought them brandies. They didn't talk much while they were drinking, but the silence that surrounded them was an easy one. 'I want to thank you for coming, for talking with Pres,' Preston said after a while. 'He said more tonight than he has in weeks. That's what we were so worried about, not so much his physical condition, but his mental state. He's been so depressed since the accident.'

'Mr. Sinclair, I didn't really do anything. . . .'

Preston patted his back quickly, a soothing fatherly gesture. 'I know you didn't. You were just being yourself. That was enough.'

'Mr. Sinclair . . .'

Humphrey felt the hand on his back again, stronger this time. 'I want you to call me Preston.' When he looked into the white man's eyes, there was a friendliness there that he hadn't seen before. No, a friendship, sitting still and deep inside those hazel eyes, just waiting for him. 'We're going to have to start talking more frequently, Humphrey. There are steps you need to take to assume the kind of future I envision for you. I want to have a closer hand, give you some guidance. Think of attaining the presidency as a three-to-five-year project. I'm getting out. Completely out. I want to spend more time with my family. Enjoy them. We'll talk soon.' The hand was still there, warm and firm and steady.

414

But if Humphrey wafted out of Preston's home on a high cloud, his spirits buoyed by the promise of both personal camaraderie and professional solidarity from his mentor, by Monday morning his mood was a lot lower. As he hung up the phone in his office, his jaw muscles were tense and his shoulders slumped forward; his second deal had just fallen through. When he left Preston Sinclair's home on Friday night, he'd imagined his career as a smooth road that led to achievement, prosperity, and power. Now he was forced to confront a grimmer reality. At the moment, his future was in the toilet. He ticked off his accomplishments in his head: The Minority Loan Program was going well; five substantial loans had been approved, and four of them had gone to African-Americans. Admittedly, his administrative skills needed honing, but the running of the regional banks was going smoothly. There had been no major fiascoes. And yet in the very area of his expertise, private placement loans, he was at a standstill. Failing. Humphrey took a deep breath. Preston Sinclair would think he was a one-deal wonder. His offers of friendship and support would evaporate. He knew the rule: he had to be twice as good as white folks to get half as far. Preston Sinclair seemed so sincere in his interest, but important white men rarely backed brothers, and the ones they did support had to be winners. Preston would find himself another up-and-coming black man, or maybe a Latino or a white woman – they were interchangeable these days – and bestow the mantle of leadership he'd promised Humphrey on another. He'd be left standing alone, with his résumé in his hand and his ass hanging out. His town house would be foreclosed; his Mercedes would be repossessed. His mother would lose her home. He'd have to sell his clothes. When he looked into the picture window, reflected in the glass was a shame-faced nine-year-old boy, weak and small, going with his mother to the welfare office.

By late morning, Humphrey was so inundated with work that he'd mentally relegated the failed deal to the back burner. He had his head buried in loan documents, but he wasn't so absorbed that he'd forgotten about his meeting with Mallory. From time to time he glanced at his watch.

His assistant rapped lightly on his door. 'Mr. Boone, Mallory Post is here to see you.' The stately black woman was beside him before he even noticed her moving. She unobtrusively shifted the papers in front of him in a way that didn't disturb the organization but made everything look much neater. She stepped behind his desk and adjusted the blinds so that they diminished the glare from the sun. 'Do you want me to bring in some coffee, Mr. Boone?'

'No, I don't think that will be necessary,' he said. Humphrey was conscious that the older woman mothered him, and he liked it. Eleanor was quiet, elegant, and efficient, the kind of mother he wished he'd had. When he was younger, he used to long to be part of the Brady Bunch, to look like them. Mrs. Brady never said, 'Get your behind up out this bed.' She didn't raise her voice at all. When he watched her on television, he had imagined that she smelled sweet.

Humphrey began smiling as soon as he saw Mallory. They hadn't really said more than hello to each other since the last time she came to his office, to complain about the Minority Loan Program memo, but he had been noticing her. Sometimes he saw her bending over to sip water from the cooler. Once, he watched her rushing from her office to the ladies' room, her face flushed, her hair streaming behind her. From his window he saw her walking to lunch, always with Esther, the wind lifting her bangs off her forehead. And when he didn't see her, he thought about her. He thought about her the way he used to think about all the pretty blondes on television.

416

He watched Mallory as she moved to the chair. Her legs were just as elegant and pale as before. She crossed them when she sat down and smiled at him with just a hint of a question in her eyes. He had asked to see her, and now he realized that he didn't have a reason for the request. Not really.

They greeted each other cordially and chatted amiably for a few minutes. He enjoyed listening to her soft, weak voice. Her eyes were the clearest gray he'd ever seen. 'Well,' he said, after they'd dispensed with pleasantries, 'I called you in because I wanted to thank you.'

'For what?' She looked genuinely puzzled.

'I wanted to thank you for your cooperation and for enlisting the cooperation of the rest of the lenders in making the Minority Loan Program such a resounding success. I know that initially you had some misgivings about the program, and you were courageous enough to share them with me. I respect your forthrightness, but even more than that, I appreciate the way you got on the bandwagon once things got under way. You're responsible for more than half the loans that have been allocated through the program. You've helped make it a success.' He stared into her eyes the entire time he was speaking, until Mallory finally looked away.

'Thank you, Humphrey.' His words seemed sincere enough, but for some reason that she couldn't figure out, his voice struck her as strange. It was low and throaty, with a seductive lilt, the kind of voice men used to pick up women.

'So since you've been such a great booster, I wanted to confer with you about a really special client that I've been considering for the program. The loan would be rather complex, and I really don't have the time to get into it right now, but maybe we could talk about it over dinner one evening this week.' He was aware that the words had been circling around his mind, but hearing himself, he was startled.

That made two of them.

'What did you say?' Mallory was sure she'd misunderstood. He saw the uncertainty in her eyes, but rather than back off, he looked at her so intently that there could be no mistaking the kind of dinner he had in mind.

Mallory looked at Humphrey for a full minute without saying a word. She was dumbfounded.

She's a little shy, Humphrey told himself.

Oh, my God, Mallory thought. Oh, my God. Her mind was at a standstill. This wasn't business; he was asking her on a date. He was black, and he was asking her on a date. He was her boss, and he was asking her out. Esther liked him, and he was asking her on a date. Oh, God. No, no, she was just imagining it was a date. It was business. Hadn't he said it was business? How could she say no without offending him? When she opened her mouth, no sound came out. She tried again, groping for calm, casual words. 'That's so kind of you. I'm so busy lately; I just don't have any time in the evenings, but anytime you'd like to meet during the day would be fine.' She smiled to let him know that she was sincerely appreciative of his offer, complimented by it, in fact.

He didn't let the refusal throw him. He knew her game. She's playing hard to get, Humphrey thought. He'd seen her looking at him during meetings; he'd noticed the way she always gave him a smile. 'Well, maybe one day you won't be so busy,' he said.

She nodded ambiguously, then flashed him another smile. 'Well, I'll just be going now,' she said. She extended her hand. Humphrey squeezed it gently.

In the space of their handshake, he imagined what it would be like to have Mallory. He had been with other white women. Being with them always made him feel successful, powerful. He glared in stony silence at the white men who dared to stare when he took these women into restaurants and bars. And the sisters, with their eye rolling and angry glances – he was getting back at them too. Weren't they just like the ones who thought that he was too dark and ugly to date when he was in high school?

Of course, he would have to be careful. Discreet. He wasn't about to risk his career by letting it become common knowledge that he was seeing a white woman he was managing. But he knew how to keep a secret. He'd done it before.

When Mallory finally pulled her hand away, she practically fled from the room. By the time she reached her office, she was panting. She sat down behind her desk and stared out the window. What had she done to suggest to Humphrey that she was interested in dating him? She reviewed every interaction she'd ever had with the man. She had done nothing. Nothing.

'What's wrong with you?' Esther asked as Mallory rushed into her office.

Mallory looked into Esther's questioning face, and for the first time it occurred to her that she couldn't tell her friend what had just happened. And she'd always told Esther practically everything. Until now. She crossed her arms defensively. 'Nothing. I just came to see what you were doing. You want to go to lunch?'

'Now? It's only eleven o'clock.'

'No,' she said quickly. 'I meant later, like around twelve-thirty.'

'That's cool.' Esther peered at her. 'You sure you don't have something on your mind? You've got that one-lip-up, one-lip-down intense look.'

'You're imagining things.' She gave Esther a fast grin that she didn't feel and then walked toward the door. 'See you later.'

28

LaKeesha counted the money into the small outstretched palm. She smiled politely at the customer, a sallow-skinned Latina with two gold teeth, who was cashing a personal check.

Angel City had been good to LaKeesha. Her six-month performance review had been excellent, and Esther had told her that she could look forward to becoming a service rep within a year or so; service reps earned nearly two thousand dollars a month.

'You got it made,' Hector had told her when he found out. His tone, almost sad, made LaKeesha search his face, look deeply into his eyes, but he gave her such a generous smile, so full of affection, that she dismissed her misgivings. He was happy for her; she was sure of that.

And Hector was right. She did have it made. Her checkbook was always balanced down to the last cent. Her J.C. Penney bill was always paid on time. Already, she'd managed to save nearly six hundred dollars. She'd seen an apartment in Inglewood: only three bedrooms, but much larger than the place they rented now. And there was a swimming pool and a playground for the children. The apartment manager told her that she needed a thousand dollars. She thought she would have that in six months. By that time, she would be a service rep. She'd done just what Mrs. Clark said she would: She had changed her life.

And things were only going to get better.

LaKeesha knew she looked nice when she got off the 103 bus at Cranston. She'd dressed carefully in one of her recent

J.C. Penney purchases, a short-sleeved yellow blouse and matching culottes. As if to confirm her own high opinion of herself, at least three young men gave her the eye as she walked up the hill to Esther's house. One of the tellers was expecting a baby, and since it was Angel City's policy not to host social events on the bank's premises, Esther had volunteered her home for the occasion. Trudging uphill, LaKeesha only wished she could walk faster.

Los Angeles was always in blossom, but this June there was a profusion of spring flowers along with the year-long blooms. The entire block smelled of roses. LaKeesha had never been in Park Crest before, although she'd heard of the neighborhood. A lot of people referred to it as the Black Beverly Hills. As she passed the large, stately homes, the beautifully kept lawns and gardens, she could see why. The only people she saw were black. LaKeesha felt a shiver of apprehension. The brothers and sisters of Park Crest barely nodded at her as she passed by. They probably knew that she belonged down the hill. By the time she reached the second street, she could feel perspiration rolling down her back. A quick glance under her arms revealed dark wet half-moons on her yellow cotton blouse. Everyone else would probably drive to the shower. They would look nice, and she'd arrive a sweaty mess. As she lifted her legs, she felt a tight pull in her calves; she slowed down. The farther she walked, the more she felt swallowed up by the neighborhood. When she reached the highest point on the hill, she looked behind her. From where she stood, she could see Cranston and, beyond that, South-Central. For a moment, she felt like running back down, but then she saw the pink and blue balloons tied to the rosebushes and realized that she was right in front of Esther's house. The door was open, and Esther was standing there, smiling. 'I saw you from the window. Come on in. Get some champagne.'

Esther led her into the living room, and her co-workers

421

greeted her, making a space for her on the sofa. She stood in front of them in a daze. Everything around her was bright and clean and nice. She could save her entire life and she would never own a home as nice as Esther's. She looked at the lovely furniture, the spotless rugs and shining windows, and knew that she would never catch up. Never. She was afraid to sit on the sofa; it looked new. She thought of her six hundred dollars and nearly laughed. She pictured the apartment in Inglewood, her dream house, and felt like crying. It was a dump. She could see that now. And she could see other things as well. LaKeesha's eyes took in the paintings on the walls, the plants in every room. Everything she saw told her the same thing: Never. And she knew that even Esther's house wasn't a mansion: she had driven through Beverly Hills with friends often enough on Saturday afternoons when they had nothing to do. That was what was so hard. She wouldn't even be able to have this. Not even a black piece of the rock.

LaKeesha's eyes grew wide when a brown-skinned woman stood in front of her with a tray full of little sandwiches. 'You like?' she asked. The black girl shook her head. A maid. Esther had a maid to make her bed and serve her guests and clean up after everybody left. A maid. Like what her grandmother had been when she used to work. LaKeesha thought about the chaotic Saturday mornings at her house, when she and her sisters ran the ancient vacuum that spread more dust and lint than it collected. Here was real china on the table. As she thought about her family's collection of mismatched and chipped dishes, LaKeesha could feel herself shrinking. She thought about the present she'd brought for Tracy, the pregnant teller, a soft yellow sweater set with matching bootees. She'd bought it at the Swap Meet in her neighborhood. Before, she wanted to see Tracy's face when she opened the box, but her gift seemed cheap and insignificant now. It wasn't good enough, and neither was she.

Someone pointed out the bathroom after she inquired. She got up and walked down the narrow hallway. There were pictures on the wall of Esther and her family; at least the older woman and man looked like her parents and the younger man looked like her brother. In every photo, the four of them were smiling, all their heads touching. That's why she has this house, LaKeesha thought, almost the instant she saw the photographs. The four of them together possessed a power she had never known. And in that same moment she realized that she hadn't seen her father in so many years that she could walk by him on the street and not know him.

She held most of her tears until she got home. She didn't cry when she told Esther that she had to go, not even when Esther said, 'But why do you have to leave? You just got here.' Didn't cry as she ran down the sloping street to Cranston. Was still holding everything in when she boarded the 103 heading east. When the driver passed the billboard of the premature baby on the blue background who couldn't take the hit, she just stared. Her face was like something carved out of stone as she got off the bus at Normandie and marched back to her house.

One look at her face, and her sisters and grandmother fell silent. Even Man didn't call her name. She spoke to no one. Once she was in her room, she closed the door and turned up 92.3 loud, very loud. And then she cried. Hot, silent tears trickled down her cheeks, turning bitter by the time they ran into her mouth.

29

Sheila was getting fatter. Prone in his bed, even a half-awake Kirk could see the additional girth in all its cellulitic glory as his wife jiggled to the bathroom wearing her baby doll pajamas. He pulled the covers over his head. Just a few more winks; he wasn't ready to face the morning yet. Or Sheila's ass. Then he heard her. 'Kirk, get up!' Sheila had doubled back and was standing right over him. 'Do you want to lose the only job you're capable of getting?' she asked maliciously. He could hear his children squabbling in their bedroom. He did not smell breakfast. Sheila had stopped cooking for him after it was clear that he wasn't going to be the regional manager. She fed the children only after he'd gone to work.

Kirk picked up the phone on the fourth ring. 'Yes,' he said tentatively. He held his breath as Sheila glared at him.

'Mr. Madison, this is Ed Brown from Visa again. When we last spoke, you promised to get up-to-date with your payments. You're behind three months, Mr. Madison.'

He mumbled a fast, incoherent excuse and then lied and said he would mail the check immediately. 'Today. Absolutely,' he said. Sheila gave him a scornful look when he hung up. For a fleeting moment he thought about how sweetly she smiled at him when he was in medical school and everything was before them. He sighed and then got out of bed. His knees felt stiff, and he stumbled as he walked toward the bathroom. He was about to step into the shower, when the phone rang again. He didn't move for five rings, until the answering machine switched on. 'This is

Sabrina with MasterCard. I'm calling to inform . . .' He turned the water on all the way.

From his office window the city was gray and overcast. Kirk had been going over a loan application and not making much headway. He looked at his watch, then got up and closed the door to his office, sat down at his desk, and turned on his radio. It was eleven o'clock, the hour of his daily visit with Lord King Clever. Yes, Lord. He knew that's who he was. Kirk barely paid attention when he heard the radio theme music, and he only half listened as Lord King Clever announced news events. Those things didn't interest Kirk. He knew that if he waited patiently, Lord Fat King Clever would come to him and him alone.

'Kirk!'

Kirk turned around, and standing right behind him was the one and only King Clever. He was a tiny man, barely five feet three, although he wore high-heeled boots in an attempt to add inches. He extended his little hand to Kirk, who bowed his head and kissed the huge diamond solitaire pinkie ring on his right baby finger.

'Stand up like a proud, red-blooded white American male,' Lord King Clever commanded. Kirk stood up. 'Amerifriend, you've got a right to be angry. You're being cheated out of your birthright. People who haven't worked as hard as you have are taking what is rightfully yours.'

'What should I do, Lord?' Kirk whispered.

'Kirk, how long have we been having our little chats? Months! It's time for you to stop being a *wimp*! Get mad! Let your anger guide you, Kirk. Look around you. Use what you have. Do something! Do you understand me?'

'Yes, I think so.'

'And Kirk . . .'

'Yes?'

'You have bought my book, haven't you?'

'Oh, yes.'

'Well, they make dandy presents!'

As soon as Lord King Clever disappeared, Kirk had barely enough time to mull over what he'd told him before he rushed down the hall to attend the loan officers' meeting that Humphrey had called. Humphrey had stood up in the front of the room just as Kirk slid into a seat next to Mallory, who whispered, 'You're late,' and gave him a quick smile. She looked so pretty in her pale-pink suit. He smiled back and stole a quick glance at her legs.

The meeting was as long and tedious as Kirk had feared it would be. Humphrey reviewed each minority loan that had been approved and then introduced the profiles of the potential ones. The longer Humphrey talked, the more pronounced the pain throbbing between Kirk's temples became. Kirk could barely look at Humphrey by the time the meeting was over. What an arrogant bastard! He approves the loans without our input, and then he rams them down our throat. He turned to tell Mallory what he thought, but he saw that her seat was empty. She was up at the front of the room, talking to Humphrey. The black man's face was animated in a way Kirk had never seen before. Mallory seemed to be trying to get away, but Humphrey just kept on talking. Sometimes he would touch her arm, as if to make a point. When he did that, Kirk had difficulty swallowing.

He waited for her outside the meeting room. 'What did the Little Emperor want with you?' he asked her.

Mallory smiled when she heard the nickname. 'Oh, we were just talking about a loan.'

As they passed the employees' lounge, Mallory said, 'I think I'll get a Coke.' She put her hand on the door and it opened and Esther came out.

'Where are you guys coming from?' Esther asked. She gave Kirk a polite nod.

'Humphrey called a loan department meeting,' Mallory said.

'How'd it go?'

Mallory shrugged. 'Okay.'

'If you ask me, he's gotten a little high-handed,' Kirk said. 'I think Homeboy needs a reality check.'

Esther froze for a moment, then whirled around to face Kirk. Stop, she told herself. But she couldn't censor the fury that she felt; the South Side wind was blowing too hard. She walked up to Kirk and put her face so close to his that he stepped back. 'Who are you calling Homeboy?'

'I . . .' Kirk was too astonished to speak.

'You better pull your collar up, Kirk; your red neck is showing.'

Kirk and Mallory didn't say a word as Esther stalked off to her office. When she'd disappeared, Kirk said, 'What the hell was that all about? I mean, what did I say that was so wrong?'

Mallory shook her head. 'I don't know.'

'Those people are getting so touchy. Why should we have to be so careful? Do you hear what they call each other? You ever listen to Richard Pryor or Eddie Murphy? Or that vulgar comedy show that comes on Friday night. Listen to the rappers. You'll hear more "niggers" than I ever even thought about saying. So why is it such a crime when I call our fearless leader Homeboy? I mean, I don't like the guy, but I'd never say anything derogatory about his or any other person's race. You know that, don't you, Mallory?'

She looked at Kirk. His face was full of sweet sincerity. He was a nice guy. 'Of course I do, Kirk.' She'd go talk to Esther. Find out what was really bothering her.

Esther was staring into the operations area when she heard the soft knock at her door. Before she could speak, the door opened and Mallory came in. 'I think you overreacted,' she said softly.

'I overreacted? Kirk calls the only other black professional in this place a homeboy, which is the same as "nigger . . ."'

'He did not say that.' How could she possibly think the two words were synonyms?

' "Homeboy" and "nigger" are interchangeable, coming out of *his* mouth.'

'Are you saying the man can't state his opinion? Kirk's not some ra-ra-racist.'

'Oh, Jesus. This isn't about the first amendment, okay? Look, you just don't get it.'

'Another black thing I wouldn't understand?'

'Actually, this is a white thing you don't understand.'

The two women stared at each other for a moment, and then Mallory said softly, 'Are you angry with me?'

'No, you're cool. It's just the rest of your people who get on my nerves from time to time. And that includes Elvis.' She moved closer to Mallory. 'Did I ever tell you that feeling guilty for crimes you didn't commit is kind of crazy?'

Mallory smiled. 'I know.'

'Get over it, will you,' Esther said softly. When she looked at Mallory, they were both smiling.

A few minutes after Mallory left, Esther was walking out the door. Even though she'd calmed down, she still wanted to talk to someone who knew where she was coming from.

'What can I do for you, Esther?' Humphrey asked, after Eleanor ushered her in. As always, she looked good, he thought.

Now, seated in front of him, Esther suddenly felt foolish to have barged in to tell Humphrey that some asshole had called him Homeboy. It had happened before; it would happen again. What did it matter?

'Humphrey, you've been around the block. I'm going to

be frank. I realize you know that everybody at Angel City isn't glad you came. I feel kind of silly telling you this, but Kirk Madison just referred to you as a homeboy who needs a reality check. I just happened to be standing there with Mallory. I thought you needed to know that.'

Humphrey began chuckling. 'I've been called a lot of things.' He laughed again, then looked at Esther's startled face. 'Listen, it's not funny. Thank you. I do need to know that.'

Esther took a deep breath. 'Humphrey, I think that under the circumstances, we need to . . .'

'Stick together.'

'Exactly.'

'And you got my back, sister?' His smile was warm.

'Brother, I got your back.'

The following Saturday morning, after a two-hour drive, Esther and Tyrone stood outside her brother's home, on the outskirts of San Diego. When Esther had awakened that morning, she told him that she wanted to see her brother, and after she called Stan and learned that the family had no plans, Tyrone offered to take her. She smiled as she looked at the huge white house with its clay-tile roof, then peeked inside a gigantic picture window with a rounded arch. 'Nice place,' Tyrone said admiringly. Esther had told him that her brother was a lawyer and his wife a dentist. It was obvious they were very successful. Looking along the street at the surrounding houses, he realized that the entire neighborhood was elegant. He suddenly felt as though he were wearing jeans at a formal affair. Esther patted his shoulder, seemingly sensing his discomfort. 'You'll like Stan. He's real cool,' she said.

Stan answered the door after the third ring. At six-feet-four and two hundred and ten pounds, her handsome older brother filled most of the spaces he stood in, and his doorway was no exception. 'Hey, baby girl,' he said, grinning at her, then kissing her on the cheek. He extended his hand to Tyrone. 'Stanley Jackson, man.'

'Tyrone Carter. Nice to meet you.'

'Well, y'all come on in. Belinda's making brunch.' He swatted Esther across her behind. 'Look at Miss Scrawny.' She grinned back at him.

The living room was sunken and sun-filled. There was a huge white baby grand piano and exquisite furniture. Tyrone stood uneasily while Esther and Stan plopped down. 'Take a seat, Tyrone,' Stan said.

'It's too gorgeous to sit on,' he said. Was it his imagination, or did he see Esther wince?

Jesus, Esther thought, don't start acting like you haven't been around the block.

A pretty, petite woman appeared. Her skin was so fair that several glances were required to verify that she was black. 'Hello, Esther,' she said. She smiled at Tyrone.

'Hello, Belinda. What's happening?' said Esther. The two women didn't hug; her sister-in-law didn't come close enough to touch Esther. 'Belinda, I'd like you to meet my friend Tyrone Jackson.'

After he and Belinda shook hands, Tyrone finally sat down. He felt like a child on his best behavior. He looked around casually. The walls were painted off-white and then stained with flecks of other colors. The lamps were made of solid brass. The pile on the Oriental carpeting was at least an inch thick. Beautiful art adorned the walls. These people have money, he thought.

A few minutes later, a little boy of about five and a smaller girl came racing into the living room and dived into Esther with the force of Tonka trucks. 'Auntie Esther,' they squealed in unison.

'Jamal and Jasmine! Stop pulling your auntie's dress,' Belinda said, shaking her head and smiling at Esther for the

430

first time. Esther grinned back, but only at the two children clamoring for her attention.

The brother and sister ignored their mother's warning and continued to grab Esther around her hips and legs. 'Chewing gum! Chewing gum! Chewing gum!' they chanted, until a laughing Esther reached into her purse and pulled out two sticks of Doublemint gum and passed them to her niece and nephew. 'Hey, give me some sugar,' she called after the boy and girl as they scrambled away, clutching their goods. The two children immediately charged back into their aunt, who bent down to receive a rapid barrage of extremely wet and slightly gooey kisses. 'Maria,' Belinda called, and a young Latina appeared. 'Would you take the kids upstairs, please. *Gracias.*'

Esther watched the two children. Every time she saw them they'd grown bigger and more independent. She was sorry she didn't get a chance to see them more often. She liked going places with her niece and nephew. Liked the feel of their small, soft hands in hers. Strangers always assumed that she was their mother, and she enjoyed pretending that Jamal and Jasmine belonged to her. The children were brown, like her and Stanley, she thought smugly, even if they did have their mother's silky hair and keen features. In the eight years that her brother had been married, she had not forgiven him for choosing someone with hair that blew in the wind, with skin the color of the inside of an almond. It was a betrayal that continued to wound.

Esther watched as Belinda picked up the pillows that the children had dropped on the floor and put them back on the sofa. She could hear a television playing in the family room and the children's intermittent squeals of laughter. The scent of spices from Belinda's fragrant brunch wafted through the rooms on the first floor. Pictures of Belinda and Stanley and the kids were propped on the baby grand piano in the living room and on the end tables. Esther stared at each one, and the longer she looked, the more she felt enveloped by the evidence of her brother's comfortable domestic life and, at the same time, squeezed out of her own contentment. Esther was suffused with the twin emotions of secondhand happiness and longing so intense that for a moment she couldn't swallow. At times like these, she couldn't bear to be in her own brother's house. Tyrone saw her face, so full of sorrow and resentment. He watched her as she walked over to where Belinda was standing and heard her say quietly, in an innocent voice, 'Are you putting on a little weight?' An expression of annoyance spread across Belinda's face. Esther enjoyed the moment. Little Miss Light Bright, she thought to herself. Everything came easy to women who looked like her. She felt a pang of guilt. Why couldn't she be nice to her brother's wife?

Belinda smiled. 'I made some mimosas. Why don't I serve them now.'

Belinda brought out the drinks and some tortilla chips and salsa as well. 'You have a lovely home,' Tyrone said. He lifted his glass. 'To family reunions and meeting new friends.' He smiled at Esther.

'Mom called me last night,' Stanley said after everyone took a first sip. 'They just got back from their vacation.'

'Your folks are the goingest people I know,' Belinda said.

Esther laughed. 'I believe they couldn't wait for us to leave so that they could start partying again. Where did they go this time?'

'They cruised the Grecian islands.'

'Damn. They're spending up all of our inheritance. I hope those Negroes have burial insurance.' Belinda chuckled and Stanley smiled at her. Tyrone watched Esther as she tried not to look at them.

After the second mimosa, some of the sharp edges of Esther's resentment softened, and by the time they sat down to brunch, she was able to be, if not friendly, cordial to

Belinda. After the meal, they sat in the backyard, around a vast swimming pool, and Belinda brought out tiny cups of foaming espresso. Stanley mentioned chess, and Tyrone asked if he'd like to play.

'I'm not that good,' he said as Stanley put the set on the table. He won the first and second games, before Esther's brother begged off.

Esther gave him a slightly awe-filled look. 'You must be really great, because Stanley has won tournaments.'

Tyrone shrugged. 'So have I,' he said.

Later, when Stanley and Esther managed to be alone for a moment, he said that Tyrone was cool. 'He treating you okay?'

'Yeah, he's really nice. It's not serious, though.'

Her brother chuckled. 'Maybe you're not serious, but he is.'

By early evening Esther and Tyrone were on the 405, headed back north to Los Angeles. They drove all the way home without speaking, and when they got to Esther's house, Tyrone hesitated. 'You want some company?' he asked. The woman seemed to be in some kind of a mood.

'Sure.'

Once they were inside, they sat on the sofa in her family room. Tyrone put his arm around her shoulder. 'Why don't you like Belinda?' he asked.

Esther tilted her head toward him. 'What do you mean? I like her. She's okay.' She didn't look him in his eyes.

'You're not a little jealous of her?'

'I am not jealous of Belinda,' Esther said, her voice sounding high and screechy. She took his arm from around her. 'Why would I be jealous of her?'

'She's got what you want,' Tyrone said quietly.

'What? My brother?'

'Yeah. Your brother the lawyer. A beautiful home. Kids. Somebody to take care of the kids and clean the house.

Looks to me like she caught the brass ring. Maybe it looks that way to you too.'

Esther faced Tyrone. Now she understood. 'Why are you into this?' she asked.

'That *is* what you want, isn't it? The big house. The big man.' He kept his eyes on hers.

'What do you want me to say: I want a little house and a little man? Why shouldn't I want someone who wants to be somebody and knows how to speak English properly.' The words just slipped out.

'I guess I'm just something to do until the real thing comes along.'

The confession was in her eyes. By the time Tyrone walked out her door, there was regret there, too, but he didn't see it.

After Tyrone left, Esther sat at her breakfast room table, sipping tea. Through her open window she could hear the Lintons' country twangs. The sound of Bessie Smith was coming from their backyard. Esther peeked out the window. Carol and Harold were reclining in matching chaise longues, the light from their back door illuminating them. Between them was a small table with a bottle of wine and a bowl of popcorn. Harold was singing, or trying to, and Carol was laughing and telling him to be quiet. Their little girl was asleep, lying across her father's knees. As soon as Bessie Smith sang the opening bars of 'Down-Hearted Blues,' Esther closed the window.

As Tyrone reached Cranston, he didn't know whether to turn left or right. Sylvia, his old girlfriend, lived to the left. His parents lived to the right. Sylvia was always his ace in the hole. He slid over into the right lane. Hell, might as well go where somebody appreciated him. But the farther north he traveled, the more slowly he drove. When he reached Sylvia's street, he passed it and made a U-turn. When he pulled in front of his parents' South-Central home, he felt relieved. He had grown up on the quiet street of neat stucco bungalows and emerald lawns. The familiarity of the old neighborhood was a comfort.

'You must have known your daddy caught some catfish,' his mother told Tyrone when she opened the door. She hugged him. 'I'm getting ready to fry them up right now.' She had on an apron over her nurse's uniform.

'You just get off work?' he asked.

'About fifteen minutes ago.'

'Where's Dad?'

'Where else? Tell him I need for him to go to the store for me before it gets too late.'

Tyrone went straight to the garage, where he found his father tinkering under the hood of his car. There was a beer within easy reach of his hand. 'Hey, boy. Whatcha know good?' his father said.

'You got it. What you doing, Dad?'

'Alternator's shot. I'm fixing to put another one in.' His father peered into his face. He turned back to the car and was quiet for a few minutes. Then he lifted his head and looked at his son. 'So what's on your mind?'

'Nothing.'

His father stared at him a little longer, then ducked his head back under the hood. 'How's that new girlfriend? When you gone bring her by?'

'I don't think she's coming by, Dad.'

He raised his head. 'She show you the door?'

'Not really; it's just not going to work out,' he said finally. He laughed a little. 'She told me I don't speak proper enough.' He gave his father a quick glance to see how he received his words, but his father's eyes were on his alternator.

'So she kinda snooty, huh?'

'No. No. Esther's real down. You'd like her, Dad. She's

pretty and smart; she has two degrees. We were having a good time being together. She didn't ask me to take her to a lot of fancy places. I mean, a lot of times we just hung out at the beach or we'd go to the movies.'

'So she's kinda down but not all the way down.' His father walked around to the other side of the car and looked under the hood.

'T.C.!' his mother called from the kitchen window.

'Oh, I forgot to tell you. Mom wants you to go to the store for her.'

'That woman always has something for me to do.'

'I'll go in a minute,' his father yelled back. 'She had me clean out the entire garage over the weekend. Week before that, she had me wash every window in the house.' He grinned. 'So you like this one, huh?'

'Yeah.'

'You like her a lot.'

'Yeah, I like her a lot. She's kind of good for me. She makes me think. I'm even thinking about going back to school myself. Getting one degree at least.'

His father turned his head, so that Tyrone didn't see the broad smile on his face. 'Most men say they want a woman who goes along with their program, but sometimes they ain't the best ones for you, especially if your program is shaky.'

'T.C.!'

He stood up, slapping his hands together and then wiping them on his pants. 'Me, I found out a long time ago that I need a woman who keeps her foot up my butt. I'm coming, Baby,' he yelled, as he walked toward the house.

Staying away from Esther was harder than Tyrone had imagined it would be. When he went into Angel City to deliver the mail, he dropped everything off at the front desk and got in and out as quickly as he could. Even so, he

436

managed to see her once or twice from a distance, although he didn't think she saw him. Each time he saw her he had the urge to shout, 'Hey, girl,' as loudly as he could. He felt silly not speaking to Esther.

'You went overboard,' Cody told him. They had just finished playing a game of chess in the locker room. Tyrone won.

'What do you mean, I went overboard?'

'The woman is outta your league. Let's start with that. Instead of being happy that this high-class sister is giving you the time of day, what do you do? You fall in love.'

'Is that what I did?'

'Sounds like it to me. Say, lemme hook up your head; you need a trim. You're looking raggedy around the edges, brother. Look in the mirror.'

There was a large mirror on the wall across from the lockers. Tyrone turned his back to it and then peered into the hand mirror that Cody gave him. He did need a trim. When he turned around, Cody was holding the clippers in the air and smiling. 'Trust me,' he said.

'Man, don't do nothing strange,' Tyrone said.

He sat on the bench in front of the lockers. He could feel the electric pulse of the clippers moving over the nape of his neck. 'Face it, Tyrone, you and this woman are never gonna make it. That princess and the pauper shit don't work out.'

'But when we're together it's cool. Her brother and I get along. He's a big-time lawyer. Man, you should see his house.'

'Nice?'

'Incredible. *Dynasty.*'

'Take my advice: Find yourself another sister.'

Cody handed Tyrone the small mirror, and Tyrone walked over to the larger one and appraised Cody's work. 'Not bad, boy.'

'I told you I could cut your kind of hair.'

'Say, why don't you just trim the rest of it. Just a little off the top and a little more off the sides.'

'I gotcha,' Cody said eagerly. 'A fade.'

I'm actually sitting here letting a crazy-ass wannabe-black white boy cut my hair, Tyrone thought. He started laughing.

'What's so funny, man?'

'Nothing. I just realized that I'm a risktaker.'

'Yeah. So what does that mean?'

'It means I'm going home and call my baby.'

As soon as Esther got home from work, she changed into her workout clothes. Three days had passed without exercise, and today, without fail, she would jog around the track and do some free weights. On her way out the door, she checked her telephone messages. Mitchell Harris had called. 'Damn!' she said when she heard his voice. He'd called her about five times since she'd seen him at the banquet. She laughed, remembering all the years she'd yearned for his attention. Now, when she didn't even return his calls, he suddenly found her irresistible.

She passed through her kitchen, which was a mistake. For no reason that she could think of, she opened the refrigerator door. The leftover carrot cake beckoned. Before she could stop herself, she was sitting at the breakfast room table, plowing into a huge hunk. She felt like hanging herself from her thumbs when she finished and less like jogging than getting into bed. But first she wanted just another little slice.

In less than five days, she'd eaten half a cake, and the most she'd moved her body was the two-minute walk from the parking lot to her office. 'You fat slob,' she whispered to herself as viciously as she could. She felt so lethargic, and it wasn't even time for her period to come on. At least a dozen times since her return from San Diego she had picked up the telephone to call Tyrone, to tell him some funny story she'd just heard, to let him sing to her, but then she remembered. After she hung up was when she ate the biggest slices of cake.

She abandoned the idea of jogging but did force herself to drive to Vanessa's house. She rang the doorbell twice before she heard the buzzer. When she opened her door, Vanessa was wearing a plain black suit and a black hat.

'What's with the suit? Did you try out for the role of an office manager?' Esther asked, as she pushed away the junk on Vanessa's couch and sat down. She laughed a little and waited for Vanessa to join in, but to her surprise she didn't.

'I just got back from a funeral,' Vanessa said.

'Who died?'

'Do you remember Helena? The old lady who lived down the hall?'

Esther had an image, months old, of the woman who appeared so frightened when she saw her coming to visit Vanessa. 'I remember her. How did she die?'

'Heart attack. They had the services over at some synagogue on Fairfax. There were only six people in the place. She left me something.'

'You're kidding. What?'

'Her china set. Her daughter came over yesterday and brought it. She said Helena told her in the hospital that she wanted me to have it. Wasn't that sweet? Her daughter said she talked about me all the time.' There were tears in Vanessa's eyes. 'She was such a nice old lady. We'd sit up here and drink wine and talk trash. My little wine-drinking partner.'

Esther stayed with Vanessa for more than an hour and listened to her sniffle and reminisce. 'So how's the acting business?' she asked, trying to change the subject.

Vanessa's eyes brightened, as they always did when she talked about her career. 'Well, I didn't get the Eddie movie, but my turn is coming. I can feel it.'

'So are you up for anything?'

'No, but I will be. I'm telling you. Something big is going to happen. I'm keeping the faith.' She looked at her friend's sad face. 'What's wrong with you?'

'I had a fight with Tyrone. I never should have started dating him in the first place. He doesn't have any potential. He doesn't have a degree. I just want to end the relationship, which I think I've done. So. That's it.'

Vanessa shook her head. 'Girlfriend, you live by too many damn rules, you know that? I mean, you have a rule for who is worthy enough for you to date. Then you have a rule for black and white people being together. You have a rule for how you have to act on your job. I mean, do you like Tyrone?'

Esther nodded.

'Does he like you?'

Esther nodded.

'Do you miss him right now?'

Esther nodded.

'Then why are you here? Now, tomorrow, when you wake up, go to the mirror and say this: I break all the rules that impede my happiness. You got that? Stop planning for the future, and live right now. Stop worrying about whether the man is good husband material and ask yourself is he a good boyfriend.'

'He's a great boyfriend.'

'Then you need to tell him that. And you need to tell yourself that too. Now repeat after me: I break all the rules that impede my happiness.'

The telephone was ringing when Esther walked in the door. As soon as she said hello, Tyrone, his voice soft and a little tentative, said, 'Hi, Esther.'

What shocked her was how enormously relieved she felt,

as though a doctor had told her that the chest pains were just gas. 'Tyrone,' she said, 'it's so good to hear your voice.'

'Listen . . .'

'Look . . .'

'What are you doing?'

'Throwing away a carrot cake that I never should have bought in the first place.'

'Have we been pigging out, sister?'

'Absolutely.' She didn't know why she wasn't embarrassed. With any other man she would have been.

'Sounds like emotional neediness to me. See, I be watching Oprah!'

'No, I was just hungry.'

'Yeah, but there's all kinds of hungers. Want me to come work you out?'

Esther hesitated for a moment. 'Well . . .'

'Just a workout,' he said casually. 'You can, uh, correct my grammar while I count the dimples on your thighs. Emergency cellulite removal is my specialty.'

She giggled a little. 'Come on over.'

30

Hayden answered the telephone on the third ring. Mallory hadn't spoken to him in a week, but she hesitated when she heard him. In all the years they'd been together, she'd never called him at home. 'Hello.' He sounded irritated, the way he became when the least little thing didn't go his way. If she spoke and his wife was around, he'd probably just hang up. Even if she wasn't there, he'd be angry. He would flare up suddenly. He'd curse and shout. Then he'd retreat until she begged him to come back. She knew the routine. Mallory bit into her bottom lip. When she looked at the hand on her lap, it was trembling. She wanted him to be glad to hear from her whenever she decided to call him. God, how had she gotten into this? When would she get out? 'Hello!' Hayden slammed down the phone, and Mallory let her receiver fall on the bed. She let only a few tears fall before she made herself stop. She was getting very controlled in the area of crying.

Mallory turned on the television loud, so that she could hear the news anchor's voice above the din of her blow dryer. He was describing the latest in a series of racial incidents in the city's high schools. Earlier in the day there had been a huge fight in the parking lot of one of the high schools in the Valley, between white, black, and Latino boys. The announcer described it as a miniriot, adding that school officials 'attribute the cause to gang rivalries'. White boys in gangs? Mallory turned off her hair dryer. The announcer must be mistaken, she thought. It was the third racial outbreak in the schools in two months. Only last week, Latino and black students had fought in the lunch-room of one of the city's oldest schools. The Latinos claimed that black students attacked them because they were playing Latin music too loud. Tonight the on-the-scene reporters interviewed several students. One black guy, a dark, gangly fellow, wearing what looked like oversize clown's clothes, said, 'Me and my homeboys were just chillin', when they started fighting.'

Homeboys. There was that word again, she thought, switching off the remote control as the sports anchor appeared. Why was it harmless when a black boy called other black people that and ra-ra-racist when someone white said it? She couldn't for the life of her understand Esther's reaction to what she thought was Kirk's joke. The day after Esther's outburst, the two women went to lunch and acted as if nothing had happened; they hadn't spoken about the incident since, but Mallory had the feeling that there was unfinished business between them. She sensed a new distance, which made her uneasy. *If she thinks that Kirk is racist, maybe she thinks I am too.* The thought frightened Mallory. She didn't want to lose Esther's friendship. Who else did she have?

As Mallory sat across from Humphrey's desk, she drew her knees together and carefully angled her legs so that it was impossible for Humphrey to see her thighs. She was very conscious of how much flesh she was showing as she waited for him to explain why he'd asked to see her at six o'clock in the evening.

But instead of explaining, he stood up and ushered her out of his office. 'Come on. It's been a long day. We can talk over drinks.'

She wanted to protest, to say that she was tired and didn't want to have a drink, but she decided not to object. After all, he was her boss. She followed Humphrey out of the building and walked with him the block to Patti's. While the waitress led them to a seat, a white man stared at them coldly. Mallory didn't notice the man, but Humphrey did.

They sat in a booth near the front. After he ordered a beer and coffee for Mallory, he smiled at her. 'Thanks for meeting with me at such short notice.'

'Was there something specific you needed to know, Humphrey?'

'Yes. When will you go out with me?'

Mallory opened her mouth and then closed it.

'Listen, I don't want to play games. I'd like to see you outside of work.'

'I don't think it's a very good idea for me to date my boss, Humphrey,' Mallory said. Jesus! She thought he'd gotten the message.

'People do it all the time.'

'Yes, I know, but . . .'

'We're adults. We can be discreet.'

'I just wouldn't feel comfortable, Humphrey.' She smiled cordially, to let him know that she wanted a friendly professional relationship.

His voice became softer, a little more insistent. 'I find you very attractive, Mallory.'

Should I tell him I'm seeing someone? she wondered. But if I do that, he might think I'd be interested in him if I didn't have a boyfriend. Maybe I should just keep saying no without an explanation. I need to leave. 'I appreciate the compliment, Humphrey,' she said, half rising, 'but— '

'Your not wanting to go out with me wouldn't have anything to do with the fact that I'm black, would it?'

Mallory's cheeks were turning cherry red by the time she sat back down. 'That is not the reason. I – I don't judge people by their skin color.'

'Are you uncomfortable sitting here with me now?' He watched her eyes closely. He could tell that he was getting

444

to her. He knew a vulnerable white woman when he saw one.

'I'm uncomfortable because you're my boss, not because you're black.' She could feel the panic squeezing through her throat. His being black didn't have anything to do with her not wanting to go out with him. It didn't. For some reason, she could feel Esther's eyes on her.

'Well, I don't want to make you uncomfortable, Mallory. I'm sorry. That wasn't my intention. Listen, let me make it up to you. Stay and have dinner with me.' He placed his hand lightly on her wrist.

Tell him no and then go home, she told herself. The words were on the tip of her tongue. But he's my boss; I don't want to offend him. Damn.

'Come on. Just one little dinner. Then we'll go back to being professionals.'

She was hungry; starving, in fact. Why should she go home and eat alone again? Maybe if she had dinner with him, he'd be satisfied. And he wouldn't think that she was a racist. 'Well, just this once,' she said. She smiled, a cordial smile, to show that she wanted a pleasant professional relationship.

Six o'clock. LaKeesha breathed a sigh of relief. Friday was the bank's late night and she was bone-tired and ready to go home. All day long she'd felt like not being there. Really, she'd been feeling like that for weeks. Just as she was about to put the Closed sign in front of her cage, a young black woman wearing a business suit appeared in front of her. LaKeesha sucked her teeth. 'What do you want?' she asked. Her tone was surly and impatient.

'Well, you don't have to be nasty!' the woman said. Her hand was on the counter. She wore a wedding ring, a large diamond solitaire that sparkled. The ring was probably worth six months' rent on the apartment she was saving for in Inglewood. Rich bitch, LaKeesha thought, seeing the way the jewel glittered. She had the urge to punch her in her smug face.

'It's after six o'clock. You lucky I'm waiting on you at all.'

'I entered this bank before closing time, and you will wait on me with courtesy or I'll go speak with your manager.' She handed LaKeesha her check. 'I'd like that in five twenties, please.'

Hector, working only a few feet away, heard LaKeesha suck her teeth, saw her flounce over to the cash drawer and then fling the money in front of the customer. He listened as the customer said, 'You need an attitude adjustment. You're lucky I don't have time to report you to your manager.'

LaKeesha was lucky, Hector thought, because he'd seen her behaving rudely a number of times lately. Only yesterday she had argued with an old white man who didn't have his ID and insisted that LaKeesha knew him well enough to cash his check. Customers' showing up without identification was a frequent problem, but instead of behaving calmly, LaKeesha was impolite. Even when the assistant operations manager intervened, she continued to suck her teeth and roll her eyes. This new LaKeesha was a stranger to him. She was hard, mean, and foolish. Twice last week she came to work late, rushing in just as the assistant operations manager was asking the tellers where she was. She didn't smile much anymore. Twice he started to ask her if everything was all right, if her son and the rest of her family were well, but he didn't want to intrude. In truth, each time he tried to shape the words in English, they felt like a strange taste in his mouth. Until he met LaKeesha, the people he cared about all spoke Spanish.

Now Hector watched her storming around behind the cage, slamming down bills on the counter as she did her final tally, and much as he cared about his friend, he couldn't help wondering how this change would affect her chances to become a customer rep. He wondered if Esther knew about LaKeesha's new behavior. Hector immediately recognized his thought as the beginning of evil, and he made a decision right then, as LaKeesha counted money not five feet from him, her lips curved into an angry scowl. She was his friend; he would not deliberately go against her. But if LaKeesha was going to throw away her opportunity for a better life, he would not hesitate to scramble after it.

And why not? He was working three jobs and still had so little money to show for all his hard labor. Every morning when he came to the bank he was tired from cleaning buildings the night before. If he became a service rep, there would be more money. He could buy things for his mother. He could marry his girlfriend, Idalia, and they could have a place of their own. He could buy a car. And he could get charge cards. Bullock's! Broadway! His breath was coming fast, the way it always did when he allowed his dreams to take over his consciousness. Stop, he told himself. Everything he imagined was years away. He was a poor man; he must remember that and act accordingly, otherwise he would drive himself crazy. Los Angeles was full of jewels, spread out for anyone to look at, to long for, to touch. On his lunch hour he passed restaurants that were filled with diners, serving meals that cost more than fifty dollars for one person to eat. Not a day passed that he didn't see beautiful cars – Mercedeses, Jaguars, BMWs – so shiny they hurt his eyes, gliding down even the most run-down streets. There were houses that were larger and more beautiful than the ones rich people on television inhabited. Even some black people were rich, which was astonishing to discover.

Hector observed that the smart and energetic learned how to service the needs of the people with glitter in their lives. In L.A., people could make a living just washing those shiny cars; detailing, they called it: fifteen dollars for washing one automobile! And men fed families from the money they received for clipping the lawns and tending the flowers of people who were too busy to do it themselves. There was a girl in his computer class, a white girl, who told him that men and women paid her fifty dollars to rub their tired shoulders and backs for only one hour! She carried a portable table to the homes of her clients. The women in his neighborhood, those with initiative, had no trouble finding jobs cleaning the houses of the wealthy, both black and white. The tales they brought home of fine furniture, beautiful rugs, lovely clothes, were enough to make their children sick. His mother often came home with boxes of clothing, shoes, even dishes, from the rich black people she worked for. All the things were like new. When his little sister went with her to clean, the child would be surly for days afterward and sometimes burst into tears over nothing. At such times, his words of comfort were useless. Money to buy what she dreamed of, enough money to have lovely, peaceful lives, that was the only thing that would stop her tears. Hector sighed. It would take so long to get that kind of money. Years. Decades. Sometimes he thought he would be an old man before he had any of the things he wanted.

But he must be patient. He'd seen the city make people go mad with greed and longing. The *cholos* on his block were so crazy to have shiny things that they shot people for the money to buy them. Even in the bank sometimes, well-dressed people, usually *blancos*, would bring him checks that were stolen or forged. People tried to pass counterfeit money so perfect it was identical to the real thing, except for the greasy feel of it. And of course there were actual bank robberies; he had been in two himself. He remembered the tattered pieces of craziness that blew into everyone's soul during the riots. People running and yelling, breaking windows, grabbing and stealing. He looked out his window, and it was like a fiesta for the insane. There were those who said it was because of Rodney King that the people became so crazy, but Hector knew better. It was Los Angeles, seducing with all her gaudy charms, promising and then reneging, that had driven the people – the blacks and Latinos, yes, and even some whites – to madness and flames.

Hector stole a quick look around him. No one was there but LaKeesha, and she was too busy sulking to notice him. He went to the computer and punched in the code. It was a secret code, but he had learned it by watching the assistant operations manager and Esther. In a few seconds, scores of names, with account numbers and, next to that, the amount in each account, appeared on the screen. They were forgotten savings, money just sitting there waiting to be claimed. When he began working as a teller, he had no idea that such a thing existed. Then one of the other tellers told him and LaKeesha how to take money from dormant accounts. 'It's easy,' the white guy said. At first Hector was afraid even to hear such a thing. But as he looked at the numbers, he thought about how he'd like to have the dollars of people so rich they'd forgotten to claim their own money. He and LaKeesha used to joke about spending dead people's money. They planned to buy huge houses for their families.

Hector turned off the computer and looked over at LaKeesha. Her face was still angry and full of pain. What did she have to be so upset about? he wondered. She was a citizen. She could vote. She spoke English. Everyone liked her. Why was she ruining her chances? He felt like warning her to be careful, but he said nothing.

By eight o'clock that evening, LaKeesha sat in bed, with the covers drawn up to her chin. The room was filled with the harsh odor of knockoff Giorgio perfume. She'd sprayed the last remnants on her wrists and behind her knees in an attempt to rise above the cloud of gloom that was rapidly descending upon her, but the sight of her last savings statement deepened her depression. She had seven hundred dollars. Hard as she was working, that's all she had to show for it. Seven hundred dollars.

She flung the piece of paper into the air and watched it sail across her bed and onto the floor. Just as it touched the rug, there was a knock at her door and her sister Shoni poked her head in. 'Dang, it stinks in here. Somebody here to see you, Miss Evilness,' she said.

King! LaKeesha bolted up from her bed and ran to the mirror. She reached in her purse, pulled out her lipstick and dabbed some on. Then she fluffed up her hair with her fingers. She needed to get it done, she thought with dismay. She gave the bangs another fluffing, then she hurried into the living room, trying not to feel too excited.

'Oh,' she said. It wasn't King; his sister, Charniece, was sitting on the sofa, waiting for her. LaKeesha's grandmother, her two sisters, their babies, and Man were all in front of the television. She smiled quickly, trying to hide her disappointment. She had no business wanting to see King anyway. She gave Charniece a hug. 'Hey, girl. How you been?'

'You don't care,' Charniece said mockingly. She was a big girl, with solid thighs and wide hips. Her round, dark face was framed by braids that hung down her back. 'Don't nobody see you no more. Where you be at all the time?'

'Working.'

'Yeah, I heard you had you a job. At a bank, right? You go 'head, girl. I brought you something.' She bent down and picked up a brown paper bag that was resting on the floor against the sofa. Pulling out two forty-ounce bottles of Colt 45, she handed one to LaKeesha. 'I figured you still drink you some Colt,' she teased.

'I ain't had the Colt in a while,' LaKeesha said, laughing. She went into the kitchen and brought back two glasses,

450

then she led her friend into her bedroom and closed the door. Charniece poured them both a drink from the first bottle, then held up her glass and tapped it lightly against LaKeesha's. 'Go 'head, Miss Keesha, working woman.'

They drank the first glass of malt liquor in big gulps. When LaKeesha's glass was empty, she said, 'I don't know, girl. It's hard. When I was getting that check, I didn't think about wanting nothing. But now that I'm working, even though I'm not making that much more money, I want more. Every time I turn around, Man needs something. I'm trying to move, but I got to come up with the deposit. Why is everything so hard?'

'Because you doing everything by yourself, that's why,' Charniece said. 'Listen, I got something to tell you, Keesha. King in jail, girl.'

LaKeesha was pouring herself another glass. She stopped and set the bottle on the floor. 'What'd he do?'

'Some dumb shit. He said he didn't do nothing, but you know, I ain't in that. They arrested him for trying to rob the liquor store on Normandie. I talked to him yesterday, and he asked me to tell you he wants you to come see him. Girl, whatchu crying for?'

LaKeesha couldn't answer her. She could feel the room whirling around her. Everything seemed to be spinning out of reach; even her own thoughts were a jumble of beginnings without endings. 'Damn,' was all she could say. 'Damn.'

'Listen, King is gone ask you for some money. Bail ain't in my mama's budget this month, you know what I'm saying? She scrambled around and got two thousand dollars together. I told her that King probably needs to stay his ass in jail, but you know how that go. He's her baby. Anyway, they need five hundred more. I know you still into my brother and shit, but Keesha, don't give him no money. Think about yourself and your baby.'

The two women talked awhile longer and drank several more rounds. After Charniece left, LaKeesha sat in her room in the dark. Pieces of her life seemed to drift by her, but she was unable to catch hold of anything. One minute she was a girl, crying for her father, and the next she was weeping again and holding Man in her arms. Her door cracked open in the middle of her reverie, and she saw Man standing in the shadows. 'What are you doing, Mommy?' he asked.

'I'm thinking.' Her voice sounded dull and far away.

'What are you thinking about?' She could feel her son climbing up on the bed. He put his head on her chest and snuggled into her. LaKeesha put one hand on his back and began rubbing his head with the other. 'What are you thinking about, Mommy?' he asked this time.

'You,' she said.

The waiting room of the county jail was packed when LaKeesha signed in. She was surrounded by mostly black women and Latinas. They were either young and dolled up for the occasion, or older, stoic, and minus the lipstick. Some women had brought children. Others had brought food and toiletries. LaKeesha came alone and empty-handed.

The room was an institutional gray – rat-colored walls and concrete floors – and smelled of disinfectant mixed in with the potpourri of colognes and perfumes that the visiting women wore. LaKeesha sat for an hour and a half before her name was called. She got on an elevator with a guard, who took her to the second floor and told her to sit down in front of a plate-glass window.

She could tell that King was happy to see her by the way he smiled. He looked a little heavier. 'How you know I was in here?' he asked.

452

'Charniece came by last night and told me what happened.'

King shrugged. 'How's my son?' he asked.

'How come you ain't been around to see him?'

King shrugged again. 'Busy, I guess.' He looked at her and laughed, and the scar on his face started dancing.

She wanted to reach through the glass and slap his face. Instead, she said, her voice louder, 'You're lucky you in jail and not stretched out in some alley with a bullet in your head. When are you going to learn? You hang around with all the rest of them dumb fools, and this is where you end up. King, when are you going to learn?'

'Aww, LaKeesha, c'mon now, baby.' He wasn't smiling anymore. He looked sorry and a little scared.

'Baby nothing!' She almost shouted. 'You have a child. I mean, you're all the time bragging about your son, but what can you do for him in jail, King?'

'Can't do shit for him in jail or out,' King said, his voice flat. When he stared at her, his dark eyes were full of pain. 'I have learned,' he said. He looked around and then pushed his face closer to the window and began whispering. 'Keesha, you right. You been right all along. All I been doing since I got in here is thinking. I been keeping to myself. Some of my homies is in here, but I ain't even kicking it with them, Keesha. When I get outta here, I'm taking control of my life, baby. That's what I been planning. Baby, when I get outta here, I'ma straight up go back to school. I'ma get my GED and then I'ma study mechanics. 'Cause you know I can fix me some cars.'

'Yeah, you're good at that.' She grinned at King for no reason at all except that the words sounded so good – so good that she had to stop herself. Believing King, that's what got her in trouble in the first place. Saying what he was going to do wasn't even close to doing it. Besides, who knew when he was going to get out of jail?

'You always had your head on straight, baby,' King said. 'You been doing it all, but I swear, that's gone change. I want to get married when I get out. I want to marry you, LaKeesha.' He put his fingers against the glass, and she pressed her fingertips to meet his. Then he took his hand away, and she knew what was coming. 'Girl, you got any money? I need five hundred dollars for the lawyer. Can you let me hold that? I'll pay you back, I swear, baby. Baby?'

When Hector arrived at the bank Monday morning, La-Keesha was sipping coffee and straightening up her area. She gave Hector a wide smile and hurried to count the fives, tens, and twenties that were in her till. When the bank opened and the first customers arrived, LaKeesha greeted them pleasantly and carried out their transactions efficiently. The brooding anger and resentment that had engulfed her for weeks had fallen away like a scab.

It didn't matter that she would never have what Esther had. She and King were going to have something together when he got out of jail. And that wouldn't be long, because as soon as she got back home from the prison, she took King's mother a check for five hundred dollars. She ignored Charniece's disdain, looked away when she said, 'Girl, you a fool.' Charniece just didn't understand. King wanted to marry her. Just his saying the words made her feel so special. He would be her husband, and there would finally be a man in her house. Five hundred dollars wasn't too much to pay for a dream like that. 'Hector,' she called, and the small bronzed man looked up at her and smiled. 'I'm going on break,' she said. 'My papusa jones is coming down on hard me.' She grinned at him.

'Don't eat my greens and corn bread,' he said.

'I wouldn't do that to you, homeboy.'

Hector kept smiling as he watched LaKeesha walk toward the employees' lounge. She seemed to be happy again; she was working hard and being polite to her customers. The other LaKeesha, the one who frowned with a tight mouth, whose eyes were like the lead in pencils, had disappeared. Hector was glad. He knew that the black girl's chances for advancement were better than his, but he tried not to think about that. It wasn't fair that LaKeesha was Esther's favorite, but nothing in life is fair, he reminded himself. For a minute, even as he was looking at LaKeesha, he was back in his country. He heard the sound of bombs falling near his village. There were soldiers shooting, and when he looked he saw the dead body of his favorite uncle. He closed his eyes, and he could hear the wailing of his grandmother and mother, their shrieks of anguish as his uncle's body was placed in the ground. There was a place inside him that was like granite. He thought: I am in America; I must make my own opportunities.

The phone wasn't picked up until the sixth ring. LaKeesha could hear her two nieces screaming in the background. 'Mother?' LaKeesha said after no one said hello.

'Uh huh. Hey, baby. Chile, these two little girls is both acting a fool over here.' She must have turned her mouth away from the phone; LaKeesha heard her say, 'All right, now. Y'all better hush.'

'Mother, did anybody call me?'

'I'm telling you, these kids is wearing me out. I'm too old to be—'

'Mother!'

'Charniece called you. Said to tell you that King is going to trial next week. Wish to God he just leave you alone.'

'Okay. I got to go now, Mama.'

'Well, come straight home, because I need me some relief, you hear me?'

It was the news she'd been waiting to hear. She got a Pepsi from the soda machine and sat down. Crossing her ankles, she took a sip, then leaned back. King had a good lawyer, some white man who, according to Charniece, 'done kept a lotta gangstas out the joint.' She could only hope that he would do the same for King.

Taking a bite of her papusa, she visualized the apartment that was now out of her reach. The three neat bedrooms weren't large, but they were bigger than what they had. There was a dishwasher in the kitchen and a small laundry room in the basement, so the girls wouldn't have to travel to wash clothes. She couldn't remember a time when one of them didn't have to bundle up the clothes in a little cart and push them two blocks to the laundromat, which was always crowded. There had been a shooting there only a few months ago. The little laundry in the apartment building was neat and clean; nobody could get in without a key. The apartment was on a quiet street with lots of maple trees. She'd seen lots of children playing in a small park directly across the street. She could have been happy there. She thought about her five hundred dollars. It had taken her months to save that money. For a moment she wondered if she'd thrown away something she could almost touch for something that might disappear like the wind. King had made promises before. No, she told herself, he was going to marry her. She wouldn't need that apartment, because she wouldn't be living with her sisters and grandmother and Annie anymore. She and King would get a place of their own. There would be just King and Man and her; they would be her family. She was going to be somebody's wife instead of just one more black woman struggling alone with a baby. And maybe she could pull it off, do what Annie hadn't been able to do: make King do right; make him stay and be her husband and Man's father.

Still, sitting in the employees' lounge, she tasted regret when she thought about the apartment, the shaded, quiet street, the nice clean rooms. How long would it take the two of them to save enough money? There was no telling when King would get a job. He had to get his GED first. We have to have our own place, she thought. I'm not giving up on that. The fierceness of her yearning spread through her like heat. She would just have to figure out a way to make it all happen.

31

Out of the corner of his eye, Kirk watched as Mallory and Humphrey chatted. The Diversity Program's long-awaited final session of the year had just concluded, and Humphrey used the occasion to speak a few words, to kind of summarize the philosophy of the program, one of those 'Where do we go from here' pep talks that reflected nothing so much as trite, redundant sentimentality. Or so Kirk thought as he applauded just enough to be polite, then watched Humphrey glad-handing his way toward the door. The black man's expression was like a politician's as he proceeded to work the room. But when he reached Mallory, his expression softened; the smile he gave her was genuine, and so was the one he got in return. They stood talking for at least three minutes – long enough for Kirk to feel suspicion gathering in his bones. He'd been watching the two of them for several weeks, noticing how Humphrey always seemed to single out Mallory for eye contact and how the white woman always looked away, as though she were afraid to look the black man in the eye. It wasn't just the way they did and didn't look at each other. There was something more.

He wants her. The thought detonated in Kirk's mind. He actually heard tiny pops. When he looked down, he realized that he was cracking his knuckles, one after the other. He fought the urge, a powerful one, to leap on Humphrey and punch him until he saw blood spurting from every opening in his face. He could feel his own fist against the black man's jaw, could taste the harsh curse words in his mouth.

He should smile at his own women.

Kirk began choking and sputtering. He felt a sudden pounding on his back and then his own hot breath, spilling from his throat. 'Are you okay?' his rescuer asked him. Kirk stiffened. Humphrey was staring at him. At first he looked anxious, but when he saw that Kirk was breathing normally, his humor returned. 'You don't need for me to do the Heimlich, do you?' he asked with a smile.

Kirk tried hard to keep the fury out of his voice. 'I'm fine. Really.'

As Kirk watched Humphrey walk away, he wanted to shout, 'You can't even save yourself.' But there was no need for that, he thought. In time everyone would know the truth.

Because Humphrey was in trouble. Oh, he was an okay manager and he ran the Minority Loan Program satisfactorily, but the skill for which he'd been hired had netted no results. In the months that he'd been at the bank, he hadn't brought in one private placement loan. And Kirk knew that he was trying. The truth was, Humphrey Boone was losing. The longer that remained true, the more hopeful Kirk became.

Kirk decided to drop in at Patti's after work and have a beer. Lately, facing Sheila without first fortifying himself demanded inner resources he no longer possessed. As soon as he walked into Patti's, Kirk saw Jason Rodgers. They'd been good friends in graduate school, where they'd both been in the M.B.A. program. Early in their careers they worked at the same bank, before Jason switched to insurance. Now they got together about once a year. At least that much time had elapsed since they'd seen each other. Kirk walked up to him and slapped him on his back. 'How the hell are you?' he asked.

'Kirk.' Jason shook his hand. 'It's good to see you. What

are you drinking? How's the family?' He smiled and revealed tiny teeth, as sharp and pointy as a rat's.

He ordered Kirk a beer and got himself another Stoly on the rocks. 'I was just thinking about you the other day. I may be cutting a deal with you guys soon. It looks pretty good.'

'Oh, really,' Kirk said. 'What kind of deal?'

'A private placement loan. I'm working with Humphrey Boone.'

Kirk was very still for a moment as he weighed the opportunity before him. There was only a split second for him to decide what he needed to convey to Jason Rodgers. He had the premonition that his words could change his life. Looking at his old friend, he laughed. Then he leaned in close and said softly, 'Don't count on it.'

Jason's expression was filled with astonishment and curiosity. 'Why not? What's going on?'

Kirk adopted a conspiratorial whisper and got even closer to Jason, who was peering at him with acute interest. 'Listen, the guy's not going to make it. They've got him on the hit list. The short hit list.'

'Are you shitting me? I heard he was the golden boy, Preston Sinclair's handpicked godson.'

Kirk recoiled at Jason's description, but he didn't change the expression on his face, which was the detached and disinterested mien of an innocent bystander. 'He's fucked up one too many times. Don't get started on anything with him, because I heard that when he goes, so do his deals. They're really pissed off with him.'

'What'd he do?'

Kirk thought quickly. 'I don't want to bad-mouth the guy, and I don't want to expose the bank. Let's just say he's not meeting their expectations. Let's just leave it at that.'

'Well, thanks for the tip, Kirk.' Jason drained his glass,

then extended his hand. 'Listen, let's do lunch soon, all right?'

'Pencil me in for two weeks from today at twelve-thirty. I'll call you that morning and we'll agree on the place. I want to talk with you about private placement loans. That's something I'm interested in.'

Jason looked a little surprised, but he dutifully took out his Wizard. 'Done deal,' he said, after he typed in the information.

'And don't forget, what I mentioned is highly confidential.'

'I won't breathe a word of it to anybody.'

Humphrey was sweating. He could feel the drops of water rolling from his armpits down his sides as he paced back and forth around his desk, waiting for Jason Rodgers of Rockford Insurance to pick up the phone. He could picture the short white man, with his tiny rat teeth. He'd been waiting at least three minutes, and the longer he held on, the more he felt like he was choking. He couldn't understand what was happening. Their initial meeting had been so promising; he could tell that Rodgers was hot for the deal. But then something happened, he didn't know what. The man simply got cold on him. This was the third time he'd called. 'Mr. Boone?' It was Jason's assistant. 'I'm sorry, but Mr. Rodgers is in a meeting. He wanted to let you know that he's a little swamped right now and that when his desk gets cleared he'll give you a call.'

Humphrey's hands were trembling as he hung up the telephone. The white boy had blown him off, just like that, he thought. Not even the decency to tell him man-to-man. He took off his jacket. The entire back of his shirt was soaked. He put his coat on again, then sat down in his chair and swiveled around and around and around.

Jason Rodgers called Kirk a few days later to tell him that

the deal was off. At noon that same day, a jubilant Kirk met Bailey Reynolds for lunch. He hadn't had a one-on-one with him since the kiss-off lunch they'd had months before. The restaurant Bailey had chosen was mediocre at best and underscored Kirk's fall from Angel City glory. There wasn't even a wine list. But as Kirk sat down at a nondescript table by the window, he didn't mind a bit. Not at all. Bailey's smile was warm, but Kirk's clandestine observation over the last few months told him that the man's heart was cold. And ambitious. Well, he had information that would further the older man's career, as well as his own.

As he faced Kirk, Bailey felt not one iota of guilt over the way the younger man had been demoted. Business was business. The truth was, Bailey had learned a long time ago that remorse was a trait that would slow him down considerably. He faced the world each day with equanimity. As he ordered his lunch, he took a quick peek at his watch. Thirty minutes was all he could spare.

'Glad we could get together like this, Kirk. It's been too long,' Bailey said amiably. 'I hope you've been well.'

'I've been fine, just fine.'

'And was there something in particular that you wanted to talk with me about?'

Bailey's smile didn't fool Kirk. The man wanted him to get to the point quickly. 'I just thought it would be good for us to keep in touch,' Kirk said.

'Well, of course.' Bailey looked around for the waiter. He'd cut the meeting short if Kirk had nothing important to say.

For his part, Kirk chatted, edging his words toward eliciting an opening from Bailey. 'Well, we had the last of the Diversity Program last Friday. There was some initial resentment at first, but I think some of the instructors really, uh, helped people to understand the nature of prejudice.'

Bailey looked bored. He glanced around the room.

Where was the waiter? 'Humphrey did a good job with that.'

Careful. Careful. Kirk gave Bailey a perfectly benign smile, full of lighthearted amusement. Casual. That was the look he wanted. He'd practised the expression in his bathroom mirror. 'It's a wonder he found time, the way he's been chasing down deals.' He waited no longer than one beat. 'He's quite a ladies' man, isn't he?'

Bailey put down his glass of water. His sharp little eyes didn't move from Kirk's face. Here was the point, and no amount of subtlety could hide it. 'Is he, now?'

32

Mallory's door was open just a crack as Kirk passed by on the way back to his office. She was sitting at her desk, talking on the telephone, her face tilted toward the wall, her perfectly shaped legs perched on top of her desk. She swiveled slightly and saw Kirk standing in the hallway, peering at her. His glance was so intense that for a moment she thought something was wrong. She looked down at her legs. When she glanced back at the door, he wasn't there. Mallory got up and closed her door.

'But when are we going away?' she asked softly into the telephone. Mallory was careful not to whine. She spoke in an even, well-modulated tone that was strained from trying to sound happy. That voice had been shaped since childhood, and as she summoned it now, resentment scraped against her throat.

She heard Hayden sighing as he fumbled for an answer that would exonerate him from his last broken promise while allowing him to mitigate his culpability by pledging something new. Mallory hated being so easy to string along, but then she always had been.

'I'll take you next week,' her father used to say as he ushered her brother out the door to some male-only adventure. Next week came and went, over and over again. Her father's excuses ran out before her hope did. Even before he'd fashioned his next lie, her heart was saying yes.

'So he's taking me to Mexico for July Fourth,' Mallory told Esther later that night. A couple of times a week, they called each other after the eleven o'clock news went off.

Sometimes, earlier in the evening, Mallory's phone would ring and it would be Esther. 'Mal, I know you're watching *Love Connection*, but turn to PBS.' Or she would call the black woman to ask her what spices she needed for her eggplant casserole. Or to talk about nothing at all.

'He's not going to do it,' Esther said after a few moments passed. Mallory was quiet. She felt like a child being chastised by her mother, and in fact, Esther's tone when she talked about Hayden Lear had become increasingly maternal and angry. 'Jesus. He's an asshole. Don't tell me it's physical, because he's old and wrinkled up, not a cute bone in his body. He lies to you all the time. Girlfriend, come on. Take a deep breath. It's brewing. Can you smell it? He's playing you. It's like my mama said: Why buy a cow when you're getting milk for free.'

Mallory giggled. 'My mother told me that too.'

'Well, *there's* one that transcends race and culture. Mamas from the South Side and mamas from the Valley, all giving their daughters the same warning. And do these little diverse girls listen. He-e-ell, no. Can't you even get mad?'

Mallory ignored the question. 'If he doesn't come through on this, I'll— '

'You need to get mad, Mallory. You need to scream and yell and throw shit.'

'I don't know how to do that,' Mallory said.

'Well, you'd better learn.' Esther knew there was an edge to her voice. I'm too involved with this, she thought, but she couldn't detach herself. Every time Mallory mentioned Hayden, she remembered her own hurt, yearning, and stupidity over Mitchell Harris in vivid detail. She felt a thirst for vengeance; misplaced aggression, without a doubt. 'Look,' she told Mallory, 'about this Mexico trip: Don't get your hopes up. Don't even pack. If he shows up, make him buy you clothes when you get there.' Even as she said the words, she knew her friend couldn't hear her.

Mallory packed and hoped. During the two weeks before the trip was to take place, Hayden called her every day and managed to see her four times. One night he stayed with her until almost four o'clock in the morning. Three o'clock the Friday before the Fourth was the appointed hour. She stood at her window until four, rubbing her palm back and forth across the sill. By five o'clock Mallory knew he wasn't coming or calling. She didn't begin unpacking until eleven. Her mind was clear and sharp as she put away the new lingerie, wrapped so carefully in scented tissue paper. The new dresses were still in plastic. She didn't cry. She folded the garment bag and set it down in the closet next to her larger luggage, then she went downstairs, poured herself a glass of wine, and sat on her couch in the dark. When she got up hours later, the blunt finger of anger was beckoning her.

Humphrey hung up the telephone and then slumped down into his chair. He couldn't understand what was happening. It was almost as if he'd been blackballed. Every lead fizzled out. He couldn't even get people on the phone whom he'd done business with in the past. Ever since Jason Rodgers reneged, nothing had been turning out right. Two of the three deals he'd been pursuing had been taken over by competitors.

To make matters worse, Preston had invited him to his country club to play tennis. At any other time, he'd have been overjoyed, but in his present state, he could only think of such an invitation as something else that was destined to slip through his fingers. How long would Preston seek his friendship if he failed to get the job done? He knew that the president was concerned. Only last week Humphrey had talked with Bailey Reynolds, who smiled during the entire meeting while asking vague but penetrating questions about the status of the private placement loans. 'Preston wants

you to know that he has every confidence in your ability,'
Bailey said, his cherubic jowls bunched up with seeming
good nature. But although his smile was amicable, his eyes
were sharp and hard. Bailey's eyes circled Humphrey's body
like a bird of prey. And there was no mistaking that stare.
They're concerned about my ability, Humphrey thought.
He could feel his shirt sticking to his back. He took his
starched coordinated handkerchief and mopped his forehead with several strong, fast swipes. 'We're expecting good
things from you,' Bailey said congenially.

'Absolutely,' Humphrey said.

Alone in the elevator after the meeting, he could feel wild,
illogical fear pressing down on his heart. He wiped his face
again and pulled his shirt away from his skin so that air
would get to it. There were clean shirts in his office, and
he tried to focus on those clean white shirts. He counted
backward from one hundred, trying to calm himself, but
the enclosed space made him want to scream. When the
elevator stopped at his floor, he was ready to fly through
the doors. He waited. They didn't open. No more than ten
seconds passed, but in that time Humphrey could feel a
howl rattling in his throat. He couldn't breathe. He
slammed his fists against the elevator doors. When they still
didn't open, he began banging on the walls around him.
Those brief moments seemed endless; he felt utterly trapped
and doomed. Even when the doors opened and the cool air
was on his face, the horror didn't quite leave him. He
suffered brief, gruesome flash-backs throughout the day,
palpable reminders that he was in a place that, at any given
moment, could close in on him like a grave.

And now, as he put down the telephone, he felt ghostlike
echoes of the dreadful panic that had seized him by the
throat in the elevator. Jason Rodgers had been his last hope.
He didn't have any more leads. He closed his eyes and saw
his scrawny nine-year-old self, standing in the welfare line

with his mama. He didn't want to go back there, back to being a nigger.

He was on his way home when he saw Mallory ahead of him, on her way out of the building. He quickened his steps, an involuntary movement. Then he slowed down. Don't press her, he told himself. Leave the woman alone. But at that moment Mallory turned around, smiled, and beckoned him with her delicate finger. She was waiting by the door when he got there.

'How was your day?' she asked once he caught up with her. There was interest in her gray eyes. Humphrey would have staked his life on that. Just looking into her friendly face lifted him somehow. He was still important, still the Man.

'My day was fine.' He looked around the empty operations area behind them to make sure they were alone. He didn't see anyone. 'How was yours?'

'Productive. Listen, I want to thank you for dinner the other night.'

'If you ever change your mind,' he said, 'I'd love to take you out again.' He spoke quickly and smoothly, putting no particular emphasis on his words. Let the chips fall where they may, he thought.

There was no mistaking the smile she gave him. It was an invitation. 'I have changed my mind,' she said softly. 'If you're available, I'd like to invite you somewhere.'

Mallory stared at herself in the full-length mirror in her bedroom. In the clingy, red-sequined gown, with her golden hair piled on top of her head, she almost looked like another woman. She certainly felt like one.

She glanced at the clock on her nightstand. In fifteen minutes Humphrey would arrive. Without thinking, she reached for the phone and began dialing Esther's number. Only when she heard the first ring did she realize what she was doing. She put the receiver down quickly. We'll have a good laugh about this one day, she thought. She imagined the two of them together somewhere, cracking up. 'You worked it, girlfriend.' That's what Esther would say. Why would she care? It wasn't as if she and Humphrey were dating. She really had no claim on the man.

'You look very wow,' Humphrey said when she opened the door. She laughed at the description. Inside the house, she got a better look at his outfit: a double-breasted tuxedo with a red bow tie and cummerbund. 'We match,' she said.

By the time they arrived at the Beverly Hills Inn, Mallory could hear music coming from the ballroom. They were in line for valet parking for at least ten minutes before their turn finally came. When they got out of the car, Mallory saw several people staring at her. She responded by peeking at her cleavage, but no, nothing was out of line. A man scowled at her. Several women frowned and stepped aside to let them pass. Others smiled solicitously, even though their eyes blinked nervously. Mallory looked at Humphrey; he was the only black person she saw. Of course, of course, she thought. Humphrey took her hand, and as they edged their way to the inn, she saw that he looked neither to the left nor to the right. She did the same until they reached the ballroom.

The Beverly Hills Society's annual dinner dance was an extravaganza like no other. Gathered together in the ballroom were the very well heeled from one of Los Angeles's wealthiest enclaves. Mallory and Humphrey had to wade through a sea of beautiful people – stars, lesser stars, usetabes, and wannabes – as they made their way across the ballroom. There were women wearing gowns that cost more than new cars and men whose millions paid for not only the trophy wives on their arms but the women who were hidden out of sight. Waiters poured Moët; the menu was filet mignon and lobster. But Mallory wasn't interested in the decorations or the designer gowns or the flashy diamonds on the age-spotted fingers of Beverly Hills matrons. She had come for something else entirely. Now she looked, oblivious to the stares that followed her and Humphrey. She was no longer conscious of the overly friendly smiles or the hidden sneers. There were more than two hundred tables, and Mallory inspected each one with ferocious precision until finally she recognized the profile she was seeking. She took Humphrey's hand and walked very close to him. She smiled and laughed loudly when people stared. She wanted to be noticed.

'Why, Hayden. How wonderful to see you. It's been a long time,' Mallory said. When she said his name, she put her hands on his shoulders. Hayden turned around to face her. He made a croaking sound, and then he cleared his throat. 'Mallory,' he said, stuttering a little. 'Mallory.' His eyes were suddenly filled with a kind of silent pleading that made her want to laugh. She extended her hand to Hayden, who shook it woodenly. She held it as she turned to his wife, who was seated next to him. His fingers became damp in her hand. 'Mrs. Lear, we met years ago, when I was working with your husband. I'm Mallory Post.'

'Oh, yes. How nice to see you again, dear. You look lovely.' She looks her age, Mallory noted with unexpected satisfaction.

'Thank you.' She was still holding Hayden's slippery fingers, even as he tried to twist them away from her. 'Hayden, Mrs. Lear, I'd like you to meet my date, Humphrey Boone.'

She let go of Hayden's hand and took Humphrey's and smiled at the older man, whose eyes shifted back and forth from Mallory to Humphrey as though he couldn't comprehend what he was seeing. His face became red, and when he tried to speak, he was overcome with a coughing fit. 'Drink some water, dear,' his wife said.

470

'Yes, Hayden, have some water,' Mallory said, watching him gag. For a moment, his face became her father's. She inhaled, imagining her father's fury if he knew she was out with a black man. When she exhaled, she was smiling.

Hayden sipped from the glass his wife offered him until he cleared his throat. His cheeks were still scarlet when he looked up at Mallory and Humphrey. He took the black man's hand and shook it quickly. Hostility flowed from his fingertips, and what Humphrey read in the white man's eyes was an unmistakable desire to inflict pain – possibly genital mutilation – upon him.

'Very nice to meet you,' Hayden said.

He's jealous, Mallory thought. She stifled an urge to raise both her fists in the air.

Humphrey saw the elation in Mallory's eyes. He looked at Hayden; his expression was full of fear and anger, which he was attempting to control. And then he glanced at Mrs. Lear, who was gazing absent-mindedly toward the crowd, her lips locked into a passive smile. He looked back at Mallory. I am being played, he thought.

Mallory pulled out the empty seat next to Hayden and motioned for Humphrey to sit next to her. 'You don't mind if we sit and chat until your friends come back, do you? Our table's way over on the other side.' Hayden, whose eyes seemed to have acquired a permanently startled expression, didn't respond. 'It's been so long. How long has it been?' She reached for Humphrey's hand, placed it in hers, and then displayed their entwined fingers on the table in front of everyone. She leaned toward Humphrey and smiled at Hayden.

Humphrey didn't know whether to stalk away or laugh. As they sat with the Lears, Hayden's crimson complexion changed to a ghostly white. From time to time he glanced at Humphrey, who could see bright flecks of anger in the white man's eyes. Now he knew what to do. The second time

Hayden looked at him that way, Humphrey stared back at him with narrowed eyes; he let go of Mallory's hand and put his arm around her shoulder. Then he glared at Hayden defiantly until he averted his glance. As Mallory and Humphrey left, Hayden attempted to rise, but his wife's arm jerked up stiffly and her hand hit him in his crotch. 'Ow!' he bellowed. Both husband and wife appeared startled. Everyone at the table looked at Hayden's crotch: his tuxedo button was caught in one of the thin gold chains his wife was wearing around her bony wrist. She smilingly pulled him toward her and said, pleasantly, 'We're stuck.'

When they finally sat down at their own table, Mallory and Humphrey were drained. They drank several glasses of Moët, picked at the dinner, danced twice, and didn't even attempt conversation. Little more than an hour after they arrived, Mallory was ready to go. 'It's a little stuffy in here, don't you think? I'm getting such a headache.'

'Let's go someplace where it's easier to breathe,' Humphrey said.

Mallory could hear the music as they pulled up to a crowded parking lot. Black music. She thought about Washington, and Traces. She really wasn't in the mood for a lot of noise. She wanted to go home. 'Aren't we overdressed?' she asked.

'It doesn't matter. Come on.'

She followed him inside. The In Town wasn't large or luxurious, and the room was more stifling than the hotel ballroom. And louder. A live band was playing, and people were trying to talk over the music. But the place seemed to get quieter when Humphrey and Mallory walked in. She was conscious of being appraised. A large man seated at the bar stood up when they came in and smiled admiringly in Humphrey's direction. 'Come on. I see a friend of mine,' Humphrey said, and they walked toward the man. Humphrey put his hand around her waist. As he introduced her, calling out her name, his voice was loud, louder than the music, louder than the talk around them. She was conscious of his hands turning her, slightly to the right, slightly to the left. He touched her hair as they stood in front of the man, a deliberate touch that seemed to have no purpose. When they left to find a table, Humphrey stopped in the middle of the floor and spoke with another friend, and again he turned her this way, that way. He spoke and laughed loudly. His chest seemed to be expanding as if someone had puffed it full of air.

They sat down at a table, and a waitress came. All the disapproval and hostility that Mallory sensed in the room seemed gathered in the woman's hard, dark face. 'What would you like?' she asked, carefully not looking at Humphrey or Mallory.

'Miss,' Humphrey said. His voice forced her eyes to meet his. Mallory felt his hand on hers. 'Let me see what my lady would like.' He turned to Mallory. 'Champagne?'

She nodded.

'Two glasses of champagne,' he said. The waitress nodded, then she pressed her lips together. The movement was familiar. Mallory had seen Esther do it, just before she made that sound that meant she was outraged and indignant. What was that sound?

As the waitress walked away, Mallory heard it. 'Umph. Umph. Umph.'

They each drank two glasses of champagne. In the front of the club, the MC announced a singer, and a tall, shapely woman came to the microphone. She crooned soft love songs in a heartfelt soprano. The crowd became quiet; all the talking was done in whispers. Listening to the woman, Mallory temporarily forgot the waitress's hostility, and the memory of Hayden's jealous wrath dimmed in Humphrey's mind. They listened quietly, and in between numbers they inclined their heads closer to each other. When they left, nearly two hours later, they were giddy from champagne and laughter.

Humphrey parked his car outside Mallory's town house and hummed the chorus of one of the love songs he'd just heard as he walked around and opened her door. Through Mallory's champagne-induced cloud of happiness, it occurred to her that Humphrey might expect to come in. She was too high to be alarmed. It was only a little after midnight. 'Would you like to come in for coffee?'

Humphrey nodded.

Once they were settled inside, she asked, 'Do you like cappuccino? I have a machine.'

'That would be great,' Humphrey said. He rested his head against the sofa and stared at the curve of Mallory's hips as she went into the kitchen.

He was asleep when she placed the steaming cups on the coffee table in front of him. Standing between his open legs, she tapped him on the shoulder. 'Humphrey. Humphrey.'

The warmth between his legs was like an alarm clock. Opening his eyes, Humphrey reached for Mallory instinctively, pulled her to his chest, and began kissing her. Her body became stiff for a moment and then went completely limp. His kisses were flashes of heat that soothed and excited. She closed her eyes, and her father was standing above her, watching, a giant, his huge face contorted with anger. She put her arms around Humphrey's neck. From the corner of his eye, Humphrey saw his own dark hand against Mallory's pale back; he felt her body grow soft and yielding. He could taste Mallory's pale-golden hair in his mouth. He reached for her zipper.

'No,' she said, when she felt his hand on her dress. She pulled away. The foam had settled on the cups of cappuccino. He smiled at her, then leaned over and kissed her again, then moved away. 'I'd like to take you out next

474

Saturday. Dinner. Movie. Whatever you want. Would you like that?'

He kissed her again, sucked her breath into his mouth. She was dizzy when he finished. She didn't think, just nodded quickly. 'Yes,' she said. She had trouble standing up. 'It's late,' she said finally. He kissed her good-bye at the door.

She took the flavor of him to bed with her, and it kept her awake. At first the sweetness of his lips lingered in her mouth, but that gradually gave way to the taste of trouble as she reviewed the evening. She had gone out with her boss, for no other reason than to make Hayden jealous. She'd kissed him, made out with him right on her couch. And now he wanted to see her again. And worst of all, she couldn't tell Esther about any of it, especially not how much she liked kissing Humphrey Boone.

Mallory woke up Sunday morning to a ringing phone. It was only six o'clock. 'Are you fucking that nigger?' Hayden's voice was a tight whisper. Where was he? she wondered. In his precious study. He had never called her from home before.

'Go to hell,' Mallory said softly. She hung up the phone.

'Are you?' he said, louder this time, when she answered after the fifth ring.

Her initially sleepiness had drained away. 'Don't ever call me again. I don't want to see you. I want you out of my life.' She was shouting; it felt wonderful.

When he called the next time, Mallory let the telephone ring until the answering machine picked it up. His tone was contrite. 'I know you're there, Mallory. Please pick up the phone. I'm sorry about what I said. Listen, I realize that you're angry. I've disappointed you so many times. I know that. Darling, please pick up the phone. I can't bear the thought of you with another man. Listen, we've got to talk. Things are going to change. I'm ready to divorce Cora. I know I've said that before, but . . . Darling, won't you please talk to me?'

Mallory picked up the telephone.

By midafternoon, every room in Mallory's town house contained flowers, long-stemmed roses that she placed in various vases as she sang cheerfully. She stood in front of her bedroom mirror and practised saying aloud the words that she'd written on the three-by-five card: 'Look, I'm really sorry. I had a great time with you last night, but I don't want to see you again outside of work. It's not that I don't enjoy your company. And it has nothing to do with your being black.' She drummed her fingers against her knee. 'I'm sorry if it appeared as though I was leading you on. I just hope that you'll accept my apology and we can continue to have a friendly professional relationship.'

Humphrey will understand that, she thought.

33

Mallory felt relief when she hung up the phone. 'Of course. No hard feelings,' Humphrey had said. All that worrying for nothing; he was a gentleman. Still, for a week after their date, she looked around cautiously when she rounded corners at the bank or went down the hall to the ladies' room. The truth was, now that the champagne-induced passion she'd shared with Humphrey was over, she was embarrassed. The man wasn't stupid; he'd probably figured everything out, including her reason for inviting him to the dance. She was ashamed that she'd used him; his apparent willingness to forgive and forget only made her feel worse.

The week after his date with Mallory, Humphrey was pursuing deals, not women. He was busy setting up a series of high-level meetings with insurance agency officials he hadn't contacted previously. This time he allowed no room for mistakes. Humphrey immersed himself in each company's history and politics, as well as the backgrounds of the executives he was wooing. He called on associates and asked for advice, listened to what was said and incorporated the best of it into his overall strategy. Every evening, he left the office with stacks of documents. Fueled with pots of black coffee, he scrutinized them until after midnight. Several nights he fell asleep at the desk in his study, only to wake up stiff and sore. He stumbled into work haggard and tired, but as soon as he sat down, he felt his adrenaline pumping. He could smell victory. Humphrey was enjoying the chase.

The series of meetings began glowingly. He took each

insurance agency representative to a power lunch at an exclusive Beverly Hills restaurant, where they chatted and he casually introduced the idea of the private placement loan. The first lunch was just the icebreaker, a chance to feel people out, to win their trust. Then he scheduled a second meeting with the likeliest candidates – there were five in all – and at these sessions he made a full-fledged presentation.

And then nothing. A week passed, and no one called him. Days later, four letters came in, all stating that they weren't interested in the deal.

Late one afternoon, the elegant, silver-haired Eleanor, who'd pieced together Humphrey's family situation but had conveyed her ability to be discreet, peeked into his office and told him that his sister Chontelle was on the line. Humphrey was prepared for another personal tragedy and, of course, a plea for money, but he was not prepared for his sister's words. 'Humptey, you need to get over here to the hospital. Mama done had a stroke.'

Chontelle was at the emergency room with their younger sister when Humphrey arrived. Humphrey wasn't surprised that his brother wasn't there. No one had seen him since he signed himself out of his drug rehab program months before. 'How is she?' he asked.

'You need to talk to the doctor, Humptey. I can't understand what he's saying, but I think it's bad,' Chontelle said.

It was bad. His mother had lost the use of her right side and could barely speak. As Humphrey stood over her narrow hospital bed and gazed down at her, for the first time in his life she looked weak to him. His mother had always been a hurricane of a woman, storming her way through life with equal parts angry bluster and religious fervor. When he was a child, it was impossible for him to tell where her rage toward him ended and her love began. Now one side of her was sagging, as though she had relinquished a part of herself. 'Oh, Mama,' he said. He wasn't calling for the unconscious, gray-haired sufferer who lay before him with tubes running in and out of her body, but for that other mother, years younger, who with her screams and slaps always failed to be Mrs. Brady.

A week later, the doctor told him that when she left the hospital, his mother would need physical therapy and twenty-four-hour nursing care for at least two months. 'I don't know how to talk to them people,' Chontelle told him immediately. So he spent hours on the phone contacting private care facilities and was forced to take a day off from work to interview prospective nurses. When he chose the service, it took days to do the paperwork, to figure out what Medicare covered and what he'd end up having to pay. Because, of course, he would be the one who was liable. His headaches began to come more frequently, and even the sight of an elevator made him freeze with terror. When he was able to sleep, he dreamed of falling.

But he wasn't falling. Not quite. The final prospect called weeks after their initial lunch, apologizing profusely for the delay. The man's name was Tom Wagner, and he said he was very interested.

Even with that good news, Humphrey couldn't shake his feelings of gloom. He told himself that he was being paranoid when he thought that Bailey Reynolds was spying on him. When Bailey invited him to lunch, Humphrey kept dropping his napkin on the floor and spilling food, even though they had a perfectly pleasant meal and didn't even discuss business. He saw a sinister gleam in Bailey's eyes, a menacing purpose in the folds of his cherubic smile, in the curve of his sharp fingers. 'You're not married, are you, Humphrey?' the white man asked him, as they were sipping coffee. His voice was smooth and congenial.

'No.'

'Haven't met the right woman?'

'I guess not.'

Bailey chuckled. 'Well, in this city there are a lot of them to meet. A man could go nuts.'

Humphrey laughed too. 'Isn't that the truth.'

Later, when Bailey sat in Preston's office, he managed to convey his own general sense of uneasiness about Humphrey Boone. 'He's not delivering, Preston,' he said. 'He's been here for months, and he hasn't landed one private placement deal. Nothing is even in the works.' His voice was well modulated. He wanted to sound indifferent, like an observer who has no stake in the game.

'A few months isn't a lot of time, Bailey,' Preston said evenly. 'Sometimes these things take much longer. I think he's doing quite well. His management skills are good and improving every day. He makes smart decisions. He's implemented a good strong minority loan program that's garnered us some good press, not to mention nearly a hundred thousand dollars in profits to date. I'm quite pleased with him. If he's taking his time on the deals, that's not a problem.'

'But isn't that why we hired him?' The smile on Bailey's face couldn't have been removed with dynamite, but beneath his informal veneer, a bit of hostility seeped out.

'No,' Preston said, responding not to the smile but to the challenge. 'We hired him because I wanted to hire him.'

The watery hazel eyes met the sharp black ones for a moment before the men turned away from each other. 'Well,' Bailey said, standing up, 'I'm sure everything will work out. Was there anything else, Preston?'

There was something else, something Preston wanted to say but didn't, because the sentiments behind the words were too personal for the office. He shook his head, and Bailey left, but after he was gone, Preston's feelings, unbusinesslike as they were, reverberated in his head: I like Humphrey.

The following weekend, Preston sat in the stands of the

tennis court of his country club and smiled as he watched Pres and Humphrey slam balls back and forth. His son was missing most of the balls. His serve was awkward, his backhand was nonexistent, and he had a pronounced limp that became even more obvious when he attempted to run. Preston was aware of his son's impediments, but he felt encouraged. Pres had gained weight, and his color was healthy. The physical therapist was so pleased with his progress that he'd dismissed him and assigned home exercises, playing tennis among them, which Pres did diligently. In a few weeks he would return to school. He was no longer the silent, morose presence he had been right after he was released from the hospital. These days, he talked and laughed with his parents and seemed to seek out Preston. The new friendship that had blossomed between father and son had begun the night Humphrey came to dinner. Pres laughed that night for the first time since the accident, and although most of his conversation was with the black man, he also talked to his mother and father. The next evening, when Preston was working in his study, he sensed a presence, and when he looked up, his son was standing at the door, watching him. The older man hesitated, then turned off his computer. 'Come in, please,' he said. Pres didn't stay long and didn't say much, but he returned the next evening and every night after that, until their evening visit had become a ritual.

The first conversation they ever had was about Humphrey. 'He's a cool guy,' Pres said. 'Are you two friends?'

'Well, he works for me.'

'Oh.'

Preston looked at his son. 'Why do you ask?'

'I like him. He said he played tennis.'

Now, as Preston watched his son's excited face, he was pleased that he had invited Humphrey. Standing in the sun, Preston felt a surge of energy as he thought of the telephone call he'd received from Dan Wilkerson, the RNC representative, only the day before. 'The committee is still anxious to meet with you,' he said. As Preston listened, he was surprised to feel himself getting excited, almost energized. He was invigorated after he hung up the phone. In the weeks since his son's accident and convalescence, he'd abandoned thoughts of a political future for himself. He focused on the newfound closeness he'd found with his family. He and Claire spoke of an early retirement. They wanted to travel together. But talking with Dan stirred up old passions. Pres was better. Claire was calm again and had even started back at the hospital. Or was it the art gallery? She wouldn't hold him to promises he'd made while he was under severe stress. After all, he was still fairly young, at least for a politician. He was younger than the new mayor of Los Angeles and the billionaire from Texas who had sought the presidency. And he'd already done the groundwork. With all the media coverage he'd received, he had a name, a good reputation. White people respected him, and the Minority Loan Program had earned him goodwill in the black community. And with Humphrey as his handpicked successor, he'd win even more support there. He felt the old yearnings to achieve, excel, climb the mountain, or at least that's how he interpreted the strange restlessness he felt.

After the game, the three men had lunch on the patio. They talked about tennis and other sports, and Preston and Humphrey even discussed a little bank business. Humphrey's eyes shifted when Preston brought up the private placement deals. Preston couldn't help but mull over Bailey Reynolds's words. In all honesty, he had expected that Humphrey would close at least one deal by now. He couldn't deny his disappointment. He was, after all, a businessman. The smooth, profitable running of Angel City was his main concern. Before he left the bank, he wanted to make sure that it was in good hands. If Humphrey wasn't capable of filling the bill . . . Well, he wouldn't be hasty. There was a lot to consider. Preston looked at Humphrey, who was just then demonstrating a swing for Pres. He smiled as he heard the black man and his son chatting amiably. Humphrey would deliver, Preston told himself. He had faith in him. He would give him time.

Humphrey slammed down his telephone right in the middle of Chontelle's third and loudest 'motherfucker,' which she screamed into his ear with all the vitriol she could muster. He could just see his sister, all three hundred pounds of her, quivering with rage and indignation because he refused to give her another cent of his money to waste on a lawyer for her son.

His head was pounding, and his thoughts came in bitter waves. He began muttering to himself. All they ever did was hold him back. Why couldn't they do what he'd done? If it weren't for his constantly trying to put out their fires, he could do more for himself. He could probably have a business of his own by now. Be as successful as any white man. They were eating him up alive.

An image of Hayden Lear slipped into his mind. He frowned. That white man was rich. Probably owned some company somewhere. Humphrey recalled the diamonds dangling from his wife's neck, her ears, her fingers and wrists. He was probably a millionaire who could snap his fingers and deals would get done. Done! Every door in America opened for a rich white man. Nobody told him no. He banged his paperweight against his desk. Shit! Hayden Lear didn't have a sister on welfare or a brother on drugs, a mother who was totally dependent on him. All he had was a silver spoon stuck up his ass. Hayden Lear could make those fast, slick deals, because he could move. There were no encumbrances tangling up his life. And the universe always told him yes.

Humphrey sat in his chair and was overcome by the intensity of his hatred and rage. He couldn't separate the pieces of his anger into specific categories. Suddenly he began laughing as he remembered Hayden's face when he saw him with Mallory. Standing next to Mallory, with Hayden's eyes on him, he felt powerful in a way he hadn't felt in months. Yeah, white boy, he should have said, she's with me. Me! He stood up and stretched, then flexed his muscles. He laughed.

Yeah, white boy. Your woman is with me.

'I deliberately stayed away for a while, to give you time to sort things out,' Humphrey said to Mallory the next day when they met in the hallway. 'I really would like to go out with you again.'

Looking into the black man's eyes, she spoke very carefully, succinctly. 'Humphrey, as I told you, I don't think that's a good idea.' She turned, and gave him a quick smile, a cordial, professional smile. She searched for something to say that wouldn't crush his ego. Men were all ego. 'You're a great-looking guy and I really enjoyed being with you. If the circumstances were different . . .' She smiled again.

He stood in the hall, reviewing her words, after she left. She said he was great-looking. That she enjoyed being with him. If the circumstances were different . . . There wasn't a no in anything she said. Not really. She was still playing her hard-to-get game.

Yeah, white boy. Your woman is with me.

He saw her again a few days later, standing at the water cooler, filling her glass. No one was around. He stood right behind her. When she turned, she almost bumped into his chest.

'Oh, excuse me,' Mallory said, moving away.

'You know, we could be having a great time together. I know a wonderful restaurant right on the beach in Malibu. Why don't you let me take you there this Saturday?'

Mallory groped for words, the firm, professional words that meant no but didn't offend. She thought he understood that everything was back to normal. Why was he still asking her out? 'I'm sorry. I just can't,' she said. She smiled quickly and then walked away.

Several nights later, he was leaving the building and saw her on her way to the parking lot. He caught up with her. 'Wouldn't you like to spend the weekend in Santa Barbara with me sometime? I've got a friend with a gorgeous time-share there. Ocean view. Me and you.' He laughed a little.

Jesus. She laughed nervously, kept laughing the entire time he repeated his request in his soft, persistent voice. 'I've got to go,' she said, when she reached the parking lot. She hurried to her car.

He's going to stop, Mallory told herself.

But a few days later, as she was leaving a loan department meeting, Humphrey asked her to stay. When everyone else had left the room, he said, 'I just wanted to tell you that you have the most beautiful legs I've ever seen.'

He watched her face closely to see the effect of his compliment. Did she like it? He couldn't tell. She turned away so quickly.

Maybe she was shy.

At home that night, Mallory sat on the edge of her bed. She had poured herself a glass of wine and was sipping it. The phone was on the bed in front of her. What she wanted to do was talk everything over with Esther. But the black woman might ask her questions she didn't want to answer.

She picked up the telephone and began dialing. Her friend Sue answered after the third ring. Mallory could hear the children in the background, a kind of low-level hum, a mixture of whining, laughing, and whimpering. 'Hi, Sue. It's Mallory.'

'Oh, Mal.' She was tired; Mallory could hear it in her coice. 'Hold on for a second.' She heard a deeper voice in the background – the jerk was home – and then Sue, pleading a little. A few seconds later, her friend was back on the line. 'Hi, Mal.' She sounded cheerful. 'How are you?'

They chatted for a few minutes, mostly about Susan's new son. Her friend had acquired a repertoire of anecdotes that illustrated every endearing quality the baby possessed. Finally there was a lull in the conversation and Mallory said, 'I need some advice, Sue.'

'What's wrong?'

Mallory hesitated. How could Sue possibly understand? But she had to tell someone. 'There's this guy at work who's coming on to me. We went out one time and then I told him I wasn't interested and now I can't get him to back off.'

'What do you mean, back off? What's he doing to you?'

'He keeps asking me out when I've told him I'm not interested. And today he told me I have beautiful legs. It's not what he says so much as the intensity. And the fact that we work together. I mean, I never should have gone out with him in the first place.'

There was silence for a moment. 'Did you sleep with him, Mal?'

'No. The one time we went out, I let him kiss me a couple of times.' Mallory thought back to when she and Sue were teenagers, how much time they spent talking on the phone about boys. They used to giggle about the way they kissed. But this was different. 'He's black, Sue.' As soon as Mallory said the words, she wished she hadn't.

She could hear Sue breathing on the phone. 'Black? You went out with a black guy, Mal?' She was whispering. There was both horror and fascination in her voice.

'It's a long story, Sue.'

'I can't believe you went out with a black guy. Why would you do that? Did you like him?'

She was silent for a moment. I went out with a black man to make my married boyfriend crazy. Could she tell that to Sue? To anyone? 'Yeah. I mean, he's okay.'

'I think you should call the police, Mal.'

'The police? Sue, it's not that ser— '

'No. You don't know them.'

'Sue, for God's sake— '

'Hold on for a minute.' Sue's baby was screaming close by the telephone.

When Sue came back to the phone, Mallory said, 'Look, I hear the baby. I'll let you go.'

'Okay, but Mal, you do what I told you. You hear?'

Mallory sat on the bed, holding the telephone in her lap. She thought about Hayden. She'd seen him only once since he sent her the flowers. He'd come that next night and made love to her, whispering, 'Who do you belong to?' the entire time he was inside her. If she told him . . . She couldn't tell him. She lifted up the telephone receiver and slammed it down into the phone. He'll stop, she said to herself. He'll stop.

At work the next day, when Humphrey passed her in the hall he stared at her with an intensity that made her avert her eyes. He thought she looked beautiful. On an impulse, he licked his tongue around his lips very slowly. Maybe he could turn her on.

Mallory stared at his mouth without moving. She was frozen. You don't know them, Sue had said. Them. She wanted to say something in a firm voice, to be in control, but she stood in front of Humphrey sputtering like a child, her eyes round and filled with disbelief.

Did she like that? Humphrey wondered as he sat in his office with the door closed, staring at the list of people who'd called while he was out. None of the names had to do with the private placement loan. He had hoped that she would laugh, or lick her lips back at him. He saw his sister's name on the list, as well as Reverend Rice's. Thinking of the minister made him feel guilty. Humphrey had canceled two manhood training workshops in the last three weeks. And he really should call Chontelle. She was staying with his mother. Something might have happened. About to reach for the phone, he heard his sister's voice in his head, the soft, slurry way she would complain and beg and complain and beg. 'You got it' – that's what she always said. He didn't have it; that was the trouble. His mother's nursing care was costing him nearly a thousand dollars a month, in addition to the fifteen hundred he paid for her bills. He didn't want to think of the needy black women in his life. He put his head down on the desk and tried to clear his thoughts, but his worries nagged him. If the deal didn't come through, what would he do? Jesus! He closed his eyes and saw Mallory, her blond hair as pale as any Brady Bunch girl's, her long, slim legs crossed neatly at her ankles. For just a moment, he felt a reassuring surge of power as he recalled Hayden's shocked face.

Yeah, white boy. Your woman is with me.

34

Esther tried not to look annoyed when her assistant operations manager ushered in a middle-aged black man and disappeared after whispering, 'Maybe you can help him.'

She smiled pleasantly and said, 'What can I do for you, Mr . . .'

'Warren. You see, Ms. Jackson, my father, Ronald Warren, and my mother were separated, and he moved out of state. We didn't hear from him in nearly five years, and during that time he developed Alzheimer's disease. To make a long story short, my sisters and I just recently found his bankbooks after we were reunited with my father.'

'Is your father still living, Mr. Warren?'

'Yes, ma'am.'

'You see, we can't release the money unless— '

'I have the power of attorney, Ms. Jackson, and in addition, each account has the name of one of the children on it. That's what I was trying to explain to your operations manager.'

'You have the passbooks with you, Mr. Warren?' He nodded and handed them to her. Esther punched in the first account number. *Ronald Warren Sr. or Ronald Warren Jr.* appeared on the screen. Next to the names was the account number and the figure $17,549.68. 'Are you Ronald Warren junior?'

'Yes, ma'am.' He handed her a driver's license and a birth certificate.

Esther looked at the total in the passbook. It was $17,748.48. She did some quick figuring, and even accounting for monthly bank fees, almost two hundred dollars was missing. She frowned. 'Let me see the other two passbooks,' she said. The man handed them to her. When she punched the numbers into the computer, the accounts came up immediately, but again there was a discrepancy. In each case, the sum in the computer was some two hundred dollars less than the passbook showed. 'Have you or your sisters come in recently and made withdrawals on these accounts?'

Mr. Warren looked astonished. 'No, ma'am. We just got the books two days ago. Is there something wrong?'

'There seems to be a difference between the amount recorded in your book and what the computer says you have. It's going to take a bit of time to straighten this out. Did you want to withdraw all the money today?'

'Oh, no. I just want to take out a thousand dollars.'

Esther nodded and passed him a withdrawal slip. 'Fill this out, please.' When he had, she initialed it. 'Take this back to the assistant operations manager. She'll help you.'

After Mr. Warren left, Esther took out a three-month-old printout of the tallies of dormant accounts, then punched in the relevant codes. She sat behind her desk, examining the numbers on the screen and then carefully matching them to the numbers on her printout. She looked back and forth from the page to the screen several times, and her frown deepened. Punching in additional codes, she stared at the totals on the computer screen and then checked the sum on her page. 'Damn.' She'd done a tally on the dormant accounts a little over three months ago, and all her totals had matched. Now, as she compared the figures on the screen with the ones she'd recorded, the sum in the actual accounts was two thousand dollars less than the total she'd recorded. She glanced at the numbers again. Most of the accounts were intact, but there seemed to be anywhere from fifty to two hundred dollars missing from nearly twenty accounts. There was probably a math mistake somewhere in her figures, she thought. No use worrying about it now. She'd go over it sometime during the week and track down the error. There was no time to investigate further. She had a meeting scheduled during lunch.

Humphrey saw Esther as soon as she walked into the restaurant. He rose from his chair and waved, then watched as she walked toward him with long, purposeful strides. After the hectic pace of the office, the black woman's rhythmic steps relaxed him. She looked strong and powerful, as if she owned the world, yet there was something about her that was as down home as his grandmother's rocking chair.

'I thought we should talk,' he said, after they ordered. 'There may be an opening in the loan department in a month or so, or rather, I may be able to make one. Are you still interested?'

'Absolutely.'

'I want you to redo your résumé and punch up anything that might build your credibility as a person with innate lending experience. You get my drift?'

She nodded.

They talked about the job possibility until their food came, and then they chatted as easily as old friends. After the restraints of the office, it felt good to both of them to be able to relax. She's fine, he thought to himself.

He grinned, and Esther was startled by how boyish he looked. He's so intelligent, she thought. She told him about the problem with the dormant accounts, and he suggested several ways that she could track the error. He can help me; he knows what I'm going through, she thought. Tyrone wouldn't have a clue.

'Listen, thanks for following up on the lender position. It feels good to know that someone is in charge who thinks I'm capable of doing the job.'

'A little cronyism never hurts,' Humphrey said with a

bitter laugh. 'God knows white folks have been playing that game for years.'

They looked at each other and began laughing. When their palms grazed, it was the high five of solidarity and understanding.

In the following week Esther and Humphrey went to lunch several times. They began calling each other, to pose a question or offer a solution, to talk. When they happened upon each other in the hallway, Esther would whisper, 'What's happening, brother?' And Humphrey would reply, 'You got it, sis.' Or they'd just smile like old friends. The more she talked with Humphrey, the more Esther began to believe that they were destined to have a relationship. He's just slow, she thought, when he failed to ask her out. 'Do you think he has a thing about not getting involved with women at work?' she asked Mallory, who said nothing. But she was sure that eventually they'd get together. Meanwhile, she was enjoying Tyrone.

But as comfortable as Humphrey felt with Esther, as much as her smile and her hips enticed him, he was also repelled. As easily as they laughed together, when he looked at her he saw the girls from the schoolyard and the high school dances who rejected him. He saw his mother's face twisted with anger, his sister with her hand held out. Esther smelled of sweet perfume, but he breathed in the scent of stale grease and beans when he was around her. When they walked down the street together, or he sat with her at lunch, people gave them admiring glances sometimes, but never envious ones. Having Esther didn't make up for his failures. Together they were just two black people, and there was no status in that. A sister was just a sister, too devalued on the common market to really matter.

He couldn't get Mallory out of his mind. But the more he gave her the eye and winked and licked, the more Mallory

492

rushed by him without speaking. Sometimes he thought she was about to say something, but then she'd pull back. He didn't know what was stopping her. Sure, she used him to make Hayden jealous, but he knew that she liked being with him, knew she enjoyed kissing him. If he had pressed her that night, she would have made love with him. Mallory wanted him; she was just playing hard to get. He was sure of that. So sure that one evening, when they were both leaving the office at the same time, he whispered, 'I know I can satisfy you.'

She stared at him; no words would come. If she'd had her wits about her, she would have tried to make her eyes hard and narrow, to push out her lips and put her hands on her hips, but she wasn't thinking, at least not clearly. 'I forgot something,' she mumbled, and went back inside the bank.

Humphrey turned to watch her walk away. He was smiling to himself. She was weakening; he could tell.

Mallory didn't pause or think; she ran right to Esther's office, so frantic that Esther was immediately alarmed. 'What happened? What's the matter?'

'Tell me what to do. Humphrey keeps bothering me.' She blurted out the words. For a moment, the room was quiet, and in that time she saw the way Esther's jaw tightened, how her eyes narrowed.

'What? What?' Esther clenched the pencil she was holding.

Mallory's eyes met Esther's; her face was full of apologies. 'He's been coming on to me, Esther.'

Each word hit the black woman like a slow-falling rock. 'What do you mean?'

'He's been inviting me out. I keep telling him no, and he keeps asking. He's always giving me compliments. And last week he . . . he . . .'

'What?' Esther could feel a hard coldness filling her chest.

'He was staring at me and licking his lips in a very suggestive way. And I just saw him a few minutes ago and he said, "I know I can satisfy you." I don't know what to do.'

Mallory's screechy wail reverberated in Esther's ears. 'What do you want me to say, Mallory?' she said coldly. 'Just tell him you're not interested.'

'I have told him that, but it doesn't stop him.'

'Well, you can't be mealy-mouthed about it. I mean, if you're telling him the same way you break up with Hayden, no wonder it doesn't stop him. Cuss him out. That is, unless you like it.' Esther felt as though she wanted to bite into each word she spoke.

'What do you mean? I told you I want him to stop.'

'Really.'

'What are you talking about?'

'Look, I've got to go home.' The black woman stood up and put on her jacket.

In the parking lot, Esther slammed her car door so forcefully that she could feel the automobile vibrate. As she sped down the freeway toward her home, her thoughts seemed like a hard ball, bouncing between the perfidy of friends and that of brothers, back and forth, until she was almost dizzy with pain and rage. Mallory knew she liked Humphrey! Just thinking the name brought his face to her mind.

Wasn't a black woman good enough for him?

Esther was still brooding by the time she reached Cranston. She had a taste for something sweet. She wanted to stuff herself full of gooey things. She turned into the strip mall parking lot in front of Diamond Donuts. Esther sensed that something wasn't right as soon as she walked inside. The air was unsettled. People were not in their regular places. There was coffee on the floor, dripping down the front of the display case from an overturned cup that lay on the counter. The back table was empty, and the old men stood together in a clump on one side of the store, their faces filled with alarm. Next to them was a black woman; her mouth was a tunnel of rage. Hyun stood across the counter, and her eyes were wide with trepidation.

'Bitch,' the woman yelled at Hyun. 'You don't come over here to my country, in my damn neighborhood, slamming my change down on the counter. You put my damn change in my hand, or you can take your ass on back to Korea.'

The old men could barely look at one another. They didn't want to see the shame in each other's eyes. 'She ain't do that on purpose,' one of them mumbled.

'I sorry. Money fall,' Hyun said. Her face was mournful and full of fear.

'You lying. That money ain't fall. If I turn around, you gone shoot me in the head? You gone kill me too?'

'I no kill,' Hyun said softly. She looked at the men, her cardplaying buddies, and there was pleading in her eyes.

But the men didn't return her glance. They stared at their shoes, at the coffee stain spreading across the shiny linoleum floor. 'You ain't right,' one of the men muttered in the dark woman's direction, but not very loudly. He looked at the woman quickly and saw the vehemence there in eyes that resembled his. He turned away.

Esther wanted to say, 'C'mon, sister, they're just trying to make a living. They're good people.' She could taste those words in her throat as she swallowed them.

'I ain't right?' the woman repeated, turning to face the old men. 'Brother, whose side you on? They ain't been in this country but three minutes and they qualify for being a minority, getting a minority loan to open up this business. Where's *your* damn bakery?' She glared at each one of the men. 'You go to the bank and try to get you a loan. I didn't see no Koreans taking part in no sit-ins, marching on no Washington. If it wasn't for us, we'd all be sitting on the back of the bus. But now here they come, gone get all the goodies. *I* ain't right? Next time this city burns, you just take your black ass over to Koreatown and see if they take you in. They ain't after nothing but the money, you hear me. At least the Jews hired us. They don't care about you. I hope you know they think you a nigger too.' She put her hand to her throat, and when she spoke again, her voice sounded tired. She whispered, pointing at Hyun. 'Y'all killed that girl. Shot her right in the back of the head. And ain't nobody spent not a day in jail.' She turned to the men. 'You want to know why? Because in this country, everybody is better than a nigger. They ain't been here but five minutes, and they know that already. And you gone take up for them?'

No one spoke. The question hung in the sweet air, mixed with the smell of coffee and doughnuts; Esther felt it in her bones. She stayed on her side of the floor. Looking out the plate-glass window, she could see the red glow of the sky. From where she was standing, it was hard to tell if the sun was setting or if there were fires in the distance.

Esther thought about the woman in the doughnut shop later that evening as she sat by her open breakfast room windows. She could hear her neighbors laughing and Bessie Smith singing in the background. She heard Carol's twangy West Virginia drawl. Bessie Smith was wailing the kind of gutbucket blues that Esther's grandmother used to play when she was a little girl. When she looked outside, she could see Harold and Carol playing Scrabble on their patio. Their little girl, her wild Bride of Frankenstein hair spiraling upward, sat between them, silently arranging the letters that her parents weren't using. As Esther watched their hands move across the board, back and forth, black and white, she could still hear the words the woman spoke in the doughnut shop: *And you gone take up for them?*

Turning into her parking space the next morning, Mallory slowed down when she saw Esther walking across the lot toward the bank. Later that day, the two women passed each other in the hall, and Esther's hello was a guarded warning, an amber light on the verge of red. Hearing it, Mallory mumbled her own greeting and walked away, swallowing the lonely feeling inside her. She didn't look back, so she didn't see Esther staring at her with that same hurt filling her eyes.

Esther worked through lunch that day, and the following afternoon she went to Patti's alone. She was surprised at how tasteless her sandwich was. She finished eating in five minutes, and it seemed to take forever for the waitress to bring her the check. As she walked back to the bank, she couldn't help but notice that the street was full of litter. L.A. used to be so clean, she thought. Now it was getting as dirty as the East Coast.

After four days of eating by herself, Mallory lifted the telephone to call Esther. Not speaking, or barely speaking – whatever they were doing – was ridiculous. We're behaving like children, she thought. She gripped the receiver. If she and Esther went to lunch, they'd have to talk, really talk. About Humphrey. About her. She hung up the phone softly.

'Are you going to lunch?' Mallory turned around. She hadn't realized that Kirk was walking behind her in the hall.

He gave Mallory a tentative smile. The papers he was holding fell from his hands. When he bent down to pick them up, he was conscious of how close his mouth was to Mallory's slim, pale legs.

'Yes.'

'Want some company?'

Eating with Esther had become such a comfortable habit that she'd never even considered filling the void with someone else. But as she nodded at Kirk, she felt relieved. She hated eating alone.

'I know a place you might like,' he said.

The restaurant, Julia's, was new, and Mallory had never

eaten there before. The decor was chic, the waiters were fawning; as Mallory scanned the prices in the menu posted inside the door, she saw that they were reflective of both. She was about to suggest that they go down the street to Patti's, when she felt Kirk's hand under her elbow, steering her toward a table in the back.

While she studied the menu, Kirk ordered two glasses of wine. 'Might as well celebrate. It's almost Friday,' he said with a grin.

She started to protest, but then she thought: What the hell.

They laughed throughout lunch. Kirk regaled her with funny stories. When she was able to catch her breath, she said, 'You remind me of my brother.'

'Really. I look like him?'

'Yes, and you act like him. He's a crack-up too.' She smiled, happy to feel so loose and relaxed.

'Another great guy,' Kirk said. He raised his glass.

'Absolutely.' She clicked her glass against Kirk's.

Lunch lasted nearly two hours, and when the check came – nearly sixty dollars without the tip – Kirk paid. 'Kirk,' Mallory said, about to protest.

He waved his hand. 'You get the next one.'

But the following week, when they went to lunch again, Kirk insisted on paying. 'You'll get your turn,' he said. When they stepped outside, he said jovially, 'And how is Esther of the dark thin skin?'

Mallory giggled.

'I couldn't believe she got so upset that time I called Humphrey homeboy.'

'Esther's a little sensitive,' Mallory said. She started laughing again, so hard that she had to grab Kirk's arm when she lost her balance.

'If you ask me,' Kirk said, lowering his voice, 'they're all a little sensitive these days. You're not allowed to joke anymore because it might be offensive to them.'

'We're supposed to be politically correct,' Mallory heard herself say. She was surprised at the intensity in her voice.

'If cops beat some drunk black guy breaking the law, it's racism. But let one of them decide to bash a white guy in the head with a brick, then somehow it's the white guy's fault and the black guys wind up being political prisoners, for chrissake. They always get to be the victim, not to mention have all the jobs set aside for them. And I'll tell you another thing: If they would get off their cans and work and stop expecting everything to be handed to them on a silver platter, they'd be a lot better off.'

'And stop being so angry about everything. I mean, other people have had it rough too. Nobody ever gave me anything.'

'Why don't they get off welfare? Why don't they stop killing each other and taking drugs? And having babies when they're twelve years old. You never hear that big shot reverend talking about that. No, he's off blaming white people for everything.'

Kirk and Mallory looked at each other and shook their heads in unison, one long coordinated motion. She glanced at Kirk again and smiled. 'You really do remind me of my brother,' she said.

35

Esther scanned the figures one last time, checking the numbers on the computer screen against those in the dormant account log. No matter how many times she compared the two, the results were the same: two thousand dollars was missing.

Someone was stealing money from the dormant accounts.

It has to be one of the tellers, Esther thought to herself. Who else would steal such a small amount? They had access. She put a legal tablet in front of her and wrote the names of the six tellers at the downtown branch. Underneath the names, she wrote the dates on which the withdrawals had occurred. Only three days were involved. She keyed a different code into the computer, and in a few minutes she pulled up the file for tellers' attendance. Only two people had been present on all of the three days: Hector and LaKeesha.

She thought of the quiet brown man. Hector had been working at the bank for nearly two years. He came early, stayed late, and did his work efficiently. He was so shy, he'd only recently begun to make eye contact with customers. He didn't seem like a thief, but maybe there'd been some family emergency. She tried to picture Hector going into the computer, punching in the numbers, putting the cash in his pocket, but the image just wouldn't come into focus. He wouldn't risk it, she thought. He'd be too afraid he'd get caught and never become an American citizen.

But LaKeesha didn't have such concerns. Esther remembered how strangely she had acted a few weeks earlier, the way she literally ran out of Esther's house during the baby shower and then barely spoke to her for weeks afterward. The assistant operations manager had reported her as being rude to customers. Maybe guilt made her act that way.

No, she wouldn't do that, Esther told herself. She knew she was in line for a promotion. Everything was going her way. She remembered LaKeesha's impassioned pleas for a job, for a new way of life. Why would she throw it away for two thousand dollars?

She hated the thoughts that filled her mind, but they came anyway. Two thousand dollars was a lot of money for a girl who'd just gotten off welfare. And maybe that was just the beginning. Maybe she planned to steal more. Face it, she told herself, the girl is from South-Central. Who knows what she grew up seeing. Besides, no thief ever thinks about getting caught.

She scanned the list of tellers again and came up with the same conclusion. Only LaKeesha and Hector were at the bank on all the days. And LaKeesha had less to lose.

She felt like crying. All the hours she'd spent with the girl, helping her with grammar, teaching her how to dress, giving her a picture of her future, a better future – and this was the result. Maybe she just ran out of faith in herself, Esther thought. Maybe she got tired of the struggle. She could understand that, but damn, why did she have to rip off the bank? She was jeopardizing both their careers. Now that Esther no longer disputed the figures and the dates that the computer revealed, the full implications of the girl's crime began to sink in with perfect clarity: If LaKeesha was a thief, Esther would look bad for hiring her. For one brief moment, she considered covering up the theft. Maybe she could change some numbers. Jesus. What was she thinking about? There was nothing she could do without becoming an accomplice to a federal crime. Besides, even if she could

501

hide the theft, someone else might still discover it. For all she knew, someone already had. The first thing anyone would ask her was why she'd ever hired LaKeesha. Her records would show that she'd passed over more qualified people.

Lawdhamercy.

The bank might bring charges against LaKeesha, and then the police would have to be brought in. Maybe she'd go to jail. She had a child. She was the only one in the family with a job. Just because the girl made one mistake, there was no reason why her entire life should go down the toilet.

White people recovered from mistakes all the time. Hadn't she seen them sweep their little indiscretions right under the rug? They scratched each other's backs. They circled up the wagons, that's what they did. Well, she could do that too, but not alone. She needed help.

The stately Eleanor gave Esther a smooth, professional smile. 'Is he expecting you?'

'No, he isn't.'

'Let me see if he's busy.'

Her stomach tightened as she waited in the reception area. She felt as though she were waiting to meet with a declared enemy. She'd been deliberately avoiding Humphrey ever since her talk with Mallory, and she didn't look forward to seeing him, but the dilemma she was facing gave her no choice. She needed greater wisdom than she possessed.

'What's going on? I haven't seen you in a while.' Humphrey stood up and smiled at her as she came in.

'I have a problem, and I need your help,' Esther said.

He motioned for her to sit down. 'You look really stressed.'

She ignored both his comment and his look of concern. No need to get personal, to talk about how she was feeling. She'd come to discuss a business problem, that was all.

502

'Someone has been stealing money from the dormant accounts. Two thousand dollars is missing. I'm sure it's one of the tellers, and I think I know which one it is.'

Humphrey let out a long whistle. 'The old dormant account routine.' He chuckled. 'Are people still doing that? God, I remember at one bank where I was working, one of the tellers stole about fifteen thousand dollars and put the money in his savings account. That's how the theft was discovered. Just transferred the money to his own savings account. Have you ever heard of anything so dumb?'

'I think LaKeesha took the money.'

'LaKeesha?'

'Dark-skinned, short hair, muscular.'

'Oh, yes. Why do you think she did it?'

'Because it has to be one of the tellers, and I checked the dates that the withdrawals were made, and she's the only teller who was there on all the dates – well, except for Hector. But my gut tells me it's LaKeesha.'

'Have you spoken to her yet?'

Esther shook her head.

'What do you want to do?'

'Well, I hired her, Humphrey. And she wasn't the most qualified candidate.'

Humphrey shook his head. 'Trying to help the sister out?' Esther looked surprised. 'Oh, you're the type,' he said. 'You gotta watch that racial solidarity stuff, Esther. It'll kick you in the butt every time.' He chuckled again.

'I don't want this to blow up in my face. And I don't want her life ruined. She's got a kid. She's the only one in her family who's working.'

Humphrey nodded. He picked up the intercom and buzzed Eleanor.

When LaKeesha walked into the room, she could feel her eyes getting bigger. She'd always thought that Esther had a nice office, but Humphrey's took her breath away. Sometimes the things that black people had amazed her. Before she came to work at the bank, every black person she'd ever known was as poor as she was. Humphrey told her to sit down. When she looked up, Esther and Humphrey were staring at her. She could feel her hands becoming moist.

Humphrey rose, walked away from his desk, and stood right in front of her. 'I'm going to make this short, La-Keesha. Esther has discovered that there is some money missing from the dormant accounts. Nearly two thousand dollars. Do you know anything about it?'

The girl had been rubbing her palms together while he spoke, and when he stopped, the only sound in the room was the soft, wispy noise her hands made. 'No.' She tilted her head a little, so that she could see Esther's face.

Esther perceived just the beginning of a question in her eyes, the tip of fear's iceberg. She spoke gently. 'Out of all the tellers, only you and Hector were there each time money was taken.'

Now LaKeesha's eyes blinked rapidly from fright. 'Hector didn't take any money, Esther. You know he wouldn't steal anything.'

'Did you take it?' Humphrey asked.

Her entire body jerked. 'No-o-o.' She looked at Esther, who was staring at her. 'No,' she repeated.

Humphrey's voice was hard and forceful, like a hammer slamming against rock. 'Listen, LaKeesha. The bank is federally regulated. When anything illegal is suspected, the federal marshals are brought in. And they don't play games. They don't give up nothing but hard times and bubble gum, and they're usually out of bubble gum. Now, I'm going to ask you once again, the same thing they're going to want to know, only they will be nastier and a lot more thorough: Did you take the money?'

'No.' She looked at Esther now, a silent appeal, but the older woman showed no emotion.

'Like I said: the federal marshals don't play. They've got all your records. They've got your whole history on the computer.'

LaKeesha's hands gripped the sides of the chair. Humphrey saw alarm in the eyes he peered into. He said slowly, as though his voice were a weapon he was aiming, 'You've been arrested before, haven't you, LaKeesha?'

She began to cry.

Esther closed her eyes, lowered her head, and groaned.

'Why were you arrested?'

LaKeesha's crying got louder. 'I helped to rob a store. I wasn't but sixteen. All I did was carry the stuff. Just that one time. I didn't . . .'

'What do you think the federal marshals will say when they find out about that? Listen to me, LaKeesha,' Humphrey said. 'Stop crying.' She looked at him, her shoulders still quivering. He loosened his tie. 'Let me tell you something, girl: If you go down, we all go down. Esther looks bad for hiring someone with a record. I look like I'm not on top of my job. And then the next black person who walks through the door looking for a job is automatically suspect. Do you understand that we're all working for white folks, and they don't want us here in the first place? You following me? You get the point?'

She nodded.

'Here's what we're going to do: I'm going to make restitution for you.'

She stared at him blankly.

'I'm going to put the money you stole back into the proper accounts. There will be no way to tell it was ever missing. And you're going to pay me back, twenty-five dollars a week, until the debt is taken care of. You got that?'

She gazed straight ahead of her for a moment. A single tear trickled down her cheek. Then she nodded at Humphrey.

'Don't mention this to anyone. And LaKeesha, if this happens again, there will be no mercy. You'll go to jail. Now go on back to work.'

'Well,' Humphrey said after LaKeesha left.

'She has a record.' Esther shook her head in disbelief.

'A juvenile record. There was no way you could have known. Don't beat yourself up. It's all over.'

He reached out and put his hand on her shoulder. Esther could feel the warmth of his fingers. 'Thanks,' she said. He squeezed reassuringly. 'Listen, I'll give you the money.'

'I'll take half,' he said with a smile. 'And I get paid back first.' Esther laughed, then stood up. 'I see you have a lot of faith.' She patted his arm. Whatever Mallory told her didn't matter. White women had been thinking that black men were trying to come on to them ever since *Birth of a Nation*. As far as she was concerned, Humphrey was a good brother.

36

Tyrone made himself as comfortable as he could on the hard wooden chair in Cody's kitchen. Letting his friend trim his hair had become a Friday evening ritual. After that first time in the locker room, he began going to Cody's apartment, which wasn't far from the job. The place was small, with more CDs than furniture. Cody seemed to have every blues, rap, and reggae recording known to mankind, Tyrone thought. From where he sat in the kitchen, he could look into the combination living room-dining room and see the vast collection of recorded music displayed on shelves that ran from the floor to the ceiling. Cody passed him his second Budweiser while he took out his scissors and electric trimmers and draped Tyrone with an old blue sheet that had faded ice cream cones and birthday cakes printed on it.

Sometimes he felt a little disloyal for not going to his usual barbershop on Cranston. He missed the camaraderie of talking trash with a roomful of black men. But Cody charged only three bucks and did a good job, and sitting with him gave Tyrone a chance to think and sometimes get a second opinion. His new barber was a good listener, and every once in a while he said something that halfway made sense. 'I gotta look good. Taking my baby to a party tonight,' he said. He didn't mention how nervous he was at the thought of Esther meeting his friends. 'Just take a little off the top and the sides and cut it close in the back,' he told Cody. It was the same thing he told him every week.

'I hear you, bro,' Cody said.

Tyrone chuckled a little. Bro. He took a sip of beer. 'You

ever think of going back to school, man?' Tyrone asked. He'd been holding in the question all week long. Now that he'd asked it, he felt a bit of tension as he waited for Cody to answer him.

Cody whistled. 'You gonna go full time or part time?'

'I wasn't talking about me, exactly. I was just thinking.'

'You talking about a four-year college or some kind of trade school?'

'College.'

'Well, that's a long haul, especially if you're working,' he said.

Tyrone felt his spirits sink. Going back to school would take forever. It was easier not to think about college or his future. The clicking of the scissors and the whirring clippers relaxed Tyrone, and he dozed. While he slept, the clippers danced to a new tune. He woke up when his friend handed him a mirror. Tyrone stood with his back to the mirror on the kitchen wall and held up the smaller one in front of him. What he saw took his breath away: A double line zigzagged up to a sharp peak, then down, then up again. Then down. Then up. The back of his head was lightning bolts on parade.

'You like it?' Cody smiled with pride.

Tyrone heard the words 'crazy motherfucker,' but they were in his head. When he tried to open his mouth to speak, nothing came out. The only sounds he was capable of were guttural animal noises, a cross between King Kong and Lassie. In the absence of speech, he did the only thing he could think of: he reached out and grabbed Cody by his collar and pulled him toward him. 'I should kick your ass,' were the first words he managed to say.

'Whatsa matter with you, man?' Cody said, with considerable difficulty. He sounded like a frog belching. 'You don't like it?' His eyes were filled with amazement.

'What the hell did you do? I told you I wanted just a little

508

off the sides and the top. A fade, man, a damn fade. You got me looking like Homey the Clown.' He tightened his grip around Cody's throat.

'Wait a minute.' Cody gasped for breath, his words sounding incoherent. 'I was just trying to hook you up, man. All the brothers wear their hair like this.'

His tone was so sincere that Tyrone was momentarily silent. He released Cody. Then he said, 'Yeah? Well, how do all the white boys wear theirs? Do y'all have a style?'

Cody's face turned red. 'I'm not a boy. Why don't you quit calling me that,' he said quietly. 'That supposed to make up for slavery and segregation, you calling me boy?'

Now it was Tyrone's turn to look surprised.

'Look, I'm sorry about your hair,' Cody said. 'I just got carried away. I thought— '

'You thought, with your wannabe-black self, that all brothers are straight-up gangstas from the 'hood.'

Cody slammed the clippers down on the table. 'In the first place, I don't want to be black. I'm not looking for an identity, dammit. I already have one.'

'You try to dress black. You try to talk black. Every piece of music you got in this joint is by somebody black. And you're gonna say you're not a wannabe?'

Cody threw up both his hands. 'What the hell is dressing black? When you put on a suit and a tie, is that dressing white? Did it ever occur to you that maybe I just admire black people? Maybe I just fucking like you guys. And you're wrong about the music. I got all the Beatles, all the Stones, and everything Frank ever recorded. So give me a fuckin' break with your hypersensitive bullshit, Tyrone. When I said all the brothers, I didn't mean to offend you. Hell, I know the difference between a gangbanger and a workaholic nerd like you. Don't put labels on me just because I gave you a bad haircut.'

Nerd?

'If you'd just chill out, maybe I can fix it,' Cody said.

The two men stared at each other briefly. Tyrone shook his head as he walked over to the chair. 'Man, why you fuck up my hair?'

'I'm sorry. I got carried away.'

'I got your carried away,' Tyrone said as he sat down. 'I told you I was taking my lady out. Now look at me.'

'I told you I can fix it,' Cody said. He was quiet for a moment. 'Hey! You want me to put a Jheri curl on the top? I got a kit in the back.'

Tyrone raised his eyes heavenward and then slowly turned to give Cody a look of pure incredulity. 'Now, do you really think . . .'

'Awrightawrightawright.'

'What the hell are you doing with a Jheri curl kit anyway?'

'I was thinking about trying it out.'

Tyrone shook his head. 'Just give me a damn Kojak, man.'

When Tyrone showed up at Esther's door later that night, he had on a black X cap, pulled down low over his forehead. He kept it on when he sat down in the living room, until Esther began eyeing the cap so hard that he took it off with a flourish. 'I can explain about the hair,' he said tersely, but before he could begin, Esther started giggling. Every time she tried to stop, she couldn't. Finally, she gasped, 'Put the hat back on.'

They could hear the music and the loud raucous laughter as they approached his friend James's bungalow. Tyrone seemed to notice the house for the first time. It was small, and the neighborhood wasn't great. He stole a quick glance at Esther, trying to determine whether or not she was turned off, but she smiled at him pleasantly. 'Hey, now! Party over here!' she said lightly, and did a little dance step as they waited for someone to open the door. That's what he liked about Esther, he thought to himself: She was big time, but she knew how to be down. You could take the woman anywhere. He put his arm around her waist and gave her a little squeeze, just as the door opened wide.

'Yo, brother, what's happening?' James said when he answered the door.

'You got it,' Tyrone said. The two men shook hands quickly.

'And who do we have here?' he asked. He stared from Esther's breasts to her face and then back to her breasts.

Jerk, she said to herself.

'James, this is my friend Esther. Esther, this is James.'

She smiled politely and shook his hand. 'Well, I sure hope I get a chance to spin you around on the floor,' James said. 'Come on in, y'all.'

Esther's heart sank the moment they stepped inside. It was worse than she'd imagined: a tiny little shoe box of a house, crammed full of sweaty dancers. She thought fleetingly of the elegant catered affairs she used to attend with Mitchell Harris. They partied on yachts in the marina, in suites at the Bel Agua Hotel. That was the kind of social life she might have had with Humphrey. Straighten up, she admonished herself as she looked at Tyrone, who was watching her intently. She grinned at him. 'Where's the wine?' she asked brightly.

The refreshments were in the kitchen, and just getting in the door was an ordeal. With every step they took, Tyrone was greeting people and introducing her. Some of the women appeared to be very young, and their conversations were filled with the latest nailshops and hairdos. They hadn't been there half an hour, and Esther's mouth ached from smiling. They finally managed to cram their bodies inside the tiny space, which smelled of beer and hot dogs, only to be told that there was no more wine or soft drinks.

511

They had to wait for nearly twenty minutes, while the host made a run to the store. He returned with several bottles of lukewarm, no-name wine.

'That's okay,' Esther said as sweetly as she could when Tyrone offered her a glass. She also declined the wilted cold cuts that were thrown together on a paper plate. All pork, she was sure. Tyrone didn't eat any either. She felt a weak throbbing in her temples, the beginning of a headache.

'Let's go outside and dance,' Tyrone said. He took Esther's hand and led her into the living room. The music was loud and fast. They found a spot and began swaying to the beat. Watching Esther's body move, Tyrone began to relax. They could always have a good time when they were dancing together.

They stayed out on the floor for eight songs straight, and then Esther spied an empty seat on the sofa and made a dash toward it. To tell the truth, she just wasn't in the mood.

Esther was silent during the ride home. When they sat down on her sofa, Tyrone kept looking at her so intently that finally she said, 'What?' She wasn't able to keep the annoyance out of her voice.

'You didn't have fun at the party,' he said lightly. 'You didn't like my friends, did you?'

'Tyrone, I didn't really get a chance to talk to anybody. I mean, everybody there seemed cool.'

'But they're not your style, are they?' His eyes stayed on her face. Go ahead and say it, he thought.

'I said they were cool.' Her voice was constrained. Please, don't go there, she thought.

'But you wouldn't hang out with them?' Just say it. Say it!

She could almost feel his hands on her shoulders, pushing her. In her mind, she searched for elbow room. 'They're your friends, not mine. Listen, Tyrone, I'm tired.'

'They're not your type, are they?'

'No.' The word was so loud, it came with an echo. 'Are you satisfied now?'

'I'm not your type, am I?'

'Tyrone . . .'

'Am I?'

She didn't say anything.

'You educated supersisters with degrees are always bitching about brothers and white women, brothers and light women, but y'all don't think regular brothers are good enough for you. You want superbrothers with M.B.A.s and white collars. How the hell do you think I feel?'

'Tyrone, I like you. We have a good time together.'

'But you just passing through. I'm nobody you could be serious about.'

Esther sighed.

He looked at her. 'I am who I am. If you think you can do better, cool. Go for it. But you just remember this, Esther: It ain't every day you gone find somebody who likes your trippy, frustrated, scaredy-cat, jealous, petty, superdriven, can't-stop-to-smell-the-roses, stuck-up self the way I do. Instead of worrying about whether I'm speaking right, you need to be glad that I'm treating you right. I may not be "all that", but I understand you and I know how to make you happy. And I'm gone tell you something else: What you see ain't all you getting. I got dreams too, girl. And if you don't want to share them with me, I'll find somebody who does.'

All Esther could do was stare as she realized for the first time that the man who was just 'something to do' might have his own agenda.

It was after eight o'clock the following Monday evening when Tyrone pulled his car into the parking lot next to Solid Rock Baptist Church. He went inside a side entrance and knocked on the door in front of him. When no one answered, he hesitated, then turned the knob; the door opened. The reception area outside the pastor's office was empty, but he could smell food. 'Hello,' he called out.

'We're back here,' a woman's voice answered. 'Come on in.'

When Tyrone opened the door to Reverend Odell Rice's office, he saw the minister and his wife and son sitting on a sofa, fried chicken dinners on their laps. 'Oh, I'm sorry,' he said. 'I didn't know . . .'

Reverend Rice waved him into the room with a chicken leg. 'Come on in, Tyrone. We're just finishing up. You know my wife, Juanita, and our son, John Henry.'

'How's everybody? I'll just wait outside while you finish,' Tyrone said.

A few minutes later, Juanita and John Henry came out. 'You go on in now,' the minister's wife said.

Tyrone could still smell the food, even though no remnants of the meal remained to be seen. 'Well, Tyrone. Haven't seen you in a while,' Reverend Rice said. 'Sit down.'

The two men sat on the small sofa. Now that Tyrone was face-to-face with the minister, he was at a loss for words. 'You said I could come talk to you,' he said, finally.

'Well, what's on your mind?'

'School,' Tyrone blurted out.

'Well, what about it?'

'I was thinking about going back. To college, I mean. I don't know how to get started.'

'Are you having trouble filling out the applications?'

'I haven't gotten them yet.'

The minister eyed Tyrone curiously. 'Well, now, son, if you want to go to college, you have to apply. That's the first step.'

'I know. It's just that it's kinda . . .' Tyrone stared at the minister, his eyes filled with anxiety.

'Kind of scares you, doesn't it, son?' The minister's

usually booming voice was very soft, as though he were speaking to a small child.

Tyrone looked startled. He thought about bolting from his seat and running out the door. Instead, he slowly nodded his head.

'That's all right. Do you know what about it scares you? Tyrone, I'm scared of the water. I'm scared of flying airplanes. I'm scared of big dogs I don't know. I got a long list of fears. What is it about going back to school that scares you?'

'I don't know,' he said softly.

'Well, me, I'm scared of drowning, crashing, and getting bit. I guess I'm scared of dying. You think school might kill you?'

'No.' Tyrone chuckled.

'Maybe it might kill your pride.' The minister waited for a few seconds, until he saw Tyrone nodding in understanding and agreement. 'You're scared you're not going to do well. You're scared of failing.' He could hear the young man's heavy breathing. 'Is that right?'

'Yeah. I'm not all that smart, Reverend. I never did well in school.'

'Okay. Okay. What do you want to study?'

'Business.'

'All right. Now, Tyrone, the world is full of successful people who never did well in school. And just because you didn't get good grades in the past doesn't mean you can't do well now. I tell you what. Why don't you just take one class. Just one class. Don't do it for credit. Just audit it. Just sit in. Get the feel of it. See if you like it. If you feel like doing the work, do it. If you don't, don't. Only thing is, you need to enroll right away. Tomorrow. Don't put it off.'

'I can do that?'

'Damn straight. Son, this is America. You can do whatever the hell you want to do.'

He watched as Tyrone nodded to himself.

'The thing is, you have to do it. You can't think about doing it. You can't just dream about doing it. You have to do it.' He gave the younger man a smile. 'Don't forget the African Family Reunion is coming up in a couple of weeks. You'll get a notice. We want you to come sell your shirts. And, boy, I sure would like to see you sitting up in church some Sunday.'

Tyrone parked his Audi in Esther's driveway then sat there for a moment. He knew she was awake, even though it was after ten o'clock. She was probably sitting up in her bed going over some work for her job. Maybe he'd be interrupting her, he thought. Maybe if he rang her doorbell, she'd think that he was some kind of lovesick wimp. He should go.

He was about to start his car when the garage door opened and Esther walked toward him. 'Hi,' she said when he rolled down the window.

'Hi.' He felt awkward, as though he were a kid and someone was reading his diary in front of his classmates. 'I, uh . . .' he said.

'I'm sorry if I hurt your feelings,' Esther said quietly. 'I'd like for us to talk.' She reached inside the window and put her hand on Tyrone's shoulder. He could feel the warmth flowing from her fingers. 'I missed you,' she said.

37

Hector knew that what he was doing was wrong, but he told himself that America was the land of opportunity. It was the country of risktakers. Well, he was willing to take a risk. And so, at seven o'clock on a Thursday evening, when everyone in the operations department had left, Hector whispered in soft Spanish to the guard, who was his friend, and the man opened the front door. A small brown woman was waiting just outside. Hector put his fingers to his lips, and Idalia gave him a look of perfect understanding. They had done this before.

Theirs was not a courtship of kisses and sighs, particularly not on this Thursday evening. Idalia's waist-length hair swayed as she followed Hector behind the tellers' station. He could smell the rose-scented hair pomade that she always wore. Some nights when she was leaning against him and her silky hair fell into his mouth, he could taste El Salvador in each strand. But this was no time for memories. 'Do you remember what I taught you last week?' he whispered.

Idalia nodded.

'Show me what you do when a customer comes to you with a check from another state.'

'Show me what you do when a customer wants to make a withdrawal and doesn't have the full amount in his account.'

'Where do you send a customer if he tells you he wishes to open a savings account?'

The testing went on for twenty minutes, and when he was

finished, Hector was satisfied. Idalia was smart, too smart to be scrubbing the floors of the rich black ladies who lived in Park Crest. 'You must get a real job,' he told her. For the past three months, he'd been training her. She learned very quickly. When an opportunity came, she would be ready. And in America, there was always an opportunity. 'Okay, let's go home,' he said. But just as they were about to leave, he heard footsteps, coming from the loan department. 'Get down,' he whispered. Quickly, the small woman crouched below him, so that anyone looking toward them from outside the tellers' cage would see only Hector. Then Hector stooped down also, although he had a right to be there. Idalia gave him a puzzled look, but he put his finger to his lips.

He heard keys rattling in a door, and judging the distance from the sound, he knew that someone was entering one of the nearby offices. He knew who the person was and where he had gone. When he heard a door close, Hector slowly stood up and looked into his boss's office. Sitting behind the desk, staring at the computer screen, was Kirk Madison. Hector knew exactly what the white man was doing: He was stealing.

It wasn't the first time he'd seen Kirk in Esther's office, punching numbers into her computer. In the last few months, Hector had seen him there several times, always at night, when he thought he was alone. At first Hector couldn't figure out what he was doing. The loan officer and his boss worked in different departments; there was no reason for him to be in her office. Hector suspected that Kirk was spying on Esther. He had heard of such things happening in big American companies. The two certainly weren't friends. He'd seen them often enough as they passed each other in the hall. They barely spoke, and Esther almost seemed angry whenever she saw Kirk.

Hector watched Kirk for weeks, sneaking into Esther's

518

office, using her computer, and then passing her in the hall and saying nothing. He became curious. He didn't understand what was happening until LaKeesha spoke with him several weeks ago. That day his friend's eyes were wet, and the dream that was once there had been washed away. He looked at her, a question in his eyes, but she shook her head, wiped her eyes, and went back to work. Later, when they were in the employees' lounge, eating their lunch, she told him what had happened. Through tears, she told him how Esther and Humphrey had called her in and accused her of stealing two thousand dollars from the dormant accounts. 'I didn't take that money,' LaKeesha said vehemently.

'But if you didn't take it, why did you say you did?' Hector asked.

'I never said I took it. When Humphrey started talking about the federal marshals, I got scared. I was in the juvenile detention center when I was younger. For robbery. It just seemed better to go along with them. Look, they said it was either you or me. We were the only ones around every time the money was moved out of the accounts.' She gave him a tentative look.

'I didn't take any money,' Hector said softly.

'That's what I told them.' She began to cry again. Awkwardly, Hector patted LaKeesha's back. He told her not to cry, that someday Humphrey and Esther would know that she was innocent. They went back to work and didn't speak of the matter again. But Hector couldn't stop thinking about it, and his suspicions grew. One evening not long after LaKeesha's tearful confession, he waited until Kirk left Esther's office. Waited until the cleaning lady came. She was his mother's friend, and although he could tell that she considered his request strange, she allowed him to go through Esther's trash can. And right on top, he found the slips of papers filled with numbers. When he punched the numbers into the computer, each one of them was a dormant account.

Whenever he saw Kirk in Esther's office, he would check the accounts. And each time, they would show less money. He added up the losses one night, and he could not believe the number he saw on the piece of paper. Kirk was stealing thousands of dollars.

At first he was tempted to tell LaKeesha about Kirk, but the more Hector pondered the situation, the more he realized that he should keep the information to himself. It wasn't his fault that Esther and Humphrey thought La-Keesha was a thief. Why should he say anything? If Esther thought LaKeesha was a thief, she wouldn't promote her. If he was quiet, he might be the one to become operations assistant. He liked LaKeesha, but her misfortune had presented him with the kind of opportunity that America offered only once in a great while. The black girl would have other chances; after all, she was a citizen.

Now, as he crouched down next to Idalia behind the tellers' cage, he pondered again what he should do. As much as he tried to harden his heart, to seize the chance that had been presented to him, he didn't feel right about not telling what he knew. He had begun to avoid LaKeesha, because he could not look into her dark eyes. As he stole another look at Kirk, he thought of a new opportunity. He could go to the white man, tell him he knew he was a thief, and demand money for his silence. He could ask for five thousand dollars, perhaps even ten thousand. He stopped breathing for a moment at the thought of having so great a sum. With that much money, he could move his family to another apartment, maybe even make a down payment on a small house. Maybe he could get more than ten thousand dollars. Growing more and more excited, he let enormous figures dance around in his mind. He glanced at Idalia; her face was serene and composed. No. No. No. If he took money, he would be as much a thief as Kirk. If the white man was found out, they would both go to jail. He would never become a citizen and never marry Idalia. The thought of his citizenship, lost before he could even reap its sweet benefits, made him shudder. No, he couldn't take any money. He felt the warmth of Idalia's body next to his, and as she put her small hand on his, a new idea entered his mind. Perhaps if he told what he knew, he would be rewarded, if not with money then with a better job. After all, he would be saving the bank thousands of dollars. Maybe Kirk hadn't spent all the money yet. There was the chance that he'd return some of it and that the bank would be grateful. Yes, Hector thought to himself, that's the best way. And he could tell his friend what he knew. He couldn't stand to see the black girl's face when it was so miserable. He heard Esther's office door open and close and then Kirk's footsteps as he went back to his own office. Hector motioned for Idalia to get up, and they quietly left the bank.

He told LaKeesha the next morning, and when he saw the light coming back into her eyes, he was glad. His story was carefully woven to make her think that he'd only just discovered the theft. They went together to tell Esther.

'You saw what?' Esther asked Hector. He repeated his story in his same emotionless tone. Esther peered first at Hector, then at LaKeesha, whose eyes flickered with indignation. 'But you said you took the money.'

'No, Esther. I kept saying I didn't take it, but you all wouldn't believe me.' LaKeesha could feel the hardness creeping into her voice as she spoke. Now, as she faced her boss, she was feeling the rage she was too frightened to acknowledge when she was initially confronted.

Hector handed Esther the slips of paper that contained the account numbers that Kirk had copied. 'I found these in your trash can after he left,' Hector said. 'They are dormant account numbers; Kirk wrote them down.'

'How did you get into my office?' Esther asked, her voice rising sharply.

'I wasn't in your office. The cleaning lady is my mother's friend. When she came out with your basket, she let me look inside.'

Esther tried to react, but the truth was, she was speechless. Her mind jumped from one question to the next. Why would Kirk steal two thousand dollars? Why would Hector lie? She wasn't ready to commit herself to affirming Hector's claims until she'd done her own investigating. 'Look, I'm grateful that you came to me, both of you,' she said, 'but I'm going to have to let one or two other people know about this and conduct some sort of investigation.'

'Kirk has stolen much more than two thousand dollars, Esther,' Hector said quietly. He tried to keep the disappointment out of his voice, but it was hard. He'd expected talk of rewards, not doubt.

LaKeesha bit her lip and lowered her head. Here the woman had accused her of being a thief and then didn't even want to apologize when she found out she was wrong. She needed to get out of Esther's office before she said something she'd regret.

Esther saw LaKeesha's rigid jaw and trembling lip. When she touched the teller's shoulder, it was tight and unyielding. She took her hand away. 'LaKeesha, if I have accused you by mistake, I offer you an apology now. But this matter must be investigated thoroughly before you can be exonerated. That's the next step.'

Esther waited until seven o'clock that night, after she watched Kirk leave and was certain that she was the only one in the bank. Usually she felt perfectly safe at night, but the mood of the city had affected her. The start of the trial of the men accused of beating Reginald Denny was imminent, and once again the city slept with one eye open. King Clever's devotees screamed for guilty verdicts and hard time for the would-be assassins. From South-Central pulpits, black clergymen prayed for mercy and freedom for society's oppressed. On the evening news, the mother of one of the accused faced the cameras. Her boy was a good boy, she swore – a God-fearing boy. She invited Denny to come to her home in South-Central and taste her greens and corn bread.

Soul food wasn't on the minds of the governor or the new mayor or the black police chief. The shouts of 'No justice, no peace' were raised once again. There will be law, order on the streets of Los Angeles, the officials promised. The National Guard was poised and ready. What would be *their* rallying cry? Shoot to kill? Outside Esther's window, the gray city sky was the color of nightmares.

The bank was eerily quiet. As Esther punched in the computer codes for the dormant bank accounts, she realized she was breathing hard. When the file appeared, she accessed the histories of ten accounts, randomly chosen, for each of the years between 1989 and 1993, and printed the figures. Placing them in a neat row on her desk, she studied the numbers carefully. There was nothing out of order until 1993. Then the totals in most of the accounts began to drop; the changes occurred within the last five months. Esther went back to the computer and had it print out monthly reports on the status of the same accounts. She began to compile a ledger sheet of the monthly withdrawals in one account. When she added up the figures, nearly $1,700 was missing. Then she calculated missing money for three other accounts, and the total became $9,287. Working very slowly, Esther computed the lost money in every dormant account. By the time she had totaled the amount, it was nearly midnight. She gasped at what she saw on the screen: Nearly $200,000 had been embezzled.

Esther sat motionless for a moment, then she punched Kirk's name into the computer, and almost immediately the numbers for four accounts appeared on the screen. The first, his savings account, had a total of $12,346.28. There had been no new deposits within the last five months. The second was a savings account with his name and Kirk Madison, Jr. – his son, she supposed – and it contained $26,984.34. That's a lot of money for a kid, she thought. Sure enough, the account had been open only five months. She punched up the third account, also savings, with Kirk's name and Heather Madison. That account had been opened at the same time as his son's and contained $34,567.89. Finally, there was a checking account with Kirk's name on it; the balance was $11,678. Following a hunch, she pulled up a five-month history. Three checks were made out to United Airlines, for more than $3,000. There were several checks of more than $1,000 made out to Regal Jewelers. A $15,000 check to Beverly Hills BMW. A down payment, she thought. A $3,700 check to Furs by Antoine. Five months' worth of conspicuous consumption, in black and white. There was no telling what he'd done with the rest of the money. The jerk didn't have the sense to open an account at another bank. Esther slumped back in her seat. She felt drained, as if she'd been digging ditches or sweeping the streets.

'Lawdhamercy,' she said to the empty room. She started to draft a memo outlining her findings, but cautioned herself. Suppose Kirk wasn't working alone? What if Kirk wasn't guilty, and her memo was viewed as slanderous? She needed to talk to someone before she attached her name to any documents. There was no hurry. The news would keep for a few days.

38

Julia's was crowded that Wednesday afternoon, thanks in no small part to the favorable review that had just run in the *Gazette Sunday Magazine*. The throng of diners within and those queuing up outside the eatery were part of its cachet. Humphrey needed chic ambience and every other advantage possible as he sat across the table from Tom Wagner, his Last Hope. When Humphrey called to confirm the meeting, he casually let Tom know that he was black. Humphrey could recall the many times he'd seen shock in the eyes of white customers when they discovered that the very proper and clipped voice they'd been hearing on the telephone belonged to an African-American. It was absolutely essential that Tom Wagner feel completely at ease. As he ordered the most expensive bottle of wine on the menu, Humphrey prayed silently: Come on, God, be on my side. Be on my side.

For the first half of the meal, they ate and chatted about everything but the deal. Humphrey could feel his temples pounding. Then, gradually, they began to discuss business. Tom had a number of questions, and Humphrey answered each one in great detail. The waiter came and cleared their plates away. His Last Hope glanced at his watch and then put his hands flat out on the table. 'Your proposal is very promising, Humphrey,' he said. 'Very promising. I tell you what: I'm not one to beat around the bush and stretch things out unnecessarily. Let me present this to my team and get back to you tomorrow afternoon. Is that fair?'

Fair enough.

Humphrey talked himself out of grinning as he walked back to the bank. If there was one thing that working in corporate America had taught him, it was that premature happiness was the deadliest sin of all. The man had promised him nothing. Still, there was no law against hoping. And so, if his lips were compressed in a tight, sensible line, his heart was feeling lighter than it had in weeks.

He stayed in his office for the rest of the day and was still seated at his desk when Eleanor poked her head in and said, her tone mellifluous and even, 'Now, don't you work too late tonight, Mr. Boone.'

'I won't,' he said, adding, 'Good night, Eleanor.'

Humphrey wasn't really working; he was brooding, shuffling through papers while he simultaneously wrestled with hope and despair. His lunchtime high had vanished, and now he was filled with gloom. Without that deal, he was finished at Angel City. He'd be just another nigger.

When Humphrey opened the door to the lounge, he saw Mallory standing next to the soda machine, drinking an RC Cola. The sight of her, so unexpected, warmed him. She looked so pretty. Pale-yellow blouse. Pale-yellow hair. Pale.

Yeah, white boy. Your woman is with me.

'Mallory,' he said softly. He was standing next to her before she could answer. 'I've been thinking about you. Thinking about that night we spent together. I was hoping you've changed your mind about going out.'

'No, Humphrey, I haven't.' Mallory wanted to sound strong, but she could hear her own voice trembling.

Just a little more coaxing, he thought, and she would give in. A little more coaxing and they would all give in, the Jason Rodgerses, the Tom Wagners, all the slick white boys who were turning him down, keeping him waiting. 'Aww, come on, baby.' Humphrey could hear the words echoing in his head – *Come on, baby* – returning to him so slowly that he didn't recognize his own voice. Come on, Jason.

Come on, Tom. He was crying out to all of them. He didn't realize that he was reaching for her until he saw his own hands stretched out before him. And in that moment he looked at her face, and there was something strange in her eyes. He thought it was fear. Jesus, what am I doing? He stepped back, because the look in her eyes was pushing him away. But he was already holding on to her. He heard the soft rip, and when he looked at his fingers he was grasping a piece of yellow silk. For a moment, both of them stared at the small opening in her sleeve, the thin expanse of pale flesh, as if they were transfixed. Then the entire room seemed to vibrate with the sound of Mallory's sobs.

Her tears alarmed and confused him. He moved toward her. He really did want to comfort her, to apologize for tearing her blouse, for being so aggressive. He'd been too aggressive; he could see that now. But as soon as he went toward her, she began screaming: 'Leave me alone! Don't you fucking touch me!' There was such anger in her voice. Such fear. He stepped back. And then she was coming after him. 'You bastard.' She kept saying that over and over again, with what seemed to him was increasing and incomprehensible hysteria. She raised her fists, and he could feel the soft thuds against his chest. So weak. And he just wanted to get her to calm down. To be rational. That was all. There might be people around. Someone might hear her and misunderstand. So he ignored her screams and reached out for her again. He was trying to get her to stop, so he grabbed her by her wrists and was going to say, 'Now, just calm down, baby.' Yes, call her baby, because they liked that. White girls liked the way brothers called them baby; it was something they couldn't get at home.

He reached for her, and she said, 'Leave me alone, you black bastard!' But before he could say anything, he heard his name, very loud, very clear, and when he looked, Esther was standing in the doorway and looking from Mallory's face to his, and her eyes were filled with what could only be described as revulsion. Yes, that was exactly what it was.

Mallory was still crying and shaking when Esther led her away. He moved forward, as if to follow them; Esther bared her teeth at him, giving him a look full of rage, and said, 'Just keep away, Humphrey.' Talked to him like she didn't know him. Like he was a criminal. Talked to him with that hurt look in her eyes.

Esther led Mallory into her office, and they stood there not speaking until Esther spat out the word that was spinning around her mind. 'Asshole.' It felt strange to say that word and mean Humphrey. And it felt traitorous to say it in front of Mallory. She almost wanted to call that word back, to hide it inside her. 'Do you want anything, Mal? Some coffee?' Their eyes met. It was the first time they'd looked at each other directly in days. Mallory shook her head so forlornly that Esther thought she was about to cry again, and she put her arms around her shoulders. 'I'm sorry I didn't believe you,' she said. She was sorry about a lot of things. 'Let's get out of here.'

It was cool and dim in Patti's. Esther ordered white wine for herself and then looked at Mallory. 'Jack Daniel's on ice,' she said, her voice dull.

'Whoa,' Esther said. 'Don't hurt yourself.'

Mallory gave Esther a sliver of a smile. 'It's been a Jack kind of day.'

'Maybe Humphrey had a bad day too.' The words slipped out.

'Don't defend him, Esther,' Mallory said sharply. 'Don't make any excuses for him. I said no. I told him no.'

'I know you did,' she said. A ten-year-old memory appeared in Technicolor and three dimensions: Her own unheeded No, gradually transformed into a scream for help, played over in her mind. She closed her eyes and could feel the thick fingers wrapped around her, pressing and

528

snatching, pressing and snatching. She began scratching her neck and arms. 'Believe me, I know you did.'

'I'm not taking this shit,' Mallory said. 'I'm going to report Humphrey to Bailey Reynolds, and you'll be my witness.'

'Mallory,' was all Esther could manage to say.

'You told me I needed to get angry, to take control. Well, I'm doing that. And I want you to help me.'

'Oh, Mal.' Her friend didn't know what she was asking her to do.

'He's been harassing me. He tore my clothes.'

Their eyes met. Esther looked away and envisioned every aspect of what she'd seen in the employees' lounge: Humphrey holding Mallory's wrists while she struggled to get away from him; the rip in her sleeve; the tiny shred of yellow fabric in his hand. The image was still fresh and had played over and over in her mind ever since she walked in on the two of them. He wanted a white woman and didn't want her. She felt the rejection so sharply that for a moment she could almost hear herself reporting him. She took a deep breath and her eyes became slits as she recalled what she had heard Mallory say when she walked into the lounge. Bastard. Black bastard. But what would Esther have called someone who was doing what Humphrey was trying to do? 'Men,' she said. Her eyes met Mallory's. She knew she spoke for both of them.

'It's so strange,' Esther told Tyrone later that night, as they ate dinner. 'I mean, I saw him holding her wrists. I saw where he tore her blouse. I'm pissed about what he did, but I don't want to get him into trouble.' She looked at Tyrone. Maybe he doesn't have a degree, but the man has good common sense, she thought. 'What do you think?'

Tyrone pictured the tall black man in his thousand-dollar suits. Suave. The brother was sophisticated, with his briefcase and shiny shoes, his Rolex. He heard the inflections in Esther's voice when she talked about him. He could feel the connection. A brother like that, educated and everything, wearing those good suits, driving that long Benz, pocket full of credit cards: that's the kind of man she wants. Ever since he and Esther had gotten back together, things had been going well between the two of them. He'd even told her about his plans to enroll in school. He didn't want to feel anger between them, but when she mentioned Humphrey, he was overwhelmed with envy and jealousy. He squeezed the back of his neck, where he could feel his muscles tensing up. 'Well, if he can't respect a woman's body, he don't need to be in that job.' His voice was louder than he meant it to be. And angrier.

Doesn't, she thought automatically. She almost said the word aloud. 'I don't think he meant to disrespect her. He just got carried away. Listen, here's a guy from the 'hood. Got a scholarship. Worked hard in his profession and volunteers in the community. He deserves his success,' Esther said.

'Why you protecting him so tough?' Tyrone asked. He placed his fork on his plate. 'I mean, she told him no, and he rips her blouse.' He was aware of his vehemence only by the shocked look in Esther's eyes. 'I mean, suppose he tries to rip somebody else's blouse. How you gone feel then?'

'I think this was a onetime thing,' Esther said.

'Why? Just because he's got a degree and drives a Benz?' Tyrone was shouting now. 'You think successful people can't act like fools?'

'He's got *two* degrees,' she said, deriving a malicious pleasure from flaunting the number in Tyrone's face. 'And that has nothing to do with it. I'm talking about the kind of person he is. I'm not talking about some Uncle Tom handkerchief head, of which there are oh so many in Corporate America. I mean, Humphrey is a brother. He was going to help me get into lending. He mentors young black men. He's a good guy.'

'It seems to me that you know Mallory better than you know him. Isn't she supposed to be your friend?'

'She is my friend, but she doesn't understand what she's asking me to do. Mallory wants me to help her get a black man fired, a man who made a mistake but is still a decent person. Would you do that? As few of us as there are in any positions of power? As hard as it took us to get there? Would you, Tyrone?'

Tyrone was quiet. He saw the passion in Esther's eyes. Humphrey Boone was the object of that passion, not him. The tall black man excited her in a way that Tyrone couldn't. Maybe he'd put his hands on Esther too. Maybe she liked it. 'Hell, yeah, I would,' he said.

After Tyrone left, he was still angry. Not with Esther. Not with the suave Humphrey Boone. He was angry with himself. Humphrey had pulled himself up by his bootstraps. What had *he* done? As he drove home, his mind kept going back to high school and community college. Why hadn't he done better? He wasn't stupid. Why hadn't he tried harder? I could have done better, he thought. Reverend Rice's words played over in his mind. He was scared. Scared of trying, scared of failing. But no more. Tomorrow he was going down to Cal State, and he didn't give a damn if he had to take remedial everything. He was starting school.

39

The two shots of Jack fueled the nascent fireball inside Mallory. After she left Patti's, she would look at her sleeve from time to time and play back the last few hours in her mind. She could see Humphrey coming toward her, hear the soft sound of her blouse being torn. She thought about the weeks and months before, when she had made it clear that she wasn't interested in dating him. She told herself it didn't matter that she went out with him once; it didn't matter that she invited him in and returned his kisses. She was his victim. And it wasn't important that she'd told Esther she would think things over; she was reporting Humphrey. She was tired of being abused. It was easy enough to let her thoughts drift back, years back, and to fill in those fleeting seasons with men whose names she couldn't remember, whose faces had blurred. And what she recalled was the waiting: for the phone or doorbell to ring; for the signal that she was not an intruder in their lives. When her inventory was completed, she admitted to herself that for as long as she could remember, she was always some man's victim. She began crying again, tears of kerosene that threatened to make the fire-ball inside her explode. When she had stopped weeping, she found herself parking her car in front of her parents' home.

Though it wasn't even eight-thirty, her first thought was that it was late, that she might disturb them. The house was lit up, but as she came up the walk, she felt like getting back in her car and driving away. She forced herself to ring the doorbell and to wait once she had done so.

'Oh, Mallory.' Her mother managed to say her name and squeal all in one breath. Her mother smelled strongly of Chloé and faintly of Scotch. 'You're so ski-i-inny.' She peered into her daughter's face. 'What's the matter, honey? What are you crying about? What's wrong?'

'Nothing's wrong.' Mallory kissed her mother lightly on the cheek and was surprised by how soft her skin was. Her mother put her arms around her, and Mallory let the older woman hold her briefly before she broke away. 'I want to see Dad.' She looked around as she walked into the house. 'Is Dad here?'

'He's in his workroom.' Of course he was. 'How have you been, Mal? We don't get to see you so much.'

'I'm fine, Mom. I need to talk with Dad.'

Her father was leaning over a sturdy wooden table. He had a piece of fine steel wool in one hand and was rubbing a very old chair with small, careful strokes. His head was so close to the wood that his nose almost touched it. For as long as she could remember, her father had been a wood-worker, spending endless hours restoring antiques. As she stood in the doorway watching him, she was struck by how lovingly his fingers touched the chair. She wiped her eyes and smoothed her hair. 'Hello, Dad,' Mallory said.

Her father looked over his shoulder at her. 'Oh, Mallory. What are you doing here?' he asked, then turned back to his work.

'I came to see you and Mom,' she said.

'Is that right?' He gently rubbed his fingers against the wood several times, then picked up the steel wool again.

'I want to talk with you, Dad,' Mallory said.

'You need money or something?' Her father dipped a soft, clean cloth into a can of walnut stain.

'Can you look at me for a minute?'

He craned his neck and glanced at Mallory, then looked back at his chair. He began wiping the stain on the wood.

'Can you *look* at me?' Her voice was a thin soprano, high as a little girl's.

He turned toward her again. 'What?' he said. 'What are you talking about?'

'I just want you to look at me.' The tears began falling before she could stop them.

Astonishment and fear filled her father's eyes, as if she'd pulled a gun on him. He threw down the stained rag and stepped away from her, shaking his head. 'Aww,' he said, lifting his hand, swatting it at the air, then letting it drop. 'Kate! Kate! Come see about Mallory.' He moved toward the door. 'Your mother's coming,' he said.

'I don't want her. I want you,' she wailed. Mallory looked up, but her father was gone.

He doesn't even get it, she thought. She could hear him calling for his wife. He'll never get it.

'I don't need him anymore,' Mallory whispered to herself as she drove home. She felt calm, cool. But her heat was only smoldering. The next day, there were renewed flare-ups, moments when she would seethe and rant, when she would cry uncontrollably. Oddly enough, during these times, she didn't think of Humphrey or feel his hands tightening around her wrists. It wasn't his dark face that she raged against; the man whom she cursed was her father.

The city held its breath as the district attorney and the lawyers for the men accused of beating the white trucker interviewed prospective jurors. Each night, the residents of South-Central collectively conducted their own tally as they watched the eleven o'clock news. They went to bed grumbling that not enough blacks were being chosen. Their lives, their histories, were too full of memories of all-white juries for them to sleep peacefully. Whites had freed Emmett's murderer and Medgar's crafty killer. The years had changed

534

nothing. They were bitter and their anger seeped into the air that blew across the city.

On Saturday afternoon Mallory was on her way to the grocery store, when she found herself on the freeway, heading toward Westwood. She used to hang out in the university community almost every weekend, but she hadn't been in the neighborhood in several years, not since a young Asian woman was murdered there, shot in broad daylight by some gangbangers. That killing, in the middle of the day, only blocks from the university, had made her as frightened of the university community as she was of Park Crest. She remembered the woman's death because up until it happened, Mallory never thought of the city's gangs as something that could ever touch her life. Before the woman died, she'd barely glance at the headlines about drive-bys and inner-city shoot-outs. After all, the violence was limited to East L.A. and South-Central; she thought the madness could be contained there.

Mallory scanned the streets, feeling a little jittery. Naturally, there was no place to park; the university was the hub of the neighborhood, and most students had their own cars. Nevertheless, it was one of the few places in the city where people actually walked. And that's what she wanted to do. After parking in the lot across the street from Bullock's, she slipped into the crowd ambling along Westwood Boulevard. She began to feel carefree as she wandered aimlessly, looking into the showcases of the clothing stores, studying the menus posted by the trendy eateries along the boulevard. The people around her didn't frighten her at all. These kinds of outings had gotten away from her; she'd sacrificed her leisure time on the corporate funeral pyre. No more, she promised herself, feeling the summer breeze in her hair. From now on, she was claiming her free time. Celebrating her life. There were at least four bookstores on the broad street, and Mallory wandered into each of them, leisurely flipping through books and magazines. She browsed in several boutiques, then ducked into a Mrs. Fields and bought a brownie. As she munched and walked, it occurred to her that she could spend more time in Westwood if she lived in the city. Maybe she'd enroll in the university's M.B.A. program. Scanning the crowd on the streets, she regretted having stayed away so long. She didn't feel frightened at all. Passing a tall, dark man, she thought about Humphrey. She'd seen him from a distance the previous day. Maybe he'd leave her alone now. Perhaps she should forget about what happened. Let it go, just the way she'd released her father. She thought about her father's hands, the rough, stained fingertips, rubbing the wood, caressing the wood, loving the wood.

Mallory turned down one of the smaller streets. It was no less traveled than the one she'd just been on and was filled with shops and restaurants as well. There were several groups of tables in front of the various restaurants, where people could eat or drink in the open air. The customers sitting at the tables chatted amiably. She heard laughter all around her. A glass of wine would be nice, she thought. She looked around and walked toward a sign that read: BLANCHE DUBOIS. The tables below the sign were painted bright green and yellow. There were wooden boxes filled with red and pink geraniums and, on either side, impatiens of various colors.

The woman's hair caught her eye. It was long, blue-black, and glossy. Mallory could see only the hair – Asian hair. The woman's face was turned away, pressed close to the cheek of her companion. Their entwined fingers were displayed on the table. Mallory walked past them, her eyes on another set of tables, farther up the street.

She didn't know what made her look back. Was it a loud squeal of brakes? A sudden shout? Laughter that pierced the air? But she did turn around, and the faces were no longer touching; the lovers were looking straight at her. The one face, young and Asian, was smiling sweetly. The other – much older and white – was smiling too, until his eyes met Mallory's.

'Hayden?' she whispered. 'Hayden!'

Mallory felt her body make a sudden spastic movement. She walked toward the table, reached out her hand, and with one grand sweep sent the two glasses of white zinfandel crashing to the pavement. The Asian mouth became a silent full moon. A tiny piece of glass lodged in Hayden's stunned face; blood trickled down his cheek. People sitting at the tables around them stared in horror. 'Trophy geisha,' she said, lunging toward the woman. Hayden grabbed Mallory by her upper arms – hours later she discovered the bruises – and led her away from the table, hustling her down the street as people gawked and stepped aside. He held her body away from him at arms' length, as if she were a bag of trash.

Mallory stomped on the birds-of-paradise and long-stemmed roses when they arrived the next day; the scent of crushed flowers permeated the house. She hung up the phone when Hayden called. Tore up his pictures and sent the few clothes of his that were hanging in the closet to the Salvation Army. Drank Jack all night long. And when the bottle was empty, heat seeped out of her every pore. Crackling inside her weren't embers but glowing flames.

40

Humphrey stood back as he watched Preston tee off. The drive wasn't a good one, and the hard white ball skittered to a stop well before it met its goal. They were both mediocre golfers, but that Saturday afternoon, they were enjoying the warmth of the sun and the beauty of the emerald-green golf course. As they putted, they talked, and that was the point. Being together on the fabulous Bel Agua Country Club golf course wasn't about playing golf at all. But of course Humphrey had always known that – he'd always known that within those exclusive precincts that were closed to him, white men were making slick, profitable deals, within reach of their golf clubs and caddies. It was the way America did business, full of trust and good sportsmanship. And now, at long last, he was part of it.

And it couldn't have come at a better time, because at last things were returning to normal. When Humphrey thought about the last few weeks, he felt like a man who had stepped back from a slippery precipice and only from that safe distance begun to comprehend the death-defying fall he had narrowly escaped. I must have been nuts, he thought when he pictured himself with Mallory's torn sleeve. Sometimes he could still feel that tiny piece of silk in his hand. He couldn't even remember how he had torn it.

But things were okay now. More than okay. Whatever madness had possessed him had drained away. He'd learned his lesson. Enough time had passed. He would apologize to Mallory on Monday. Thank God she wasn't a vindictive woman. When he thought about what might have happened . . . Well, no need to dwell upon that.

He'd rather consider his deal. That was the best news of all. The deal was about to happen. After all the false starts, he finally had a real player on his hook. Tom Wagner had called late yesterday afternoon to tell him that he and other insurance agency officials would be signing the documents that would lock up the private placement loan in one week.

'It's going to be beautiful,' he said to Preston as they ate lunch in the country club's dining room. 'Angel City stands to make well over a million dollars.'

'A million sounds good,' Preston said. He couldn't help feeling pleased for the tall black man sitting across from him. He had to admit that Humphrey had gotten off to a slow start. But now he was back on track. Preston felt vindicated, especially when he recalled how Bailey had urged him to fire the black man. But then Bailey had never been enthusiastic about Humphrey.

Preston was also pleased for himself. His son had returned to school; his wife had resumed her volunteer work. Their lives had fallen back into comfortable old patterns and familiar rhythms, as though the frenzy of Pres's accident and recuperation had never occurred. Interestingly enough, only recently he'd attended a meeting in a room full of men who told him that he had a political future. He didn't know why he had gone, except that Dan Wilkerson had been so persuasive. Preston had just about given up on the idea of getting into politics. He and Claire were discussing a new way of life; the feasibility of his retiring, really calling it quits. They had several lengthy talks about where they might like to live. As he sat at the meeting, listening to the men, he waited for the old ambition to rush through him. But it didn't. And although Dan privately urged him to make a commitment, he told the people gathered in the room that he would take everything they said 'under consideration'.

He got home late that night, and Claire met him at the door. She put her arms around him and they kissed. She actually cried and told him that she was lonely, that she wanted to be held. They went upstairs and made love, and when he looked down at her face, there was that flush of ecstasy. She fell asleep, and he rolled over to his side of the bed and switched on the night-light. He opened his Bible to the beginning of the New Testament. He'd read it before, of course, and now, as he sat in bed, he paused to contemplate the words, to let the meaning of them resonate in his mind. And as he read, he found himself growing more and more excited, more and more touched in a way he'd not experienced before.

Now, however, Preston wasn't contemplating Bible verses. He was watching Humphrey Boone and thinking that whatever he chose to do, he had someone who could take over the reins, a choice that made good business sense. If he did choose to run for office, how many potential Republican candidates could boast that they had a cadre of middle-class black voters in their hip pocket? Humphrey was president of the black bankers group, and he was tied in with some of the city's old-guard civil rights leaders. The man was connected. So it had taken him a while to get going. Preston knew a winner when he saw one.

Mallory had just picked up the telephone in her office on Monday morning when she heard a soft knock. The door opened, and Humphrey stepped inside, closing it behind him. 'Mallory,' he said. His face was somber, his voice full of regret and high principles.

She dropped the receiver and jumped up, hitting the back of her leg against her chair. The pain radiated upward to her knee. 'What the hell do you want?' she said.

When their eyes met, he stepped back. Why was she still frightened? 'I should have waited for you to invite me in.'

'Stay away from me!'

'Mallory, I'd like to— '

'You fucking ripped my blouse.' When she said the words, she could remember the tearing sound. As she spoke, she could feel the heat of her words, feel the fireball expanding inside her. She spoke slowly, deliberately. 'Do you think you can get away with that?' Mallory watched Humphrey's eyes widen.

He saw her chest heave in and out, slowly at first, and then faster. The rhythm of her breathing echoed her words. *Do you think you can get away with that?*

She dabbed at her forehead, where tiny beads of perspiration gathered near her hairline. 'Get out of here!'

Humphrey nodded and left, taking the echo of her warning – yes, there was no mistaking what it was – with him. As he walked back to his office, his shoulders were hunched and his lip was already bleeding where his teeth had torn through the skin.

Kirk watched Humphrey as he left Mallory's office. The black man's eyes were filled with the kind of dread he'd seen in deer right before they were shot. Kirk wasn't surprised when he sidled up to Mallory's door and heard muffled crying. He stood outside, then turned the knob softly and went in.

Mallory didn't know she wasn't alone until she felt his hand on her shoulder. Her body jumped a little, and then she saw who it was standing in front of her, smiling gently. He could see the fear in her eyes, and when he looked closer, he could see the anger there too. 'Oh, Kirk,' she said, and began crying again. It was just that she felt so empty and alone. She leaned her head against Kirk's chest. He put his hands on her shoulders and started kneading them, very softly, almost imperceptibly, until he could feel her tension diminishing and his excitement growing. 'You want to talk about it?' he asked.

His hands were rhythmic and soothing. 'Close the door,' she said.

A few hours later, Bailey Reynolds stood up behind his desk and beamed at Mallory when she was ushered in by his receptionist. Earlier that afternoon, he'd received a call from Kirk. The mutual recognition that Humphrey Boone was an impediment to both men's professional ascendancy had bound them together. For the last few weeks, they'd been checking in with each other regularly. This afternoon, the younger man could hardly contain the enthusiasm in his voice as he described what had transpired between the white woman and Humphrey. When he'd heard the entire story, Bailey was even more excited. 'Is she willing to report him?' he asked.

'I think she's angry enough, but she's vacillating,' Kirk said.

'You can't talk her into it?'

'I've been trying. I guess the thought of filing sexual harassment charges is intimidating to her. I tell you what: If you haven't heard from her by four o'clock, why don't you call her in and . . .'

'Do what I do best,' Bailey said with a chuckle.

'Exactly.'

When Kirk hung up the telephone, King Clever appeared in the visitors' chair. As usual, Kirk was excited to see the living deity. Today he had something very important to tell him. 'I've begun,' he said softly.

'What's that, Amerifriend?' King Clever asked.

'I've begun to reclaim what's mine,' Kirk whispered.

The tiny man yawned. 'That a fact?'

Kirk leaned in closer. 'You remember that job I told you about? The one that I lost because of affirmative action?

Well, I've begun taking the necessary steps, the ones you talk about in your book . . .'

At the word 'book,' King Clever sat up straight and focused his eyes on Kirk. 'How many copies did you say you bought?'

Kirk was taken aback. 'Three,' he mumbled.

King Clever nodded briskly. 'Listen, Kirk Amerifriend, I've gotta go.'

'But you haven't heard my story. You see, there's this woman, a very pretty woman. Her name is Mallory, and the man in the affirmative action job was attracted to her. Only she didn't care for him, of course, and, well, the guy just wouldn't take no for an answer. And I reported him.'

King Clever waved his hand in disgust. 'Don't tell me this is a sexual harassment complaint. If there's anything I hate, it's women who scream harassment every time a man so much as looks at her. That's un-American.'

'But in this case, the harasser is a black man in a very high position, which, of course, he's jeopardized.'

'On the other hand, sexual harassment can often serve the greater good.' King Clever grinned at Kirk. 'Kirk, you've done well.'

Kirk beamed. He was still smiling long after King Clever had disappeared back inside the portable radio.

'Don't you count me out,' he said, his eyes ferocious as he faced Sheila's portrait, with its accusing gaze. All those fancy Jew doctors in Beverly Hills, with their marble offices, their mansions from hell, and their slim, Wonder Bread wives, wouldn't be able to look down on him anymore. He was smarter and more capable than any of them. He was making a comeback.

At five after four, Bailey made the call.

'Good to see you. Good to see you,' he said, watching Mallory as she sat and crossed her slim, pale legs, folded her hands in her lap. He appraised the light-blue suit, the way the fabric clung to her body. She has a nice figure, he thought. And a pretty face. All in all, she's a very attractive woman. Enticing, definitely enticing. Observing her golden hair and her soft gray eyes, Bailey could certainly understand how a man could get carried away. He smiled at Mallory, who looked at him questioningly. 'I've heard some disturbing rumors, Mallory.'

The woman stared at him. 'What kind of rumors, Mr. Reynolds?'

He stood up. 'I'll get right to the point. Has Humphrey Boone been bothering you?'

As Mallory sat there, she could feel tiny snatches of anger assembling in her mind. She closed her eyes and heard the sound of her blouse ripping. The fury rose inside her. 'Yes,' she said.

Bailey smiled charmingly. 'Sexual harassment in the workplace is a crime, and the bank looks at that crime very seriously. We can't afford to brush it under the rug. It is the policy of this bank that everyone has the right to a work environment that is free from the oppression of racial discrimination or sexual misconduct. The latter is every bit as serious as the former. The bank is financially liable if we continue to knowingly harbor a person who is guilty of sexual harassment.'

Mallory hadn't thought of that. Suppose Humphrey chose to force his attentions on someone else? She shut her eyes, and again she could hear her sleeve tearing, feel the large black hands gripping her wrists. And now she could feel other hands: Hayden's tightening around her arms, pulling her away from his Asian lover. She saw her father's thick fingers, sanding the wood, polishing the wood, slowly, steadily, lovingly. When she looked up at Bailey, his face was a blur. 'I didn't mean to upset you, Mallory,' he said soothingly. She wiped away the tears that were coursing down her cheeks. Her sobs, soft at first, gradually grew louder. Bailey patted her back awkwardly.

'I'm all right,' she said after a while. She took a deep breath.

'Start at the beginning, my dear,' Bailey said.

Mallory nodded. Slowly, she described how Humphrey began asking her out and how she refused. She talked about the night they went to a restaurant after work. 'I assumed the dinner was a meeting, an extension of the workday,' she said. From time to time, she looked at Bailey. His eyes were fixed on her. He seemed to be taking everything she said very seriously. The more she talked, the fresher her anger seemed, as though talking about it revived it somehow. She described their date. 'I invited him as a friend,' was how she put it. Wanting to be fair, she admitted they kissed after the dance: 'Several goodnight kisses,' as she described it. 'But after that, I told him that I'd changed my mind and didn't want to date him,' she said.

Bailey nodded his head. 'A woman's prerogative.'

That was when the harassment began to increase, she told him, describing the kinds of things Humphrey would say and do to her. How he complimented her, how he licked his lips and made suggestive comments. And then the fateful evening. 'I told him I didn't want to date him, and the next thing I knew, he had ripped my blouse and was grabbing me by my wrists. And then Esther came in.'

She stopped and looked across the desk at Bailey Reynolds. He had been nodding, saying 'I see,' over and over again, and 'Go on,' in a thoughtful way, always keeping his sharp eyes on her face. And while he nodded and murmured solicitously, Bailey was sifting through the information, committing to memory what could be used and discarding what could not. And what could be used was all the pertinent information that underscored Humphrey Boone's culpability and cried out for his removal. And not just

Humphrey. Mallory's accusation was the rock that could kill the two birds who stood in his way. If Humphrey was forced to resign because of scandal, then Preston's days were numbered too. After all, he was the man responsible for hiring him. And if the number one man was removed, it was possible for the number two man to move up.

He was so tired of being second in command.

Now he leaned toward Mallory. 'You said he ripped your blouse. And then he grabbed your wrists. And someone saw this?'

Mallory nodded. 'Yes,' she said.

'My dear, I think we're talking about more than sexual harassment.'

'What do you mean?' There was the faint glow of alarm shining in Mallory's eyes.

'He ripped your blouse. He grabbed you. And by your own words, you don't know what might have happened if someone hadn't come in.' He recited the events in sequence. Bailey was, after all, a details man, and in this instance not one detail had escaped him. 'What you're describing is attempted rape.'

Mallory looked shocked. 'Oh, no. I don't think he meant to— '

'He tore your clothes and grabbed you. You told him no and he wouldn't stop.'

'But— '

'You are telling the truth, aren't you, Mallory?'

'Yes, of course.'

'Because it would be a very serious matter if you weren't telling the truth.'

'Everything I've said is true, but— '

'Is there anything that you've said that you would like to change?'

'No. I told you everything that happened. It's just that— '

'I'm sure you were very frightened, Mallory. Sometimes

the mind tries to protect us from the full force of dreadful experiences. Perhaps you're blocking on the gravity of the situation you faced. As an officer of this bank, I have an obligation to protect you and other women from future attacks. Do you understand that you were being attacked and that only the intervention of your witness saved you?'

His eyes were like two smooth stones. Mallory slumped back against her seat. It was true. She didn't know what Humphrey would have done. She heard Sue's voice: *You don't know them.* 'I guess you're right,' she said.

Bailey smiled to himself. Preston Sinclair had put a rapist in charge of Angel City. The board wouldn't like that at all. And the board would hear about it.

It was a little after four when Esther saw Humphrey standing outside her door. She watched him as he weighed whether or not to knock, as he tried to gauge her mood, to figure out if there was a welcome for him behind the door. She didn't want to see him, but there was no way to pretend he wasn't there. 'Come in,' she said at last.

'I think I left you with a bad impression of me the other evening,' he said quietly.

She didn't return the smile he offered so tentatively, didn't unclench her fists or invite him to sit down. He wants me to reassure him, to tell him that everything's all right, she thought. I'm supposed to make him feel okay. 'I was taken by surprise,' she said. It took every bit of strength she had to control her voice, to keep it soft and even. Earlier, her loyalties had seemed so fixed. He was black; she was black. But now nothing seemed sure. 'You walk into the employees' lounge for a soda, you don't expect to see the regional manager standing there with a piece of the senior loan officer's blouse in his hand,' she said dryly.

'Look, I know what you're thinking.'

'I'm not thinking anything,' she said sharply. 'What you

do with your personal life isn't my business. But for your own sake, I don't think you ought to go around displaying your personal life at this bank. Especially if your attentions aren't wanted.'

'I didn't realize they weren't wanted.'

'When you have to rip a woman's blouse to get her to notice you, that's a pretty good sign she's not interested.'

'When a woman asks me to a formal affair and then invites me into her home and comes on to me, I take that as a sign that she is interested.'

Esther dropped the pen she was holding. She didn't attempt to pick it up from the floor. 'You and Mallory dated?' she managed to whisper.

'Look, we had a good time. We kissed. I thought she was interested. I got a little carried away.'

Esther's lips felt frozen, and her eyes couldn't focus. The angry rumblings of the South Side were churning inside her. The next thing she knew, she was spitting out hot words, as sharp as broken bottles. 'I guess black women aren't good enough for you anymore.'

'What?' Humphrey stepped back a little. Her words put him in a lineup, under a glare of light that made him want to cover his face.

'Did you outgrow us?'

Outgrow? 'No.' Outgrow? 'I . . . Look, she came on to me.' He stared at the floor.

'So did I.' His shocked eyes slowly found her face. Now it was her turn to want to look away. She felt naked standing in front of him, naked and bruised. She fought the urge to wrap her arms around her own body. It was the body of a thin brown girl with wide nostrils and full lips, with hair that wouldn't grow, whose mirror told her that she wasn't beautiful because she didn't resemble a Brady Bunch girl. Looking into a brother's eyes wasn't supposed to feel like staring in that mirror. 'Mallory wants me to go with her to

Bailey Reynolds and report what you did. Did you know that?' she said coldly.

Humphrey stared at her, and then he groaned. 'Esther. Come on, now.' His voice was soft, his words slurred.

She knew what he was saying: Protect me. Be on my side. Help me. Be my sister. Now, when I'm in trouble.

'Black folks have got to stick together,' he said. She didn't answer, just stood staring at him, feeling her outrage. 'Sister, do you still have my back?'

'Do you have mine?'

Humphrey sat in his office and waited for the call to come from Bailey Reynolds. He'd decided that his strategy would be to minimize the whole affair. Just a misunderstanding. These things happen. It wouldn't happen again. He trembled as he whispered fragments of these sentences aloud in the empty room. Finally, at half past five, there was a soft knock at the door, and then Eleanor peeked in. 'Mr. Reynolds would like to see you, Mr. Boone. He said now, if you're available.' Her usually tranquil eyes were full of fear.

Every time Humphrey had been in Bailey Reynolds's presence, he'd sensed that he was being appraised. He couldn't put his finger on one specific thing that the man ever said or did, but when he was around him, he felt stalked. The sensation overwhelmed him now as he faced the brilliance of the older man's fixed smile.

'Good to see you, Humphrey,' Bailey said. 'I understand things are going quite well.'

'Quite well,' Humphrey repeated. He nodded his head.

'Yes, the word is out that you're in line to be quite the fair-haired . . . well, that your private placement deal is virtually in the bag, as they say. That's quite an accomplishment.'

'Well, quite a bit of hard work, Bailey.'

'Of course, of course. You are a hard worker. One of the

hardest I've ever come across. That's why I'm perplexed, Humphrey, just damned confused. Why would a hard worker like you risk his entire future on an indiscretion?' Bailey smiled broadly. And then waited.

'I don't know what you mean,' Humphrey said. His heart began to pound in his chest.

Bailey stood up and walked around to Humphrey. 'You don't?'

Humphrey was quiet. Then he said slowly, 'Would you tell me exactly what you're talking about?'

Bailey began circling the desk and the chair where Humphrey sat. He walked around the room so fast that the back of his black suit coat flapped in the breeze he created. 'I'm talking about Mallory Post, and I'm talking about your asking her out repeatedly after she told you no.' The circle was getting smaller. 'I'm talking about a torn blouse. I'm talking about your grabbing her. I'm talking about a boss harassing his employee. I'm talking about a very serious offense.' Bailey's jacket brushed against Humphrey's shoulders. He stopped walking and placed a hand on the black man's shoulders. Humphrey could feel his sharp nails digging in.

Perspiration dripped along Humphrey's sides and rolled down his back. He leaned forward, sprang forward really, like a cornered rat trying to fight his way out. 'Did Ms. Post inform you that we dated?'

'Yes; as a matter of fact, she did. She went out with you, and then she changed her mind. It's a woman's prerogative, Humphrey.'

'This is all a misunderstanding. I never harassed her.' He laughed awkwardly.

'Oh, it's a little more serious than that,' Bailey said, his dark pebble eyes fixed on Humphrey.

'What do you mean? I categorically deny that I ever did anything improper.'

550

'You tore her blouse. You grabbed her wrists.'

Humphrey winced as the older man spoke.

'That sounds more like attempted rape than sexual harassment.'

When he heard the words, Humphrey was filled with such a swell of instant panic that the force of it almost toppled him from his chair. The room was an elevator that refused to open. He couldn't breathe. Bailey bent over him. He said, 'She has a witness.'

Esther, he thought, through the haze that was rapidly descending upon him. His sister. He spoke slowly and with as much conviction as he could muster. 'I don't think she does.'

After Humphrey had left her office, Esther stood up and breathed in and out as slowly as she could. One minute she believed Mallory, and the next she was convinced that Humphrey was telling the truth. She found no peace in either version of the story.

Esther would recall later that she was standing in the employees' lounge, drinking a fruit punch, when she first heard the whispering around her. Heard Humphrey's and Mallory's names floating by. She turned and stared at the people who were talking. Two tellers. Their young faces froze when she looked at them. 'What are you saying?' she asked.

The two young women glanced at each other and tittered just a bit. The older of the two said, 'Oh, nothing,' then grinned at the other girl.

She didn't wait for more. Esther left the room, the drink, the giggles, all behind. As she passed people in the hall, she heard other whispers, more covert laughter. Mallory. Humphrey. The two names were as entwined as ivy leaves. Everyone knew. But how? When Esther opened the door to her office, Humphrey was standing inside, his dark face creased with tension and fear. 'What happened?' Esther asked him.

'Bailey Reynolds found out about Mallory and me.'

'How?'

Humphrey shrugged his shoulders dejectedly. 'She must have told him.'

Esther shook her head. 'She told me she would think it over.'

The telephone rang. Still shaking her head and staring at Humphrey, Esther picked up the receiver. 'Yes. Certainly,' she said.

'He wants to see me,' she said, after she hung up.

'I told him I never did anything improper. He said that Mallory has a witness.'

Their eyes met.

'Esther, he's saying I tried to rape her.' The last came out as a kind of hoarse whimper.

'Lawdhamercy,' Esther whispered. She could see the anguish filling his eyes.

'Save me,' he said.

Mallory was at the computer when Esther came in. She was concentrating so intensely that she didn't hear the black woman until she said, 'You lied to me.'

Mallory looked up. 'What do you mean?' Her face bleached out to a sudden pallor.

'I mean you didn't tell me that you dated him. That's the part that you left out.'

Mallory held her breath. For a moment, she was frightened. She could not only see Esther's rage; she could feel it engulfing her. It was a living thing, this anger she faced, threatening her like a swarm of wasps.

'I didn't want to hurt you,' she said, her voice rising in a wail of despair. 'I only did it to get back at Hayden. But that's not how it started.' There was no way she could read

Esther's mind, whether the eyes that glared at her so coldly wanted her to continue or stop. 'He began paying me compliments at first. Then he started asking me out and I told him no, that I didn't want to date my boss, but he kept asking me. Then he accused me of not wanting to go out with him because he was black. And I felt guilty about that. So when Hayden didn't take me to Mexico, I invited Humphrey to a big formal affair that I knew he'd be attending. But it was just to make Hayden jealous.'

'And when you invited him in and kissed him, was Hayden around to get jealous about that?' Esther watched as Mallory opened her mouth and then closed it. 'You've been screwing another woman's husband for – what? – a million years; a husband, I might add, who eased your climb up the corporate ladder considerably. And now you turn around and try to come on to another man in power, a man you knew I liked, only when you change your little Valley Girl mind, then you have the nerve to yell rape, which is like the universal rallying cry of the white woman, as far as black men are concerned.'

For a moment, Mallory's lips were trembling so badly that she couldn't speak. She felt guilty and remorseful. But at the same time, she had her own growing fireball, and she could feel it inside her, spurring her on. All her life, she'd been some man's victim. No more. 'I'm not seeing Hayden anymore. Anyway, what I did with him has nothing to do with Humphrey. I did kiss Humphrey, but only that one night. After that, I told him I didn't want to go out with him anymore. And he kept asking me, and when I refused he started getting nasty.' Her voice wasn't strong, but it was firm, and she didn't flinch when her eyes met Esther's.

'Why can't you stay with your own men?'

Mallory's voice rose. 'What the hell do you mean, "my own men"? Is that what this is about? You're jealous, because he's a black man and I'm a white woman? He's fucking harassing me and you're jealous. I never knew that you were so bitter. I thought we were friends.'

'Any black person in America who isn't bitter is either dead or psychotic. You're my friend if I smile at waitresses who ignore me and act like I don't see sales clerks following me around. Get this through your airhead: I'm not having as good a time as you are in this god-damned country.' The two women stared at each other. Then Esther added quietly, 'You've never even come to my house.'

'What?'

'You've never come to my house, Mallory. You're afraid to come to my neighborhood.'

'I don't . . .' Her words sputtered into meaningless sounds. 'You saw what he did.'

'I saw what Charles Weber did too. You never reported him.'

'I didn't report Humphrey. Bailey Reynolds sent for me. And when he asked me what happened, I told him the truth. And you know what: I'm glad I did.' Her voice began to rise. 'Maybe you think Humphrey is innocent, but you weren't in the room with him. He didn't rip your blouse. He didn't grab you and frighten you. I didn't know what he was going to do to me.'

'You're trying to make him the scapegoat for your entire life.'

'I am trying to get justice. Suppose he does this to someone else?'

Esther shook her head wearily. 'Bailey Reynolds has sent for *me*.'

'Just tell the truth, Esther. Just tell him what you saw.'

'I didn't see him try to rape you. I didn't see that.'

'I never said he tried to rape me,' Mallory shouted.

'But that's what Bailey's accusing him of.'

'I don't deserve this. If you don't tell the truth, it makes me look like a liar. I'm asking you to back me up. Esther, you're my friend.'

'So few of us ever make it to the top. I can't knock him down.'

'Do you know how it feels to be grabbed, to have your clothes torn? To have someone treat you like a piece of meat? We're both women, Esther.'

'I'm a black woman,' Esther said slowly. 'There is a difference.'

But misgivings began crowding Esther's mind as she tried to organize her thoughts while riding the elevator to the thirty-fourth floor. In the two minutes that it took for her to get upstairs, she tried to separate out what she needed to say from what couldn't be said. But opposing facts and feelings kept colliding in her mind.

Blood was thicker than water; she had to protect Humphrey. He was a brother, and Mallory came on to him; she asked for it.

Humphrey rejected her for a white woman. Why should she care what happened to him?

Mallory was her friend. She told Humphrey no. How many damn ways did you have to say no for them to understand? He ripped her blouse; he made her cry. The words echoed in her mind in their own discordant rhythm.

But how many of us make it that far? she asked herself. Her friend Titilayo was right. Every time one of us does succeed, white people are always trying to figure out ways to take it back. And they always use the same strategy: get a black person to crush another black person. Well, she wasn't the one to use. No. If Humphrey left, Angel City would never have a black man rise that high again.

And she would never get to be a lender.

Mallory wasn't hurt, not really. She'd survive. But if this accusation stuck, Humphrey would be destroyed. What black man could recover professionally from this kind of accusation? Esther thought about his work with black bankers, how he volunteered with young brothers. He was too valuable to throw to the wolves. For a fleeting moment, she stiffened as she remembered Humphrey and Mallory together. She recalled Mallory's sobs. But she couldn't think about Humphrey's preferring a white woman to her, and she had to put her friendship with Mallory out of her mind. Humphrey had covered for her and LaKeesha when they thought that she was stealing. They had to stick together now as well.

'I got your back, brother,' she whispered to herself.

'So, Esther,' Bailey said when she sat down. 'May I call you Esther?' he asked, barely waiting for her to nod her head before he continued. 'We've not had the opportunity to chat before. I'm sorry we have to meet under rather unfortunate circumstances.'

Esther didn't acknowledge what he said; she just watched him. She saw his eyes of stone and recalled the schoolyard brawls of her youth. She suddenly realized that Bailey was going to try to jump her.

'You're from Chicago, aren't you, Esther? That's my hometown.'

'Really? What part?'

'North end of town.'

She nodded, picturing a quiet neighborhood of shaded streets and wide rectangular lawns. 'I'm from the South Side.'

Bailey nodded amiably. 'Let me get right to the point. There have been certain allegations.'

'Allegations?'

Bailey paused and looked at the woman again. Something about her cautioned him to be wary. Her alert eyes warned him that he was dealing with an adversary. He hadn't expected that. For some reason, he thought that she'd align herself with the other woman, but looking at her face, the way her chin jutted defiantly forward, he suspected that her loyalties lay elsewhere. 'It's come to my attention that Humphrey Boone has behaved offensively toward one of the female employees.'

Esther stared at him without a flicker of recognition in her eyes. 'I don't understand,' she said.

'Mallory Post said that Humphrey Boone attempted to force himself on her.'

Force himself. Esther let the words slam together inside her mind. Those words were weapons, loaded and aimed.

Bailey watched Esther's eyes. There was no mistaking the outrage he saw there.

'Force himself? What exactly does that mean?' she asked, in a tight, hard voice.

'It means that Mr. Boone doesn't appear to understand the word "no" when it comes to women. Now, the reason I asked you to have this little chat with me is because I understand that you saw Ms. Post when she was struggling to get away from Mr. Boone. That is, you were a witness to that struggle. Is that true?'

A tiny muscle in Esther's neck began pulsating. Bailey kept his eye on it. He smiled pleasantly.

A witness? The word sounded so cold and legal, so frightening, like an awful beginning to something truly dreadful. She put her hand on her neck and began rubbing the jumping muscle. 'I don't know what you're talking about,' she said. 'I was under the impression that they liked each other. I know that they dated.' As she spoke the words, she saw Mallory's face and she felt guilty.

Bailey seemed suddenly lost in contemplation, and watching him, Esther thought that her surprise blow had stunned him into submission, that he would look at her and say, 'I see I've made a mistake,' and send her on her way. But she'd underestimated the North Side.

Bailey's eyes were glittering not with remorse but with anticipation. He could feel the dark woman's rebellion, the fight in her spirit. But he could smell her fear also. 'Yes, I know that they went out one time,' he said smoothly. 'I supposed that's when he got carried away.'

'Or maybe she got carried away,' Esther said coolly. She felt the same twinge of disloyalty, but again she ignored it.

'Perhaps I should have prefaced my question with some essential information, Esther. As you know, Angel City National Bank, like most banks, is a very conservative company. Our public persona has been carefully shaped so that our customers trust us with their money. Trust is the cornerstone of banking, Esther. The people who represent us, our employees, must be an extension of the bank's public persona. In short, they must be trustworthy. When we detect that there are employees in our midst who don't fit that mold, they must be ejected, for the good of the whole. And we expect the full cooperation of our loyal staff to assist us in that weeding-out process. People who don't cooperate are suspect and eventually are subject to the same kind of weeding-out process as those other perpetrators of nonconformity. Are you following me, Esther? Now, I want you to tell me exactly what you saw.'

His cold, dark eyes stared into hers. Hold your ground, she told herself. Admit nothing. She tried not to feel like a cornered schoolgirl. Bailey hadn't been there. It was still Mallory's word against hers and Humphrey's.

And whose word will they believe?

'I saw the two of them in the lounge and . . .' She tried to make her voice sound strong, but she barely managed a whisper.

'And what was he doing to her?'

Bailey leaned across his desk, and she could see how brightly his eyes glittered with malice and envy. What did it matter? He wants to get rid of Humphrey, Esther thought.

If it isn't this thing with Mallory, he'll think of something else. She could cooperate or she could be history.

Esther had the sudden urge to laugh. The situation was far too pitiful not to crack up. Here she thought she was bad enough to save Humphrey and she couldn't even save herdamnself. That's what Bailey was telling her: you're black and you're pathetic. I've got the power.

All he had to do was pick up the damn telephone and her ass would be gone. She let that thought sink in. And she could pray to whatever God she chose: Malcolm, Martin, the Republicans, the Democrats, Jehovah's Witnesses – didn't change a goddamn thing. She was expendable, like black folks in the Motor City who hadn't worked in ten years; like brothers in the aerospace industry whose names were on the short list for layoffs, like most black people in America since 1865. She looked at Bailey's smug face. Esther could hear his thoughts: Gal, you get sassy with me and you'll be looking at a welfare check.

Not a damn thing has changed, she thought. I'm still at the same plantation.

'What was he doing to her?' Bailey repeated.

When she raised her eyes to meet his, Bailey could clearly identify the surrender, even though it was still mingled with defiance. She's weakening, he told himself. In less than two minutes, she will roll over. There was nothing left to say; no further persuasion was needed. Everything would go his way. Tomorrow he would have lunch with several of the board members, those who opposed the addition of so many women so quickly to their ranks, who didn't like the Diversity Program and thought that Preston's leadership was flawed. He would carefully mention the problems with Humphrey and suggest that he be terminated immediately. Then he would discuss how Preston's poor judgment placed the bank in jeopardy. He made a mental note to keep tabs on Kirk Madison. The man was ambitious, and that could be as much a curse as a blessing to him. Bailey glanced at the dark woman in front of him. Her eyes were closed, and her head seemed to be lowered. He slowly circled her chair, and then he leaned in toward her.

41

Bailey went to see Preston first thing the following morning. 'I believe that Ms. Post is fully prepared to sue Angel City and bring criminal charges against Humphrey Boone if we don't get rid of him immediately,' he told the president. 'This isn't something that can be put off. The woman is hysterical, and she's ready to take action. Frankly, I don't think the bank can bear up to the kind of scrutiny it will have to undergo if the press gets wind of this. And of course she's threatening to go to the media. The best thing for the bank is to let him resign and go away quietly.' Bailey smiled at Preston, wondering if the president would question any part of what he'd been told. He liked Humphrey, that much Bailey knew, but how hard would he fight to keep him? There were holes in Bailey's story. If Preston called Mallory Post, he'd know the truth in five seconds flat. And the truth was that the woman simply wanted Humphrey to leave her alone. She hadn't insisted on having the black man's head on a platter, or revenge of any kind. He'd goaded the girl into demanding that Humphrey be fired. A person with less nerve than Bailey would have suffered at least mild trepidations about Preston's response, but Bailey had nerves of steel. Besides, he knew that the last thing on Preston's mind was picking up the telephone. The president just wasn't a details man.

Preston sat behind his desk, trying to let everything that Bailey told him sink in. The man made it sound as if Humphrey were a rapist, or at least had attempted rape. He could scarcely believe his ears. The Humphrey he knew was refined, a true gentleman. How had he misjudged him so? He thought fleetingly of their time together at the country club, the way Pres took to him. It seemed such a shame. If he did decide to run for office, he'd been looking forward to Humphrey's support. And then there was the private placement deal he was working on, finall going well after so many false starts.

Bailey read his boss's mind. 'You needn't worry about his project. There is someone here who is prepared to take it over completely. I've already spoken with him about it. It's absolutely not a problem. Don't give it a thought.'

But Preston was disturbed. In the past, he'd never gotten personally involved with his employees, and so when they left, he never felt the full impact of their absence. But Humphrey was different. As he sat in front of Bailey, he tried to think of a way to salvage his protégé, to resurrect him, but he couldn't come up with a course of action that seemed logical. Suppose they did manage to be able to keep him on. What if he then turned around and did the same thing all over again? Bailey was right. If the press got wind of it . . . Well, it just didn't make good business sense to keep Humphrey. The man simply had to go.

He realized that, but still something nagged at Preston. He didn't like to fire anyone, and, of course, he never had, not directly. That's why he kept people like Bailey Reynolds in his employ. Bailey was good at that sort of thing. He had the ability to remain detached. Preston genuinely liked Humphrey and wished that things had worked out. Part of him wished that he could talk with him, ask him exactly what happened. There might have been extenuating circumstances. There was always that possibility. But then to talk with the man would be awkward. He had a fleeting thought: What would Jesus do in this situation? He pondered the question for a moment and then put it out of his mind. The answer, whatever it was, would certainly not be businesslike.

Bailey smiled. 'I plan on asking Humphrey for his resignation tomorrow morning.'

Preston nodded. 'I trust you to take care of everything.' There was just a bit of tension between his eyebrows and sadness in his eyes. 'All the details, I mean.'

'Of course.'

On his way out, Bailey instructed Preston's secretary not to put through any calls from Humphrey to Preston and under no circumstances to allow the man in Preston's office. 'If he comes up here, call security immediately,' he told her.

As he stepped on the elevator, Bailey was filled with such an extreme sense of satisfaction that he laughed out loud.

By the end of the day, the news of Humphrey Boone's resignation had spread all over the bank. Details of his demise, mostly embellishments and distortions, drifted up and down the halls in whispered tones. Esther sat in her office with her door closed; she put her head down on her desk and tried to collect her thoughts. Then she heard the soft knock. By the time she sat up, Humphrey was standing in front of her. 'I came to say good-bye,' he said.

'Humphrey, I'm so sorry. I tried, but . . .'

He waved his hand slightly. 'I know you did. It's nobody's fault but mine. I had no business trying to date Mallory. For the record, though, I wasn't going to rape her.'

'I never believed that.'

'The threat of criminal charges did drift into the conversation I had with Bailey Reynolds,' Humphrey said dully. 'Anyway, it's all over. I'm history at Angel City. I wanted to let you know that I'm sorry I let you down.'

'Humphrey, you didn't— ' She lowered her eyes.

'I thought about what you said. I wanted you to know that I find black women very beautiful, especially you.'

563

Esther looked up and stared at him, her astonishment showing plainly on her face.

'If this seems like bad timing for me to start rapping, believe me, I'm not. I'm trying to make some sense of what I did.' He looked at her and said softly, 'Sometimes the hardest thing in the world is to love your own kind. I have some painful memories of black women, Esther. Memories of rejection and hurt feelings. When I was growing up I remember being black and ugly. And there were black girls who made me feel that to the core of my being. And I still feel it to this day. When I got older, I found out that other women judged me by different standards. Being exotic is a lot less hurtful than being black and ugly. And it's easy to be exotic to strangers. Maybe it's too easy.'

Esther hesitated for a moment. 'Who you care about and why you care about them isn't my business,' she said slowly.

'I didn't mean to hurt you.'

'I shouldn't let myself be hurt because of who you choose,' she said quickly. 'Sometimes I think black folks are carrying an ugly demon inside of us, some monster that's always telling us we're not okay.'

Humphrey smiled quickly. 'So how do you get rid of it?' He looked at her as though he really expected her to tell him what to do.

'My color is my joy and not my burden,' she said softly.

'What?'

'I break all the rules that impede my happiness.' She smiled at him. 'A friend of mine told me to look in the mirror every morning and say that. It's supposed to be a way to exorcise the demons.'

'Does it work?'

'I don't know. I haven't tried it.' They smiled at each other for a moment. 'What do you think you're going to do, Humphrey?'

'Maybe sell some of my suits,' he said, laughing a little. 'I

564

don't know. I think I need to go sit under a tree and figure out a few things.'

'I believe you can do that, Humphrey,' she said, taking his hand and squeezing it. 'You take care of yourself.'

He nodded. 'I wish you well, my sister.'

As Humphrey Boone waited for the red light on the Spring Street corner to change, he felt a gust of hot, soot-filled air against his face. Grit and smog temporarily blinded him, and for a moment the only thing he could feel was the smarting in his eyes. The rest of him was numb. Seconds later, he saw that the traffic signal had changed to green. But even though his sight had returned, he walked toward the parking lot in slow, halting steps, like a man who wasn't quite sure what lay in front of him.

'Dumb black nigger.' The words he spoke cut through the still hot air in his car and echoed in his mind. 'Dumb. Black. Nigger.' That's what he was. As soon as he heard the words, he realized that he'd been running from them all his life. He'd been hiding from them while he made straight As in high school and at Yale. He'd dodged them while he played pro ball and ducked them when he was successful in business. He'd hidden from them with Armani suits, Rolexes, Mercedeses, and blondes. But the words had always been on the lookout for him; they'd followed him everywhere he went. And now they had come to claim him. His early triumphs had merely covered up the truth he could no longer hide: He was inferior. And now everyone would know.

His career was over. Bailey Reynolds had promised that Angel City wouldn't divulge the reason for his resignation, but Humphrey knew that the word would filter out. He'd never get another job in banking. Black men didn't recover from mistakes like his. Comebacks were for rich white men. Sitting in his car, Humphrey began to tremble. He could see his house and car, his entire life, slipping away from him. How would he take care of his mother? She would have to go back on welfare. His groans filled the silence, and he thought of his sister's words: 'One of these days you gone remember exactly what it's like to be a nigger.' Well, that day had come.

'You fool!' he shouted, staring at his face in the rearview mirror. He could feel the energy seeping out of his body; a heavy torpor settled in his bones and made his mind go blank. He felt as immobilized as a dead man. He might as well be dead, he thought. He had a fleeting image of the white truck driver at the moment when he was first seized from his truck. Whenever that segment of the video appeared on television, Reginald Denny seemed to have a permanently startled expression, as though he'd just been pitched into the middle of a nightmare and he couldn't figure out how to escape. Humphrey knew the feeling.

He had been sitting in his car for nearly thirty minutes when he was startled by light tapping against his window. When he looked up, a neatly dressed man was standing beside his car, holding up a bottle of Windex in one hand and several pieces of newspaper in the other. Below the man's left eye was a strange kind of dark birthmark that reminded Humphrey of a cauliflower. He was wearing a red-black-and-green T-shirt. SOLID ROCK CLEANUP, INC. was printed across the front. 'Clean your glass, mistuh?' the man asked when Humphrey rolled down the window. 'I can make it shine,' he added.

'Sure,' Humphrey whispered. He watched as the man sprayed the glass cleaner on the lower left corner of the front window. Using small, circular motions, he carefully wiped away the dirt with the paper. He repeated the same painstaking movements on each window. When he was finished, the glass was spotless.

'Right on, brother,' the man said when Humphrey

handed him a ten-dollar bill. His grin revealed several missing teeth. As he walked away, Humphrey saw the back of his T-shirt. It read: WORKING FOR A NEW BEGINNING. DAMN STRAIGHT.

'My man Odell,' Humphrey said softly. He began to laugh. The sound was still in his throat as a calm, lucid thought slowly surfaced in his mind: Maybe. He started the car and took off slowly in the direction of Solid Rock.

Later, Kirk would marvel to himself how everything fell into place so smoothly. Two days after Humphrey Boone left, Bailey Reynolds called to tell Kirk that he had been appointed acting regional manager, and exactly one week later, the position became permanent. He completed the private placement deal in record time, and Bailey took him out to lunch to celebrate. They went to a posh downtown private club and stayed there nearly two hours.

'You've had an auspicious beginning,' Bailey said, taking a generous sip of brandy. 'You've come in during a turbulent time and managed to excel. I want you to know that Preston is impressed and so am I.' The older man leaned his head toward Kirk's and nodded, his teeth gleaming. 'You know, you will be the one creating the agenda for next year. It's not too soon to think about themes and various programs. For instance, this recent Diversity Program was quite enhanced. Do you intend to make it as prominent in the future?'

Kirk began to frown, unaware that Bailey was watching his expression closely, that his grimace was exactly what the older man wanted to see. 'Well, if you ask me, far too much time was given to that program. I don't think that kind of politically correct claptrap does anyone any good. This is a business. It's not the function of this bank to conduct socially conscious, politically correct sensitivity sessions. Nor should it be our purpose to show favoritism to certain groups. People must compete on an equal basis.'

'So I hear you saying that you'd like to downplay the program,' Bailey said eagerly.

Kirk detected the enthusiasm in his voice. 'That's the direction I'm leaning toward.'

'And eventually phase it out?'

The two men smiled at each other. 'Exactly,' Kirk said.

Bailey felt deeply satisfied. He liked the way the young man thought, but he talked himself out of becoming too enthusiastic. Kirk had yet to prove himself an ally. Of course, he'd known from the start that he couldn't confide in Humphrey. The black man was an adversary who wanted exactly what Bailey wanted: to be president of Angel City National Bank. And after his recent talks with several board members, there was no doubt in his mind that he was headed in that direction. 'We should get together more often now,' he told Kirk. 'We need to keep each other informed.'

Kirk nodded. He understood that Bailey had invited him to become his confidant, and he appreciated the offer. He felt successful and redeemed as they were chauffeured back to the bank in the company limousine. Kirk let his mind drift as the city passed by. In the stifling August air, he could smell the fires that burned to the north of the city. He would let Bailey mentor him, not that he needed guidance; King Clever was the only adviser he needed. Still, it would be good to have an ally as he made his way to the top. And that was where he was headed; he was sure of it. He sighed and allowed himself to slip into a brandy-induced languor. In a few moments he'd be back in his office, and he would carry out his first order of business as regional director: the removal of the remaining obstacles in his path.

Esther walked into Kirk's office later that afternoon and

was startled to see him pacing back and forth in front of his desk with his head lowered and his lips moving rapidly. He tilted his head and then nodded, as if he were listening to someone. When he realized that Esther was in the room with him, he jerked his head a little and then stared at her coldly. Esther felt a sudden and terrible trembling all over her body. Recent events had distracted her from completing the memo on the dormant accounts. She hadn't alerted the proper authorities. Now, looking at Kirk, she had a premonition that she was too late. Just as she sat down in one of the two chairs in front of Kirk's desk, the door behind her opened. To Esther's surprise, LaKeesha quietly took the seat beside her.

Kirk could see the apprehension in their eyes as the two women glanced first at each other and then at him. He wanted to laugh in their stupid faces. He was ahead of them, just as he was ahead of everyone. The last time he went into the dormant accounts, he could tell that someone else had been in the files; two thousand dollars had been deposited in accounts from which he'd taken money. When he checked the computer, sure enough, he saw the entry dates logged. There were far too many entries – three and four in a single day – to be business as usual: normally, dormant accounts were checked every three months. He realized then that someone knew about the missing money. He smiled now, remembering how quickly he had panicked, thinking that there was a chance that the person who had identified the theft could blame him. He checked the code – whoever had gone into the computer had stupidly logged in an ID – and found out that it belonged to Esther. At first he was frightened. It occurred to him that the rest of the world would think of him as a thief, even though he'd only taken what he deserved. He stayed in the bank one night and juggled the figures in the computer, so that all but twenty-five hundred dollars of the stolen money was covered up.

But after the business with Humphrey came out, he realized that he didn't have to be afraid anymore. When he was returned to the position of regional manager, he'd have the power not just to absolve himself but to make sure that he was never accused. He could shift the blame to one of the tellers and accuse Esther of a cover-up. LaKeesha was black; it made sense that her boss would help her.

'I know you're probably wondering why I called you two in,' Kirk said. His voice was cold and hard. He didn't look directly at either of the women. He took two pieces of paper off his desk and handed a copy to each of them.

He watched quietly as Esther and LaKeesha read the page. 'What the hell is this all about, Kirk?' Esther finally said. She tried to stand up, but she felt oddly off balance, as though she might fall. She remained seated, rubbing her hands together, clenching and unclenching her fists.

'I think the letter is pretty self-explanatory,' Kirk said. 'LaKeesha has stolen twenty-five hundred dollars from dormant accounts. You've been covering up for her. I want both of you to get your personal belongings and be out of here in fifteen minutes.'

Esther was so stunned that she couldn't make a sound. She had a fleeting sense of déjà vu, but nothing solid enough to grab on to. Then she heard a low, guttural moan. It was LaKeesha. Her lips were trembling.

'You son of a bitch,' Esther said. 'We all know who's been ripping off the bank.' Just looking at Kirk made her feel weak and drained, as if she'd been knocked down and couldn't get back up. She felt frightened as soon as she said the words.

Kirk could feel the women's shock; he could smell their fear clogging the air like heavy perfume. The scent excited him. 'If you're threatening me, you'd better think twice,' Kirk said. 'I have copies of all the computer entries for the last six months. Every time there has been a theft, LaKeesha has been on duty. And, Esther, your code is entered so frequently over the last few weeks that there is no way you couldn't have known. You could be prosecuted. Both of you. You could go to jail. I have proof. What do you have?'

LaKeesha and Esther exchanged glances, and now, like Kirk, they could sense the fear they shared. The air around them was laden with it. The longer they stared at each other, the weaker they felt.

'By the way, Esther, the bank is prepared to offer you a severance package and a good recommendation, provided that you sign a release form. Think about it. I'll give you a few days to make your decision.'

Esther and LaKeesha walked down the hall in a daze. Finally, LaKeesha broke their silence. 'Can he fire us like that?'

'He just did,' Esther said dully. She glanced at the younger woman's face, and she saw a nascent anger in her eyes. She knew that some of the emotion she saw was directed toward her. 'Go ahead and say it,' she said quietly.

'Why didn't you report him like you said you would?' LaKeesha asked.

'There was so much going on at the time, and I wanted to talk things over with a lawyer. I just thought it would be better to wait.'

'Why'd you have to think that I did it? Why me?'

It was hard for Esther to look into LaKeesha's eyes. 'I'm sorry I accused you of stealing.'

'Why me?' There was a child in her eyes, whimpering and damaged.

'I guess I thought you had more reasons. I don't know. I'm sorry.'

'Yeah. I have reasons. I live in South-Central. I have a baby. I've been on welfare. I don't use good grammar. Those the reasons you're talking about?' When Esther didn't respond, LaKeesha kept staring at her. 'You know me,' she said, her voice full of a child's sorrow. 'You're not supposed to think like them.' Esther watched her walk away.

'LaKeesha, I'm so sorry,' she whispered over and over. Long after LaKeesha disappeared down the hall, she was still repeating the words.

This isn't happening, Esther told herself as she emptied her desk drawers. She was a banker in the midst of the worst state and industry recession in history. How was she going to find another job? How was she going to pay her mortgage?

'Is it true?'

Esther stiffened when she heard the white woman's voice. She scarcely looked at Mallory. 'Is what true?'

'Are you leaving?'

'That's true. Kirk fired me. What else did you hear?'

'That LaKeesha was stealing and that you covered up for her.'

'That's not true. LaKeesha never stole anything, and I never covered up for her. Kirk's the thief. He's stolen more than two hundred thousand dollars from the dormant accounts. I don't know how he's done it, but he's tampered with the computers so that LaKeesha looks guilty. But she's not.'

Mallory stared back at her. Esther could see the stark disbelief in her eyes. 'You can't believe that.' The Valley Girl tone was grating.

'His kids have an awful lot of money in their savings accounts, more than sixty thousand dollars. And Kirk's been writing checks to a lot of jewelry stores and a rather large one to a BMW dealership. You think that's a coincidence?'

'He recently inherited some money. His grandfather died,' Mallory said. She was surprised at how defensive her tone was. But why shouldn't she defend him? 'Kirk has no reason to steal.'

572

'But LaKeesha does? Why, Mallory?'

She could feel her face redden. 'Esther, why do you make everything a racial incident? Just look at things logically.'

Esther sighed. How could she blame Mallory for something she herself was guilty of? 'Here's the real deal: I don't expect you to side with me against the man you're screwing.'

Mallory's face flamed red.

Esther let out a harsh chuckle. 'I know you, girlfriend. I know you well.'

'Esther . . .'

The black woman collected the last of her things and shoved them into her briefcase. She looked at Mallory. 'It's been real. I must say that.'

'I don't want to get in trouble, Keesha,' Hector said softly.

'You won't get in trouble. Just tell that you saw Kirk in Esther's office at night. Just tell that.' LaKeesha stared at the brown man's eyes, her friend's eyes. She couldn't understand why he wouldn't help her.

Hector shook his head. The movement was a difficult one, because his head was heavy. He wished that LaKeesha weren't standing in front of him, that he didn't have to look at her. 'If they think I'm lying, they might fire me too. I have a big family.' Why did she have to look at him that way? He wasn't the cause of her problems. She had no right to make him feel guilty. After all, he'd helped her once. Now he was helping himself.

'You think I don't? Come on, homeboy. Why can't you help me out?'

Hector shook his head. 'I'm sorry. I can't.'

LaKeesha sighed. When she began crying, Hector looked away. He didn't want to see the black girl when she was so sad. Seeing her tears made him think of all the times when they'd laughed together, the times when they brought each other food and played games. But life was not a game. Life in his new country was serious, and he had to be serious as well. The black girl wiped her eyes. He had to think of himself, of his family. 'Well, you take care of yourself. Tell your mama I said she can really burn on those papusas.' She flashed him a sad half-smile, then gave him a quick kiss on his cheek. He wanted to call after her, but he swallowed her name as she walked out the door. He had no time to mourn his friendship with the smiling black girl. An opportunity had been given to him.

After LaKeesha left, Hector caught himself looking at the clock every five minutes. He gave two customers the wrong change. When there was no one in line, he simply paced back and forth. He kept his eyes on the clock. At eleven forty-five, he rushed out of the cage and raced through the door. He had only one hour for lunch, and his girlfriend lived a little over two miles away. He ran all the way, and when he banged on the door, she answered. He was grateful that she was at home, that she had no rich black family's house to clean that day. He could see into the small, crowded room. Her mother and two grandmothers, her three aunts, were watching *The Price Is Right* on a tiny portable television that was propped up on a small wooden box in the middle of the dining room table. 'Comb your hair up. Put on your good dress,' he told her.

She knew the one.

He told the assistant operations manager that Idalia was his cousin. That she was trained and could replace La-Keesha. 'She is ready to start working today,' he said. The woman leaned forward and nodded and smiled at Idalia, who smiled back. And Idalia repeated what he had told her: 'I live only five minutes away. I will be very prompt. I know that I would enjoy working for you.'

Hector could feel his courage rising as he listened to Idalia. When there was a break in the conversation, he turned to his boss. 'I would like to talk with you about being a customer rep.'

Hector and Idalia took the bus back to her house that evening. As they rode through the city, he looked at his girlfriend and smiled. They would have a future together, he thought. They would marry. Have their own place and make babies. But not too many. They would have an apartment. And then a small house. And one day they would live in the beautiful neighborhood where the rich black people lived. He said to Idalia, 'With your first and second paychecks, you must buy a black skirt, a jacket, a pair of black shoes, and several blouses of different colors. Everything must go together.'

She nodded at him.

'Remember to be very careful. Don't make any mistakes. Mistakes are for white people. If we mess up, we're gone. History. No second chances. That's the first thing you must learn in this country: There's two sets of rules. So we gotta stick together.'

When she opened the door to her apartment, LaKeesha could see the surprise in her grandmother's eyes. 'What you doing home so early?' the older woman called from the kitchen.

'Anybody call me?' LaKeesha asked as she sat down at the table.

'King's mama called. She say to tell you that there's been a delay in King's trial.'

LaKeesha nodded slowly and thought about the five hundred dollars she had given up so easily. She had thought then that everything would be so simple, that with a good lawyer King would get out of jail. Now she wondered if anything was ever going to work out for her.

'What's wrong, baby?' The old woman walked over to her. 'Did something happen?'

She heard a dragging sound, and then she smelled the harsh grainy odor of malt liquor. When she turned around, Annie was standing near the doorway, her rheumy eyes fixed on her daughter.

'I got fired,' LaKeesha said softly.

'Lawdhamercy!' her grandmother said, and then she sighed. They were silent for a long while, holding on to each other.

There was a gagging sound, like someone choking. When LaKeesha looked at her mother, her face was contorted as she coughed.

LaKeesha saw Man peeking at her from behind the door. 'Come on over here, boy,' she called. Her grandmother let go of her arms.

Man shuffled toward his mother, as he sucked on a finger. When he reached LaKeesha, he put his head in her lap. 'Man, I got something to tell you,' she said. She watched as he raised his head and stared at her with round, inquisitive eyes. 'Remember how I was telling you that we're going to move? Well, Mommy lost her job and we can't move now. We have to stay here for a while.'

Man nodded at her solemnly. 'What happened to your job?'

'I don't have that one anymore.'

'You gonna find another one?'

LaKeesha paused for a moment, not knowing what to say. In the short space of time that she was groping for the right words, her mother slowly walked over and stood beside her. She put her hand on her grandson's head.

'Yeah,' Annie whispered.

As Esther trudged up the hill, she could hear Vanessa panting behind her. It was nearly ten o'clock in the morning, much later than she usually jogged. But of course, since she no longer had a job, she could run whenever she felt like it.

Running had been Vanessa's idea. 'Exercise will make you feel better,' she told Esther when she dropped in on her that morning. She practically had to push her into the shower to get her out of bed. Lately, Esther had been sleeping a lot.

The run did wake her up, and now, as the two women walked back to her house, Esther realized that she was actually feeling good for the first time since she'd been fired, three days earlier. 'Thanks for making me get my butt out of bed,' she said to Vanessa.

'Aww, girl, no sense in being down. You're going to get a job.'

'Vanessa, this is a terrible market for the banking industry. People are getting laid off all over town.'

Vanessa shrugged. 'Have some faith. You're going to get a job. Trust me. Oh, did I tell you that I got another commercial? MCI. It's national.'

'Oh, that's great. Congratulations.'

'Yeah. And I'm up for another movie. Great role. I play this superstar singer who falls in love with her bodyguard. Is that deep?'

Esther glanced over at her friend, who was grinning. 'Vanessa. Maybe . . .'

'What?'

'Maybe you shouldn't get your hopes up.'

Her friend's face was filled with incredulity. 'But that's what it's all about. Why do you think I came to L.A.? I love getting my hopes up.' She grinned. 'It's an actress thing; you wouldn't understand.'

As they got closer to her house, Esther could see her neighbor Carol and her little girl. The woman was putting in impatiens across the front of her lawn, as her daughter, with her finger-in-the-electric-socket hair, played around her. Esther felt a twinge of guilt. She'd never invited the family over; she knew she had hurt their feelings.

As they got closer, Vanessa whispered, 'What does that woman do to that child's hair?'

'Who knows,' Esther said.

As soon as they were in front of the white woman, Vanessa marched over to her. 'Hi,' she said. 'I'm Vanessa, Esther's friend.'

Carol looked surprised but pleased. 'Hello. I'm Carol.'

'Yeah. Your daughter's hairstyle is so, uh, unusual. What do you do to get it like that?'

Carol was silent for a full minute, and then her lower lip began to tremble. 'I don't know how to fix it,' she whispered. 'And my husband doesn't know how either. And so I gave her a Tani home permanent and . . .'

Vanessa put her hand on Carol's shoulder. 'Girlfriend, you're lucky the child's hair didn't blow up. Put those flowers down. Go get some money. We're going to go to the beauty supply store and show you what to buy. Then Esther and I are going to teach you something your mother never told you about.'

By the time the three women left the store, Carol had spent nearly fifty dollars on hair care products. At Esther's house, Vanessa washed Sarah's hair in the sink, put conditioner in it, and then parted it down the middle. Esther braided one side and Vanessa did the other. When they were finished, the little girl grinned and spun around, while her thick braids twirled in the air around her. 'The child needs a sister auntie,' Vanessa whispered to Esther. Esther had to admit that Sarah did look pretty. It felt good to stand next to Carol, admiring their handiwork.

'I can't thank you enough,' Carol said to the two women as she and her daughter were leaving. 'It's been so hard, not knowing anybody. All our relatives are back home. It's not easy to make friends in L.A.'

'Well, you've got one living right next door,' Vanessa said jovially.

Esther smiled.

Moments after her neighbors and then Vanessa left, Esther could feel gloom descending upon her. She went upstairs, took a bath, and got into bed, where she stared at the television screen without really knowing what she was watching. Every once in a while, she would reach for the remote control and change the channel, then settle into an even deeper stupor. She slept on and off, catnaps full of bad dreams. Each time she awakened, she felt drunk and strangely dislocated. Several times, she thought about calling her parents or her brother but changed her mind. For some reason that she couldn't begin to explain, she wanted to talk with Mallory. She wanted it to be like old times, the two of them giggling on the phone, liking each other. Even after all that had happened, she missed Mallory.

The thought that everyone at Angel City would believe that she and LaKeesha had been involved in robbing the bank made her cringe with shame and rage. She knew there had to be some way for her to make things right, but every time she tried to think, her mind seemed to shut down. Why had she given up so easily?

Sitting in her rumpled bed, she recalled a time when she was eight years old. It was her first year at the white private school on the North Side. She and her brother had made very few friends and had attracted a number of enemies. Her particular nemesis was an older girl named Suzanne, who seemed to delight in tormenting her. One day when she yanked her braids, Esther punched her in the stomach. 'How dare you come to our school and behave that way,' her teacher said as she marched her to the principal's office.

Suzanne was brought in, and they listened to her side of the story, but Esther never got a chance to tell hers. She recalled how furious and helpless she felt, sitting in the principal's office while her fate was decided. 'This is our

school,' the principal told her. 'We just let you come here.'
Those words lacerated her soul.

Now, weeping silent tears, she understood why she had
felt so powerless in Kirk's office. She realized there what she
had learned so many years ago: It was their world; they just
let her live in it. And they could decide to kick her out
anytime they chose.

She fell asleep and woke up an hour later, hearing her
doorbell ring. The clock beside her bed said ten o'clock. She
had no idea who would be visiting so late. Going downstairs, she looked out the window; Tyrone's Audi was
parked in front of her house. She could feel a smile rising up
from inside her.

'What's happening?' he asked, when she opened the door.
He held out two bottles of wine and two bags of microwave
popcorn.

'I got fired,' she said after he came in.

'Yeah, I heard. I figure you're an unemployed supersister
with two degrees and I'm an underemployed regular
brother with a high school diploma. That should make us
about equal, don't it? I thought maybe we could sit around,
pop some corn, and split a few verbs together.'

Esther laughed until her chest hurt. 'You know, you're
crazy. Certifiable.' She began to cry, and before she knew
what she was doing, she was in his arms, holding him,
holding on.

'Whoa, baby. It ain't the end of the world. Take it easy.
Tell me what happened.'

She cried a little longer, and then they sat down on the
sofa in the family room and she told Tyrone the entire story.
When she finished, there was a look of incredulity on his
face. 'Wait a minute. You not going out like that, are you?'
he asked. 'You not gonna tell nobody? Shi-i-it.'

'Who's going to believe me? And if I don't sign the release
form by tomorrow, I won't get the severance package.'

'Baby, you just can't let him do you like this.'

'Kirk's got all the proof. He rearranged computer files. He switched things around. Nobody will believe me.'

'How do you know that? They'd have to investigate. There's gotta be some proof. Dude had to be spending some money somewhere. You have to tell.'

Esther shook her head. 'Who could I tell?'

'That old guy who sits in that big-ass office, that's who.'

'Are you talking about Preston Sinclair, the president?'

'Yeah. The president. Tell the damn president.'

'The president?'

'He-e-ell, yeah.'

42

This will be the last time, Kirk said to himself as he punched in the computer codes for the dormant accounts. He had told himself that he would stop taking the money when he became regional director, but he'd made at least three transactions since then, totaling more than fifty thousand dollars. It was so easy to take the money. And he felt so incredibly good every time he did. He always had the urge to call up one of his old medical school classmates and say, 'Do you know that I just took twenty-five thousand dollars?'

He'd transfer the funds into one of his kids' accounts in the evenings, after everyone had left. The next day, he'd withdraw the cash he wanted. It was as simple as that. Sometimes, after he had the money, he would tell his assistant that he was going to a meeting, then he would get into his new car, go to Beverly Hills, and drive past the marble medical building. Several times he had the urge to shout at the building, to yell at the top of his lungs, 'I'm as good as you are! I'm as good as you are!' One time he actually did scream out those words, although he kept his windows rolled up tight. While he was yelling, he saw, out of the corner of his eyes, the man in the car next to his staring at him.

Kirk completed the transaction, then turned off the computer in Esther's old office. He began to chuckle, remembering the look of astonishment on the two black women's faces, remembering the fear in their eyes. Esther was trying to destroy him, and he'd gotten rid of her as easily as flicking away a pesky insect. He'd already begun interviewing for her replacement. Only yesterday he spoke with two women and a man – all white – and he was leaning toward the man. It just so happened that he had attended the same undergraduate school and even pledged the same fraternity as he had. He felt very comfortable with him, especially after the man confided that he liked King Clever.

Bailey had told him to hire whoever he wanted. 'The city has calmed down. I think we can soft-pedal affirmative action. After all, it's not as though we haven't tried,' he said.

Kirk took a quick look around the office before he turned off the lights. Satisfied that everything was in order, he closed the door. When he looked up, he was startled to see the security guard, a short, slender Latino. 'Oh, Mr. Madison. I know that Esther, she go. I wondering who it was.' He smiled.

'Yes, I left something in her office.' He gave the guard a wave as he left the bank.

In the time it took him to cross the street and get his car from the parking lot, he'd convinced himself not to worry. 'Nothing can harm me,' he whispered to himself. He said it three times, and then he forgot about the security man.

The jewelry store in the Beverly Hills Mall didn't close until nine. The saleslady, an older woman with rain-colored hair, smiled when she saw Kirk come in. 'I have your bracelet ready, Mr. Madison,' she said.

The deference in her voice pleased him. She knows my name, he thought. He'd always imagined the doctors he studied with going into fancy establishments where the proprietors fawned all over them and called them by name.

The saleslady brought over a small box and then opened it. He took out the diamond tennis bracelet and held it up. Perfect. She would love it. He smiled at the woman. 'Shall I wrap it for you, Mr. Madison?'

'Please,' he said.

583

When he got the raise, he told Sheila that the bank had given him a bonus as well. He bought his wife a mink coat and, of course, the new BMW. Now they were looking for a house on the west side of the city. Since the promotion, Sheila no longer screamed at him. In the morning, she made him breakfast. When he came home at night, dinner was waiting for him. For the first time in years, she seemed hot for him in bed.

But he was no longer hot for Sheila.

Sunday night, Mallory stared at her face in the mirror as she combed her hair. Downstairs in her living room, the lights were dim. Champagne was chilling in the refrigerator. She was clad in silk pajamas, and her skin was lightly perfumed. 'What the hell are you doing?' she asked herself.

It was all so familiar, this ritual of seduction. Every detail was memorized, from the music to the wine, from the transparent pajamas to the wrong man. And Kirk was the wrong man, the last in a long line. 'What the hell are you doing?' she repeated, staring at herself in the mirror. But she couldn't stop. Couldn't stop applying scarlet lipstick or teasing her hair, couldn't stop being glad that for at least one night, he'd chosen her and left another woman waiting. She gave her hair a yank that made her wince. Esther was almost right. Mallory was seeing Kirk, but she hadn't slept with him. At least not yet.

She dropped her lipstick when the doorbell rang.

Mallory invited Kirk in. They went into the living room, and she poured him a glass of wine. She listened to him talk about himself and his plans. But all the while she was noticing things she'd never paid attention to before. His new suit. His new shoes. A diamond pinkie ring. She thought about the BMW outside her door, the wad of cash Kirk always carried.

'I brought you a little something,' he said, placing a small jewelry box on her lap.

She was used to receiving gifts from him, but as soon as she saw the diamond bracelet, she felt the urge to run. She looked at the wedding band on Kirk's finger. 'I can't take this,' she said, handing the box back to him. She stood up. 'I'm sorry. I can't do this anymore. I want you to leave.'

'But, Mallory . . .'

'Kirk, go home.'

After Mallory closed the door behind Kirk, she returned to the living room and sat on the sofa, sipping her wine slowly. As much as she didn't want to, she couldn't stop thinking about the thick wad of bills that Kirk always pulled out when they went to lunch. Against her will, the memory of a Friday afternoon not long ago intruded into her thoughts. That day, Kirk took her shopping on Rodeo Drive and bought her a purse that cost six hundred dollars. He paid for it with cash. The bracelet that she'd just returned must have cost a thousand dollars. He drove a new BMW and seemed to have acquired a wardrobe of Italian suits. She took another sip of wine and stared at the thick Oriental carpet beneath her feet. She had to face the truth: Kirk was spending money as though he had an endless supply. 'Jesus,' she said.

The only right thing to do was to go see Bailey Reynolds on Monday morning and tell him her suspicions. And if he didn't believe her, she would talk to someone else. But she didn't know if she had the courage to do the right thing. If she told the people in upper management what she suspected about Kirk, she'd have to confess that he'd spent a lot of money on her. To reveal her relationship with a married man right after her problems with Humphrey had become known would hardly help her career. She would be risking her professional reputation. And for what? She wasn't even sure that Esther was still her friend.

Kirk was a thief. Two innocent people had been fired because of him. Even if Esther wasn't her friend anymore, she did deserve to be exonerated.

Kirk was her friend. He'd been kind to her when she was lonely. Maybe he wasn't stealing. Maybe there was a plausible explanation for his walking around with large sums of cash. And even if he was taking money from the bank, she didn't have to be the one to turn him in.

Mallory poured herself another glass of wine and drank it in several nervous gulps. She sat on the sofa, mulling over her options, becoming more and more frustrated. Making decisions alone had always been hard for her. She needed to talk things out.

Mallory looked at her watch. It wasn't even eight o'clock. She ran upstairs, took off her silk pajamas, and put on jeans and a T-shirt. When she passed the telephone, she started to dial the familiar number but then hung up and dashed out the door to her car instead. She didn't want to risk being told not to come.

Mallory got off the Santa Monica Freeway at the Cranston exit. Her instincts told her to go south. She hadn't been on this side of town in years, not since she was a little girl. The street was definitely the worse for wear – some buildings were still in a state of disrepair, and here and there she saw litter scattered about. But Cranston didn't look as horrible as she'd imagined. Some parts were still quite nice. When she passed the mall, she almost cried out for joy. She remembered shopping there with her mother. There were people milling about on the street, going in and out of fast-food restaurants. They were mostly black and brown, and they weren't very scary-looking. The most frightening thing was a huge billboard with a blue background. Mallory gasped when she saw it. There was a scrawny baby on it, with tubes all over his body and the words: HE COULDN'T TAKE THE HIT. She shuddered, then turned up the hill. The beauty of Park Crest, even in the twilight, stunned her. The neighborhood looked as if it had been plucked from Beverly Hills or Hancock Park. Some of the houses were mansions. The streets were quiet and clean, the lawns all had precision cuts. When she looked in the rearview mirror, she saw a picture-perfect view of downtown. We traded all this for an hour's commute and ten extra degrees in the summer, she thought. What were we so scared of?

When Esther opened the door, she was shocked to see Mallory standing in front of her. 'Come in,' she said, then led the white woman into the breakfast room. 'I was just having dinner. Would you like something?' What does she want? Esther thought. What the hell is she doing here?

'Sure.' Mallory could feel the black woman's resentment.

Esther fixed her a plate, and both women sat down at the table.

'Your house is neat. I used to live in Park Crest when I was a kid. Two streets over.' Was she gushing?

Esther nodded. She could feel herself slipping into the friendly comfort zone that she and Mallory had shared. She tried to stop herself from going there. Mallory wasn't her friend, she reminded herself. And she didn't trust her anymore. 'What brings you here?' she asked abruptly.

Mallory sensed the suspicion in Esther's voice. For a moment she was sorry she'd come. She hadn't thought things through. If she told Esther about Kirk, she'd have to report everything she knew. He would go to jail. She might be implicated in some way. 'I think you're right about Kirk,' she said slowly.

Esther's eyes locked onto hers.

'I know that you're right. He's been spending money on me like it's water.'

Esther felt herself stiffen. 'When did you finally figure everything out?' she asked. 'Did you know when I got fired?'

Esther's eyes were hard when Mallory looked into them. 'No.' The word came out in a gasp. 'Please don't think that of me,' Mallory said. She looked at Esther, who turned away.

Esther wanted to say something hurtful, but it was hard to be mean to Mallory. 'So how long have you known?'

'He's been taking me to lunch for a while, always to the most expensive restaurants. I never really paid that much attention. I mean, sometimes the tab for the two of us was more than a hundred dollars, but I figured he was trying to impress me. And he told me that he'd inherited some money, that some relative had died. Last weekend, he took me shopping. Paid cash for everything. The man must have spent five thousand dollars in three hours. Then, tonight, he brought me a diamond bracelet. I wouldn't take it . . . He acts guilty, maybe even a little crazy.'

'So what are you going to do with this information, Mallory?'

'I want to help you and LaKeesha get your jobs back.'

'You mean you want to report Kirk?'

'Yes.'

'If you tell what you know and how you know it, you won't look like a very nice girl, Mallory. Are you aware of that?'

'It's crossed my mind. I'm not a nice girl, but for the record, I didn't go to bed with Kirk.' She paused, waiting for some response from Esther, but there was none. 'I figured we could go together, tomorrow morning.'

Esther looked deep into Mallory's eyes; she didn't smile. 'Two is always better than one,' she said.

43

Preston and Bailey stood at the back door of Angel City and watched as the federal marshals led Kirk out to a waiting car. He had gone peacefully enough. Only now was Preston aware that the younger man's lips were moving and his head was nodding, as though he were in deep conversation with some invisible being. He is a nut, Preston thought to himself. Amazing, simply amazing, he thought as the car took off. As he glanced at Bailey, a scowl spread across his face and settled into the lines that ran on either side of his mouth. Each time he looked at his assistant's plump, congenial expression, he felt another surge of anger. It was the man's job to troubleshoot. He should have known what was going on, and instead he promoted Kirk Madison, exposing the bank and Preston to the glare of potentially ruinous publicity. Bailey put a whacko and a thief in charge of the entire region. His own mistake in judgment – choosing for his successor a man who lacked the self-control to leave his female co-worker alone – paled in comparison.

Bailey's jaw ached from grinning so much, but it was his only shield to ward off Preston's wrath, an unholy anger that he could feel in his bones. When the women had first come to him, making their accusation so forthrightly, he didn't want to believe them. Even when the night security guard was willing to swear that he had seen Kirk Madison sitting at Esther Jackson's computer at least twenty-five times after the black woman had left for the day, Bailey tried to get the women to back down. But they only threatened to go above his head if their allegations weren't investigated.

The recent deposits in Kirk's children's accounts, the list of checks that he'd written in the last five months, Mallory's statement about his lavish spending, left Bailey little room for wriggling. To think that an inside job of that magnitude had been carried out right under his nose! For the first time in his career, Bailey felt overwhelmed – and frightened. He'd just approved the promotion of a man who'd stolen nearly three hundred thousand dollars from the bank. And he had to be the one to tell Preston.

Preston had been furious. 'Why weren't you aware of what was going on sooner?' he shouted. Of course, the president's biggest concern was that the theft be kept out of the papers. 'Contain it, Bailey,' is how he put it. Thank God he managed to do that. Everything had been handled rather expeditiously, Bailey thought, considering the delicacy of the matter. He glanced sheepishly at Preston's glacial profile, realizing that he now had to focus his attention on the rather pressing matter of doing damage control for his own career.

If the paper had gotten hold of this . . . Preston cringed at the thought as he watched the unmarked car speed away. Only last week, one of the reporters from the *Gazette* had wanted to know why Humphrey Boone had left Angel City. Before he could answer, the woman told him that Humphrey's name had been mentioned as the possible chief operating officer of Solid Rock National Bank, chartered only last week by a group affiliated with the church of the same name. When asked about the black man's record, Preston, without hesitating, told the reporter that Humphrey's tenure with the bank had been marked by unparalleled excellence.

Preston shot Bailey a look of disgust as they stepped into the express elevator to the thirty-fourth floor. Only two days ago, one of the board members had pulled him aside and told him that Bailey had been 'wooing' certain fellow members. He'd received a letter, signed by both Mallory Post and Esther Jackson, describing how Bailey had tried to talk them out of making their claims. What the circumstances required was obvious. He would do what was necessary. He would see to the details.

As the elevator door opened, he said to Bailey, 'You've set things in motion to rehire the two women who were fired?'

Bailey smiled. He could barely hold his lips in position, he was so nervous. 'It's all been taken care of, Preston,' he said.

'You offered them their jobs back with a raise? I want the paperwork on my desk as soon as possible.'

'Of course, Preston.' Bailey's forlorn smile didn't hide the anxiety in his eyes.

'Well then, only one thing remains to be done, Bailey. Gather your things together. I want your resignation on my desk in one hour.'

Smile about that, Preston thought as he strode away.

Preston felt a surge of excitement as he sat down at his desk. He opened the *Gazette* to the business section. The article about the new black bank was on the front page. It was while he was perusing the story that the idea came to him: I can be of help to them. Why shouldn't Angel City play a part in the development of the new black bank? Angel City's Minority Loan Program had succeeded in increasing the number of black loan recipients to three percent of the total, but that was still a pretty poor showing. Many of their black customers would undoubtedly go to Solid Rock and take their savings accounts with them. Still, there could be a win in it for the bank. He could start a program, send his best executives to Solid Rock for three-month stints to help train the new bank's people. Yes. An arrangement like that would be sure to attract coverage. He could just see the photograph, the three of them smiling: Humphrey,

Reverend Rice, and himself, their hands in one solid clasp. That kind of publicity would help both banks. He pressed his intercom. 'Beatrice? Call Reverend Odell Rice and make an appointment at his earliest convenience.'

Strong grip, Reverend Rice thought as he shook Preston Sinclair's hand two days later. When his wife had told him that the personal assistant to the president of Angel City National Bank had called, he almost laughed out loud. He had made up his mind only that morning that he needed to contact the man. But then God did work in mysterious ways.

Reverend Rice sat back and listened as Preston explained the kind of big brother-little brother partnership that Angel City was interested in developing. He succeeded in not smiling as the president spoke, only because he could hear the sincerity in Preston's voice as he explained his idea of having Angel City's senior managers train the new bank's employees. In his years in the ministry, he'd learned that nearly everything could be feigned except sincerity.

When the president had finished, the minister leaned forward. 'Well, sir,' he said, 'that's an intriguing idea you have. And I do appreciate your interest. However, I assure you that the banking professionals at Solid Rock National are highly trained. They come from some of the top colleges and business schools in the country, and they've cut their teeth on some of the largest banks in the area, including yours.' He tried to speak as gently as possible and watched Preston's expression as he did. He didn't want to offend or embarrass the man.

But as the minister was speaking, Preston recognized his mistake and feared that he'd insulted Reverend Rice. He had assumed that black professionals weren't as well trained as white ones. Now his face reddened slightly as the minister mildly corrected his inaccurate assumption. 'Well,

592

is there any role that Angel City might play in the new bank?' he asked, as soon as the minister paused.

Reverend Rice smiled broadly. 'As a matter of fact, there is a way that you can participate in Solid Rock's progress. Mr. Sinclair, Humphrey Boone, our new chief operating officer, speaks highly of you. He and I were wondering if you'd be willing to serve on the board.'

Now, here was an opportunity for goodwill. And the chance to work with Humphrey pleased Preston. 'I'd be honored,' he said. 'I admire what you're trying to do. Angel City and the other major banks haven't served our minority communities very well, I'm afraid. The least we can do is assist those who will be able to do a better job. I think the future of this city depends upon that. I hope to God that this trial will end reasonably. Maybe after this is over the city will calm down. Perhaps the worst is behind us.'

'We are going to live with the worst for a very long time,' Reverend Rice said quietly.

Preston didn't respond immediately. Looking into the black man's solemn face, he felt naive and foolish. 'It seems never to end,' he finally mumbled.

Reverend Rice smiled. 'I think I'll enjoy working with you, Mr. Sinclair,' he said. 'You'll be receiving a letter informing you of the date and location of our first board meeting.' He stood up to leave and extended his hand. 'I'm afraid I've got to get back to church. We're planning a huge bazaar for tomorrow, our annual African Family Reunion.'

Preston nodded. 'Reverend Rice, mind if I ask you something?'

The minister sat back down. 'Not at all,' he said.

'My father was a minister. Baptist. He always spoke in terms of getting the "call". I never asked him what that meant. How do you know when you get it?'

'A call is nothing more than God nudging you. It's an

irresistible urge to submit to the will of the Lord for the good of all, Mr. Sinclair.'

'By preaching the gospel?'

'That. Sometimes by writing a check. Sometimes by tutoring kids. You can serve the Lord in a number of ways.'

'I see.'

'Do you think you've had the call?'

Preston looked startled. 'Me? Oh, no.'

Reverend Rice smiled and then stood up again. He extended his hand to the president. 'Well, Mr. Sinclair. Listen to your heart. If you've received the call, you'll know it soon enough. And by the way, If you ever want to try out your preaching skills, you can come to Solid Rock on the fourth Sunday at the noon service. That's when we let laypeople give minisermons. We call it Karaoke Sunday.'

44

When she opened the door on Sunday morning, Esther saw Harold and Sarah standing there. The little girl carried a brightly colored backpack. She barreled into Esther, hugging her around the knees. 'Good morning, Miss Sarah,' Esther said, smiling, as the child released her and scampered into the family room.

'I think you have a buddy for life,' Harold said, chuckling. 'You're sure this is no trouble?'

'I'm happy to do it. You guys have a good time. Sarah and I are going to hang out.' She smiled at Harold, a tranquil smile that was full of goodwill.

Later, after Esther and Sarah waved good-bye to the little girl's parents from the picture window in the living room, they walked down to Cranston Boulevard. The air around them seemed fresh. It had rained the night before: one of those unexpected, out-of-season downpours that never could be predicted in Los Angeles. Now the sidewalks glistened, and even the dingiest buildings seemed clean. That was the allure of the place: even though the city blew apart from time, from any number of natural and unnatural disasters, there were those days when L.A. could deceive, times when it stood still and seemed perfect and peaceful.

As she neared Diamond Donuts, Esther was assailed by the sweet, yeasty odor. Inside, the old regulars were sitting in their corner, their coffee cups in front of them. Their voices were low, guarded. Hyun stood at the counter, watching them with cautious eyes.

'Hello, may I help you?' she said carefully. Her face was solemn.

'How are you doing, Hyun?' Esther said. The Korean woman nodded stiffly. 'Let me have three apple bran muffins, please.' She picked up Sarah. 'What would you like?'

The small girl pointed to the jelly doughnuts. 'What's that?' she said, looking at the small table with its fruit, doughnuts, and candle, on the floor behind the counter.

'That's her table for Buddha. That's her religion,' Esther said.

'No,' Hyun said.

Esther and Sarah looked at her.

'Buddha table for father. I Baptist.'

'You're Baptist?' Esther asked.

Hyun nodded.

'Oh.'

There was a sudden roar of laughter at the corner table. One of the men stood up, letting loose with a barrage of friendly insults directed toward his companions.

As Hyun handed Esther her bag, she said, 'Every day. Same thing. Same thing.'

Sarah dallied as they walked up the hill, and by the time they got back to the house, they were both hungry. Inside her kitchen, Esther poured herself a cup of peppermint tea and put the warmed muffins and jelly doughnuts on the breakfast room table. She gave Sarah a glass of milk.

They had finished eating when Esther heard her bell ringing. She left Sarah and answered the front door.

Tyrone was standing in front of her, wearing a bright-red X cap and an even brighter smile. Damn, she looks good, he thought. 'Hey,' he said, stepping inside.

'Hey.' Esther gave him a long hug, full of friendship and affection.

'How'd it go?'

'They offered LaKeesha and me our old jobs back, with

596

raises, if we want them. Mallory helped a lot. She reported to upper management all the times she saw Kirk with lots of cash.' She kissed him quickly on his lips. 'Thank you for making me go.'

Tyrone grinned at her.

'And Solid Rock National Bank called me today. They want to interview me for an operations position, and they're offering the possibility of my becoming a loan officer in the future. They offered LaKeesha a job as a teller, for slightly more money. She's going to take it.'

Tyrone clapped his hands and let out a long chortle. 'My baby's in demand. I was just on my way over to Solid Rock. The church is having their African Family Reunion today. Thought you might want to go with me. I've got some shirts and caps to sell. You can help me. You like counting money, don't you?'

Esther looked over his shoulder and saw a thin young white man sitting in Tyrone's car. 'Who's that?' she asked.

'Cody. He's coming.'

Esther's eyebrows rose slightly. 'To the African Family Reunion?'

'Trust me. He's a long-lost cousin.'

'I'm baby-sitting,' Esther said.

'Whose kid?'

'Little girl from next door.'

'She can come,' Tyrone said. 'You like kids?'

They both walked over to the car, and Tyrone introduced her to Cody. She looked inside. On the backseat were several boxes without tops filled with T-shirts. Next to them was a blank application for Cal State Los Angeles. Just as Esther was about to open the car door to examine the shirts, she heard a squeal of brakes. A car was pulling up right behind Tyrone's. Before Esther's surprise had time to register, Mallory was standing next to her.

'Hi,' Mallory said, walking toward them. 'I was fooling

around in Westwood, so since I wasn't that far, I took the chance that you'd be home.' She suddenly felt self-conscious. Maybe I shouldn't have come, she thought.

Esther's expression was guarded. She could feel the old anger rising up in her, but she could feel something else fighting that emotion. 'Hi. You remember Tyrone,' Esther said. 'And this is Cody.'

Mallory greeted the two men.

'We'll be right back,' Esther told Tyrone. 'Come on in,' she said to Mallory. In the kitchen, Sarah was finishing her doughnut.

'Oh,' Mallory said. 'Who's this?'

'This is Sarah. She lives next door. Sarah, say hello to Mallory.'

'Hello,' the little girl said solemnly.

'Do you want some coffee or juice or anything?' Esther asked Mallory.

'No.'

The two women stood facing each other awkwardly. 'I just came by to ask you a question,' Mallory suddenly blurted out. Standing in front of Esther, she felt jittery. 'Are we still friends?'

The question startled Esther. For a moment, she didn't speak. 'I don't know,' she said finally.

Mallory chewed on her bottom lip. 'I want us to be friends,' she said softly. 'It's so weird. I have so much more in common with you than I do with Susan, a woman I grew up with, but it's easier being her friend.'

'Because she's white?'

Mallory nodded. 'I'm not scared of offending her. I don't feel guilty when I'm around her. She doesn't get angry for reasons I can't comprehend.'

'It's a white thing, and you understand,' Esther said.

The two women smiled at each other.

'Yeah, I guess so,' Mallory said. 'Sometimes when I'm

around you I feel like "the white people". You get so mad all the time.'

'Don't you think I get tired of being angry?' Esther said. 'I am so sick of being angry, but every time I walk out my door there's somebody reminding me that I'm not quite as good as white folks.'

'But *we* like each other.'

Esther looked at her friend. 'Yeah, we do. But it's still hard being friends.'

'Maybe it's supposed to be hard.'

Tyrone's car horn blared from the street.

Esther sighed and turned to Sarah. 'You finished, Miss Missy? We're going somewhere.'

'Oh,' Mallory said. 'I didn't mean to interrupt anything.'

'We're going to the African Family Reunion. It's at a church just south of here.' Esther hesitated for a moment. 'You can come if you like.'

'Thanks,' Mallory said easily. 'Actually, I was thinking about exploring the neighborhood. Anything interesting to see?'

Esther's eyebrows rose just slightly. Then she smiled. 'There're some good restaurants on Cranston. Jamaican. Japanese. Vegetarian. There's a soul food place called Duley's that's really good. The African art museum is in the mall. If you cross Cranston, there's a bunch of galleries, coffeehouses, and little shops, and around the corner are a couple of really nice dress shops and bookstores. We have five zillion places to get your nails done. And if you need a wig . . . Girlfriend, Cranston is the wig shop capital of the Western world.'

Mallory grinned. 'I don't need a wig, but that soul food sounds good. Maybe I'll just wander around for a while and work up an appetite.' .

'Call me tomorrow. Tell me how you liked everything,'

Esther said as the two women walked to the front door. Sarah tagged along behind them.

Tyrone was leaning against his car, laughing about something Cody had said, when the two women came outside. As Mallory headed for her car, he came over to Esther. 'She didn't want to go with us?' Tyrone asked, watching the white woman drive away.

'She had something else to do,' Esther said. 'Something important. Maybe we'll all hang out another time.' She grinned at him. 'Let me see your shirts.'

Esther and Tyrone walked over to the car and opened the back door. She pulled out a few of the shirts from one of the boxes. 'These are great, but do you have them arranged by size?' she asked.

Tyrone stood behind her. 'So do you want to work with me?'

'I can't believe you didn't sort these.' She held up a bunch of T-shirts.

Tyrone put his hands on her shoulders and spun her around to face him. 'Do you?'

'Do I what?'

'Do you want to work with me, sister?'